J.W Forte

A History of the British Army
Volume 2

outlook

J.W Fortescue

A History of the British Army
Volume 2

1st Edition | ISBN: 978-3-75235-339-6

Place of Publication: Frankfurt am Main, Germany

Year of Publication: 2020

Outlook Verlag GmbH, Germany.

Reproduction of the original.

A History of

The British Army

BY

THE HON. J. W. FORTESCUE

VOL. II

BOOK VII

CHAPTER I

1713.
1714.

The work of disbanding the Army began some months before the final conclusion of the Peace of Utrecht. By Christmas 1712 thirteen regiments of dragoons, twenty-two of foot, and several companies of invalids who had been called up to do duty owing to the depletion of the regular garrisons, had been actually broken. The Treaty was no sooner signed than several more were disbanded, making thirty-three thousand men discharged in all. More could not be reduced until the eight thousand men who were left in garrison in Flanders could be withdrawn, but even so the total force on the British Establishment, including all colonial garrisons, had sunk in 1714 to less than thirty thousand men. The soldiers received as usual a small bounty on discharge; and great inducements were offered to persuade them to take service in the colonies, or, in other words, to go into perpetual exile.

But this disbandment was by no means so commonplace and artless an affair as might at first sight appear. One of the first measures taken in hand by Bolingbroke and by his creature Ormonde was the remodelling of the Army, by which term was signified the elimination of officers and of whole corps that favoured the Protestant succession, to make way for those attached to the Jacobite interest. Prompted by such motives, and wholly careless of the feelings of the troops, they violated the old rule that the youngest regiments should always be the first to be disbanded, and laid violent hands on several veteran corps. The Seventh and Eighth Dragoons, the Thirty-fourth, Thirty-third, Thirty-second, Thirtieth, Twenty-ninth, Twenty-eighth, Twenty-second, and Fourteenth Foot were ruthlessly sacrificed; nay, even the Sixth, one of the sacred six old regiments, and distinguished above all others in the Spanish War, was handed over for dissolution like a regiment of yesterday.[1] There were bitter words and stormy scenes among regimental officers over such shameless, unjust, and insulting procedure.

Aug. $\frac{1}{12}$

All these designs, however, were suddenly shattered by the death of Queen Anne. The accession of the Elector of Hanover to the throne was accomplished with a tranquillity which must have amazed even those who desired it most. Before the new King could arrive the country was gladdened by the return of the greatest of living Englishmen. Landing at Dover on the very day of the Queen's death, Marlborough was received with salutes of artillery and shouts of delight from a joyful crowd. Proceeding towards London next day he was met by the news that his name was excluded from the list of Lords-Justices to whom the government of the country was committed pending the King's arrival. Deeply chagrined, but preserving always his invincible serenity, he pushed on to the capital, intending to enter it with the same privacy that he had courted during his banishment in the Low Countries. But the people had decided that his entry must be one of triumph; and a tumultuous welcome from all classes showed that the country could and would make amends for the shameful treatment meted out to him two years before.

On the 18th of September King George landed at Greenwich, and shortly afterwards the new ministry was nominated. Stanhope, the brilliant soldier of the Peninsular War, became second Secretary-of-State; William Pulteney, afterwards Earl of Bath, Secretary-at-War; Robert Walpole, Paymaster of the Forces; while Marlborough with some reluctance resumed his old appointments of Captain-General, Master-General of the Ordnance, and Colonel of the First Guards. He soon found, however, that though he held the titles, he did not hold the authority of the offices, and that the true control of the Army was transferred to the Secretary-at-War.

| 1715. |
| May 24. |

How weak that Army had become was presently realised at the outbreak of the Jacobite rebellion in the autumn of 1715. The estimates of 1714 had provided for a British establishment of twenty-two thousand men, of which two-thirds were stationed in Flanders and in colonial garrisons, leaving a dangerously small force for the defence of the kingdom. Even this poor remnant the Jacobite Lords had tried to weaken, by introducing a clause in the Mutiny Act to confine all regiments to the particular districts allotted to them in the British Isles. This insidious move, which was designed to prevent the transfer of troops between Ireland and England, was checked by the authority of Marlborough himself. The King, it seems, had early perceived the perils of such a situation; and accordingly, in January, the Seventh Dragoons were recreated and restored under their old officers, together with four more of the old regiments.[2] In July the prospect of a rising in Scotland made further increase imperative, and orders were issued for the raising of thirteen regiments of dragoons and eight of foot, some few of which must for a brief moment detain us.

4

The first of the new regiments of dragoons was Pepper's, the present Eighth Hussars, which for a time had shared the hard fate of the Seventh, and was now, like the Seventh, restored to life. The next six, Wynn's, Gore's, Honeywood's, Bowles's, Munden's, and Dormer's, are now known respectively as the Ninth Lancers, the Tenth and Eleventh Hussars, the Twelfth Lancers, and the Thirteenth and Fourteenth Hussars, regiments which have made their mark on many a field in the Peninsula and in India, while two of them bear on their appointments the name of Balaclava. The remaining six were disbanded in 1718.[3] Of the foot six regiments also perished after a short life in 1718;[4] the remaining two were old regiments, the Twenty-second and the Thirty-fourth, each of which was destined in due time to add to its colours the name of a victory peculiar to itself.

It may be asked whether no use was made of the hundreds of veterans who had returned from the wars of Flanders. The answer gives us a curious insight into the old conception of a reserve. On the first alarm of a rising, the whole of the officers on half-pay were called upon to hold themselves ready for service;[5] and concurrently twenty-five companies of Chelsea pensioners were formed to take over the duties of the garrisons and to release the regular troops for work in the field. For many years after as well as before this date the same system is found in force; and of this, as of so many obsolete institutions, there is fortunately a living relic still with us. In March 1719 ten of these veteran companies were incorporated into a regiment under Colonel Fielding, and having begun life with the name of Fielding's Invalids, survive to this day as the Forty-first Foot.[6]

I shall not detain the reader with any detailed account of the abortive insurrection of 1715. The operations entailed by an invasion of England from the north are always the same. The occupation of Stirling cuts off the Highlands from the Lowlands, and bars any advance from the extreme north. An invasion from the Lowlands may be checked on either flank of the Cheviots, on the east coast at the lines of the Tweed or the Tyne, or, if headed back from thence, on the west coast at the line of the Ribble. If both Highlands and Lowlands are in revolt, there is the third resource of a simultaneous attack from north and south upon Stirling. This last course lay open to the insurgents on this occasion but was not accepted. The two decisive engagements were accordingly fought, one at Sheriffmuir, a little to the north of Stirling, the other at Preston, whither the insurgents of the Lowlands, checked by an insignificant force on the east coast, made a hopeless and futile march to the west, and were enveloped by English forces marching simultaneously from east, west, and south. None the less the peril to England was great. The force at Stirling was far too weak for the duty assigned to it; and Sheriffmuir was one of those doubtful actions from which each army emerges with one wing defeated and the other victorious. The English force on the Tweed was made up of raw recruits, and was so weak in numbers that General Carpenter, a veteran of Flanders and Spain, who commanded it, accomplished his work chiefly by the bold face with which he met a dangerous position. Such was the military impotence of England after a bare two years of peace.[7]

| 1716. |
| 1717. |

The panic caused by the insurrection swelled the military estimates of 1716 very considerably. Apart from the new regiments raised for the occasion, the strength of every existing troop and company had been augmented, while the addition of a battalion to each regiment of Guards increased the brigade to the total of seven battalions, which constituted its strength unaltered almost for the next two centuries. The full establishment voted by Parliament for Great Britain was thirty-six thousand men, exclusive of course of troops in Ireland, and of six thousand Dutchmen, who had been sent over by the States-General in fulfilment of obligations by treaty. The very next year, however, saw the establishment diminished by one-fourth, and in May the King announced that he had given orders to reduce the army by ten thousand men more. The estimates for 1718 accordingly provided for but sixteen thousand men in Great Britain, while those for 1719 diminished even that handful by one-fourth, and brought the total down to the figure of twelve thousand men.

| 1718. |
| 1719. |

Then as usual the numbers were found to be dangerously weak. A quarrel between Spain and the Empire, and the ambitious designs of Cardinal Alberoni brought about a breach between England and Spain, which finally culminated in the attack and defeat of the Spanish fleet by Admiral Byng off Cape Passaro. The action was fought before war had actually been declared, and Byng affected to treat it as an unfortunate accident; but Alberoni was too much incensed at the subversion of his designs to heed such empty blandishment as this. He prepared to avenge himself by making terms with the Jacobites and by fitting out an expedition from Cadiz for the support of the Pretender. The force was to be commanded by Ormonde, the same poor, misguided man who had supplanted Marlborough in Flanders; but the menace was formidable none the less. At the meeting of Parliament the King gave warning that an invasion must be looked for, and received powers to augment the Army to meet it. Nevertheless, it was thought best once more to borrow six thousand foreigners from the Dutch and Austrian Netherlands; and England's contribution to her own defence consisted in no more than the transfer of four weak battalions from the Irish to the British establishment. The King's ministers took credit, when the danger was over, for the moderation with which they had exercised the powers entrusted to them, failing to see that resort to mercenary troops at such a time was a policy wanting as much in true statesmanship as in honour.

| April 16. |
| June 10. |

For the rest the peril vanished, as four generations earlier had the peril of a still greater Spanish invasion, before wind and tempest. The Spanish transports were dispersed by a gale in the Bay of Biscay, and the great armament crept back by single ships to Cadiz, crippled, shattered, barely saved by the sacrifice of guns, horses and stores from the fury of the storm. Two frigates only reached the British coast and landed three Scottish peers— Lords Tullibardine, Marischal and Seaforth—with three hundred Spanish soldiers, at Kintail in Ross-shire. Here the little party remained unmolested for several weeks, being joined by some few hundred restless Highland spirits, but supported by no general rising of the clans. At length, however, General Carpenter detached General Wightman with a thousand men from Inverness, who fell upon the insurgents in the valley of Glenshiel and, though their force was double that of his own, dispersed them utterly.[8] The campaign ended, like all mountain-campaigns, in the burning of the houses and villages of the offending clans; and thus ignominiously ended this hopeless and futile insurrection. Its most remarkable result was that it drove Lord Marischal and his brother into the Prussian service, and gave to Frederick the Great one of his best officers and most faithful friends—that James Keith who fell forty years later on the field of Hochkirch.

| Sept. 21. |

Such aggression, failure though it was, naturally led the English to make reprisals; and in September a British squadron sailed from Spithead with four thousand troops on board for a descent on the Spanish coast. The original object of the expedition had been an attack on Corunna, but Lord Cobham,[9] who was in command, thought the enterprise too hazardous, and turned his arms against Vigo. The town being weakly held was at once surrendered, and the citadel capitulated after a few days of siege. A considerable quantity of arms and stores, which had been prepared for Ormonde's expedition, was captured, and with this small advantage to his credit, Cobham re-embarked his troops for England.[10] Shortly afterwards Alberoni opened negotiations for peace, which he purchased at the cost of his own dismissal. The treaty was signed on the 19th of January 1720, and England entered upon twenty years of unbroken peace.

But before I touch upon the history of that peace I may be allowed to advance two years to record an event which may fittingly close the first thirty years of conflict with Jacobitism and its allies. On the 16th of June 1722 died John, Duke of Marlborough. Constantly during his later campaigns he had suffered from giddiness and headache, and in May 1716 the shock caused by the death of his daughter, Lady Sunderland, brought on him a paralytic stroke. He rallied, but was struck down a second time in November of the same year; and although, contrary to the received opinion, he again rallied, preserving his speech, his memory, and his understanding little impaired, yet it was evident that his life's work was done. In the few years that remained to him he still attended the House of Lords, spending the session of 1721 as usual in London, and retiring at its close to Windsor Lodge. There at the beginning of June in the following year he was smitten for the third time, and after lingering several days, helpless but conscious, he at dawn of the 16th passed peacefully away.

On the 14th of July the body was brought to Marlborough House. In those days London was empty at that season, and only in Hyde Park, where the whole of the household troops were encamped, was there sign of unusual activity. Day after day the Foot Guards were drilled in a new exercise to be used at the funeral; the weeks wore on, the day of Blenheim came and went, and at length on the 9th of August all was ready. From Marlborough House along the Mall and Constitution Hill to Hyde Park Corner, from thence along Piccadilly and St. James's Street to Charing Cross and the Abbey, the way was lined with the scarlet coats of the Guards. The drums were draped in black, the colours wreathed with cypress; every officer wore a black scarf, and every soldier a bunch of cypress in his bosom. Far away from down the river sounded minute after minute the dull boom of the guns at the Tower.

The procession opened with the advance of military bands, followed by a detachment of artillery. Then came Lord Cadogan, the devoted Quartermaster-General who had prepared for the Duke so many of his fields, and with him eight General Officers, veterans who had fought under their great Chief on the Danube and in Flanders. Among these was Munden, the hero who had led the forlorn hope at Marlborough's first great action of the Schellenberg, and had brought back with him but twenty out of eighty men. Then followed a vast cavalcade of heralds, officers-at-arms and mourners, with all the circumstance and ceremony of an age when pomp was lavished on the least illustrious of the dead; and in the midst, encircled by a forest of banners, rolled an open car, bearing the coffin.[11] Upon the coffin lay a complete suit of gilt armour, above it was a gorgeous canopy, around it military trophies, heraldic devices, symbolic presentations of the victories that the dead man had won and of the towns which he had captured, strange contrast to the still white face, serene beyond even the invincible serenity of life, that slept within.

As the car passed by there rang out to company after company of the silent Guards a new word of command. "Reverse your arms." "Rest on your arms reversed." The officers lowered their pikes, the ensigns struck their colours, and every soldier turned the muzzle of his musket to the ground and bent his head over the butt "in a melancholy posture." The procession moved slowly on, and the troops, still with arms reversed, formed up in its rear and marched with it. Fifty-two years before, John Churchill, the unknown ensign of the First Guards, had marched in procession behind the coffin of George Monk, Duke of Albemarle; now he too was faring on to share Monk's resting-place.

At the Horse Guards the Guards wheeled into St. James's Park and formed up on the parade-ground, where the artillery with twenty guns was already formed up before them. The car crept on to the western door of the Abbey, and then rose up for the first time that music which will ever be heard so long as England shall bury her heroes with the rites of her national Church. Within the Abbey the gray old walls were draped with black, and nave and choir and transept were ablaze with tapers and flambeaux. Of England's greatest all were there, the living and the dead. The helmet of Harry the Fifth, still dinted with the blows of Agincourt, hung dim above his tomb, looking down on the stolid German who now sat upon King Harry's throne, and on his heir the Prince of Wales, who had won his spurs at Oudenarde. And at the organ, humble and unnoticed, sat William Croft, little dreaming that he too had done immortal work, but content to listen to the beautiful music which he had made, and to wait till the last sound of the voices should have died away. [12]

Then the organ spoke under his hand in such sweet tones as are heard only from the organs of that old time, and the procession moved through nave and choir to King Henry the Seventh's chapel. By a strange irony the resting-place chosen for the great Duke was the vault of the family of Ormonde, but it was not unworthy, for it had held the bones of Oliver Cromwell.[13] Then the voice of Bishop Atterbury, Dean of Westminster, rose calm and clear with the words of the service; and the anthem sang sadly, "Cry ye fir-trees, for the cedar is fallen." The gorgeous coffin sank glittering into the shadow of the grave, and Garter King-at-Arms, advancing, proclaimed aloud, "Thus has it pleased Almighty God to take out of this transitory world unto his mercy the most high, mighty and noble prince, John, Duke of Marlborough." Then snapping his wand he flung the fragments into the vault.

As he spoke three rockets soared aloft from the eastern roof of the Abbey. A faint sound of distant drums broke the still hush within the walls, and then came a roar which shook the sable hangings and made the flame of the torches tremble again, as the guns on the parade-ground thundered out their salvo of salute. Thrice the salvo was repeated; the drums sounded faintly and ceased, and all again was still. And then burst out a ringing crash of musketry as the Guards, two thousand strong, discharged their answering volley. Again the volley rang out, and yet again; and then the drums sounded for the last time, and the great Duke was left to his rest.[14]

From such a scene I must turn to the further work that lies before me in the events of the next twenty years; and it will be convenient to deal first with the political aspect of the Army's history. England, it must be observed, had not yet recovered from the indiscipline and unrest of the Great Rebellion. Since the death of Elizabeth the country, except during the short years of the Protectorate, had not known a master. William of Orange, who had at any rate the capacity to rule it, was unwilling to give himself the trouble; Marlborough, while his power lasted, had been occupied chiefly with the business of war; and during the reign of both war had been a sufficient danger in the one case and a sufficient cause of exultation in the other to distract undisciplined minds. Now, however, there was peace. A foreign prince had ascended the throne, a worthy person and very far from an incapable man, but uninteresting, ignorant of England, and unable to speak a word of her language. The tie of nationality and the reaction of sentiment which had favoured the restoration of Charles the Second were wanting. The country too, after prolonged occupation with the business of pulling down one king and setting up another, had imbibed a dangerous contempt of all authority whatsoever.

Other influences contributed not less forcibly to increase the prevalent indiscipline. Many old institutions were rapidly falling obsolete. The system of police was hopelessly inefficient, and the press had not yet concentrated the force of public opinion into an ally of law and order. In all classes the same lawlessness was to be found; showing itself among the higher by a fashionable indifference to all that had once been honoured as virtue, an equally fashionable indulgence towards debauchery, and an irresistible tendency to decide every dispute by immediate and indiscriminate force. Among the lower classes, despite the most sanguinary penal code in Europe, brutal crime, not of violence only, was dangerously rife. No man who was worth robbing could consider himself safe in London, whether in the streets or in his own house. Patrols of Horse and Foot Guards failed to ensure the security of the road between Piccadilly and Kensington;[15] and further afield the footpad and the highwayman reigned almost undisturbed. Nor did great criminals fail to awake lively sympathy among the populace. The names of Dick Turpin and Jack Sheppard enjoy some halo of heroism to this day; and frequently, when some desperate malefactor was at last brought to Tyburn, it was necessary to escort him to execution and, supposing that the gallows had not been cut down by sympathisers during the night, to surround him with soldiers lest he should be rescued by the mob. All over England the case was the same. Strikes, riots, smuggling, incendiarism and general lawlessness flourished with alarming vigour, rising finally to such a height that, by the confession of a Secretary-of-State in the House of Commons, it was unsafe for magistrates to do their duty without the help of a military force.[16]

Against this mass of disorder the only orderly force that could be opposed was the Army. It will presently be seen that the Army had grave enough faults of its own, but the outcry against it was levelled not at its faults but at its power as a disciplined body to execute the law. So far, therefore, the unpopularity of the Army was fairly universal. But its most formidable opponents were bred by faction, the Jacobites who wished to re-establish the Stuarts naturally objecting to so dangerous an obstacle to their designs. The howl against the Army was raised in the House of Commons as early as in 1714, and in 1717 a Jacobite member who, being more conspicuous for honesty than for wisdom, was known as "Downright Shippen," opened a series of annual motions for the reduction of the forces. This self-imposed duty, as he once boasted to the House, he fulfilled on twenty-one successive occasions, though on thirteen of them he had found no seconder to support him.[17] If this had been all, no great harm could have resulted; but the watchword of a baffled opposition, artfully stolen from old times of discontent, was too useful not to be generally employed, and "No Standing Army" became the parrot's cry of every political adventurer, every discontented spirit, every puny aspirant to importance. Walpole himself did not disdain to avail himself of it during the four years which he spent out of office between 1717 and 1721, and the stock arguments of the malcontents were never urged more ably nor more mischievously than by Marlborough's Secretary-at-War.[18] The Lords again were little behind the Commons, and Jacobite peers who had commanded noble regiments in action were not ashamed to drag the name of their profession through the dirt.

| 1714-1739. |

In such circumstances, where the slightest false step might have imperilled the very existence of the Army, the administration of the forces and the recommendation of their cost to the House of Commons became matters of extreme delicacy. It has already been told how the King, as the alarm of the first Jacobite rebellion subsided, voluntarily reduced the Army by ten thousand men at a stroke. Such policy, dangerous though it was from a military standpoint, was undoubtedly wise; it was the sacrifice of half the cargo to save the ship, an ingenious transformation of a necessity into a virtue. Even before the Spanish War was ended but fourteen thousand men were asked for as the British establishment, the remainder of the Army being hidden away in Ireland; and the same number was presented on the estimates up to the year 1722. In the autumn of that year, however, the administration insisted that the number should be raised to eighteen thousand. The spirits of the Jacobites had been raised by the birth of Prince Charles Edward; there had been general uneasiness in the country; troops had been encamped ready for service all the summer, and six regiments had been brought over from Ireland. The augmentation was bitterly opposed in Parliament, but was carried in the Commons by a large majority, and was judiciously executed, not by the formation of new regiments but by raising the strength of existing corps to a respectable figure.[19] Until this increase was made, said Lord Townsend in the House of Lords in the following year, it was impossible to collect four thousand men without leaving the King, the capital, and the fortified places defenceless.[20]

Having secured his eighteen thousand men, Walpole resolved that in future this number should form the regular strength for the British Establishment. In 1727 the menace of a war with Spain brought about the addition of eight thousand men, but in 1730 the former establishment was resumed and regularly voted year after year until the outbreak of the Spanish War in 1739. Year after year, of course, the same factious motives for reduction were put forward and the same futile arguments repeated for the hundredth time. "Slavery under the guise of an army for protection of our liberties" was one favourite phrase, while the valour of the untrained Briton was the theme of many an orator. Men who, like Sir William Yonge and William Pulteney, had held the office of Secretary-at-War, were, when in opposition, as loud as the loudest and as foolish as the most foolish in such displays. "I hope, sir," said the former in 1732, "that we have men enough in Great Britain who have resolution enough to defend themselves against any invasion whatever, though there were not so much as one red-coat in the whole kingdom." On the side of the Government the counter arguments were drawn from an excellent source, namely, from the disastrous results of wholesale disbandment after the Peace of Ryswick. The establishment was, in fact, far too small. It would have been impossible (to use Walpole's own words) even after several weeks' time to mass five thousand men at any one point to meet invasion, without stripping the capital of its defences and leaving it at the mercy of open and secret enemies.

Foiled in its attempts to reduce the numbers of the Army, the Opposition sought to weaken it by interference with its administration and discipline, for which mischief the discussion of the Mutiny Act gave annual opportunity. Here again it was Walpole who set the evil example. He it was who maintained that the Irish Establishment must be counted as part of the standing Army, who insinuated that the British regiments, with their enormous preponderance of officers as compared with men, were potentially far stronger than they seemed to be, who encouraged the Commons to dictate to the military authorities the proportion that should be observed between horse, foot, and dragoons.[21] He too it was who imperilled the passing of the Mutiny Act by advancing the old commonplace that a court-martial in time of peace was unknown to English law, and that mutiny and desertion should be punished by the civil magistrate. He it was once more who blamed the ministry for sending the fleet to the Mediterranean instead of keeping it at home to guard the coast, and gave his authority to the false idea that the function of a British fleet in war is to lie at anchor in British ports. Such were the aberrations of a conscience which fell blind directly it moved outside the circle of office.

The Opposition was not slow to take advantage of such powerful advocacy, but fortunately with no very evil results. An address to the King was carried, praying that all vacancies, except in the regiments of Guards, should be filled up by appointment of officers on the list of half-pay. The King willingly acceded, for indeed he had already anticipated the request; and this rule was conscientiously adhered to, both by him and by his successor. It made for economy, no doubt, but it also weakened what then counted as the most efficient form of military reserve; and the result was that officers were forbidden to resign their commissions, being allowed to retire on half-pay only, so that their services might still be at command.[22] The Articles of War were also sent down to the Commons, and may still be read in their journals. [23] It must suffice here to say that they made careful provision for the trial of all but strictly military crimes by the civil power. Here, however, was a new precedent for allowing Parliament a voice not only in the broad principles, but in the details of discipline.

The Opposition in both Houses did not at once take advantage of this innovation, but confined itself to discourses on the inutility and danger of a Mutiny Act at large. It was not surprising that the ignominious Robert Harley, Earl of Oxford, should have declaimed against the Act, but it was a sad revelation of factious feeling to find an old colonel, Lord Strafford, declaring that the country got on very well without it in King William's time. Nor must it be thought that, because the Act was ultimately passed every year, no inconvenience resulted from the obstruction in Parliament. On at least one occasion it was not renewed in sufficient time. The courts-martial held after its expiration were therefore invalid, and as prisoners could not be tried twice for the same offence, a number of them escaped scot-free.[24] It was not until 1726 that the attacks upon the measure began to subside, and even then the Government was afraid to introduce necessary amendments, lest by calling attention to the Act it should blow the dull embers of hostility anew into flame.[25]

The next attempted encroachment of Parliament was of a more dangerous nature, though it was more than a little excused by extreme provocation. In the heat of resentment against the opposition to his favourite scheme of an Excise Bill, Walpole in 1733 persuaded the King not only to dismiss his opponents from their places about the court, but to deprive the Duke of Bolton and Lord Cobham, Colonels of the King's Dragoon Guards and of the Blues, and Cornet William Pitt of the King's Dragoon Guards[26] of their commissions. This was to inflict the severest of military punishments short of death for a political disobligation, and was justly seized upon by the Opposition as a monstrous abuse. Lord Morpeth accordingly brought forward a motion in the Commons to make officers of the rank of lieutenant-colonel or above it irremovable except by sentence of court-martial or upon address of either House. The issue thus raised was direct, since by the Articles of War no officer could be dismissed except by Royal Order or sentence of a general court-martial. The debate was very ingenious on both sides, but the motion was lost without a division. The most remarkable speech was that of General Wade, who opposed Lord Morpeth on the ground that he had the greatest difficulty in collecting officers for a court-martial, and that they would be still more negligent if they could be dismissed only by sentence of their fellows. "In short, sir," he said, in words of significant warning, "the discipline of our army is already in a very bad way, and, in effect, this alteration will only make it worse."

The study of the mingling of political and military influence on the Army will enlighten us as to the cause of this indiscipline. In the first place, it will be noticed that there was no Commander-in-Chief. Lord Cadogan had succeeded Marlborough as captain-general, but even Marlborough had been powerless since his restoration, and he was not in the modern sense of the word a commander-in-chief. The result was that the whole of the authority attached to the office fell into the hands of the Secretary-at-War. That functionary still received as heretofore a military commission, and was nominally a mere secretary, not a minister nor secretary-of-state; and early in the reign he took the opportunity in the person of William Pulteney to repudiate anything approaching to a minister's responsibility.[27] So far as any one was answerable for the Army, it was that secretary-of-state whose duties were later apportioned to the Home Office; and hence we find the Secretary-at-War, though really in control of the whole Army, sending daily requests to the Secretary-of-State for the preparation of commissions,[28] since he himself in theory could sign documents not as the King's adviser, but only as his clerk. As a mere matter of routine this arrangement was most inconvenient, but this would have signified little had it not also been dangerous.[29]

Peculiar circumstances, now long obsolete, gave this irresponsible secretary peculiar powers. In the first place, it must be remembered that as yet barracks were almost unknown. There were, it is true, barracks at the Tower, at the Savoy, at Hull, and at Edinburgh, wherein there was accommodation for the half or even the whole of a battalion; and there was also a barrack at every garrisoned town capable of holding at least the handful of men who were supposed to keep the guns in order. But for the most part the Army was scattered all over the country in minute detachments,[30] for inns were the only quarters permitted by the Mutiny Act, and the number of those inns was necessarily limited. In Ireland the paucity of ale-houses had led comparatively early to the construction of barracks, with great comfort alike to the soldiers and to the population, but in England the very name of barrack was anathema. [31] It was in vain that military men pointed to the sister island and urged that Great Britain too might have barracks. The Government was afraid to ask for them, and the opposition combated any hint of such an innovation, "that the people might be sensible of the fetters forged for them."[32]

The apportionment of quarters fell within the province of the Secretary-at-War; and it is obvious that whether the presence of soldiery were an advantage to a town or the reverse, the power to inflict it could usefully be turned to political ends. A frequent accusation was that troops were employed to intimidate the voters at elections; and indeed the newspapers, not very trustworthy on such points, assert that at the election at Coventry in 1722 the foot-soldiers named two persons and the sheriff returned them.[33] Whether this be true or false it was not until 1735 that the Mutiny Act provided for the withdrawal of the troops to a distance of at least two miles from the polling-place during an election. But it was not so much for their interference with the free and independent voter as for the burden which they laid on the innkeeper that the soldiers were disliked. Whether this burden was really so grievous or not is beside the question; it was, at any rate, believed to be intolerable.[34] As early as in 1726 the King had asked for additional powers in the Mutiny Act to check the evasion by the civil authorities of their duty of quartering the men, and it was just after this date that municipalities began to abound in complaints.[35] The question was one of extreme difficulty for the Secretary-at-War, since the outcry of the civilians was balanced by a no less forcible counter-cry of officers. Municipalities seemed to think that no military exigency could excuse the violation of their comfort. Riots, for instance, were expected at Bath which, as a watering-place, was exempt from the duty of finding quarters for soldiers. The Secretary-at-War, though he did not shrink from sending troops thither to put down the rioters, looked forward to a disturbance between the civil and military elements as inevitable.[36] Southampton, again, cried out bitterly against the arrival within her boundaries of a whole regiment of dragoons. The colonel retorted that the regiment in question had been dispersed in single troops ever since its formation, and that this was actually his first opportunity of reducing it to order and discipline.[37] On some occasions the officers were certainly to blame, though they appear rarely to have misbehaved except under extreme provocation. Thus we find an officer, who had been denied a guard-room at Cirencester, solving the difficulty by the annexation of the town hall,[38] another still more arbitrary putting the Recorder of Chester under durance,[39] and a cornet of dragoons revenging himself upon an innkeeper by ordering eight men to march up and down before the inn for an hour every morning and evening, in order to disturb the guests and spoil the pavement.[40] On one occasion, indeed, we see two officers making the wealthiest clothier of Trowbridge drunk and enlisting him as a private.[41] These are specimens of the petty warfare which was waged between soldiers and civilians all over the kingdom, actions which called forth pathetic appeals from the Secretary-at-War to the offenders not to make the Army more unpopular than it already was. The warning was the more necessary, since, to use Pulteney's words, giddy insolent officers fancied they showed zeal for the Government by abusing those whom they considered to be of the contrary party. This, however, was but the natural result of making the Army a counter in the game of party politics. The only moderating influence was that of the King, who, if once convinced of any abuses committed by the soldiery was inexorably severe.[42]

Yet, on the whole, it should seem that soldiers were far less aggressive towards civilians than civilians towards soldiers. It is abundantly evident that in many places the civil population deliberately picked quarrels with troops in order to swell the clamour against the Army;[43] and officials in high local and municipal station, in their rancour against the red-coats, would stoop to lawlessness as flagrant as that of the mob. Lord Denbigh falsely accused the soldiers employed against the famous Black Gang of poachers, a sufficiently dangerous duty, of leaguing themselves with them for a share in the profits. [44] The Mayor of Penzance deliberately obstructed dragoons, who had been sent down to suppress smuggling, in the execution of their duty; the inference being that his worship was the most notorious smuggler on the coast.[45] The

Mayor of Bristol threw every obstacle, technical or captious, that he could devise, in the way of recruiting officers.[46] The Mayor of St. Albans, most disgraceful of all, took the Secretary-at-War's passes from certain discharged soldiers, whipped them through the streets, and gave them vagrant's passes instead, with the result that the unhappy men were stopped and shut up in gaol for deserters.[47] Redress for such injuries as these was not easily to be obtained; for of what profit could it be to these poor fellows to speak to them of their legal remedy? The soldiers were subject to a sterner and harder law than the civilians, and the civilians never hesitated to take advantage of it. They thought nothing of demanding that an officer should be cashiered unheard, solely on their accusation, and that too when redress lay open to them in the courts of law.[48] The difficulties of the Secretary-at-War in respect of these complaints are pathetically summarised by Craggs: "If I take no notice of such things I shall be petitioned against by twenty and thirty towns; if I inquire into them the officers think themselves discouraged; if I neglect them I shall be speeched every day in the House of Commons; if I give any countenance to them I shall disoblige the officers. My own opinion is that I can do no greater service to the Army than when, by taking notice of such few disorders as will only affect a few, I shall make the whole body more agreeable to the country and the clamour against them less popular in the House of Commons.[49]"

With traps deliberately laid to draw the troops into quarrels, with occasional experience of such brutality as has been above described, and with members of the House of Commons incessantly branding soldiers as lewd, profligate wretches, it is hardly surprising that there should have been bitter feeling between the Army and the civil population. But even more mischievous than this was the tendency of civilians, as of the House of Commons, to interfere with military discipline. It is tolerably clear, from the immense prevalence of desertion, and from the effusive letters of thanks written to magistrates who did their duty in arresting deserters, that the great body of these functionaries were in this respect thoroughly disloyal. Men could hardly respect their officers when they saw the civil authorities deliberately conniving at the most serious of military crimes. But this was by no means all. We find Members of Parliament interceding for the ringleaders of a mutiny,[50] for deserters,[51] for the discharge of soldiers, sometimes, but not always, with the offer to pay for a substitute;[52] and finally, as a climax, we see one honourable gentleman calmly removing his son from his regiment on private business without permission either asked or received.[53] And the Secretary-at-War liberates the mutineers, warns the court-martial to sentence the deserter to flogging instead of death, since otherwise interest will procure him a pardon, and begs General Wade, one of the few officers who had the discipline of the Army at heart, to overlook the absence of the member's son without leave.

A parallel could be found to all these examples at this day, it may be said. It is quite possible, for such ill weeds once sown are not easily eradicated, but the roots of the evil lay far deeper then than now in the overpowering supremacy of the Secretary-at-War. That official throughout this period continued to correspond directly with every grade of officer from the colonel to the corporal, whether to give orders, commendation, or rebuke, wholly ignoring the existence of superior officers as channels of communication and discipline.[54] His powers in other directions are indicated by the phrase, "Secretary-at-War's leave of absence,"[55] which was granted to subalterns, without the slightest reference to their colonels, to enable them to vote for the Government's candidate at by-elections.[56] We find him filling up a vacancy in a regiment without a word to the colonel,[57] instructing individual colonels of dragoons when they shall turn their horses out to grass, [58] and actually giving the parole to the guard during the King's absence from St. James's.[59] All these orders, relating to purely military matters, were issued, of course, by the King's authority, though not always in the King's name; and, indeed, as the volume of work increased, directions, criticisms, and reproofs tended more and more to be communicated by a clerk by order of the Secretary-at-War. In fact, the absolute control of the Army was usurped by a civilian official who, while arrogating the exercise of the royal authority, abjured every tittle of constitutional responsibility.

The result of such a system in such an age as that of Walpole may be easily imagined. All sense of military subordination among officers was lost. Their road to advancement lay, not by faithful performance of their duty for the improvement of their men and the satisfaction of their superiors, but by gaining, in what fashion soever, the goodwill of the Secretary-at-War,[60]—by granting this man his discharge, advancing that to the rank of corporal, pardoning a third the crime of desertion. "Our generals," said the Duke of Argyll in the House of Lords at the opening of the Spanish War, "are only colonels with a higher title, without power and without command … restrained by an arbitrary minister…. Our armies here know no other power but that of the Secretary-at-War, who directs all their motions and fills up all vacancies without opposition and without appeal."[61] Well might General Wade be believed when he asserted that the discipline of the Army was as bad as it could be.

CHAPTER II

From the political I turn to the purely military side of the Army's history. Treating first of the officers, it has, I think, been sufficiently shown that there were influences enough at work to demoralise them quite apart from any legacies of corruption that they might have inherited from the past. Against their indiscipline and dishonesty George the First seems to have set his face from the very beginning. He had a particular dislike to the system of purchasing and selling commissions. If (so ran his argument) an officer is unfit to serve from his own fault, he ought to be tried and cashiered, if he is rendered incapable by military service, he ought to retire on half-pay; and so firm was the King on this latter point that the Secretary-at-War dared not disobey him.[62] As early, therefore, as in June 1715 the King announced his intention of putting a stop to the practice, and as a first step forbade all sale of commissions except by officers who had purchased, and then only for the price that had originally been paid. One principal cause that prompted him to this decision appears to have been the exorbitant price demanded by colonels, on the plea that they had discharged regimental debts due for the clothing of the men, and suffered loss through the carelessness of agents.[63] It should seem, however, that as the rule applied only to regiments on the British and not to those on the Irish Establishment, the desired reforms were little promoted by this expedient. In 1717, therefore, the King referred the question to the Board of General Officers, with, however, a reservation in favour of sale for the benefit of wounded or superannuated officers, which could not but vitiate the entire scheme. He thought it better, therefore, to regulate that which he could not abolish, and in 1720 issued the first of those tariffs for the prices of commissions which continued to appear in the Queen's Regulations until 1870. At the same time he subjected purchase to certain conditions as to rank and length of service, adding somewhat later that the fact of purchase should carry with it no right to future sale.[64] Evidently ministers kept before his eyes not only the usefulness of the system from a political standpoint, since every officer was bound over in the price of his commission to good behaviour, but still more the impossibility of obtaining from Parliament a vote for ineffective men. They followed, in fact, the precept of Marlborough, and it is hard to say that they were not right.

Concurrently the King took steps, not always with great effect, to check the still existing abuse of false masters.[65] A more real service was the prevention of illegal deductions from the pay of the men, a vice from which hardly a regiment was wholly free, by the regulation of all stoppages by warrant.[66] As part of the same principle, he endeavoured also to ensure honesty towards the country and towards the soldiery in the matter of clothing. In fact, wherever the hand of King George the First can be traced in the administration of the Army, it is found working for integrity, economy, and discipline; and it is sufficiently evident that when he gave decided orders the very officials at the War Office knew better than to disregard them.

It is melancholy to record the fact that he was ill supported by the General Officers of the Army. The Board of Generals, to which the settlement of all purely military questions was supposed to be referred, seems to have been lazy and inert, requiring occasionally to be reminded of its duty in severe terms.[67] It may well be that this supineness was due to the general arrogation of military authority by civilians, but even so it remains unexcused. Colonels again appear to have been scandalously negligent and remiss in every respect; and it may have been as a warning to them that the King on one occasion dismissed seven of their number in one batch from his service.[68] But issue orders as he might, the King could never succeed, owing to the prevailing indiscipline, in making a certain number of officers ever go near their regiments at all. This habit of long and continued absence from duty, especially on colonial stations, is said to have troubled him much, and to have caused him greater uneasiness than any other abuse in the Army. It will be seen when we read of the opening of the Seven Years' War that he had all too good ground for misgiving. Yet the regimental officers must not be too hardly judged. In foreign garrisons, as shall presently be shown, they were exiles, neglected and uncared for; at home they were subject to incessant provocation, to malicious complaints, and in every quarter and at all times to the control of civilians. Lastly, though frequently called out in aid of the civil power, they had the fate of Captain Porteous before their eyes, and indeed took that lesson so speedily to heart that for want of their interposition the life of that unlucky man was sacrificed.[69]

When officers flagrantly neglected their duty and civilians deliberately fostered indiscipline, it is hardly astonishing that there should have been much misconduct among the men. It was natural, in the circumstances, that after the Peace of Utrecht the profession of the soldier should have fallen in England into disrepute. The greatest captain of his time, and one of the greatest of all time, had been rewarded for his transcendent services with exile and disgrace. Many officers had quitted the service in disgust, some of them abandoning even regiments which they loved as their own household. Wholesale and unscrupulous disbandment did not mend matters; and the survivors of that disbandment were confronted with the railings of the House of Commons, the malice of municipalities, the surliness of innkeepers and the insults of the populace. The most honest man in England had but to don the red coat to be dubbed a lewd profligate wretch. Small wonder that, clothed with such a character, ready made and unalterable, soldiers should have made no scruple of living their life in accordance with it.

The standard of the recruit, socially and morally, appears at the accession of George the First to have sunk to the level of the worst days of Elizabeth, of the Restoration, or of William the Third. It is abundantly evident that the ranks were filled in great measure by professional criminals, who passed from regiment to regiment, spreading everywhere the infection of discontent, debauchery, and insubordination. The noxious weeds of desertion and fraudulent enlistment flourished with amazing exuberance, and no severity of punishment had power to root them out. Week after week deserters were brought out into Hyde Park, tied up to the halberds, or simply to a tree, and flogged with hundreds of lashes. Every variety of scourging was tried that ingenuity could suggest. Sometimes the instrument employed was the cat, sometimes the rod, sometimes a twig, varied in the case of the cavalry by cloak-straps and stirrup-leathers. Sometimes the whole regiment did the part of executioners,[70] sometimes the guard, sometimes the drummers only. Sometimes the culprit ran the gantlope, accomplishing the unpleasant journey as quickly as he could, sometimes he walked it with a halberd's point before him, lest he should hurry unduly. Sometimes he took the whole of his punishment at one time and place, sometimes in instalments of a hundred lashes before the quarters of each detachment of his regiment, a practice akin to "flogging round the fleet."[71] Often he received two or three floggings in as quick succession as the state of his back would permit, the execution of the sentence being followed in many cases by "drumming out," with every circumstance of degradation.[72] The sentence of death was often pronounced by courts-martial and not unfrequently carried out, a deserter convicted for the third time rarely escaping with his life. Many a man was shot in Hyde Park during the twenty years of peace, and no opportunity was lost to enhance the terror of the penalty, the firing party sometimes consisting solely of fellow-deserters, who were spared in consideration of the warning given by the ghastly body which their own bullets had pierced.[73]

The newspapers record such matters with little ceremony, dwelling with greater relish on incidents of the cart's tail, of the pillory, or of Tyburn. The picketing of a soldier was indeed for a time a sufficient novelty to attract crowds,[74] but the interest in the process appears to have been short-lived. People were not squeamish in those days, and men would lay a wager to receive so many hundred lashes without flinching, as calmly as if it were to run so many miles or drink so many pots of ale. It is, however, noteworthy that both of the first of the Guelphic kings were prone to lighten the sentences of courts-martial, constantly reducing the number of lashes and remitting the penalty of death. Whether this was due to policy or humanity it is a little difficult to determine, for the populace certainly sympathised with deserters, and would help to rescue them, while there were "malicious persons" who were glad to denounce the severity of military punishments as a reproach against the Government.[75] I am, however, inclined to believe that both kings were inspired by the higher of the two motives, and should receive due honour for the same. The like, I believe, can hardly be said of the malicious persons above named, considering that the House of Commons had the scandalous evils of the London prisons before it in 1729, but left the whole work of reform to be done by John Howard in 1774.

The consequences of filling the ranks with rogues, together with the evils of indiscipline and neglect, did not end with desertion and fraudulent enlistment. That soldiers in their private quarrels should have fought desperately, wounding and killing each other on the slightest provocation, is nothing remarkable, for such encounters were common in the poorer classes of the urban population. But the newspapers report a sufficient number of mishaps through the use of loaded instead of blank cartridges at drill, to show that such occurrences were not wholly accidental. Again, we find a corps so much favoured as the First Troop of Horse Grenadier Guards breaking into open mutiny, because one of their number was sentenced to the picket.[76] On one very scandalous occasion the officers in command of the Prince of Wales's guard were so careless as to allow the troopers to get drunk when actually in attendance on His Royal Highness. The guard was turned out, and after some delay three troopers appeared who, though egregiously tipsy, were able to stagger to their places and stand more or less firmly on their legs. "This," we read, "the Prince complained of as shameful, as well he might"; but at this distance of time the reader, with the self-important figure of the prince who became King George the Second before him, will have no eye except for what was probably the most ludicrous spectacle ever witnessed at the Horse Guards.[77] But the climax of scandal was reached when a burglary was actually committed in Kensington Palace, and when, on the calling of the roll of the guard, but two men were found to be present, the rest being engaged apparently in rendering assistance to the burglars.[78] Certainly the soldiers of some regiments did their best to merit the bad name which was attached impartially to all who wore the red coat.

It may be asked why the system of enlistment for three years, which had produced such excellent results in Queen Anne's time, should have been abandoned. The reply, judging from the arguments of a later time, is that there was apprehension lest men should pass through the ranks of the British Army to strengthen those of the Pretender. There are signs that a reintroduction of the system was talked of in 1731, and was received by at least one observer with joy at the prospect of converting the whole nation into a sort of militia, [79] but I can find no official trace of such a revival. If it be asked how the Army survived a period of such discouragement and distress at all, the answer, I cannot doubt, is that it was saved, as it has often been saved, by the spirit, the pride, and the self-respect of individual regiments. There were always officers who worked hard and conscientiously for the credit of their own corps, and always men who were proud to take service with them and help them to maintain it. After the Peace of Utrecht, as at the present day, the War Office did its best to subvert regimental feeling by a return to the practice, expressly condemned by Marlborough, of strengthening the weaker corps by drafts from the stronger, but then as now regimental traditions preserved the War Office from the consequences of its own incapacity, and the Army from total dissolution.

So much for purely British affairs: but the British Empire, then as now, was not bounded by the shores of the British Isles, and it is necessary to examine next the broader question of Imperial defence. As the reader will have gathered in the course of my narrative, the system of home defence, up to the birth of the New Model and beyond it, had, apart from the fleet, been always the same. A few gunners and a few weak independent companies were maintained rather as caretakers than as defenders of the fortified places; in the event of an invasion there was the militia; while in case of an expedition beyond sea, a special force was raised, and disbanded as soon as its work was done. The standing Army gradually swept the independent garrison-companies out of existence, though there were still a few at Hampton Court, Windsor, and one or two similar places in the last year of King William the Third; but as has already been seen, the standing Army voted by Parliament just sufficed to furnish garrisons for the most important British fortresses and no more. Practically, therefore, the new system differed little from the old: if England were called upon to fight an enemy outside her own borders she must still raise a new army before she could send a man beyond sea. The only difference was that there were sufficient skeleton regiments, with their officers complete, to absorb several thousand men.

In our possessions abroad the old English system was followed exactly. British colonies were expected to raise their own militia and to provide for their own defence, as though each one of them had been an England in herself; and they fulfilled that expectation with a readiness which in those days seems astonishing. In the case of the American colonies, and in particular of the northern provinces, the problem of forming a national militia presented little difficulty; for theirs was a country where the white population could increase and multiply, and where white children could grow up to a vigorous manhood. The reader will shortly be able to judge the American militia by test of active service. But in the tropical islands of the West Indies, and to some extent in the southern provinces of Virginia and Carolina, the conditions were different. There the white man could not thrive and rear a healthy progeny, while a horde of negro slaves, sound, strong, and prolific, made an element of danger which was only kept in awe by systematic intimidation of almost incredible severity.[80]

Failing the natural increase of a white population, the ranks of the militia in the West Indies were kept full by continual exportation of white "servants" from England, that is to say, of men, women, and children saved from the gaol or the gallows, plucked naked and starving out of the gutter, trepanned by scoundrelly crimps, or kidnapped bodily in the streets and spirited, as the phrase went, across the Atlantic. From the earliest days of English colonisation the seeds to be sown in the great continent of the West had been gathered from the weeds that grow by the roadside. In 1610 three hundred disorderly persons were sent to Virginia, in 1617 and 1618 a cargo of poor and impressed emigrants, in 1620 "a parcel of poor and naughty children." New England, with higher ideals and a deeper insight than her sisters, resolved to accept only youths untainted by vice, but even so did not escape an infusion of the very scum of the earth.[81] An enlightened Frenchman did indeed formulate a scheme for recruiting old soldiers as emigrants for Virginia, but for the most part the white servants were drawn almost exclusively from the unprofitable classes.

The Civil War, the conquest of Ireland, the subdual of Scotland, and the crushing of royalism introduced a new element into the exported white servants. Irish men and Irish girls, grouped under the generic name of Tories, were shipped off to the West Indies by hundreds and even thousands.[82] English and Scottish prisoners of war, the vanquished of Dunbar and of Worcester among them, followed the Irish; and, finally, all ranks of the Royalists who dashed themselves in vain against the iron will of the Protector, many of them men of birth and high character, were, in the phrase of the day, Barbadosed. After the Restoration the supply of white servants, though swelled for a moment by the rebellion of Monmouth and by the innocent victims of Jeffreys, reverted to its dependence on the gaol, the crimp, and the "spirit." Transportation, though not long obsolete, has been well-nigh forgotten as a means of penal discipline, and quite forgotten as the first foundation of our system of colonial defence.

The white servants might, in the majority of cases, have been termed white slaves. They were frequently sold for money at so much a head without the least concealment, and were granted away in scores both by Oliver Cromwell and by James the Second as a means of profit and reward to good servants or to favourites. The practice was thoroughly recognised; and not a voice, except that of the younger Vane, was ever raised against the principle.
[83] Theoretically the white servants were bound apprentices for a term of years, rarely exceeding ten, at the close of which they received their freedom with, as a rule, a grant of Crown-land to encourage them to settlement.[84] During their period of servitude they were obliged to serve in the ranks of the colonial militia, not as free men, but as the subjects of their masters. Every planter was bound by law to furnish his quota of men, and old colonial muster-rolls frequently consist only of a list of masters, with a figure showing the number of servants to be supplied by each of them, not unlike the provincial muster-rolls of Queen Elizabeth's day in England. Having furnished their men to the ranks, the masters took their places at their head, in such numbers as were required, as their officers.

Three causes conspired to clothe the colonial militia with an efficiency unknown to the militia of England,—the presence of powerful neighbours, native or European; the knowledge that little help was to be expected from the mother country; and, in the tropics, the eternal dread of a rising of the negroes. Barbados, an island no larger than the Isle of Wight, could at the close of King Charles the Second's reign show six regiments of foot and two of horse, or a total of six thousand men; while Jamaica, a less fortunate island and a full generation later in settlement, produced in the same year seven regiments of four thousand men. Jamaica, it may be observed, owing to the presence of wild tribes of runaway slaves called Maroons, lived in more than ordinary terror of a servile war, and therefore kept her militia up to a high standard of efficiency. The reader should take note, in passing, of these Maroons, for we shall meet with them again at a very critical time. Even so, colonies frequently observed the true English spirit of apathy.[85] The main point, however, is that each colony, tropical or temperate, made provision for its own defence in respect of trained men and of fortification. Magazines were replenished partly by local laws, which compelled all vessels trading regularly from England to pay dues of gunpowder in proportion to their tonnage; the mother country making frequent grants of guns and of other stores from the depots of the Ordnance in England, and occasionally doling out even a small subvention of money. As a rule, moreover, the Crown was careful to appoint men of some military experience to be governors, in order that the local forces might not want a competent commander; and it is noteworthy, as a curious survival of old military traditions, that the civilian who performs the functions of sheriff in the West Indian Islands still bears, in a great many cases, the title of provost-marshal.

But even in the days of Charles the Second this primitive method of colonial defence showed signs of breaking down. At St. Kitts, which island was shared by the French and English until the Peace of Utrecht, the French kept a small permanent garrison. The English were of course bound to do likewise, and accordingly two independent companies of red-coats were stationed there at the cost of the Crown—stationed, not maintained, for they were left at first without pay, clothing, or attention of any kind from home, for whole years together.[86] In times of emergency such companies were quartered also in other colonies, such as Jamaica and Virginia, but these were never retained for longer than could be helped, the colony receiving the option of maintaining them at its own expense or of dispensing with them altogether. As the men were generally mutinous for want of pay, they sometimes proved to be an element of danger rather than of security.[87] Where settlements were granted out by charter to companies or to proprietors, the burden of defence of course fell on them, and was almost invariably borne by a local militia. There were, however, exceptions, notably the East Indian and African Companies, which, as they concerned themselves not with colonisation, but solely with trade, will be more conveniently discussed elsewhere. New York, from its supreme importance as a commercial and strategic station, was provided by its proprietor, James, Duke of York,[88] with two regular independent companies of English.

Time went on, and the system of defence by transportation became more and more unstable. White men, chafing against servitude, ran away from the West Indian Islands by scores to join the pirates that swarmed in the Caribbean Seas. The long war from 1689 to 1714 finally cut off the supply of white servants altogether for a time, every possible recruit having been seized by the press-gang or by the parish constable to serve in the regular army or navy. At the accession of King William the only British garrisons in the colonies were one company at the Leeward Islands and two at New York; by 1692 the West Indies alone had one complete regiment[89] and four independent companies of red-coats. At the accession of Queen Anne the independent companies for a time disappeared from the West Indies, and gave place to regular regiments of the Line, which have furnished the garrison ever since.[90] Elsewhere, however, the old principle still held its own. In 1695 two companies at New York were increased to four, and in 1696 another company took charge of Bermuda and Newfoundland. The close of the War of the Spanish Succession found England in exclusive possession of Newfoundland,

Nova Scotia, Minorca, and Gibraltar, all of them requiring permanent garrisons, and not one with the means of providing a militia of its own.

A situation so novel called for an entirely new departure in English military policy, but no one appears to have perceived any necessity for the same, possibly from the conviction that, however clearly a soldier's eye might see, the eyes of the country and of the House of Commons would certainly be blinded. The authorities, therefore, held fast to the tradition of the Tudors, that the garrison of a strong place must be irremovably attached to it. Nova Scotia and Newfoundland required special attention, and were accordingly furnished with four independent companies apiece, which in 1717 were merged, by some brilliant inspiration at headquarters, into a single regiment of ridiculous weakness, now living in our midst as the Fortieth Foot. The Leeward Islands having received their regiment of the Line during the war, were allowed to keep it during the peace, on condition of providing barracks and extra pay for all ranks; but a colonial garrison, even though it were a regiment of the Line, was still a garrison, and therefore irremovable; and so it came to pass that the Thirty-eighth Foot remained in the Leeward Islands unrelieved for sixty years. But meanwhile it was found indispensable to keep a small garrison also at Jamaica. The temptation to revert to the old system was irresistible, so two independent companies took charge of Port Royal.[91] Then Carolina was perceived to require defence, and in 1720 another independent company was sent there; then the Bahamas and Bermuda, which had hitherto shared a company between them, asked for a company apiece and received them; and at this strength the colonial garrisons remained until 1735. Then Jamaica was seen to be in serious peril from a rising of negroes, and everything pointed to the permanent quartering of a whole regiment in the Island; but still the old expedient was followed. Six independent companies were drafted from the regiments at Gibraltar, making with the two already in existence a total of eight independent companies; nor was it until 1743 that these were at last combined into Trelawny's regiment, or, to give it its modern name, the Forty-ninth Foot.

But meanwhile, in 1737-38, the needs of a new colony forced the War Office to provide yet another garrison for the defence of Georgia; and it was boldly resolved to form a whole regiment for that service and for that alone. Its colonel was the governor and founder of Georgia, General James Oglethorpe; and it was formed by the simple process of turning over the whole of the effective privates of the Twenty-fifth Foot to that estimable man. [92] This incident marks the furthest limit to which the principle of separating Colonial and Imperial service was pushed by the War Office. Another quarter of a century was to see, not the impressment of English soldiers for a colonial regiment, but the embodiment of colonists into an English, and a famous

English, regiment.

But it was not in respect of the localisation of foreign garrisons only that the War Office showed itself hide-bound by ancient tradition. The authorities were amazingly slow to recognise that the conditions of service at Portsmouth and Annapolis, at Hull and at Gibraltar, were not and could not be identical. In a previous chapter I hinted at the neglect which drove the garrison of Gibraltar to burn their huts for fuel. The experience of twenty years seems to have taught the War Office but little, for in 1730 the men were still without a roof over their heads and suffering terribly from exposure and from dysentery. [93] In Minorca the quarters of the troops were equally bad, the fortifications were in as ill condition as the quarters, and the unhappy soldiers begged in vain for new bedding to replace that which they had fairly worn out by ten years of service.[94] At Annapolis and Placentia the barracks were falling down; and from Bermuda came complaints in 1739 that no stores of any kind had been received since 1696. In New York the tale of misery and hardship almost passes belief. There, men on the frontier-guards marched to their posts knee-deep in snow and lay down in their clothes, for want of bedding, when relieved: the sergeant having orders to wake them from time to time, lest they should be frozen to death in the guard-room. Yet the officers begged in vain for the supply of their wants. The Office of Ordnance, in abject fear of swelling the sum of its estimates, pleaded that Parliament had made no provision for such services: and the result was that forty-nine men out of two weak companies perished in a single winter for lack of a blanket to cover them.[95]

But the story of helplessness and neglect does not end here. The War Office appears to have imagined that all the world over there were, as in England, not only alehouses, wherein troops could be quartered, but landlords who would provide them, according to the tariff of the Mutiny Act, with food, fire, and candle. It would seem not to have occurred to it that supplies in an isolated barren fortress like Gibraltar must of necessity be limited; nor was it until 1720 that, at the King's instance, it was ordered that Gibraltar should be provided always with victuals for two months in advance. The feeding of the garrisons there, in Minorca, in Nova Scotia and in Newfoundland was entrusted to contractors, but in the contracts the most obvious necessities were overlooked. Thus, though Minorca was supplied with brandy, oil, bread, salt, and tobacco, the item of meat was entirely omitted, and it was actually necessary for the governor to explain that the five articles above enumerated were insufficient for the nourishment of the British soldier.[96] At Annapolis —loneliest, dullest, and dreariest of quarters—the soldiers were expected to content themselves with water for their only beverage. Not unnaturally they mutinied; and their officers were fain to purchase molasses at their own expense and brew them beer.[97] Deadly though the climate of the West Indies then was, men could think themselves fortunate to be quartered there, for Jamaica and the Leeward Islands showed far more generosity to the British soldier than the British Parliament.[98]

The greatest hardship of service on foreign stations remains yet to be noticed, namely, the absence of any system of periodic reliefs. Englishmen did not accept exile so readily in those days as in these. Ordinary soldiers did not conceive that they enlisted for service in foreign garrisons; that duty was for men especially recruited, as they thought; and they constantly deserted in sheer despair of ever returning home.[99] A distinguished officer, the Duke of Argyll, went the length of saying that a long term of duty at Mahon was equivalent to a punishment, and that his only surprise was that the troops had not mutinied both at Minorca and Gibraltar.[100] The Board of General Officers urged the question at least once upon the King,[101] but without result. A still more cruel matter was that the War Office refused to grant to invalided soldiers a free passage home. Even in these days of sanitary science the amount of sickness among our troops in the tropics is sufficiently great: the reader may calculate for himself what it must have been when malarial fever, yellow fever, and smallpox[102] were allowed to run their course unchecked. But the only answer of the War Office to an appeal from the Governor of Jamaica for the return of invalided soldiers was the usual plea of no funds, urged with something more than the usual warmth of indignation.

Such petty economies, of course, cost the country incredibly dear. The hardships of foreign service led not only to desertion but to extreme difficulty in obtaining recruits for the independent companies abroad. To overcome these obstacles three separate devices were employed. The first was to offer large bounties, which from between 1720 and 1739 grew swiftly from thirty shillings to seventy-five.[103] This proving very costly, recourse was made to the mischievous practice of drafting men from regiments at home, thereby transferring the expense from the state to the regimental officers, who were compelled to pay as much as five pounds a head for the men drafted to them.[104] The system being simple was soon carried to outrageous lengths. The bounty failing to attract recruits for Carolina, a draft of pensioners was sent out in their place, and the same principle was shortly after extended to Gibraltar.[105] Thus not only was cruel hardship inflicted on the pensioners, but the one reserve which England possessed for her defence in time of emergency was frittered away in service abroad. Finally, on the rare occasions when a relief was sent to the Mediterranean garrisons, the relieving regiment was generally so much weakened by desertion before its departure that it was necessary to turn over to it bodily the two junior companies of the relieved, and to call for volunteers from the remaining companies. If the requisite men could not be obtained by these means, the orders were to select as many more as were required by lot.[106] The inevitable result was that the garrison was composed mainly of discontented men, ready to desert at the first opportunity, with an infusion of lazy, cunning old soldiers, who had contracted an attachment to the wine or the women of the country, and were content to pass the rest of their lives in chronic insobriety.

The difficulties of the whole situation became so pressing that the Board of General Officers advised the King to make transportation to service abroad an alternative penalty for desertion, and to show no mercy in inflicting it.[107] The King declined, nor can it be denied that there was wisdom in his decision; but it is none the less certain that abundance of deserters received pardon on condition of enlisting in corps that were quartered in the colonies, and particularly in Carolina.[108] The principle of sending off bad characters to wear their red coats on the other side of the Atlantic received final sanction in 1742, when over a hundred mutinous deserters from a Highland regiment were divided between the Mediterranean garrisons, the West Indies, and Carolina.[109] Such a windfall did not come everyday.

It is now easy to see why foreign service should have been no less unpopular with officers than with men. Their soldiers were discontented and miserable through evils which they had no power to remedy; their regiments were filled with the worst characters, for whom they were obliged to pay an extravagant price; no better provision was made for their comfort than for that of the men: and the life was insufferably dull and monotonous. Nothing, however, can excuse the systematic evasion of duty which was so common among them, still less the hopeless indiscipline which nullified the King's repeated orders for their attendance. Altogether it is clear that England was not yet the least awake to the fact that she had entered upon possession of an Empire, and that an Empire must be defended by the sword. There was no definite scheme of defence, no attempt to realise the extent of the country's military resources, no effort to discover how they might be turned to most effective account. To live from hand to mouth, from budget to budget, was sufficient for Robert Walpole, while the King, if ever he looked beyond the sea, gazed eastward and not westward, and then not at India, but at Hanover.

It remains for me to mention such improvements as were effected in the Army during the period under review, which, though they were few, were none the less far-reaching. The first was the permanent organisation of the Artillery. As has been seen, the Commonwealth latterly maintained a field-train ready and equipped for the field, while William the Third improved upon this by distributing the train into two companies. In the chaos which followed upon the Peace of Utrecht this organisation was suffered to collapse, and the Board of Ordnance, when ordered to fit out a train in 1715, was absolutely unable to do so. It was therefore determined to revert to the system of King William by the establishment of four permanent companies of Artillery, which was duly ordained by Royal Warrant of 26th May 1716. Two companies only were created at first, with a total strength of nine officers and ninety-two men, but the number was increased to four companies in 1727, with the title of the Royal Regiment of Artillery, a designation which still covers about a hundred companies and over a hundred batteries of garrison, field, and horse artillery. The first colonel was a foreigner, Albert Borgard by name, who had entered the British service in time to fight at Steenkirk, and had afterwards served through the War of the Succession in Spain, distinguished more than once by grievous wounds and always by excellent and honourable service. We shall see that the career of the corps has been like unto that of its first colonel.[110]

A second novelty in the Army during this period has enwoven itself even more closely into its traditions. In 1725 General Wade was sent up to Scotland armed with instructions for the disarmament of the Highland clans, and with statutory powers to send all clansmen that did not surrender their arms to serve the King in a red coat beyond sea. Whether any recruits were obtained by those means is uncertain, for Wade exercised his authority in a judicious and tactful spirit, and earned immortality by employing his troops in the construction of roads, whereby he not only kept them from the idleness which begets indiscipline, but endowed the country with a lasting benefit. To enforce the disarmament, overawe the disaffected, and preserve order among the clans, there were raised in that same year four companies of Highlanders, under Captains Lord Lovat, Sir Duncan Campbell, John Campbell, and George Grant.[111] There had been independent companies for service in the Highlands since 1710, but these had been disbanded in 1717, though the officers were subsequently reappointed. The new companies wore their national dress, which, as it consisted principally of black, blue, and green tartan, presented a sombre appearance, and gained for its wearers the name of the Black Watch.[112]

The ranks were filled with a number of young men of respectable families who had joined the corps to gain the Highlanders' beloved privilege of bearing arms, and many were wealthy enough to keep their gillies to attend them in their quarters and to carry their arms and kits on the march. The privates were taken indiscriminately from all the clans, but the officers from the Whig clans only. The service seems to have been popular, for the companies, though increased almost immediately from four to six, were within eighteen months raised to a strength of one hundred and ten men each.

The fact that within the same period they had worn out their arms by sheer hard work proves sufficiently that their life was no easy one. At length, on the 7th of November 1739, orders were issued for the raising of four additional companies, and for the formation of a Highland regiment, seven hundred and eighty strong. The colonel appointed to command them, John, Earl of Crawford, was suffering at the time from a wound received in battle against the Turks five months before at Krotzka,[113] and was therefore unable to take immediate charge of them. Finally, a few weeks later, a sergeant and a private[114] were brought down to London, the first kilted soldiers ever seen in the capital, and were duly exhibited to the King, presumably with satisfaction to his sartorial mind. Thus came into being the famous regiment which, ranking originally as the Forty-third of the Line, is still with us as the Forty-second Highlanders.[115]

For the rest, it must be noted that with the accession of a foreign dynasty the Army began early to show signs of subjection to foreign influence. In not a few directions the strict German precision of George the First worked decidedly for good. Before he had been on the throne two years he instituted a regular system of inspection of all regiments by General Officers,[116] and shortly after, observing that every corps used such methods of drill as happened to be preferred by the colonel, he ordered an uniform exercise to be drawn up for all.[117] More curious, however, was his interference with the arming of the infantry, for while on the one hand he insisted that every man should carry a sword as well as a bayonet, a curious old-fashioned prejudice, [118] yet within two years he introduced the steel ramrod, which was the newest of new improvements.[119] This steel ramrod is emblematic of much, since it was the invention of a veteran who had fought among the Prussian troops throughout Marlborough's campaigns, Prince Leopold of Anhalt-Dessau, famous in Prussian history as the "Old Dessauer."

Perforce we must turn our eyes for a moment towards the military reforms which were going forward in Prussia under that half-demented, half-inspired monarch, King Frederick William. Of the really important lessons which the British learned from him and from his far greater son, it is not yet time to speak: for our present purpose it must be remarked, and remarked not wholly with a light heart, that he was the first great military tailor that sat on a throne. He was also, unfortunately, an admirable soldier into the bargain, and thus has led many monarchs into the delusion that the most important military manual is the book of patterns, and that a soldier is made not by training and discipline but by tape, goose, and shears. His influence soon made itself felt in England, for as early as 1718 we find Colonel Cosby of the Eighteenth Royal Irish insisting that every man of his regiment should wear ruffles at the sleeves and bosom of his shirt;[120] and three years later, when Frederick William visited England in person, the grenadiers of the Guards were bidden to let their whiskers grow, to do him honour on his arrival.[121] Thus dawned the era of powder, pigtail, and tight clothing.

With the accession of King George the Second the reign of the military tailor in England began in good earnest. George did not love his brother-in-law, Frederick William, but he envied him not a little the reputation of his army. He had little capacity for military duties beyond the sphere of a sergeant-major, though he had won his spurs gallantly enough at the head of a squadron at Oudenarde, but being ambitious of military distinction he threw himself with all the enthusiasm of a narrow nature into the pleasing excitement of dressing his army. Before he had been on the throne four months he announced his desire that every regiment should have "fixed clothing," and by a single edict swept away all lace from the buff belts of the cavalry.[122] In the following year the headdress of the Horse-Grenadiers was altered,[123] and in the next year again the Foot Guards were prohibited from wearing perukes except in case of sickness.[124] And so the process went on, barely interrupted even by war, until finally it culminated in an elaborate table of regulations as to colours, clothing, facings, and lace,[125] and, to the great good fortune of posterity, in the depiction of a private of almost every regiment in the Army.

In such trifles were the great lessons taught by Marlborough forgotten. The great Duke's mantle had descended on one man, but even if he had been suffered to wear it, the Secretary-at-War would not have heeded him the more. Until 1742 he remained obscure, and meanwhile the better known officers died fast. Cadogan, the Duke's successor, died in 1726, and was laid with his great chief in Henry the Seventh's chapel, not with military pomp, but, by his own express desire, with all possible privacy. It should seem that he shrank above all things from even the semblance of a share in his master's glory. Of the veterans who outlived him, Lord Orkney and the Duke of Argyll were made field-marshals in 1736, while Wade, the kindly administrator of the Highlands, and Lord Stair took their part, as shall be seen, in the next war. Beyond them no one knew whither to look for an English general. Some perhaps counted on little Prince William who, dressed as a corporal, was often to be seen drilling a miniature company of the Coldstream Guards,[126] not yet dreaming that he would one day be called the butcher of Culloden. None thought of looking into a little house at Westerham, in Kent, where Colonel Edward Wolfe, a veteran of Flanders, was educating his little son James, a remarkably ugly boy with a shock of red hair and a turned-up nose, who had been born to him in 1727. None guessed again that a natural genius for war lay in another boy two years older than Wolfe, who was the scourge of every orchard, the terror of every tradesman, and the ringleader of all mischief in and about Market Drayton, and who bore the name of Robert Clive. Yet these two, the one frail and delicate, the other an incorrigible scapegrace, were the instruments appointed to carry on the work begun by Cromwell and by Marlborough. Marvellous to relate there were still alive in 1731 two old men, the one a Royalist officer aged one hundred and eighteen, the other a Puritan soldier aged one hundred and eleven, who had fought at the battle of Edgehill and yet shared some few years of the world with Wolfe and Clive. They had seen Oliver Cromwell as a simple captain, and they lived to see William Pitt gazetted a cornet of horse.[127]

CHAPTER III

The long reign of Walpole and of peace had endured for full seventeen years. Session after session, through difficulty after difficulty, the minister had handled his charge with consummate dexterity, as a horse-breaker handles an unbroken colt; lunging or riding the nation round and round sometimes in a larger, sometimes in a smaller circle, but except in a circle never permitting it to move at all. It was a change, and doubtless a wholesome change, from the erratic course which England had pursued for the past century, but after a time it became wearisome. Conscious of health, vigour, and strength, the nation began to pant for a wider field and for a rider that would guide it on some more adventurous career. But though there was abundance of aspirants to the saddle it was no easy matter for them to unseat Walpole; their only chance was to rouse the dumb creature, which he had so cleverly mastered, to throw him. The terrors of a standing Army, notwithstanding persistent brandishing of the old flag and howling of the old cries, had ceased to terrify, and it was necessary to discover some excitement of a more formidable kind.

The first signs of coming trouble were seen in Parliament in the spring of 1738, when there was a great debate, culminating in an address of both Houses, respecting Spanish depredations in the South American seas. The newspapers thereupon did their utmost to make matters worse by furious attacks upon Spain. Into the merits of the question it is unnecessary to enter here. The grievances of the English against the Spaniards in respect of restrictions on trade and of the right of search, and of Spaniards against English for evasion of those restrictions, were at least half a century old; and it is sufficiently evident that both sides alike had good ground of complaint. The English, in fact, chafed less against the restrictions themselves than against the arbitrary and capricious fashion in which they were enforced, owing to the dishonesty and corruption of the Spanish authorities. It was a complaint, as early as in the reign of Charles the Second, that Spanish governors would encourage British vessels to violate the regulations for a time in order to make a sudden swoop on them for their own profit, when they had been enticed in sufficient numbers to make a remunerative prize. Altogether, it is only surprising that it should have needed fifty years, an unscrupulous Opposition, and a fable of Jenkins's ear to set the two nations fighting over the question of American trade.

1739.
Oct. $\frac{19}{30}$.

Walpole, for his part, strove his hardest to avert war, and even came to a convention with Spain as to the damages which she should pay for injuries inflicted on British ships; but this was not what the nation desired. The convention was furiously denounced in both Houses as a half-hearted measure, and by no man more vehemently than by William Pitt. The animosity against Spain was inflamed to the highest pitch; but amid all the clamour for war the Opposition did not fail to produce and to support the annual motion for the reduction of the Army.[128] The estimates provided only for a small increase of the garrisons in the West Indies, Minorca, and Gibraltar; yet this most obvious of precautions in the prospect of a rupture with Spain was opposed by the very men who were shrieking loudest for war. Walpole's unfailing dexterity, however, carried him triumphantly through the session; and though half a million was voted for the augmentation of the forces, he still hoped to prolong the years of peace, and with them of his own tenure of office. But meanwhile the proud spirit of Spain had taken offence at the invectives and insults of the self-styled patriots in the English Parliament; and when the plenipotentiaries met in pursuance of the convention to adjust the regulation of commerce between the two nations, the Spaniards refused to proceed with the business unless the right of search, the very point which had been denied in Parliament, were first admitted. Walpole had now to choose between resignation and war, and to his shame he chose war. The open declaration of hostilities was proclaimed in London on the 19th of October, amid the pealing of joy-bells from every steeple in the city. "They may ring their bells now," muttered Walpole, doubtless with memories of the War Office in Marlborough's day strong upon him, "they will be wringing their hands before long."

Nov. $\frac{15}{26}$.

Already, in the course of the summer, an augmentation of some five thousand men had been made to certain regiments of horse and foot both at home and in colonial garrisons.[129] Recruits offered themselves in such abundance that officers could pick their men, and the enthusiasm for the war spread to all parts of the kingdom.[130] Seven hundred men were enlisted in Edinburgh alone; and the Irish, attracted by the offer of a bounty, came over in numbers to take service, though only to be met by an order that, as papists, they should not be admitted.[131] The people were, in fact, intoxicated at the prospect of plundering New Spain. Not a man called to mind the expedition of Venables and Penn, nor thought of the thousands who started with them, big with expectation of gold told up in bags, and had never returned. In November the King opened Parliament, and, having announced the increase already made to the forces, declared his intention of raising several corps of marines, and left the Commons to debate upon the same. Then the old instinct of faction at once recovered strength. Though war had actually been declared, the proposal was severely criticised as an insidious augmentation of the standing Army. Pulteney declined to distinguish between marines and land-forces, as if the point could at the moment have been of the slightest importance; several members expressed their hope that the marines would at least be drafted from the standing Army, and an address to the King to that effect actually found ninety-five supporters. Finally, old Shippen, for the twenty-third time, brought forward his annual motion for the reduction of the Army. These were the men who had brought on the war, and this was the way in which they prepared to support it.[132] When it is remembered that these creatures claimed the name of patriots, it is hardly surprising that patriotism should have found a definition as the last refuge of a scoundrel.

| Nov. 21 |
| Dec. 2. |
| 1740. |
| March $\frac{3}{14}$. |

However, orders were issued for the formation of six regiments of marines,[133] under Colonels Wolfe, Robinson, Lowther, Wynyard, Douglas, and Moreton, with a strength of eleven hundred men apiece; and either in deference to the House of Commons, or possibly for greater despatch, these corps were actually filled mainly by drafts from existing regiments, as the event was to prove, with disastrous results.[134] Meanwhile Admiral Vernon's squadron in the West Indies attacked Porto Bello, and having blown up the defences returned triumphant to Jamaica. This piece of work was undoubtedly well done, but the exploit was magnified in England as though Vernon had captured the whole of Spanish America. When a nation goes to war with a light heart it must needs exaggerate the most trifling success; and Vernon became the hero not only of the hour but of the whole war, once again with disastrous results. Elated by his good fortune, the Admiral three months later made an attempt on Carthagena, but found that the capture of the port was a task beyond the strength of his squadron, or indeed of any squadron without the assistance of seven or eight thousand troops. His report, however, indicated the spot where a blow might be struck in earnest at Spain, and to his influence must be ascribed the choice of the field of operations.

The Government now girded itself for a serious effort against New Spain, and decided, like Cromwell, that New as well as Old England should take a share in the conflict. Directions were accordingly issued for the raising of four battalions of Americans under the colonelcy of Deputy-Governor Spotswood of Virginia; the recruiting sergeant was set to work on both sides of the Atlantic; and all through the summer preparations went forward for a secret expedition. It was hoped that it would sail for its destination at the end of June or the beginning of July, that being declared by experts to be the latest possible date at which operations could be conducted with any hope of success.[135] In April the regiments appointed for the service began to assemble in the Isle of Wight, and all was bustle and activity. There was not a little difficulty with these troops, for the new regiments of marines were remarkable neither for drill nor discipline; but by the energy of Brigadier-General Wentworth they were licked into shape with creditable rapidity. Lord Cathcart, who had been selected for the chief command, was indefatigably vigilant, and indeed he had good cause, for the ignorance and stupidity of the authorities with whom he had to deal was almost incredible. Thus, for instance, the War Office, having depleted regiments of the Line to make up the new corps of marines, did not hesitate to order one of the regiments so depleted upon active service; and Cathcart, bound as he knew to a deadly climate in the heart of the tropics, found that part of the force allotted to him consisted of boys who had not strength to handle their arms.[136] Such were the first-fruits of the cry of "No Standing Army."

Aug. $\frac{3}{14}$

By intense labour the military officers sifted out this unpromising material and turned the residue to the best account, struggling manfully and not unsuccessfully to have all ready for the expedition to start in July. Moreover, on the death of Colonel Spotswood, the intended second in command, Lord Cathcart begged that his place might be filled by Brigadier Wentworth, as a reward for the diligence and the capacity which he had shown in the camp.[137] The request was duly granted, with very tragical consequences. At the same time, however, the General discovered that, although it was now late in July, the Admiral who was to escort his transports had no orders to sail, while his fleet was not even so much as manned.[138] None the less he pushed his preparations strenuously forward, and, choosing the anniversary of Blenheim as a day of good omen for the embarkation, put eight regiments of six thousand men on board ship.[139] Then came vexatious delays, due partly to foul winds, partly to official blundering. Three times the ships got under way, the men cheering loudly at the prospect of sailing at last, and three times the wind failed them or turned foul. Cathcart grew more and more anxious. The favourable season was slipping away fast. The men had been cooped up in the transports for six weeks and had consumed most of the victuals intended for the voyage. Scorbutic sickness was seriously prevalent, and there had already been sixty deaths. "Surely," wrote the General, "some fresh meat might be given to the troops"; but the authorities had given no thought to such matters. August passed away and September came, bringing with it the news that a Spanish fleet had put to sea, and that a French fleet also was about to sail from Brest. France had already manifested sympathy with Spain, as was natural from one Bourbon king to another, and the intentions of the ships from Brest might well be hostile. Such a contingency might have been foreseen, but it was not; so there was further delay while the British fleet was reinforced. Then, when the ships were ready, men could not be found to man them. Two old regiments of the Line, the Thirty-fourth and Thirty-sixth, were turned over to the fleet to make up its complement; but these were insufficient, and Cathcart was ordered to send six hundred of his marines also to the men-of-war. He obeyed, not without warning the Government that an infectious fever, which had already proved terribly fatal, was raging in the fleet; but his warning was not heeded, possibly in the pressure of business could not be heeded. So the days dragged on; the transports waited, and the men died. Cathcart's patience was strained almost beyond endurance. Apart from the trouble with army and fleet, an endless shower of vexations poured on him from Whitehall. His instructions were constantly altered, and no effort was made to keep his destination unknown. One statement which was communicated to him as an important secret had been the talk of all the coffee-houses in Portsmouth long before it reached him. The newspapers published details of every ship-load of arms and stores that was sent to the West Indies, and as a climax printed in full a proclamation which had been prepared for Cathcart to issue on his arrival in South America.[140] Such were the English ideas of organising victory.

| Oct. 24 |
| Nov. 4. |
| 1740, Dec. 23. |
| 1741, Jan. 3. |

At length, on the 4th of November, the fleet sailed, just four months too late, and after a very stormy passage, which scattered the ships in all directions, the bulk of the transports arrived at St. Rupert's Bay, Dominica, on the 3rd of January 1741. Already the force had suffered heavy losses. The fleet was very sickly, over one hundred soldiers had died, and worst of all, Lord Cathcart himself had been seized with dysentery and was also dead.[141] Wentworth assumed the command in his stead; and the fleet after a day or two proceeded to St. Kitts, where all the missing ships were found at anchor safe and sound. But among them too sickness had made sad havoc, and of the six hundred marines transferred despite Cathcart's warnings to the men-of-war, many were dead and few fit for duty. From thence the fleet sailed, as had been appointed, for Jamaica, where it found Vernon's squadron awaiting it in the harbour, and the American battalions, now regimented under the command of Colonel Gooch, in camp on the island. The Americans were in a very bad state. Their ranks had been filled without difficulty, but with bad material: they were guiltless of drill or discipline, and on arrival at Jamaica had at once become disorderly and mutinous. There was good excuse for their discontent, for the English Government, though it had made arrangements for the payment and victualling of the British troops, had made none whatever for the Americans, who were thus compelled to fall back on such meagre resources as Jamaica could provide.[142] Moreover, the Americans were even more sickly than the British, and had buried scores of men since their disembarkation. By the first returns sent home from Jamaica it appears that of the nine thousand soldiers who had started from England and America in October, seventeen officers and six hundred men had died before the end of the year, while fifteen hundred more were actually on the sick-list.[143]

| Feb. 24 |
| March 7. |

Still the survivors remained in good spirits. There was for the present all possible harmony between army and navy,[144] and the losses could to some extent be made good by embarking the four independent companies which lay in garrison in Jamaica. But meanwhile the French fleet was concentrated off the coast of Hispaniola, and until it should be dispersed the commanders dared not undertake any operations against the Spanish Main. It is true that France and England were not at open war; but this, as shall presently be seen, was no reason why the fleets and armies of the two nations should not fight each other. When, therefore, the fleet at last sailed from Jamaica on the 7th of March, Vernon was fully resolved to attack the French if he should fall in with them.[145] He was, however, relieved of any such responsibility. Sickness had driven the French fleet back from the Caribbean Sea to Brest, and the British were free to go whither they would. It was thereupon decided to attack Carthagena without delay, for though Cathcart's instructions gave Wentworth the option of first attempting Havana, yet the Cuban port was considered to be too well defended, whereas Carthagena would, it was hoped, fall an easy prey. The fact was that Vernon had set his heart on Carthagena, and he found little difficulty in carrying his point.

| March $\frac{4}{15}$ |

On the 15th of March, accordingly, the fleet anchored at Playa Grande, two leagues to windward of Carthagena, and the English commanders could judge of the work before them. The city of Carthagena lies at the head of an inland lake, which extends at its greatest length for some seven miles north and south. To this lake there are two entrances, of which the eastern, known from its narrowness as the Boca Chica or Little Mouth, alone was practicable for line-of-battle ships. The western side of the Boca Chica was defended by three forts—St. Jago and San Felipe at the entrance from the sea, and Fort Boca Chica, a far more formidable work, half way up the passage. On the eastern side a fascine-battery had been thrown up at the entrance, while another stronghold, Fort St. Joseph, sealed up the inner end. To force the Boca Chica so as to admit the fleet to the harbour was the first task to be accomplished by Wentworth and Vernon.

March $\frac{9}{20}$.
March $\frac{11}{22}$.

On the 20th of March a portion of the squadron, under Admiral Sir Chaloner Ogle, battered down the forts of St. Jago and San Felipe; three hundred grenadiers were successfully landed on the western shore of the Boca Chica; and on the 22nd the whole of the land-forces were disembarked excepting the Thirty-fourth, the Thirty-sixth, and the Americans, of which last, owing to their indiscipline, but three hundred were trusted ashore. From the moment of disembarkation Wentworth seems to have lost his head. He knew his profession by book, but he was wholly without experience. Though encamped on an island surrounded everywhere by at least a league of water, he lived in mortal terror of a surprise, and posted guards so numerous and so strong that he could hardly find men to relieve them. Vernon and Ogle watched him with amazement for two days, and then losing all patience sent him a letter, the first of a very remarkable series that was to pass between Admirals and General before Carthagena. "Push forward part of your force to Fort Boca Chica," they said in effect, "put the rest of your men under canvas, hasten your engineers to the siege of the fort, and choose a few picked men for your guards instead of harassing your whole army."[146] It was excellent if elementary advice, though hardly such as a General looks for from an Admiral.

March $\frac{12}{23}$.
March 22
April 2.

Wentworth, to do him justice, seems to have taken this counsel in good part, but the delay in opening the siege of Fort Boca Chica was not altogether his fault. There was but one engineer in the whole army who was the least competent to carry on a siege, and there seems to have been considerable difficulty, first in getting him to the scene of action at all, and secondly in making him work when he reached it.[147] Ground was broken at last on 23rd

March, but when the batteries had been built, there were so few efficient artillerymen with the army that Vernon's seamen were perforce borrowed to work the guns. Finally, on the 2nd of April Wentworth opened fire; and then it was discovered that by some mistake the camp had been pitched directly in the same straight line with the battery, so that every shot from Fort Boca Chica that flew over the British guns fell among the tents, killing and wounding over a hundred men on the first day. Nevertheless, with the help of a furious cannonade from some of the men-of-war, the guns of Fort Boca Chica were silenced, and then Vernon and Ogle began again to stir up Wentworth to action. "We hope," they wrote on the 3rd of April, "that you will order your troops to make a lodgment under Boca Chica to-night … the longer you delay, the harder your work will be." Wentworth hesitated, and nothing was done. "You ought to storm the fort to-night before the moon rises," they wrote again on the 4th. Wentworth still hesitated, and another day was lost. Then the naval officers became more peremptory. "Diffidence of your troops," they wrote, "can only discourage them. In our opinion you have quite men enough for the attack of so paltry a fort. You should have built another battery, for your men would be all the healthier for more work. Knowing the climate, we advise you to pursue more vigorous measures in order to keep your men from sickness."

The tone of the two sailors towards the soldier was rather that of a contemptuous nurse towards a timid child, but the last letter had the desired effect, for Wentworth ordered the fort to be stormed on the very same day. The English no sooner mounted the breach than the Spaniards fled almost without firing a shot, and the dreaded fort of Boca Chica fell into Wentworth's hands at the cost of two men wounded. Moreover, the Spaniards in the forts on the other side of the channel also partook in the panic and abandoned them, leaving the entrance to the harbour open to the British. The operations so far had cost one hundred and thirty men killed and wounded, but two hundred and fifty had perished from sickness, and over six hundred were in hospital. The rest of the work needed to be done quickly if it were to be done at all.

April $\frac{5}{16}$,
April.

It was, however, first necessary to re-embark all the troops in order to carry them to the head of the harbour for the attack on the city of Carthagena. This process occupied more than a week, and did not improve relations between army and navy. Vernon had already complained loudly, and probably with some justice, of the laziness of the soldiers: the blue-jackets had done all the hard work at the first landing of the regiments, and they were now called upon to do it again. At length, however, the transports got under way and proceeded towards the inner harbour, the entrance to which, like that of the outer port, lay through a narrow channel with a large fort, called the Castillo Grande, on one side, and a small redoubt on the other. The passage was more effectually blocked by a number of sunken ships which the Spaniards had scuttled after the forcing of Boca Chica. The fleet, however, quickly disposed of all these obstacles. The Spaniards abandoned Castillo Grande, and the naval officers, with their usual deftness, contrived to find a channel through the sunken ships. A few broadsides cleared the beach for the disembarkation, and on the 16th of April Wentworth landed. He had begged hard for five thousand men, but had been answered curtly, though not unjustly, by the naval commanders that, while they were ready to land them if required, they thought fifteen hundred men quite sufficient, since time above all things was precious.[148] So with fifteen hundred men Wentworth proceeded to the further task before him. There was now but one outwork between him and Carthagena, a fort standing on an eminence about seventy feet above the plain, and called Fort St. Lazar. The approach to it from the head of the harbour lay through a narrow defile, at the mouth of which the Spaniards offered some slight resistance. They soon gave way on the advance of the British, but poor Wentworth, always a General by book, with his head full of ambuscades and other traps for the unwary, halted his men instead of pushing on boldly, or he would almost certainly have carried Fort St. Lazar then and there, and broken into Carthagena itself on the backs of the fugitives. Vernon had urged upon him on the day before that he had only to act vigorously to ensure success, but Wentworth was far too much oppressed by the responsibilities of command to avail himself of such sound advice. He advanced no further than to within a league of St. Lazar, encamped, and pressed the Admiral to send him the remainder of his men.

Vernon acceded to the request, but with no very good grace. "I send the men," he wrote, "but I still think such a number unnecessary. Delay is your worst enemy; their engineers are better than yours, and a vigorous push is your best chance. No time should be lost in cutting off the communication between the town and the surrounding country. We hope that you will be master of St. Lazar to-morrow." The advice was sounder than ever, but Wentworth could not nerve himself to act on it. Shielding himself behind the vote of a council of war, he replied that the escalade of St. Lazar was impossible; the walls were too high and the ditch too deep. Would it not be possible, he asked, for the ships to batter the fort and sweep the isthmus that divided the town from the surrounding country for him. This was too much. The fleet had borne the brunt of the work so far, but it could not do everything. Vernon's tone, always overbearing, now became almost violent.

"Pointis,[149] who knew the climate, tried the escalade and succeeded," he retorted, "the ships can do no more. If you had advanced at once when the Spaniards fled from you, we believe that you would have taken St. Lazar on the spot."

After digesting this unpalatable document for a day Wentworth decided after all for an escalade. Though he lacked Vernon's experience of the tropics he had a sufficient dread of the rainy season, which had already sent sickness into his camp to herald its approach. By some mischance, for which he disclaimed responsibility, neither tents nor tools were landed with the men; [150] and for three nights the troops, young, raw and shiftless, were compelled to bivouac. On the third day they began to fall down fast. A council of war was held, and although General Blakeney, an excellent officer, opposed the project to the last, it was decided to carry St. Lazar by assault. The fort indeed was nothing very formidable in itself, and could have been knocked to pieces without difficulty from another eminence called La Popa, about three hundred yards from it. The only engineer, however, had been killed before Boca Chica was taken, the artillerymen were wholly ignorant of their duty, and the tools had not been landed; so that although a battery on La Popa would have served the double purpose of destroying St. Lazar and battering the walls of the city, no attempt was made to erect it. And meanwhile the Spaniards had made use of their respite to strengthen St. Lazar by new entrenchments which were far from despicable, and had reinforced the garrison from the town. There, however, the matter was; and the problem, though it might be difficult in itself, was so far simple in that it admitted of but one solution. St. Lazar was practically inaccessible except on the side of the town, where it was commanded by the guns of Carthagena. The fort must, therefore, be carried from that side before daylight, and carried as quickly as possible.

April $\frac{9}{20}$.

Early in the morning of the 20th of April the columns of attack were formed. First came an advanced party of fifty men backed by four hundred and fifty grenadiers under Colonel Wynyard, then the two old regiments, the Fifteenth and Twenty-fourth, jointly one thousand strong; after them a mixed company of the Thirty-fourth and Thirty-sixth; then the Americans with woolpacks and scaling-ladders, and finally a reserve of five hundred of Wolfe's marines. The design was to assault the north and south sides of St. Lazar simultaneously, Wynyard taking the southern or weaker face, while Colonel Grant with the old regiments, on which Wentworth principally relied, assaulted the northern. A couple of Spanish deserters were at hand to guide the columns to their respective positions.

At four o'clock the march began, the fireflies still flickering overhead against the darkness, the air close and still, and alive with the chirping, whistling, and croaking of the noisy tropic night. Within the camp men were lying in scores under the scourge of yellow fever, some tossing and raving in delirium, some gasping in the agonies of the last fatal symptom, some prostrate in helpless and ghastly collapse, waiting only for the dead hour before the dawn when they should die. These were left behind, and the red columns disappeared silently into the darkness. Before long Wynyard's men reached the foot of the hill and began the ascent. The ground before them was so steep that they were forced to climb upon their hands and knees, and the officers began to doubt whether their guides might not have played them false. Still the grenadiers scrambled on almost to the top of the hill, and then suddenly, at a range of thirty yards, the Spaniards opened a deadly fire. Now was the time for a rush, which would have swept the Spaniards pell-mell from their entrenchments. One man with the traditions of Cutts the Salamander would have carried the fort in two minutes; a few score of undisciplined Highlanders with naked broadswords would have mastered it even without a leader; but the officers had no experience except of the parade ground. They were conscious of a heavy fire in front and flanks, so they wheeled their platoons outwards to right and left for "street-firing," as it was called, and advanced slowly in perfect order, the men firing steadily at the flashes of cannon and musketry that blazed before them over the parapet. Raked through and through by grape and round shot, the soldiers stood without flinching for a moment, and loaded and fired as they had been taught, while the grenadiers lit their fuses coolly and hurled their hand-grenades into the belt of flame before them. They did not know, poor fellows, that the grenades provided for them were so thick, owing to the negligence of the authorities of the Ordnance, that not one in three of them would burst. So Wynyard's column fired dutifully on, though the men that composed it were mown down like grass.

On the northern face of the hill, where Grant's column was engaged, a like tragedy was enacted. Grant himself was shot down early, and after his fall no man seemed to know what should be done. The men faced the fire gallantly enough and returned it with perfect order and steadiness, but without effect. There were calls for the woolpacks and scaling-ladders, but the undisciplined Americans had long since thrown them down and fled; and even had the ladders been forthcoming they were too short by ten feet to be of use. There were appeals for guns to silence the Spanish artillery, but these had been placed in the rear of the columns and were not to be brought forward. So for more than an hour this tragical fight went on. Day dawned at length; the light grew strong, and the guns of Carthagena opened fire on Grant's column with terrible effect. Still the English stood firm and fired away their ammunition. It was all that they had been bidden to do, and they did it. Wynyard, his grenadiers once thrown into action, seemed incapable of bringing up other troops to support them. General Guise, who was in charge of the combined attack, showed magnificent courage and set a superb example, but it was something more than courage that was wanted. It was now broad daylight, and the Spaniards began with unerring aim to pick off the English officers. Finally, a column of Spanish infantry issued from the gates of Carthagena to cut off the English from their ships, and at last at eight o'clock Wentworth gave the order to retire, Wolfe's marines coming forward to cover the retreat. The troops had been suffering massacre for close on three hours, but until that moment not a man turned his back. There was no pursuit and the retreat was conducted in good order; but the troops, who had borne up hitherto against hardship and sickness, were thoroughly and hopelessly disheartened.

April $\frac{10}{21}$.

April $\frac{14}{25}$.

The losses in the assault were very heavy. Of the fifteen hundred English engaged, forty-three officers and over six hundred men were killed and wounded, and the Fifteenth and Twenty-fourth both lost over a fourth of their numbers. The treachery of the guides was answerable for much, but the mismanagement of the officers was responsible for more. Colonel Grant was picked up alive, indeed, but desperately wounded. "The General ought to hang the guides and the King ought to hang the General," he gasped out in his agony; and a few hours later he was dead. Wentworth, striving hard to put a good face on the disaster, ordered a battery to be erected against Fort St. Lazar on that same evening; but by this time yellow fever had seized hold of the army in good earnest, and it was a question not of building batteries but of digging graves. On the 21st the General called a council of war and announced to the Admiral its decision that the number of men was insufficient for the work, and that the enterprise must be abandoned. "Since the engineers or pretended engineers of the army declare that they do not know how to raise a battery, we agree," answered Vernon and Ogle, "though if our advice had been taken we believe that the town might have fallen." Then with studied insolence of tone they proceeded to offer a few obvious suggestions for the withdrawal of the troops. The military officers, not a little hurt, remonstrated in mild terms against the taunt, and after a short wrangle Wentworth requested a general council of war, by which it was finally determined that the attack on Carthagena must be given up as impracticable.

It was indeed high time. Between the morning of Tuesday the 18th and the night of Friday the 21st of April the troops had dwindled from sixty-six hundred to thirty-two hundred effective men. The two old regiments had been much shattered in the attack of St. Lazar, and the residue of the British force consisted chiefly of young soldiers, while the twelve hundred Americans who still survived were distrusted by the whole army, and were in fact little better than an encumbrance. On the 28th the troops were re-embarked, poor Wentworth being careful to carry away every scrap of material lest the Spaniards should boast of trophies. The naval officers grudgingly consented to blow up the defences of Boca Chica, and then for ten terrible days the transports lay idle in the harbour of Carthagena.

The horrors of that time are quite indescribable. By the care of Cathcart hospital-ships had indeed been provided for the expedition, but these had neither nurses, surgeons, cooks, nor provisions. "The men," wrote Smollett, himself a surgeon on board a man-of-war, "were pent up between decks in small vessels where they had not room to sit upright; they wallowed in filth; myriads of maggots were hatched in the putrefaction of their sores, which had no other dressing than that of being washed by themselves in their own allowance of brandy; and nothing was heard but groans and lamentations and the language of despair invoking death to deliver them from their miseries." So these poor fellows lay in this sickly, stifling atmosphere, with the raging thirst of fever upon them, while the tropical sun burnt fiercely overhead or the tropical rain poured down in a dense, gray stream, filling the air with that close clammy heat which even by a healthy man is grievous to be borne. The sailors also suffered much, though less heavily, being many of them acclimatised; and surgeons could have been spared from the men-of-war for the transports could Wentworth have been brought to ask them of Vernon, or Vernon to offer them to Wentworth. So while the commanders quarrelled the soldiers perished. Officers died as fast as the men, all discipline on the transports came to an end, and the men gave themselves up to that abandoned listlessness which was seen in Schomberg's camp in Ireland, when the bodies of dead comrades were used to stop the draughts in the tents. Day after day the sailors rowed ashore to bury their boats' loads of corpses, for there was always order and discipline in the ships of war; but the raw soldiers simply dragged their dead comrades up on deck and dropped them overboard, without so much as a shroud to their bodies or a shot to their heels. Vernon railed furiously at this nastiness, as he called it,[151] not reflecting that men untrained to the sea might know no better. So after a few hours the bodies that had sunk beneath the water came up again to the surface and floated, hideous and ghastly beyond description, about the transports, while schools of sharks jostled each other in the scramble to tear them limb from limb, and foul birds with ugly, ragged wings flapped heavily above them croaking for their share. Thus the air was still further poisoned, sickness increased, and the harbour became as a charnel-house. At length, on the 5th of May, it was resolved to return to Jamaica; and two days later the fleet sailed away from the horrors of Carthagena. By that time the men nominally fit for service were reduced to seventeen hundred, of whom not above a thousand were in a condition to be landed against an enemy.[152]

August $\frac{12}{23}$.
August $\frac{18}{29}$.

Arrived at Jamaica the commanders deliberated as to what should next be done. There were still men enough, it was thought, for a successful descent upon Cuba, though the British regiments were terribly short of officers, having lost over one hundred since they had left England. But the plague was not stayed by the removal to Jamaica. Within the month that elapsed after the abandonment of Carthagena eleven hundred men died; the strength of the British was reduced to fourteen hundred, and of the Americans to thirteen hundred, men.[153] For the next three weeks the troops continued to die at the rate of one hundred a week, the Americans, as always throughout this expedition, perishing even more rapidly than the British. At last, after long disputes, it was decided to make an attempt upon Santiago de Cuba. The fleet sailed on the 23rd of August, and on the 29th anchored on the north coast of the island, in a bay which Vernon, in honour of Prince William, named Cumberland Haven.

Then the Admiral again came forward with the same advice as he had offered at Carthagena. He urged Wentworth to take a picked force of a thousand men only, together with a thousand bearers, and with this column to make a forced march and take Santiago by surprise, the fleet meanwhile co-operating by sea. In the hands of an enterprising commander it is possible that such a plan might have succeeded; it was in fact just such a stroke as had been beloved of Drake and of the greatest of the buccaneers, but it was beyond the spirit of Wentworth. The risk indeed was great. The town lay ninety miles distant from Cumberland Haven, the only road was a path cut through the jungle, and there were rivers on the way which a few hours of rain might render impassable whether for advance or retreat. In a word Wentworth would have none of such ventures. The ill-feeling between army and navy was embittered; the troops lay idle in their camp, and, worst of all, sickness increased rather than abated at the close of the rainy season. By the middle of November there were hardly sufficient men to supply reliefs for the ordinary guards, and at the beginning of December there were less than three hundred privates fit for duty. A council of war was called, and it was decided to re-embark the troops for Jamaica, whither Wentworth, despite violent protests from Vernon, decided to accompany them.

| 1742. |
| March $\frac{9}{20}$. |
| May. |

Still the curtain was not yet to fall on this awful drama. The military force was now so much reduced that four of the eight regiments were drafted into the other four, and only the Fifteenth, Twenty-fourth, Wolfe's, and Fraser's were left. The yellow fever continued to rage unchecked. Two hundred and fifty of the men left in hospital by Wentworth on his departure for Cuba died in a single fortnight.[154] Then in February 1742 there came a reinforcement of three thousand men, namely, one battalion of the Royal Scots, the Sixth, and the Twenty-seventh Foot. They arrived healthy, but began to sicken at once.[155] All kinds of new projects were now debated, an attack on Guatemala, on Yucatan, on Panama; but the troops continued to die at the rate of fifteen men a day, and it was of little profit to discuss plans in the presence of such a general as yellow fever. At length, after much delay, the expedition put to sea for the third time, and sailed against Porto Bello. The voyage was protracted by inclement weather to nineteen days, and at the end of those nineteen days, although none but healthy and selected men had been embarked, the Sixth regiment alone had thrown ninety-eight corpses overboard, and of the whole force nearly a thousand were sick or dead.[156] In such circumstances the enterprise was abandoned, and the expedition, once more delayed by unfavourable weather, returned again to Jamaica. There the hospitals were emptier and the graveyards fuller than at Wentworth's departure, for five hundred of the sick which he had left behind him had succumbed. The survivors who returned from Porto Bello soon filled up the hospital again, and by the end of July it was crowded with eight hundred men. One hundred and fifty of these died in August, and three hundred more were dead by the middle of October. By this time such few men as remained of the four thousand Americans had been discharged, the survivors numbering little more than three hundred, and all hope of further operations had been abandoned. The commanders indeed still met and discussed their plans with each other and with Governor Trelawny, the contention growing so hot between them that Trelawny and Sir Chaloner Ogle drew their swords upon each other, and were with difficulty prevented by Wentworth from adding to the death-roll. But when yellow fever is killing men before they can arrive within range to kill each other, councils of war are even less than ordinarily profitable. Of the regiments that had sailed from St. Helen's under Cathcart in all the pride and confidence of strength, nine men in every ten had perished. [157]

A great historian has asked, When did this Spanish war end?[158] and the answer is that it ended imperceptibly in the gradual annihilation of the contending armies by yellow fever. The French fleet was driven back to France by it, the Spaniards were left defenceless by it, the English were palsied for attack by it. There was indeed desultory fighting, not without incidents of signal gallantry, between the colonists of Carolina and Georgia and their Spanish neighbours in Florida, but the operations were too trifling to merit record in this place. The one gleam of light in the whole dark history is the heroic voyage of Anson, who had been sent round Cape Horn, with some vague idea that his fleet and Vernon's should co-operate in attacks on Central America. In Anson's fame the Army also has some faint though melancholy share, for about three hundred Chelsea pensioners, weak, aged, and infirm, were barbarously driven on board his ships, nominally to man them, but in reality only to find at sea the grave which past service should have ensured them on English soil. Whether with Anson or with Vernon, whether on the Atlantic or the Pacific, the war had nothing but failure and death for the red-coats.

It remains to say something of the human share in the catastrophe of the expedition to Carthagena. Wentworth has hitherto been made the scapegoat for every misfortune, and it is probable that he must remain so; yet the blame of the avoidable disasters must not be laid wholly to his charge. So far as he had been tried up to the time of his command he had proved himself a diligent and painstaking officer; he had been installed as Cathcart's second by Cathcart's own request, and could he have remained a subordinate would probably have done well enough. Though lacking experience of active service, in or out of the tropics, he did his best to make good the deficiency by consulting those officers who knew more than himself. He tried his hardest to work in concert with the naval officers, and never wrote home a word of complaint against Vernon until he had endured his arrogant and overbearing tone for more than a year. But his own training, like that of his men, had been mechanical only, and he could neither rise above the stiff formalities of his profession himself, nor raise his men above them. It will be seen that this same mechanical training could produce astonishing results on the familiar battlegrounds of Flanders, but it was out of place on the Spanish Main, as it was soon to prove itself out of place on the Ohio. Again, poor workman though Wentworth was, the tools to his hand were not good. He himself had only with great difficulty taught six of his regiments the rudiments of discipline in the Isle of Wight. His regimental officers were, without exception, young and inexperienced, while some few of them, who had obtained commissions through political jobbery, are described as the most abandoned wretches of the town. The American troops, which formed a third of the whole force, were incomparably worse than the worst of the English, and being made up to some extent of Irish papists were more than a little untrustworthy. Again, although the least foresight must have shown that the brunt of the work would fall upon the artillery, the gunners furnished to Wentworth were raw yokels, just caught up from the plough and wholly ignorant of their duty, while their commander was incapable, and his second a drunkard. Of the engineers it is sufficient to repeat that after the chief was killed not one could be found with the slightest knowledge of his duty. Moreover, of the eight battering cannon furnished to him one was found to be unserviceable and the rest were all of different patterns, while the shells, like the hand-grenades, were of bad quality. Again, the stores of all kinds were so unspeakably bad as to call forth the bitterest complaints from Wentworth; and beyond all doubt bad food contributed to increase the sickliness of the Army and to weaken the men against the attacks of yellow fever. In fact, the trail of the incompetent Newcastle is over the whole expedition; but these blunders and deficiencies only the less excuse Wentworth for failing to adopt a swifter and more dashing system of operations.

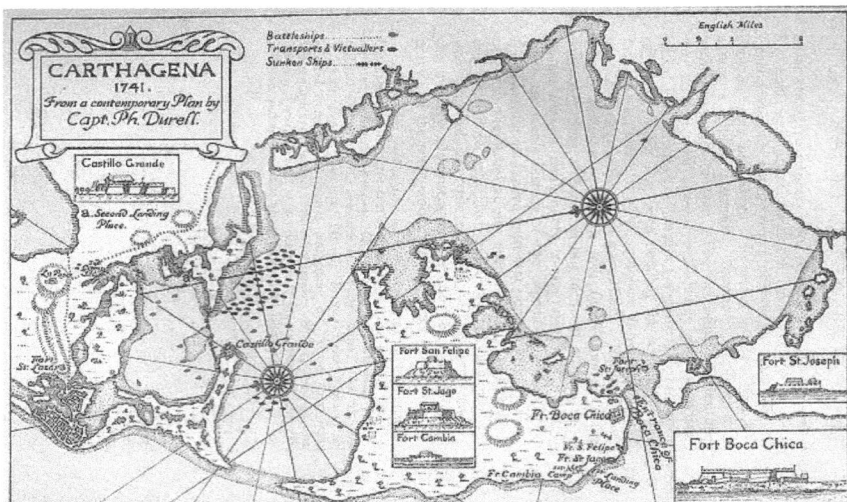

Walker & Boutall del.

To face page 78.

CARTHAGENA 1741.
From a contemporary plan by
Capt. Ph. Durell.

Vernon, on his side, boasted loudly that had he been invested with the sole command he would have accomplished every object at a far lower sacrifice of life; and it is probable that he spoke truth. Certainly he never ceased to impress upon Wentworth the necessity for bold and active measures. Nevertheless it was Vernon who was mainly responsible for the fatal friction between army and navy. He seems to have been by nature a bully; imperious, conceited, insolent, and without an idea of tact. The ill-feeling between the two services had shown itself before the expedition joined Vernon's fleet at Jamaica; and the Thirty-fourth regiment, which had been detailed for service on the men-of-war, lost half of its numbers through ill-usage on board ship before a shot was fired. It would have been a sufficiently difficult task for Vernon to have composed these differences, but far from attempting it he set himself deliberately to aggravate them. Still, when the whole history of the expedition is examined the blame for its failure must rest not with the General, not with the Admiral, not even with the Government, but with those benighted and unscrupulous politicians who gambled away the efficiency of the Army and of the military administration for the petty triumphs of party and the petty emoluments of place and power.

AUTHORITIES.—The most familiar account of the expedition to Carthagena is of course that of Smollett, a great part of which is repeated in *Roderick Random*. Other sources are the *State Papers, Colonial Series*, "North America and West Indies," No. 61, and *Admiralty Papers*, "Jamaica," No. 1.

There is indeed more to be gleaned from the enclosures sent home by Vernon than from Wentworth's despatches. All the returns, however, are in the *Colonial Series*, as well as a criticism of the conduct of the expedition, and an excellent narrative by Lord Elibank.

CHAPTER IV

Long before the enterprise against the Spanish Main had worn itself out to its tragical end, all Europe had been kindled into a blaze of war. On the 20th of October 1740, while Cathcart was still impatiently awaiting the fair wind which should carry him from Spithead, the Emperor Charles the Sixth died, leaving his daughter Maria Theresa sole heiress of his dominions. Her succession had already been recognised by the powers of Europe through their guarantee of the Pragmatic Sanction, but on such guarantees little trust was to be reposed. The principal rival to the Queen of Hungary was the Elector of Bavaria, and France, mindful of her old friendship with Bavaria, was ready enough to wreak her old hostility upon the House of Austria by upholding him. England and Holland alone, commercial nations to whom a contract was a thing not lightly to be broken, felt strongly as to their duty in supporting the young Queen. The various states of Germany were as usual self-seeking and disunited, watching greedily to make what profit they could out of the helpless House of Hapsburg. Frederick of Prussia, not yet named the Great, was the first to move. He had but recently come to the throne, inheriting together with it the most efficient army in Europe, and a large stock of ready money. Moving, as ever, promptly, swiftly, and silently, he invaded Silesia, and by a signal victory over the Austrians at Mollwitz called the whole of Europe to arms.

France, with visions not only of acquiring new territory in Germany, but of paying off old scores against England through Hanover, had begun to weave great schemes even before the fight of Mollwitz. The most remarkable of living French statesmen, Marshal Belleisle, having thought out his plans and obtained the royal sanction for them, started off in March 1741 on a tour of visits to the courts of Europe; his object being to persuade them, first to renounce the Pragmatic Sanction, and secondly to support the candidature of the Elector Charles Albert of Bavaria against that of Maria Theresa's husband, the Grand Duke Francis of Lorraine, for the imperial crown. This done, he seems to have hoped to partition Austria proper between Saxony and

Prussia, and to divide all Germany and the Empire into four weak kingdoms, Bavaria, Saxony, Prussia, and Hungary, which by careful fostering of jealousies and quarrels should be kept dependent on France.

<table>
<tr><td>Dec. $\frac{4}{15}$;</td></tr>
<tr><td>1742.</td></tr>
<tr><td>February.</td></tr>
</table>

Charles Albert of Bavaria, Augustus of Saxony, Frederick of Prussia and the Queen of Spain were gained over by Belleisle with little difficulty; but Hanover, with England at its back, stood out for the Pragmatic Sanction. In England the sympathy with Maria Theresa was strong, and Walpole in the session of 1741 obtained from Parliament a pledge to maintain her succession, a subsidy of three hundred thousand pounds to tide her over financial difficulties, and an acknowledgment of England's obligation to assist her with a force of twelve thousand men. He also attempted to detach Frederick from Belleisle's confederacy, but with conspicuous ill-success. Meanwhile King George went over to Hanover to assemble troops for the support of Maria Theresa; and then France, always ready to strike the first blow, sent two armies across the Rhine, one to join hands with the forces of Bavaria and carry the war to the gates of Vienna, the other straight upon Hanover itself. Thus surprised, the King could do nothing but stipulate for one year's neutrality for Hanover, promising also that during the same period he would neither give help to the Queen of Hungary nor cast his vote as an Elector of the Empire in her husband's favour. Bound by this humiliating agreement, which had excited no less scorn in England than in Austria, the King returned home to meet a new parliament, which had been elected amid no ordinary excitement owing to the disasters on the Spanish Main. Furious attacks were made upon Walpole, who was held responsible for a war which he had always deprecated, and for which he knew the nation to be unprepared; and in less than two months he was driven from office. Lord Wilmington succeeded him as nominal head of the Treasury, and Lord Carteret, one of the few living Englishmen who could speak German, took charge of foreign affairs. Parliament showed itself more zealous than ever in the cause of Maria Theresa, and voted her a subsidy of half a million, while Carteret prevailed with his colleagues to send sixteen thousand British troops to Flanders to act as her auxiliaries in arms. Finally, five millions were granted for the prosecution of the war.

Notwithstanding that all these preparations could be aimed at no power but France, the two nations were not supposed to be at war with each other. The French had invented the phrase auxiliaries, and had marched their armies into Germany under the shelter of that innocent designation; and the English were foolish enough for a time to follow their example. The movements of the French fleet at the outset of Wentworth's expedition had, however, left little doubt as to the hostility of France towards England, and the fact had been settled beyond all dispute by some French despatches intercepted by Vernon. The past year therefore had not passed without additional military preparations on the part of England. In January 1741 four more regiments of marines were raised over and above those sent out with Wentworth; and simultaneously orders were issued for the formation of seven new regiments of foot under Colonels Fowke, Long, Houghton, Price, Cholmondeley, and De Grangue. Of these the first six still remain with us, numbered the Forty-third to the Forty-eighth. Throughout the summer also a force of some five thousand men had been kept in camp near Colchester under General Wade, in readiness to take the field. Finally, the estimates for 1742 provided for a force on the British establishment of sixty-two thousand men. Sufficient troops being therefore presumably to hand, the next thing was to appoint a commander, and the choice fell on John, Earl of Stair.

Stair was now close on seventy years of age, but despite a very early beginning of a soldier's life, was still active and efficient enough. At the age of nineteen he had fought at Steenkirk, already with the rank of colonel; in Marlborough's first campaign he had been the foremost in the breach in Cutts's mad assault upon Venloo; he had served as a regimental officer at Blenheim, as a brigadier at Ramillies, on Marlborough's staff at Oudenarde, and had been present also at Malplaquet. He had been distinguished by particular kindness and attention both from the great Duke and from Prince Eugene, and had not failed to take to heart their teaching in the art of war. Altogether he was not ill-qualified to command a British army in its first active service on the continent since the death of Marlborough.

May $\frac{6}{17}$.

His first duties, however, were diplomatic, namely to induce the States-General to permit the occupation of Nieuport and Ostend by the British, as their bases of operations against the French in the Austrian Netherlands. He was further instructed to allay any feeling of distrust that might have been roused by Hanover's declaration of neutrality, and if possible to engage the Dutch to take an active part as auxiliaries of Queen Maria Theresa. It was no easy task, for endless faction joined to an impossible form of government had reduced the Dutch to the lethargy, inefficiency, and helplessness which was their ruin; while, moreover, recollections of the Peace of Utrecht were still strong enough to make them diffident and cold towards any overtures from England. The proposal to quarter a British garrison in the Netherlands was therefore ill-received, until, in the nick of time, there came the news that the

Austrians, having made a desperate push to expel Frederick of Prussia from Silesia, had been totally defeated by him at the battle of Chotusitz. Such a blow to the Austrian cause might bring about great results. Marshal Maillebois, with a French army of forty thousand men, lay in Westphalia, blocking the march of the Hanoverian troops if they should try to join the British, and at the same time ready to pierce into Holland at any moment. In such circumstances a contingent of British troops could not but be valuable to the States, so leave was granted for the disembarkation of the first British battalions at Ostend; and arrangements were made, though with no very good grace, to find them quarters in Bruges and Ghent. But as to throwing in their lot with the British for the defence of the Pragmatic Sanction, the machinery of the Dutch Government was too complicated, the minds of men too cautious, and the spirit of those in authority too corrupt, to permit the settlement of a matter of such importance without delay of months or even years.

The British troops continued to arrive in driblets from England, and Stair meanwhile, knowing that his movements must depend upon those of the French, watched the situation with the keenest interest. The French army of Bavaria, after a few trifling successes on the Danube, had been rapidly swept back by the energy of the Austrian General Khevenhüller. A portion of it, which had penetrated into Bohemia and captured Prague, was still lying in that kingdom under an incompetent commander, Marshal Broglie, with Prague for its base. Little was to be feared from Broglie: the really formidable enemy was Frederick of Prussia, whom Stair was for detaching from Belleisle's confederacy at any cost. The Prussian army once out of the way, the whole armed force of Austria could be turned upon the French in Bohemia, who, owing to Khevenhüller's successes on the Danube, must either be sacrificed altogether, or rescued with great difficulty at the price of denuding the whole French frontier of troops. It would then be open to the Austrians to advance through the Palatinate and up the Moselle into France, while the Dutch and English might either join them or break straight in from the north upon Paris and put an end to the war and to the mischief of French ambition for ever.

| May 31 |
| June 11. |

So counselled Stair, with a clearness of judgment, alike as soldier and statesman, that was not unworthy of his great master; but unfortunately Maria Theresa would not come to terms with Frederick without striking a last blow for Silesia, which ended, as has been told, in the disaster of Chotusitz. Then at last she gave in; and the Treaty of Breslau purchased the friendship of Frederick at the cost of Silesia. Stair was instantly on the alert, for the game seemed now to be in his hand. The French frontier towards the Netherlands was but weakly defended; a feint of invasion in that direction must certainly bring back Maillebois from Westphalia to guard it, and then the road would be open for the junction of the Hanoverians with the British. The Austrians had already fourteen thousand troops in the country, which, added to the British and their Allies, would make up a force superior to any that Maillebois could bring together.[159] Carteret entered warmly into the plan; and meanwhile events elsewhere had fallen out exactly according to Stair's prevision. The Austrians, relieved from the pressure of Frederick and his Prussians, turned all their strength against the French in Bohemia, and swept them out of all their posts except Prague, wherein they held the wreck of the French force closely besieged. Maillebois was called away to Bohemia to save the beleaguered army if he could, and the whole of the French frontier towards Flanders lay open, with little more than twenty thousand men to protect it. This was the moment for which Stair had waited, hardly daring to hope that it would ever come, and he urged that the whole of the forces present, alike of England, Hanover, and Austria, should be concentrated for an immediate attack on Dunkirk, where the best of the French troops were known to be gathered together. These troops once beaten, the road would be clear for a march to Paris.[160]

But just at this moment King George suddenly turned lukewarm. He was not at war with France, he said, and his troops were acting simply as auxiliaries to the Queen of Hungary. France could take no offence at their presence, as her troops were likewise employed only as auxiliaries to the Elector of Bavaria.[161] Again, there were sundry arrangements to be adjusted before the troops of the Allies could be concentrated. It was, therefore, not until the 24th of August that orders were despatched to the Hanoverians to march; and even then King George was inclined rather to bar the return march of Maillebois from Bohemia at the Meuse than to strike at the heart of his enemy at Dunkirk. Then, again, the men of skill in England, as Stair contemptuously called the council of war at Whitehall, thought the attack on Dunkirk too venturesome; and the plan was disapproved, chiefly, it should seem, because the King had some idea of taking command of the Army in person.[162] Stair meanwhile was chafing with impatience, concerting new plans with the Austrian commanders, and promising himself that his winter quarters should be in Normandy. His design now was to march straight for the head of the Oise, which would give him a navigable river for his transport, and to move from thence direct upon Paris. The French troops on the spot were few in number and would not dare to leave Dunkirk. The road for two-thirds of the journey to the Oise was paved, and the short distance that remained, therefore, constituted the only difficulty, by no means insuperable, in the way. Arrived at Paris the army could take artillery from the arsenal there, and move down the Seine to the siege of Havre. Finally, Stair promised that, if the King would give him a free hand, he would enable him before the 12th of October to dictate his own terms.[163]

The plan was daring enough, but Stair was neither a visionary nor an idle boaster, and there appears no reason to doubt that it was perfectly feasible. The French had recently fortified Dunkirk anew, and, as was not uncommon with them, had elaborated the works to such excess that forty thousand men were required to defend them. Unless, therefore, they chose to abandon Dunkirk, which they could hardly afford to do, there remained no troops to check an advance on Paris. But the design did not commend itself to the King. He submitted it to General Wade, slowest and most cautious of generals, who criticised it adversely; and meanwhile, whether through jealousy or treachery or sheer mismanagement, the orders for the Hanoverians to march were on one pretext or another delayed until all hopes of a campaign of 1742 were banished by the coming of the winter.[164]

| 1743. |
| February. |

Stair was deeply chagrined; and the discipline of his troops, who had been long kept idle in quarters which they detested, suffered so much that it was only restored by the strongest measures.[165] The winter set in with unusual severity, making the ground easy for purposes of transport and neutralising the value of the inundations on which the fortresses of the north-west frontier of France depended chiefly for their defence. Stair was eager to pounce upon some of them while the frost lasted, but the Austrian generals would not hear of it. He then proposed to attack one or other of the fortresses in Lorraine, Metz, Longwy, or Thionville, preparatory to an invasion of France by the Moselle; but again the Austrians dissented.[166] Their great object was to move King George's army into Germany, in order to frighten some of the minor German princes into alliance with Austria; and Stair, as he bitterly complained, was so much hampered by his instructions that he felt absolutely helpless.[167] The Hanoverians again, though supposed to be under his command, received independent orders from the King which were not communicated to Stair, and they declined to obey any other.[168] At last, after many struggles with Austrian generals and English ministers, the British army in February 1743 began its march eastward, as the Austrians had desired. The regiments were sadly distressed by the absence of multitudes of officers, who had gone home on leave for their duties in Parliament or for more private and trivial objects. "I thought it hard to refuse them leave," wrote Stair with biting sarcasm, "when they said that their preferment depended on the interest of their friends at Court. They had no notion that it depended on their exertions here."[169] To such a pass had twenty years of peace under Walpole brought the discipline of the Army.

Nevertheless Stair's recent severity had borne good fruit, and the conduct both of officers and men in a winter's march of extreme hardship and discomfort was such as to call forth his warmest praise.[170] As the spring drew near, the question as to the plan of the coming campaign became urgent. Fifty thousand French troops had been moved to the Moselle to bar any invasion through Lorraine, while all their forces in Flanders had been stationed on the Meuse ready either to join their comrades on the Moselle, or to advance to the Neckar in case the Allies should cross the Rhine to the south of Cologne. Stair, with the spirit of his master strong upon him, hinted at the desirability of a march to the Danube. The Austrians, as he guessed, would certainly resume their advance from the east against the French on that river as soon as the weather permitted, and his plan was to close in upon them from the west and fall upon their rear while the Austrians attacked them in front. Such a project, however, was too bold for the caution of King George, and, moreover, as he was always reminding Stair, though the French were to be treated as enemies he was not at war with France.[171] His final orders, given after immense delay, were that Stair should occupy the heights of Mainz and command the junction of the Rhine and Main.[172] Such a disposition was from a military point of view sufficiently obscure; and indeed it had no military object whatever, being designed simply to secure the choice of King George's nominee for the vacant electorate of Mainz.

| May. |
| May 23 |
| June 3. |

Very slowly, owing to the extreme difficulty of obtaining forage, the forces, both native and mercenary, of England, Hanover, and Austria were assembled on the north bank of the Main. Their position extended from the Rhine to Aschaffenburg, and faced to the south, while a bridge of boats was kept ready at Frankfort for the passage of the river.[173] Meanwhile, a French army of seventy thousand men, under Marshal Noailles, had quietly taken up its station on the Upper Rhine near Spires, and was seeking to establish communication with Bavaria and the Neckar, in order to save what was left of Broglie's army while still it might; though, at the same time, not without apprehensions as to the danger of leaving the Palatinate and Lorraine open behind it. Stair took in the situation at a glance. He was for crossing the Main, following the left bank downward and taking up a position between Oppenheim and Mainz. There he could threaten Noailles so closely that he would not dare to detach any part of his army to Bavaria. He would, moreover, have it in his power to attack the French on the Neckar whenever he pleased; and finally, he could in due time cross the Rhine westward, and force the French to retire on Landau and Alsace, leaving Lorraine and the Netherlands open to invasion. After some trouble Count d'Arenberg, a general neither very enterprising nor very capable, who commanded the Austrians, appears to have been converted to his views; and though the entire army was even now not yet arrived at the rendezvous, the Allies on the 3rd of June began the passage of the Main. A day or two later Stair received intelligence that Noailles had left the Neckar and was advancing along the high road from Darmstadt to Frankfort to attack him. This road passed for a considerable distance through a forest, and it was at its outlet from this forest that Stair took up his position to await the French. D'Arenberg so strongly disapproved of the whole proceeding that he withdrew the whole of the Austrian dragoons to the right bank of the Main, in order to rescue the shattered remnants that should be left of Stair's army after the battle. Marshal Neipperg, his second, however, led the Austrian infantry to the position of Stair's choice: and when Noailles arrived on the following morning he withdrew without venturing to attack.

| May 30 |
| June 10. |

Meanwhile King George, who had arrived at Hanover a fortnight before, was perfectly frantic. On Stair's first proposal to cross to the south bank of the Main he had sent positive orders, which reached Stair too late, that he was not to stir. The King was surrounded by nervous Austrians who, having information of Noailles's intended advance, were, or professed to be, in terror lest the Allies should be beaten in detail, and did not fail to represent how dreadful it would be if the army should be defeated before His Majesty could take command. Letter after letter therefore was despatched to Stair, bidding him above all things to be careful, and finally ordering him to repass the Main. Stair at first had prepared to obey orders, though not without speaking his mind. "I am too careful of the King's interest," he wrote, "to be rash, but I am sure of two things, that the French are far more occupied with Bavaria than with us, and that we are superior to them even in numbers. The importance of giving an army to a person who is trusted is now evident. Had my plan been followed, we should now be in a position to fall on the head of the French army which, after sending away a detachment to Bavaria, is now taking post along the Rhine." In truth, during the months of May and June, the Austrians on the Danube had swept Broglie right out of Germany; and Noailles's detachment no sooner reached him than it was ordered forthwith to retreat. But when Stair heard of Noailles's advance to attack him he quietly suppressed the King's orders to repass the Main until he had offered battle to the French. When Noailles refused it, Stair recrossed the river as he had been bidden, unwillingly indeed, yet not a little satisfied that after all the King's orders and all the Austrian predictions of disaster, he had successfully proved the soundness of his views. "But," he added significantly on arriving on the northern bank, "it will be impossible for us now to find forage. The French being masters of one side of the river, forage cannot be brought down to us by water, so we must move upward." It was just this question of supplies which had made him so anxious for a general action; and the event proved that he was right.[174]

| June $\frac{8}{19}$. |
| June $\frac{15}{26}$. |

On the 19th of June King George at last arrived from Hanover and took over the command of the army, which was encamped, as he had ordered, on the right bank of the Main, the English and Hanoverians lying about Aschaffenburg. In the hope of securing forage on the other bank, a battery had been erected on the bridge of Aschaffenburg, but Noailles, moving up to the river, erected a redoubt at his own end of the bridge and put an end to all such hopes. Meanwhile he seized a post further up the river to intercept all supplies from Franconia, and threw two bridges over it below Aschaffenburg at Seligenstadt, by which his troops could cross and cut off the Allies from their magazines at Hanau. For a week the King remained helpless in this camp, unwilling to retreat though his peril increased every day. The result was that he found himself in command of a starving army. It was impossible to keep the soldiers from plunder, and discipline became seriously relaxed. At last, on the 26th of June, it was perforce resolved that the army must retreat to Hanau that very night.

| June $\frac{16}{27}$. |

Meanwhile Noailles had not been idle. The ground on which the Allies were encamped is a narrow plain pent in between the Spessart Hills and the Main. These hills are densely wooded, and the forest appears at that time to have descended lower into the plain than at present. When therefore the Allies retired to Hanau, as Noailles knew that inevitably they must, it would be impossible for them to keep out of range of cannon posted on the opposite bank of the Main, and accordingly the marshal had erected five different batteries to play upon them during their march. At one o'clock on the morning of the 27th intelligence was brought to him that the Allies were in motion. This was the moment for which he had been waiting. Instantly galloping to Seligenstadt, he ordered Count Grammont to cross the Main with twenty-eight thousand men by the two bridges which he had laid for the purpose, and to take up a position about a mile up the river by the village of Dettingen. At that point a rivulet runs down across the plain from the Spessart Hills to the Main, through a little boggy dale which was uncrossed by any bridge except by that of the high road to Hanau. There Grammont was bidden to wait and to make an end of the Allies as they defiled over the bridge. He took up his position accordingly, and Noailles returned to the opposite bank of the Main to direct his operations against King George's flank and rear.

It was four o'clock in the morning before the Allied army was fairly in motion. The British cavalry led the way, followed by the Austrian, then came the British infantry and the Austrian infantry after them; and last of all came a strong rear-guard composed of the British Guards, the choicest of the German infantry, and the Hanoverian cavalry; for it was in the rear that an attack of the French was most looked for and most to be dreaded. The apprehensions of a French advance on Aschaffenburg were soon seen to be well founded. The march of the Allies from that town lay across a bend of the Main to the village of Klein Ostheim, and as they approached the river they could see the French on the opposite bank in full march to cross the river behind them and cut off their retreat up the stream. Thus Noailles's dispositions were complete. These troops were to block the Allies to the south, impenetrable woods shut them off from the east, the Main barred their way on the west, and Grammont stood before them at Dettingen on the north. Noailles had caught them, as he said, in a mouse-trap, and might reasonably feel certain that they could not escape.

On arriving about seven o'clock at Klein Ostheim, the whole army of the Allies was obliged to file through it by a single road. The cavalry, therefore, when it had passed through the village was halted and wheeled round with its face to the river to wait till the infantry should come up. This again Noailles had foreseen, and he had planted his cannon in exactly the right place to play upon the Allies when they should advance beyond the village. For an hour the cavalry stood halted before the march could be resumed; and now came intelligence from an advanced party in Dettingen that Grammont was in order of battle in front and that an immediate engagement was inevitable. King George hastened to set his army likewise in order of battle; but all the baggage had been massed between the first and second divisions of the column of route, and the confusion for a time was very great. Meanwhile the French troops bound for Aschaffenburg had by this time cleared the front of the first of Noailles's batteries and left the guns free to open fire. The shot soon came humming thick and fast into the heavy mass of waggons and baggage-animals, and the confusion increased. Guns were sent for in frantic haste to silence the French cannon, but the artillery being far in the rear was long in making its appearance: and meanwhile the King capered about on horseback in great excitement, staff-officers galloped to and fro, and the troops marched and counter-marched into their positions, always under the deadly fire of the French battery. Gradually, though with infinite difficulty, the troops were shuffled into their places, for the stereotyped order of battle was useless in a plain that permitted a frontage only of twenty-three battalions and a few squadrons at most. So passed a terrible hour and more, until at last the British guns came into action and replied effectively to the French batteries; and then a push was made to shift the baggage into a place of safety. In the middle of the plain between Klein Ostheim and Dettingen stood a wood flanked on each hand by a morass. Two lines of cavalry were moved forward towards this wood, the baggage followed them, the infantry followed the baggage, and the troublesome waggons were at last stowed away securely under cover of the trees, while the cavalry and the Austrian infantry made haste to form the right of the Allies' line of battle.

It was high time, for it was now almost noon, and Grammont, tired of remaining where he had been bidden to wait on the north side of Dettingen, or believing (as he himself said) that the Allies had already passed him and that only their rear-guard was left, had advanced beyond the ravine to take up a fresh position. So far as the Allies could see, he was manœuvring to move troops down under cover of the forest upon their right flank. By this time, however, King George's line was formed, and on its extreme left were seen the scarlet coats of the British battalions. To the left of all, and within a furlong of the river, stood the Thirty-third Foot, and to its right in succession the Twenty-first Fusiliers, Twenty-third Fusiliers, Twelfth, Eleventh, Eighth and Thirteenth Foot. On the right of the Thirteenth stood an Austrian brigade, and then in succession the Blues, Life Guards, Sixth Dragoons, and Royal Dragoons. All of these were in the first line. In the second line, in rear of their comrades on the left, were posted the Twentieth, Thirty-second, Thirty-seventh, Thirty-first, and the Buffs; and in rear of the cavalry on the right, the Seventh Dragoon Guards, King's Dragoon Guards, Fourth and Seventh Dragoons, and the Scots Greys. Opposite to them the French were ranged in two lines with a reserve in third line, the infantry being in the centre and the cavalry on the flanks, so that the famous French Household Cavalry,[175] in its place of honour on the extreme right, stood opposed to the British battalions on the Allied left. General Clayton, who commanded on the left, observing the mass of cavalry that confronted him, sent hastily for the Third Dragoons to fill up the gap between the Thirty-third and the river, and therewith the British dispositions were complete.

The whole of the first line then advanced, the King, who had with difficulty been prevented from stationing himself on the extreme left, waving his sword and shouting words of encouragement with a broad German accent. Fortunately the French were themselves in great disorder and confusion. The corrupt dealing in the appointment and promotion of officers, which fifty years later was to set the French army on the side of the Revolution, was already undermining efficiency and discipline. Grammont on advancing beyond the ravine had thought out no new order of a battle. Not a brigadier was competent to draw up his brigade, and the Household Cavalry kept manœuvring about in front of the infantry without a thought except for the fine figure that it was cutting in the sight of both armies. The advance of the Allies was necessarily slow, for some of the English regiments, whose way lay through the morasses, were knee-deep in mire. The whole line was presently halted to take breath, and the British, evidently a little shaken by the previous hurry and confusion and by the gesticulations of the King, broke into a feeble and irregular cheer, a sound which Lord Stair heard with great displeasure. The line was dressed and the advance was resumed in better order, though the French batteries on the other bank of the Main never ceased to rain destruction on the Third Dragoons and on the unfortunate battalions on the left. The men were not yet quite steady, for some undisciplined spirits, fretting at the incessant parade of the French Household Cavalry, opened an irregular fire all along the line. Then, as it seems, came the most comical incident of the day. King George's horse, frightened by the crackle of the musketry, took the bit in his teeth and bolted away to the rear, His Majesty, with purple face and eyes starting out of his head, pulling desperately at him with both hands but unable to stop him. Ultimately the animal's career was checked, and the King returning to the right of the line dismounted and resumed his gestures on foot, utterly fearless, as are all of his race, and confident that his own legs, at least, would carry him in the right direction. The line was again halted to load, there being fortunately still time to repair previous faults, and the advance was again resumed with greater steadiness.

Then the French infantry of the Guard on Grammont's right centre advanced likewise, cheering loudly, and opened a fitful and disorderly fire. The British, now thoroughly in hand, answered with a regular, swift, and continuous fire of platoons, the ranks standing firm like a wall of brass and pouring in volley after volley, deadly and unceasing—such a fire as no French officer had ever seen before.[176] The French Guards staggered under it and the British again raised an irregular cheer. "Silence," shouted Stair imperiously, galloping up. "Now one and all together when I give the signal." And as he raised his hat the British broke into the stern and appalling shout which was to become so famous on the fields of the Peninsula. The French Guards waited for no more when they heard it, but shrank back in disorder in rear of their horse, which now advanced in earnest against the extreme British left.

Clayton saw the danger. His left flank in the general confusion had never been properly secured, and though the fire of the French batteries by the river had ceased lest it should destroy their own troops, yet the Third Dragoons and the Thirty-third had been much weakened by it during their advance. Despatching urgent messages for reinforcements of cavalry, he put a bold face on the matter, ordered the Dragoons, Thirty-third, Twenty-first, and Twenty-third forward to meet the French attack, and prepared to stand the shock. Down came the flower of the French cavalry upon them, sword in hand, at high speed. The Third Dragoons were the first to close with them. They were but two weak squadrons against nine squadrons of the enemy, their depth was but of three ranks against eight ranks of the French; but they went straight at them, burst into the heart of them and cut their way through, though with heavy loss. The Thirty-third faced the attack as boldly, never gave way for an inch and brought men and horses crashing down by their eternal rolling fire. Next to them the two regiments of Fusiliers were even more hardly pressed. The Gendarmerie came down upon them at full trot with pistols in both hands and swords dangling by the wrist. Arrived within range they fired the pistols, dashed the empty weapons in the faces of the British, and then fell in with the sword; but the Fusiliers, as it was said, fought like devils, their platoon-fire thundering out as regularly as on parade, and the French horse fell back repulsed.

Still, gallantly as this first attack had been met, the numerical superiority of the French cavalry was formidable, and there was imminent danger lest the British left flank should be turned. The Third Dragoons had suffered heavily, after their first charge, from the bullets of a battalion posted in support of the French horse, but they rallied, and twice more, weak and weary as they were, they charged ten times their numbers and cut their way through them. But after the third charge they were well-nigh annihilated. All the officers except two, and three-fourths of the men and horses had been killed or wounded; two of the three standards had been cut to atoms, both silk and staves, by shot and shell, and in the last charge the third had dropped from a cornet's wounded hand and lay abandoned on the ground. A trooper of the regiment, Thomas Brown by name, was just dismounting to recover it when a French sabre came down on his bridle-hand and shore away two of his fingers. His horse, missing the familiar pressure of the bit, at once bolted, and before he could be pulled up had carried his rider into the rear of the French lines. There Dragoon Brown saw the standard of his regiment borne away in triumph by a French gendarme. Disabled as he was he rode straight at the Frenchman, attacked and killed him; and then gripping the standard between his leg and the saddle he turned and fought his way single-handed through the ranks of the enemy, emerging at last with three bullet-holes through his hat and seven wounds in his face and body, but with the standard safe.

But now the First and Seventh Dragoons, which had been summoned from the right, came galloping up and fell in gallantly enough upon the French Household Cavalry. These were, however, repulsed, partly, it should seem, because they attacked with more impetuosity than order, partly because the French were armed with helmets and breastplates heavy enough to turn a pistol shot. The Blues followed close after them, but sacrificing order to speed were, like their comrades, driven back in confusion; and the French Gendarmes, flushed with success, bore down for the second time upon the Twenty-first and Twenty-third and succeeded in breaking into them. But the two battalions were broken only for a moment. Quickly recovering themselves they faced inwards, and closing in upon the French in their midst shot them down by scores. The Fourth and Sixth British Dragoons, together with two regiments of Austrian dragoons, now came up and renewed the combat against the French Household Cavalry, but it was not until after they had been twice repulsed that at last they succeeded, with the help of their rallied comrades, in forcing back the intrepid squadrons of the French horse.

Meanwhile the battle elsewhere had flagged. A feeble attack of the French against the right of the Allies had been easily repelled, and in the centre the second line of the French infantry had cared little more than the first to face the terrible English fire. But while the Gendarmerie were still pressing the British hard on the left, the French Black Musketeers suddenly broke away from their place by their side, and wheeling to their left galloped madly between the fire of friendly and hostile infantry to make a dash upon the British Royal Dragoons at the extreme right of the Allied line. The Austrian Marshal Neipperg no sooner saw them than he exclaimed: "Now is the time. The British horse will attack in front, and our horse in flank, and the thing is done." British and Austrians at once closed in upon the Black Musketeers, cut them to pieces, and then bore down upon the flank of the French infantry. The French foot, which had behaved very unworthily of itself all day, now took to its heels and fled in confusion towards the Main. The British horse on the left, one regiment in particular burning to wipe out the humiliation of its first failure, pressed the French Household Cavalry harder than ever in front, and the Scots Greys plunging in upon their flank threw them into utter rout. The whole French army now made headlong for the fords and bridges of the Main, the infantry in their panic plunging madly into the stream and perishing by scores if not by hundreds in the water. Now was the moment for a vigorous pursuit, and had Stair been left to work his own will the French would have suffered very heavily; but the King was too thankful to have escaped from Noailles's mousetrap to think of turning his good fortune to account. The Marshal was allowed to retreat in peace, and thus, after four hours of sharp work, ended the battle of Dettingen.

Seldom has a commander found more fortunate issue from a series of blunders than King George. Had Grammont obeyed his orders it is difficult to see how a man of the Allied Army could have escaped; but even allowing for Grammont's ill-timed impatience it is strange that Noailles should have allowed the day to go as it went. It is true that he had sent the best of his troops across the Main with Grammont, but he had still from twenty to thirty thousand men on his own side of the river whom he left standing idle, without an attempt to employ them. He seems, in fact, to have been paralysed with dismay over the wreck of his very skilful combinations. The action itself deserves the name of a combat rather than a battle, for on neither side was more than half of the force really engaged; yet Dettingen was decidedly a victory, for the French were badly beaten and lost little, if any, less than five thousand men, killed, wounded, and prisoners. The loss of the Allies was about half of that number, of which the British share was two hundred and sixty-five killed and five hundred and sixty-one wounded, the most valuable life taken being that of General Clayton. As the brunt of the action fell wholly on the first line, the greatest sufferers among the infantry were the regiments chiefly exposed to the flanking fire of the French batteries. These were the Thirty-third, Twenty-first, Twenty-third, and Twelfth of the Line, but in not one of them did the casualties exceed one hundred men, or about an eighth of their strength. The cavalry suffered far more heavily in comparison, though here again the losses of the heroes of the day, the Third Dragoons, were more than twice as great as those of any other regiment: one hundred and fifty men and as many horses forming a terrible proportion of casualties in two squadrons. The most noticeable points in the engagement were the disgraceful behaviour of the French infantry, by no one more severely censured than by Noailles himself, and the deadly accuracy of the British fire. A smaller but curious fact is that both the King and the Duke of Cumberland were run away with by their horses, the former, as has been told, to the rear, the latter to the front, and indeed into the midst of the French infantry, from which, however, he emerged with no greater hurt than a bullet in the leg. At the close of the day the King was so much elated by his success as to revive the creation of knights banneret in the field, a proceeding which ceases to seem ridiculous when we learn that Lord Stair was the first and Dragoon Thomas Brown the last of the new knights. Such a scene was never to be seen again, for Dettingen was the last action in which a king of England actually commanded his army in person.

The ceremony of knighthood completed, the King left his wounded on the ground to the care of Noailles, and hastened away as quickly as possible with the army to his magazine at Hanau. The battle virtually closed the campaign, so far as the British were concerned, and King George returned home with his laurels fresh upon him, to be hailed with acclamation as a victor, and hear his praises sung in endless stanzas of most execrable verse. A few months later Lord Stair also returned home, without recrimination and without complaint, but with resolute and scornful determination to resign the command, since he was not trusted with the conduct of operations. General Wade was appointed field-marshal, to command in his stead. Finally, some weeks later the ridiculous fiction, that the principal combatants were acting only as auxiliaries to rival claimants to the Empire, was abandoned, and open war was declared against France. Had this straightforward course been adopted two years before, Stair would probably have turned the date of the declaration of war into that of the conclusion of an honourable peace. As matters stood the war was prolonged, and the time of its avowed inception was chosen as the moment for discarding the ablest of living British Generals.

AUTHORITIES.—The best accounts of the battle of Dettingen will be found in a collection of letters entitled *British Glory Revived*, in the British Museum, and in a great number of letters printed in the *Gentleman's Magazine*. There are accounts also in the *Life of the Duke of Cumberland*, and in the anonymous *Memorial of the E[arl] of S[tair]*. The best known of the French accounts is that of Voltaire in *Siècle de Louis Quinze*, which should be read with Noailles's report to the King in *Correspondance de Louis XV. et du Maréchal Noailles*. The exploits of Thomas Brown are to be found in the newspapers, and in Cannon's *History of the Third Dragoons*. The best plan of the battle that I have seen is in the *Memorial of the E. of S.* As a specimen of the doggerel effusions, I transcribe one stanza from a broadsheet in the British Museum:—

Our noble generals played their parts,

Our soldiers fought like thunder,

Prince William too, that valiant heart

In fight performed wonders.

Though through the leg with bullet shot

The Prince his wound regarded not,

But still maintained his post and fought

    For glorious George of England.

CHAPTER V

However fortunate might be the issue of Dettingen, it served at least its purpose in preventing the despatch of French reinforcements to the Danube and to Bohemia; and the campaign of 1743 closed with the utter collapse of Belleisle's great schemes and with the expulsion of the French from Germany. It was now clear that the war would be carried on in the familiar cockpit of the Austrian Netherlands. Such a theatre was convenient for France, since it lay close to her own borders, and convenient for the Allies, because the Dutch had at last been persuaded to join them, and because the British would be brought nearer to their base at Ostend. Marshal Saxe, whose fine talent had hitherto been wasted under incompetent French Generals in Bohemia, was appointed to the chief command of the French in Flanders; and every effort was made to give him a numerous and well-equipped army, and to enable him to open his campaign in good time.

1744.

In England the preparations by no means corresponded with the necessities of the position. The estimates indeed provided for a force of twenty-one thousand British in Flanders in 1744 as against sixteen thousand in the previous year, but only at the cost of depleting the weak garrison left in England; for the actual number of men voted for the two years was the same. All British officers of experience strongly urged upon the Government the importance of being first in the field,[177] but when an army was to be made up in different proportions of English, Dutch, Germans, and Austrians it needed a Marlborough to bring the discordant Courts into harmony as well as to make ready the troops for an early campaign. By the beginning of April eighty thousand French soldiers had marched from their winter quarters, and were concentrated on the frontier between the Scheldt and the Sambre, while the Allies were still scattered about in cantonments, not exceeding even then a total strength of fifty-five thousand men. Wade, the English commander, delayed first by confusion at home and next by contrary winds, was still in England while the French were concentrating, and not a single English recruit to repair the losses of the past campaign had arrived in Flanders. Then arose disputes as to the disposition of the Allied forces, both Austrians and Dutch being nervously apprehensive of leaving their towns on the frontier without garrisons. When in the second week in May the Allied Army was at last collected close to Brussels, it was still weaker by twenty thousand men than it should have been, and found itself confronted with the task of holding Flanders, Brabant, Hainault, and the Sambre against a superior force of French.[178] May passed away and June came, but the Allies remained helpless and motionless in their camp, while Saxe, after a short march westward, turned north and advanced steadily between the Scheldt and the Lys. His principal object was not very difficult to divine. By the middle of June his detachments had seized Ypres and Fort Knock, which commanded the canal from Nieuport to Ypres, thus cutting off the British from one of their bases on the coast. It remained to be seen whether he would aim next at Ostend, where the whole of the British stores of ordnance were accumulated, or whether he would attempt Bruges and Ghent in order to secure the navigation of the Bruges Canal as well as of the Scheldt and Lys. Again, it was always open to him, if he pleased, to besiege Tournay, a fortress which the Allies would not willingly lose. Thus the problem set to the Allies was not easy of solution; but of all solutions they chose the worst. The Dutch and Austrians could not bear the notion of forsaking any one of their darling strongholds, and insisted that the strength of the army should be frittered away in providing weak garrisons for the defence of all.[179] Wade, to do him justice, was for keeping all the troops together, crossing the Scheldt, and taking up a strong position to cover Ghent; but the Austrians would not consent lest they should expose Brussels.[180] Wade was certainly not a strong man, but he must not be too hardly judged. Marlborough had spent the most anxious days of all his campaigns in distraction between the safety of Ghent and of Brussels, and had only extricated himself by the march that preceded the battle of Oudenarde.

July.

Meanwhile King George had been exerting himself with great energy, but two months too late, to provide Wade with additional troops, both British and Dutch, and had begged that Prince Charles of Lorraine might cross the Rhine with his whole army, and direct the operations in Flanders as Commander-in-Chief of all the Allies. It was a wise step in every way, since the Prince's relationship to Queen Maria Theresa assured to him the seniority in rank which was needed to hold so heterogeneous a host in coherence. Prince Charles did his share of the work admirably, forcing his passage across the Rhine with great skill in the face of the French, and taking up a strong position on the frontier of Alsace. A few days later the British reinforcements reached Wade, and King George issued positive orders to him to take the offensive and "commence hostilities of all kinds."[181]

July $\frac{20}{31}$.

It seemed, indeed, as if the time were come for pressing home upon the French; but just at this critical moment Frederick of Prussia intervened in favour of France, and by a threat to invade Bohemia brought Prince Charles back quickly over the Rhine. None the less Wade and his fellows held a council of war and resolved to bring Saxe to action if possible. King George gave his gracious approval to their plan, and on the 31st of July the Allies turned westward and crossed the Scheldt. It still remained to be seen, however, whether Saxe would allow an action to be forced on him; for he lay now, entrenched to the teeth, on the Lys between Menin and Courtrai, which was a pretty clear indication that he would not. At this moment Lord Stair, who had followed the course of operations carefully from England, came forward, like a true pupil of Marlborough, with a new plan of campaign. His advice was that the Allies should turn Saxe's tactics against himself. They should march south to Orchies, between Lille and Tournay, and there encamp, where they would be within reach of half a dozen French fortified towns. The French would not dare to leave the fortresses defenceless; and the garrisons necessary to render them secure would absorb the whole of their force in the field. Then the Allies could send detachments into France and lay Picardy under contribution, or possibly carry out the plan, rejected two years before, of a march to the Seine. The King of Prussia's action only made some bold stroke of the kind the more imperative.[182]

Stair had gained over the Austrian general D'Arenberg to this project in 1742; but it was hardly likely to be accepted by him now. Carteret, in forwarding Stair's memorandum to Wade, gave him no positive orders except at least to do something; but poor Wade found it impossible to make the Austrians do anything. The Allies having crossed the Scheldt halted inactive for weeks, and no persuasion could induce D'Arenberg to move. At last the army did march down to the plains of Lille, but without its artillery, so that it could not be said seriously to threaten the French fortresses. The Dutch and Austrians had undertaken to furnish a siege-train, but had taken no step to procure one of the ten thousand horses that were required to transport it. After a short sojourn in the south the Allies marched helplessly northward once more. August passed away and September came, but even in the fourth month of the campaign the Dutch and Austrians were still without their artillery.[183] Wade boldly proposed to force Saxe's lines on the Lys: the Austrians refused. He proposed to pounce on a detachment of fourteen thousand men which Saxe had imprudently isolated from his main army: D'Arenberg carefully sent a weak body of cavalry to reveal to the detachment the danger of its position. Finally, in the first week of October, the Allies retired into winter-quarters, which was precisely the object for which D'Arenberg had been working from the first. Despite the English subsidies, he had no money with which to pay his troops, and he wished to spare the Austrian Netherlands the burden of furnishing forage and contributions. Wade, sick in body and distressed in mind, at once resigned his command. He had had enough of the Austrian alliance, and King George before long was to have enough of it also.[184]

| 1745. |

Once again, despite the endless length to which the war was dragging on, the establishment of the British forces remained virtually unaugmented for the year 1745. The troops allotted for service in Flanders were indeed raised to a strength of twenty-five thousand men, but this was effected only by reducing the garrison of Great Britain to fifteen thousand, which, as events were to prove before the year's end, created a situation of perilous weakness. Moreover, the past campaign had revealed a failing in one of the confederated powers which was hardly less serious than the impecuniosity and selfishness of Austria. The Dutch army, which under Marlborough had done such brilliant service, was become hopelessly inefficient. The competition of rival demagogues for popular favour had reduced it to such weakness in numbers that it hardly sufficed to find efficient garrisons for the fortified towns. Concurrently its discipline had suffered, and General Ligonier had already complained that the Dutch troops which served with the Allies in 1744 were intolerably insubordinate and disorderly, setting a bad example to the whole army.[185] In February 1745 Ligonier again brought the matter to the notice of the English Government. The Dutch, he said, would probably keep all their men in garrison, and if the Allies were so weak that they could only find garrisons for the fortresses on the frontier, the French would be free to go where they pleased. It would be far better, therefore, to make a great effort, collect a hundred thousand men, take the offensive, and end the war in a single campaign. Ten thousand men would be required to guard the line of the Bruges Canal, and the remainder should besiege Maubeuge and Landreçy and enter France by the line of the Sambre, making the Meuse the main line of communication, as open alike to the passage of reinforcements from England, from Holland, and from Germany.[186] Such counsel was not likely to find acceptance with the men who had mismanaged the war so far. One important change, however, was made by the appointment of the Duke of Cumberland to be Commander-in-Chief in Flanders, and also in Great Britain.[187] The Duke at the time of this promotion still wanted a month to complete his twenty-fifth year, but he had from his boyhood been an enthusiastic soldier, he had studied his profession, he had shown bravery at Dettingen, and, young though he might be, he was older than Condé had been when he first gained military fame. Finally, it was an immense advantage that a prince of a reigning family should preside over so motley an army as that of the Allies, since there would be the less disposition to cavil at his authority.

April 22
May 3.
April $\frac{19}{30}$.
April 28
May 9.

Cumberland entered upon his work energetically enough, crossed over to Flanders early in April, made all his arrangements for concentration at Brussels on the 2nd of May, and actually began his march southward on the following day.[188] Even so, however, Marshal Saxe had taken the field before him, assembling his troops in Hainault, as in the previous year, so that it was impossible to divine which of the fortresses of the barrier he might intend to attack. After a feint which pointed to the siege of Mons, he marched rapidly upon Tournay and invested it on the 30th of April, screening his movements so skilfully with his cavalry that not a word of his operations reached Cumberland until nearly a week later. Cumberland, after leaving Soignies on the 3rd of May, moved slowly south-westward by Cambron, Maulbay, and Leuse, and arrived on the evening of the 9th at Brissoel, within sight of Saxe's army. The ground immediately in front of the Allies was broken by little copses, woods, and enclosures, all of them crammed with mercenary irregular troops—Pandours, Grassins, and the like—which, imitated first from the Austrians, had by this time become a necessary part of the French as of every army. Beyond this broken ground a wide plain swept in a gentle, almost unbroken slope to the village of Fontenoy, which formed the centre of Saxe's position. The advanced parties of irregulars, together with twelve squadrons drawn up on the slope before Fontenoy, forbade Cumberland's further advance for that day, and the Allies encamped for the night. Headquarters were fixed at Maubray, a village in full sight of Fontenoy, and a bare mile and a half to the south-eastward of the French camp.

April 29
May 10.

On the next day the French advanced posts were pushed out of the copses, and Cumberland, together with the Prince of Waldeck and the Count of Königseck, who commanded the Dutch and the Austrians respectively, went forward to reconnoitre the position. Saxe's army occupied the crest of the slope, lying astride of the two roads that lead from Condé and from Leuse to Tournay. His right rested on the village of Anthoin and on the Scheldt, the tower of Anthoin Castle marking the western boundary of his position with clearness enough. From thence his line extended due east along the crest of the height for nearly two miles to the village of Fontenoy. A few hundred yards before Fontenoy stands the hamlet of Bourgeon, but this was now veiled in smoke and flame, having been fired by the Pandours as they retired.

From Anthoin to Fontenoy Saxe's front faced due south, but eastward from Fontenoy it turned back almost at right angles to the forest of Barry and the village of Ramecroix, fronting considerably to eastward of south. The village of Vezon, however, which lies in the same straight line with Fontenoy due east of Anthoin, was also occupied by the French as an advanced post. This was quickly cleared by Cumberland's troops, and the Allied Generals completed their reconnaissance. The position was undoubtedly strong by nature and had been strengthened still further by art. Beyond Anthoin the French right flank was secured by a battery erected on the western bank of the Scheldt, while the village itself was entrenched, and held by two brigades. Between Anthoin and Fontenoy three redoubts had been constructed, and the space was defended by three brigades of infantry backed by eight squadrons of horse. Fontenoy itself had been fortified with works and cannon, and made as strong as possible; and from Fontenoy to the forest of Barry ran a double line of entrenchments, the first line held by nine and the second by eleven battalions of infantry. At the edge of the forest of Barry were two more redoubts, the foremost of them called the Redoubt d'Eu, both armed with cannon to sweep the open space between the forest and Fontenoy; in rear of the forest were posted nine more battalions, and in rear of all two strong lines of cavalry. The flower of the French army, both horse and foot, was stationed in this space on Saxe's left, for the English had the right of the line in the Allied Army, and Saxe knew the reputation of the red-coats.

The Allied Generals decided to attack on the following day. Königseck, it is said, was for harassing Saxe's communications and compelling him to raise the siege of Tournay; but finding himself overruled by Cumberland and by Waldeck he gave way. Cumberland's force was decidedly inferior in numbers, being less than fifty thousand against fifty-six thousand men, but he was young and impetuous, and had been strongly impressed by the disastrous inaction of the preceding campaign. It was agreed that the Dutch and Austrians should assail the French centre and right, the Dutch in particular being responsible for Fontenoy, while the British attacked the French left between that village and the forest of Barry.

| April 30 |
| May 11. |

At two o'clock on the following morning the British began to move out of their camp upon Vezon, the cavalry leading. The advance took much time, for there were many narrow lanes to be traversed before the force could debouch upon the slope, and when the slope was passed it was still necessary to defile through the village of Vezon. Cumberland's order of attack was simple. Brigadier Ingoldsby, with the Twelfth and Thirteenth Foot, the Forty-second Highlanders, a Hanoverian battalion, and three six-pounder cannon, was to assault the Redoubt d'Eu on the right flank of the line of the British advance, and to carry it with the bayonet. The remainder of the infantry was simply to march up across the thousand yards of open ground between it and Fontenoy and sweep the enemy out of their entrenchments.

Before five o'clock the advanced squadrons of the British horse, fifteen in all, under General Campbell, had passed through Vezon and deployed in the plain beyond, to cover the formation of the infantry for the attack. The French batteries in Fontenoy and the redoubt at once opened fire on them, but the cavalry endured the fire for an hour unmoved, until at length a shot carried away General Campbell's leg. The gallant veteran, who had fought at Malplaquet, and was now seventy-eight years of age, was carried dying from the field, full of lamentation that he could take no further part in the action. No one but himself seems to have known for what purpose his squadrons had been brought forward, and accordingly after his fall they were withdrawn. The infantry then moved up to the front, where General Ligonier proceeded to form them in two lines, without further interruption, to use his own simple words, than a lively and murderous cannonade from the French. Cumberland meanwhile ordered up seven six-pounders to the right of the British front, which quickly came into action. Conspicuous before the French front rode an officer on a white horse, and the English gunners at once began to lay wagers who should kill him. The second or third shot brought the white charger to the ground, and his rider was carried, shattered and dying, to the rear. He was Count Grammont, the gallant but thoughtless officer who had spoiled the combinations of Noailles at Dettingen. Then, turning to their more legitimate work, the gunners quickly made their presence felt among the French field-batteries; but the round shot never ceased to plough into the scarlet ranks of the British from Fontenoy and from the Redoubt d'Eu. Ligonier's two lines of infantry were soon formed, with the cavalry in two more lines in their rear, and the General presently sent word to Cumberland that he was ready to advance as soon as Waldeck should lead his Dutch against Fontenoy. The name of the aide-de-camp who carried this message should not be omitted, for he was Captain Jeffery Amherst of the First Guards.

Thereupon the Dutch and Austrians, in the centre and left, advanced against Fontenoy and Anthoin, but flinching from the fire in front, and above all from that in their flank from the battery on the other side of the Scheldt, soon shrank back under cover and could not be induced to move forward again.[189] Worst of all, the Dutch cavalry was smitten with panic, galloped back on to the top of some of the British squadrons, and fled away wildly to Hal crying out that all was lost. Things therefore went ill on the Allied left; and meanwhile on the right there was enacted a blunder still more fatal. For Ingoldsby, misconceiving his instructions, hesitated to make his attack on the

Redoubt d'Eu, and despite repeated orders from Cumberland never delivered it at all. Cumberland, however, was impatient. Without further delay he placed himself at the head of the British, who were standing as Ligonier had arrayed them, in most beautiful order. In the first line, counting from right to left, stood a battalion of the First Guards, another of the Coldstreams, and another of the Scots Guards, the First, Twenty-first, Thirty-first, Eighth, Twenty-fifth, Thirty-third, and Nineteenth; in the second line the Buffs occupied the post of honour on the right, and next to them came in succession the Twenty-third, Thirty-second, Eleventh, Twenty-eighth, Thirty-fourth, and Twentieth. Certain Hanoverian battalions joined them on the extreme left. The drums beat, the men shouldered arms, and the detachments harnessed themselves to the two light field-guns that accompanied each battalion. Ingoldsby saw what was going forward and aligned his battalions with them on the right. Then the word was given to advance, and the two lines moved off with the slow and measured step for which they were famous in Europe.

Forward tramped the ranks of scarlet, silent and stately as if on parade. Full half a mile of ground was to be traversed before they could close with the invisible enemy that awaited them in the entrenchments over the crest of the slope, and the way was marked clearly by the red flashes and puffs of white smoke that leaped from Fontenoy and the Redoubt d'Eu on either flank. The shot plunged fiercely and more fiercely into the serried lines as they advanced into that murderous cross-fire, but the gaping ranks were quietly closed, the perfect order was never lost, the stately step was never hurried. Only the Hanoverians in the second line, finding that they were cramped for space, dropped back quietly and decorously, and marched on in third line behind the British. Silent and inexorable the scarlet lines strode on. They came abreast of village and redoubt, and the shot which had hitherto swept away files now swept away ranks. Then the first line passed beyond redoubt and village, and the French cannon took it in reverse. The gaps grew wider and more frequent, the front grew narrower as the men closed up, but still the proud battalions advanced, strewing the sward behind them with scarlet, like some mass of red blossoms that floats down a lazy stream and sheds its petals as it goes.

At last the crest of the ridge was gained and the ranks of the French battalions came suddenly into view little more than a hundred yards distant, their coats alone visible behind the breastwork. Next to the forest of Barry, and exposed to the extreme right of the British, a line of red showed the presence of the Swiss Guards; next to them stood a line of blue, the four battalions of the French Guards, and next to the Guards a line of white, the regiments of Courtin, Aubeterre, and of the King, the choicest battalions of the French army. Closer and closer came the British, still with arms shouldered, always silent, always with the same slow, measured tread, till they had advanced to within fifty yards of the French. Then at length Lord Charles Hay of the First Guards stepped forward with flask in hand, and doffing his hat drank politely to his enemies. "I hope, gentlemen," he shouted, "that you are going to wait for us to-day and not swim the Scheldt as you swam the Main at Dettingen. Men of the King's company," he continued, turning round to his own people, "these are the French Guards, and I hope you are going to beat them to-day"; and the English Guards answered with a cheer. The French officers hurried to the front, for the appearance of the British was a surprise to them, and called for a cheer in reply, but only a half-hearted murmur came from the French ranks, which quickly died away and gave place to a few sharp words of command; for the British were now within thirty yards. "For what we are about to receive may the Lord make us truly thankful," murmured an English Guardsman as he looked down the barrels of the French muskets, but before his comrades round him had done laughing the French Guards had fired; and the turn of the British had come at last.[190]

For despite that deadly march through the cross-fire of the French batteries to the muzzles of the French muskets, the scarlet ranks still glared unbroken through the smoke; and now the British muskets, so long shouldered, were levelled, and with crash upon crash the volleys rang out from end to end of the line, first the First Guards, then the Scots, then the Coldstreams, and so through brigade after brigade, two battalions loading while the third fired, a ceaseless, rolling, infernal fire. Down dropped the whole of the French front rank, blue coats, red coats and white, before the storm. Nineteen officers and six hundred men of the French and Swiss Guards fell at the first discharge; regiment Courtin was crushed out of existence; regiment Aubeterre, striving hard to stem the tide, was swept aside by a single imperious volley which laid half of its men on the ground. The British infantry were perfectly in hand; their officers could be seen coolly tapping the muskets of the men with their canes so that every discharge might be low and deadly, and nothing could withstand their fire; while the battalion guns also poured in round after round of grape with terrible effect. The first French line was utterly shattered and broken. Even while the British were advancing Saxe had brought up additional troops to meet them and had posted regiments Couronne and Soissonois in rear of the King's regiment, and the Brigade Royal in rear of the French Guards; but all alike went down before the irresistible volleys. The red-coats continued their triumphant advance for full three hundred yards into the heart of the French camp, and old Ligonier's heart leaped within him, for he thought that the battle was won.

Saxe for his part thought little differently from Ligonier; but though half dead with dropsy, reduced to suck a bullet to assuage his intolerable thirst, so weak that he could not ride but was carried about the field in a wicker litter, the gallant German never for a moment lost his head. Sending a message to the French King, who with the Dauphin was watching the action from a windmill in the rear, to retire across the Scheldt without delay, he strove to gain time to rally his infantry. On the first repulse of the French Guards Cumberland had detached two battalions to help the Dutch by a flanking attack on Fontenoy. Seeing that this movement must be checked at all hazards, Saxe headed these troops back by a charge of cavalry; whereupon one of the battalions extended itself along the left flank of the British. Partly in this way, partly owing to the incessant play of the French artillery on both flanks, the two British lines assumed the form of two huge oblong columns which gradually became welded into one. The change was not untimely, for now the first line of the French cavalry, which had been posted in rear of the forest of Barry, came down upon the British at full gallop, but only to reel back shivered to fragments by the same terrible fire. Then the second line tried its fortune, but met with no better fate. Finally, the Household Cavalry, the famous Maison du Roi, burning with all the ardour of Dettingen unavenged, was launched against the scarlet columns, and like its predecessors, came flying back, a mob of riderless horses and uncontrollable men, decimated, shattered and repulsed by the never-ending fire. "It was like charging two flaming fortresses rather than two columns of infantry."[191]

Nevertheless some time was hereby gained for the broken French infantry to reform. The British, once arrived within the French camp, came to a halt, and looked at last to see how the Dutch were faring on their left. As has already been told, Waldeck's attack had been a total failure, and the British, unsupported and always under a cross-fire of artillery, fell back to the crest of the ridge and were reformed for a second attack. Waldeck undertook to make another attempt on Fontenoy, and Cumberland in reliance upon his help again advanced at the head of the British. But meanwhile Saxe had brought forward his reserves from Ramecroix, and among them the Irish brigade, to meet him, while artillery had also been brought up from the French right to play upon the British front. The French Guards and the rest of the troops of the French first line had also been rallied, and the task of the British was well-nigh desperate. The Irish brigade, which consisted of six battalions, was made up not of Irish only but of Scots and English also, desperate characters who went into action with a rope round their necks, and would fight like devils. Yet, even in this second attack the British carried their advance as far as in the first, the perfection of their fire-discipline enabling them to beat back even the Irish brigade for a time. But their losses had been frightfully heavy; the Dutch would not move one foot to the attack of Fontenoy, and the cannonade in front added to that in the flanks became unendurable. The French infantry likewise closed round on them in superior numbers on both flanks, and it became apparent that there was nothing for it but a retreat.

Ligonier sent back two battalions to secure the roads leading through Vezon, and the retreat then began in perfectly good order. The French Household Cavalry made a furious charge upon the rear of the column as it faced about, but found to its cost that the infernal fire was not yet quenched. The three battalions of Guards and a battalion of Hanoverians turned sternly about to meet them, and gave them a few parting volleys, which wholly extinguished one regiment and brought down every officer of another. A few British squadrons, the Blues conspicuous among them, pushed forward, in spite of heavy losses, through the cross-fire to lend what help they could, and the remnant of the heroic battalions retired, facing about in succession at every hundred yards, as steadily and proudly as they had advanced.

Their losses in the action were terribly severe. Of the fifteen thousand infantry, English and Hanoverian, for the Hanoverians bore themselves not less nobly than their Allies, nearly six thousand were killed or wounded, the casualties of the twenty English battalions just exceeding four thousand men. The heaviest sufferers were the Twelfth and Twenty-third regiments, both of which lost over three hundred men, the Twenty-first and Thirty-first, which lost rather less than three hundred men apiece, and the three battalions of Guards, which lost each of them about two hundred and fifty. Of the Generals of Foot, Cumberland, Ligonier, and Brigadier Skelton, though in the hottest of the fire, alone came off unhurt; all of the rest were either killed or wounded. Many regiments of cavalry also suffered not a little, in particular the Blues and Royal Dragoons; and the total loss of the British cavalry exceeded three hundred men and six hundred horses. The loss of the French was never made public, but was certainly at least equal to that of the Allies. Contemporary accounts set it down, with no great improbability, at fully ten thousand men. As an example of the prowess of British infantry, Fontenoy stands almost without a parallel in its history. The battalions formed under a cross-fire of artillery, remained halted under the same fire, advanced slowly for half a mile in perfect order under the same fire, and marched up to within pistol-shot of the French infantry to receive their volley before they discharged a shot. They shattered the French battalions to pieces, repulsed three separate attacks of cavalry, halted under a heavy cannonade, retired for some distance and reformed under a cross-fire, advanced again with both artillery and musketry playing on front and flanks, made the bravest brigade in the French service recoil, repelled another desperate attack of cavalry, and retired slowly and orderly under a cross-fire almost to the end. By consent of all the British commanders it was Ingoldsby's misunderstanding of his orders and his failure to capture the Redoubt d'Eu that lost the battle; and Ingoldsby was duly tried by court-martial for his behaviour. He was, however, acquitted of all but an error in judgment; and indeed there was no question of cowardice, for he accompanied the remainder of the infantry in its advance with his own detachment and was severely wounded. It is customary to blame Cumberland for dashing his head against a wall in attempting such an attack, but he could hardly have been expected to count on such bad luck as the failure of Ingoldsby on one flank and of the Dutch on the other. The sheer audacity of his advance went near to give him the victory. Saxe owned that he never dreamed that any General would attempt such a stroke, or that any troops would execute it. Cumberland is blamed also for not attacking either the Redoubt d'Eu or Fontenoy after he had penetrated into the French camp. This charge is less easy to rebut, for the French always know when they are beaten, and seeing their left rolled up and troops advancing on Fontenoy in flank and rear would probably have given up the game for lost, and that the more readily since their ammunition in Fontenoy was for the moment nearly exhausted. Even so, however, Saxe's reserves were always at hand at Ramecroix, and would have required to be held in check. Another puzzling question, namely, why Cumberland did not make greater use of his artillery in the action, is answered by the fact that the contractors for the horsing of the guns ran off with the horses early in the day. Such an occurrence was by no means unusual, and yet it never happened to Marlborough, not even at Malplaquet. Altogether, the conclusion seems to be that Cumberland stumbled on to a brilliant feat of arms by mistake, and, though seconded by his troops with bravery equal to his own, was not a General of sufficient capacity to turn his success to account.

At the close of the action Cumberland retreated to Ath and encamped under the guns of that fortress, leaving his wounded to the mercy of the French, who, by a strange perversion of their usual chivalry, treated them with shameful barbarity. Among the wounded, strangely enough, were a few of the new sect of Methodists founded by John Wesley, who faced death and wounds with the stern exultation that had once inspired the troopers of Cromwell. One of them wrote to Wesley, that even after a bullet in each arm had forced him to retire from the field, he hardly knew whether he was on earth or heaven, such was the sweetness of the day. This man and a few more of his kind probably helped their fellow-sufferers through the misery of the days following the battle, until Cumberland's furious remonstrances with Saxe procured for them better treatment.

| June 30 |
| July 11. |
| August. |

From Ath Cumberland fell back to Lessines and drew out such British corps as were in garrison in Flanders to replace those which had suffered most heavily in the action. Meanwhile Tournay, very shortly after the battle, fell by treachery into the hands of the French; and Saxe's field-army being thus raised to a force nearly double that of the Allies, Cumberland was reduced to utter helplessness. The mischief of Fontenoy lay not in the repulse and the loss of men, for the British did not consider themselves to have been beaten, but in the destruction of all confidence in the Dutch troops. The troubles which had harassed Wade to despair now reappeared. Cumberland, despite his inferiority in strength, was expected somehow to defend Flanders, Brabant, and above all Brussels, and yet simultaneously to keep an active army in the field. Worse than this, he attempted to fulfil the expectation. Against his better judgment he weakened his force still further by detaching a force for the garrison of Mons,[192] and then, instead of taking up a strong position on the Scheldt to cover Ghent at all hazards, he yielded to the pressure of the Austrians and crossed the Dender to cover Brussels.[193] Halting too long between two opinions he at last sent off a detachment for the defence of Ghent, half of which was cut off and turned back with heavy loss, while the other half, after enduring much rough usage on the march, entered Ghent only to see the town surprised by the French on the following day. Four British regiments took part in this unlucky enterprise and suffered heavy loss, while the Royal Scots and the Twenty-third, which had been despatched to Ghent after Fontenoy, of course became prisoners.[194] Moreover, a vast quantity of British military stores were captured in Ghent, although Cumberland had a week before ordered that they should be removed.[195] After this blow Cumberland retired to Vilvorde, a little to the north of Brussels, still hoping to cover both that city and Antwerp, and so to preserve his communications both with Germany and with the sea. Here again he sacrificed his better judgment to the clamour of the Austrians, for he would much have preferred to secure Antwerp only. His position was in fact most critical, and he was keenly alive to it.[196] Just when his anxiety was greatest there came a letter from the Secretary of State, announcing that invasion of England was imminent, and hoping that troops could be spared from Flanders without prejudice to his operations. "What!" answered Ligonier indignantly, "Are you aware that the enemy has seventy thousand men against our thirty thousand, and that they can place a superior force on the canal before us and send another army round between us and Antwerp to cut off our supplies and force us to fight at a disadvantage? This is our position, and this is the result of providing His Royal Highness with insufficient troops; and yet you speak of our having a corps to spare to defend England!"[197]

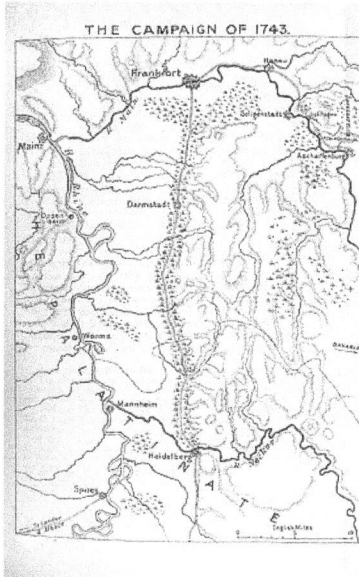

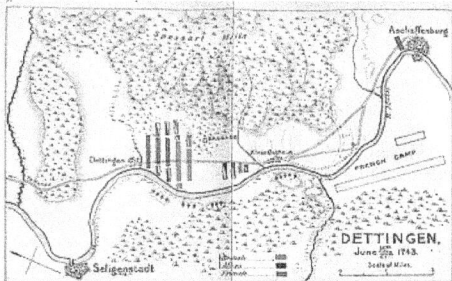

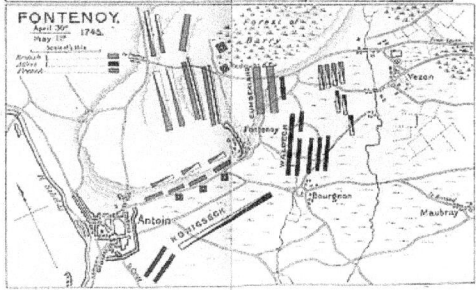

Walker & Boutall del.

To face page 122.

THE CAMPAIGN OF 1743.

DETTINGEN, June $\frac{16^{th}}{27^{th}}$ 1743.

FONTENOY, $\frac{April\ 30^{th}}{May\ 11^{th}}$ 1745.

Aug. $\frac{13}{24}$.
Sept.
Oct.

Saxe's plan for reducing the Allies was in fact uniformly the same throughout the whole of the war, namely to cut off their communications with the sea on one side and with Germany on the other. Even before he began to press Cumberland northward toward Antwerp he had detached a force to lay siege to Ostend, which was the English base. Cumberland, on his side, had advised that the dykes should be broken down and the country inundated in order to preserve it, and both Dutch and Austrians had promised that this should be done; but as usual it was not done, and before the end of August Ostend had surrendered to the French. The English base was then perforce shifted to Antwerp. But by this time the requests for the return of troops to England had become urgent and imperative orders. First ten battalions were recalled, then the rest of the foot, and at last practically the whole of the army, including Cumberland himself.[198] It is now time to explain the causes for the alarm in England.

AUTHORITIES.—The official account of Fontenoy was drawn up by Ligonier in French and translated into English, with some omissions, for publication. The French version is far the better and will be found in the State Papers. The account in the *Life of the Duke of Cumberland* is poor, though valuable as having been drawn up from the reports of the English Generals. Of the French accounts Voltaire's is the best known, and, as might be expected from such a hand, admirably spirited. More valuable are the accounts in the *Conquête des Pays Bas*, in the *Mémoires du Maréchal de Saxe*, where Saxe's own report may be read, in the *Campagnes des Pays Bas*, and in Espagnac. The newspapers furnish a few picturesque incidents of some value.

CHAPTER VI

Ever since the death of Cardinal Fleury, in January 1743, the hopes of the Jacobites for French help in an attempt to re-establish the Stuarts by force of arms had been steadily reviving. Cardinal Tencin, Fleury's successor, was warmly attached to the cause of the exiled house; the feeling between France and England was greatly embittered; the beginning of overt hostilities could be only a matter of time; and an invasion of Britain was the most powerful diversion that could be made to divide the forces of the partisans of the Pragmatic Sanction. In the autumn of 1743 preparations for a descent upon England from Dunkirk under Marshal Saxe were matured, and a French fleet, with Saxe and Prince Charles Stuart on board, actually sailed as far as Dungeness. There, however, it was dispersed by a storm, which wrecked many of the transports, and for the present put an effectual end to the enterprise.

July 25
August 5.

Prince Charles returned to Paris not a little disappointed, but receiving no further encouragement from France nourished the hope of landing in Scotland and making his attempt with the aid of his British adherents only. Those adherents for their part had warned him that success was hopeless unless he should bring with him at least six thousand men and ten thousand stand of arms; but Charles was none the less determined to try his fortune. The defeat of the British at Fontenoy doubtless strengthened his resolution: in June 1745 he came to a definite decision, and on the 25th of July he landed at Loch-nan-Uamh, between Moidart and Arisaig, with seven companions, of whom one only besides himself, Sir John Macdonald, had any experience of the military profession. Three weeks before his actual arrival a rumour of his landing had reached Sir John Cope, the General commanding in Scotland, who recommended that all officers should be recalled to their posts, and that every precaution should be taken.[199] Even so, however, Charles had been on Scottish soil a full week before Cope could believe the rumour to be true.

August $\frac{19}{30}$.

The three persons on whom the Government chiefly relied for the safety of Scotland were Cope himself, Andrew Fletcher, the Lord Justice-Clerk, and Duncan Forbes, the Lord President: but the only man in authority who at once betrayed serious apprehension was the Lord Advocate Craigie, who had been dreading some such complication ever since Fontenoy. Cope also was uneasy, owing to the extreme weakness of the force at his disposal. He had not, in all, more than three thousand men, for the most part new and raw regiments upon which he could repose little trust, and which in spite of his representations in the previous year were not even properly armed.[200] He resolved, however, to march northward at once in order to overawe any waverers by a display of force: and on receiving at last, after long delay, absolute confirmation of the news of the Pretender's disembarkation, he threw his most trustworthy regiment, the Sixth Foot, with two companies of the Royal Scots, into the forts which protected the line of Loch Lochy and Loch Ness.[201] It was, however, impossible for him to move without first making provision for the subsistence of his little army, and this was a work of much time and difficulty. It was not until the 19th of August that he finally marched from Edinburgh for Fort Augustus with fifteen hundred men of the Forty-fourth, Forty-sixth, and Forty-seventh Foot, and a convoy of stores so large as greatly to impede his movements.

Meanwhile affairs had assumed a far more dangerous complexion. Charles had been active in summoning the leaders of the clans on which he counted; and though less favourably received than he had hoped he had secured Cameron of Lochiel, Macdonald of Keppoch, Macdonald of Glengarry, and others. On the 16th of August a party of Keppoch's and Lochiel's men succeeded in cutting off two companies of the Royal Scots which were on their way to Fort Augustus, killed a dozen of them, and took the rest prisoners: and on the 19th, the very day of Cope's departure from Edinburgh, Charles raised his standard at Glenfinnan, to find himself on the next day at the head of sixteen hundred men.

Cope had not yet received full intelligence of these transactions, but it was pretty evident to him that his advance to the north was likely to be something more than a mere military promenade, and he became extremely unwilling to execute it. Yielding, however, to positive orders from the Lords-Justices[202] he continued his march upon Fort Augustus, not a little disgusted to find that, though he had encumbered his train with several hundred stand of arms for distribution to loyal volunteers, no such volunteers were forthcoming to receive them. Charles, for his part, on receiving information of Cope's approach, with great promptitude made a forced march to Corry Arrack, the worst pass on the road, and having disposed his troops with great skill, waited exultingly for the coming of the red-coats that he might overwhelm them during their passage of the defile.[203] To his surprise not a man appeared.

Cope had been made aware of his dispositions and had turned aside from Dalwhinnie to Inverness, leaving the road to the south open to the rebels. From Inverness he despatched urgent messages to Edinburgh for transports to convey his troops southward by sea.

Cope has always been greatly blamed for this movement, the contention being that he should either have maintained his ground in front of Charles or have fallen back on Stirling. All critics, however, overlook the crucial points, that not only was his force inferior to that of the rebels but that he could not trust a man of them. Charles's Highlanders could march two miles to Cope's one, and would have made short work of a large convoy in charge of undisciplined troops. Again, if Cope had halted, the rebels would have been on him in a few hours before he had had time to entrench himself, even supposing that he could have found entrenching tools. The fact that he sent for transports shows that he would not rely upon his troops in a retreat; the advance northward was undertaken contrary to his advice, and the misfortune that followed was simply the usual result of civilians' interference with military operations.

| Aug. 30 |
| Sept. 10. |
| Sept. $\frac{4}{15}$; |
| Sept. $\frac{11}{22}$. |

Charles, on his side, lost no time in following up his advantage, and at once pushed rapidly southward. One of his parties was, indeed, repelled by the minute English garrison which held the post at Ruthin,[204] but his men indemnified themselves by bringing in Macpherson of Cluny a prisoner, and thereby gaining Lord Lovat and the Frasers to the cause. By the 30th of August Charles had reached Blair Athol, and on the 4th of September he entered Perth, where he was joined by James Drummond, titular Duke of Perth, and Lord George Murray, both of them valuable acquisitions for the following that they brought with them, while Murray was, in addition, a very skilful officer. Resuming his march on the 11th, he avoided the guns of Stirling Castle by fording the Forth eight miles above the fortress, and took up his quarters in the town of Stirling, which had opened its gates to him. By the 15th he was within eight miles of Edinburgh.

| Sept. $\frac{16}{27}$. |
| Sept. $\frac{17}{28}$. |

The city was in consternation over his approach. The Castle of Edinburgh was, indeed, provided with an adequate garrison, but the town was absolutely defenceless; nor were there any regular troops at hand excepting the Thirteenth and Fourteenth Dragoons, both of them young regiments, raw and untrained. On the morning of the 16th these two corps, together with a party of the town-guard, were drawn up at Coltbridge, when their picquets were suddenly driven in by the pistol-shots of a few mounted gentlemen of the rebel army. The picquets were seized with inexplicable panic, which presently communicated itself to the main body; and in a few minutes both regiments, despite the entreaties of their officers, were off at full gallop to the south, never stopping until they reached Preston. They had not been there long before the panic was rekindled. One of the dragoons, while in search of forage after dark, fell into a disused coal-pit full of water and shouted lustily for help. Instantly the cry was raised that the Highlanders were on them, and the men, rushing to their horses, galloped away once more through the night, and could not be halted till they reached Dunbar. The "Canter of Coltbrigg," as this ludicrous but shameful flight was dubbed, was the source of all the subsequent success of the Pretender. So petty are the causes that will go near to overset a throne. Probably, if the truth of the matter could be known, it would be found that a few raw horses, unbroken to fire-arms, among the picquets were the cause of the whole disaster.[205] For the moment, however, the panic was decisive in its results. Charles entered Edinburgh without resistance on the following day and took up his quarters at Holyrood; but halting for no more than twenty-four hours in the capital he pursued his march to the south. His troops by this time had swelled to twenty-five hundred men, though many of these were indifferently armed, and the force was absolutely destitute of artillery. Still happy chance had sent panic in advance of him, and he wisely followed it with all possible speed.

Sept. $\frac{19}{30}$.

<u>Sept. 20</u>
October 1.

Cope, meanwhile, on hearing of the march of the rebels southward had moved from Inverness to Aberdeen, where, on the arrival of transports from Edinburgh, he embarked his men and arrived safely on the 16th of September at Dunbar. On the two following days the troops were disembarked, and the army, being reinforced by two hundred Highland levies under Lord Loudoun, and by the Thirteenth and Fourteenth Dragoons, was raised to a total of twenty-three hundred men, with six guns. On the 19th Cope marched northward along the coast road, and on the following day caught sight of the rebels, not, as he had expected, to westward, but to southward of him, quietly halted on the brow of Carberry Hill. He at once took up a strong position, with his rear resting on the sea, his left being covered by a marsh and his right by two enclosures with walls seven feet high, between which ran the road to the village of Prestonpans. In his front lay another enclosure surrounded by a ditch from ten to twelve feet broad; and thus naturally entrenched, Cope's force might well have seemed unassailable. The rebels, however, moved down from the hill and took up their position opposite to the marsh on Cope's right. Cope therefore changed front to the left so as to rest his right on the ditch and his left on the sea, thus presenting his front to the marsh, an alteration which appeared to offer the rebels little advantage. In the course of the evening, however, a man well acquainted with the marsh pointed out to the rebel commanders a passage by which it might safely be traversed; and in the course of the night Charles threw his army safely across and formed it for attack in two lines—twelve hundred men in the first, and the remainder, who were but ill-armed, in the second line. His new position was not more than two hundred yards from the English camp, for Cope, deeming the marsh impassable, had omitted to post a single guard or sentry on that side.

| Sept. 21 |
| October 2. |

A little before daybreak the alarm was given in Cope's camp, and the General hastened to form his line of battle, with his infantry, as usual, in the centre, the Thirteenth Dragoons on his right wing, and the Fourteenth Dragoons on his left. The Highlanders were no sooner formed than Charles gave the signal for attack. They rushed forward with a yell upon the artillery before Cope's front, and drove the gunners, who were seamen from the fleet, away from their guns. Then, firing a volley at the dragoons, they rushed straight upon them with the broadsword and slashed furiously at the noses of the horses. The dragoons, already too well inured to panic, at once wheeled about in confusion. The infantry, though uncovered on both flanks, remained steady and poured in a destructive fire, but the Highlanders immediately closed with them, and the bayonet was no match for broadsword and target. In a few minutes the English were broken and flying for their lives. Four hundred were cut down on the spot and over a thousand more were taken prisoners, one hundred and seventy only succeeding in making their escape. The loss of the rebels was no more than thirty killed and seventy wounded. The whole action did not last ten minutes, and yet never was victory more complete. The dragoons were so thoroughly scared that, after galloping first to Edinburgh, where the Governor indignantly refused to admit them to the Castle, they turned round and hurried south to Berwick, where Cope had already arrived before them.

The moral effect of Prestonpans was prodigious. Twice the English troops had faced the Highlanders, and each time they had fled in panic. On the first occasion no blood had been shed, but Prestonpans brought with it a memory and a tradition of horror, for all of the slain English had perished by the sword, and the field presented a frightful spectacle of severed limbs and mutilated bodies. Charles was for taking advantage of the moment and marching immediately upon London; and if he had done so it is probable that he would at least have reached the capital. There was little or no enthusiasm among the English for the cause of the Guelphs, and there were few or no troops to stand in Charles's way; there was only one fortified place, Newcastle, to trouble him to the south of the Tweed, and the whole district was profoundly scared. But the Highlanders were already hurrying homeward with the plunder gained by the action, diminishing the strength of his force by one-half; so that it was deemed more prudent to return to Edinburgh.

Charles's great object now was the reduction of Edinburgh Castle, which with Stirling Castle and the forts in the Highlands was practically all of Scotland that remained to the Guelphs. A blockade of a few weeks would have forced it to submission by famine, but General Guest, the Governor, threatened to lay the town in ashes if his supplies were cut off. A few shots from his cannon showed that he was in earnest, and, in deference to the entreaties of the townsfolk, Charles was fain to let him have his way. The circumstance might in itself have sufficed to show the futility of military operations on such terms, but the gain of certain prominent Scottish nobles to the cause, and the addition of several hundred volunteers to the rebel army, seemed to afford some compensation for this enforced inactivity. By the end of October Charles's force was augmented to six thousand men, five-sixths of them excellent material, while its efficiency was further heightened by the arrival of several French and Irish officers, who brought with them money, five thousand stand of arms, and six pieces of field artillery.

Meanwhile military preparations went forward in England with feverish activity. Cumberland, as has already been told, received orders to send back first a part, and then the whole of his army: and now the full peril of the situation in Flanders can be realised. It is plain from Ligonier's letters that Saxe had it in his power to destroy the British force encamped at Vilvorde, and that one good soldier at least lived in daily dread of the catastrophe. Had Ligonier's apprehension been fulfilled the throne of the Guelphs must have fallen: and the fault would have been King George's own, for his folly in trifling with the war for two campaigns instead of pursuing it vigorously as Stair had advised. As things were, however, the British passed the North Sea in safety, together with certain Dutch and Hessians who had been summoned, as in 1715, the help of England in pursuance of the Treaty. The Dutch indeed arrived before the British could be despatched, and thus of ten battalions placed under the command of Marshal Wade for the defence of the kingdom no fewer than seven were foreign.[206] Pending the arrival of the troops from over sea frantic efforts were made to fill the ranks, as usual much depleted by drafts, of the regiments at home. On the 6th of September a bounty of no less than six pounds was offered to every recruit who would join the Guards before the 24th, and of four pounds to any enlisting between the 24th and the 1st of October.[207] The spirit of the country also began slowly to kindle: and the newspapers fanned the rising flame by an incessant blast of "No popery, no arbitrary power, no wooden shoes."[208] Fifteen leading noblemen offered to raise and equip two regiments of horse and thirteen of foot at their own expense. The gentlemen of Yorkshire raised a Royal Regiment of Hunters, first germ of our present Yeomanry, which served without pay. Companies of volunteers were formed in London. The peaceful Quakers combined to present every soldier with a flannel waistcoat for the coming winter campaign: and a subscription was started in the City to provide a blanket and two paillasses to each tent, thirty watch-coats to each battalion, and a pair of worsted gloves to every man.[209] The militia also was called out in several counties: and finally Cope was removed from the command in Scotland and replaced by General Handasyde.[210]

| Oct. 31 |
| Nov. 11. |

Charles in the meantime was anxious to move southward with the least possible delay, and fight the motley force which was gathered together under Wade at Newcastle;[211] but his Scottish adherents were most unwilling to move, and it was only when he declared his determination to enter England alone, if no one would follow him, that they grudgingly consented to march for a little distance over the border. Lord George Murray with great wisdom advised that the advance should be through Cumberland rather than Northumberland, which would compel Wade to harass his troops by marches along bad roads through a difficult country. If Wade should remain inactive, which his previous behaviour in command suggested to be more than likely, the rebels would be at liberty to move whither they pleased. The better to conceal the true direction of the advance the army was divided into two columns, the one under Charles himself to march by way of Kelso and the other by way of Moffat, both to converge ultimately on Carlisle. Thus at length, on the 31st of October, the rebels began their advance southward, but still in no very good heart. The letters of the chiefs show that they looked upon the whole enterprise as desperate, and that they longed to be at their homes reaping their harvest, and looking to the wintering of their herds.[212] The rank and file of the Highlanders did not write letters, but simply betook themselves in scores to their homes.

| Nov. $\frac{8}{19}$. |

Nov. $\frac{17}{28}$.
Nov. 20
Dec. 1.

Murray's plan of invasion succeeded admirably. On his arrival at Kelso Charles sent forward an advanced party to order quarters at Wooler, and having thus alarmed Wade for Newcastle turned sharply to the westward and entered Cumberland by Liddesdale. On the following day he was joined by the other column, and the united army, some five thousand strong, proceeded to the investment of Carlisle. The town was held only by a garrison of militia, but the commander and the mayor refused to surrender, and the siege was delayed by a false alarm that Wade was marching to rescue. On the 13th of November, however, batteries were raised by the rebels, whereupon the mayor's courage evaporated and his worship requested a capitulation for the town. Charles refused to grant it unless the Castle also was included, and the result was that he gained both Castle and town with the loss of hardly a man. Wade, when it was too late, started to relieve Carlisle, but, being stopped by a fall of snow, returned again to Newcastle, and sent General Handasyde with two battalions of foot and a regiment of dragoons to re-occupy Edinburgh. This movement increased the anxiety of the Highlanders to return home: but after some debate it was decided to continue the advance. Two hundred men were left to garrison Carlisle, and with a force greatly reduced by desertion Charles, on the 20th, renewed his march to the south without the least molestation from Wade. On the 27th he passed the Ribble, that barrier so often fatal to Scottish invasion, at Preston, where he was well received, and a few recruits were added to his army. Acclamations, too, greeted him on his way to Wigan and Manchester, but the people refused to accept the arms that were offered to them or to enlist themselves for his cause. Only at Manchester the exertions of Mr. Francis Townley, a Roman Catholic of a very old family in the county, availed to raise a couple of hundred men. It was but a trifling addition compared with that expected by the Highland chiefs, and served to confirm their misgivings as to the desperate character of the enterprise.

Dec. 4.

English troops now began to close in upon the little rebel army from every side. Wade was moving down upon it from the north; Cumberland lay before it with eight thousand men at Lichfield, while a still larger force of militia, stiffened by battalions of the Guards, was in process of concentration at Finchley Common for the defence of London. Still the rebels pursued their march southward, the people staring at them as they passed, amused but indifferent, and apparently hardly able to take the matter seriously. At Cambridge sensible middle-aged men talked of taking a chaise to go and see them on the road;[213] and Hogarth, to the great good fortune of posterity, could see nothing in the march of the Guards to Finchley but an admirable subject for the exercise of his pencil and the indulgence of his satire. Yet there was still a panic in store for London. From Macclesfield Lord George Murray sent forward a small force to Congleton, which pushed away a party of horse that lay there and pursued it for some way along the road to Newcastle-under-Lyme. Cumberland, thinking that the rebels were about to advance by that line or turn westward into Wales, turned also westward to Stone to intercept them, and Murray, making a forced march eastward, reached Ashbourne and on the following day entered Derby. By this manœuvre the rebel army had gained two marches on Cumberland and successfully passed by the most formidable force interposed between it and London. The capital was in consternation. Business was suspended, all shops were shut, and the Bank of England only escaped disaster by making its payments in sixpences in order to gain time. Cumberland on discovering his mistake hurried his cavalry by desperate marches to Northampton in order to regain, if possible, the ground that he had lost, but the only result was utter exhaustion of the horses; and the Duke of Richmond, who was in command of this cavalry, frankly confessed that he did not see how the enemy could be stopped. The rapidity of the rebels' movements, the difficulty of moving regular troops during the winter along execrable roads, and above all the want of an efficient head at Whitehall to replace the timid and incompetent Newcastle, served to paralyse the whole strength of England.

| Dec. $\frac{6}{17}$. |
| Dec. $\frac{18}{29}$. |
| Dec. 26. |
| 1746. |
| Jan. $\frac{3}{14}$. |

On the night of his arrival at Derby Charles discussed at length the question of the dress which he should wear on his entry into London; but on the following day his officers represented to him the danger of further advance, with Wade and Cumberland closing in upon his rear. News had arrived of the landing of French troops at Montrose; it would be better, they urged, to retreat while there was yet time and to join them. Charles combated the proposition hotly for the whole day, but yielded at last; and on the morrow the retreat was begun. Cumberland, who had fallen back to Coventry, at once caught up four thousand men and followed the rebels by forced marches, but did not overtake them until the 18th, when his advanced parties made an attack on Murray's rear-guard at Clifton Moor, a few miles to the south of Penrith. The English, however, were repulsed with the loss of a hundred men, a misadventure easily explained by the fact that the action was fought after dark, when the musket was a poor match for the claymore. Still the repulse was not creditable to the royal troops nor encouraging for further attempts upon the rebel rear-guard. Wade meanwhile made no attempt to intercept the northward march of Charles, who crossed the Esk into Scotland unmolested on the 20th of December, and six days later occupied Glasgow. His force, despite many days of halt, had covered the distance from Edinburgh to Derby and from Derby back to Glasgow in exactly eight weeks. A few days later he resumed his march to Stirling, where he was joined by the French, who had landed at Montrose, and by other levies which, notwithstanding General Handasyde's entreaties that they might be attacked from Edinburgh and Inverness, had been allowed to assemble in the north. These reinforcements augmented his strength to nine thousand men: and since the French had brought with them battering guns Charles resolved to besiege the Castle of Stirling and so to secure for himself, if possible, all Scotland north of the Firths of Forth and Clyde.

Meanwhile Cumberland after recovering Carlisle had been recalled to the south of England with most of his infantry to guard the southern coast in case of a French invasion. Wade, who was quite worn out with age and infirmity, was also removed from his command, and at Cumberland's nomination General Hawley was appointed to be Commander-in-Chief in Scotland. Hawley was a man of obscure origin, rough and brutal in manners, but a strict disciplinarian of the ruder school which was beloved of Cumberland, and very far from an incapable soldier. On his arrival at Edinburgh he found himself entrusted with twelve battalions and four regiments of dragoons, and with absolute liberty to do with them as he thought best. Still his difficulties were considerable. Artillery had been given to him but no gunners, his instructions being that he should draw the latter from the garrisons of Berwick and of Edinburgh. On being summoned, however, these gunners proved to be civilians who had been foisted on to the establishment for the sake of their votes, and were not intended to be of any other service.[214] The same principle could be traced in every other detail relating to these two garrisons, for the trail of corruption was over all.[215] Many of the battalions again were no better than militia, and the infantry generally was in so bad a state that it was hard to raise above three or four thousand men fit for service from the whole of it. "I hope we shan't be blamed," wrote Hawley, in explaining his inaction, "but it is not the name of twelve battalions that will do the business. No diligence in me shall be wanting, but a man cannot work without tools. The heavy artillery is still at Newcastle for want of horses, which were sent to Carlisle for no use. The major of artillery is absent through sickness. I suspect his sickness to be a young wife: I know him. I have been obliged to hire a conductor of artillery, and seventy odd men to act as his assistants for the field-artillery. I was three days getting them from the Castle to the Palace-yard and now they are not fit to march."[216] At length by great exertion the whole force of twelve battalions and three regiments of dragoons, with its artillery, was made ready for the field. Hawley then moved up to Falkirk on the way to relieve the beleaguered Castle of Stirling, and encamped on the western side of the town.

Jan. $\frac{17}{28}$.

The rebels so far had made little progress with the siege. The French engineer with them, who was a coxcomb of little skill, had chosen wrong sites for his batteries, and General Blakeney, who was in command of the garrison, had made him sensible of the fact by a most destructive fire. On the 16th of January Charles, hearing of Hawley's march upon Falkirk, left a few hundred men to maintain the blockade of the Castle, and advanced with the remainder to Bannockburn, where he drew them up, as on a field of good omen, in order of battle. Hawley, however, declined to move, his artillery being but just come up: so on the following day Charles determined to attack him. While he was moving forward Hawley was enjoying the hospitality of Callendar House from Lady Kilmarnock, wife to one of the rebel leaders, having left General Huske, an excellent officer, in command. Manœuvring with a small detachment to distract Huske's attention to the northward along the road that leads to Stirling, Charles led his army to the south of the English camp, and then advanced upon it towards a ridge of rugged upland known as Falkirk Muir. The English drums promptly beat to arms, and urgent messages were despatched to Callendar House for Hawley, who presently galloped up at speed without his hat. Hastily placing himself at the head of the three regiments of dragoons he hurried with them in the teeth of a storm of rain and wind to the top of Falkirk Muir, ordering the foot to follow with bayonets fixed. The rebels however reached the summit of the ridge before him; and Hawley then formed his army on the lower ground, drawing up the infantry in two lines, with the cavalry before them on the left of the first line. His left was covered by an impassable morass, and thus it came about that the left of the rebels, who were also formed in two lines, stood opposite to his centre. The numbers of each army were about nine thousand men. The formation of the British being complete, Hawley, who had great faith in the power of cavalry against the Highlanders, ordered the dragoons to attack. They advanced accordingly. The Highlanders waited with perfect coolness until they were within ten yards of them, and then poured in an effective volley. Therewith the evil tradition of panic seized at once upon the Thirteenth and Fourteenth Dragoons, which turned about and galloped off in disorder. The Ninth Dragoons showed more firmness, but the Highlanders throwing themselves on the ground thrust at the bellies of the horses with their dirks, and they also were beaten back. Then the Highlanders advanced, and the foot, shaken by the defeat of the horse and blinded by wind and rain, fired an irregular volley. One-fourth of the muskets missed fire owing to the rain, and every regiment excepting two at once turned and fled. No efforts of their officers, who behaved with the greatest gallantry, had the least effect in stopping them, though many were regiments of famous reputation; and the Highlanders pursuing with the claymore made not a little havoc among the fugitives. On the right of the first line, however, the Fourth and Forty-eighth stood firm, their front ranks kneeling with bayonets fixed while the middle and rear ranks fired, and repulsed the left wing of the rebels: the Fourteenth soon rallied and joined them, the Royal Scots and Buffs rallied also, and these troops keeping up a steady fire made, with the Ninth Dragoons, an orderly retreat. The losses did not exceed two hundred and eighty of all ranks, killed, wounded or missing, the two regiments that stood firm coming off with little hurt, the Forty-eighth indeed without injury to a man.

The action cannot be called a great defeat if a defeat at all, but it was a disgrace, and Hawley felt it to be so. "My heart is broke," he wrote to Cumberland, "I can't say we are quite beat, but our left is beat and their left is beat.... Such scandalous cowardice I never saw before. The whole second line of foot ran away without firing a shot." It may well be that Hawley's absence during the preliminary manœuvres of the rebel army and his hurried arrival immediately before the action contributed to make the troops unsteady, but in reality there was nothing to excuse their precipitate flight except that, as Hawley had himself written from Edinburgh, they were little better than militia. The truth was, that by constant talk of the desperate prowess of the Highlanders and by endless gloating, such as the ignorant delight in, over the horrors of the field of Prestonpans, the men had worked themselves into a state of almost superstitious terror.[217] Such a thing is not rare in military history and has, unless I am mistaken, been seen again in our own army within our own time.[218]

Hawley was soon able to report that the whole of his force had recovered itself with the exception of the Thirteenth and Fourteenth Dragoons, which appear to have been hopelessly demoralised. Nor can it be denied that the General's remedies were stern enough. "There are fourteen deserters taken," he wrote, a fortnight after the action, "shall they be hanged? Thirty-one of Hamilton's dragoons are to be hanged for deserting to the rebels, and thirty-two of the foot to be shot for cowardice."[219] Still it was felt that there was but one way thoroughly to restore the spirit of the troops, namely that the Duke of Cumberland should take command of them in person. The Duke no sooner received his orders than he hurried to Edinburgh, travelling night and day with such speed that he accomplished the journey from London in less than six days. Neither he nor the King blamed Hawley. Indiscipline was in his opinion the reason for the failure, and he came up to Scotland fully resolved to put an end to it. He seems in fact to have joined the army, asking in scornful and indignant surprise what was the meaning of this foolish flight of English infantry before wild Highlanders: and this attitude was almost sufficient in itself to put the soldiers upon their mettle.

Feb. $\frac{1}{12}$

Hawley had made all preparations for an advance against the Duke's arrival, and on the 31st of January Cumberland moved forward to Falkirk with twelve battalions of foot, two regiments of dragoons, in which neither the Thirteenth nor the Fourteenth was included, and several companies of loyal Highlanders. The rebels thereupon raised the siege of Stirling and retired, much against the will of Charles, to Inverness, leaving their battering guns in the trenches behind them. Cumberland at once sent forward his dragoons in pursuit, and pushed on as rapidly as possible to Perth. He was in no amiable mood, and gave an indication of his feelings towards the rebels by granting his troops licence to plunder the estates of rebel leaders on the march.[220] Arriving at Perth he was detained for several days by the difficulty of collecting supplies and transport. Nevertheless the campaign was at last to be conducted with common sense. Cumberland was careful to give his troops special training against their enemy, prescribing for the infantry the formation so successfully adopted by the Fourth and Forty-eighth at Falkirk, and directing that when at close quarters with Highlanders each soldier should turn his bayonet not against the enemy immediately before him, but against the man on his own right front, where the target could not parry the thrust. But this, though creditable to Cumberland, was of small importance compared to the change in the general situation. The rebels were in full retreat from the fertile lowlands into the barren mountains, and their supplies from France were cut off by British ships of war, while Cumberland's force was fed from the sea. When one army is full and another starving, lead and steel are hardly needed to decide the victory.

Feb. 18
March 1.

Nevertheless, even after his retreat from Stirling Charles met with some trifling successes. Inverness, when he reached it, was held by Lord Loudoun with some raw Highland levies. Loudoun made a night march in the hope of seizing Charles's person at Moy Castle, some ten miles distant; but half a dozen of the rebel Highlanders, firing a few shots and raising the war-cry of their clans, kindled the inevitable panic, and Loudoun's men ran away to

Inverness in such disorder that he decided to evacuate the town, and retired across the Moray Firth. In the course of the evacuation panic again overtook his men, and fully a third of them deserted.[221] Charles occupied the town on the following day, and thus obtained a port into which such French ships as might elude the British cruisers could bring him supplies. Another of his parties, again, contrived to capture Fort Augustus, together with three companies of the Sixth Foot which formed its garrison. But his attempts against Fort William and Blair Castle were fruitless, for both posts though besieged, and the latter indeed hard pressed, held out with the greatest firmness and determination. Thus the barrier of Loch Lochy and Loch Ness was never wholly broken through.

During all this time Cumberland's temper was steadily rising. For all his impatience, his operations were delayed by bad weather and difficulties of transport; though his troops scoured the country overawing and disarming the inhabitants he could obtain no intelligence of the rebels whatever; and the petty defeat of Loudoun, though of no very great importance, was from its moral effect extremely irritating. Throughout the month of March he remained at Aberdeen unable to move; and meanwhile a further revival of the spirit of panic exasperated him beyond measure. Five thousand Hessians under Prince Frederick of Hesse-Cassel had been taken into British pay, landed in Scotland, and posted at Perth to check any attempt of the rebels to return to southward. On the intelligence of a petty inroad of rebel parties upon Blair and Rannoch Prince Frederick actually decided to evacuate Perth and fall back to Stirling. Cumberland was no sooner apprised of this decision than he ordered the Hessians forward to relieve Blair Castle, but the Prince from sheer timidity shrank from any attempt to execute the command. Fortunately Blair was able to defend itself: but Cumberland did not fail to let the Prince know what he thought of his conduct.

April $\frac{15}{26}$.

At length on the 8th of April the Duke was able to advance from Aberdeen, and having crossed the Spey successfully on the 12th, pushed forward by forced marches upon Nairn. On the evening of the 14th his advanced parties had a brush with the rebels' rear-guard, and he knew that his enemy lay at last within his reach. Charles lodged for that night at Culloden House, some twelve miles from Nairn, while his troops, now reduced to five thousand starving, dispirited men, bivouacked on Culloden Moor. On the following day he drew up his army in order of battle; but the Duke had granted his troops a halt at Nairn after their exertions, and the more readily since the 15th was his birthday. Charles therefore formed the bold design of surprising him in his camp on that same night; but though his troops were actually set in motion for the purpose, the men were too weak from privation to traverse the distance within the appointed time; and they fell back weary and despondent, having fatigued themselves to no purpose. Charles's officers were now for moving to some stronger position, but the young Prince's head seems to have been turned by his previous successes, and he resolved to accept battle where he stood.

April $\frac{16}{27}$.

Between four and five in the morning of the next day the Duke broke up from Nairn, and after a march of eight miles received intelligence from his advanced parties that the rebels were in his front. He at once formed in order of battle, but finding that the enemy did not come forward, continued his march. The rebels were formed in two lines, their right resting on some straggling park walls and huts, their left extending towards Culloden House. The Duke's army was disposed in three lines, the two first consisting each of six battalions of infantry and two regiments of dragoons, while the Highland irregulars formed the third line. The entire force numbered about ten thousand men with ten guns, which were stationed in pairs between the battalions of the first line. "Now," said the Duke, turning to his men when all was in order, "I don't suppose that there are any men here who are disinclined to fight, but if there be, I beg them in God's name to go, for I would rather face the Highlanders with a thousand resolute men at my back than with ten thousand half-hearted." The men answered with cheers, and there could be little doubt as to the issue of the battle. Hawley and the dragoons were then sent forward to break down the enclosures on the enemy's right, and at ten o'clock the rebels opened the action with a discharge from their artillery.

The Duke's cannon instantly took up the challenge; but the duel could not last long, for Charles's guns were ill-aimed and ill-served, whereas the British fire was most accurate and destructive. The right and centre of the Highlanders, unable to endure the grape, presently rushed forward, swept round the left of the British line upon the flank and rear of the Fourth and Twenty-seventh Regiments, and for a short time threw them into some confusion. At every other point, however, they were speedily driven back by a crushing fire, and the Fourth and Twenty-seventh, recovering themselves, turned bayonet against claymore and target for the first time with success. In utter rage at this repulse the rebels for a few minutes flung stones at the hated red-coats; but by this time Hawley had broken through the enclosures and turned four guns upon Charles's second line. On the left of the rebels the Macdonalds, sulking because they had not the place of honour, refused to move, and now the English dragoons burst in upon the Highlanders from both flanks, and, charging through them till they met in the middle, shivered them to fragments. The rout of the enemy was complete and the dragoons galloped on to the pursuit. One thousand of Charles's troops were killed on the spot, and five hundred prisoners, of whom two hundred were French, were taken. The remainder fled in all directions. The loss of the Duke's army was slight, barely reaching three hundred men killed and wounded, of whom two-thirds were of the Fourth and Twenty-seventh. The victory was decisive: the rebellion was crushed at a blow, and all hopes of a restoration of the Stuarts were at last and for ever extinguished.

The campaign ended, as a victorious campaign against mountaineers must always end, in the hunting of fugitives, the burning of villages, and the destruction of crops. To this work the troops were now let loose, as they had already been in the march to Perth, though now with encouragement rather than restraint, and with no attention to "proper precautions." But enough and too much has been written of the inhumanity which earned for Cumberland the name of the butcher; his services were far too valuable to be overlooked, and himself of far too remarkable character to be tossed aside with the brand of a single hateful epithet. Charles Edward, and Murray, the ablest of his officers, had turned the gifts which fortune gave them, and the peculiar powers of their little force in rapidity of movement and vigour of attack, to an account which entitles them to very high praise as commanders. It was by such bold actions as Falkirk and Prestonpans, and by such skilful manœuvres as left Wade astern at Newcastle and Cumberland at Stone, that our Indian Empire was won. Thus it was against no unskilful leaders that Cumberland was matched; and on taking the command he found the British regular troops in a state of demoralisation, through repeated panic, which is almost incredible. Whole regiments were running away on the slightest alarm, in spite of the heroism of their officers; and even a General, a foreigner and a royal prince, Frederick of Hesse-Cassel, prepared to retreat at the mere rumour of the approach of a few score of Highlanders. To all this, Cumberland, by the prestige of his position and rugged force of character, put an end. He was called up, young as he was, to a duty from which almost every General in Europe, of what experience soever, would have shrunk—a winter campaign in a mountainous country. Ninety-nine men out of a hundred would have waited for the summer, and indeed such delay was expected of Cumberland, but he pressed on to his task at once. He restored the confidence of his troops partly by the dignity of his station, partly by his own ascendency as a man, partly by his skill as a soldier, encouraging them not by mere words only, but also by training them to meet the peculiar tactics of a peculiar enemy by a new formation and a scientific, if simple, method of using the bayonet. He pursued his work persistently, despite endless difficulties, disappointments, and vexations, and did not rest until he had achieved it completely. Jacobitism, which had been the curse of the kingdom for three quarters of a century, was finally slain, and the Highlanders, who had been a plague for as long and longer, were finally subjugated, for no one's advantage more than for their own. The methods employed were doubtless harsh, sometimes even to barbarity, being those generally used by barbarians towards each other and therefore held inexcusable among civilised men; but it is not common for half-savage mountaineers—and the Highlanders were little else—to be brought to reason without some such harsh lesson. Military execution, as it was called, was not yet an obsolete practice in war, whether for injury to the enemy or indulgence of the troops, while Tolpatches, Pandours, and other irregular bands, whose barbarities were unspeakable, were esteemed a valuable if not indispensable adjunct to the armies of the civilised nations of Europe. Moreover, French regular troops behaved quite as ill in Germany during the Seven Years' War as any of the irregulars. Still wanton brutality and outrage, however excused by the custom of war, must remain unpardoned and unpardonable, on the score not only of humanity but of discipline. But though the blot upon Cumberland's name must remain indelible, it should not obscure the fact that, at a time of extreme national peril, the Duke lifted the army in a few weeks, from the lowest depth which it has ever touched of demoralisation and disgrace, to its old height of confidence and self-respect.

AUTHORITIES.—The literature of the rebellion of 1745 is of course boundless, but the military operations and the state of the Army can hardly be better studied than in the *S.P., Dom., Scotland*, vols. xxvi.-xxxi., in the Record Office. On the other side, the Narrative of the Chevalier Johnstone, though frequently inaccurate, throws useful light on divers points.

CHAPTER VII

| 1746. |
| May $\frac{20}{31}$. |

The virtual evacuation of the Low Countries by the British in consequence of the Jacobite Rebellion was an advantage too obvious to be overlooked by the French. At the end of January, though winter-quarters were not yet broken up, they severed the communication between Antwerp and Brussels, and a week later took the town of Brussels itself by escalade. The citadel, after defending itself for a fortnight, went the way of the town, and the capital of the Spanish Netherlands was turned into a French place of arms.[222] The consternation in Holland was great, and it was increased when the French presently besieged and captured Antwerp. Meanwhile the British Commander, Lord Dunmore, who had been left in the Netherlands with a few squadrons of cavalry, could only look on in utter helplessness. It was not until June that the Hessian troops in British pay and a few British battalions could be embarked, together with General Ligonier to command them, from England; and it was not until July, owing to foul winds, that they were finally landed at Williamstadt. The change of base was significant in itself, for since the capture of Ostend and Antwerp there was no haven for British ships except in the United Provinces. Even after the disembarkation these forces were found to be still unready to take the field. The Hessians had not a grain of powder among them, and there were neither horses for the artillery nor waggons for the baggage. Again, to add small difficulties to great, the Austrian General, Batthyany, having no British officer as his peer in command, denied to the British troops the place of honour at the right of the line. It was a trifling matter, but yet sufficient to embarrass counsel, destroy harmony, and delay operations.[223]

| June 30 |
| July 11. |
| July $\frac{13}{24}$. |

While the Allies were thus painfully drawing their forces together, the activity of the French never ceased. The Prince of Conti was detached with a considerable force to the Haine, where he quickly reduced Mons and St. Ghislain, thus throwing down almost the last relics of the Austrian barrier in the south. Thence moving to the Sambre, Conti laid siege to Charleroi. It was now sufficiently clear that the plan of the French campaign was to operate on the line of the Meuse for the invasion of Holland. Maestricht once taken, the rest would be easy, for most of the Dutch army were prisoners in the hands of the French; and with the possession of the line of the Meuse communication between the Allied forces of England and of Austria would be cut off. But before Maestricht could be touched Namur must first be captured; and the campaign of 1746 accordingly centred about Namur.

July $\frac{6}{17}$.
July $\frac{16}{27}$.
July 21
Aug. 1.

For the first fortnight of July the Allies remained at Terheyden, a little to the north of Breda, Saxe's army lying some thirty miles south-westward of them about Antwerp. On the 17th of July the Allies at last got on march, still with some faint hopes of saving Charleroi, and proceeded south-eastward, a movement which Saxe at once parried by marching parallel with them to the Dyle between Arschot and Louvain. Pushing forward, despite endless difficulties of transport and forage, through a wretched barren country, the Allies, now under command of Prince Charles of Lorraine, reached Peer, turned southward across the Demer at Hasselt, and by the 27th of July were at Borchloen. They were thus actually on the eastern side of the French main army, within reach of the Mehaigne and not without good hope of saving Namur if not Charleroi. On the 1st of August they crossed the Mehaigne, only to learn to their bitter disappointment that Charleroi had surrendered that very morning. Saxe meanwhile, with the principal part of his army, still lay entrenched at Louvain with detachments pushed forward to Tirlemont and Gembloux. The Allies continued their march before the eyes of these detachments to Masy on the Orneau, and there took up a position between that river and the head-waters of the Mehaigne, fronting to the north-east. This was the line approved through many generations of war as the best for the protection of Namur.[224]

Aug. $\frac{18}{29}$.
Sept. $\frac{2}{13}$.

Saxe now drew nearer to them, and the two armies lay opposite to each other, in many places not more than a musket-shot apart, both entrenched to the teeth. The Allies so far had decidedly scored a success, but they were outnumbered by the French by three to two, and they were confined within a narrow space wherein subsistence was extremely difficult; while if they moved, Namur was lost. Ligonier, who was most uneasy over the situation, longed for five thousand cavalry with which to make a dash at Malines and so call the enemy back in haste to defend Brussels and Antwerp.[225] Prince Charles, however, was averse to operations of such a nature. His hope was that Saxe would offer him battle on the historic plain of Ramillies where, notwithstanding the disparity of numbers, he trusted that the quality of his troops and the traditions of the field would enable him to prevail. But Saxe had no intention of doing anything of the kind. He did indeed shift his position further to the north and east, with the field of Ramillies in his rear, but it was not to offer battle. Pushing out detachments to eastward he captured Huy, and cutting off the Allies' communications with Liége and Maestricht forced them to cross the Meuse and fall back on Maestricht from the other side of the river. Cross the Meuse the Allies accordingly did, unmolested, to Ligonier's great relief, by twenty thousand French who were stationed on the eastern bank of the stream. They then opened communication with Maestricht, five leagues away, while Saxe extended his army comfortably with its face to the eastward along the line of the Jaar from Warem to Tongres, waiting till want of forage should compel the Allies to recross the Meuse. Back they came over the river within a fortnight, as he had expected, and the Marshal, without attempting to dispute the passage, retreated quietly for a few miles, knowing full well that his enemy could not follow him from lack of bread. Ligonier never in his life longed so intensely for the end of a campaign.[226]

| Sept. $\frac{6}{17}$. |
| Aug. 30 |
| Sept. 10. |
| Sept. 27 |
| Oct. 7. |

On the 17th of September the Allies advanced upon the French and offered battle. Saxe answered by retiring to an impregnable position between Tongres and the Demer. There was no occasion for him to fight, when his enemies were short of provisions and their cavalry was going to ruin from want of forage. So there the two armies remained once more, within sight of each other but unwilling to fight, since an attack on the entrenchments of either host would have entailed the certain destruction of the attacking force. But meanwhile the trenches had been opened before Namur by a French corps under the Prince of Clermont, and within nine days the town had fallen. Ligonier again urged his design, for which he had prepared the necessary magazines, to upset Saxe's plans by a dash upon Antwerp, but he could find no support in the council of war; so there was nothing for the Allies to do but to wait until some further French success should compel them to move. Such a success was not long in coming. The castle of Namur surrendered after a miserable defence of but eleven days; Clermont's corps was released for operations in the field, and the Allies were forced to fall back for the protection of Liége. Accordingly, on the 7th of October they crossed the Jaar, not without annoyance from the enemy, and took up a new position, which gave them indeed possession of Liége, but placed them between the Meuse in their rear, and an enemy of nearly twice their strength on the Jaar before their front.[227]

Sept. 29
Oct. 10.

Now at last Saxe resolved to strike a blow. On the 10th of October he crossed the Jaar with evident intention of an attack, and the Allied army received orders to be ready for action before the following dawn. The Allies' position faced very nearly due west, the army being drawn up astride of the two paved roads leading into Liége from Tongres and St. Trond. Their extreme right rested on the Jaar and was covered by the villages of Slins, Fexhe, and Enick, all of which were strongly entrenched and occupied by the Austrians. South of Enick extended an open plain from that village to the village of Liers, and in this plain was posted the Hanoverian infantry and four British battalions, the Eighth, Nineteenth, Thirty-third, and Forty-third Foot, with the Hessian infantry on their left in rear of Liers. The Hanoverian cavalry prolonged the line southward to the village of Varoux, and the Sixth and Seventh Dragoons and Scots Greys continued it to the village of Roucoux, from which point Dutch troops carried it on to the village of Ance, which formed the extreme left of the position. Ligonier did not like the situation, for he did not see how the turning of the left flank could be prevented if, as would certainly be the case, the French should seriously attempt it. Prince Charles, knowing that if his right were turned his retreat to Maestricht would be cut off, had taken care to hold the right flank in real strength and dared not weaken it; but the position, with the Meuse in its rear, was perilously shallow, while the convergence of two ravines from the Jaar and Melaigne into its centre allowed of but one narrow way of communication between the right and left of the army. The defects of the Allies' dispositions were in fact not unlike those which had proved fatal to King William at Landen, and Ligonier's anxiety was proved to rest on all too good foundation.

Sept. 30
Oct. 11.

The morning of the 11th of October opened with bad news for the Allies. The French had been admitted into Liége by the inhabitants behind the backs of the Dutch, so that the Prince of Waldeck, who, commanded on the left, was obliged to withdraw eight battalions from Roucoux and post them *en potence* on his left flank, with his cavalry in support. Thus the defence of Roucoux, as well as of Liers and Varoux, was left to eight battalions of British, Hanoverians, and Hessians only. This made the outlook for the Allied left the worse, since it was evident that the brunt of the French attack would fall upon it. Saxe gave Prince Charles little time for reflection. He had one hundred and twenty thousand men against eighty thousand, and he knew that of the eighty thousand at least one-third were tied to the Austrian entrenchments about the Jaar. He opened the action by a furious assault upon the Dutch on the left flank, his infantry being formed in dense columns, so that the attack could be renewed continually by fresh troops. Simultaneously fifty-five battalions in three similar columns were launched upon Liers, Varoux, and Roucoux. Outmatched though they were, Dutch, Germans, and British all fought splendidly and repelled more than one attack. But, to use Ligonier's words, as soon as two French brigades had been repulsed in each village, a third brigade ran in; and the eight battalions, though they still held Liers, were forced to withdraw both from Roucoux and Varoux. Being rallied, however, by Ligonier, they advanced again and recaptured both villages; and the Nineteenth and Forty-third took up a position in a hollow road which they held to the last. The Dutch now began to retire across the rear of the position from the left, in good order despite heavy losses, while Ligonier checked the enemy in the plain with the British cavalry. When the Dutch had passed he ordered his own men to retreat in the same direction, still covering the movement with the cavalry and with the Thirteenth and Twenty-sixth Foot, which had been sent to the field from the garrison of Maestricht. The Austrians formed a rear-guard in turn when the British and their German comrades had passed, and thus the whole army filed off, unpursued and in perfect order, and crossed the Meuse in safety on the following morning.

The action may be looked upon as a fortunate escape for the Allies, since it was impossible, humanly speaking, that it could have issued favourably for them. Prince Charles, in seeking to cover both Liége and Maestricht, had attempted too much. His army thus occupied too wide a front, the villages in the centre were too weakly held, there was hardly anywhere a second line of infantry, and the left flank could not be sustained against so superior an enemy. The total loss of the Allies was about five thousand men, which was sufficiently severe considering that but a third of the army was engaged. The casualties of the British were three hundred and fifty killed and wounded, of whom no fewer than two hundred belonged to the Forty-third. The French lost as many men as the Allies, or more, and gained little by the action except eight guns captured from the British, Hanoverians, and Hessians. Had not the Allied troops been far better in quality and discipline than the French, they must have been lost during their retreat with superior numbers both in flank and rear. Both armies presently retired into winter-quarters, and the campaign ended far less disastrously than might have been feared for the Allies.[228]

| Sept. 20 |
| Oct. 1. |
| Oct. $\frac{1}{12}$. |

Unfortunately, however, it was not in Flanders only that discredit fell upon the British arms. At the end of September a force of six battalions[229] was sent, under command of General St. Clair, to the coast of Brittany to attack Port L'Orient and destroy the stores of the French East India Company there. The enterprise was conducted with amazing feebleness. The troops landed at Quimperle Bay practically unopposed, but, being fired at on their march on the following day, were turned loose to the plunder of a small town as a punishment to the inhabitants for their resistance. On the following day they reached L'Orient, which the Deputy Governor of the East India Company offered to surrender on good terms. His overtures, however, were rejected and a siege was begun in form; but after a few days of firing and the loss of about a hundred men killed and wounded, St. Clair thought it prudent to retreat; and on the 12th of October the troops re-embarked and returned to England. Anything more pointless than the design or more contemptible than the execution of this project can hardly be conceived, for it simply employed regiments, which were badly needed in Flanders and America, in useless operations which did not amount to a diversion.

| 1747. |

If the cause of Queen Maria Theresa was to be saved, it was evident that great efforts were imperative in the coming campaign of 1747. To meet the vast numbers brought into the field by the French the Austrians promised to have sixty thousand men at Maseyck on the Meuse by April; the British contributed four regiments of cavalry and fourteen battalions of infantry; and it was hoped that the Allies would take the field with a total strength of one hundred and ten battalions, one hundred and sixty squadrons, and two hundred and twenty guns, besides irregular troops, the whole to be under command of the Duke of Cumberland.[230] Unfortunately the weather was adverse to an early opening of the campaign; and the French, by the seizure of Cadsand and Sluys, which were shamefully surrendered by the Dutch, closed the southern mouth of the Scheldt below Antwerp. This was a sad blow to the arrangements for the transport of the Allies, since it brought about the necessity of hauling all the forage for the British overland from Breda. Had Cumberland been in a position to open the campaign before the French, he meant to have laid siege to Antwerp; as things were, he was compelled, thanks chiefly to the apathy of the Dutch, to attempt to bring Saxe to a general action. His last letter before beginning operations has, however, an interest of another kind. It contains a recommendation that Major James Wolfe may be permitted to purchase a vacant lieutenant-colonelcy in the Eighth Foot, that officer having served constantly and well during the past two years as a major of brigade and proved himself capable and desirous to do his duty.[231]

| May $\frac{15}{26}$. |
| June $\frac{15}{26}$. |
| June $\frac{18}{29}$. |
| June $\frac{19}{30}$. |
| June 20 |
| July 1. |

The French being encamped between Malines and Louvain, Cumberland collected his troops at Tilburg and advanced straight upon them, encamping on the 26th of May on the Great Nethe, a little to the east of Antwerp, between Lierre and Herenthout. Saxe, entrenched as usual to the teeth, remained immovable for three weeks, and Cumberland despaired of bringing him to action. At length the news that a detached corps of thirty thousand French, under the Prince of Clermont, was on the old ground about Tongres, moved Cumberland to march to the Demer, in the hope of overwhelming Clermont before Saxe could join him. Saxe, however, was on his guard, and on the 29th of June prepared to concentrate the whole of his army at Tongres. Cumberland thereupon decided to take up Saxe's camp of the previous year, from Bilsen, on the head-waters of the Demer, to Tongres. So sending forward Count Daun, afterwards well known as an antagonist of Frederick the Great, with a corps of Austrians to occupy Bilsen, he ordered the rest of the army to follow as quickly as possible on the next day. Riding forward at daybreak of the morrow, Cumberland was dismayed to see the French advancing in two columns from Tongres, as if to fall upon the head of his own army. This was a surprise. Cumberland knew that Saxe was in motion but had not expected him so soon; and indeed Saxe had made a notable march, for his army had not left Louvain until the 29th of June and had traversed little less than fifty miles in two days. The Duke lost no time in setting such troops as were on the spot in order of battle, and hurried away to see if those on the march could be brought up in time to force back the French, and to secure the position of his choice. But the French cavalry was too quick for him, and, before Ligonier could bring up the English horse, had occupied the centre of the ground which Cumberland had intended for himself. Ligonier drew up his squadrons before them to bar their further advance, and the Allied infantry, as it came up, was formed in order of battle, fronting, however, not to eastward, as had been originally designed, but almost due south. In fact, owing to Saxe's unexpected arrival and to deficient arrangements by the staff of the Allies, there seems to have been considerable delay in putting the Allied army into any formation at all, or the French might certainly have been forced back to Tongres. Saxe's rear had not yet come up and the men were fatigued by a long and harassing march; but Cumberland was not the man to fight an action of the type of Oudenarde, and the opportunity was lost. [232]

The position now occupied by the Allies extended from some rising ground known as the Commanderie, a little to the south-east of Bilsen, along a chain of villages and low heights to the Jaar, a little to the south of Maestricht. The Commanderie being the right of the line was held by the Austrians, with a strong corps thrown back *en potence* to Bilsen to protect the right flank; for it was as important on this field as on that of Roucoux that the retreat into Holland should not be cut off. The ground possessed natural features of strength which were turned to good account, so good account indeed that the Allied right, like the French left at Ramillies, could neither attack nor be attacked. Eastward from the Commanderie the Austrians occupied the heights of Spaeven, together with the villages of Gross and Klein Spaeven; next to them the Dutch formed the centre of the line, while the Hanoverians and British held the villages of Val, or Vlytingen, and Lauffeld, and prolonged the line to its extreme left at the village of Kesselt.

| June 21 |
| July 2. |

There the Allies lay on their arms until nightfall, while Saxe's weary battalions tramped on till far into the night up to their bivouacs. At daybreak the French were seen to be in motion, marching and countermarching in a way that Cumberland did not quite understand; the fact being that Saxe, as at Roucoux, was doubling the left wing of his army in rear of the right, for the formation of those dense columns of attack which he could handle with such consummate skill. After observing them until nine o'clock Cumberland came to the conclusion that the Marshal meditated no immediate movement and retired to the Commanderie for breakfast; but he had hardly sat down when an urgent message arrived from Ligonier that the enemy was on the point of attacking. Cumberland at once returned and moved the left of his line somewhat forward, setting fire to the village of Vlytingen and occupying Lauffeld with three British and two Hessian battalions. Lauffeld was a straggling village a quarter of a mile long, covered by a multitude of small enclosures with mud walls about six feet high, topped by growing hedges. It was thus easily turned into a strong post for infantry, and cannon were posted both in its front and flanks. The remainder of the British were drawn up for the most part in rear of Lauffeld in order to feed and relieve its garrison, the brigade of Guards being posted in the hedges before Vlytingen. The British cavalry stood on the right of the infantry and joined their line to that of the Dutch.

Meanwhile Saxe, sending forward a cloud of irregular troops to mask his movements, had despatched Count d'Estrées and the Count of Segur with a strong force of infantry and cavalry to seize the villages of Montenaken and Wilre on the left flank of the Allies. This service was performed with little loss. At the same time he directed the Marquis of Salières, with six brigades of foot and twenty guns, to attack Vlytingen, and launched five brigades, with as many guns, backed by a large force of cavalry, against Lauffeld. The assault of the French infantry upon Lauffeld was met by a furious resistance. It was just such another struggle as that of Neerwinden, from hedge to hedge and from wall to wall; and the French, for all their superiority of numbers, were driven back headlong from the village with terrible loss. Salières met with little better success against the brigade of Guards in the hedges of Vlytingen; but with great readiness he turned half of his guns to his right against Lauffeld and the remainder against a ravine on his left, with most destructive effect. Cumberland, observing the fury with which Saxe had concentrated his attack against these two villages, asked the Austrians to relieve him by a diversion upon his right; but the Austrian troops could not face the fire of Salières' guns, and it became clear that Vlytingen and Lauffeld must be held by the British and Hanoverians alone.

Saxe's first attack had been brilliantly repulsed. He at once replaced the beaten troops by two fresh brigades of infantry, with cavalry to support them, and renewed the assault, but with no better success. The British were driven back from the outer defences only to stand more fiercely by those within, and Lauffeld remained unconquered. But Saxe was not to be deterred from his purpose. Two more brigades, including the six Irish battalions that had saved the day at Fontenoy, were added to those already on the spot, and the whole of them launched for a third attack against Lauffeld. They were met by the same stubborn resistance and the same deadly fire; and the Irish brigade lost no fewer than sixty officers in the struggle. Nevertheless Irish impetuosity carried the rest of the troops forward; the British were borne back to the rearmost edge of the village and the French began to swarm up the slope beyond it. Cumberland promptly ordered the whole of his line of infantry to advance; and the French at once gave way before them. The French cavalry was obliged to drive the foot forward at the sword's point, but Cumberland continued steadily to gain ground despite their efforts. Then at an unlucky moment, some Dutch squadrons in the centre were seized with panic and came galloping straight into the British line, carried away the Hessians and one squadron of the Greys and fell pell-mell upon the Twenty-first and Twenty-third Fusiliers. The Twenty-first, anticipating the treatment of the Belgians at Waterloo, gave the Dutchmen a volley and partly saved themselves, but the Twenty-third suffered terribly and the whole line was thrown into confusion. Before order could be restored Salières had thrown three more brigades upon Lauffeld, which closed in round it, blocking up a hollow road which formed the entrance into it from the rear, and barring the way for all further reinforcements of the Allies. The few troops that were left in the village were speedily overpowered, and Lauffeld was lost.

Some of Daun's Austrians now advanced to Cumberland's help from the right; but three French brigades of cavalry that were waiting before Vlytingen at once moved forward to check them, and charging boldly into them succeeded in turning them back, though themselves roughly handled when retiring from the charge. Meanwhile Saxe had brought up ten guns to right and left of Lauffeld, and reinforcing the cavalry of D'Estrées and Segur extended it in one long line from Lauffeld to Wilre, for a final crushing attack on the Allied left. Order had been restored among the British infantry, who were now retreating with great steadiness, but they were wholly unsupported. Ligonier, determined to save them at any cost, caught up the Greys, Inniskillings, and Cumberland's dragoons, and led them straight against the masses of the French cavalry. The gallant brigade charged home, crashed headlong through the horse, and fell upon the infantry beyond, but being galled by their fire and attacked in all quarters by other French squadrons, was broken past all rallying and very heavily punished. Ligonier himself was overthrown and taken prisoner. Cumberland, who had plunged into the broken ranks to try to rally them, was cut off by the French dragoons, and only with difficulty contrived to join the remainder of his cavalry on the left. With these he covered the retreat of the army, which was successfully effected in good order and with little further loss.

So ended the battle of Lauffeld, in which the British bore the brunt with a firmness that extorted the praise even of Frenchmen, but of which few Englishmen have ever heard. The troops, in Cumberland's words, behaved one and all so well that he could not commend any one regiment without doing injustice to the rest. The total loss of the five regiments of horse and fourteen battalions of foot was close upon two thousand men.[233] The three devoted regiments which charged with Ligonier were the worst sufferers, the Greys losing one hundred and sixty men, the Inniskillings one hundred and twenty, and Cumberland's dragoons nearly one hundred. The loss of the whole of the Allies was about six thousand men, that of the French decidedly greater, amounting indeed, according to Saxe's account, to not less than ten thousand men. The British, moreover, had nine French colours and five

French standards as trophies for their consolation. Finally, the French failed to accomplish the object of the action, which was to cut off the Allies from Maestricht.

After the battle the Allies crossed the Meuse and encamped at Heer, a little to the east of Maestricht, while Saxe returned to his quarters at Tongres. The French then detached a corps for the capture of Bergen op Zoom; but the most important transactions of the war still went forward on the Meuse, where constant negotiations were carried on between Saxe and Cumberland. The campaign closed with the fall of Bergen op Zoom and the capture of most of the strong places in Dutch Brabant.

> **1748.**
> April $\frac{19}{30}$.
> **October.**

By this time King George and his people in England were thoroughly sick of the war. The British had suffered severely in every action, but had reaped no success except in the fortunate victory of Dettingen. The Dutch had proved themselves useless and contemptible as Allies, their Government feeble and corrupt in council, their troops unstable if not dangerous in action. The Austrians, in spite of lavish subsidies, had never furnished the troops that they had promised, and had invariably obstructed operations through the obstinacy of their Generals and the selfishness of their ends. The opening of the campaign of 1748 was even more unpromising for the Allies. Saxe, strong in the possession of a superior force, kept Cumberland in suspense between apprehensions for Breda and for Maestricht, and when finally he laid siege to Maestricht could match one hundred and fifteen thousand men against Cumberland's five-and-thirty thousand. War on such terms against such a master as Saxe was ridiculous. Moreover, the Dutch, despite a recent revolution, were more supine than ever; the Prince of Orange, who was the new ruler, actually keeping two thousand of his troops from the field that they might adorn the baptism of one of his babies. In the face of such facts Cumberland pressed earnestly for peace;[234] and on the 30th of April preliminaries were signed, which six months later were expanded into the definite treaty of Aix-la-Chapelle.

The peace left matters practically as they had stood before the war, with the significant exception that Frederick the Great retained Silesia. Not a word was said as to the regulation of trade between England and Spain, which had been the original ground of quarrel; and as between England and France it was agreed that there should be mutual restitution of all captures. Yet this could not set the two countries in the same position as before the war. The French were utterly exhausted; but the British, though not a little harassed by the cost of maintaining armies and producing subsidies, had received a military training which was to stand them in good stead for the great struggle that lay before them. To understand this struggle aright it must first be seen what was implied by the mutual restitution of all captures, for among the possessions that had changed hands during the war were Cape Breton and Madras. The time is now come to watch the building up of empire in distant lands to east and west. Let us turn first to the great Peninsula of the East.

AUTHORITIES.—The official correspondence in the Record Office. *F. O. Military Auxiliary Expeditions. Campagnes de Louis XV. Espagnac. Life of the Duke of Cumberland.* Some useful details as to Lauffeld are to be found in the *Gentleman's Magazine.*

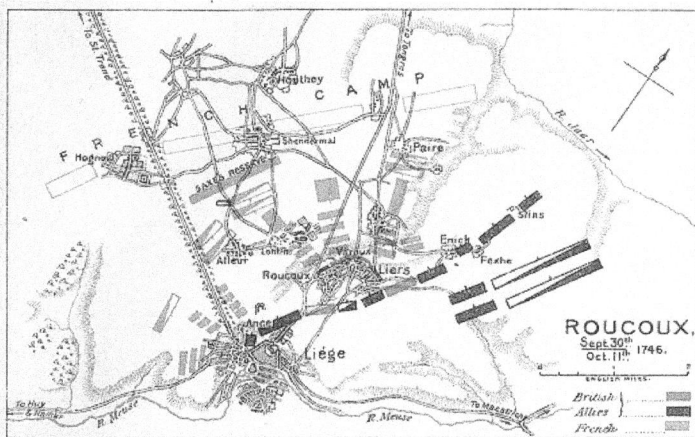

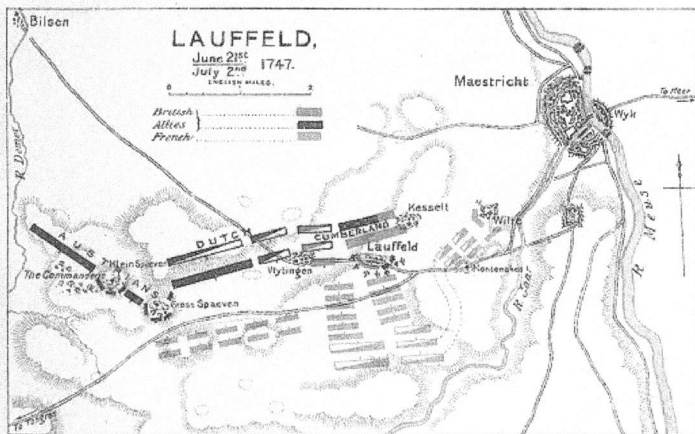

Walker & Boutall del.

To face page 164.

113

ROUCOUX. Sept. 30th 1746.
Oct. 11th
LAUFFELD. June 21st 1747.
July 2nd

■

BOOK VIII

CHAPTER I

| 1023. |
| 1193. |
| 1526, |
| April 20. |
| 1672. |
| 1680. |
| 1687. |
| 1707. |

As English history to the vast majority of Englishmen begins with the Norman, so does also the modern history of India begin with the Mohammedan, conquest. As early as in the eighth century Arab conquerors made incursions into Scinde as far as Hyderabad, only to be driven back by a revolt of Hindoos; but it was not until the eleventh century that Sultan Mahmoud, the second of the House of Ghuznee, established a Mohammedan garrison to the south of the Indus at Lahore, nor until the end of the twelfth century that Shahab-ud-din penetrated as far as Benares and fixed the seat of government at Delhi. It was at his death that India assumed the form of an independent kingdom distinct from the governments to the north of the Indus; and it was only a few years later that the invasion of the Moguls under Zinghis Khan heralded the approach of the race that was first to gather the greatest portion of the peninsula into a single empire, and to found a dynasty which should rule it. The battle of Delhi placed Baber, the first of this dynasty, in possession of the capital, and set up therein the throne of the Great Mogul. Baber's grandson, Akbar, after fifty years of conquest, wise policy and incessant labour, reduced the whole of Hindostan and great part of the Deccan under the Mogul Empire, dividing it for administrative purposes into eighteen provinces, each under the rule of a governor or *subahdar*. But the Deccan had never been firmly secured; and even after the Hindoos had submitted there were Mohammedan chieftains who refused to acknowledge the supremacy of the Moguls. Too jealous, however, to unite in resistance, these chieftains allowed themselves to be crushed in detail; and in 1656 the Emperor Shah Jehan seemed to have established his authority over all the Mohammedan kingdoms of the Deccan. But even so the work of Shah Jehan did not endure. In the reign of his son Aurungzebe a new power appeared to dispute the rule of the Moguls in the Deccan. A race of Hindoo mountaineers, the Mahrattas, came down from their fastnesses in the Western Ghauts and hired themselves out as mercenary soldiers to the Mohammedan chiefs. Led by a man of genius, the famous Sevajee, the Mahrattas grew continually in strength, and at length fairly defeated the army of the Moguls in the open field. It was not until after the death of Sevajee that Aurungzebe was able to drive his followers back to the hills, and push his Empire to its farthest limits to southward, so far indeed as to include in it even a portion of Mysore. Never before, it should seem, had so much of the peninsula been united under the dominion of one man; but the Mahrattas none the less had laid the axe to the root of the Mogul Empire, and from the death of Aurungzebe the tree, though destined to totter for yet another fifty years, was already doomed. It must now be told how the foundation of a new Indian Empire fell not to the Mahrattas but to invaders from Europe.

| 1498. |
| 1600, |
| Dec. 31. |

The first of the European nations to gain a footing in the peninsula was of course the Portuguese. In 1493 Bartholemew Diaz doubled the Cape of Good Hope, and five years later Vasco da Gama arrived on the Western or Malabar coast, and after a second voyage obtained permission to establish a factory at Calicut. His work was continued by Albuquerque, under whose care the Portuguese power in India was more widely extended than at any time before or since. To him it was due that Goa was made the chief centre of Portuguese influence, and that Ceylon became tributary to Portugal's king. It was not, however, conceivable that Portugal should long be allowed to enjoy the monopoly of this lucrative traffic; and competitors soon presented themselves from the maritime powers of Europe. Moreover, in 1580, Portugal passed under the crown of Spain, so that any encroachment on her East Indian trade inflicted also some damage on the detested Spaniard. In 1582 an Englishman, Edward Fenton, led the way by attempting a voyage direct to the east. The venture, however, was a failure, as was also a second attempt made by James Lancaster in 1589. Finally, a Dutchman, James Houtmann, sailed from the Texel in 1595, and presented himself as the first rival of the Portuguese by the establishment of a factory at Bantam in Java. But though thus distanced for a moment in the race for a new market the English speedily resolved to make up the lost ground; and in 1599 an association of Merchants Adventurers was formed in London with the object of prosecuting a voyage to the East Indies. In the following year they received a charter from Queen Elizabeth, and thus came into being the famous East India Company.

| 1607. |
| 1611. |
| 1612. |
| 1628. |
| 1651. |

The two first voyages of the new Company followed the track of the Dutch to Sumatra and Java, but in the third the ships were driven by stormy weather into Sierra Leone, whence one of them under Captain Hawkins sailed direct to Surat, and found there good promise of opening trade. In 1609 Hawkins visited Agra in person and obtained privileges from the reigning Mogul, eldest son of the great Akbar; but his influence was soon undermined by Portuguese Jesuits, and he was fain to return with little profit. Two years later, however, an English vessel touched at Point de Galle, sailed up the Coromandel, or eastern, coast of India as far as Masulipatam and founded the nucleus of a factory at Petapolee, the germ from which was to spring the trade of England in the Bay of Bengal. The jealousy of Dutch and Portuguese had by this time risen so high that the Company was obliged to employ force against them. In 1612 Captain Best boldly attacked a superior Portuguese fleet in the Bay of Surat, and defeated it so thoroughly that the reigning Mogul disallowed the Portuguese claim to a monopoly of the trade, agreed to a treaty granting important privileges to the English, and consented to receive an ambassador from them at his Court. One formidable rival was thus crippled, but the Dutch were not so easily to be dealt with, more particularly since the troubles which followed on the accession of Charles the First in England left them little to fear from an armed force. The affairs of the Company began to languish, but fresh outlets for trade were none the less sought for. One factory was definitely established at Masulipatam, a second on the coast further northward, and finally, in 1640, a third was settled at Madras under the name of Fort St. George. This was the one gleam of sunshine at that period amid all the troubles of England at home and abroad. Then at last the cloud of the Civil War passed away; the power of England began to revive, and the Company addressed a petition to Parliament for redress of injuries received from the Dutch. Thereupon followed the Dutch war and the seven furious actions of Blake and Monk, which dealt Dutch maritime ascendency a blow from which it never recovered. A piece of unexpected good fortune, namely the recovery of Shah Jehan's daughter from dangerous sickness under the care of an English surgeon at Surat, procured for the Company free trade with Bengal. At the close of the Protectorate the Company had organised its markets into three divisions. A supreme presidency was established at Surat with special charge of the Persian trade, a subordinate presidency at Madras with control of the factories on the eastern coast and in Bengal, and a third presidency at Bantam for direction of the traffic with the Eastern Islands.

1660.
1661.

Then came the Restoration, and with it a new charter empowering the

118

Company to send ships of war, men, and arms to their factories for defence of the same, and to make peace or war with any people not Christians. Authority was also granted for the fortification of St. Helena, which since 1651 had become the port of call on the voyage to India, and stringent provision was made for the maintenance of the Company's monopoly. The following year brought Bombay by dowry to the British Crown, and in 1662 Sir Abraham Shipman was sent out with four hundred soldiers to take possession and to remain as governor. These were the first British troops to land in India, but as there was a dispute with the Portuguese as to whether the word Bombay, as inscribed in the treaty of marriage, signified the island only or included its dependencies also, the poor fellows were landed on the island of Anjediva, near Goa, where they at once began to sicken. In 1664 they were transferred to Madras, in view of the war with Holland; but by the end of the year Shipman and a vast number of the men were dead, and when at last they landed in Bombay, in March 1665, the four hundred had dwindled to one officer and one hundred and thirteen men. Such was the first experience of the British Army in India.[235]

| 1668. |

In 1668 Bombay, together with the whole of its military stores, was made over to the Company for a rent of ten pounds a year; and authority was also given for the Company to enlist officers and men for their own service, as well as to call in certain garrisons of the King's troops at Bombay and Madras to fill up vacancies. Further, in order to form a local militia, half-pay was granted to all soldiers who would settle on the island, new settlers were promised from England, and a rule was made that not more than twenty soldiers should return to Europe in any one year. The men and officers of the King's troops at once took service with the Company under its own military code and articles of war, and thus was founded the first military establishment in Bombay. The men agreed, it seems, to serve for three years only, which gives them an additional interest as the first English soldiers ever enlisted for short service. Having thus provided itself with men the Company proceeded next to the improvement and fortification of Bombay itself, and with such vigour that by 1674 no fewer than one hundred cannon were mounted for its defence. Finally, in 1683-84 the garrison was increased from four hundred to six hundred men, two companies of Rajpoots were embodied as an auxiliary force, and Bombay was made the headquarters of the Company in India.

| 1685. |

The Company thus strengthened forthwith became ambitious. Hitherto it had addressed the native princes in terms of humble submission: it now assumed the tone of an equal and independent power, able to command respect by force of arms. It also equipped a fleet of twelve powerful men-of-war, which was first to capture Chittagong and then to proceed up the eastern branch of the Ganges to seize Dacca. Hostilities were precipitated by a quarrel between English and native soldiers in the bazaar at Hooghly, wherein the forces of the nabob of the province were defeated. The nabob, however, avenged himself by pouncing upon the British factory at Patna; and the approach of Aurungzebe caused the British to withdraw from Hooghly to Chuttamuttee, the site of the present Calcutta. Thus the war against the Moguls ended in the utter humiliation of the Company. The period of conquest was not yet come.

| 1642. |
| 1668. |
| 1669. |
| 1697. |
| 1701. |

Meanwhile a new rival had sprung up in the East Indies. In 1609 a French East India Company had been formed, which after thirty years of ineffectual life at last gave definite evidence of vitality by the formation of a settlement at Madagascar. The venture was not a success; but the great minister Colbert, quickly awake to the advantages of an Indian trade, granted the help of the Government to form a new Company, which, after wasting some time and money on a second experiment in Madagascar, sent an expedition to Surat. There in 1668 was established the first French factory in India, which was quickly followed by the erection of a second at Masulipatam. But, if the Company were to prosper, something more than a factory with a rival factory alongside it was needed; and this want was made good by the foundation of Pondicherry by François Martin in 1674. Two or three years later a French fleet entered the Hooghly and disembarked a body of settlers at Chandernagore, which was finally granted to them by Aurungzebe in 1688. Meanwhile the foolish quarrel of the English Company with the Moguls had given the French an opportunity to take a share of the Indian trade, of which they did not fail to make good use. Their further progress was, however, checked for the moment through the capture of Pondicherry by the Dutch in 1693; but the settlement was restored at the Peace of Ryswick, and no time was lost in improving and fortifying it. Shortly afterwards the French abandoned their factory at Surat and transferred their headquarters to Pondicherry. On the whole they had made good use of their time. The settlements of the British Company after one hundred years of existence were set down, in contemporary spelling, as follows: Bombay, with factories at Surat, Swally, Broach, Amadavad, Agra, and Lucknow; on the Malabar coast the forts of Carwar, Tellicherry, and Anjengo, with the factory of Calicut; on the Coromandel coast Chinghee, Orixa, Fort St. George or

Madras, Fort St. David (which had been purchased in 1692 as a counterpoise to Pondicherry), and the factories of Cuddalore, Porto Novo, Petapolee, Masulipatam, Madapollam, and Vizagapatam; in Bengal, Fort William (Calcutta), with factories at Balasore, Cossimbazar, Dacca, Hooghly, Moulda, Rajahmaul, and Patna. The French could show Pondicherry, with a factory at Masulipatam on the eastern coast, and Chandernagore and Cossimbazar on the Hooghly as the result of barely five-and-thirty years of work.

Such competition as this might not at first appear formidable to the English, but the comparative strength of the rival nations in India was not to be measured by mere counting of forts and factories. François Martin had shown considerable dexterity in handling the native authorities during the negotiations by which he acquired Pondicherry, and had established good traditions for the management of similar business in future. All Frenchmen had and still have a passion for interference with the internal politics of any barbarous or semi-civilised races with which they may be brought into contact, and will spare no pains to gratify it. The emissaries of the most insolent nation in Europe approached the Indian princes with flattery of their self-esteem, deference for their authority, respect for their prejudices, conformity with their customs and imitation of their habits; while the French love of dramatic action and of display brought them at once into touch with the oriental character. They gave sympathy, sometimes in reality, always in appearance; and they obtained in return not only toleration but friendship and influence. Mere trading was sufficient for the English; it was not so for the French. Their ambition rose above the mere bartering of goods to the governing of men and the swaying of them by subtle policy to the glory of France. It was no ignoble aim, and might well lead to the making, if not to the keeping, of an Empire.

| 1707. |
| 1719. |

Aurungzebe at his death divided his dominions among his three sons, who at once fell to fighting for the succession to the entire realm. The contest was decided after a year in favour of the eldest of them, Bahadur Shah, who hastened to make terms with the Mahrattas in the south, but secured a precarious peace in that quarter only to find himself confronted with an insurrection of Rajpoots and with the sudden and alarming rise of the Sikhs in the Punjaub. He died in 1712, when the succession after the inevitable dispute passed to his grandson Farokshir, who succeeded in crushing the Sikhs but made little head against the Mahrattas, whose territory continued to increase in the south. Finally, on Farokshir's death in 1719 Nizam-ul-Mulk, the Governor of Malwa, rose in revolt against his successor, made terms with the Mahrattas, and was soon virtually master of the Deccan; to which, after a short-lived reconciliation with the Court of Delhi, he returned in 1724, openly and avowedly as an independent monarch.

```
1725.
1735.
```

During this period the English Company acquired from Farokshir an extension of territory on the Hooghly, amounting to a tract of nearly ten miles on both sides of the river. The French, on the other hand, were declining owing to the virtual insolvency of the Company; nor was it until 1723, five years after the reconstruction of a new Company, that their prospects in India began to revive. But already, in 1720, a man had been appointed to high station in Pondicherry who was destined to raise French influence in India to a height undreamed of by friend or foe. This was Joseph François Dupleix, son of a director of the French East India Company, who, though in boyhood averse to a mercantile life, had been converted by travel at sea to a passion for commercial enterprise and to a longing for a field wherein to indulge it. Such a field was now opened to him, when no more than twenty-three years of age, in India. His idea was to extend the operations of the Company beyond the mere trade between Europe and Pondicherry, and, by opening up traffic with the cities both inland and on the coast, to make Pondicherry the centre of the commerce of Southern India. To show, by example, that such a scheme was feasible, he embarked his own fortune in the trade and made a handsome profit. In 1731 he was sent to Chandernagore, then fast sinking into stagnation and decay, and by his energy soon raised it to the most important European centre in Bengal. Concurrently a second great Frenchman, who was also to leave his mark on India, had made his appearance in 1725. The occasion was the capture of Mahé, a little town on the western coast, where the French desired a port to compensate them for the abandonment of Surat. The feat was accomplished by a captain in the French navy named Bertrand de la Bourdonnais. His next duty, though not performed in India, was none the less of high importance to it, namely the improvement of the island of Mauritius. The French attempts at colonisation in Madagascar had been foiled alike by the climate and by the hostility of the natives; and the settlers had perforce betaken themselves to the adjacent island of Bourbon. La Bourdonnais found Mauritius a mere forest, yet within two years he converted it into a flourishing settlement, well cultivated and well administered, with arsenals, magazines, barracks, fortifications, dockyards, and all that was necessary to make it not only a commercial station but a base for military operations in India.

Meanwhile the confusion that accompanied the gradual dissolution of the Mogul Empire was turned to useful account by yet another Frenchman, Dumas, the Governor of Pondicherry. In 1732 the Nabob of the Carnatic died and was succeeded by his nephew Dost Ali, who however was on such ill terms with his superior, the viceroy Nizam-ul-Mulk of the Deccan, that he could not obtain from him authentic confirmation of his succession. He therefore courted the support of the Governor of Pondicherry, conceding to him substantial privileges in return, and soon formed intimate relations with him. Dost Ali, moreover, had a son, Sufder Ali, and two sons-in-law, Mortiz Ali and Chunda Sahib, of whom the last named was imbued with a particular admiration for the French. The extension of French influence through these new friendships advanced rapidly. In 1735 the death of the Hindoo Rajah of Trichinopoly was followed, as usual, by a quarrel over the succession. The widow of the Rajah, who was one of the claimants, took the fatal step of invoking the help of Dost Ali, who sent Chunda Sahib with an army to her assistance. Chunda Sahib, however, once admitted to the city refused to leave it, but assumed the government in the name of Dost Ali; and thus Trichinopoly passed into the hands of a friend to the French. Adjoining Trichinopoly and between it and the eastern coast lay the Hindoo kingdom of Tanjore; the Coleroon river, which formed its northern boundary, running within thirty miles of Pondicherry. Here again the death of the Rajah in 1738 led to a dispute over the succession, and one of the competitors, named Sauhojee, offered Governor Dumas the town of Carical in the delta of the Cauvery and Coleroon, as the price of French assistance. Dumas promptly supplied money, arms, and ammunition; and when Sauhojee, having thus gained his kingdom, declined to fulfil his agreement, Chunda Sahib stepped in unasked to compel him. Thus Carical also was added to the French settlements in India.

| 1739. |
| 1740. |
| 1741, |
| March. |

But now the Mahrattas, jealous of the advance of the Mohammedans in the south, gathered themselves together for the conquest of the Carnatic, defeated and killed Dost Ali, and spread panic from end to end of the province. Sufder Ali, thus become Nabob, and Chunda Sahib fell back on their French allies and sent their families and goods for security to Pondicherry. Dumas gave them asylum without hesitation, nor could all the threats of the Mahrattas shake his loyalty to his friends. He answered their menaces by strengthening the defences of the town, formed a body of European infantry, and by a happy inspiration armed four or five thousand Mohammedan natives and trained and drilled them after the European model. Thus was conceived in danger and emergency the embryo, now grown to such mighty manhood, of a Sepoy Army. Meanwhile Sufder Ali, after the Oriental manner, succeeded in purchasing immunity from the Mahrattas by secretly betraying Chunda Sahib into their hands; but none the less his gratitude to the

French was extreme. He declared that from henceforth they should be as much masters of the Carnatic as himself, and granted to them additional territory on the southern bounds of Pondicherry. The Mahrattas, pursuant to their agreement with Sufder Ali, then beleaguered Chunda Sahib in Trichinopoly, captured the city after a siege of three months, and carried him off as their prisoner. This done they turned again upon Dumas, and required of him, among other demands, the surrender of Chunda Sahib's property. Dumas received the Mahratta envoy with courtesy but refused inflexibly to comply; and having shown him the preparations which he had made for the defence of Pondicherry he dismissed him with the assurance that he would stand by the city so long as a man was left with him. This resolute bearing had its effect. The further wrath of the Mahratta chief was allayed by a present of French liqueurs; and the danger passed away. Dumas, as the man who had defied the dreaded Mahrattas, became the hero of Southern India. Presents and eulogies were showered on him by Sufder Ali and Nizam-ul-Mulk; and even the effete Mogul Emperor at Delhi conferred on him the title of Nabob, adding thereto the favour, conferred at Dumas's own request, that the rank should descend to his successor.

Oct.

Dumas then resigned and returned to France, leaving Dupleix to reign in his stead. The latter, after ten years' administration of Chandernagore, had raised it to the head of the European settlements in Bengal, and had concurrently amassed for himself an enormous fortune by private trading. He at once assumed all the pomp and circumstance of his rank of Nabob, caused himself to be installed with great ceremony at Chandernagore, and took pains to impress upon the neighbouring princes that he was one of themselves and armed with like authority from the court of Delhi. He could wear the dignity of his position the more naturally since he had an innate passion for display, and could turn the outward glitter to the better account for that he loved it for its own sake. But his was no spirit to be content with the mere robes of royalty. The weakness of the court of Delhi and his own remoteness from it left him free from all restraint. He had the power, and he knew how to use it; and it had come to him in the nick of time, when hostilities between France and England were hastening to their development into avowed and open war.

1742,
Sept.
1744.

But meanwhile native affairs had undergone their usual swift changes in the Carnatic. Sufder Ali, once established as Nabob, refused to pay the revenue due from him to the viceroy Nizam-ul-Mulk, and, having little hope of French support in such defiance of authority, transferred his treasures from

Pondicherry to the custody of the English at Madras. Shortly afterwards he was assassinated by his brother-in-law, Mortiz Ali, who thereupon proclaimed himself Nabob. His principal officers then appealed to the Mahratta chief, Morari Rao, to drive him out, and Mortiz Ali fled, leaving Sufder Ali's infant son to reign in his place. The whole province fell into anarchy, and in 1743 the viceroy Nizam-ul-Mulk appeared with a large army to restore order. The Mahrattas therefore retired from Trichinopoly; and, the infant ruler having been made away with, Anwarudeen, one of the viceroy's officers, was installed as Nabob. By this time Dupleix had received intelligence that war had been declared between France and England, and that a British squadron was on its way to destroy Pondicherry. The French squadron in East Indian waters had been recalled to France; the fortifications of the city were open to destruction by the cannon of men-of-war; and there were less than five hundred Europeans in garrison to defend it against a joint attack by sea and land. At this crisis Dupleix appealed to Anwarudeen for protection, pleading the friendship of the French with the Nabobs of the Carnatic in the past. The Nabob responded by sending a message to Madras that he intended to enforce strict neutrality within his province, and would permit no attack to be made on the French possessions on the coast of Coromandel.

1745.
1746,
June 25
July 6.

At the close of 1745 the British squadron duly arrived, but found itself, through Anwarudeen's action, limited exclusively to operations by sea. Meanwhile, also La Bourdonnais, aided partly by the arrival of a few weak ships from France, but chiefly by his own amazing energy and resource, had fitted out a squadron at Mauritius, with which he appeared in July 1746 off the southern coast of Ceylon. An indecisive engagement followed, at the close of which the British commander, Commodore Peyton, with strange pusillanimity sailed to Trincomalee to repair the trifling damage sustained in the action, leaving Pondicherry untouched and Madras unprotected from French attack. The French therefore had won a first and most important point in the game: if the Nabob could be persuaded to let that game proceed without interference, the ultimate victory must lie with France.

Aug. $\frac{18}{29}$.
Sept. $\frac{3}{14}$;
Sept. $\frac{10}{21}$.

The town of Madras at that time consisted of three divisions; that on the south side, which was known as the White Town or Fort St. George, being inhabited by Europeans, that next to northward of it being given up to the wealthier class of Indian and Armenian merchants, while a suburb to the north of all was filled with all other classes of natives. Of these divisions the White Town, which was about four hundred yards long by one hundred broad, alone possessed defences worthy the name, being surrounded by a slender wall with four bastions and as many batteries. The total number of English did not exceed three hundred, two-thirds of which was made up of the soldiers of the garrison. The Directors of the East India Company had too often been neglectful of defences in the past, and had improved little in this respect during the past half century. They relied upon the British fleet and upon that alone. The Governor, Mr. Morse, was simply a merchant, a man of invoices and ledgers, with little knowledge of affairs beyond the scope of his business, and ignorant of the very alphabet of intercourse with native princes. There was, it is true, a clerk in his office named Robert Clive, who had arrived in India two years before; but this clerk was known only as a quiet, friendless lad, not without spirit when provoked, but lonely and out of harmony with his environment, and grateful to be able to escape from it to the refuge of the Governor's library. On receiving intelligence of hostile preparations by the French at Pondicherry, Governor Morse appealed to the Nabob Anwarudeen to fulfil his determination of enforcing neutrality within the Carnatic; but his envoy, being unprovided with the indispensable credentials of a present, met with little success in his mission. On the 29th of August the French squadron appeared before Madras, cannonaded it for a time with little effect and sailed away again; but a fortnight later it reappeared with eleven hundred European soldiers and four hundred drilled natives, under the command of La Bourdonnais in person. The troops were at once landed, batteries were erected, and after a short bombardment Madras was forced to capitulate. The terms agreed on were, that all the English inhabitants should be prisoners on parole, and that negotiations might be reopened later for ransom of the town.

Oct. $\frac{3}{14}$;
Oct. $\frac{10}{21}$.

The Nabob Anwarudeen no sooner heard that the French were actually besieging Madras than he sent a message to Dupleix that unless further operations were suspended he would put an end to them by force. Dupleix answered astutely that he was conquering the town not for France but for the Nabob himself, and would deliver it to him immediately on its surrender. Fortunately for England La Bourdonnais's views as to the future treatment of Madras differed materially from those of Dupleix. As conqueror of the settlement he claimed that the ultimate disposal of it lay with himself:

Dupleix, intent above all things on conciliating the Nabob, as vehemently contended that his authority as Governor-General was supreme in such matters. The two masterful men fell bitterly at variance over the question, and lost sight of all greater interests in the acrimony of their quarrel. La Bourdonnais, fully aware of the danger of waiting on the coast when the northern monsoon was due, but bent none the less on having his own way, lingered on and on before Madras, until on the 14th of October the monsoon suddenly burst upon him with the force of a hurricane, destroyed four of his eight ships utterly, and disabled the remainder. A week later he signed a treaty for the ransom of Madras and for its subsequent evacuation by the French; and this done he returned, as soon as his ships could be made seaworthy, to Pondicherry. There the quarrel with Dupleix was resumed face to face; and after only ten days' stay La Bourdonnais sailed from India never to return.

| Oct. 22 |
| Nov. 2. |
| Oct. 24 |
| Nov. 4. |

Dupleix was now left in sole and unhampered command, with moreover a force of three thousand trained Europeans ready to his hand, some of them left behind by La Bourdonnais, some taken from the French squadron. Such an accession of strength was all important to him, for he had now to reckon with the Nabob, who growing suspicious over the long delay in the delivery of Madras had sent ten thousand men under his son Maphuze Khan to invest the town. Dupleix, who, if he had ever meant to give it up, had determined first to dismantle the fortifications, sent orders to D'Espréménil, the officer in command, to hold the town at all hazards. D'Espréménil finding himself hard pressed made a sortie with four hundred of his garrison, and boldly facing the masses of the enemy's cavalry opened on them so effective a fire from his field-guns that they fled with precipitation, abandoning their camp to the victor. With their own clumsy artillery, not yet advanced beyond the stage attained by European nations in the sixteenth century, the natives thought it good practice if a gun were discharged four times in an hour; and they were utterly confounded and dismayed by the rapidity with which the French pieces were served. This was one great lesson for Europeans in Indian warfare, but a second and a greater was to follow. After lingering for another day in the vicinity of Madras Maphuze marched to St. Thomé, some four miles to southward of it, to intercept a French force which was on its way to relieve D'Espréménil's garrison. On the morning of the 4th of November the expected detachment appeared, a mere handful of two hundred and thirty Europeans and seven hundred Sepoys, which had been sent up from Pondicherry under a Swiss officer named Paradis. The situation of Paradis was sufficiently perilous to have alarmed him. His orders were to open communications with Madras; and here was an army of ten thousand men, with artillery, drawn up on the bank of a river before him to bar his advance. Now, after a century and a half of fighting in India, no British officer would be for a moment at a loss as to the course to be pursued, but Paradis had neither tradition nor experience to guide him. However, whether by inspiration or from despair, he did exactly what he ought. Knowing the river to be fordable, he led his men without hesitation across it and straight upon the enemy, scrambled up the bank, gave them one volley, and charged with the bayonet. The effect of this bold attack was instantaneous. The Nabob's army was at once transformed into a disorganised mob, which fled headlong into the town of St. Thomé, only to be crowded and jammed in hopeless confusion in the streets. Paradis, following up his success, poured volley after volley into the struggling mass; while, to perfect the victory, a party which had been detached from Madras to join hands with him came up in rear of the fugitives and cut off their retreat. This attack in rear, always dreaded by Oriental nations, completed the rout. Maphuze Khan, who was mounted on an elephant, was one of the first to fly; and his army streamed away to westward, a helpless, terrified rabble, never pausing in its flight until it reached Arcot.

With this action it may be said that the dominance of an European nation in India was assured. Hitherto the native armies had been treated with respect. Their numbers had given the impression of overwhelming strength; and it had not occurred to Europeans that they could be encountered except with a force of man for man. Consequently all dealings of Europeans with native princes had been conducted in a spirit of humility and awe. Even Dupleix, while flaunting his dignity among his brother Nabobs, had courted the ruler of the Carnatic with deference and submission. Now the spell was broken, and Dupleix from the courtier had become the master; so momentous was the change wrought by a single Swiss officer, whose very name is hardly known to the nation which now rules India. Of all the fruits of the long friendship which French and Swiss sealed with each other's blood in the furious struggle of Marignano, none is more remarkable than this. The memory of Paradis should be honoured in England since he taught us the secret of the conquest of India.

| Nov. |
| Dec. $\frac{6}{17}$, |

The victory swept away Dupleix's principal difficulties at a blow. He at once appointed Paradis to the chief command at Madras and bade him issue a manifesto repudiating La Bourdonnais's treaty as null and void, and declaring Madras to belong to the French by right of conquest. The English protested, but in vain. Morse and the rest of the officials were conducted to Pondicherry.

A few only contrived to make their escape to Fort St. David, among them the man who was soon to make Dupleix smart for his ill-faith, the young writer Robert Clive. Fort St. David, situate about twelve miles south of Pondicherry, now became the rallying-point of the English. Since the fall of Madras the authorities there had taken over the general administration of British affairs on the coast of Coromandel; the fort, though small, was the strongest for its size that the British possessed in India; and they were determined to defend it to the last extremity. Dupleix on his side was equally resolved to strike at it without delay, and with this object he instructed Paradis to return to Pondicherry as soon as he should have settled the affairs of Madras. This duty, however, detained Paradis until December; and meanwhile the British officials had invoked the aid of the Nabob Anwarudeen, who, smarting under the defeat of St. Thomé, agreed to send a force under Maphuze Khan and his brother Mohammed Ali to Fort St. David. Maphuze Khan, eager to wipe out his disgrace, attacked Paradis on his march down from Madras; but the French, though they were but three hundred strong and encumbered with the plunder of Madras, beat off his attack with little difficulty, and made their way, with trifling loss, to their destination of Ariancopang, a mile and a half from Pondicherry.

Dec. $\frac{8}{19}$.
1747.
Feb.

The total force now gathered together by Dupleix at Ariancopang for the attack on Fort St. David consisted of about sixteen hundred men, nine hundred of them Europeans, with six field-pieces and as many mortars. Against these the British garrison could muster but two hundred Europeans and half as many natives. Unluckily, however, for the success of Dupleix's schemes, there were several French officers senior to Paradis, the chief of whom, General de Bury, took the command. On the 19th of December De Bury crossed the river Pennar and encamped in a walled garden about a mile and a half from Fort St. David. Though the Nabob's army was not five miles distant, neither picquets nor sentries were posted; and the French were dispersed and cooking their dinners when they were suddenly alarmed by the approach of the enemy. Panic-stricken the whole force rushed out of the garden to the river, each man anxious only to place the water between himself and the foe; and had not the artillery stood firm De Bury's troops would have fared badly indeed. As things fell out they escaped with the loss of a dozen Europeans killed and one hundred and twenty wounded, and made good their retreat to Ariancopang. For three weeks after this reverse the French remained inactive in their camp, but in January 1747 a squadron of French ships arrived on the coast, and Dupleix seized the opportunity offered by this display of force to reopen negotiations with the Nabob Anwarudeen. With his usual dexterity he pointed out that the condition of the British was hopeless; and his arguments were not the less cogent for an accompaniment of gifts to the value of fifteen thousand pounds. The Nabob, already weary of the war, concluded a peace with the French and withdrew his army from Fort St. David.

| Feb. 19 |
| Mar. 2. |
| Mar. $\frac{2}{13}$. |

Dupleix seemed now to hold his rivals in his hand; and undoubtedly for the moment the outlook for the British was dark. One or two isolated ships despatched by the Company had arrived on the coast, but had either been captured or frightened away; and it was not until March that one of them succeeded in landing twenty men and sixty thousand pounds in silver at Fort St. David. Ten days later the French began a second attempt against the fort, but were compelled to beat a hasty retreat by the arrival of Admiral Griffin with a British squadron in the roadstead. Griffin landed a company of one hundred soldiers, and lent also marines and sailors from the fleet, as a temporary measure, to strengthen the garrison while he sailed with the fleet to blockade Pondicherry. Fresh reinforcements arrived at Fort St. David both from Europe and from some of the Company's settlements during May and June; and by July the garrison, including the naval brigade, had risen to twelve hundred Europeans and eight hundred natives.

| June $\frac{11}{22}$. |
| 1748. |

The restoration of British supremacy at sea turned the tables against Dupleix, but he contrived none the less to despatch a message to Mauritius for reinforcements. The letter did not reach the island until December, nor was it possible until May 1748 to send off a squadron, which even then was inferior in strength to the blockading fleet under Griffin. By great dexterity, however, the French Admiral contrived to entice Griffin to sea and to slip past him in the night to Madras, where having landed three hundred European soldiers and a large sum of money he put to sea again, leaving Griffin to hunt for him where he would. Dupleix thereupon snatched the opportunity afforded by Griffin's absence to make an attack on Cuddalore, an English fortified station about two miles south of Fort St. David, which he had already attempted once without success. The force that he had collected for this enterprise was large judged by the minute scale of the armies employed in these early Indian wars, consisting of eight hundred Europeans and one thousand Sepoys. But by this time the British had been strengthened not only by the reinforcements of the previous year but by the arrival in January of a competent commander. This officer, whose fame is far below his deserts, was Major Stringer Lawrence.

June $\frac{17}{28}$.

Dupleix's idea was to surprise Cuddalore by night, and with this view he sent his army by a circuitous route to some hills within three miles of the station, with orders to halt and remain concealed until the time should come for the attack. Lawrence, who had full intelligence of the design, ostentatiously removed the garrison and the guns from Cuddalore to Fort St. David during the day; but at nightfall sent them back again, with due precautions to conceal the fact from the French, together with a reinforcement of four hundred Europeans. At midnight the French advanced to the walls without thought of meeting with resistance, but had no sooner planted their scaling-ladders than they were saluted by a withering fire of musketry and grape. The whole body was instantly smitten with panic. Most of them flung down their arms without firing a shot, and one and all took to their heels and fled, not halting until they reached Pondicherry. So ended the first brush between French and English troops in India.

June 23
July 4.
July 31
Aug. 11.

The result was a sad blow to Dupleix, for news had reached them that a powerful armament was on its way from England. In effect the British Government had determined to help the East India Company both with ships and men, and in November 1747 Admiral Boscawen had sailed with eight men-of-war and a convoy of fourteen hundred regular troops. By a novel arrangement, due doubtless to the sad experience of Carthagena, the Admiral held sole command both of army and navy. The first object prescribed to the expedition was the capture of Mauritius and Bourbon, which islands, being within a month's sail of the coast of Coromandel, were of unspeakable value to the French as a base for their operations in India. The British possessed no such station. St. Helena was too remote, even supposing that a harbour comparable to Port Louis could have been found in it, and the Cape of Good Hope was in the hands of the Dutch. Boscawen arrived before Port Louis on the 4th of July, but found Mauritius strongly defended by forts and batteries at every spot which was suitable for a landing. After three days spent in vain endeavour to discover a weak point, the Admiral decided to push on without further loss of time to the ulterior goal appointed him by his instructions, Pondicherry. He set sail, therefore, for Fort St. David, and early in August effected his junction with Griffin. The combined squadrons formed the most powerful armament yet seen in East Indian waters.

A fleet of thirty ships set Boscawen at ease as to his communications by sea; and as every preparation had been made at Fort St. David against his arrival, he was able within a week to march to the siege of Pondicherry. The King's regular troops consisted of twelve independent companies each one hundred strong, eight hundred marines, and eighty of the Royal Artillery, which, added to the Company's soldiers and a naval brigade, brought up the total to a strength of thirty-seven hundred Europeans. Two thousand Sepoys also accompanied the expedition, though as yet neither trained nor disciplined. But meanwhile Dupleix had not been idle. Desperate though his situation might appear, he had resolved to make the best of it, and had not only strengthened the defences of Pondicherry itself, but had added a strong fort at Ariancopang, which was constructed under the care of the indefatigable Paradis. This latter work was the first obstacle that presented itself to Boscawen's advance. No one in his camp knew anything about it, because no one had been at any pains to find out. A deserter reported that it was held by a hundred natives only, and Boscawen without further ado resolved to carry it by storm. Seven hundred men were therefore launched against it, only to find that the defences were decidedly formidable and the garrison four times as strong as had been supposed. Moreover, owing to a neglect which, after the failure before St. Lazaro, seems perfectly unpardonable, no scaling-ladders had been prepared for the storming party. The troops, therefore, as at St. Lazaro, tried stubbornly to do impossibilities until nearly a fourth of their number had been killed or wounded, and then fell back not less mortified than dispirited by their repulse.

It was then resolved to besiege Ariancopang in form; but here as at Carthagena the engineers proved to be utterly ignorant of their business, and blunder succeeded blunder. Paradis, who had a troop of sixty horse in addition to the infantry of his garrison, judged astutely of the moral effect which cavalry might produce on seafaring men, and sent his handful of troopers, with infantry in support, straight at the trenches of the naval brigade. The sailors were seized with panic; the panic spread to the regular troops, and the whole rushed headlong back to the camp, leaving their best officer, Stringer Lawrence, to be taken prisoner. Accident, however, came to the help of the British. A magazine at Ariancopang caught fire and exploded, disabling over one hundred men; and the garrison having dismantled the fortifications withdrew into Pondicherry. Boscawen accordingly moved forward from Ariancopang and opened his trenches against the north-western corner of the town. Then once more the ignorance of the engineers led to blunders and waste of time, for they opened their first parallel at a distance of fifteen hundred yards, or twice the distance prescribed by rule and common sense, from the covered way. Still fortune for the present favoured the British. A sortie made by the French was brilliantly repulsed, and Paradis, the ablest of the French both as officer and engineer, was wounded to the death. The Englishman most distinguished in this affair was to prove himself Paradis's most brilliant pupil, an ensign in the Company's service, taken only twelve months before as a clerk from the Company's desks, Robert Clive.

The success of the British now appeared so certain that the Nabob Anwarudeen, yielding to the repeated gifts and appeals of Boscawen, decided to throw in his lot with them and promised to furnish a body of two thousand horse. Still Dupleix was not discouraged. By the death of Paradis the chief burden of military as well as of civil command was thrown upon his shoulders, but he did not shrink from it. After all, if he were no soldier, neither was Boscawen. By immense labour the British trenches were carried forward to the position from which they should have been opened, eight hundred yards from the wall, and early in October two batteries at last opened on the town. They were answered by twice as formidable a fire from the guns of the besieged. Boscawen then ordered the fleet to open fire from the sea, but the ships being prevented by shoal water from approaching nearer than a thousand yards from the works, the cannonade was wholly ineffective. The fire of the British batteries ashore continued for three days with little result, while that of the besieged increased rather than languished. The rainy season then set in earlier than usual; the trenches were flooded, and disease began to rage in the British camp. Finally, on the 11th of October, Boscawen decided to raise the siege and the British retreated, leaving over one thousand Europeans dead behind them, while Dupleix remained proud and unconquered in Pondicherry.

The failure of this enterprise was due to the same causes that had wrecked the expedition to Carthagena. In the first place, Boscawen arrived on the coast too late. In the second, he wasted nearly three weeks over the capture of Ariancopang, which was not essential to the capture of Pondicherry. In the third, the unskilfulness of the engineers prolonged the operations, and occupied the troops with duties which kept them from active service in the trenches and harassed them to death for no purpose. The experiment of setting a naval officer in charge of highly technical military operations was probably due to the influence of Vernon; to which also maybe traced Boscawen's readiness to attempt the storm of Ariancopang after Vernon's rough-and-ready manner. Against Spaniards in South America such methods might have succeeded; against Frenchmen they could not, least of all when commanded by a Dupleix with a Paradis for his military adviser. If the failure before Pondicherry had ended with the raising of the siege, the reverse would have been comparatively a trifling matter; but it told far and wide over India as a blow to British influence and prestige, and Dupleix was not the man to neglect to magnify the success and the greatness of his nation.

The news of the peace of Aix-la-Chapelle some months later brought about a cessation of overt hostilities and the re-delivery of Madras to Boscawen; but still the war did not end. As in Europe French and English could fight fiercely as auxiliaries of an Elector of Bavaria and a Queen of Hungary, so in Asia they could carry on, as allies of native princes, the contest which was to determine the fate of India.

CHAPTER II

1749.

The first of the native states in which the British initiated their new policy of intervention was one with which the French had busied themselves ten years earlier, the kingdom of Tanjore. There the ruler favoured by Governor Dumas, Sauhojee, had, after some years of misrule, been deposed; he now came to the British Company for assistance, offering to pay the expenses of the war and to give the fort and territory of Devicotah as the price of his re-establishment on the throne. The Company accordingly detailed a force of five hundred Europeans and fifteen hundred Sepoys, which started at the end of March 1749 for Trichinopoly. Sauhojee had engaged that its operations could be seconded by a general rising in his favour, but this promise was found to be illusory, and the expedition returned without effecting anything. Undismayed, however, by this first failure, the Company equipped a second force, and resolved this time to push straight for the prize offered by Sauhojee, the fort of Devicotah. Eight hundred Europeans and fifteen hundred Sepoys under command of Major Stringer Lawrence embarked for the mouth of the Coleroon, and landing on the south side of the river succeeded after a few days' cannonade in battering a breach in the wall of the fort. A ship's carpenter then contrived a raft on which troops could be conveyed across the river, and Lawrence resolved to storm the fort forthwith. Clive led the storming party, which consisted of thirty-four Europeans and seven hundred Sepoys, but, the Sepoys failing to support him, his little party of British was cut to pieces by the cavalry of the Tanjorines, and he himself narrowly escaped with his life. Lawrence thereupon resolved to throw the whole of his Europeans into the breach. The Tanjorine horse again attacked them as they advanced, but were crushed by their fire; and the British on entering the breach found the fort deserted. Lawrence accordingly took possession of the fort and territory, and the Company, having obtained all that it desired, promised Sauhojee a pension if he would undertake to give no more trouble in Tanjore. It was destined to pay dearly for this evil precedent, and for the paltry acquisition so ignobly gained.

July 23
Aug. 3.

Meanwhile momentous events elsewhere had led to fresh complications. In 1748 Nizam-ul-Mulk, the Viceroy of the Deccan, died, and his death was followed as usual by a quarrel over the succession to his throne. The successor nominated by the dead ruler was his grandson, Murzapha Jung; the rival was his second son, Nasir Jung; and, as was natural, both claimants cast about them for allies. It has already been related how Chunda Sahib, the devoted admirer of the French, had been captured by the Mahrattas in Trichinopoly in 1741. Ever since that time he had been kept in close confinement at Satara; the Mahrattas, who knew him by reputation as the ablest soldier that had been seen for years in the Carnatic, refusing to release him except for an impossible ransom. He had, however, a friend in Dupleix, who throughout his imprisonment had protected his wife and family in Pondicherry, and had contrived further to maintain with him a friendly correspondence. Murzapha Jung while travelling in search of help from the Mahrattas encountered Chunda Sahib at Satara, and at once perceived the value of such a man for an ally. Dupleix was called in, and took in the whole situation at a glance. If the force of the French arms could enthrone Murzapha Jung as viceroy, there would be little or nothing to hinder French influence from becoming predominant in the Deccan, or, in other words, to prevent Dupleix from becoming practically if not nominally viceroy himself. He at once pledged himself to discharge Chunda Sahib's ransom, and immediately after his release allowed him to take into his pay two thousand Sepoys from the garrison of Pondicherry; agreeing also, on receipt of a further cession of territory near the town, to give him the assistance of four hundred European soldiers. With these and with the troops that he had collected, in all some six thousand men, Chunda Sahib joined himself to Murzapha Jung's army of thirty thousand men, and advanced with them against Arcot. The capture of this, the capital town of the Carnatic, would place the resources of that province at their disposal and win for them the first step to the throne of the Deccan. The old Nabob Anwarudeen had collected a force to oppose them, but he could bring forward no troops to match the disciplined infantry of the French. After a sharp action at Amoor he was defeated and slain: the victorious army entered Arcot on the following day, and the Carnatic was won.

Murzapha Jung having proclaimed himself Viceroy of the Deccan, and taken steps to assert his sovereignty, proceeded next with Chunda Sahib to Pondicherry, where they were received in great state by Dupleix, and in return rewarded him with yet another grant of the neighbouring territory. Meanwhile the English looked on, indignant but helpless, having barred their right to protest by their own foolish action at Tanjore. Boscawen did indeed take advantage of Anwarudeen's death to hoist the British flag over St. Thomé, as a masterless town which might be of profit to the Company; but for the rest the arm of the British seemed paralysed. Mohammed Ali, son of the dead

Nabob Anwarudeen, who had fled from the field of Amoor to Trichinopoly, invoked the aid of the East India Company; but though profoundly distrustful of the friendship between Chunda Sahib and Dupleix, the authorities sent but one hundred and twenty men to help him. This done, they actually permitted Boscawen to return to England with his fleet and transports, retaining but three hundred of his men in India to strengthen the British garrison. This was the moment for which Dupleix had longed. The one force which he dreaded was removed. It remained only for Murzapha Jung and Chunda Sahib to march to Trichinopoly and crush Mohammed Ali; and Southern India was gained once for all.

Dec. $\frac{20}{31}$.

Dupleix did not fail to urge this step upon his two allies; but they had spent so much money over their own enjoyment at Pondicherry that they had exhausted the treasure necessary for the decisive campaign. Judging that the easiest and speediest method of replenishing their empty purse would be to extort funds from the Rajah of Tanjore, they led their armies against that city and summoned it to surrender. The Rajah, Partab Singh, gained time by astute negotiation to summon the English and Murzapha Jung's rival, Nasir Jung, to his assistance; but the English hardly responded, and the Rajah, cowed by an attack of the French infantry on the defences of the city, agreed to pay the sum required of him. None the less, by continual haggling he continued to keep his enemies inactive before the walls until the news of Nasir Jung's approach, with a force of overwhelming strength, caused them to fall back in panic upon Pondicherry.

1750.
April $\frac{1}{12}$.

The favourable moment in fact had been lost, despite Dupleix's pressing entreaties that it might be seized. Nasir Jung had not only invaded the Carnatic with his own forces but had called Mohammed Ali and the British to his standard; and the East India Company, roused by the imposing numbers of his army, had sent him six hundred European soldiers under command of Stringer Lawrence in person. At the end of March the hostile armies stood within striking distance of each other midway between Pondicherry and Arcot, near the fortress of Gingee; but no blow was struck. A mutiny of the French troops practically broke up Murzapha Jung's army; Murzapha himself surrendered to Nasir Jung; and the whole of Dupleix's grand combinations seemed to be shattered beyond repair. With inexhaustible energy, however, the French Governor set himself to restore the discipline of the troops, and meanwhile opened negotiations with Nasir Jung. Finding his overtures rejected he boldly surprised his camp by night with a handful of men, and with such effect that Nasir Jung retreated hurriedly to Arcot. The British, thus abandoned, retired likewise to Fort St. David, and the field was left open once more to the ambition of Dupleix.

```
Aug. 31
Sept. 11.
Dec. 5
     16
```

Thoroughly understanding the Oriental character, he hastened to follow up this first blow with another. First he turned upon Mohammed Ali, who had been left in isolation near Pondicherry, dispersed his army, though vastly superior to his own, almost without loss of a man, and sent him flying northward. He then detached one of his best officers, M. de Bussy, with a handful of troops against the fugitives of Mohammed Ali's force which had rallied under the walls of Gingee; and Bussy not only routed them in the field but actually carried the fort of Gingee itself, for generations deemed an impregnable stronghold, by escalade. This feat, one of the most brilliant and marvellous ever achieved by Europeans in India, provoked Nasir Jung anew to try his fortune in the field and lured him on to his destruction. Notwithstanding the lateness of the season he collected a vast unwieldy host of a hundred thousand men and moved down to Gingee, only to find military operations absolutely impossible owing to the breaking of the monsoon. For three months he remained perforce inactive, while Dupleix sedulously fostered sedition and conspiracy in his camp. At last, in December, the French attacked and utterly defeated his army, while the conspirators made an end of Nasir Jung himself. Murzapha Jung was at once saluted as Viceroy of the Deccan, and a few days later was solemnly installed as such at Pondicherry; Dupleix, in all the splendour of Oriental robes, sitting by his side as one of equal rank, to receive with him the homage of the subordinate princes. The French Governor was declared Nabob of the whole of the country south of the Kistnah to Cape Comorin, and Chunda Sahib was appointed Nabob of Arcot and of its dependencies under him; his former rival, Mohammed Ali, being only too glad to gain Dupleix's favour by renouncing all pretensions of his own. Finally, new privileges and concessions were showered on the French East India Company. To such a height indeed had French ascendency risen that Dupleix gave orders for the erection of a city with the pompous title of the Place of the Victory of Dupleix.

```
1751.
Jan. 4
     15
June 18 .
     29
```

Nothing now remained but to escort the new Viceroy of the Deccan to his capital at Aurungabad, a duty which was entrusted to Bussy. At one point in the march some opposition was encountered, which, though easily swept aside by the French artillery, proved fatal to Murzapha Jung. His vindictive temper led him forward to a personal contest of man to man, and while actually within reach of the goal of his ambition he was struck dead. The incident, untoward though it might appear at such a time, proved to be of little moment. One puppet would serve as well as another for Viceroy of the Deccan, so the actual sovereignty rested with Dupleix. Salabat Jung, a younger brother of Nasir Jung, was accordingly released by Bussy from the prison in which he was confined, and was elevated with general approval to the place of the potentate whose career had been so unfortunately cut short. Needless to say, he at once confirmed all former privileges to the French and added yet others to them. Finally, in June, the poor creature entered Aurungabad in state, attended by Bussy and his troops, who did not omit to take up their quarters permanently in the capital. Thus from the Vindhya mountains to the Kistnah the country was practically under the control of Bussy, while from the Kistnah to Cape Comorin Dupleix ruled as actual vicegerent of the Mohammedan sovereign of the Deccan. The moment marks the zenith of French power in India.

| March. |
| May. |

Throughout these transactions the British had remained open-mouthed and inactive, so inactive that in October 1750 they had permitted their ablest soldier, Stringer Lawrence, to return to England. Thoroughly alarmed at the rapid progress of Dupleix's influence, and irritated by the ostentatious display of his sovereignty on its boundaries, the Company at last resolved to initiate a steady policy of opposition to the French in all quarters. There was but one pretext for intervention. Mohammed Ali, the son of the late Nabob Anwarudeen, while negotiating with Dupleix for the surrender of Trichinopoly, had never ceased to make piteous appeals for British assistance. Rather, therefore, than allow this last excuse for interference to be taken from them, the British authorities consented to give him help, and as a first instalment despatched three hundred British and as many Sepoys to Trichinopoly in February 1751. The main issue now turned on the possession of Trichinopoly, and Dupleix was not slow to recognise the fact. Chunda Sahib was already preparing to march upon the city with a native army of about eight thousand men, and to these Dupleix added four hundred French under an able officer. The British replied by equipping a further force of five hundred Europeans, one hundred Africans, and a thousand Sepoys, under the command of Captain Gingen, with Lieutenant Robert Clive for his commissariat-officer. Not daring to act as principal, for French and English were still nominally at peace, Gingen waited at Fort St. David until the middle of May, when he was joined by sixteen hundred of Mohammed Ali's troops. Vested by the advent of this rabble with the character of a legitimate auxiliary, he then marched southward to seize the pagoda of Verdachelum, which commanded the communications between Fort St. David and Trichinopoly. This was successfully accomplished; and having received further reinforcements he moved south-westward to Volconda, on the road between Arcot and Trichinopoly, to intercept the advancing army of Chunda Sahib.

July $\frac{17}{28}$.

The result was disastrous for Gingen. After the exchange of a few cannon-shots the British troops were seized with panic, flung down their arms, and could not be rallied even by Clive himself. Gingen, finding them much shaken, thereupon fell back upon Trichinopoly. Chunda Sahib immediately followed them; and after three days of skirmishing the British crossed the river Coleroon and finally took refuge under the walls of the city. The enemy lost no time in closing in around them, and now the French could look upon their success as well-nigh assured. Almost the whole of the British force in India was cooped up in the city before them; there seemed to be no prospect of relief for them from any other quarter, and it was therefore necessary only to keep them strictly blockaded to make them prisoners in a body.

The British authorities in Fort St. David saw the danger, but could not divine how to avert it. A small force of Europeans had lately arrived from England, but every military officer was shut up in Trichinopoly, and there was not one at hand to take charge of a relieving force. None the less a convoy was equipped at the end of July and sent off with an escort of eighty Europeans and three hundred Sepoys under command of a civilian, Mr. Pigot, with Robert Clive, who had returned from the army after the retreat from Volconda, as second in command. Pigot conducted his convoy safely as far as Verdachelum and passed his reinforcement successfully into Trichinopoly, but both he and Clive were cut off while returning to Fort St. David, and only with the greatest difficulty evaded capture. Clive, now raised to the rank of captain, was presently sent into Tanjore with a second reinforcement, which, like its predecessor, contrived to make its way into Trichinopoly, and raised the strength of the British battalion therein to six hundred men. But the French on their side could bring nine hundred Europeans to meet them; and the salvation of Trichinopoly, and of British power in India which lay bound up in it, seemed to be hopeless.

August.

Clive grasped at once the significance of the situation, and without wasting further time over the blockaded city returned with all haste to Madras. The only hope for Trichinopoly, as he pointed out, lay in a vigorous diversion which should carry the war into the enemy's country. Though the bulk of the British forces might be shut up in Trichinopoly, the bulk of Chunda Sahib's army was equally tied down before it, and therefore the capital of the Carnatic must be left unguarded. Let a bold stroke be aimed at Arcot, and Chunda Sahib must either raise the siege of Trichinopoly to save it, or suffer a loss for which the gain of Trichinopoly would be poor compensation. The plan was audacious beyond measure, but the Governor, Mr. Saunders, a resolute and far-seeing man, perceived its merit; so reducing the garrisons of Madras and Fort St. David to the lowest point he equipped a force of two hundred Europeans and three hundred Sepoys, together with three field-guns, and placed Clive in command with unlimited powers. With this handful of men and eight officers, of whom four had like himself been taken from desk and ledger, Clive marched on the 6th of September from Madras.

Arcot, the capital of the Carnatic, and then the seat of Chunda Sahib's government, lies sixty-four miles to south and west of Madras. It was then an open town of about one hundred thousand inhabitants, with no defences but a ruined fort, which was held by a garrison of a thousand natives. Five days, including a halt of one day at Conjeveram, sufficed to bring Clive within ten miles of the city. At this point he again made a short halt, but resuming his march through a terrific thunderstorm pushed forward to the gates on the same evening. Rumour of his approach had gone before him. Spies had reported that the British were striding on unconcerned through lightning, rain, and tempest; and the garrison, afraid to oppose a man who set the very elements at defiance, evacuated the fort without firing a shot.

Clive at once occupied the deserted fort, repaired the defences, mounted the guns that he found there, and made every preparation to resist a siege. The native garrison having encamped about six miles from the city, Clive made two successful sorties against them, in order to keep them in a becoming state of alarm; and hearing a week later that they had been reinforced to a strength of three thousand men, he burst suddenly upon their camp by night, killed several, sent the rest flying away in panic terror, and returned to the fort without the loss of a man. But by this time Chunda Sahib had heard of the misfortune to his capital, and had detached four thousand men from before Trichinopoly to recapture the fort. Dupleix, though greatly averse to any diminution of the blockading army, added one hundred French soldiers to this detachment, while other levies raised it to a total of ten thousand men. With this force Raju Sahib, Chunda Sahib's son, entered Arcot on the 4th of October and began the investment of the fort.

Sept. 24
Oct. 5.
Sept. 25
Oct. 6.
Oct. 30
Nov. 10.
Nov. $\frac{13}{24}$.
Nov. $\frac{14}{25}$.

On the very next day Clive made a bold sally with the object of driving the enemy from the town, but was driven back with the loss, very serious in view of his numbers, of two officers and thirty-one European soldiers killed and wounded. On the morrow the besiegers received further reinforcement, which raised their numbers to eleven thousand natives and one hundred and fifty Europeans; whereas Clive's garrison was by this time reduced to six score Europeans and two hundred Sepoys only. A fortnight later the enemy's battering train arrived, and on the 10th of November, a practicable breach having been made in the walls, Raju Sahib summoned Clive to surrender. He was answered by a message of contemptuous defiance; but knowing that the supplies of the fort were running low, he hesitated to storm, in the hope of reducing the garrison by starvation. Meanwhile, however, Governor Saunders was pushing forward reinforcements, and had induced the Mahrattas, under the redoubtable Morari Rao, to throw in their lot with the British. Intelligence of this last put an end to Raju Sahib's inaction, and on the 24th of November he laid his plans for an assault. The day chosen was the festival of the brothers Hassan and Hussein, an anniversary on which Mohammedan fanaticism is inflamed always to its fiercest heat. Fortunately Clive had been warned by a spy of the intended attack, and had made such preparations as he could by training cannon on to the breach, and keeping relays of muskets loaded for the maintenance of a continuous fire. At dawn the enemy's troops swarmed up to the breach, while elephants, with their heads armoured by plates of iron, were brought forward to batter down the gates. But the fire of the British was too hot and deadly to be endured, and the elephants, galled by wounds, swerved back and trampled all around them under foot. Once only the storming-party seemed likely to gain ground, and then Clive, taking personal charge of one of the field-guns, dispersed them effectively with three or four rounds. After maintaining the attack for an hour the enemy fell back defeated. The French for some reason held aloof, and the bravest of the native leaders were killed. How hot the affair was while it lasted may be judged from the fact that Clive's garrison, though reduced to eighty Europeans and one hundred and twenty Sepoys, expended twelve thousand cartridges during the assault. The loss of the defenders was but six killed and wounded; that of the enemy was reckoned at not less than four hundred. On the following day Raju Sahib raised the siege and marched away, abandoning several guns and a great quantity of ammunition; and Clive was left in Arcot triumphant. The siege had lasted fifty days and had cost the little garrison one-fourth of its number in killed alone, besides a still greater number wounded; but this was no heavy price to pay for the re-establishment of British prestige. The feast of Hassan and Hussein may justly be accounted the birthday of our empire in India.

On the evening of the day of the assault Clive was joined by a reinforcement of men and of four guns, which enabled him, after leaving a garrison in the fort, to take the field with two hundred Europeans and seven hundred Sepoys. Raju Sahib's army had in great measure disbanded itself during his retreat, none remaining with him except his small party of French and the men which he had brought with him from Trichinopoly. With these he retired westward to Vellore. There a reinforcement from Pondicherry increased the number of his French to three hundred, while the successful repulse of a rash attack of Mahrattas had served to raise the spirits of his troops. But Clive, though inferior in numbers, was not the man to let them escape scot free. Picking up six hundred Mahratta horsemen he made a forced march in pursuit of them and caught them as they were about to cross the river Arnee. The enemy could show three hundred Europeans against two hundred, fifteen hundred Sepoys against seven hundred, and three thousand native levies against the Mahratta horse; but they were out-manœuvred and defeated, with the loss of fifty Europeans, thrice as many natives, and the whole of their artillery, while Clive's loss did not exceed eight Sepoys and fifty Mahrattas. After this action Clive marched on Conjeveram, captured it after a siege of three days and dismantled the fort. Then, having thrown a strong garrison into Arcot, he returned at the end of December to Fort St. David to concert measures for the relief of Trichinopoly.

1752.
Feb. $\frac{2}{13}$;

143

No sooner was his back turned than the scattered levies of Raju Sahib reassembled; and having first restored the defences of Conjeveram and thrown a garrison into it to cut off communication between Madras and Arcot, ravaged the country to within a few miles of Madras itself. This diversion, which was brought about at the instigation of Dupleix, had the effect which he desired. The preparations for the relief of Trichinopoly were suspended, and on the 13th of February Clive marched from Madras with three hundred and eighty Europeans and thirteen hundred Sepoys, together with six guns; the troops being drawn in great part from the garrison at Arcot. The enemy, though superior in strength of Europeans and very far superior in native troops and artillery, would not await his coming, but retired to an entrenched camp at Vendalore, about five-and-twenty miles south-westward of Madras. Clive hurried after them, but arriving at Vendalore at three o'clock in the afternoon found that they had disappeared, no one knew whither. A few hours later he received certain information that they were gone to Conjeveram. It was now nine o'clock in the evening, and the men had already marched twenty-five miles on that day, but Clive without a moment's hesitation called them out for another forced march, and by four o'clock next morning had reached Conjeveram. The garrison of the fort surrendered at the first summons, but gave the bad news that the enemy had marched on Arcot. Clive's troops were too much exhausted to follow them at once, but at noon the march was resumed. At sunset Clive had reached Covrepauk, sixteen miles on his road, when his advanced guard was surprised by a sudden fire of nine field-guns upon its right flank. The enemy, failing in their design against the fort of Arcot, had retraced their steps by a forced march and laid an ambush for Clive; and Clive, quite unsuspectingly, had marched straight into it.

The position taken up by the enemy was well fitted for their purpose. About a furlong to the north of the road, or on the right of Clive as he advanced, was a dense grove of mango-trees covered in front by a ditch and a bank; and here were stationed the nine field-guns of the French with a body of infantry in support. On Clive's left, or to the south of the road, and about one hundred and fifty yards from it ran a dry water-course, in the bed of which troops were well sheltered from fire; and here was massed the remainder of the enemy's infantry. Between the road and the water-course and beyond the water-course to the southward was drawn up the enemy's cavalry, some two thousand in all, ready to bar the British advance to the front or to sweep round upon their rear. The peril of Clive's position, already formidable enough, was enhanced by his inferiority in numbers, for the French could match four hundred Europeans against his three hundred and eighty, and two thousand Sepoys against his eighteen hundred; while against their two thousand horsemen Clive could not produce a man. Without losing his presence of mind for an instant Clive at once brought up three of his field-guns to reply to the French artillery, ordered the main body of his infantry to take shelter in the water-course, directed the baggage to be drawn back for half a mile with one gun and a small guard to defend it, and posted his two remaining guns, with forty Europeans and two hundred Sepoys, to the south of the water-course to check the enemy's cavalry. The rapidity with which he grasped the situation, surprised as he was in the waning light, and the readiness with which he made his dispositions to meet the danger, suffice in themselves to distinguish Clive as a man almost unmatched for steadfastness and resource.

Meanwhile the sun went down, and the moon shone cold and white to light the combatants to battle. In the water-course the French infantry, six abreast, encountered the English, and exchanged a savage fire at close range; but both sides, worn out with long marching, recoiled from a fight with the bayonet. On the other flank the British gunners, though outnumbered by three to one, stood to their guns and fell by them under the ceaseless rain of fire from the French pieces. And all the time the enemy's cavalry careered restlessly backward and forward, now pressing on the guns to the south of the water-course, now swooping on the infantry that guarded them, now making a dash upon the baggage, but never charging home, for they dared not face the white man. So the combat went fitfully on for three full hours under the silver moon, but the red flashes never ceased to leap from the shadow of the grove, and the British artillerymen were at last so much thinned that there were scarce enough of them to work the guns. It was plain that unless the French battery could be silenced the battle was lost. Clive bethought him that the mango-grove, though protected by the ditch in front, might be open in the rear, and sent a native sergeant round to reconnoitre. The sergeant returned to report that the rear of the battery was unguarded; and Clive, withdrawing two hundred of the British from the water-course, marched off stealthily at their head, with the sergeant for his guide. Like Cromwell at Dunbar he wished to direct the turning movement that was to decide the day; but no sooner was he gone than the troops in the water-course began to waver. The whole of them ceased firing and prepared for flight: some of them, indeed, did actually make off. Perforce Clive returned to rally them and appointed Lieutenant Keene to command the turning movement in his place.

Making a wide circuit to avoid discovery, Keene stole round to the rear of the mango-grove, halted within three hundred yards of it and sent Ensign Symmonds forward to examine the French dispositions. Symmonds was not gone far when he came upon a deep trench, in which a detachment of infantry was taking shelter until its time for action should come. He was challenged as he drew nearer, and could see muskets pointed at him, but answering calmly in French he was allowed to pass and to enter the grove in rear of the French guns. Behind the battery stood a detachment of one hundred French soldiers, all gazing eagerly towards the failing fire of the British cannon in their front, and without any precaution against attack from the rear. Symmonds stole back to his men, avoiding the trench; and the two hundred British advanced silently and noiselessly, by the track of his return, into the grove, halted under the deep shadow of the mangos within thirty yards of the French detachment and fired a volley. The effect was instantaneous. Many of the French fell, the rest of them broke, the artillerymen abandoned their guns, and the whole fled away in confusion, they knew not whither, through the trees, with the British in pursuit. A building in the grove presented a refuge, and there the fugitives crowded in, not knowing what they did, one on the top of another until they were packed so tightly that they could not use their arms. The British presently came up with them and offered quarter, whereupon the whole of them surrendered as prisoners of war. Meanwhile the silence of the French battery told Clive of Keene's success, and his troops in the water-course regained their confidence. Presently a few of the fugitive French who had escaped capture came running up to their comrades with news of the disaster in the grove, and therewith the whole of the enemy's infantry in the water-course incontinently took to flight. The native cavalry was not slow to follow the example, and very soon all sign of an enemy had vanished and the victory was won. Clive gathered his men together, and the exhausted army lay under arms until the moon paled and the sun rose up to show what manner of victory it had won. On the field fifty French soldiers and three hundred Sepoys lay dead; sixty more French had been captured in the grove, and the whole of the French artillery was abandoned to the British. Of Clive's force forty Europeans and thirty Sepoys were killed and a still greater number wounded, no extravagant price to pay for so far-reaching a success.

For by Covrepauk not only was the work begun at Arcot completed but Trichinopoly was saved; not only was British military reputation established but supremacy in the south of India was wrenched from the French. It was essentially a general's action, Clive's action; and when we reflect on the hours that preceded it, hours of continuous marching, doubtful information, and incessant anxiety, we can only marvel at the moral and physical strength which enabled him to present instantly a bold front, to keep his weary soldiers together during those four hours of fighting by moonlight, and to devise and execute the counterstroke which won the day.

From Covrepauk Clive marched on to Arcot, and was proceeding southward from thence when he was recalled to Fort St. David, to command an expedition which was preparing for the relief of Trichinopoly. On his way he passed the growing city which was to commemorate the victories of Dupleix and razed it to the ground;[236] but he met with no trace of an enemy. Raju Sahib's army had dispersed; the French and their Sepoys had been recalled to Pondicherry; and Raju Sahib himself, on returning thither from the scene of his defeat, was received by Dupleix with a displeasure and contempt which showed how deeply the dart of Clive's victory was rankling in the breast of the ambitious Frenchman.

Meanwhile, through all these months the French had maintained the siege of Trichinopoly, feebly indeed but persistently. In September 1751 their battering train had arrived and batteries had been erected before the town, but, like Boscawen's before Pondicherry, at too great a distance to do effectual damage. In fact the French commander, Law, a nephew of the famous Scottish financier, had proved himself both unenterprising and incompetent. The force under his orders comprised the unparalleled number of nine hundred French troops and two thousand Sepoys, over and above the thirty thousand native levies of Chunda Sahib; yet he had effected little or nothing. He was now to be put to a sterner test than the mere blockading of an inferior force under an inactive leader. The supreme command of the expedition for the relief of Trichinopoly was indeed taken from Clive at the last moment, but only to be transferred to Stringer Lawrence, who had just returned from England. Moreover Clive was to accompany Lawrence as a trusted subordinate, so that the change signified only the presence of two officers of conspicuous ability instead of one. Dupleix's instructions to Law were explicit: to leave the least possible number of his troops to continue the blockade of Trichinopoly, and to march out with the rest to intercept the relieving army.

March $\frac{17}{28}$.

On the 28th of March Lawrence started from Fort St. David at the head of four hundred Europeans and eleven hundred Sepoys, together with eight guns and a large convoy of stores. The distance to be traversed was about one hundred and fifty miles, and the way was barred by several rivers. The most important of these was the Coleroon, which a few miles above Trichinopoly parts itself into two branches, the northern branch retaining the name of Coleroon while the southern becomes the Cauvery. It is on the south bank of the Cauvery, and about three miles below the parting of the streams, that Trichinopoly stands. The long narrow strip of land between the two branches is called the island of Seringham, on which, about fifteen miles below and to eastward of Trichinopoly, stood the fort of Coilady, barring the advance of any enemy from that side. About six miles up the river from Coilady the Cauvery splits again into two branches, and it was along the narrow delta between these two branches that the advance of Lawrence must necessarily be made. The ordinary road passed within range of the guns of Coilady across the Cauvery; and Law, assuming that the British would certainly follow it, threw the whole of his intercepting army into the fort. Lawrence, on learning of this disposition, naturally looked for another road, and although, by an error of his guides, the British did come under the fire of Coilady and suffer some loss, yet Law took no advantage of the favourable moment. Lawrence therefore was able to cross the river and to advance on the same evening to within ten miles of Trichinopoly.

On the following day Law took up a position astride of the direct road to Trichinopoly, extending obliquely from the village of Chukleypollam on the south bank of the Cauvery past a rocky eminence known as French Rock, whereon he had mounted cannon, and thence to another almost inaccessible rock called Elimiseram. Lawrence, apprised of these dispositions, made a circuit to southward which carried him outside Elimiseram, and a mile beyond it effected a junction with a detachment of the garrison which had been sent forward to meet him under Captain Dalton. Law now made a feeble and half-hearted attempt at an attack; but the action soon resolved itself into a duel of artillery, from which the French retired with heavy loss, leaving Lawrence to enter Trichinopoly unmolested.

| April $\frac{1}{12}$. |
| April $\frac{6}{17}$. |

A few days later Law, taking fright at a threatening movement of the British against some of his native levies, resolved forthwith to withdraw from the south of the Cauvery to the island of Seringham. In such haste did he execute this pusillanimous decision that he abandoned most of his baggage, destroyed vast quantities of stores, and left a small garrison isolated at Elimiseram, which was promptly captured by the British. Clive then proposed to cut matters short by dividing the British forces into two bodies, one to remain to the south of the Cauvery, the other to cross without delay to the north bank of the Coleroon, in order to cut off the supplies of the French and sever their communications with Pondicherry. Lawrence assented, and on the night of the 17th of April four hundred British, seven hundred Sepoys and four thousand Mahratta and Tanjorine horse, together with six field-guns, crossed the Cauvery and Coleroon under Clive himself, and took up a position at Samiaveram, about nine miles north of Seringham, on the road to Pondicherry.

| March 30 |
| April 10. |

Meanwhile Dupleix with unconquerable energy had, on the news of Law's retreat, despatched one hundred and twenty Europeans and four hundred Sepoys to him under M. d'Auteuil. Leaving Pondicherry on the 10th of April, D'Auteuil marched to within fifteen miles of Clive's position at Samiaveram, and resolved to advance from thence by a circuitous route to the Coleroon in order to avoid him. Clive, however, having intercepted one of the messengers sent by D'Auteuil to apprise Law of his intentions, moved out to meet him; whereupon D'Auteuil, learning in turn of Clive's advance, retreated to Uttatoor, while Clive on his side hastened back to Samiaveram. Meanwhile Law, hearing of Clive's departure from Samiaveram but not of his return, sent a force of eighty Europeans, forty of whom were British deserters, and seven hundred Sepoys to attack his camp, as he supposed, during his absence. At midnight of the 26th of April Law's party approached the English encampment. Clive, never dreaming of such enterprise on the part of the French commander, was in bed and asleep. As the French drew nearer they were challenged by a sentry of the British Sepoys; but the officer of the deserters, an Irishman, stepped forward and explained that he was come with a reinforcement from Major Lawrence, and the sentry, hearing the deserters speak English, allowed them, after some hesitation, to pass. The British troops at Samiaveram occupied two pagodas a quarter of a mile apart, and the native troops were encamped around them. The French marched through the heart of the natives' camp and came to the smaller of the two pagodas, near which Clive was sleeping under an open shed in his palanquin. Here they were again challenged. They answered by firing a volley into both pagoda and shed, and then, pressing into the pagoda, put all within it to the sword.

Clive, startled out of his sleep, and never doubting but that the fire was the result of a false alarm, ran to the greater pagoda, turned out two hundred of his Europeans and hurried back with them to the shed. Here he found a large body of French Sepoys drawn up before it and firing incessantly at they knew not what, but in the direction of Seringham. Confirmed by this circumstance in the idea that these were his own men, for the darkness obliterated all distinctions of dress, he drew up his Europeans in their rear and ran in among them, rebuking and even striking them for what he supposed to be their panic. For some minutes this absurd position remained unchanged, until one of the Sepoys discovering at last that Clive was a Englishman, attacked him and wounded him in two places with his sword. Clive turned upon him instantly, and the Sepoy finding himself overpowered fled into the pagoda pursued by Clive, who was now in the highest pitch of exasperation over what he conceived to be the mutinous behaviour of one of his own men. To his amazement Clive was accosted at the gate by six Frenchmen; and then at last he was undeceived. With astonishing composure he told them that he was come to offer them terms, and invited them to see his whole army drawn up ready to attack them. Completely deceived by his confidence the French surrendered; and Clive then prepared to attack the Sepoys, but found that they were already withdrawn out of reach of his Europeans. There still remained, however, the larger force of the enemy's Europeans, including the British deserters, which had occupied the greater pagoda. These last refused to surrender, and made so desperate a resistance that at daybreak Clive approached them to open a parley. Owing to weakness from loss of blood he was obliged to lean on the shoulders of two sergeants; but the officer of the deserters, whether through desperation or sheer brutality, at once presented a musket at him and fired. The bullet missed Clive but wounded both of the sergeants to death; whereupon the French soldiers, fearing that their apparent connivance with such an act might debar them from any claim to quarter, immediately laid down their arms. All the Europeans of the enemy's force being now secured, the Mahratta horse was despatched in pursuit of the retreating Sepoys, whom they overtook before they had reached the Coleroon and cut down to a man. Thus for the second time did Clive's marvellous presence of mind not only pluck himself and his troops out of deadly peril, but turn his enemies' devices with terrible retribution upon their own head.

| April 26 |
| May 7. |
| April 28 |
| May 9. |
| June $\frac{2}{13}$ |

After this repulse the toils closed rapidly round the French in Seringham. On the 7th of May Lawrence captured the fort of Coilady together with all the stores therein and cut off Law from communication with the east; and after this little remained to be done except to dispose of D'Auteuil, who still lingered at Uttatoor waiting for an opportunity to effect a junction with Law. On the 9th of May Lawrence detached Captain Dalton with five hundred Europeans and Sepoys and as many Mahratta horse to oust him; a task which Dalton accomplished by making such a display of his force that D'Auteuil, conceiving Clive's whole army to be upon him, retreated after a faint resistance to Volconda. In the course of the next few days Clive captured an important post which severed Law's communications with the north and commanded the camp of Seringham. Thereupon the greater part of Chunda Sahib's army deserted, some of the men even taking service with Clive.

Shortly afterwards the British crossed the Cauvery and established themselves on the island of Seringham itself, hemming the French in closer and closer. Then D'Auteuil, roused by the desperate state of his comrade, took courage and again moved southward from Volconda. Clive was at once despatched with a force to Uttatoor to meet him; but D'Auteuil's heart again failed him when he arrived within seven miles of that position, and he retreated hastily towards Volconda. He was not, however, to escape thus easily. Clive at once pushed forward the Mahrattas to harass him on the march; his Sepoys, veterans of Arcot, marched their swiftest after the Mahrattas and opened the attack by themselves; and last of all the British, who had been unable to keep pace with the Sepoys, arrived at the scene of action, when D'Auteuil, seeing resistance to be hopeless, surrendered. His force consisted of but one hundred Europeans and less than eight hundred Sepoys and natives, of whom the latter were at once disarmed and released. Thus vanished Law's last hope of relief. Chunda Sahib in vain urged him to make a sally against the divided forces of the British, and to cut his way out to Carical. Law would not move. On the 13th of June he surrendered; and eight hundred French troops and two thousand Sepoys became prisoners of war, while forty-one pieces of artillery passed into the hands of the victors. A few days later Chunda Sahib, who had made terms of surrender for himself, was treacherously assassinated by order of the Tanjorine General, and his head was sent to his successful rival, Mohammed Ali. Thus for the present ended the long agony of the contest for Trichinopoly. To all appearance Dupleix was really beaten at last; but his resources were not yet exhausted, and the last battle had not yet been fought before the city on the Cauvery.

CHAPTER III

1752.
June $\frac{7}{18}$.

No sooner was the victory gained at Trichinopoly than the Nabob Mohammed Ali and his allies the Mysoreans and Mahrattas fell at variance over the division of the spoil. This complication, which was due in great measure to the intrigues of Dupleix, thoroughly answered his purpose; for the British, who had marched northward as far as Uttatoor to prosecute the campaign in the Carnatic, found themselves obliged to return to Trichinopoly. Finally two hundred Englishmen and two thousand Sepoys under Captain Dalton were left in the city to keep the peace; the Mahrattas and Mysoreans still keeping their former position to westward of the city, and occupying, by leave of Mohammed Ali, the pagoda which formed the strongest post on the island of Seringham. The remainder of the British army then resumed its march to northward, but with all hope of future operations frustrated by this untoward diminution of its strength. Advancing by Volconda and Verdachelum Lawrence on the 17th of July took Trivady, which was held by a small party of French Sepoys, and there left the army, to return to Fort St. David on sick-leave. Clive had already proceeded thither for the same reason, and the British force was left under the command of Major Gingen, an officer of tried incapacity.

Meanwhile Dupleix's activity had never ceased. While the native confederates were quarrelling over the success at Trichinopoly the annual reinforcement of troops arrived from France, and these, by dint of taking sailors from the ships, he increased to a strength of five hundred European soldiers. This done he waited only for an opportunity for retrieving the reputation of the French arms. Such an opportunity soon came. Yielding to the fanciful representations of Mohammed Ali, but contrary to the wishes of Lawrence, Governor Saunders ordered Gingen to detach a portion of his force against the fortress of Gingee. Gingen accordingly told off two hundred Europeans, fifteen hundred Sepoys and six hundred native cavalry for the task, the command being entrusted to Major Kinnear, an officer only recently arrived from Europe and wholly without experience of India. What the object of such an enterprise can have been it is difficult to divine. Gingee, it is true, was above all fortresses in India bound up with the glory of France, and its capture would therefore have dealt a blow at French military reputation; but Gingee, held by trained troops under an European commander, was not to be taken again as Bussy had taken it, when defended by undisciplined natives only. Kinnear on approaching the fortress perceived his task to be hopeless, and while still hesitating as to his movements found that Dupleix had moved a French force, under command of his nephew, M. Kerjean, in his rear, to cut off his communications with Trivady. Nothing daunted Kinnear faced about and attacked Kerjean, but was repulsed with heavy loss; and the native princes, finding their faith in the invincibility of the British thus disappointed, began again to veer round to the side of the French. Most opportunely also for himself Dupleix received at this time the confirmation from Delhi of his appointment of Nabob of the country south of the Kistnah. With his usual cleverness he selected Raju Sahib, the son of Chunda Sahib, to hold the post subject to himself, thus reasserting himself as Dupleix the king-maker. Strengthened by this accession of dignity he renewed his intrigues with the Mysoreans and Mahrattas, who engaged themselves to embrace the side of the French if Dupleix would find means to distract the principal British army from Trichinopoly and leave them free to do what they would with the city. Dupleix accordingly as a first step reinforced Kerjean to a strength of two thousand trained men, one-fourth of them Europeans, and five hundred native horse, and sent him to blockade Fort St. David and cut its communications with Trichinopoly.

| Aug. $\frac{17}{28}$. |
| Aug. 26 |
| Sept. 6. |

Lawrence on learning of this movement at once embarked from Fort St. David for Madras, and marched from thence with a force nearly equal to Kerjean's to attack him. Kerjean, however, fell back, closely followed by Lawrence, until he was within a league of Pondicherry and on French soil, where Lawrence's instructions forbade him to take aggressive action. Lawrence thereupon, as though in dread of a regular engagement, retreated with precipitation to Bahoor, two miles from Fort St. David, in the hope that Kerjean would pursue him. Kerjean and his master Dupleix with him both fell into the snare; and the French force advancing in pursuit of the British encamped within two miles of Bahoor. At three o'clock on the following morning the British force marched off to attack him, the Sepoys seventeen hundred strong in the first line, the English four hundred strong in the second, while four hundred native horse advanced parallel to them on the farther side of a high bank which ran from the right of Lawrence's position to the French camp. A little before dawn the British Sepoys struck against the French outposts and skirmished with them until daylight, when the battalion of

French soldiers, stronger by fifty men than that of the British, was discovered drawn up between the bank and a large pond. The British halted to extend their front to equal that of the French, a French battery of eight guns playing upon them vigorously as they executed the movement, and then advanced firing, platoon after platoon. Closer and closer they came, still firing; but the French never shrank for a moment until, rarest of rare incidents, the bayonets crossed and the two battalions engaged each other fiercely hand to hand. At length, however, a company of British grenadiers, the choicest troops in India, forced its way though the French centre; upon which the whole of the French gave way, flung down their arms and fled. Had the native cavalry then charged as they were bidden they would utterly have annihilated Kerjean's troops, but according to their custom they preferred to plunder the French camp. The loss of the French in killed and wounded is unknown, but Kerjean himself with fifteen other officers and one hundred men were taken prisoners. The British battalion lost four officers and seventy-eight men killed and wounded, a sufficient proof of the stubbornness of the fight.

Signal though this victory might be, Lawrence did not think it prudent to venture on further operations until he could ascertain whether the Mahrattas, always wavering since the dispute after the expulsion of the French from Trichinopoly, would finally attach themselves to the British or to their enemies. He therefore moved to Trivady, designing to reduce the country northward between Pondicherry and the river Paliar. Meanwhile the Nabob Mohammed Ali requested that the forts of Chinglapet and Covelong, which commanded a considerable tract of country north of the Paliar, might be captured. The only troops that could be furnished from Madras for the purpose were two hundred English recruits, the sweepings of the streets of London, and five hundred newly raised Sepoys as untrained as the English. It was unpromising material, but Clive volunteered to take the command, and to Clive the task was entrusted. The force accordingly marched, taking four siege-guns with it, from Madras on the 10th of September; its first destination being Covelong, a walled fort on the coast, which was held by fifty Europeans and three hundred Sepoys. On arriving before it Clive sent forward a detachment to a garden within a short distance of the fort, where it was attacked by the French. Unfortunately the officer commanding the British was killed, whereupon the men at once took to their heels. By good luck they ran against Clive and the main body in their flight, and by dint of blows and curses they were with some difficulty rallied and brought back to the garden, which was evacuated by the French on their approach. On the following day Clive began the erection of a battery, but it was only with the greatest trouble and by constant exposure of himself to the enemy's fire that he could induce his men to stand. On the third day of the siege intelligence reached Clive that a French force, little inferior in numbers to his own, was advancing from Chinglapet to the relief of Covelong. With his usual audacity he at once led half of his miserable troops forth to meet it; but the terror of his name sufficed to awe the French commander into a precipitate retreat. Thereupon the garrison of Covelong surrendered, and Clive on taking possession of the fort found therein fifty guns which had been taken from Madras by La Bourdonnais.

| Oct. 31 |
| Nov. 11. |

At daybreak of the following morning Ensign Joseph Smith discovered a considerable force moving forward upon Covelong, and concluding that it must be the French again advancing from Chinglapet, posted such troops as were with him in ambuscade and hastened to inform Clive. The conjecture proved to be correct. The French marched straight into the ambuscade, where the troops, which Clive had taken over less than a week before as a spiritless, undisciplined rabble, poured in so deadly a fire that within a few minutes they struck down a hundred men. The attack was so unexpected that half of the French force stood rooted to the ground with fear. The commanding officer, with a score more of Europeans, two hundred and fifty Sepoys and two guns were captured, and the remainder, throwing down their arms, rushed away in terror to Chinglapet. Clive resolved to follow them while the panic was still alive. The fort of Chinglapet, though of native construction, was designed with more than ordinary native skill; it mounted fifteen guns and was held by forty Europeans and five hundred Sepoys. Clive hastened to traverse the thirty miles that separated it from Covelong, and after four days' cannonade succeeded in making indeed a breach, though not such a breach as in the least to endanger the safety of the fort. But the terror of his name was again potent, and the garrison surrendered the place on condition that it should march out with the honours of war, terms which Clive was very well content to grant. Thus the country to the north of the Paliar, from the mouth of the river to Arcot, was subjected to the allies of the British, all by a handful of men who, starting as raw and villainous recruits, returned, under the magic of Clive's leadership, as heroes. This instance of his power is the more remarkable inasmuch as throughout the expedition he was in bad health, which indeed forced him to sail for England as soon as he had completed the work. His departure from India was more valuable than a victory to Dupleix.

| 1753. |
| Jan. 3. |

Meanwhile, despite these successes and Lawrence's brilliant action at Bahoor French influence was, on the whole, decidedly on the gaining hand. Within six weeks of Bahoor, thanks to the indefatigable intrigues of Dupleix, both Mysoreans and Mahrattas had alienated themselves from the English and openly attached themselves to the French cause. Dalton had from the first been troubled by conspiracies and other mischievous designs of the Mysoreans in Seringham, which compelled him to take precautions in Trichinopoly as elaborate as though he were in presence of an enemy. Dupleix, seeing that affairs were going as he wished, promised to send some Europeans to help the Mysoreans in Seringham; and the Mysoreans, thus encouraged, moved a step further forward and suborned the Mahrattas to cut off supplies from the city. It was now useless for the authorities at Madras longer to pretend to treat the Mysoreans otherwise than as enemies. Accordingly, early in January 1753 Dalton attempted a surprise of their camp in Seringham, which though at first successful was eventually repulsed with the serious loss of seventy Europeans and three hundred of the best Sepoys. Thus the struggle for Trichinopoly, the darling object of Dupleix's ambition, was reopened, and reopened by a reverse to the British. Dalton, undismayed though fully alive to the significance of his failure, now turned all his attention to the defence of the city.

March.

His situation indeed was most critical. Even before his sortie he had discovered that but three weeks' supplies were left to him, and had urged Lawrence to march to his relief; and now not only were his communications with the north severed by the hostile occupation of Seringham, but a force of eight thousand men had entrenched itself at a place called Fakir's Tope, four miles to south-west of the city, to intercept all supplies from the south. Meanwhile, to divert the British from Trichinopoly, Dupleix had skilfully engaged Lawrence in a campaign of petty, harassing operations on the river Pennar; while the Mahrattas scoured every part of the Carnatic from the Paliar to the Coleroon, insulting even the fortifications of Fort St. David. Lawrence in vain strove to bring the French to action. They were following the tactics of Saxe in the Low Countries, always present and therefore always a danger, but always entrenched to the teeth against attack. Finally, after an unsuccessful attempt to storm their entrenchments, Lawrence resolved to adopt the course so often urged by Ligonier in Flanders, to carry the war into some other quarter. So far his operations had proved a failure, and the reputation of the British had accordingly waned paler than ever in the eyes of the native princes. He was still hesitating as to the choice of a new theatre of operations when his mind was made up for him by the receipt of Dalton's letters from Trichinopoly.

April 21
May 2.
May $\frac{6}{17}$

Throwing a garrison of one hundred and fifty British and five hundred Sepoys as a garrison into Trivady, he marched with the remainder by Chillumbrum, Condoor, and Tanjore for Trichinopoly, and entered the city unmolested on the 17th of May. Dalton had not been inactive during the interval, and had done his best to clear the way for his coming by scaring the enemy from their position at Fakir's Tope. Nevertheless Lawrence's men had suffered greatly on the march. Several died from the effects of the heat, others were sent back to Fort St. David, and no less than a hundred were carried straight into hospital at Trichinopoly. Finally, there was much desertion, in particular from a company of Swiss which had been sent down from Bengal. Thus, even including such men of the garrison as could be spared from duty in the city, he could muster no more than five hundred Europeans, two thousand Sepoys, and three thousand native horse for service in the field. To add to his difficulties Dupleix, on hearing of his march, had with his usual promptitude despatched M. Astruc with two hundred Europeans, five hundred Sepoys and four guns to join the Mahrattas and Mysoreans at Seringham, which force arrived at its destination only one day later than Lawrence himself. None the less, after granting his troops three days' rest Lawrence took the initiative with his wonted energy, crossed the river to Seringham with his infantry only, and made a daring attempt to drive the enemy from the island. Success was almost within his grasp, and the French were actually about to retreat when, by an unfortunate misadventure, the British troops were recalled just at the critical moment, and the enemy recovering themselves forced him to fall back. His loss was but slight, but he had seen sufficient to convince him that for the present he must confine himself to the defensive.

Meanwhile matters went ill with the British farther north. The French attacked Trivady and though twice repulsed succeeded, thanks to a mutiny among the garrison, in capturing it. A British detachment was also obliged to evacuate Chillumbrum through the treachery of the native governor. Thus the control of these districts was lost, and communication between Trichinopoly and Fort St. David was hampered, while swarms of banditti, pretending commissions from Dupleix, levied contributions and spread lawlessness through the country. Finally Mortiz Ali, called from obscurity by Dupleix to replace Raju Sahib as Nabob of the Carnatic, commenced hostilities in the neighbourhood of Arcot and even destroyed a small British force. He was only restrained from further operations in that quarter by Dupleix who, always with his eye on Trichinopoly, persuaded him to detach three thousand of his Mahrattas to Seringham and added to them three hundred Europeans and a thousand Sepoys. The total force on the island after the arrival of this reinforcement amounted to four hundred and fifty Europeans, fifteen hundred well-trained and over a thousand imperfectly trained Sepoys, eight thousand

Mysorean and over three thousand Mahratta horse, and a rabble of fifteen thousand native infantry. After many failures it seemed that Dupleix at last held the coveted Trichinopoly within his grasp.

As soon as these troops had joined them the French quitted Seringham, and crossing to the south side of the Cauvery encamped in the plain three miles to the north of Fakir's Tope. A mile to the south of Lawrence's position some mountains known as the Five Rocks rise out of the plain, on which he had always maintained a guard to secure the passage of his supplies from the south. Unfortunately Lawrence was obliged by sickness to withdraw from the camp to the city, and during his absence this guard was withdrawn. The French thereupon at once seized the Five Rocks and encamped there with their entire force, thus cutting Lawrence off not only from his supplies but from seven hundred of his Sepoys, who were on their way to him from the south with a convoy. The British commander's position was now almost desperate. His troops lost heart in the presence of overwhelming numbers, and desertion became frequent; Dupleix seemed to be nearer than ever to the capture of Trichinopoly.

| June 26 |
| July 7. |

Lawrence had now but one post by which to communicate with the south, a rocky eminence known as the Golden Rock, about half a mile to south-west of his camp, which he had occupied with two hundred Sepoys. On the 7th of July Astruc sallied forth from the French camp with his grenadiers and a large force of Sepoys to attack it, knowing that, if he could capture it, his artillery would force Lawrence to take refuge under the walls of Trichinopoly, where his surrender or retreat would be only a question of days. The Sepoys on the Golden Rock made a stout resistance, and Astruc presently ordered out the whole of his army to support the attack. Lawrence observing this detached a hundred Europeans to guard the camp, and marched with the rest of his force, a bare three hundred European infantry, eighty British artillerymen and five hundred Sepoys, to gain the position before the French army; but ere he could reach it Astruc by a desperate effort carried the Golden Rock and killed or captured every Sepoy of the guard. Lawrence saw the white flag of France flutter from the summit, and halted. Before the rock itself stood the French Sepoys with the grenadiers in support; on either flank of them the French artillery was playing on his own troops, in rear of the rock was the battalion of French, with the entire Mysorean army drawn up a cannon-shot behind him, while the Mahratta horse scoured the plain in small parties, continually menacing Lawrence's flanks and rear. The courage of the British rose to the occasion. After the tedious disappointing work with the French entrenchments on the Pennar they asked for nothing better than a brush with their old enemy in the open field. Lawrence saw with joy the spirit that was in them. A few words from him served to heighten it; and then he gave the order to his grenadiers to fix bayonets and storm the Golden Rock, while he himself with the rest of the troops should engage the entire army of the enemy. The men replied with three cheers: the bayonets sprang flashing from their scabbards, and the word was given to advance.

Forward strode the grenadiers, at great speed but in perfect order, with the best of the Sepoys after them, forward to the base of the Rock, heedless of the spattering fire from above them, forward to the ascent of it, forward without dwelling or firing a shot to the summit; while the enemy, not daring to await the shock of their onset, scrambled headlong down in terror to the plain. Meanwhile Lawrence, with his men in beautiful order, was moving in column round the western side of the Rock, with the design of falling on the left flank of the French battalion. Astruc thereupon changed front to the left to meet him, resting his right flank upon the Rock; but the movement was hardly completed when the British column with admirable precision wheeled into line to its left and halted squarely before him, not more than twenty yards away. Astruc called to his men to reserve their fire till the rest of his troops should deploy and encompass Lawrence's handful of infantry; when to his amazement, for he had not seen the advance of the British grenadiers, a heavy fire from the Rock struck full and true against his right flank and flung it staggering back. The French line wavered. Lawrence's men poured in one crushing volley, and before the French ranks could be closed the British bayonets came gleaming through the smoke, and Astruc's battalion was broken up in hopeless confusion. A few rounds of grape from a British field-gun completed the disorder, and the whole of the French infantry fled for refuge to the rear of the Mysoreans, leaving their guns in the hands of their victors. The Mahratta cavalry dashed forward to cover their retreat, and cut down a few of the British grenadiers who had run forward to secure the captured guns; but they strove in vain to pierce the phalanx of bayonets about the main body and were repulsed with heavy loss. Lawrence halted at the foot of the Rock for three hours, anxious only to renew the fight, and then prepared to retire to his camp, leaving the French to occupy the Golden Rock again if they dared.

Then came the critical operation of a retreat across the plain among the swarms of the enemy's horse. The three captured guns were placed in the centre, the infantry was formed in platoons on each flank, the British field-guns distributed in the front, rear and intervals of the column. Against these two parallel lines of eight hundred resolute men not even the rush of ten thousand cavalry could prevail. The infantry halted at the word with ordered arms as coolly as on parade, and the gunners waited calmly, linstock in hand, while the wild horsemen whirled up to them, till the signal was given and a shower of grape laid men and horses in scores upon the plain. The havoc wrought by the British artillery and the sight of the infantry steady and immovable, reserving their fire, was too much for the native cavalry. They broke and fled in all directions, and Lawrence marched proudly back to his camp, having fought an action as skilful, as gallant, and as daring as ever was won by British officer on the blood-stained plains of India.

The victory not only ensured the safe arrival of Lawrence's convoy from the south, but set the French and their allies at variance, Mysoreans and French mutually reproaching each other, and the Mahrattas impartially blaming both. Astruc resigned his command and was succeeded by M. Brennier, who continued the blockade of Trichinopoly. Lawrence being weak in numbers resolved not to hazard another general action, but marched with his army into Tanjore, with the double object of meeting a reinforcement that was on its way from Madras, and of persuading the wavering king to take his side and to furnish him with some native horse. He was successful in both matters, and after a month's absence turned back towards Trichinopoly, having obtained three thousand horse and two thousand foot from Tanjore, and one hundred and seventy Europeans and three hundred Sepoys from Fort St. David.

August $\frac{9}{20}$.

On entering the plain with a large convoy Lawrence was warned by signals from Trichinopoly that the French were awaiting him. Their cavalry was drawn up between the Golden Rock and another eminence, called the Sugar-loaf Rock, about a mile to the east of it. The Golden Rock itself was occupied by a detachment, but the main body of the enemy's infantry and the whole of their artillery was formed up by the Sugar-loaf Rock, that being the point where Lawrence, whose advance was from the south-east, would first come within their reach. Lawrence on perceiving their dispositions resolved to hold on his course straight westward, keeping his convoy wide on his left or unexposed flank, and so to move round the Golden Rock and wheel northward upon the city. It was, however, imperative that he should capture the Golden Rock at whatever cost, since that position commanded the entire space between it and Trichinopoly. To conceal his intention he halted the army a mile to south-east of the Sugar-loaf and bade the convoy march on alone, at the same time detaching his grenadiers and eight hundred Sepoys with orders to defile westward under cover of the convoy, and at the right moment to move as swiftly as possible to the attack of the Golden Rock.

Brennier, with no eyes for anything but Lawrence's menacing attitude before the Sugar-loaf Rock, hastily recalled most of the detachment from the Golden Rock to his main position. Then, perceiving too late the advance of the British grenadiers, he despatched a thousand native horse at full gallop to check them, and sent three hundred infantry to reinforce the party on the Rock. But the cavalry dared not charge home upon the grenadiers, who without slackening their pace for an instant swarmed up the Rock, drove out the enemy, and planted their flag on the summit. The French reinforcement lost heart at the sight and halted, and Brennier, who was advancing with the main army, halted likewise, giving time to Lawrence to bring the whole of his force up to the Golden Rock. Brennier then opened a destructive fire of artillery upon the British, but for some reason left the reinforcement, which had failed to reach the Golden Rock, still standing alone and unsupported. Lawrence therefore detached the grenadiers and five hundred more Europeans and Sepoys to cut off this isolated party before Brennier's main body could reach it, giving orders that it should be broken up with the bayonet. These troops suffered much from the fire of the French cannon during their advance, and the officer in command hesitated to attack; whereupon Lawrence himself galloped to their head, and the French not caring to await the shock turned and fled. Dalton, who had been watching the fight from Trichinopoly, now came up in their rear with a couple of field-guns and completed their discomfiture. Then too late Brennier set the main body in motion; but these seeing the defeat of their comrades ran off in confusion to the Five Rocks, with the British guns from the Golden Rock playing on them all the way. This little combat cost the French about one hundred and the British about forty killed and wounded; but its moral effect was great, since it showed Brennier to be as helpless as a child in presence of such a commander as Lawrence.

| Aug. 24 |
| Sept. 4. |
| Aug. 26 |
| Sept. 6. |

After the action the French retreated to Weycondah, a strongly fortified post some two miles west of the city, where they entrenched themselves; but quitted this stronghold in confusion at the mere menace of an attack by Lawrence, and retired to the south bank of the Cauvery. A few weeks more under Brennier would probably have brought the French to a pitch of demoralisation which would have simplified Lawrence's task not a little; but just at this moment the energy of Dupleix again turned the tables against the British. Four hundred Europeans, two thousand Sepoys, and several thousand native troops arrived to reinforce the French, and, more important still, Astruc arrived with them to take the command out of Brennier's hands. Once more, therefore, Lawrence was thrown on the defensive, and forced back to his old position at Fakir's Tope. The French likewise moved round to southward of him, resuming their old position between the Golden and Sugar-loaf Rocks; and in this posture the two armies remained, looking at each other across two miles of open plain without firing a shot. At last on the 30th of September Lawrence moved round to the French Rock, off the south-east side of the town, to meet a reinforcement which was on its way to him from the eastward, and brought it in successfully on the same evening. The reinforcement consisted of three hundred Sepoys and of two hundred and thirty-seven Europeans, which latter had just arrived from England, together with an officer who was soon to become famous, Captain Caillaud. Small though it was, and very far from sufficient to equalise the disparity of numbers between the British and the enemy, its arrival raised the army's spirits not a little; and Lawrence, straitened for supplies and fuel, resolved to bring the enemy to a general action and, if necessary, to attack them in their camp.

| Sept. 20 |
| Oct. 1. |

Sending his baggage under cover of night to Trichinopoly, he withdrew from the garrison every European that could be spared, a bare hundred men, appeared at daybreak at his old position of Fakir's Tope, and offered battle. The enemy declining to meet him, he determined to attack them on the morrow. The French camp fronted towards the north, extending both east and west of the Sugar-loaf Rock. The Mahrattas were encamped to the east, and the French close to the west of the Sugar-loaf, while beyond the French the Mysoreans prolonged the line westward almost to the Golden Rock. The rear of the camp was covered by jungle and rocky ground; the front of the French quarters was protected by an entrenchment, as was also that of the Mahratta camp; but along the rest of the line the field-works, though marked out, were still unfinished. The Golden Rock itself was held by one hundred Europeans, six hundred Sepoys, and two companies of native infantry, with two guns. The total strength of the French forces would seem to have been about six hundred Europeans, three thousand Sepoys, and from twenty to thirty thousand Mahrattas and Mysoreans, both horse and foot. Against them Lawrence could pit an equal number of Europeans, two thousand Sepoys and three thousand Tanjorine horse. The battle therefore, if won, must be won by the General.

| Sept. 21 |
| Oct. 2. |

The moon was shining brightly over the plain when Lawrence's army fell into its ranks before the camp and marched away in profound silence towards the Golden Rock. The British battalion, five hundred strong, led the van in column of three divisions, the grenadiers in the front; while six field-guns, with a hundred British artillerymen, were distributed equally on the flanks of each division. In rear of the British followed the Sepoys in two lines, and echeloned to the left rear of the Sepoys rode the Tanjorine horse. The troops had not proceeded far on the march when a heavy cloud floated across the moon and shrouded the plain in darkness. Still silently the columns pushed on through the gloom, and the grenadiers drew closer and closer to the familiar Rock which they had so often stormed; but no sign came from the enemy, until at last, when they were arrived within pistol shot, a challenge and a flash told them that they were discovered. Firing one volley they swarmed up the Rock on three sides at once, while the French, having barely time to snatch up their arms, emptied their muskets in a feeble, irregular fire, and fled hurriedly down to the plain. Such was their haste that they left their two field-guns undischarged, though these were ready and loaded with grape. The left of the French position being thus overpowered, Lawrence ordered the Tanjorine horse to move up before the French entrenchments; then wheeling his three divisions into line to the left, he formed the Sepoys in echelon in rear of each flank and ordered the whole to advance through the Mysorean camp upon the left flank of the French battalion. The men received the order with loud cheers, and the troops stepped off, the drums of the British beating the Grenadiers' March, the gunners advancing with lighted port-fires on the flanks of the divisions, and the Sepoys making wild music on their native instruments in rear.

The Mysoreans fled in all directions before the din, and the Sepoys kept up a constant fire on the swarms of fugitives before them; but the British, disdaining such ignoble game, marched proudly on with recovered arms and bayonets fixed. But the formation of the British was soon broken by the obstacles that confronted them in that dark march through the Mysorean camp; and presently the grenadiers, who kept the right of the line, were striding away in their old place in the front, having out-marched the second division, while the second division in its turn out-marched the third. The Sepoys having clear ground before them also came forward from their places in rear, and the artillery being unable to keep up was left to toil along as it might. Then broad spurts of flame flashed out from the darkness in the front, and the round shot from the French guns flew humming overhead far away to the west, where wild yells told that they had fallen among the hapless Mysoreans, their own allies. Onward marched the British, and soon the gleam of port-fires showed them more clearly where their enemy stood.

Meanwhile Astruc, perceiving by the flight of the fugitives from what quarter the attack was coming, was busy changing front to his left. His French battalion had already been drawn up with its face to the west, and two divisions, each of two thousand Sepoys, were hastening into their positions to support it on either flank; but in the darkness and confusion the division designed for his right flank mistook its direction and took post on the Sugar-loaf Rock. And now the dawn flushed up in the east and showed the white coats of the French battalion conspicuous in their line of battle, and the scarlet of the British, not, as they should have been, in line, but broken into echelon. The rear divisions quickened their pace to align themselves with their comrades in front, but before the formation could be completed the Sepoys on their right came into action and swept the Sepoys opposed to them off the ground with their very first volley. Then at last, when within twenty yards of the enemy, the British battalion got into line, while Astruc, galloping backward and forward, repeated again and again the order that not a French musket must be discharged until the red-coats had fired. In the volleys that followed, Captain Kilpatrick, who commanded the grenadiers on the right, was desperately wounded; but Caillaud, instantly taking his place, wheeled the grenadiers round and fell upon the left flank of the French, which had been uncovered by the flight of their Sepoys. A crushing volley on this flank, followed by a charge with the bayonet, drove the French left crowding upon its centre, and a second deadly volley from the British centre and left completed the discomfiture of the whole line. Astruc strove in vain to rally his men; the grenadiers pressing on with the bayonet gave them no respite. Meanwhile also the British Sepoys on the left had pushed on against the Sugar-loaf Rock and dispersed the French Sepoys there, and the whole of the French army fled scattered and in disorder towards Seringham. Had the Tanjorine horse done its duty, the enemy would have suffered past recovery, but as usual it was far too busy with plunder to give a thought to pursuit. None the less the losses of the French were heavy. Of their Europeans a hundred were killed and wounded, and two hundred more, together with Astruc and ten of his officers, were taken prisoners; while the whole of their tents, baggage and ammunition, and eleven guns remained in Lawrence's hands. The loss of the British amounted to no more than forty killed and wounded, Lawrence himself being slightly hurt in the arm. So ended his third and most important victory before Trichinopoly.

Sept. 22
Oct. 3.
Oct., end.

On the very same evening Lawrence moved westward to besiege the fortified post of Weycondah, which was assaulted next day without orders by the Sepoys and carried by the resolution of an English sergeant belonging to one of their companies. Such was the spirit which Lawrence had infused into them that they emulated the exploits of King Harry's army after Agincourt. Being assured of abundance of supplies by his victory, Lawrence now put his troops into cantonments at Coilady for the rainy season, detaching four hundred Sepoys and one hundred and fifty Europeans to strengthen the garrison of Trichinopoly. At about the same time Captain Dalton returned to Europe, resigning the command of the city to Lieutenant Harrison.

Nov., beginning.
Nov. 28
Dec. 9.

The French at Seringham being thoroughly cowed, Dupleix resorted as usual to intrigue to regain his lost ground, and by threats and promises contrived to detach the Tanjorines from the British alliance. The next step was to gain their active assistance for the French, and to this end he strengthened the troops at Seringham by a reinforcement of three hundred Europeans and matured preparations for a blow, great and daring in conception, which should neutralise all the successes of Lawrence; namely to surprise and storm Trichinopoly by night. On the morning of the 9th of December the attempt was made, and was within an ace of success. Six hundred Frenchmen escaladed the walls and surprised and bayonetted the Sepoys on guard; and had they obeyed their orders not to fire a shot, they must infallibly have taken the city. But in the elation of their first success they fired a volley which aroused the garrison. Lieutenant Harrison, with perfect presence of mind, made effective dispositions, and the attack was beaten back with a loss to the French of forty Europeans killed and nearly four hundred taken prisoners.

1754.

This reverse was a fatal blow to Dupleix, for, apart from the loss of so large a body of Europeans, the King of Tanjore determined to reject his overtures and reverted to his original predilection for the British. At the opening of 1754 therefore Dupleix approached Governor Saunders with proposals for peace in the Carnatic; for despite his misfortunes in the south he had, thanks to the skill of Bussy, good compensation in the spread of French influence in the northern provinces of the Deccan. The negotiations, however, soon broke down and the war was renewed.

Meanwhile the position of Lawrence before Trichinopoly was still, for all his victories, both anxious and critical. Owing to the numbers of French prisoners in the city he could muster but six hundred Europeans and eighteen hundred Sepoys for service in the field; whereas the enemy's European battalion was as strong as his own, their Sepoys thrice as numerous, and the Mahrattas and Mysoreans still with them in undiminished strength. Moreover, in February a stroke of good fortune revived the drooping spirits of the French. A British convoy destined for Trichinopoly was attacked by them and by their allies in overwhelming force and captured, the whole of its escort being either killed or wounded. This was by far the most serious reverse suffered by the British during the whole course of the war, for among the troops that were lost was the entire company of grenadiers which had done such magnificent service before Trichinopoly. This defeat greatly increased Lawrence's difficulty in obtaining supplies. He applied to the King of Tanjore for assistance in vain; and having lost one-third of his Europeans and five hundred Sepoys, his situation became perilous in the extreme.

May $\frac{12}{23}$.

A still greater misfortune followed. Lawrence himself fell dangerously ill, and it was not until after weeks of anxiety, by which time the army could hardly hold its ground for want of supplies, that there came at last a gleam of hope for the British. A convoy of stores being expected, Captain Caillaud was sent southward on the night of the 23rd of May with one hundred and twenty Europeans, five hundred Sepoys, and two guns to escort it into camp. The French having gained intelligence beforehand of this movement, despatched double that number of trained troops and guns, together with four thousand picked Mysorean horse, to occupy the position which Caillaud had designed for himself and to lie there in wait for him. Fortunately Caillaud made timely discovery of their whereabouts and decided to attack them forthwith, which he did with success, driving them from a tank in which they were posted and occupying it himself. Not until the day broke did he realise the odds against which he had fought in the darkness and the numbers by which he was still menaced; but fortunately the sound of the firing had been heard in Trichinopoly, and Captain Polier, who commanded during Lawrence's illness, at once started with every man that could be spared to Caillaud's assistance. A French force started at the same time with him to intercept him; but Polier out-marching it, effected his junction with Caillaud without mishap. The British force thus united amounted to but three hundred and sixty Europeans and fifteen hundred Sepoys, with five guns: the task that lay before it was to fight its way back over the plain against seven hundred Europeans, five thousand Sepoys, and ten thousand horse, of which last fortunately none were Mahrattas. Forming two sides of a square the little force marched, not without loss but without serious molestation, over a mile of the plain to a second tank; and here the enemy closed round it, the Sepoys and cavalry on three sides and the French battalion on the fourth. But when the French advanced to the attack they were met by a fire of grape which in a few minutes laid a hundred of them on the ground and so staggered the rest that they wavered and halted. "Never, I believe," says Lawrence, "were two field-pieces better served than these." Caillaud, who was again in command owing to the disabling of Polier by two wounds, seized the moment to make a counter-attack, and the British poured in so deadly a volley of musketry that the French gave way and fled.

Their officers exerted themselves to the utmost to rally them, but they would not stop until they were beyond range of cannon, nor even then would they return to the attack. After this there was little impediment to Caillaud's retreat. The loss of the French amounted to five hundred killed and wounded, of whom two hundred were Europeans; that of the British slightly exceeded two hundred, of whom rather more than a third were Europeans. Thus the much-needed convoy was brought safely into camp; and the French were not a little disheartened by their repulse.

Lawrence accordingly took the opportunity to march into Tanjore, at once to confirm the vacillating king in his allegiance and to pick up a slender reinforcement which was waiting for him at Devicotah. Thereupon the French as usual moved round to the south side of Trichinopoly to cut off its supplies. Fortunately the garrison had now provisions for three months, for the Tanjorines, though quickly gained over to the British side, showed no eagerness to give active assistance; nor was it until the 17th of August that Lawrence re-entered the plain of Trichinopoly with twelve hundred Europeans, three thousand Sepoys, and five thousand of his hardly won allies. For the fourth time the French prepared to fight him, but would not carry the action beyond a duel of artillery, wherein they suffered much from the superiority of the British fire. In a few days they were again shut up in Seringham; and Lawrence went into cantonments for the rainy season.

| Oct. 11. |
| 1755. |

At this time a squadron arrived on the coast from England under Admiral Watson, having on board the Thirty-ninth Foot, a small party of the Royal Artillery, and recruits for the Company's forces. The French likewise received reinforcements from Europe; but meanwhile they had lost the life and soul of their enterprise in India. At the beginning of August Dupleix was recalled to France, and three months later, in accordance with orders received from London and Paris, Governor Saunders and M. Godeheu, Dupleix's successor, agreed to a suspension of arms, which in the following January was expanded into a conditional treaty. The revenue of the territory gained by France during the war was computed at over eight hundred thousand pounds; the gains of the English were set down at less than a tenth of that sum. There could be no question as to the side which had reaped the greater advantage, thanks to the energy of Bussy and of Dupleix.

Yet Dupleix was now recalled; himself, the most indefatigable of intriguers, falling a victim to obscure intrigues and jealousies at Versailles. This is no place wherein to treat of the grandeur of his ambition, the vast range of his designs, the incomparable adroitness with which he handled native princes, the insight with which he foresaw every danger, the constancy with which he faced every reverse, the resource whereby he repaired every misfortune, and the unfailing tenacity with which he clung to his purpose. Excepting Napoleon England has known no such dangerous and uncompromising enemy, nor can it be said that he was beaten even at the last. Yet after reading the story of the long struggle for Trichinopoly, it is difficult to believe that he would not have been beaten even had he remained in India. His panegyrists complain, not unjustly, that he was hampered by a dearth of able subordinates. It would be nearer to the truth to say that he was checked by an extraordinary abundance of able British officers, not one of them bearing high rank; by clerks such as Clive, by majors such as Lawrence, by captains such as Dalton, Kilpatrick, and Caillaud, lieutenants such as Harrison, ensigns such as Joseph Smith. These were the men who thrust the cup of success from his lips as often as he raised it to drink, until his own countrymen finally dashed it from his hand. And this is the true significance of our early wars in India to the student of British military history—the vast wealth of ability that lay, and doubtless still lies, latent among the junior officers of the British Army.

Authorities.—Orme's *Military Transactions* is the principal authority for the history of the war on the English side, next to which the *Memoirs* of Stringer Lawrence and Wilks's *History of Mysore* are the most valuable works in elucidation. Colonel Malleson has treated the subject from the French side in *The French in India*, to which may be added his two short lives of Clive and Dupleix, and his *Decisive Battles of India*. Malleson's work, however, requires to be carefully checked, since it contains more than a few inaccuracies of detail, and betrays marks of haste if not of carelessness. The French sources of information are enumerated by him.

BOOK IX

CHAPTER I

1506.
1535.
1608.

From the East the course of our history leads us by rapid transition to the great continent of the West. The English claim to the sovereignty of North America dated from the reign of Henry the Seventh, under whose patronage Sebastian Cabot had made his great discoveries; but it was the Spaniards who first approached the unknown land and gave it the name of Florida, and it was a Frenchman, Denis of Honfleur, who first explored the Gulf of St. Lawrence. So also it was a Frenchman, Jacques Cartier, who gave its name to that noble river, and the name of Mount Royal or Montreal to the hill on which the city now stands. Full sixty years passed away before further attempt was made to found European settlements on the North American continent, and then English and French took the work in hand well-nigh simultaneously. In 1603 De Monts obtained permission from the French king to colonise Acadia,[237] discovered and planted the harbour called by him Port Royal and by the English at a later date Annapolis Royal, and explored the coast southward as far as that Plymouth where the Pilgrim Fathers were to land in 1621. The attempt of De Monts was a failure, and it was left to Samuel Champlain to begin the work anew by the founding of Quebec and by the establishment of Montreal at once as a gateway for Indian trade and a bulwark against Indian invasion. To him was due the exploration of the river Richelieu and of the lake which bears his name, as far as the two headlands which were afterwards to become famous under the names of Ticonderoga and Crown Point. In Champlain's wake followed the Jesuit missionaries, whose history presents so curious a mixture of that which is highest and lowest in human nature. Lastly, to Champlain must be ascribed not only the final settlement of the French in Canada but the initiation of the French policy of meddling with the internal politics of the Indian tribes.

1613.

Meanwhile an English Company of Adventurers for Virginia had established a first settlement on the James river, just three-and-twenty years after Raleigh's abortive attempt to accomplish the same feat. The rival nations had not been settled in North America five years before they came into collision. The English claimed the whole continent in virtue of Cabot's discoveries, and the English Governor of Virginia enforced the claim by sending a ship to Acadia, which demolished the Jesuit settlement at Port Royal and carried the settlers prisoners to Jamestown.

1621.

A few years later a Scottish nobleman, Sir William Alexander, afterwards Earl of Stirling, obtained a grant from James the First of the territory which, in compliment to his native land, he christened Nova Scotia, and planted a colony there. Finally, in 1627, during the war with France, a company of London merchants, inspired chiefly by two brothers named Kirke, sent an expedition up the St. Lawrence, which captured Quebec, established settlements in Cape Breton, and in a word made the conquest of Canada. Unfortunately, however, Charles the First, then as always impecunious, allowed these important acquisitions to be restored to France at the Peace of 1632 for the paltry sum of fifty thousand pounds. The conquering merchants protested but in vain, pleading passionately for the retention at any rate of Quebec. "If the King keep it," they wrote, "we do not care what the French or any other can do, though they have an hundred sail of ships and ten thousand men."[238] So truly was appreciated, even in the seventeenth century, the strategic value of that famous and romantic fortress.

1654.
1667.

Still even so Acadia[239] was not yet permanently lost, for in 1654 Major Sedgwicke, who had been sent by Cromwell to attack the Dutch settlements on the Hudson, took the opportunity to capture the French ports at St. Johns, Port Royal and Penobscot, and restored Acadia to England once more. With England it remained until 1667, when it was finally made over to France by the Treaty of Breda. Thus was established the French dominion in what is now called Canada.

1621.

Meanwhile, in the same year as had seen the first British settlement in Nova Scotia, English emigrants had landed at New Plymouth and founded the New England which was destined to swallow up New France. King James granted the infant settlement a charter of incorporation, encouraged it, and in 1625 declared by proclamation that the territories of Virginia and New England should form part of his empire.[240] The next step was the foundation of a distinct colony at Massachusetts Bay in 1628, which was erected into a corporation two years later and soon increased to a thousand persons. In 1635 yet another settlement was formed at Connecticut by emigrants from Massachusetts; and in the same year the intolerance of his fellow-settlers in Massachusetts drove Roger Williams afield to found the colony of Rhode Island. Finally, in 1638, another secession brought about the establishment of New Haven. The settlers had left England, as they pleaded, to find liberty of conscience; but as the majority understood by this phrase no more than licence to coerce the consciences of others, the few that really sought religious liberty wandered far before they found it.

1644.

A very few years sufficed to assure the preponderance of Massachusetts in the Northern Colonies. It widened its borders, absorbed the scattered settlements of New Hampshire and Maine, and in 1644 took its place at the head of the four federated colonies of New England.[241] The distraction caused by the Civil War in Britain left the colonies practically free from all control by the mother country, and Massachusetts seized the opportunity to erect a theocracy, which was utterly at variance with the terms of her charter, and to assume, together with the confederacy of New England, the airs and privileges of an independent State. The ambitious little community coined her own money, negotiated with the French in Acadia without reference to England, refused to trade with other colonies that were loyal to the King's cause, resented the appointment by the Long Parliament of Commissioners for the administration of the colonies, and hinted to Cromwell that the side which she might take in the Dutch war of 1653 would depend entirely on the treatment which she might receive from him. As her reward she received the privilege of exemption from the restrictions of the Navigation Acts.

1660.
1684.

Then came the Restoration; and the confederacy of New England quickly fell to pieces. Connecticut received a separate charter, under which she absorbed New Haven; and Rhode Island obtained a separate charter likewise. Massachusetts being thus left isolated, Charles the Second determined to inquire into the many complaints made against her of violation of her charter. The colonists replied by setting their militia in order as if for armed resistance; but on reconsideration decided to fall back on smooth words, false promises, false statements, and skilful procrastination. Such methods might seem at first sight to be misplaced in a community of saints, such as Massachusetts boasted herself to be, but at least they were never employed without previous invocation of the Divine guidance. For twenty years the colonists contrived to keep the Royal authority at arm's length, till at last, after long forbearance on the side of Whitehall, the charter was cancelled by legal process, and Massachusetts was restored to her dependence on the mother country.

In the course of these years the English settlements in North America had multiplied rapidly. Maryland had been granted to Lord Baltimore in 1632; Carolina was planted by a company in 1663; Delaware with New Jersey was assigned by patent to the Duke of York, afterwards James the Second, in 1664, and Pennsylvania to William Penn in 1680. In fact, by the close of Charles the Second's reign the British seaboard in North America extended from the river St. Croix[242] in the north to the river Savannah in the south. But of all England's acquisitions during this period the most momentous was that of the Dutch settlements on the Hudson, captured in 1664 by Colonel Nicolls, who gave to the town of New Amsterdam its now famous name of New York.[243] One chief advantage of New York was that it possessed a direct way to the west from Albany, on the Hudson, up the Mohawk River to Lake Oneida and so to Lake Ontario, whereby it had access to the great fur-trade with the Indians. But this consideration, important though it was commercially, paled before the strategical significance of the port of New York. No more simple method of explaining this can be found than to quote the belief held by many of the English emigrants before they sailed, that New England was an island. In a sense this is almost true, the country being surrounded by the sea, to north, east, and south, and by the rivers Hudson and St. Lawrence to the west. Champlain had already paddled up the Richelieu to Lake Champlain with the design of passing through Lake George, carrying his canoes to the head-waters of the Hudson and re-embarking for a voyage down the river to the sea. He had in fact chosen the highway of lakes and rivers on which the principal battles for the possession of the New World were to be fought. The northern key of that highway was Quebec, the southern New York. France possessed the one, and England the other. The power that should hold both would hold the whole continent.

| 1670. |
| 1673. |
| 1678. |
| 1680. |

Let us now turn for a moment to the proceedings of the French during these same years. Unlike the English, who stuck sedulously to the work of making their settlement self-supporting by agriculture, they were intent rather on trading with the Indians for fur and exploring the vast territory which lay to south and west of them. To these objects may be added the salvation of the souls of the Indian tribes; for beyond all doubt it was zeal for the conversion, or at any rate for the baptism, of these savages that led the Jesuits through endless hardship and danger into the heart of the continent. As early as 1613 Champlain had travelled up the Ottawa by way of Lake Nipissing and French

River to Lake Huron, returning by Lake Simcoe and Lake Ontario. Jesuit missionaries followed the same track in 1634, and established a mission on the peninsula that juts out from the eastern shore of Lake Huron. From thence they spread to Lakes Superior and Michigan, erecting mission-houses and taking possession of vast tracts of land and water in the name of King Lewis the Fourteenth. Shortly after the restoration of King Charles the Second, Jean Talon, Intendant of Canada, formed the resolution of getting in rear of the English settlements and confining the settlers to a narrow strip of the seaboard; his plan being to secure the rivers that formed the highways of the interior, and to follow them, if they should prove to flow thither, to the Gulf of Mexico, so as to hold both British and Spaniards in check. A young adventurer, named Robert Lasalle, appeared at the right moment as a fit instrument to his hand. In 1670 Lasalle passed through the strait, still called Detroit, which leads from Lake Huron to Lake Erie, reached a branch of the Ohio and made his way for some distance down that river. Three years later a Jesuit, Joliet, striking westward from the western shore of Lake Michigan, descended the Wisconsin and followed the Mississippi to the junction of the Arkansas. In 1678 an expedition under Lasalle explored the passage from Lake Ontario to Lake Erie, and discovered the Falls of Niagara, where Lasalle, with immediate appreciation of the strategic value of the position, proceeded to build a fort. Finally, in 1680, Lasalle penetrated from the present site of Chicago on Lake Michigan to the northern branch of the River Illinois, paddled down to the Mississippi, and after five months of travel debouched into the Gulf of Mexico. He took nominal possession of all the country through which he passed; and the vast territory between the Alleghanies and the Rocky Mountains from the Rio Grande and the Gulf of Mexico to the uppermost waters of the Missouri were annexed to the French crown under the name of Louisiana.

The next step was to secure the advantages that should accrue from the discoveries of Lasalle. To this end the fort at Niagara had already been built; and Fort Frontenac was next erected at the northern outlet of Lake Ontario to cut off the English from trade with the Indians. At the strait of Michillimackinac, between Lakes Huron and Michigan, a Jesuit mission sufficiently provided for the same object. Besides these there were established Fort Miamis by the south-eastern shore of Lake Michigan, to bar the passage from the lake to the Upper Illinois, Fort St. Louis, near the present site of Utica, to secure the trade with the tribes on the plains of the Illinois, and yet another fort on the Lower Mississippi.

1682.
1687.
1688.
1689.

Such a monopoly of the Indian trade was by no means to the taste of the British and Dutch, nor of the Five Indian Nations, better known by the French name of Iroquois, whom they had taken under their special protection. Nevertheless, in their simple plodding industry, their zeal for religious controversy and their interminable squabbles over their boundaries, the English colonies took little heed to what was going on in the continent behind them. One man alone saw the danger from the first, namely, Colonel Thomas Dongan, an officer who had begun his career in the French army, but had left it for the British, and after some service at Tangier had been sent out as Governor to New York. Dongan, however, was at first unsupported either by the Government at Whitehall or by the neighbouring colonies. His protests were vigorous to discourtesy, but he had small means for enforcing them. One resource indeed he did possess, namely the friendship of the Iroquois, who were the dominant tribes of the continent; for with all their subtle policy and their passion for interference with native affairs, the French had never succeeded in alienating the Iroquois—who covered the flank of New York and New England towards Canada—from their alliance with the British. Dongan therefore assiduously cultivated a good understanding with these Indians against the moment when he should be allowed to act. Meanwhile the French went yet further in aggression. They destroyed the factories of the Hudson's Bay Company; they treacherously entrapped and captured a number of Iroquois at Fort Frontenac, plundered English traders, and repaired and strengthened the fort built by Lasalle at Niagara. Dongan's indignation rose to a dangerous height; and now at last came a reply from England to his previous reports, and an order to repel further aggression on the Iroquois by force. Assembling a force of local militia at Albany he first insisted on the destruction of the fort at Niagara; and then the Iroquois burst in upon Canada and spread terror to the very gates of Montreal. It was just at this crisis that William of Orange displaced James the Second on the throne of England, and that war broke out between England and France. Therewith New England and New France entered upon a conflict which was to last with little intermission for the next seventy years.

Judging from mere numbers the contest between the rival colonies should have been short, for the population of New England was over ninety thousand, whereas that of Canada did not exceed twelve thousand. But this disparity was more than equalised by other advantages of the French. In the first place, they were compact, united, and under command of one man, who was an able and experienced soldier. In the second, a large proportion of the inhabitants had undergone long military training, the French king offering bounties both of money and of land to officers and soldiers who should consent to remain in the colony. The chief delight of the male population was not the tilling of the soil; they loved rather to hunt and fish, and live the free and fascinating life of an Indian in the forest. Every man therefore was a skilful woodsman, a good marksman, a handy canoe-man, and in a word admirably trained for forest-fighting. Finally, there was a permanent garrison of regular troops, which never fell below, and very often exceeded, fifteen hundred men.

The English settler, on the other hand, knew little of the forest. When not engaged in husbandry he was a fisherman in his native heritage, the sea. Every colony had its own militia, which legally included, as a rule, the whole male population between the ages of sixteen and sixty. In the early days of North American settlement the colonists had been at pains to bring with them trained officers who could give them instruction in the military art. Such an officer was Miles Standish, who had served with the English troops in the Dutch service; such another was Captain John Underhill, who had fought in Ireland, Spain, and the Low Countries, and was reputed a friend of Maurice of Nassau. Under such leaders, in 1637, seventy-seven colonists had boldly attacked an encampment of four hundred Indian warriors and virtually annihilated them; giving, in fact, as fine an exposition of the principles of savage warfare as is to be found in our history.[244] In 1653 again, New England, once assured of Cromwell's favour, made great and expensive preparations for an attack on the Dutch; and Massachusetts supplied two hundred volunteers to Nicolls for the capture of New York in 1664.

| 1680. |
| 1686. |

But as time went on the military efficiency of the colonies decreased; and in the war against the Indian chief, Philip, in 1671, the settlers suffered disaster upon disaster. The officers possessed neither skill nor knowledge; and the men, though they showed no lack of bravery and tenacity, were wholly innocent of discipline. Moreover, they shared the failing of the English militia of the same period, that they were unwilling to go far from their own homes. Again, since the confederacy of New England had been broken up, the jealousy and selfishness of the several provinces had weakened them for military efficiency. In the great peril of 1671 Rhode Island, being full of Quakers, would not move a finger to help her neighbours, and Connecticut, exasperated by extreme provocation, actually armed herself a few years later to inflict punishment on the cantankerous little community.[245] Within the several provinces again there was no great unanimity, and in fact in the event of a war with France every advantage of skill, of unity, and of prompt and rapid action lay with the French. James the Second, who saw the peril of the situation, tried hard to mend matters during his brief reign by uniting New England, New York, and New Jersey under the rule of a single governor, Sir

Edmund Andros, an officer of the Guards. The experiment from one point of view was statesmanlike enough, but as it could not be tried without abolishing the representative assemblies of the various states, it defeated its own object by its extreme unpopularity.

The military aid furnished to the American colonies from home throughout this early period was infinitesimal. New England had never appealed to the mother country for help even in her utmost need. An independent company of regular troops was formed for the garrison of New York while the Duke of York was proprietor, and another company was also maintained for a short time in Virginia; but the first troops of the standing army to visit America were a mixed battalion of the First and Coldstream Guards, which crossed the Atlantic to suppress the Virginian rebellion of 1677. When Andros assumed his government in 1686 he brought with him a second company of soldiers from England. These were the first red-coats ever seen in Boston, and they have the credit of having taught New England to "drab, drink, blaspheme, curse and damn," a lesson which, as I understand, has not been forgotten. Thus though the militia of the colonies under Andros might muster a nominal total of ten or twelve thousand men, these two companies were all that he could have brought to meet the thirty-two or more companies of regular troops in Montreal and Quebec.

1689.

The outbreak of the war in 1689 brought back an efficient soldier, Count Frontenac, to the government of Canada. He knew the country well, having already served there as Governor from 1672 to 1682, and in that capacity seconded the great designs of Lasalle. On his arrival he at once made preparations for an advance on Albany by Lakes Champlain and George and for a rapid movement against New York. The project fortunately issued in no more than a general massacre of the inhabitants on the northern frontier of New York; but when that province called in alarm upon New England for assistance, it was found that Massachusetts had risen in revolution at the news of King James's fall, had imprisoned Andros, and through sheer perversity had cancelled all his military dispositions for the protection of New Hampshire and Maine. The Indians accordingly swept down upon the defenceless borders and made frightful havoc with fire and sword.

1690.
1691.

In the following year the colonies of New York and New England met in congress and agreed to make a counter-stroke against Canada. More remarkable still, Massachusetts for the first time appealed to England for military aid in the furtherance of this enterprise; though, as may be guessed by those who have followed me through the story of King William's difficulties, the appeal was perforce rejected. The colonies therefore resolved to act alone, and despatched fifteen hundred troops by the usual line of inland waterways against Montreal, and thirty-two ships under Sir William Phips against Quebec. The expedition by land soon broke down on its way through dissension, indiscipline, and disease; and the fleet, though it made an easy conquest of Acadia, failed miserably before Quebec. The next year a small force from New York made a second futile raid into Canada; but for the most part the English colonies were content to hound on their Indian allies against the French. The French on their side retaliated in kind, and, as circumstances gave them opportunity, with still greater barbarity. Hundreds of defenceless settlers on the border were thus slaughtered without the slightest military advantage. Frontenac wrote repeated letters to his master urging him to determine the possession of the continent once for all by sending a fleet to capture New York; but either Lewis's hands were too full or he failed to appreciate the wisdom of Frontenac's counsel, for in any case, fortunately, he left New York unmolested.

| 1697. |

The sphere of operations widened itself over Acadia and Newfoundland, and the war dragged on in a desultory fashion with raid and counter-raid, generally to the advantage of the French. To the last the English colonies were blind to the importance of the issue at stake. Jealous, self-centred, and undisciplined, many of them took no part whatever in the war; two only, New England and New York, rose to aggressive action, which, though the stroke was wisely aimed against the tap-root of French power, failed utterly from lack of organisation and discipline. The French struck always at strategic points where their blow would tell with full force and weight. The colonists in their insane jealousy of the crown neglected the defence of these strategic points simply because it was enjoined by the mother country, and refused to provide the contingents of troops requested by the English commander-in-chief.[246] In fine, when the Peace of Ryswick ended the war, the French could reckon that they had achieved one great success; they had broken the power of the most formidable of the Indians, the Iroquois.

Massachusetts, which had suffered heavily from the war, found herself at its close obliged once more to invoke the assistance of England. In an address to the King she prayed for his orders to the several colonial governments to give their assistance against French and Indians, for a supply of ammunition, for the protection of a fleet, and for aid in the reduction of Canada, "the unhappy fountain," as they wrote, "from which issue all our miseries." So far, therefore, the war had taught one useful lesson; but, indeed, even at the time of her greatest disloyalty to the English crown Massachusetts had always soundly hated the French. Obviously closer union of the colonies for military purposes could not but be for the general advantage, and sundry schemes were prepared to promote it; but all alike were unsuccessful, though nothing could be more certain than that further trouble was ahead.

| 1702. |
| 1707. |
| 1709. |

The renewal of war in 1702 brought the usual raids of Indians, stirred up by the French, upon the borders of the English colonies. These barbarous inroads, which meant the massacre and torture of innocent settlers, could serve no military end except to commit the Indians to hostility with the English, and naturally aroused the fiercest resentment. The colonies, however, once again showed neither unity nor zeal for the common cause. New York evinced an apathy which was little short of criminal, Connecticut long held aloof, Rhode Island only after infinite haggling supplied grudging instalments of men and money. Massachusetts alone, true to her traditions, showed some vigour and spirit and actually made an attack on Port Royal in Acadia, choosing that point because it could be reached by sea. The expedition, however, failed with more than usual discredit owing to ignorance and unskilfulness in the commanders and utter indiscipline among the troops. Then the colonies wisely decided that it was useless to attempt to choke the fountain of all their miseries except at its head. An address was sent to Queen Anne praying for help in the conquest of Nova Scotia and Canada, which was favourably received; and for the first time operations were concerted for a joint attack of imperial and colonial troops upon the French in North America. England was to supply a fleet and five regiments of the regular Army, Massachusetts and Rhode Island were to furnish twelve hundred men more, and these forces united were to attempt Quebec; while fifteen hundred men from the other colonies, except from New Jersey and Pennsylvania, which selfishly kept apart, were to advance upon Montreal by Lake Champlain. The troops of Massachusetts were mustered and drilled by British officers sent across the Atlantic for the purpose, and all signs pointed to a great and decisive effort. In due time the western contingent advanced towards Lake Champlain, by way of Albany and the Hudson, building on their way a fort at the carrying-place from the Hudson, which we shall know better as Fort Edward, and a second fort at Wood Creek, where the journey by water to Lake George was recommenced, called Fort Anne. There the little column halted, for the brunt of the work was to fall on the fleet which was expected from England. The weeks flew on, but the fleet never appeared. The disaster of Almanza had upset all calculations and disconcerted all arrangements; and the great enterprise was perforce abandoned.

In July of the following year, however, an expedition on a smaller scale met with more success. A joint fleet of the Royal Navy and of colonial vessels, together with four regiments from New England and one of British marines, sailed against Port Royal, captured it after a trifling resistance, and changed its name to that which it still bears, of Annapolis Royal. Nova Scotia had changed hands many times, but from henceforth it was to remain British. Thus for the first time a British armament interposed seriously in the long strife between French and English in America. It was the beginning of the end, and of the end of more than French rule over the continent. "If the French colonies should fall," wrote a French officer at the time, "Old England will not imagine that these various provinces will then unite, shake off the yoke of the English monarchy, and erect themselves into a democracy."[247] The idea of the capture of Canada, however, took root just at this time in the new English Ministry, where Bolingbroke and Harley had succeeded in ousting Marlborough from office. The conquest of New France would, they conceived, be a fine exploit to set off against the victories of the great Duke. Massachusetts seconded the project with extraordinary zeal, and in July 1711 a British fleet with seven regular regiments on board sailed into Boston harbour. The disastrous issue of this enterprise has already been told. Bad seamanship cast eight of the transports on the rocks in the St. Lawrence, and seven hundred soldiers were drowned. General Hill and Admiral Walker were not the men to persist in the face of such a mishap, and the whole design was abandoned with disgraceful alacrity. The expedition was in fact simply a political move, conceived by factious politicians for factious ends instead of by military men for the benefit of the country, and accordingly it fared as such expeditions must inevitably fare.

Finally came the Peace of Utrecht, which gave England permanent possession of Newfoundland and of Acadia, though still without settlement of the vexed question as to the boundaries of the ceded province. These acquisitions entailed an increase of the British garrisons in America, as has already been told; but the entire strength of the British regular troops in New York, Nova Scotia, and Newfoundland did not exceed nine hundred men. The French, for their part, after the loss of Acadia betook themselves to Cape Breton, or, as they called it, L'Ile Royale, and set themselves forthwith to establish in one of the harbours a post which should command the access to Canada, and form a base for future aggression against New England and Nova Scotia. A haven, named Port à l'Anglais, on the east coast was selected, and there was built the fort of Louisburg, the strongest on the Atlantic coast, and as the French loved to call it, the Dunkirk of America. The establishment of this fortress was one of those costly follies to which the French are prone, when failure and defeat allow them no outlet for their vexation and their spite. The climate absolutely forbade the construction of an elaborate stronghold of masonry. Fog and rain prevented mortar from setting all through the short spring and summer, fog and frost split mortar and stones and demolished walls every winter. Repairs were endless, yet the fortress was never in good repair, and the expense was intolerable. Lastly, such a stronghold was worthless without supremacy at sea.

| 1724. |

But the French did not stop here. They lost no opportunity of stirring up the Acadians to discontent and of inflaming the Indians against the British both in Acadia and in New England. The result was a series of raids on the Kennebec, where the French, in order to guard the line of advance on Quebec by that river and Lake Chaudière, had established a chain of mission-stations. The colonists, goaded to exasperation, at last rooted out these missions by force, though not until after long delay owing to the perversity of the Assembly of Massachusetts, which, always jealous of the English Governor, wished to take the control of operations out of his hand into their own, never doubting that their rustic ignorance would be as efficient as the tried skill of one of Marlborough's veterans.

| 1727. |

So this state of outward peace and of covert war continued. France, despite the concessions made at the Peace of Utrecht, still claimed the whole of the North American continent, with some few trifling exceptions, and took every measure to make good her claim. A new fort was erected at Niagara; another fort was built at Chambly to cover Montreal from any English attack by way of Lake Champlain, and in 1731 a massive stronghold of masonry was constructed at Crown Point, on the western shore of the same lake, and christened Fort Frédéric. The ground on which this last fort stood was within the bounds claimed by New York, but the province was too busy over quarrels with her neighbour, New Jersey, to interpose. So although New York and New England alike denounced the encroachment furiously, neither the one nor the other would lift a finger to prevent it. The one movement made by the colonists in counterpoise to the ceaseless activity of the French was the establishment of a fortified trading station at Oswego on Lake Ontario, as a rival to the French post at Niagara. Even this work was done not by the colonists but by Governor Burnet of New York at his own expense; and the debt due to him from the province on this account has never been liquidated to this day.

Thus matters drifted on until the war of the Austrian Succession. Then, as usual, the French at Louisburg received warning of the outbreak before the English at Boston, and the imperial garrisons at Annapolis Royal and at Canseau were overpowered and captured by the French without an effort. But now the colonists with superb audacity resolved to take the bull by the horns and to attack the French in the most formidable of their strongholds, Louisburg itself. The moving spirit in the enterprise was Governor William Shirley of Massachusetts, an Englishman by nationality and a barrister by training, who thought himself a born strategist; and the commander whom he selected was one William Pepperrell, a prosperous merchant of New England, whose father had emigrated as a poor man from his native Devon and had made his fortune. Pepperrell had neither education nor experience in military matters, but he had shrewd good sense; while, being popular, he was likely to command the respect and obedience of his undisciplined troops. After some trouble the Provincial Assemblies were coaxed into approval of the design; four thousand men were raised in New England, a small fleet of armed vessels was collected for the protection of the transports, and the little expedition sailed to its rendezvous at Canseau, some fifty miles from Louisburg. Here by good luck it was joined by a British squadron under Commodore Warren, which threw in its lot with it; and the army of amateurs with its escort of hardy seamen proceeded with a light heart to the siege of the Dunkirk of America. The account of the operations is laughable in the extreme, though the French found them no matter for laughter. Skilled engineers the besiegers had none, and few if any skilled artillerymen, but they went to work with the best of spirits and good humour in their own casual fashion, which puzzled the French far more than a regular siege in form. To be brief, with the help of gunners from the fleet and of extraordinary good fortune they succeeded in capturing the fortress after a siege of six weeks. The performance is certainly one of the curiosities of military history, but must be passed over in this place since it forms no part of the story of the British Army.[248] The colonists were not a little proud of the feat, and with right good reason. Nor did their gallant efforts pass without recognition in England. Pepperrell, who had amply justified Shirley's choice, was created a baronet; and on Warren's suggestion[249] the remains of the colonial troops were taken into English pay and formed into two regiments, with Pepperrell and Shirley for their colonels.

1746.

Though the colonial garrison suffered terribly from pestilence during the ensuing winter,[250] Shirley was anxious to complete the conquest of Canada in 1746; and Newcastle received his proposals with encouragement at Whitehall. Three British regiments—the Twenty-ninth, Thirtieth, and Forty-fifth—arrived in April to occupy Louisburg, and Newcastle promised five battalions more under Lieutenant-General St. Clair, together with a fleet under Warren, to aid in the operations. It was agreed that the British and the levies of New England should sail up the St. Lawrence to attack Quebec, while the remainder should, as usual, march against Montreal by way of Lake Champlain. The colonists took up the enterprise with great spirit, and the Provincial Assemblies of seven colonies voted a total force of forty-three hundred men. The French in Canada took the alarm and made frantic preparations for defence; but though the colonists were ready and eager at the time appointed, the British troops never appeared; Newcastle having detained them in Europe for the ridiculous descent, already described elsewhere, upon L'Orient. Shirley, undismayed, then decided to turn his little force against Crown Point; when all New England was alarmed by intelligence of a vast French armament on its way to retake Louisburg, recapture Acadia and burn Boston. Then the colonists took fright in their turn and equipped themselves for defence with desperate energy; but once again there was no occasion for panic. The French fleet sailed indeed, but after a voyage of disasters reached the coast of Nova Scotia only to be shattered and dispersed by a terrible storm. The Commander-in-Chief died of a broken heart, his successor threw himself on his own sword in despair, and after some weeks of helpless lingering in the harbour which now bears the name of Halifax, the fragments of the French fleet returned almost in a state of starvation to France.

| 1747. |

Not discouraged by this terrible reverse the French Government in the following year sent out a second fleet, which was met off Rochelle by a superior fleet under Admirals Anson and Warren and utterly defeated. It was fortunate, for the British Government with Newcastle at its head gave the Americans no further help. Three hundred soldiers were indeed shipped off to Annapolis, but more than half of them died on the voyage, and many of the remainder, being gaol-birds and Irish papists, deserted to the French. The situation in Acadia was perilous, for the French population did not love their new masters, and the Canadians, particularly the Jesuit priests, never ceased to stimulate them to revolt. Shirley resolved that, though the security of Acadia was the charge of the mother country, the colonists must protect the province for themselves sooner than abandon it. Massachusetts responded to his appeal with her usual spirit, and notwithstanding one severe reverse of the colonial troops, Acadia was still safe at the close of the war. For the rest, the French pursued their old method of hounding on the Indians against the

British; and petty but barbarous warfare never ceased on the borders. For once, too, this warfare produced, though indirectly, an important result, since it brought to the front a young Irishman named William Johnson who, having shown an extraordinary power and ascendency over the Indians, was chosen as agent for New York in all dealings of the British with them. We shall see more of this Johnson in the years before us. Finally came the Peace of Aix-la-Chapelle, when the Americans to their huge disgust learned that Louisburg, their own prize, had been restored to France—bartered away for the retention of an insignificant factory called Madras.

CHAPTER II

| 1748. |

The conclusion of the Peace of Aix-la-Chapelle was followed by the usual reduction of the forces in Britain. The ten new regiments and several other corps were disbanded, leaving for the cavalry all the regiments now in the Army List down to the Fourteenth Hussars, and in the infantry the Foot Guards and the First to the Forty-ninth Regiments of the Line. The strength of all corps was of course diminished and the British Establishment was fixed at thirty thousand men, two-thirds of them for service at home and one-third for colonial garrisons. The rest of the Army, thirty-seven regiments in all, but very weak in numbers, was as usual turned over to the Irish Establishment. Efforts were of course made in both Houses of Parliament to cut down the numbers of the Army to a still lower figure, and the antiquated arguments in favour of such a step were repeated as though they had not already done duty a thousand times within the past forty years. Nay, so vigorous is the old age of folly and of faction that men were still found, when the Mutiny Act was brought forward, to urge the needlessness of courts-martial in time of peace. These childish representations, however, received little notice or encouragement; while, on the other hand, divers projects for reform in the Army were brought forward which, even though they led to no result, received at least careful attention and intelligent debate. Of these matters it will be more convenient to speak when the narrative of the war is concluded. For although peace had been proclaimed, and estimates and establishment had been accordingly reduced, the struggle with France, far from being closed, was not even suspended abroad. It would seem that not a few members of both Houses were alive to the fact; while fugitive notices in the newspapers, announcing that "Mr. Clive, a volunteer, had the command given to him to attack a place called Arcourt," may have suggested it even to the gossips of the coffee-houses. The Government, however, was not one which could be expected to take thought for the morrow, or indeed for anything beyond the retention of power. It was that Administration which had been formed by Henry Pelham in 1744, and is generally identified with the name of his brother, the Duke of Newcastle, who is remembered chiefly through his ignorance of the fact that Cape Breton is an island. This deplorable person possessed no talent beyond an infinite capacity for such intrigue as lifts incompetence to high office, and was only less of a curse to England than

Madame de Pompadour was to France. One able man, however, there was in the lower ranks of the Administration, William Pitt, who, after a vain effort to become Secretary at War, had accepted the post of Paymaster of the Forces. He now lay quiet, though not without occasional outbursts of mutiny, abiding his time and fulfilling the duties of his place with an integrity heretofore unknown in the Paymaster's Office.

| 1749. |

One important military measure, meanwhile, the Government did take. The number of men disbanded from fleet and army was so large that it was deemed prudent, in the interests alike of humanity and of public security, to make some provision for them. Accordingly fifty acres of freehold land, with an additional ten acres for every child, were offered to all veterans who would emigrate as settlers to Nova Scotia; their passage outward being likewise paid, and immunity from taxation guaranteed to them for ten years. The system was copied from the model given by the French in Canada, and by them doubtless borrowed from ancient Rome; but it was successful. Four thousand persons, with their families, took advantage of the offer, embarked under the command of Colonel Cornwallis and landed at the harbour of Chebucto, from thenceforward called, in honour of the President of the Board of Trade and Plantations, by the name of Halifax. Three companies of rangers were formed for the defence of the settlement, in addition to which two battalions of regular troops were detailed for the garrisons of Nova Scotia and Newfoundland. For it was intended that Halifax should be not only a refuge for disbanded soldiers, but a fortified station in counterpoise to the French fortress at Louisburg.

The French in Canada instantly took the alarm, and after their unscrupulous manner incited the Indians to murder the settlers, sparing no pains meanwhile to alienate the hearts of the Acadians from the British. The priests were their instruments in this treacherous policy, and their proceedings were fully approved at Versailles. What was called an Indian war was, in the plain words of Governor Hopson of Nova Scotia, no other than a pretence for the French to commit hostilities on British subjects. Yet through the trying years that followed, the British officials behaved always with exemplary patience and forbearance, though, owing to the incessant intrigues of the French, occasional skirmishes between French and English were unavoidable. But British settlers had touched French America elsewhere on a more tender point even than in Acadia. British traders had found their way across the Alleghanies to the Ohio, and had stolen the hearts of the Indians on the river from their French rivals. To Canada this was a serious matter, for the chain of French posts that was designed to shut off the British from the interior ran from the Gulf of St. Lawrence to the Gulf of Mexico, and if the British should sever this chain at the Ohio French America would be parted in twain. In 1749 a French emissary was despatched from Montreal to vindicate French rights on the river and to bid the English traders depart from it. His reception by the Indians was not encouraging, and even while he was on the spot a company was formed by some capitalists in Virginia to settle the country about the Ohio. The Governors of Pennsylvania and Virginia quickly perceived the importance of the position on the fork of the river where Pittsburg now stands, and were anxious to secure it by a fortified station; but unfortunately the public spirit of the colonies was less intelligent than the private enterprise. The Provincial Assemblies quarrelled with their governors and with each other, and refused to vote a farthing either for building a fort or for presents to conciliate the Indians in the valley of the Ohio.

1752-1753.

Then, as usual, while the colonies debated and postponed the French took prompt and decisive action. In the summer of 1752 a new Governor, Duquêsne, had arrived in Canada, who, as soon as the spring of 1753 was come, sent an expedition of fifteen hundred men through Lake Ontario to Lake Erie, where they landed on the eastern shore and built a fort of logs at Presquile, the site of the present Erie. Thence cutting a road for several leagues southward to French Creek (then called Rivière aux Bœufs), they constructed there a second fort named Fort le Bœuf, from which, when the water was high, they could launch their canoes on the creek and follow the stream downward to the Alleghany and the Ohio. The expedition was to have built a third fort at the junction of French Creek and the Alleghany, and descended the Ohio in order to intimidate the Indians, but the project was defeated by the sickliness of the troops. Garrisons were therefore left at Fort le Bœuf and Presquile, and the remainder of the force returned to Montreal, having thus secured communications between the St. Lawrence and the Ohio.

1753.
Dec. 11.

Governor Dinwiddie of Virginia no sooner heard of this movement on the part of the French than he sent a summons to the commanders of the forts to withdraw forthwith from the King of England's territory. The bearer of the message was the Adjutant-General of the Virginian militia, a young man of twenty-one with a great destiny before him, George Washington. There were two British trading stations on the Ohio, Venango, at the junction of French Creek and the Alleghany, and Logstown, some miles below the site of Pittsburg. On arriving at Venango, Washington found it converted into a French military station, the officers of which received him hospitably, but told him that they had orders to take possession of the Ohio, and that "by God they would do it." Making his way from thence to Fort le Bœuf, Washington delivered Dinwiddie's letter, and returned with the reply that it should be forwarded to Montreal, but that the garrisons had no intention of moving until orders should arrive from thence. Dinwiddie meanwhile had again appealed to the Virginian Assembly to vote money to build forts on the Ohio. He could show a letter from the Board of Ordnance in England approving of the project and offering arms and ammunition, as well as a letter from the King authorising the execution of the work at the colony's expense and the repelling of force by force; but the Assembly, though alive to the danger, would not vote a sixpence.

| 1754. |
| February. |

Such obstinacy was enough to drive a Governor to despair, but Dinwiddie was blessed with considerable tenacity of purpose. A renewal of his appeal in the ensuing session was more successful, and the Assembly grudgingly voted a small and insufficient sum, with which the Governor was forced to be content. Urgent applications to the neighbouring colonies for aid met with little response. The remoter provinces thought themselves in no way concerned; those nearer at hand refused help chiefly because their governors asked for it. It was in fact a principle with the Provincial Assemblies to thwart their governor, whether he were right or wrong, on every possible occasion; they being, as is so common in representative bodies, more anxious to assert their power and independence than their utility and good sense. North Carolina alone granted money enough for three or four hundred men. However, the British Government had sanctioned the employment of the regular companies at New York and in Carolina, and Dinwiddie having raised three hundred men in Virginia, ordered them to the Ohio Company's station at Will's Creek, which was to be the base of operations. Meanwhile he despatched a party of backwoodsmen forthwith to the forks of the Ohio, there to build, on a site selected by Washington, the fort for which he had pleaded so long. Forty men were actually at work upon it when, on the 17th of April, a flotilla of small craft came pouring down on the Alleghany with a party of five hundred French on board. The troops landed, trained cannon on the unfinished stockade, and summoned the British to surrender. Resistance was hopeless. The backwoodsmen perforce yielded; and the French having demolished their works erected a much larger and better fort on the same site, and called it Fort Duquêsne. The name before long was to be altered to Pittsburg, but the change was as yet hidden behind the veil of years. For the present the French had stolen a march on the British, and Dinwiddie was chagrined to the heart. "If the Assembly had voted the money in November which they did in February," he wrote, "the fort would have been built and garrisoned before the French approached."

The Governor, however, was by no means disposed meekly to accept this defeat. The French had expelled a British party from British territory by force of arms, and both he and Washington treated the incident as equivalent to a declaration of war. Washington, though but half of his troops had yet joined him, presently advanced over the Alleghanies to the Youghiogany, a tributary of the Monongahela; and there on the 27th of May he came upon a small party of French and fired the shots which began the war. A few weeks later he with his little force, something less than four hundred men, was surrounded by twice that number of Frenchmen, and after a fight of nine hours and the loss of a fourth of his men, was compelled to capitulate.

Dinwiddie was vexed beyond measure by this second reverse, and by the delay in the arrival of the reinforcements which had caused it. The two companies of regular troops from New York came crawling up to the scene of action in a disgraceful state. Their ranks were thin, for their muster-rolls had been falsified by means of "faggots"; they were undisciplined; they had neither tents, blankets, knapsacks, nor ammunition with them, nothing, in fact, but their arms and thirty women and children.[251] The troops from North Carolina were still worse than these in the matter of discipline, so much so that they mutinied and dispersed to their homes while yet on the march to the rendezvous. The peril was great; yet the colonies remained supine. The Assembly of Virginia only after a bitter struggle granted Dinwiddie a competent sum; that of Pennsylvania, being composed chiefly of Quakers and of German settlers, who were anxious only to live in peace and to cultivate their farms, refused practically to contribute a farthing. New York was unable to understand, until Washington had been actually defeated, that there had been any French encroachment on British territory; Maryland produced a contribution only after long delay; and New Jersey, safely ensconced behind the shelter of her neighbours, flatly declined to give any aid whatever. New England alone, led as usual by Massachusetts, showed not only willingness but alacrity to drive back the detested French. United action was as yet inconceivable by the colonists or, as the English more correctly called them, the Provincials. It was only in deference to representations from the British Government that New York, Pennsylvania, Maryland, and the four colonies of New England met in congress to concert for joint action in securing the unstable affections of the Indians. A project for colonial union broached by Benjamin Franklin at this same congress was wrecked by the jealousy of Crown and Colonies as to mutual concession of power.

| September. |

In such circumstances the only hope lay in assistance from the mother country; and Dinwiddie accordingly sent repeated entreaties to England for stores, ammunition, and two regiments of regular infantry. The Ministry at home was not of a kind to cope with a great crisis. Henry Pelham was dead; and the ridiculous Newcastle as Prime Minister had succeeded in finding a fool still greater than himself, Sir T. Robinson, to be Secretary of State in charge of the colonies. Nevertheless, in July ten thousand pounds in specie and two thousand stand of arms were shipped for the service of the colonies, [252] and on the 30th of September orders were issued for the Forty-fourth and Forty-eighth regiments, both of them on the Irish Establishment, to be embarked at Cork. Each of these regiments was appointed to consist of three hundred and forty men only, and to take with it seven hundred stand of arms, so as to make up its numbers with American recruits.[253] But the nucleus of British soldiers was presently increased to five hundred men, the augmentation being effected, as usual, by drafts from other regiments; not, however, without difficulty, for the service was unpopular, and there was consequently much desertion. The next step was to appoint a commander; and the choice fell upon General Edward Braddock, sometime of the Coldstream Guards. He was a man of the same stamp as Hawley, and therefore after the Duke of Cumberland's own heart,—an officer of forty-five years' service, rough, brutal,[254] and insolent, a martinet of the narrowest type, but wanting neither spirit nor ability, and brave as a lion. His instructions were sufficiently wide, comprehending operations against the French in four different quarters. The French were to be driven from the Ohio, and a garrison was to be left to hold the country when captured; the like was to be done at Niagara, at Crown Point, and at Fort Beauséjour, a work erected by the French on the isthmus that joins Nova Scotia to the Continent. This plan had been suggested by Governor Shirley of Massachusetts; and in furtherance thereof the British Government had ordered two regiments, each one thousand strong, to be raised in America under the colonelcy of the veterans Shirley and Pepperrell, and to be taken into the pay of Great Britain.[255] There might well be doubt whether the means provided would suffice for the execution of the scheme.

| 1755. |
| April. |

It was January 1755 before the Forty-fourth and Forty-eighth were embarked at Cork, and past the middle of March before the whole of the transports arrived in Hampton Roads. Good care seems to have been taken of the troops on the voyage, for Braddock was able to report that there was not a sick man among them.[256] The transports were ordered to ascend the Potomac to Alexandria, where a camp was to be formed; and there on the 14th of April several of the governors met Braddock in council to decide as to the distribution of the work that lay before them. All was soon settled. Braddock with the two newly arrived regiments was to advance on Fort Duquêsne; Shirley with his own and Pepperrell's regiments was to attack

Niagara; William Johnson, on account of his influence with the Indians, was chosen to lead a body of Provincial troops from New England, New Jersey, and New York against Crown Point; and to Lieutenant-Colonel Monckton, an officer of whom we shall hear more, was entrusted the task of overpowering Fort Beauséjour. The first and second of these operations were designed to cut the chain of French posts between the St. Lawrence and the Ohio, and may be described as purely offensive. Why, however, it should have been thought necessary to sever this chain at two points when one point would have sufficed, and why therefore the whole strength of the blow was not aimed at Niagara, are questions not easily to be answered. The capture of Crown Point would serve alike to bar a French advance southward at Lake Champlain and to further a British advance on Montreal, and hence combined objects both offensive and defensive. The reduction of Fort Beauséjour having no other purpose than the security of Acadia, was a measure wholly defensive.

The Council broke up; the commanders repaired to their several charges, and Braddock was left to cope with his task. A great initial blunder had been made by the military authorities in England in sending the troops to Virginia and ordering them to advance on the Ohio by the circuitous route from Wills' Creek. This was, it is true, the line that had been taken by Washington; but Washington, like Shirley, was but an amateur, and a sounder military judgment would have shown that the suggestions of both were faulty. Disembarkation at Philadelphia, and a march directly westward from thence, would have saved not only distance and time but much trouble and expense; for Pennsylvania, unlike Maryland and Virginia, was a country rich in forage and in the means of transport. It was the collection of transport that was Braddock's first great difficulty. The Pennsylvanians showed an apathy and unwillingness which provoked even Washington to the remark that they ought to be chastised. It was only by the mediation of Benjamin Franklin, of all persons, that Braddock at last obtained waggons and horses sufficient for his needs. The General's trials were doubtless great, but his domineering temper, and the insolent superiority which he affected as an Englishman over Americans and as a regular officer over colonial militiamen, could not tend to ease the general friction between British and Provincials. His example was doubtless followed by his officers, the more so since it had been ordained that the King's commission should confer superiority in all grades, and that Provincial field-officers and generals were to enjoy no rank with Imperial officers of the same standing. Nevertheless Braddock was too capable a man to blind himself to the merit of the ablest of his coadjutors; and it was in terms honourable to himself that he invited and obtained the services of Colonel George Washington upon his staff.

| May. |

On the 10th of May Braddock reached his base at the junction of Wills' Creek with the Potomac, where the former trading station had been supplanted by a fort built of logs and called, in honour of the Commander-in-Chief, by the name of Fort Cumberland. It was a mere clearing in a vast forest, an oasis, as it has happily been termed, in a wilderness of leaves.[257] Here the troops had already been assembled, the Forty-fourth and Forty-eighth, each now raised by recruits from Virginia to a strength of seven hundred men, a detachment of one hundred of the Royal Artillery, thirty sailors lent by Commodore Keppel, helpful men as are all of their kind, and four hundred and fifty Virginian militia, excellently fitted for the work before them but much despised by the regular troops. The whole force amounted to about twenty-two hundred men. Fifty Indian warriors, a source of unfailing interest to the bucolic British soldiers, were also seen in the camp in all their barbaric finery of paint and feathers; for Braddock, whatever his bigotry in favour of pipe-clay, was far too wise to underrate the value of Indian scouts.

May 3.
June 7.

A long month of delay followed, for the cannon did not arrive until a week later than Braddock, and the arrangements were still backward and confused. The General, doubtless with good reason, railed furiously at the roguery and ill-faith of the contractors; but it is sufficiently evident that what was lacking at headquarters was a talent for organisation. And meanwhile, though Braddock knew it not, events of incalculable moment were going forward elsewhere during those very weeks. The French had not failed to take note of the reinforcements sent by England to America, and had replied by equipping a fleet of eighteen ships and embarking three thousand troops to sail under their convoy to Canada. The departure of this fleet was long delayed, and the dilatory British Government had time to despatch two squadrons to intercept it; but the French, putting to sea at last in May, contrived to elude the British cruisers and arrived safely at Louisburg and Quebec. Three only of their ships, having lagged behind the rest, found themselves off Cape Race in the presence of Admiral Boscawen's squadron. The two nations were nominally at peace, but the fleets opened fire, and the engagement ended in the capture of two of the French ships. Whether Newcastle desired it or not, England by this act was irrevocably committed to war.

June 10.
June 16.

It was just three days after this action that Braddock's force moved out of Fort Cumberland for its tedious march through the forest. Three hundred axemen led the way to cut and clear the road, which being but twelve feet wide was filled with waggons, pack-horses and artillery, so that the troops were obliged to march in the forest on either hand. Scouts scoured the ground in advance and flanking parties were thrown out against surprise, for Braddock was no mere soldier of the parade-ground. The march was insufferably slow, the horses being weak from want of forage, and the column dragged its length wearily along, "moving always in dampness and shade,"[258] through the gloomy interminable forest. Who can reckon the moral effect wrought on the ignorant and superstitious minds of simple English lads by that dreary trail through the heart of the wilderness? Day after day they toiled on without sight of the sun, and night after night over the camp-fire the Provincials filled them with hideous tales of Indian ferocity and assured them, in heavy jest, that they would be beaten.[259] The Forty-eighth had stood firm at Falkirk; but the Forty-fourth had suffered heavily at Prestonpans, and such preparation could be wholesome for no regiment. Eight days' march saw the column advanced but thirty miles on its way, many of the men sick and most of the horses worn out, with no prospect ahead but that of a worse road than ever. Then came a report that five hundred French were on their way to reinforce Fort Duquêsne; and by Washington's advice Braddock decided to leave the heavy baggage, together with a guard under Colonel Dunbar, to follow as best it could, and himself to push on with a body of chosen troops. Twelve hundred men were accordingly selected, and with these and a convoy reduced to ten guns, thirty waggons, and several pack-horses, the advance was resumed. Still progress continued to be wonderfully slow. The traditions of Flanders were strong in Braddock, and by dint of halting, as Washington said, to level every molehill and to throw a bridge over every brook, he occupied four whole days in traversing the next twelve miles.

| July. |

At length, on the 7th of July, the column reached the mouth of Turtle Creek, a stream which enters the Monongahela about eight miles from its junction with the Alleghany, or in other words from Fort Duquêsne. The direct way, though the shorter, lay through a difficult country and a dangerous defile, so Braddock resolved to ford the Monongahela, fetch a compass, and ford it once more, in order to reach his destination. The French meanwhile had received intelligence of his advance on the 5th, and were not a little alarmed. The force at the disposal of M. Contrecoeur, the commandant of Fort Duquêsne, consisted only of a few companies of regular troops, with a considerable body of Canadians and nearly nine hundred Indians. He resolved, however, to send off a detachment under Captain Beaujeu to meet the British on the march, and told off to that officer a force of about seventy regulars, twice as many Canadians, and six hundred and fifty Indians, or about nine hundred men in all. Early in the morning of the 8th this detachment marched away from Fort Duquêsne, intending to wait in ambush for the British at some favourable spot, and by preference at the second ford of the Monongahela.

| July 8. |

Braddock also had moved off early in the same morning, but it was nearly one o'clock when he forded the Monongahela for the second time. He himself fully expected to be attacked at this point, and had sent forward a strong advanced party under Lieutenant-Colonel Gage, to clear the opposite bank. No enemy however was encountered, for Beaujeu had been delayed by some trouble with his Indians, and had been unable to reach the ford in time. The main body of the British therefore crossed the river with perfect regularity and order, for Braddock wished to impress the minds of any Frenchmen that might be watching him with a sense of his superiority. The sky was cloudless, and the men, full of confidence and spirit, took pride in a movement nearer akin than any other during their weary march to the displays of the parade-ground in which they had been trained. On reaching the farther bank the column made a short halt for rest, and then resumed the march along a narrow track parallel to the river and at the base of a steep ridge of hills. Around it on all sides the forest frowned thick and impenetrable; and Braddock took every possible precaution against surprise. Several guides, with six Virginian light horsemen, led the way; a musket-shot behind them came an advanced party of Gage's vanguard followed by the vanguard itself, and then in succession a party of axemen to clear the road, two guns with their ammunition-waggons, and a rear-guard. Then without any interval came the convoy, headed by a few light horsemen, a working party, and three guns; the waggons following as heretofore on the track, and the troops making their way through the forest to right and left, with abundance of parties pushed well out on either flank.

At a little distance from the ford the track passed over a wide and bushy ravine. Gage crossed this ravine with his advanced guard, and the main body was just descending to it when Gage's guides and horsemen suddenly fell back, and a man dressed like an Indian, but with an officer's gorget, was seen hurrying along the path. At sight of the British, Beaujeu (for the figure so strangely arrayed seems to have been no other) turned suddenly and waved his hat. The signal was followed by a wild war-whoop from his Indians and by a sharp fire upon the advancing British from the trees in their front. Gage's men at once deployed with great steadiness and returned the fire in a succession of deliberate volleys. They could not see a man of the enemy, so that they shot of necessity at haphazard, but the mere sound of the musketry was sufficient to scare Beaujeu's Canadians, who fled away shamefully to Fort Duquêsne. The third volley laid Beaujeu dead on the ground, and Gage's two field-pieces coming into action speedily drove the Indians away from the British front.

Meanwhile the red-coats steadily advanced, the men cheering lustily and shouting "God save the King"; and Captain Dumas, who had succeeded Beaujeu in the command of the French, almost gave up the day for lost. His handful of regular troops, however, stood firm, and he and his brother officers by desperate exertions succeeded in rallying the Indians. The regulars and such few of the Canadians as stood by them held their ground staunchly, and opened a fire of platoons which checked the ardour of Gage's men; while the Indians, yelling like demons but always invisible, streamed away through the forest along both flanks of the British, and there, from every coign of vantage that skilful bushmen could find, poured a deadly fire upon the hapless red-coats. The cheering was silenced, for the men began to fall fast. For a time they kept their ranks and swept the unheeding forest with volley after volley, which touched no enemy through the trees. They could see no foe, and yet the bullets rained continually and pitilessly upon them from front, flank, and rear, like a shower from a cloudless sky. The trial at last was greater than they could bear. They abandoned their guns, they broke their ranks, and huddling themselves together like a herd of fallow-deer they fell back in disorder, a mere helpless mass of terrified men.

Just at this moment Braddock came up to the front. On hearing the fire he had left four hundred men under Colonel Sir Peter Halket of the Forty-fourth to guard the baggage, and had advanced with the remainder to Gage's assistance. As the fresh troops came up, Gage's routed infantry plunged blindly in among them, seeking shelter from the eternal hail of bullets, and threw them likewise into confusion. In a short time the whole of Braddock's force, excepting the Virginians and Halket's baggage-guard, was broken up into a succession of heaving groups, without order and without cohesion, some facing this way, some facing that way, conscious only of the hideous whooping of the Indians, of bullets falling thickly among them from they knew not whence, and that they could neither charge nor return the fire. The Virginians alone, who were accustomed to such work, kept their presence of mind, and taking shelter behind the trees began to answer the Indian fire in the Indian fashion. A few of the British strove to imitate them as well as their inexperience would permit; but Braddock would have none of such things. Such fighting was not prescribed in the drill-book nor familiar in the battlefields of Flanders,[260] and he would tolerate no such disregard of order and discipline. Raging and cursing furiously he drove British and Virginians alike back to their fellows with his sword; and then noting that the fire was hottest from a hill on the right flank of his advance, he ordered Lieutenant-Colonel Burton to attack it with the Forty-eighth. The panic had already spread far, and it was only with infinite difficulty that Burton could persuade a hundred men to follow him. He was presently shot down, and at his fall the whole of his men turned back. The scene now became appalling. The gunners stood for a time to their guns and sent round after round crashing uselessly into the forest; but the infantry stood packed together in abject terror, still loading and firing, now into the air, now into their comrades, or fighting furiously with the officers who strove to make them form. Braddock galloped to and fro through the fire, mounting fresh horses as fast as they were killed under him, and storming as though at a field-day. Washington, by miracle unwounded though his clothes were tattered with bullets, seconded him with as noble an example of courage and devotion; but it was too clear that the day was lost. Sixty out of eighty-six officers had fallen, and Braddock, after the slaughter had continued for three hours, ordered the wreck of his force to retreat.

He was still struggling to bring the men off in some kind of order when he fell from his horse, the fifth that the Indians' fire had compelled him to mount on that day, pierced by a bullet through arm and lungs. The unwounded remnant of his troops instantly broke loose and fled away. In vain Washington and others strove to rally them at the ford; they might as well have tried to stop the wild bears of the mountains.[261] They splashed through the river exhausted though they were, and ran on with the whoops of the Indians still ringing in their ears. Gage succeeded in rallying about eighty at the second ford; but the rest were not to be stayed. Braddock, stricken to the death, begged to be left on the battlefield, but some officers lifted him and carried him away, for not a man of the soldiers would put a hand to him. Weak as he was, and racked with the pain of his wound and the anguish of his defeat, the gallant man still kept command and still gave his orders. On passing the Monongahela he bade his bearers halt, and sending Washington away to Dunbar for provisions and transport he passed the night among the handful of men that had been rallied by Gage.

July 9.
July 10.

On the next morning some order was restored, and the retreat was continued. Meanwhile stragglers had already reached Dunbar's camp with wild tidings of disaster and defeat, and many of the teamsters had already taken to their heels. After one more day of torture Braddock himself was carried into the camp. On the march he had issued directions for the collection and relief of stragglers, and now he gave, or is said to have given, his last order, for the destruction of all waggons and stores that could not be carried back to Fort Cumberland. Accordingly scores of waggons were burned, the provisions were destroyed, and guns and ammunition, not easily to be replaced in the colonies, were blown up or spoiled. Then the relics of the army set out in shame and confusion for the return march of sixty miles to Fort Cumberland. Braddock travelled but a little distance with it. His faithful aide-de-camp, Captain Orme, though himself badly wounded, remained with him to the end and has recorded his last words; but there was little speech now left in the rough, bullying martinet, whose mouth had once been so full of oaths, and whose voice had been the terror of every soldier. It was not only that his lungs were shot through and through, but that his heart was broken. Throughout the first day's march he lay white and silent, with his life's blood bubbling up through his lips, nor was it till evening that his misery found vent in the almost feminine ejaculation, "Who would have thought it"? Again through the following day he remained silent, until towards sunset, as if to sum up repentance for past failure and good hope for the future, he murmured gently, "Another time we shall know better how to deal with them." And so having learned his lesson he lay still, and a few minutes later he was dead.

With all his faults this rude indomitable spirit appeals irresistibly to our sympathy. He had been chosen by the Duke of Cumberland, whose notions of an officer, in Horace Walpole's words, were drawn from the purest German classics, the classics initiated by Frederick William and consecrated by Frederick the Great. It was the passion of the Hohenzollerns, great soldiers though they were, to dress their men like dolls and to manipulate them like puppets; but, dearly though they loved the mechanical exercise of the parade-ground, they knew that the minuteness of training and the severity of discipline thereby entailed were but means to an end. In the eyes of Cumberland, though he was very far from a blind or a stupid man, powder, pipe-clay, and precision loomed so large as to appear an end in themselves. He could point too to the initial success of his attack at Fontenoy, which was simply an elaborate parade-movement; but he forgot that the battlefields of a Prussian army and the adversaries of a Prussian general were to be found on the familiar lands of Silesia, Brandenburg, and Saxony, whereas the fighting-grounds of the British were dispersed far and wide among distant and untrodden countries, and their enemies such as were not to be encountered according to the precepts of Montecuculi and Turenne. It was as a favourite exponent of Cumberland's military creed that Braddock was sent to North America. He was born and trained for such actions as Fontenoy; and it was his fate to be confronted with a difficult problem in savage warfare. His task was that which since his day has been repeatedly set to British officers, namely to improvise a new system of fighting wherewith to meet the peculiar tactics of a strange enemy in a strange country. Too narrow, too rigid, and too proud to apprehend the position, he applied the time-honoured methods of Flanders, and he failed. Other officers have since fallen into the like error, owing not a little to a false system of training, and have failed likewise; and vast as is our experience in savage warfare, it may be that the tale of such officers is not yet fully told. Nevertheless, though Braddock's ideal of a British officer may have been mistaken, it cannot be called low. In rout and ruin and disgrace, with the hand of death gripping tightly at his throat, his stubborn resolution never wavered and his untameable spirit was never broken. He kept his head and did his work to the last, and thought of his duty while thought was left in him. His body was buried under the road, that the passage of the troops over it might obliterate his grave and save it from desecration from the Indians. But the lesson which he had learned too late was not lost on his successors, and it may truly be said that it was over the bones of Braddock that the British advanced again to the conquest of Canada.

The losses in this disastrous action were very heavy; the devotion of the officers, whose conduct was beyond all praise, leading them almost to annihilation. Among the wounded were two men who were to become conspicuous at a later day, Gage the leader of the advanced guard and Captain Horatio Gates of the garrison of New York. Of thirteen hundred and seventy-three non-commissioned officers and men, but four hundred and fifty-nine came off unharmed; and the wounded that were left on the field were tortured and murdered by the Indians after their barbarous manner. The loss of the French was trifling. Three officers were killed and four wounded, all of them at the critical moment while their men were wavering; nine white men also were killed and wounded, and a larger but inconsiderable number of Indians. It was in fact a total and crushing defeat. Yet Count Dieskau, an officer high in the French service in Canada, expressed no surprise when he heard of it, for it was the French rule, founded on bitter experience, never to expose regular troops in the forest without a sufficient force of Indians and irregulars to cover them. The Virginians, whose admirable behaviour had been the one creditable feature in the action, had shown that abundance of good irregular troops were to be found in America; and it was evident that the British needed only to learn from their enemies in order to defeat them.

CHAPTER III

The first blow against the French in America had failed; it must now be seen how it fared with the operations entrusted to Shirley, Johnson, and Monckton. Shirley, at Massachusetts, had been busy since the beginning of the year in calling the Northern provinces to arms, and they had responded nobly, Massachusetts alone raising forty-five hundred men, and the rest of New England and New York nearly three thousand more. The point first selected for attack was Fort Beauséjour on the Acadian isthmus, for which object two thousand volunteers of New England were sent up to Monckton. Adding to them a handful of regular troops from the garrison,[262] Monckton sailed away without delay to his work. On the 1st of June the expedition anchored in the bay before Fort Beauséjour, which after a fortnight's siege and the feeblest of defences fell, together with a smaller fort called Fort Gaspereau, into Monckton's hands. This success was followed by the expulsion of the greater part of the French population from Acadia, a harsh measure necessitated entirely by the duplicity of the Jesuit priests and of the Canadian Government, who had never ceased to stir up the unhappy peasants to revolt. From henceforth, therefore, Acadia may be dismissed from the sphere of active operations.

The attack on Crown Point was a more serious matter, for which the force entrusted to William Johnson included some three thousand Provincial troops from New England and New Hampshire, and three hundred Indians. Johnson had seen no service and was innocent of all knowledge of war, but his influence with the Indians was very great, and as he came from New York his appointment could not but be pleasing to that province. His men were farmers and farmers' sons, excellent material but neither drilled nor trained. With the exception of one regiment, all wore their own clothes, and far the greater number brought with them their own arms. After long delay, owing to the jealousies of the various provinces and to defective organisation, the force was assembled at Albany, and in August began to move up the Hudson towards Lake George, a new name bestowed by Johnson in honour of his sovereign. At the carrying-place, where the line of advance left the Hudson, was built a fort, which was first called Fort Lyman but subsequently Fort Edward, by which latter name the reader should remember it. Here five hundred men were left to complete and to man the works, while the remainder, moving casually and leisurely forward, advanced to the lake and encamped upon its southern border.

Meanwhile the French, warned by papers captured from Braddock of the design against Crown Point, had sent thither thirty-five hundred regular troops, Canadians and Indians, under the command of Count Dieskau, an officer who had served formerly under Marshal Saxe. There were two lines by which Johnson could advance against them, the one directly up Lake George, the other by the stream named Wood Creek, which runs parallel with it into Lake Champlain. The junction of both passages is commanded by a promontory on the western side of Lake Champlain, called by the French Carillon, but more famous under its native name of Ticonderoga. To this point Dieskau advanced with a mixed force of fifteen hundred men, and from thence pushed forward to attack Johnson in his camp. The sequel may be briefly told. Johnson had imprudently detached five hundred men with some vague idea of cutting off Dieskau's retreat; and these were caught in an ambuscade and very roughly handled. But when, elated by this success, Dieskau advanced against Johnson's camp he was met by a most stubborn resistance; and finally his troops were driven back in disorder and he himself wounded and taken prisoner. Johnson, however, did not follow up this fortunate success. Shirley repeatedly adjured him to advance to Ticonderoga, but was answered that the troops were unable to move through sickness, indiscipline, bad food, and bad clothing. Johnson lingered on in his camp until the end of November, with his men on the verge of mutiny, and having built a fort at the southern end of the lake, which he called Fort William Henry, retreated to the Hudson. He was rewarded for his victory by a vote of five thousand pounds from the British Parliament and by a baronetcy from the King; but none the less his enterprise was a failure, and Crown Point was left safely in the hands of the French.

The expedition against Niagara was undertaken by Shirley himself, in all the pride of a lawyer turned general. Hitherto he had but planned campaigns on paper; now he was to execute one in the field. His base of operations was, like Johnson's, the town of Albany, and his force consisted of his own regiment and Pepperrell's, which, although the King's troops and wearing the King's uniform, consisted none the less of raw Provincial recruits, together with one regiment of New Jersey militia, in all twenty-five hundred men. From Albany the force ascended the river Mohawk in bateaux to the great carrying-place, where the town of Rome now stands; from which point the bateaux were drawn overland on sledges to Wood Creek,[263] where they were again launched to float down stream to Lake Oneida and so to the little fort of Oswego on Lake Ontario. As might have been expected with an amateur,

Shirley's force arrived at its destination long before his supplies, so that his force was compelled to wait for some time inactive and on short rations. The French, too, having learned of this design also from the papers taken at the Monongahela, had reinforced their garrisons not only at Niagara but at Fort Frontenac at the north-eastern outlet of the lake. This materially increased Shirley's difficulties, for unless he first captured Frontenac the French could slip across the lake directly he was fairly on his way to Niagara, take Oswego and cut him off from his base. To be brief, the task, rendered doubly arduous by dearth of provisions, was too great for Shirley's strength; and at the end of October he abandoned the enterprise, having accomplished no more than to throw a garrison of seven hundred men into Oswego.

So amid general disappointment ended the American campaign. Of the four expeditions one only had succeeded; all of the rest had failed, one of them with disaster. Nor did this disaster end with the retreat from the Monongahela, for no sooner had Dunbar retired from the frontier than the Indians, at the instigation of the French, swarmed into Virginia, Maryland, and Pennsylvania to the massacre and pillage of the scattered settlements on the border. Washington with fifteen hundred Virginian militia did what he could to protect three hundred miles of frontier, but with so small a force the duty was far beyond his power or the power of any man. Reinforce him, however, the Assembly of Pennsylvania would not. They closed their ears even to the cry of their own settlers for arms and ammunition, and for legislation to enable them to organise themselves for defence. The Assembly was intent only on fighting with the Governor. The members would yield neither to his representations nor to the entreaties of their fellow-citizens; and it was not until the enemy had advanced within sixty miles of Philadelphia that, grudgingly and late, they armed the Governor with powers to check the Indian invasion. It was none too soon, for the French had taken note of the large population of pauperised Germans, Irish, "white servants," and transported criminals in Pennsylvania, and were preparing to turn it into a recruiting-ground for the French service.[264]

Thus closed the year 1755, with hostilities in full play between English and French in North America. Yet war had not been declared, nor, though it was certain to come, had any preparation been made for it. The measures taken at the beginning of 1755 sufficiently indicate the feebleness and vacillation of a foolish and effete Administration. In February some addition had been made to the infantry by raising the strength of the Guards and of seven regiments of the Line; and in March the King sent a message to Parliament requesting an augmentation of the forces by land and sea. The Ministry employed the powers thus given to them in raising five thousand marines in fifty independent companies, and placing them expressly under the command of the Lord High Admiral. It is said[265] that Newcastle refused to raise new regiments from jealousy of the Duke of Cumberland's nomination of officers, and there is nothing incredible in the assertion. But though this measure pointed at least to activity on the part of the fleet, never were British ships employed to less purpose. The squadron sent out under Boscawen to intercept the French reinforcements on their way to Louisburg was considerably inferior to the enemy's fleet, and required to be reinforced, of course at the cost of confusion and delay, before it was fit to fulfil its duty. Fresh trouble was caused in May by the King's departure for Hanover, a pleasure which he refused to deny himself despite the critical state of affairs in England. During his absence his power was delegated, as was customary, to a Council of Regency, a body which was always disposed to reserve matters of importance for the King's decision, and was doubly infirm of purpose with such a creature as Newcastle among its ruling spirits. A powerful fleet under Sir Edward Hawke was ready for sea and for action; and the Duke of Cumberland, remembering the consequences of peaceful hostility in 1742 and 1743, was for throwing off the mask, declaring open war and striking swiftly and at once. He was, however, overruled, and Hawke's fleet was sent to sea with instructions that bound it to a violation of peace and a travesty of war. The King meanwhile was solicitous above all things for the security of Hanover. Subsidiary treaties with Bavaria and Saxony for the protection of the Electorate had for some time existed, but were expired or expiring; and now that some return for the subsidies of bygone years seemed likely to be required, the contracting States stood out for better terms. The King therefore entered into a new treaty with Hesse-Cassel for the supply of eight thousand men, and with Russia for forty thousand more, in the event of the invasion of Hanover.

| Sept. 15. |

With these treaties in his pocket he returned to England, to find the nation full of alarm and discontent. Nor was the nation at fault in its feelings. In August the news of Braddock's defeat had arrived and had been received with impotent dismay. Yet nothing was done to retrieve the disaster, and two full months passed before a few thousand men were added to all three arms of the Army.[266] Meanwhile Newcastle, after vainly endeavouring to persuade Pitt to serve under him, had strengthened his ministry somewhat by securing the accession of Henry Fox; and on the 13th of November the King opened Parliament, announcing, as well he might, the speedy approach of war. A long debate followed, wherein Pitt surpassed himself in denunciation of subsidiary treaties and contemptuous condemnation of Newcastle; but the party of the Court was too strong for him, and the treaties were confirmed by a large majority. Pitt was dismissed from his office of Paymaster, and Fox having been promoted to be Secretary of State was succeeded by Lord Barrington as Secretary at War. Lastly, some weeks later, General Ligonier was most unjustly ousted from the post of Master-General of the Ordnance, to make way for a place-hunter who was not ashamed thus to disgrace his honoured title of Duke of Marlborough. It seemed, in fact, as though there were a general conspiracy to banish ability from high station.

| Nov. 27. |
| Dec. 5. |
| Dec. 8. |

A fortnight later the estimates for the Army were submitted to Parliament. Notwithstanding the urgent danger of the situation, the number of men proposed on the British Establishment little exceeded thirty-four thousand men for Great Britain and thirteen thousand for the colonies. A few days afterwards the question was debated, and Barrington then announced a further increase of troops; whereupon Pitt very pertinently asked the unanswerable question why all these augmentations were made so late. The House, however, was in earnest as to the military deficiencies of the country. Fox had taunted Pitt by challenging him to bring forward a Militia Bill, and Pitt seized the opportunity offered by a debate on the Militia to give the outlines of a scheme for making that force more efficient. His proposals were embodied in a Bill, which formed the basis of the Militia Act that was to be passed, as shall be seen, in the following year. So far therefore the Commons forced upon the Government and the country at least the consideration of really valuable work.

| 1756. |

On the re-assembly of Parliament after Christmas an estimate was presented for the formation of ten new regiments, to be made up in part of certain supplementary companies which had been added to existing battalions in 1755. These new regiments were, in order of seniority, Abercromby's, Napier's, Lambton's, Whitmore's, Campbell's, Perry's, Lord Charles Manner's, Arabin's, Anstruther's and Montagu's, and they are still with us numbered in succession the Fiftieth to the Fifty-ninth.[267] At the same time a new departure was made by adding a light troop apiece to eleven regiments of dragoons, both men and horses being specially equipped for the work which is now expected of all cavalry, but which was then entrusted chiefly to irregular horse formed upon the model of the Austrian Hussars. Yet another novelty was foreshadowed in February when a Bill was introduced to enable the King to grant commissions to foreign Protestants in America. The origin of this measure, according to Horace Walpole, was a proposal made by one Prevost, a Protestant refugee, to raise four battalions of Swiss and Provincials in America, with a British officer for colonel-in-chief but with a fair number of foreigners holding other commissions. Quite as probably this new step was quickened, if not suggested, by the news that the French contemplated the enlistment of recruits among the foreign population of British America. The vote for these four battalions was passed without a division, though Pitt opposed the Bill with all his power and was supported by a petition from the Agent of Massachusetts. He was vehement for the employment of British soldiers to fight British battles; whereas so far the most important military measure of King and ministers had been the hiring of Germans. The Bill was none the less passed, and on the 4th of March the order for the enlistment of the four battalions was given. Lord Loudoun was to be their Colonel-in-Chief, Pennsylvania their recruiting-ground, and their title the Royal Americans, an appellation long since displaced by the famous number of the Sixtieth.

| March 23. |

Amid all these preparations, however, the nation throughout the first months of 1756 lived in abject terror of an invasion. France on her side had not been backward in equipping herself for the approaching contest. Great activity at Toulon had been followed by equal activity at Dunkirk, and despite good information as to the true object of the armaments fitted out at these two ports, the people naturally, and the Government most culpably, persisted in the belief that they were designed for a descent upon Britain herself. Few troops were ready to meet such a descent, for votes cannot improvise trained officers and men, and the folly of the Administration had done its worst to discourage enlistment. When the danger seemed nearest, many great landowners had interested themselves personally and with great success to obtain recruits; and among others Lord Ilchester and Lord Digby in Somerset had attracted some of the best material to be found in rural England, promising that the men so enlisted should not be required to serve outside the Kingdom. Notwithstanding this pledge, however, these recruits were by order of the Ministry forcibly driven on board transports and shipped off to Gibraltar. Never was there more brutal and heartless instance of the ill-faith kept by a British Government towards the British soldier. Having thus checked the flow of recruits at home, the Ministry turned to Holland and asked for the troops which she was bound by treaty to furnish. The request was refused; whereupon a royal message was actually sent to Parliament announcing that the King in the present peril had sent for his contingent of Hessian troops from Germany, for the defence of England. The message was received with murmurs in the Commons, as well it might be, but it was not opposed; and indeed the climax of disgrace was not yet reached. Whether from desire to embarrass Newcastle or to pay court to the King, Lord George Sackville, an officer whom before long we shall know too well, expressed a preference for Hanoverians over Hessians, and proposed an address praying the King to bring over his own electoral troops. Pitt left his sickbed and came down, ill as he was, to the House, to appeal to the history of the past and to the pride of every Englishman against the motion; yet it was passed by a majority of nearly three to one. The Lords consented to join the Commons in this address, the King granted their prayer, and the result was that both Hanoverians and Hessians were imported to defend this poor Island that could not defend herself.

| Jan. 16. |

The next business brought before Parliament furnished new evidence of the general confusion of affairs. As might have been foreseen, Frederick of Prussia had viewed with no friendly eye the treaty made by King George with Russia; and he now proposed, as an alternative, that Hanover and England should combine with Prussia to keep all troops whatsoever from entering the German Empire. Since Frederick had already announced his intention of attacking the Russians if they moved across the frontier, and since there was good reason to apprehend that, if driven to desperation, he might join with the French in overrunning Hanover, the Russian treaty was thrown over, and the new arrangement accepted by King George. The pecuniary conditions attached to the agreement were duly ratified by the House of Commons in May, with results that were to reach further than were yet dreamed of. Then at last, apparently as an after-thought, war was formally declared. The country being thus definitely committed to a struggle which might be for life or death, the Lords supported by Newcastle seized the opportunity to reject the Militia Bill, which was the one important military measure so far brought forward. The general helplessness of the moment, owing to the absence of a strong hand at the helm, is almost incredible.

| April 8. |
| April 18. |

Meanwhile the French had struck their first blow, not on the shores of Britain, but at Minorca. As early as in January the Ministry had received good intelligence of the true destination of the enemy's armaments, but had made no sufficient preparation to meet the danger; nor was it until the 7th of April that it sent a fleet of ten ships, ill-manned and ill-found, under Admiral Byng to the Mediterranean. On the day following Byng's departure twelve ships of the line under M. de la Galissonière, with transports containing sixteen thousand troops under the Duke of Richelieu, weighed from Toulon, and on the 18th dropped anchor off the port of Ciudadella, at the north-western end of Minorca. General Blakeney, the governor, had received warning of the intended attack two days before, and had made such preparations as he could for defence; but the means at his disposal were but poor. He had four regiments, the Fourth, Twenty-third, Twenty-fourth, and Thirty-fourth of the

Line; to which Commodore Edgcumbe, who was lying off Mahon with a squadron too weak to encounter the French, had added all the marines that he could spare before sailing away to Gibraltar. Even so, however, Blakeney could muster little more than twenty-eight hundred men. But his most serious difficulty was lack of officers. He himself had won his ensigncy under Cutts the Salamander at Venloo, and he had maintained his reputation for firmness and courage at Stirling in 1745, but he was now past eighty, crippled with gout and unfit to bear the incessant labours of a siege. Nevertheless he was obliged to take the burden upon him from sheer dearth of senior officers. The lieutenant-governor of the Island, the governor of its principal defence, Fort Philip, and the colonels of all four regiments were absent; nineteen subalterns had never yet joined their respective corps, and nine more officers were absent on recruiting duties. In all five-and-thirty officers were wanting at their posts. It was the old evil against which George the First had struggled in vain, and it was now about to bear bitter fruit.

| April. |
| May. |

Richelieu landed on the 18th, and Blakeney at once withdrew the whole of his force to Fort St. Philip in order to make his stand there. This fortress, which commanded the town and harbour of Mahon, was probably the most elaborate possessed by the British, and was inferior in strength to few strongholds in Europe. Apart from the ordinary elaborations of the school of Vauban, it was strengthened by countless mines and galleries hewn out of the solid rock, which afforded unusual protection to the defenders. Blakeney had little time to break up the roads or otherwise to hinder the French advance; and Richelieu, marching into the town of Mahon on the 19th, was able a few days later to begin the siege. His operations, however, were unskilfully conducted, and the garrison defended itself with great spirit. An officer of engineers, Major Cunningham by name, while on his way to England from Minorca on leave, had heard of the French designs upon the Island and had instantly hurried back to his old post to assist in the defence; and his skill and resource were of inestimable value. So clumsily in fact did the French manage their operations that it was not until the 8th of May that their batteries began to produce the slightest effect.

Byng meanwhile had arrived at Gibraltar and had learned what was going forward. He carried the Seventh Fusiliers on board his fleet for Minorca, and had orders to embark yet another battalion from Gibraltar as a further reinforcement. General Fowke, however, who was in command at the Rock, urged that his instructions on this latter point were discretionary only and that he could not spare a battalion, having barely sufficient men to furnish reliefs for the ordinary guards. He therefore declined to grant more than two hundred and fifty men, to replace the marines landed from the fleet by Commodore Edgcumbe. It is instructive to note the difficulties imposed upon the commanders by the neglect of the Government. Hitherto one of the first measures taken in prospect of a war had been the reinforcement of the Mediterranean garrisons. Now, after a full year of warning, they were left unstrengthened and unsupported. Nay, Richelieu had lain in front of Fort St. Philip for three whole weeks before three battalions were at last ordered to sail for Gibraltar.[268] Byng's fleet was so slenderly manned that he required the Seventh Fusiliers for duty on board ship, and therefore asked Fowke for a battalion for Minorca; Fowke's position was so weak that he dared not comply; and Blakeney's force was so inadequate that, though he could indeed hold his own in the fortress, he dared not venture his troops in a sortie.

| June 6. |
| June 9. |
| June 14. |
| June 27. |
| June 28. |

At length on the 19th of May Byng came in sight of Fort St. Philip, and on the following day fought the indecisive action and made the unfortunate retreat which became memorable through his subsequent fate. The besieged, though greatly disappointed by his withdrawal, still defended themselves stoutly and with fine spirit. The fortress was well stored and the batteries were well and effectively served. Six more battalions were now sent to Richelieu, and the French plan of attack was altered. New batteries were built, which on the 6th of June opened fire from over one hundred guns and mortars, inflicting much damage and making a considerable breach. The British repaired the injured works and stood to their guns as steadily as ever; but on the 9th the French fire reopened more hotly than before and battered two new breaches. Matters were now growing serious; and on the 14th a party of the garrison made a sally, drove the French from several of their batteries and spiked the guns, but pursuing their success too far were surrounded and captured almost to a man. Still Richelieu hesitated to storm; nor was it until the night of the 27th that he nerved himself for a final effort and made a grand attack upon several quarters of the fortress simultaneously. The defence was of the stubbornest, and the successful explosion of a mine sent three companies of French grenadiers flying into the air; but three of the principal outworks were carried, and the ablest officer of the garrison, Lieutenant-Colonel Jefferies, while hurrying down to save one of them, was cut off and made prisoner with a hundred of his men. Cunningham also was severely wounded and rendered unfit for duty. With hardly men enough left to him to man the guns, Blakeney on the 28th capitulated with the honours of war, and the garrison was embarked for Gibraltar. The siege had lasted for seventy days and had cost the French at the least two thousand men. The losses of the garrison were relatively small, amounting to less than four hundred killed and wounded, and the surrender was no dishonour to the British Army; but there was no disguising the disgraceful fact that Minorca was gone.

On the 14th of July the news reached England, and the nation, frantic with rage and shame, looked about savagely for a scapegoat. Bitter and cruel attacks were made even upon poor old Blakeney, who for all his fourscore years had never changed his clothes nor gone to bed during the ten weeks of the siege. Fowke was tried by court-martial for disobedience of orders in refusing to send the battalion required of him from Gibraltar, and though acquitted of all but an error in judgment and sentenced to a year's suspension only, was dismissed the service by the King. Finally, as is well known, the public indignation fastened itself upon Byng; and the unfortunate Admiral was shot because Newcastle deserved to be hanged. Old Blakeney alone, as was his desert, became a hero and was rewarded with an Irish peerage. Amid all the disgrace of that miserable time men found leisure to chronicle with a sneer that the veteran went to Court in a hackney coach with a foot-soldier behind it. St. James's would not have been the worse for a few more courtiers and lacqueys of the same rugged stamp.

More disasters were at hand; but the general paralysis in England continued. Such troops as the country possessed were still distributed as though an invasion were imminent. There was a camp at Cheltenham under Lord George Sackville, and another in Dorsetshire; the Hessians were at Winchester, the Hanoverians about Maidstone, the artillery massed together under the Duke of Marlborough at Byfleet; all doing nothing when there was so much to be done. The news of Braddock's defeat was nearly eight months old when Byng sailed for the Mediterranean, but not a man had been embarked to America. Up to the end of March the only step taken had been the despatch of Colonel Webb to supersede Shirley as Commander-in-Chief, but with instructions to yield the command to General Abercromby, who was also under orders for America, on his arrival; while Abercromby in turn was to give place to Lord Loudoun. At last, towards the end of April the Thirty-fifth Foot and the Forty-second Highlanders were embarked and reached New York late in June; and a month later Lord Loudoun arrived and assumed the command. Pitt before its departure had described the force under Loudoun's orders as a scroll of paper, and the description was little remote from the truth. Of the Sixtieth hardly one battalion was yet raised; Shirley's and Pepperrell's regiments, or what was left of them, were in garrison at Oswego; and the levies of the various colonies as usual were long in enlisting, late in arriving, and not too well supplied. Finally, each several contingent was jealously kept by its province under its own orders and control.

Shirley, undismayed by the failures of the previous year, meditated further operations in the direction of Fort Frontenac and Niagara, and against Crown Point; and with this view he had accumulated supplies along the route to Oswego on the one hand, and at Forts Edward and William Henry on the other. The troops which he had appointed for Niagara were the shattered remains of the Forty-fourth and Forty-eighth, part of his own and of Pepperrell's regiments, four independent regular companies from New York, and a small body of Provincials. The enterprise against Crown Point was assigned to the Provincial forces of New England and New York. Loudoun's instructions seem to have prescribed for him much the same line as Shirley had marked out for himself; but the new Commander-in-Chief conceived an immense and not wholly unreasonable contempt for Shirley and for all his works. In the first place, he found that his predecessor had emptied the military chest, and that there was remarkably little to show for the outlay. Oswego, on inspection by a competent engineer, was declared incapable of defence, being ill-designed and incomplete, while the garrison through sickness and neglect was in a shocking condition.[269] The fact was that the King's boats had been used to transport merchandise for sale by private speculators to the Indians, instead of food for the nourishment of the King's troops. Fort William Henry again was found to be in an indescribably filthy state. Graves, slaughter-houses, and latrines were scattered promiscuously about the camp; no discipline was maintained; provisions were scandalously wasted; and the men were dying at the rate of thirty a week. Loudoun decided almost immediately to abandon the attack on Niagara and to turn all his strength against Ticonderoga and Crown Point.

| August 12. |
| August 9. |
| August 14. |

Meanwhile there were sinister rumours that the French were likely to attack Oswego, and Loudoun sent Colonel Webb with the Forty-fourth regiment to reinforce the garrison. Webb had hardly reached the Great Carrying-place on his way, when the news met him that Oswego had already been captured. On the night of the 9th the Marquis of Montcalm, an energetic officer who had arrived in Canada in May 1755, had swooped down swiftly and secretly upon the fort with three thousand men, and after three days' cannonade had forced it to surrender. Webb at once retired with precipitation, and in alarm at a report that the French were advancing upon New York, burned the fort at the Great Carrying-place and retreated down the Mohawk.

Such timidity was worthy of Newcastle's nominee; and this disaster brought the whole of the operations to a standstill. Montcalm having burned Oswego retired to Ticonderoga, where with five thousand men he took up a position from which Loudoun could not hope, with the troops at his disposal, to dislodge him. The British General therefore contented himself with improving the defences of Fort Edward; and therewith ended the campaign of 1756 in North America. Everything had gone as ill as possible. Loudoun had shown great impatience with the Provincials, and the Provincials had taken no pains to help him. In Pennsylvania every conceivable obstacle was thrown in the way of recruiting; in New York there was not less friction over the quartering of the King's troops. There were reasons sufficient in the jealousy, the inexperience, and occasionally the corruption of the Provincials to excuse impatience in the General, but Loudoun was not conciliatory in manner nor had he the ability which commands confidence. He was, in fact, one more of the incompetent men nominated by an incompetent Administration. All that he could show for his first campaign was the loss of Oswego, the station which bound the British colonies to the great Indian trade with the West, the place of arms from which the chain of French posts was to be cut in two, in a word the sharpest and deadliest weapon in the armoury of British North America. Small wonder that the French were filled with triumph and the British colonies with dismay.

The news of yet another reverse heaped fuel on the flame of the nation's indignation against Newcastle; but meanwhile the cloud of war which had hung so long in menace over Europe burst at last in one tremendous storm. For some months past a league had been forming between France, Austria, Saxony, Russia, and Sweden to crush Frederick the Great and partition Prussia. France had been launched into this strange alliance by Madame de Pompadour, in revenge for Frederick's disdainful rejection of a friendly message; the Czarina likewise sought vengeance for an epigram; Austria burned to recover Silesia; Saxony had been enticed by Austria with the lure of a share in partitioned Prussia; and Sweden had been attracted by the bait of Pomerania. Frederick, fully aware of all that was going forward, resolved to meet the danger rather than await it, and boldly invading Saxony began the Seven Years' War. Where it should end no man could divine. All that was certain was that Frederick, far from protecting Hanover, would have much ado to defend himself. Thus, then, on the one side there was Hanover open to attack, and on the other Minorca lost, British naval reputation tarnished, and France triumphant in America. Further, though as yet men knew it not, the news of the loss of Calcutta and of the tragedy of the Black Hole was even then on its way across the ocean. The outcry against the Government rose to a dangerous height; Fox deserted Newcastle, and resigned; and at length, in

November, the shifty old jobber himself, after endless intrigues to retain office, reluctantly and ungracefully made way, nominally for the Duke of Devonshire, but in reality for William Pitt.

On the 2nd of December Parliament met, and the spirit of the new minister showed itself at once in the speech from the throne. The electoral troops and Hessians were to be sent back forthwith to Germany; and it was now the royal desire, which it had not been before Pitt took office, that the militia should be made more efficient. In a word, England was from henceforth to fight her battles for herself. Two days later leave was granted for the introduction of a Militia Bill, and on the 15th estimates were submitted for a British Establishment of thirty thousand men for the service of Great Britain and nineteen thousand for the colonies, besides two thousand artillery and engineers; the absence of Minorca from its usual place in the list of garrisons providing a significant comment on the whole. Of the additional troops fifteen thousand had already been appointed for enlistment in September, when orders had been issued for the raising of a second battalion to each of fifteen regiments of the Line.[270] These battalions were erected two years later into distinct regiments, of which ten still remain with us, numbered the Sixty-first to the Seventieth. This addition showed marks of Pitt's influence, but after the Christmas recess his handiwork was seen in a new and daring experiment, namely the formation of two regiments of Highlanders, each eleven hundred strong, which, though afterwards disbanded, became famous under the names of their Colonels, Fraser and Montgomery.[271] The idea was a bold one, for it struck the last weapon from the dying hands of Jacobitism and turned it against itself; and the result soon approved it as a success. The existing Scottish regiments were required to contribute eighty non-commissioned officers who could speak Gaelic;[272] and the Highlander from henceforth took his place not as a subverter of thrones but as a builder of empires. It is remarkable, concurrently, to note the sudden wave of energy which swept over the entire military administration in the first weeks of 1757, when the breath of one great man had once broken the springs and set the stagnant waters aflow. Shirley's and Pepperrell's regiments, which had been crippled and ruined at Oswego, were struck off the list of the Army to make room for more efficient corps.[273] Newcastle's feeble ministers had directed the embarkation of a single battalion only, besides drafts, to America: Pitt, without counter-ordering these, ordered the augmentation and despatch of seven battalions more.[274] The Forty-ninth regiment, which was serving in Jamaica, was increased to nearly double of its former strength, to hearten the colonists in that Island. The Royal Artillery was raised to a total of twenty-four companies and distributed into two battalions, and a company of Miners, first conceived of six months before, was incorporated with it.[275] Finally, the Marines, which had been creeping up in strength ever since the beginning of the war, were augmented from one hundred to one hundred and thirty companies, so that men should not be lacking for the fleet. Nor was it only in the mere activity of departments and ubiquity of recruiting sergeants that the spirit of the master was seen. The nation was stirred by such military ardour as it had not felt since the Civil War, and there was a rush for commissions in the Army.[276]

On the re-assembling of Parliament the Militia Bill was again brought forward, and, though it did not pass the Lords until June, was so essential a feature of Pitt's first short Administration that it may be dealt with here once and for all. The measure was introduced by George Townsend and was practically identical with that which had been rejected in the previous year, though Henry Conway, an officer of some distinction, had prepared an alternative scheme which was preferred by many. The Bill as ultimately passed appointed a proportion of men to be furnished for the Militia in every county of England and Wales, from Devonshire and Middlesex, which were to provide sixteen hundred men apiece, to Anglesey, which was called upon for no more than eighty. These men were to be chosen by lot from lists drawn up by the parochial authorities for the Lords-Lieutenants and their deputies; and every man so chosen was to serve for three years, at the close of which period he was to enjoy exemption until his time should come again. Thus it was designed that every eligible man in succession should pass through the ranks and serve for a fixed term. Special powers were given to justices and to deputy-lieutenants to discharge men from duty on sufficient reason shown, or after two years of service if they were over five-and-thirty years of age. The possession of a certain property was required as a qualification for officers, who likewise were entitled to discharge after four years' service, provided that others could be found to take their places. Provision was also made for the appointment by the King of an adjutant from the regular Army to every regiment, and of a sergeant to every twenty men. The organisation was by regiments of from seven to twelve companies, in which no company was to be of smaller strength than eighty men. The Lord-Lieutenant of each county was in command of that county's militia; and in case of urgent danger the King was empowered to embody the whole force, communicating his reasons to Parliament if in session, when officers and men became entitled to the pay of their rank in the Army and subject to the articles of war. It had been part of the original design, favoured with reservations by Pitt himself, that Sunday should be a day of exercise, as in Switzerland and other Protestant countries;

but this clause was dropped in deference to petitions from several dissenting sects, and it was finally enacted that the men should be drilled in half-companies and whole companies alternately on every Monday from April to October. The Act was not passed without much opposition in the Lords, who indeed reduced the numbers of the force to thirty-two thousand men, or one-half of the strength voted by the Commons, and added clauses which clogged the working of the measure. Nor was it at first enforced without dangerous riot and tumult in some quarters, due principally to the unscrupulous employment, already narrated, of men enlisted for duty at home on foreign service. Nevertheless the great step was taken. A local force had been established for domestic defence, and the regular Army was set free for service abroad, or more truly for the service of conquest.

During the early debates on the Militia Bill Pitt himself was absent, being confined to his house by gout; nor was it until the 17th of February that he appeared in his place to support the royal request for subsidies for Hanover and for the King of Prussia. The occasion drew upon him not a few sarcasms, for no man had more vehemently denounced the turning of Great Britain into a milch cow for the Electorate; but he waived the sneers aside in his wonted imperious fashion, for, consistent or inconsistent, he knew at least his own mind. It was one thing for British interests to be subordinated to Hanoverian; but it was quite another for Britain and Hanover to march shoulder to shoulder against a common enemy for their common advantage. The conquest of America in Germany was, as shall be seen, no idle phrase, though few as yet might comprehend its purport. But suddenly at this point Pitt's career was for the moment checked. Notwithstanding this proof of his loyalty to the cause of Hanover, the King was still unfriendly towards his new minister, and actually found, in the peril which threatened his beloved Electorate, a pretext for dismissing him from office. In March 1757 a French army of one hundred thousand men poured over the Rhine; and it was necessary to call out the Hanoverian troops to oppose it. The King was urgent for the Duke of Cumberland to command these forces, but the Duke was by no means so anxious to accept the trust. The memory of past failure oppressed him; and, since he hated Pitt, he was unwilling to correspond with him or to depend on him for instructions and supplies. To obviate this difficulty the King agreed to remove Pitt; and thus a minister of genius was discarded that an unskilful commander might take the field. It was a proceeding worthier of Versailles than of St. James's.

On the 5th of April Pitt, having refused to resign, received intimation of his dismissal; but by this time the nation had been roused to such a pitch that it would suffer no return to the imbecile and disgraceful administration of the past two years. The stocks fell; all the principal towns in England sent the freedom of their corporations to Pitt, and, in Walpole's phrase, for weeks it rained gold boxes. The King turned to Newcastle, but the contemptible old intriguer tried in vain to form a government with Pitt or without him. For eleven whole weeks the negotiations continued and the country was left virtually without a government of any kind, until at length it was seen that Pitt's return to office was inevitable, and on the 27th of July, though Newcastle still retained the post of First Lord of the Treasury, Pitt was finally reinstated as Secretary of State on his own terms, that is to say, with full control of the war and of foreign affairs. "I will borrow the Duke's majority to carry on the Government," he had said, "I am sure that I can save this country and that no one else can."

This was the turning-point of the whole war; but during the political struggle much precious time had been lost, all enterprise had been paralysed, and all arrangements dislocated. Thus fresh misfortunes were still at hand to increase the new minister's difficulties. In January Loudoun had received the Twenty-second regiment and the draft sent out to him by Newcastle's Government; but in April he was still awaiting his instructions as to the coming campaign, and meanwhile had little to report but the difficulties thrown by the Provincial authorities in the way of recruiting.[277] Pitt's intention, in deference to Loudoun's own representations, had been that he should attack Louisburg; and the seven battalions already referred to had been ordered to sail to Halifax with that object. These troops had been embarked on the 17th of March but had been detained by contrary winds until after the date of Pitt's dismissal; and though there seems to have been some effort to get them to sea a few days later, it is none the less certain that for one reason or another they did not reach Halifax until July.[278] Meanwhile Loudoun's position was most embarrassing. He had withdrawn all his troops from the frontier to New York, and was waiting only for news of Admiral Holburne's squadron and the reinforcements that he might embark and sail to Halifax to join them. Not a word as to Holburne reached him; and all that he could discover was the unwelcome fact that a French fleet, strong enough to destroy his own escort and sink the whole of his transports, had been seen off the coast.[279] He decided at last that the risk must be run, embarked his troops and arrived safely at Halifax, where ten days later he was joined by Holburne's squadron. The troops were landed, and then, but not till then, steps were taken to obtain intelligence as to the condition of Louisburg. This fact alone enables us to judge of Loudoun's efficiency as a commander. The first reports received, though meagre, were encouraging, and the troops were re-embarked for action; but directly afterwards an intercepted letter revealed the fact that twenty-two French sail of the line were in Louisburg harbour, and that the garrison had been increased to seven thousand men. The French naval force was so far superior to Holburne's that any attempt to prosecute the enterprise was hopeless. The expedition was therefore abandoned, and the troops sailed back to New York.

Meanwhile the disarming of the frontier afforded Montcalm an opportunity for striking a telling blow. At the end of July eight thousand French, Canadians and Indians were assembled at Ticonderoga, and on the 30th twenty-five hundred of them under command of an officer named Lévis started to march to North-West Bay on the western shore of Lake George, while Montcalm with five thousand more embarked in bateaux on Lake Champlain. On the following day both divisions united close to Fort William Henry, and on the 3rd of August Montcalm, mindful of the defeat of Dieskau, laid siege to the fort in form. Fort William Henry was an irregular bastioned square, built of crossed logs filled up with earth and mounting seventeen guns. On the northern side it was protected by the lake, on the eastern side by a marsh, and to south and west by ditches and *chevaux de frise*. The garrison, which had been reinforced a few days before in view of coming trouble, counted a total strength of twenty-two hundred men, including regular troops, sailors and mechanics, under the command of a veteran Scottish officer, Lieutenant-Colonel Monro of the Thirty-fifth Foot. On the night of the 4th the trenches were opened on the western side of the fort, and two days later the French batteries opened fire. The fort returned the fire with spirit, but it was evident that unless it were speedily relieved its fall could be only a question of time. Colonel Webb lay only fourteen miles away at Fort Edward, and by summoning troops hurriedly from New York and from the posts on the Mohawk had collected a force of over four thousand men; but Montcalm was reported to have twelve thousand men, and Webb did not think it prudent to advance to Lake George until further reinforced. He therefore sent a letter to Monro, advising him to make the best terms that he could, which was intercepted by Montcalm and politely forwarded by him to its destination. The siege was pushed vigorously forward, and by the 8th the besieged were in desperate straits. Over three hundred men had been killed and wounded, all the guns excepting a few small pieces had been disabled, and, worst of all, smallpox was raging in the fort. On the 9th, therefore, Monro capitulated on honourable terms, which provided, among other conditions, that the French should escort the garrison to Fort Edward. On the march the Indian allies of the French burst in upon the unarmed British, unchecked by the Canadian militia, and despite the efforts of Montcalm and of his officers massacred eighty of them and maltreated many more. This, however, though it might well stir the vengeful feelings of the British, was but an episode. The serious facts were the loss of the post at Lake George, and yet another British reverse in North America.

| July 26. |
| Sept. 5. |

Such were among the last legacies bequeathed by Newcastle's feebleness; and meanwhile the King's perversity in driving Pitt from office had brought speedy judgment upon himself and upon Cumberland. The Duke was defeated by the French at the battle of Hastenbeck, and retreating upon Stade concluded, or rather found concluded for him, the convention of

Klosterzeven, whereby he agreed to evacuate the country. Such were the discouragements which confronted Pitt on resuming office. It was hard to see how he could initiate any operations of value at so late a period of the year, but there was one species of diversion which, though little recommended by experience of the past, lay open to him still, namely a descent upon the French coast. A young Scottish officer, who had travelled in France, gave intelligence based on no very careful or recent observation, that the fortifications of Rochefort were easily assailable; and Pitt on the receipt of this intelligence at once conceived the design of surprising Rochefort and burning the ships in the Charente below it. Somewhat hastily it was determined to send ten of the best battalions and a powerful fleet on this enterprise, and the military command was offered to Lord George Sackville, who not relishing the task found an excuse for declining. Pitt was then for entrusting it to General Henry Conway, but the King objected to this officer on the score of his youth, and insisted on setting over him Sir John Mordaunt, a veteran who had showed merit in the past, but had now lost his nerve and was conscious that he had lost it. He and Conway alike objected to the project as based on flimsy and insufficient information, but both thought themselves bound in honour to accept the trust confided to them.

Sept. 8.
October.

Though the expedition had been decided upon in July, it was not until two months later that it sailed from England, and meanwhile the troops waited as usual in the Isle of Wight.[280] There was much delay in providing transports, and the embarkation was so ill-managed that the troops were obliged to row a full mile to their ships. On the 8th of September, however, the vessels put to sea under convoy of sixteen sail of the line under Sir Edward Hawke, and after much delay from foul winds and calms anchored in Basque Roads, the haven which was to become famous half a century later for an attack of a very different kind. On the 23rd the fortifications of the Isle d'Aix were battered down by the fleet and the island itself captured; but therewith the operations came abruptly to an end. Fresh information revealed that the French were fully prepared to meet an attack on Rochefort; and a council of war decided that any attempt to take it by escalade would be hopeless. It was therefore decided to attack the forts at the mouth of the Charente, but the order was countermanded by Mordaunt; and after a week's delay Hawke gave the General to understand that unless operations were prosecuted forthwith he would return with the fleet to England. The military commanders thereupon decided that they would return with him, which on the 1st of October they did, to the huge indignation of both fleet and army. A court of inquiry was held over this absurd issue to such extensive and costly preparations, and Sir John Mordaunt was tried by court-martial but honourably acquitted. The incident gave rise to a fierce war of pamphlets. It is certain that Mordaunt showed remarkable supineness, and he was suspected of a wish to injure the influence of Pitt by turning the enterprise into ridicule; but with such men as Wolfe, Conway and Cornwallis among the senior officers, the only conclusion is that, in the view of military men, no object of the least value could have been gained by any operations whatever. Military opinion had been against the expedition from the first. Ligonier, a daring officer but of ripe experience and sound judgment, wrote of it in the most lukewarm terms as likely to lead to nothing. On the whole it seems that the troops were sent on a fool's errand, and that the blame lay solely with Pitt. The nation was furious, and the King showed marked coldness towards the generals who had taken part in the failure; but Pitt, who was more hurt and disappointed than any one, took no step except to promote Wolfe, who had advocated active measures, over the heads of several other officers, and thus in one way at least extracted good from evil.

So ended the campaigning season of 1757 with an unbroken record of ill success in every quarter. But the right man was now at the head of affairs and was looking about him for the right instruments. The long period of darkness had come to an end and the light was about to break, at first in flickering broken rays, but soon to shine out in one blaze of dazzling and surpassing splendour.

∎

BOOK X

CHAPTER I

Pitt had now a free hand for the execution of such enterprises as he might desire, a freer hand indeed than any of his predecessors for ten years past had enjoyed; for Cumberland, being ill-received by the King on his return from Hastenbeck, had resigned the Commandership-in-Chief and all his military appointments of whatever description. Pitt, conscious that the Duke had been hardly treated, made no secret of his sympathy with him; but there can be no doubt that Ligonier, who succeeded him as Commander-in-Chief, was infinitely more competent as a military adviser and more sympathetic as a military colleague. And there was need for sound military capacity to deal with all the projects that were ripening in the minister's teeming brain.

Parliament met on the 1st of December, and the King's speech, after announcing vigorous prosecution of the war in America and elsewhere, begged for support for the King of Prussia. Frederick fortunately stood just at that moment at his highest in the public view, for his two masterly victories at Rossbach and Leuthen; and Parliament did not hesitate to confirm a subsidy to him to enable him to carry on the struggle. But in other respects Pitt could find little to boast of in the past year, and he was obliged to confine his eulogy to Frederick and to Clive, whose victory at Plassey, now just become known in England, could not be ascribed to any extraordinary efforts on the part of a British Ministry. The word "elsewhere" in the King's speech was understood to signify Hanover, though Pitt warmly disclaimed any such interpretation of the term; but the Commons did not quarrel with it nor with the estimates that were submitted in support of the policy. These were presented on the 7th of December and showed a force for the British Establishment of eighty-six thousand five hundred men, thirty thousand of them for Gibraltar and the colonies, and the remainder nominally for service at home. Four thousand of this number, however, were invalids, who were kept for duties in garrison only, a system wisely copied from earlier days and followed from the beginning to the end of the war. One new regiment only had been raised since the formation of Fraser's and Montgomery's Highlanders, namely Colonel Draper's, which had been created for service in India and which brought up the number of the regiments of the Line to seventy-nine. Adding the troops on the Irish to those on the British Establishment the full numbers of the Army may be set down roughly at one hundred thousand men. It was soon to be seen what Pitt could accomplish with them, when he had found officers who would fulfil his instructions.

America first occupied his attention and was dealt with summarily. The first thing to be done was to recall Lord Loudoun from the command, a resolution which was carried out before the year's end,[281] and to appoint a new General in his place. The choice fell upon General James Abercromby, who had been sent out by Newcastle's Administration; and the selection was not a fortunate one. The next step was to summon Colonel Jeffery Amherst from Germany, where he had been employed since 1756 as Commissary to the Hessian troops in the pay of England. Amherst, it will be remembered, was a Guardsman, and was last seen by us as Ligonier's aide-de-camp on the field of Fontenoy; so it is at least probable that his appointment was due to Ligonier's influence. Three new brigadiers were nominated to serve under him, Lawrence, Whitmore, and James Wolfe. The operations to be undertaken in America were threefold. First and foremost Louisburg was to be besieged; and this duty was assigned to Amherst with fourteen thousand regular troops. Concurrently an advance was to be made upon Crown Point, and pushed forward if possible to Montreal and Quebec; which service was entrusted to Abercromby, aided by Brigadier Lord Howe, with about ten thousand regulars and twenty thousand Provincial troops. Lastly, nineteen hundred regular troops and five thousand Provincials under Brigadier-General Forbes were to repair Braddock's failure and capture Fort Duquêsne.[282] The number of Provincial troops to be employed was five times as great as that provided by the colonies in any previous year; but Pitt, while asking for so formidable a force, agreed to supply the troops with tents, provisions, arms, and ammunition, leaving to the provinces the expenses of raising, clothing, and paying them only. Moreover, he had readjusted the former regulations as to the seniority of Provincial and Imperial officers, which had given much offence, in a spirit somewhat less to the prejudice of the Provincials. True to his principle that British battles should be fought by British subjects he grudged no expense to gather recruits from the new British beyond sea.

The troops were to be escorted to America by a fleet under Admiral Boscawen, which was strong enough to overpower any French fleet in American waters. A squadron was also sent under Admiral Osborne to the Mediterranean to intercept any French reinforcements from Toulon, while yet another squadron under Sir Edward Hawke cruised with the like object before

Rochefort. Osborne's name has been forgotten, and Hawke's lesser services have been swallowed up in the fame of his action before Quiberon; but it may be said here once for all that both officers performed their parts with admirable ability and signal success. The reader may now begin to judge of Pitt's talent for organising victory.

1758.
Feb. 19.

Boscawen, with twenty-three ships of the line and several smaller vessels, sailed with his convoy of transports on the 19th of February. It had been Pitt's hope that the siege of Louisburg should have been begun by the 20th of April;[283] but fate was against him, and the Admiral did not reach Halifax until the 9th of May. Amherst, who had sailed with Captain George Rodney in H.M.S. *Dublin* on the 16th of March, was not less unlucky in his passage; and Boscawen, after waiting for his arrival at Halifax until the 28th of May, at last put to sea without him, but fortunately met the *Dublin* just outside the harbour. The huge fleet, one hundred and fifty-seven sail in all, with eleven thousand troops on board, then steered eastward, and on the 2nd of June sailed into Gabarus Bay, immediately to westward of the tongue of land whereon stood Louisburg. Here there were three possible landing-places: Freshwater Cove, four miles from the town; Flat Point, which was rather nearer; and White Point, which was within a mile of the ramparts. East of the fortress there was yet another landing-place named Lorambec. It was determined to threaten all these points simultaneously, Lawrence and Whitmore with their respective brigades moving towards White Point and Flat Point, with one regiment detached against Lorambec, while Wolfe's brigade should make a true attack upon Freshwater Cove.[284] Nothing very clear was known of the French defences erected to cover these landing-places, and it so happened that the point selected for attack was the most strongly defended of all.

June 8.

For five days all attempts at disembarkation were frustrated by fog and storm; but at two o'clock on the morning of the 8th the troops were got into the boats, and at daybreak the frigates of the fleet stood in and opened a fierce fire upon the French entrenchments at all of the threatened points. A quarter of an hour later the boats shoved off and pulled for the shore. Wolfe's party consisted of five companies of grenadiers, a body of five hundred and fifty marksmen drawn from the different regiments and known as the Light Infantry, and a body of American Rangers, with Fraser's Highlanders and eight more companies of grenadiers in support. The beach at Freshwater Cove, for which they were making, was a quarter of a mile long, with rocks at each end; and on the shore above it more than a thousand Frenchmen lay behind entrenchments, which were further covered by abatis. Eight cannon and swivels had been brought into position to sweep every portion of the beach and of its approaches, but were cunningly masked by young evergreen shrubs planted in the ground before them. The French had not been at fault when they selected the point remotest from the town as the most likely to be attacked by an enemy.

The boats were close in-shore before the French made any sign, when they suddenly opened a deadly fire of grape and musketry. Wolfe, seeing that a landing in face of such a tempest of shot would be hopeless, signalled to the boats to sheer off; but three of them, filled with Light Infantry on the extreme right, being little exposed to the fire, pulled on to a craggy point just to eastward of the beach, which was sheltered from the enemy's cannon by a small projecting spit. There the three officers in charge leaped ashore followed by their men, and Wolfe hastened the rest of his boats to the same spot. Major Scott, who commanded the Light Infantry, was the first to reach the land; and though his boat was stove in against the rocks he scrambled ashore, and with no more than ten men held his own against six times his numbers of French and Indians, till other troops came to his support. The rest of the boats followed close in his wake. Many were stove in and not a few capsized; some of the men too were caught by the surf and drowned; but the greater part made their way ashore wet or dry, Wolfe, who was armed only with a cane, leaping into the surf and scrambling over the crags with the foremost. Arrived at the firm ground beyond, the men formed, attacked the nearest French battery in flank, and quickly carried it with the bayonet. Lawrence's brigade now rowed up, and finding the French fully occupied with Wolfe, landed at the western end of the beach with little difficulty or loss. Amherst followed him; and the French seeing themselves attacked on right and left, and fearing to be cut off from the town, abandoned all their guns, some three-and-thirty pieces great and small, and fled into the woods in the rear of their entrenchments. The British pursued, until on emerging from the forest they found themselves in a cleared space with the guns of Louisburg opening fire upon them. Then the pursuit was checked, for the first great object had been obtained. The total loss of the British little exceeded one hundred in killed, wounded, and drowned; that of the French was not much greater, but the British had gained a solid success.

Amherst pitched his camp just beyond range of the guns of the fortress, and selected Flat Point Cove as the place for landing his guns and stores. The disembarkation of material was a task of extreme difficulty and danger owing to the surf, so much so that over one hundred boats were stove in during the course of the siege. The General, therefore, had ample leisure to examine the ground before him. The harbour of Louisburg is a land-locked bay with an extreme width from north-east to south-west of about two and a half miles. The entrance is rather more than a mile wide, but is narrowed to less than half of that distance by a chain of rocky islets. The defences of the entrance were a battery on a small island on the west side of the channel and a fort on the eastern shore at the promontory of Lighthouse Point. Within the harbour on the northern shore had stood a battery known as the Grand battery, but this was destroyed by the French on the night of Amherst's landing; and on the western shore on a triangular peninsula stood Louisburg itself, the Dunkirk of America, the apex of the triangle pointing towards the harbour, the base towards the land where Amherst's force now lay encamped. The full circuit of its fortifications was about a mile and a half, and the number of cannon and mortars mounted thereon and on the outworks exceeded two hundred. The garrison consisted of five battalions of regular troops, numbering about four thousand men, together with several companies of colonial troops from Canada; the whole being under command of a gallant officer named Drucour. Finally, at anchor in the harbour lay five ships of the line and seven frigates. The strongest front of the fortress was on the side of the land, running from the sea on the south to the harbour on the north: it was made up of four bastions called in succession, from north to south, the Dauphin's, King's, Queen's, and Princess's bastions. The King's bastion formed part of the citadel, and before it the glacis sloped down to a marsh which protected it completely; but at both extremities of the line there was high ground favourable for the works of a besieging force. It was towards the northern extremity, from a hillock at the edge of the marsh, that Amherst resolved to push his first attack.

| June 25. |
| June 29. |

Meanwhile the labour to be accomplished before the guns and stores could be brought to the spot was immense. The distance from the landing-place was a mile and a half, every yard of it consisting of deep mud covered with moss and water-weeds, through which it was necessary to make not only a road but an epaulement also, to protect the road; for a French frigate, the *Aréthuse*, lay in a lagoon called the Barachois at the extreme western corner of the harbour, and swept all the ground before the ramparts with a flanking fire. While, therefore, this work was going forward Wolfe was ordered with twelve hundred men and artillery to the battery at Lighthouse Point, which had been abandoned by the French, in order to fire upon the Island battery and upon the ships in the harbour. After some days the Island battery was silenced with the help of the fleet, and the men of war were driven under the guns of the main fortress. The entrance to the harbour being thus laid open to the

British fleet, the French commander under cover of a foggy night sank six large ships in the channel to bar the passage anew.

```
July 9.
July 14.
July 21.
```

On the very day when Wolfe succeeded in silencing the Island battery Amherst's preparations were at last completed; and the British began to break ground on the appointed hillock. From thence the trenches were carried, despite the fire of the *Aréthuse*, towards the Barachois; and it was soon evident that the frigate would be repaid for all the mischief that she had wrought. At the same time Wolfe broke ground to the south opposite to the Princess's bastion, and despite a fierce sortie made by a drunken party of the garrison, pushed his works steadily forward against it. Another three weeks saw the net closing tighter and the fire raining fiercer about the doomed fortress. The *Aréthuse*, after sticking to her moorings right gallantly under an ever increasing fire, was compelled at last to shift her position. Two days later Wolfe, as busy at the left as at the right attack, made a dash at nightfall upon some rising ground only three hundred yards before the Dauphin's bastion, drove out the French that occupied it, and would not be forced back by the fiercest fire from the ramparts. On the 21st a lucky shell fell on one of the French line-of-battle ships and set her on fire. The scanty crew left on board of her could not check the flames. She drifted from her moorings upon two of her consorts and kindled them also; and all three were burned to the water's edge. The two remaining line-of-battle ships survived them but a little time, for a few nights later six hundred sailors rowed silently into the harbour and surprised and captured both of them. One, being aground, was burned, and the other was towed off, in contempt of the fire from the fortress, to a safe anchorage.

```
July 27.
```

By this time Amherst's batteries had reduced Louisburg almost to defencelessness. The masonry of the fortress had crumbled under the concussion of its own guns and was little able to stand the shot of the British. A new battery erected on the hill to the north of the Barachois raked the western front of the French works from end to end, and there was no standing against its fire. On the 26th of July the last gun on that front was silenced and a practicable breach had been made. Drucour then made overtures for a capitulation. Amherst's reply was short and stern: the garrison must surrender as prisoners of war, and a definite answer must be returned within one hour. Drucour replied at first with defiance, but, before his messenger could reach Amherst he sent a second emissary to accept the terms; and on the following day the British occupied the fortress. The casualties of the besiegers were not heavy, little exceeding five hundred killed and wounded of all ranks. The loss of the French is unknown, but must have been very great, from sickness not less than from shot and shell. The number of soldiers and sailors made prisoners amounted to fifty-six hundred, while over two hundred cannon and a large quantity of munitions and stores were surrendered with the fortress. So Cape Breton, and Prince Edward's Island with it, passed under the dominion of the British for ever.

The siege over, Amherst proposed to Boscawen to proceed to Quebec, but the Admiral did not consider the enterprise to be feasible. Drucour's gallant defence, indeed, had accomplished one object, in preventing Amherst from co-operating with Abercromby in the attack on Canada; though, could the siege have been begun at the date fixed by Pitt, his efforts would have been of little avail. Amherst therefore left four battalions to garrison Louisburg,[285] and sent Colonel Monckton, Colonel Lord Rollo, and Wolfe, each with a sufficient force, to complete the work of subjugation on Prince Edward's Island, the Bay of Fundy, and the Gulf of St. Lawrence. Wolfe having accomplished his part of the task went home on sick leave, and Amherst sailed with five battalions[286] for Boston, where he arrived on the 14th of September and was received with immense though rather inconvenient enthusiasm by the inhabitants.[287] His presence was but too sorely needed to repair the mischief wrought by Abercromby's incapacity.

The prospects of Abercromby at the opening of the campaign were such as might have encouraged any General. Vaudreuil, the Governor of Canada, a corrupt and incapable man, knowing of the intended advance of the British by Lakes George and Champlain upon Ticonderoga and Crown Point, had proposed to avert it by a counter-raid along the Mohawk upon the Hudson. This plan, being vague, and indeed impracticable, was abandoned; and the defence of the approaches to Montreal was committed to Montcalm, who was stationed at Ticonderoga with an insufficient force of about four thousand men, and without support from the posts higher up the lake. To Abercromby, with seven thousand regular troops and nine thousand Provincials, the exposure of this weak and isolated force should have been welcome as the solution of all his difficulties. It must now be seen to what end he turned so excellent an opportunity.

The early months of the summer were occupied with the task, always vexatious and troublesome, of collecting the Provincial troops, and of sending supplies up the Mohawk and the Hudson to Fort Edward. The latter work was tedious and harassing, despite the facilities of carriage by water, for there were three portages between Albany and Fort Edward, at each of which all boats had to be unladen, and dragged, together with their stores, for three or even more miles overland before they could be launched again for easier progress. None the less the business went forward with great energy; and notwithstanding the danger of convoys from the attack of Indians when passing through the forest, the work of escorting was so perfectly managed that not one was molested. These admirable arrangements were due to Brigadier Lord Howe, the eldest of three brothers, all of whom were destined to leave a mark for good or evil on English history.

Howe had been appointed by Pitt to make good the failings which were suspected in Abercromby. He was now thirty-four years of age, and having arrived in America with his regiment, the Fifty-fifth, in the previous year, had been at pains to learn the art of forest-warfare from the most famous leader of the Provincial irregulars. He threw off all training and prejudices of the barrack-yard, joined the irregulars in their scouting-parties, shared the hardships and adopted the dress of his rough companions and became one of themselves. Having thus schooled himself he began to impart the lessons that he had learned to his men. He made officers and men, alike of regular and of Provincial troops, throw off all useless encumbrances; he cut the skirts off their coats and the hair off their heads, browned the barrels of their muskets, clad their lower limbs in leggings to protect them from briars, and filled the empty space in their knapsacks with thirty pounds of meal, so as to make them independent for weeks together of convoys of supplies. In a word, he headed a reaction against the stiff unpractical school of Germany so much favoured by Cumberland, and tried to equip men reasonably for the rough work that lay before them. Such ideas had occurred to other men besides him. Colonel Bouquet of the Sixtieth wished to dress his men like Indians, and Brigadier Forbes went cordially with him, for, as he wrote emphatically, "We must learn the art of war from the Indians." Washington, again, said that if the matter were left to his inclination he would put both men and officers into Indian dress and set the example himself.[288] There was in fact a general revolt of all practical men against powder and pipeclay for bush-fighting, and Howe was fortunately in a position to turn it to account. Possibly it is to his influence that may be traced the formation in the same year of a regiment which, being designed for purposes of scouting and skirmishing only, was clothed in dark brown skirtless coats without lace of any description. This corps ranked for a time as the eightieth of the Line, and was known as Gage's Light Infantry.[289] It must not be supposed that these reforms were accepted without demur. Officers were dismayed to find that they were expected to wash their own clothes without the help of the regimental women, and to carry their own knives and forks with them according to Howe's example; and the German soldiers, of whom there were many in the Sixtieth, sorely resented the cropping of their heads. But Howe was a strict disciplinarian, and not the less, but rather the more, on this account was adored by the men.[290]

July 5.

By the end of June the whole of Abercromby's force, with all its supplies, was assembled at the head of Lake George. On the 4th of July the stores were shipped, and on the following day the men were embarked. The arrangements were perfect: each corps marched to its appointed place on the beach without the least confusion, and before the sun was well arisen the whole army was afloat. The scene was indescribably beautiful. Overhead the sky was blue and cloudless; the sun had just climbed above the mountain tops, and his rays slanted down over the vast rolling slope of forest to the lake. Not a breath of air was moving to ruffle the still blue water or stir the banks of green leaves around it, as the twelve hundred boats swept over the glassy surface. Robert Rogers, most famous of American partisans and instructor of Howe, with his rangers, and Gage with part of his new Light Infantry led the way. John Bradstreet of New England followed next with the boatmen, himself the best boatman among them; and then in three long parallel columns came the main body of the army. To right and left blue coats showed the presence of the Provincial troops of New England and New York, and in the centre flared the well-known English scarlet. Howe led this centre column with the Fifty-fifth, his own regiment; and after him followed the first and fourth battalions of the Sixtieth, the Twenty-seventh, Forty-fourth, Forty-sixth, and last of all the Forty-second with their sombre tartan, each regiment marked by its flying colours of green or buff or yellow or crimson. Then, unmarked by any flag, for colours they had none, came more of Gage's brown coats. Two "floating castles" armed with artillery also accompanied this column, towering high above the slender canoes and whale-boats; and in the rear came the bateaux laden with stores and baggage, with a rear-guard made up of red coats and of blue. So the great armament, stretching almost from shore to shore, crept on over the bosom of the lake, the strains of fife and drum mingling with the plashing of ten thousand oars, till the narrows were reached and the broad front dwindled into a slender procession six miles in length, still creeping on like some huge sinuous serpent on its errand of destruction and death.

July 6.

By five in the afternoon the flotilla had travelled five-and-twenty miles, and a halt was made for the baggage and artillery, which had lagged behind. At eleven o'clock it started again, and at daybreak reached the narrow channel that leads into Lake Champlain by the headland of Ticonderoga. A small advanced post of the French on the shore was driven back, and the work of disembarkation was begun. By noon the whole army had been landed on the western shore of the lake; Rogers with his rangers was sent forward to reconnoitre, and the troops were formed in four columns for the march. The route proposed was to follow the western bank of the channel which connects Lake George with Lake Champlain, since the French had destroyed the bridge over it, and to fall upon Ticonderoga from the rear. The way lay through virgin forest, encumbered with thick undergrowth and strewed with the decaying trunks and limbs of fallen trees. All order became impossible; the men struggled forward as best they could; the columns got mixed together; the guides lost all idea of their direction in the maze; and the army for a time was lost in the forest.

Meanwhile the French advanced party, some three hundred and fifty men, which had fallen back before the British, found its retreat cut off, and had no resource but to take to the woods. They too lost themselves among the trees, and the two hostile bodies were groping their way helplessly on, when the right centre column of the British, with Lord Howe and some rangers at its head, blundered unawares full upon the French party. A sharp skirmish followed, and in the general confusion the main body of the British, hearing volleys but unable to see, became very unsteady. Fortunately the rangers stood firm, and Rogers' advanced guard, turning back at the sound of shots, caught the French between two fires and virtually annihilated them. The British loss in this affair was trifling in numbers but none the less fatal to the expedition; for Lord Howe lay dead with a bullet through his heart, and with his death the whole soul of the army expired.

| July 7. |

Abercromby's force was for the moment paralysed. Half of his army was lost, nor did he know where to find it. So much of it as he could collect he kept under arms all night, and next morning he fell back to his landing-place, where to his great relief he found the rest of his troops awaiting him. Montcalm meanwhile had been devoured by anxiety. The channel between Lake George and Lake Champlain being impassable by boats owing to rapids, the usual route to Ticonderoga lay across it by some saw-mills at the foot of the rapids, where he had already destroyed the bridge. Nevertheless it was not by these saw-mills but on the western bank of the channel that he had determined to make his stand; nor was it until the evening of the 6th that, yielding to the advice of two of his officers, he decided to retire to Ticonderoga. Accordingly, at noon of the 7th, Abercromby sent Rogers forward with a detachment to occupy the saw-mills. The bridge was rebuilt; and the army, crossing the channel late in the afternoon, occupied the camp deserted by the French. Abercromby was now within two miles of Ticonderoga.

But meanwhile Montcalm had not been idle. The peninsula of Ticonderoga consists of a rocky plateau with low ground on each side, standing at the junction of Lakes George and Champlain. The fort stood near the end of this peninsula; and half a mile to westward of the spot the ground rises and forms a ridge across the plateau. On this ridge Montcalm decided at the last moment to throw up abatis and accept battle. The outline of the works had already been traced, and at the dawn of the 7th every man of his force was at work, cutting down the trees that covered the ground. The tops were cut off and the logs piled into a massive breast-work nine feet high, which was carefully loop-holed. The forest before the breast-work was also felled and left lying with the tops turned outwards, as though, to use the words of an eye-witness, it had been laid low by a hurricane. Between these felled trees and the breast-work the ground was covered with heavy boughs, their points being sharpened and the branches interlaced, so as to present an almost impenetrable obstacle. The French officers themselves were amazed at the work which had been accomplished in one day.

| July 8. |

Still the position was no Malplaquet, and there was no occasion for Abercromby to dread it. It was open to him either to attack Montcalm in his flanks, which were unfortified; or to bring up his artillery and batter the breast-work to splinters about his ears; or better still to post his guns on a height, called Mount Defiance, which commanded the position, and to rake the breast-work from end to end; or best of all to mask this improvised stronghold with a part of his force and push on with the rest northward up Lake Champlain and so cut off at once Montcalm's supplies and his retreat. The French General had but thirty-six hundred men and only eight days' provisions with him, so that this movement would have ensured his surrender without the firing of a shot. Abercromby's intelligence, however, told him that the French were six thousand strong and that three thousand more were expected to join them at any hour; and he was nervously anxious to make his attack before this reinforcement, which had in reality no existence, should arrive on the spot. Accordingly, at dawn of the 8th, Abercromby sent his engineers to reconnoitre the enemy's position from Mount Defiance. The duty was most perfunctorily fulfilled, and the chief engineer, Lieutenant-Colonel Clark, reported that the works could be captured by direct assault. This was enough for Abercromby. Without further inquiry he resolved that the artillery should be left idle at the place where it had been landed, and that the abatis should be carried with the bayonet.

It was high noon, and the French were still busily strengthening their wooden ramparts with earth and sandbags when shots in the forest before them gave warning that the British advanced parties had struck against their picquets. Instantly they fell in behind the breast-work, three deep, eight battalions of regular troops and four hundred and fifty Canadians, numbering in all little more than a fourth of the British force. The advance of the British was covered by the Light Infantry and rangers while the columns of attack were forming under shelter of the forest. Then the skirmishers cleared the front and the scarlet masses came forward, solid and steady; the picquets leading, the grenadiers in support, the battalions of the main body after the grenadiers, and the Fifty-fifth and Forty-second Highlanders in reserve. It was little that they could see through the tangle of fallen trees and dying leaves; possibly they caught a glimpse of the top of the breast-work but of not a white coat of the defenders behind it. On they came in full confidence, knowing nothing of the obstacles before them, when suddenly the breast-work broke into a sheet of flame and a storm of grape and musketry swept the ranks from end to end. Abercromby's instructions had been that the position should be taken with the bayonet, but all order was lost in the maze of fallen trees, and very soon the men began to return the fire as they advanced, but with little effect, for not an enemy could they see. Nevertheless, though riddled through and through, they scrambled on over the prostrate trunks straight upon the breast-work, when they were stopped by the tangled hedge and sharpened boughs of the inner abatis. Strive as they might they could not force their way through this under the terrible fire that rained on them in front and flank from the angles of the breast-work; and after an hour's struggle they fell back, exclaiming that the position was impregnable. Reports were sent to Abercromby, who throughout the action had never moved from the saw-mills, two miles away, and for all answer there came back the simple order to attack again.

And then came such a scene as had not been witnessed since Malplaquet nor was to be seen again till Badajoz. The men stormed forward anew, furious with rage and heedless of bullets or grape-shot, through the network of trunks and boughs against their invisible enemy. Behind the breast-work the French were cheering loudly, hoisting their hats occasionally above the parapet and laughing when they were blown to pieces, but pouring in always a deadly and unquenchable fire; while the British struggled on, grimed with sweat and smoke, vowing that they would have that wooden wall at any cost. The Highlanders broke loose from the reserve with claymores drawn and slashed their way through the branches to the breast-work, and the British rushed after them to its foot but could advance no further. They had no ladders, and as fast as they hoisted one another to the top of the breast-work they were shot down. Montcalm, cool and collected, moved to and fro among his men in his shirt-sleeves, always at the point of greatest danger, to cheer them and keep them to the fight. The French fire was appalling in its destruction. Men who had passed through the ordeal of Fontenoy declared that it was child's play compared with Ticonderoga. Nevertheless not once only, but thrice more, the British and the Americans with them hurled themselves desperately against the French stronghold, only to be beaten back time after time, until the inner abatis was hung with wisps of scarlet, like poppies that grow through a hedge of thorn, some swaying with the contortions that told of living agony, some limp and still in the merciful stillness of death. The fight had endured for five hours, when some officer of more intelligence than his fellows formed two columns and made a fifth attack upon the extreme right of the French position. The men hewed their way to the breast-work, and for a time the fate of this unequal day hung trembling in the balance. Montcalm hurried to the threatened quarter with his reserves, but only by desperate exertion held his own, for the Highlanders fought with a fury that would yield neither to discipline nor to death. Captain John Campbell and a few of his men actually scaled the wooden wall and dropped down within it, but only to be pierced at once by a score of bayonets. Finally at six o'clock a last attack was delivered, as heroic, as hopeless, and as fruitless as the rest; and then the order was given to retreat. The Highlanders were with the greatest difficulty forced away from their fallen comrades, and under cover of the skirmishers' fire the British withdrew, shattered, exhausted, and demoralised.

And then came one of those strange and dreadful scenes which break an officer's heart. Hardly was the retreat sounded when the very men who for six hours had faced the mouth of hell without flinching were seized with panic and fled in wild disorder through forest and swamp to the landing-place, leaving their arms, their accoutrements, the very shoes from their feet to mark the track of their flight. Fortunately Bradstreet and his armed boatmen mounted guard over the boats and prevented the fugitives from setting themselves afloat. Abercromby came up, as abject as the worst, despatched orders for the wounded and the heavy artillery to be sent back to New York, and followed himself so speedily with his humiliated troops that he arrived at the head of Lake George before his messenger. There he entrenched himself and sat still, while the reckoning of his ignorance and folly was made up. Of the Provincial troops three hundred and thirty-four had fallen before Ticonderoga; of the seven British battalions no fewer than sixteen hundred. The Forty-second lost close on five hundred men and officers killed and wounded, the Forty-fourth and Forty-sixth each about two hundred, the Fifty-fifth and the fourth battalion of the Sixtieth each about one hundred and fifty, the Twenty-seventh and first battalion of the Sixtieth each about a hundred. The loss of the French was less than three hundred and fifty, and Montcalm might well praise his gallant soldiers and hug himself over his victory, for he had fended off attack on Canada for at least one year.

The French General contented himself with strengthening the defences of Ticonderoga and sending out parties of irregulars to harass Abercromby's communications with Fort Edward. Abercromby for his part remained throughout July and the first days of August glued to his camp at the head of Lake George, losing many men from dysentery but attempting nothing. At last he made over to Bradstreet a force of twenty-five hundred men, Provincial troops for the most part, and sent him to attack the French post of Fort Frontenac, which guarded the outlet of Lake Ontario into the St. Lawrence. The project was Bradstreet's own and had been favourably regarded some time before by Loudoun; but it was only under pressure of a council of war that Abercromby's assent to it was wrung from him. Bradstreet accordingly dropped down to Albany, and advanced by the Mohawk and Onandaga to the site of Oswego, where he launched out on to the lake on the 22nd of August, and on the 25th landed safely near Fort Frontenac. The French garrison being little over one hundred strong could make small resistance, and on the 27th surrendered as prisoners of war, leaving nine vessels, which constituted the entire naval force of the French on the lake, in Bradstreet's hands. The fort was dismantled, two of the ships were carried off, the remainder were burned since there was no fort at Oswego to protect them, and Bradstreet returned triumphant to Albany. The service that he had rendered was of vast importance. The command of Lake Ontario was lost to the French, their communications north and south were severed, the alliance of a number of wavering Indian tribes was secured for the British, and Fort Duquêsne, the point against which Pitt had levelled his third blow, was left isolated and alone.

Heartened by this success and by the news of Louisburg, Abercromby began to write vaguely of a second attempt upon Ticonderoga[291] as soon as Amherst should have reinforced him; but it was October before the conqueror of Louisburg reached Lake George, and then both commanders agreed that the season was too far spent for further operations. The troops were accordingly sent into winter quarters, and Canada was saved for another year. It now remains to be seen how matters fared with Brigadier Forbes at Fort Duquêsne.

Forbes himself had arrived at Philadelphia early in April, to find that no army was ready for him. The Provincial troops allotted to him from Pennsylvania, Virginia, Maryland, and North Carolina had not even been enlisted; Montgomery's Highlanders were in the south, and only half of Colonel Bouquet's battalion of the Sixtieth was within reach. It was the end of June before the various fractions of his force were on march: and meanwhile the General was seized with a dangerous and agonising internal disease, against which he fought with a courage and resolution which was as admirable as it was pathetic. Forbes's career had been somewhat singular. He hailed from county Fife and had begun life as a medical student, but had entered the Scots Greys as a cornet and had risen to command the regiment. He had served in Flanders and Germany on the staff of Stair, Ligonier, and General Campbell, and finally as Cumberland's quartermaster-general.[292] But though all his training had been in the old formal school he had recognised, as has been seen, that in America he must learn a new art of war. He had studied Braddock's failure, and had perceived that even if Braddock had succeeded he must inevitably have retired from Fort Duquêsne from want of supplies. Instead, therefore, of making one long march with an unmanageable train of waggons, he decided to advance by short stages, establishing fortified magazines at every forty miles, and at last, when within reach of his destination, to march upon it with his entire force and with as few encumbrances as possible. This plan he had learned from a French treatise, [293] though he might have gathered it from a study of Monk's campaign in the Highlands had the opportunity been open to him. Nor was Bouquet, a Swiss by nationality, less assiduous in thinking out new methods. His views as to equipment have already been noticed; but knowing the value of marksmanship in the woods, Bouquet obtained a certain number of rifled carbines for his own battalion, and thus turned a part of the Sixtieth into Riflemen before their time.[294] He also introduced a new system of drill for work in the forest, forming his men into small columns of two abreast which could deploy into line in two minutes. Under such commanders the mistakes of Braddock were not likely to be repeated.[295]

July.

Then came the question whether Braddock's route should be followed, or a new but shorter line of advance from Pennsylvania. Virginia was furiously jealous lest Pennsylvania should reap the advantage of a direct road to the trading station on the Ohio, and Washington was urgent in recommending the old road; but Forbes had no respect for provincial squabbles and decided for Pennsylvania. He had much difficulty in shaping the Provincials into soldiers, the material delivered to him being of the rawest, and destitute of the remotest idea of discipline. It was not till the beginning of July that Bouquet with an advanced party encamped at Raystown, now the town of Bedford, on the eastern slope of the Alleghanies, and that Forbes was able to move to the frontier village of Carlisle and thence to Shippensburg. There his illness increased, with pain so excruciating that he was unable to advance farther until September. Bouquet meanwhile pushed forward the construction of a road over the Alleghanies with immense labour and under prodigious difficulties. The wildness and desolation of the country seems somewhat to have awed even the stern resolution of Forbes. "It is an immense uninhabited wilderness," he wrote to Pitt, "overgrown everywhere with trees or brushwood, so that nowhere can one see twenty yards." Through this with its endless obstacles of jungle, ravine, and swamp Bouquet's men worked their way. The first fortified magazine had been made at Raystown and named Fort Bedford; the next was to be on the western side of the main river Alleghany at a stream called Loyalhannon Creek. Progress was necessarily slow, but Forbes's advance was not made so leisurely without an object. The French had collected a certain number of Indians for the defence of Fort Duquêsne; but if the attack were delayed it was tolerably certain that these fickle and unstable allies would grow tired of waiting and disperse to their homes. Forbes meanwhile lost no opportunity of conciliating these natives; and by the efforts of his emissaries the most powerful tribes were persuaded to join the side of the British, and scornfully to reject the rival overtures of the French.

But at this critical time a rash exploit of one of Bouquet's officers went near to wreck the whole enterprise. Major Grant of the Highlanders entreated permission to go forward with a small party to reconnoitre Fort Duquêsne, capture a few prisoners, and strike some blow which might discourage and weaken the French. Eight hundred men of the Highlanders, Sixtieth, and Provincial troops were accordingly made over to him; so setting out with these from Loyalhannon he arrived before dawn of the 14th of September at a hill, since named Grant's hill, within half a mile of the fort. With incredible rashness he scattered his force in all directions. Leaving a fourth of his men to guard the baggage, he sent parties out to right and left, took post himself two miles in advance of the baggage with a hundred men, and sent an officer forward with a company of Highlanders into the open plain to draw a map of the fort. Finally, as if to call attention to his own folly, he ordered *reveillé* to be beaten with all possible parade. The French and Indians at once swarmed out of the fort and drove all the parties back in confusion upon one another. The Highlanders were seized with panic at the yells of the Indians and took to their heels, and but for the firmness of the Virginians of the baggage-guard the whole force would probably have been cut to pieces. As it was, nearly three hundred men were killed, wounded, or taken, and Grant himself was among the prisoners. Forbes, who amid all torments, troubles, and reverses preserved always a keen sense of the ridiculous, declared that he could make nothing of the affair except that his friend Grant had lost his wits; which indeed was a concise and accurate summary of the whole proceeding.

But such paltry success could avail the French little, for Bradstreet's capture of Fort Frontenac had already decided the fate of Fort Duquêsne. The French commander, his supplies being cut off, was obliged to dismiss the greater number of his men; otherwise Forbes could hardly have penetrated to the Ohio in that year. The elements fought for the French. Heavy rain ruined Bouquet's new road; the horses being underfed and overworked kept breaking down fast; the magazines at Raystown and Loyalhannon were emptied faster than they could be replenished; and Forbes was in despair. All through October the rain continued until at length it gave place to snow, and the roads became a sea of mud over which retreat and advance were alike impossible. At the beginning of November the General, though now sick unto death, was carried to Loyalhannon, where he decided that no attack could be attempted for that season. Intelligence, however, was brought that the French were so weak in numbers as to be defenceless; and on the 18th, twenty-five hundred picked men marched off without tents or baggage, Forbes himself travelling in a litter at their head. At midnight of the 24th the sentries heard the sound of a distant explosion, and on the next day at dusk the troops reached the blackened ruins of what had been Fort Duquêsne. The fortifications had been blown up; barracks and store-houses were in ashes; there was no sign of anything human except the heads of the Highlanders who had been killed in Grant's engagement, stuck up on poles with their kilts hung in derision round them. Their Highland comrades went mad with rage at the sight; but the French and their allies were gone, having evacuated and destroyed the fort and retired to the fort of Venango farther up the Alleghany river. Forbes planted a stockade around a cluster of huts that were still undestroyed, and named it Pittsburg in honour of the minister. Arrangements were then made for leaving a garrison of two hundred Provincials to hold the post, for there could be no doubt that the French would collect a force from Venango and Niagara to endeavour to retake it. The garrison indeed was far too small, but there was not food enough for more; so this handful of poor men was left perforce to make the best of its solitude during the dreary days of the winter.

One duty still remained to be done before Forbes's column turned homeward,—to search for the bones of those who had fallen with Braddock. A party of Pennsylvanians made their way through the forest to the Monongahela, Major Halket of Forbes's staff accompanying them. Among the multitude of ghastly relics two skeletons were found lying together under one tree. Halket recognised the one by a peculiarity of the teeth as that of his father, Sir Peter Halket of the Forty-fourth; and in the other he thought that he saw his brother, who had fallen by his side. The two were wrapped in a

Highlander's plaid and buried in one grave, under a volley fired by the Pennsylvanians. The rest of the remains were buried together in one deep trench; and then at the beginning of December the troops marched back to Pennsylvania with the dying Forbes in their midst. With great difficulty the General was brought still living to Philadelphia, where he lingered on through the winter and died in the following March. Though no brilliant action marked his advance to the Ohio he had accomplished his work against endless difficulties and in extremity of bodily torture; and that work was the taking from France of half of her Indian allies, the relief of the western border from Pennsylvania to Maryland from Indian raids, and the opening to the British of the vast regions of the West.

So ended the American campaign of 1758. The French had been struck hard on both flanks, at Louisburg in the north and on the Ohio in the south, but in the centre they had held their own. Two parts out of three of Pitt's design had been accomplished; but the most important success of all was that achieved by Bradstreet in severing the French communications at Fort Frontenac. It may be that Pitt thought best to adhere to the plan of operations mapped out for him by Loudoun, or it may be that he wished to retrieve the reputation lost by Braddock's defeat; but the fact remains that he meditated no attack on Niagara or Fort Frontenac, the capture of either of which would have entailed that of Fort Duquêsne, and that despite the industry of Bouquet and the tenacity of Forbes the advance to the Ohio would have been impossible but for the brilliant and successful enterprise of Bradstreet.

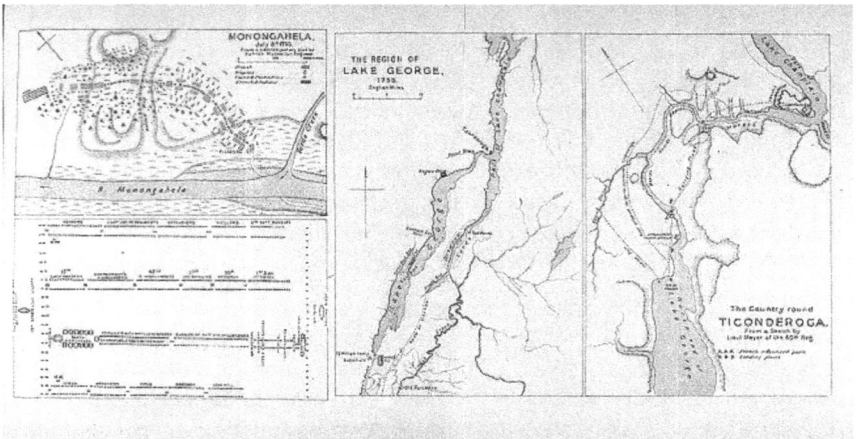

to face page 338

MONONGAHELA, July 8th 1755.
FORMATION OF AMHERST'S FLOTILLA JULY 1759.
From a contemporary plan.

THE REGION OF LAKE GEORGE, 1755.

The Country round TICONDEROGA,
From a Sketch by Lieut. Meyer of the 60th Reg.

CHAPTER II

1757.
1758.
Feb. 15.
March 31.

The reader will probably have been struck during the narrative of the American campaign of 1758 with the inferiority of the French in numbers to the British at every point. The French colonies were in fact allowed to take their chance, while French soldiers were poured by the hundred thousand into Germany to avenge King Frederick's sarcasm against Madame de Pompadour. A Pitt was hardly needed to perceive that the more employment that could be found for French armies in Europe, the fewer were the men which could be spared for the service of France's possessions beyond sea; and Pitt resolved accordingly to keep those armies fully occupied. By the convention of Klosterzeven, as has already been told, it was agreed that the Hanoverian army should be broken up; but even before Cumberland's return to England, the question of repudiating that convention had been broached, and a fortnight later a message was despatched to Frederick announcing that the army would take the field again, and requesting the services of Prince Ferdinand of Brunswick as General-in-Chief. Frederick assented; and on the 24th of November Ferdinand arrived at Stade, fresh from the victory of Rossbach in which he had taken part three weeks before, to assume the command. The whole aspect of affairs changed instantly, as if by magic. Setting his force in motion at once Ferdinand by the end of the year had driven the French back to the Aller, and renewing operations after six weeks spent in winter-quarters pressed the enemy still farther back, even across the Rhine.

June 5.
June 7.
June 29.
July 1.

It is said that even before Ferdinand had achieved this success Pitt had resolved to reinforce him with British troops, but for the present the minister reverted to his old plan of a descent on the French coast, which might serve the purpose of diverting French troops alike from America and from Germany. The first sign of his intention was seen in April, when the officers of sixteen battalions received orders to repair to the Isle of Wight by the

240

middle of May. Such long notice was a strange preliminary for a secret expedition, for the troops themselves did not receive their orders until the 20th of May; and it was the end of the month before the whole of them, some thirteen thousand men,[296] were encamped on the island. The Duke of Marlborough was selected for the command, and, since his military talent was doubtful, Lord George Sackville, whose ability was unquestioned, was appointed as his second, with the duty of organising the whole of the operations. Two squadrons, comprising twenty-four ships of the line under Lord Anson, Sir Edward Hawke, and Commodore Howe, were detailed to escort the transports, and on the 1st of June the armament set sail, arriving on the 5th at Cancalle Bay, about eight miles from St. Malo. A French battery, erected for the defence of the bay, was quickly silenced by the ships, and on the following day the entire army was landed. One brigade was left to guard the landing-place, and the remainder of the force marched to St. Malo, where the light dragoons under cover of night slipped down to the harbour and burned over a hundred privateers and merchant-vessels. The Duke of Marlborough then made dispositions as if for the siege of St. Malo, but hearing that a superior force was on the march to cut off his retreat, retired to Cancalle Bay, re-embarked the troops, and sailed against Granville, a petty town some twenty miles to north-east of St. Malo. Foul weather frustrated the intended operations; and on the 27th the expedition arrived off Havre de Grace. Preparations were made for landing, but after two days of inactivity Marlborough decided against an attack, and the fleet bore up for Cherbourg. There once more all was made ready for disembarkation, but the weather was adverse, forage and provisions began to fail, and the entire enterprise against the coast was abandoned. So the costly armament returned to Portsmouth, having effected absolutely nothing. It is, however, doubtful whether blame can be attached to the officers, either naval or military, for the failure. Pitt had procured no intelligence as to the dispositions of the French for defence of the threatened ports; so that a General might well hesitate to run the risk of landing, when he could not tell how soon he might find himself cut off by a superior force from the sea.

| June 23. |
| Aug. 21. |

Meanwhile Ferdinand following up his success had pursued the French over the Rhine and gained a signal victory over them at Creveld. This action appears to have hastened Pitt to a decision, for within four days he announced to the British Commissary at Ferdinand's headquarters the King's intention to reinforce the Prince with two thousand British cavalry. The troops were warned for service on the same day; but within three days it was decided to increase the reinforcement to six thousand troops,[297] both horse and foot, and a week later the force was further augmented by three battalions. The first division of the troops was shipped off to Emden on the 11th of July, and by the second week in August the entire reinforcement had disembarked at the same port under command of the Duke of Marlborough, joining Prince Ferdinand's army at Coesfeld on the 21st.[298] There for the present we must leave them, till the time comes for Ferdinand's operations to engage our whole attention. Meanwhile the reader need bear in mind only that the British Army is definitely committed to yet another theatre of war.

| August. |

Even so, however, Pitt remained unsatisfied without another stroke against the French coast. While the troops were embarking for Germany he had formed a new encampment on the Isle of Wight and was intent upon a raid on Cherbourg. So intensely distasteful were these expeditions to the officers of the Army that the Duke of Marlborough and Lord George Sackville used their interest to obtain appointment to the army in Germany, so as to be quit of them once for all. The result was that when Lieutenant-General Bligh, who had been originally selected to serve under Prince Ferdinand, arrived in London from Ireland to sail for Emden, he found to his dismay that his destination was changed, and that he must prepare to embark for France. He accepted the command as in duty bound, the more so since Prince Edward was to accompany the expedition, but he was little fit for the service, having no qualification except personal bravery and one great disqualification in advanced age. Accordingly, obedient but unwilling, he set sail on the 1st of August with twelve battalions[299] and nine troops of light dragoons, escorted by a squadron under Commodore Howe. Not yet had the gallant sailor learned of his succession to the title through the fall of his brother Lord Howe at the head of Lake Champlain.

| Aug. 16. |
| September. |

The expedition began prosperously enough. The fleet arrived before Cherbourg on the 6th and at once opened the bombardment of the town. Early next morning it sailed to the bay of St. Marais, two leagues from Cherbourg, where the Guards and the grenadier-companies, having landed under the fire of the ships, attacked and drove off a force of three thousand French which had been drawn up to oppose them. The rest of the troops disembarked without hindrance on the following day and advanced on Cherbourg, which being unfortified to landward surrendered at once. Bligh thereupon proceeded to destroy the docks and the defences of the harbour and to burn the shipping, while the light cavalry scoured the surrounding country and levied contributions. This done, the troops were re-embarked; and after long delay owing to foul winds the fleet came to anchor on the 3rd of September in the Bay of St. Lunaire, some twelve miles east of St. Malo. There the troops were again landed during the two following days, though not without difficulty and the loss of several men drowned. Bligh's instructions bade him carry on operations against Morlaix or any other point on the coast that he might prefer to it, and he had formed some vague design of storming St. Malo from the landward side. This, however, was found to be impracticable with the force at his disposal; and now there ensued an awkward complication. The weather grew steadily worse, and Howe was obliged to warn the General that the fleet must leave the dangerous anchorage at St. Lunaire, and that it would be impossible for him to re-embark the troops at any point nearer than the bay of St. Cast, a few miles to westward. Accordingly he sailed for St. Cast, while Bligh, now thrown absolutely on his own resources ashore, marched for the same destination overland.

| Sept. 9. |

The army set out on the morning of the 7th of September, and after some trouble with small parties of French on the march encamped on the same evening near the river Equernon, intending to ford it next morning. It speaks volumes for the incapacity of Bligh and of his staff that the passage of the river was actually fixed for six o'clock in the morning, though that was the hour of high water. It was of course necessary to wait for the ebb-tide; so it was not until three in the afternoon that the troops forded the river, even then waist-deep, under a brisk fire from small parties of French peasants and regular troops. Owing to the lateness of the hour further advance on that day was impossible; and on resuming the march on the following morning the advanced guard encountered a body of about five hundred French troops. The enemy were driven back with considerable loss, but their prisoners gave information of the advance of at least ten thousand French from Brest. Arrived at Matignon Bligh encamped and sent his engineers to reconnoitre the beach at St. Cast in case he should be compelled to retreat. Deserters who came in during the night reported that the French were gathering additional forces from the adjacent garrisons; and in the morning Bligh sent word to Howe that he intended to embark on the following day.

| Sept. 11. |

Constant alarms during the night showed that the enemy was near at hand; and it would have been thought that Bligh, having made up his mind to retreat, would in so critical a position have retired as swiftly and silently as possible. On the contrary, at three o'clock on the morning of the 11th the drums beat the assembly as usual, to give the French all the information that they desired; while the troops moved off in a single column so as to consume the longest possible time on the march. It was nine o'clock before the embarkation began, and at eleven, when two-thirds of the force had been shipped, the enemy appeared in force on the hills above the beach. For some time the French were kept at a distance by the guns of the fleet, but after an hour they found shelter and opened a sharp and destructive fire. General Drury, who commanded the rear-guard, consisting of fourteen hundred men of the Guards and the grenadiers, was obliged to form his men across the beach to cover the embarkation. Twice he drove back the enemy, but, ammunition failing, he was forced back in turn, and there was nothing left but a rush for the boats. The French bringing up their artillery opened a furious fire; and all was confusion. So many of the boats were destroyed that the sailors shrank from approaching the shore and were only kept to their work by the personal example of Howe. In all seven hundred and fifty officers and men were killed and wounded, General Drury being among the slain, and the rest of the rear-guard were taken prisoners. The fleet and transports made their way back to England in no comfortable frame of mind, for the French naturally magnified their success to the utmost; and so ended Pitt's third venture against the coast of France.

There can be little doubt but that Bligh must be held responsible for the failure. It should seem indeed that he was ignorant of the elements of his duty, even to the enforcing of discipline among the troops, who at the first landing near Cherbourg behaved disgracefully. The Duke of Marlborough had met with the same trouble at Cancalle Bay, but had had at least the strength to hang a marauding soldier on the first day and so to restore order. But after all Pitt was presumably responsible for the selection of Bligh; or, if he was aware that he could not appoint the right man for such a service, he would have done better to abandon these raids on the French coast altogether. The conduct of Marlborough and Sackville in shirking the duty because it was distasteful to them does not appear commendable; but Sackville at any rate was no fool, and Pitt might at least have recognised the military objections that were raised against his plans. The truth of the matter is, as Lord Cochrane was to prove fifty years later, that sporadic attacks on the French coast are best left to the Navy; for a single frigate under a daring and resolute officer can paralyse more troops than an expedition of ten or fifteen thousand men, with infinitely less risk and expense. Pitt had not yet done with his favourite descents, but his next venture of the kind was to be directed against an island instead of the mainland, when the British fleet could interpose between his handful of battalions and the whole population of France. Meanwhile Cherbourg had at any rate been destroyed, so like a wise man the minister made the most of this success, by sending some of the captured guns with great parade through Hyde Park to the Tower.

April 30.
Oct. 26.
Dec. 29.

The operations already narrated of the year 1758 were of considerable scope, embracing as they did the advance of three separate armies in America, two raids on the French coast, and the despatch of British troops to Germany; but these by no means exhaust the tale. There were few quarters of the globe in which the British had not to complain of French encroachment, and to this insidious hostility Pitt had resolved to put a stop once for all. Five years before, the merchants of Africa had denounced the unfriendliness of the French on the Gambia, who were building forts and stirring up the natives against them. The Royal African Company also, with its monopoly of the slave-trade, was anxious for its line of fortified depôts on the West Coast, and prayed to be delivered from its troublesome neighbours at Senegal and in the island of Goree.[300] One of Pitt's first actions in 1758 was to order an expedition to be prepared against Senegal, a duty for which two hundred marines and twenty-five gunners were deemed a sufficient force. On the 23rd of April Captain Marsh of the Royal Navy sailed into the Senegal river, and by the 30th Fort Louis had surrendered and was flying the British flag. Two hundred men of Talbot's regiment[301] were at once sent to garrison the new possession, and then for some months there was a pause, while the troops for Germany and Cherbourg were embarking for their destinations. But no sooner was Bligh's expedition returned than a new enterprise was set on foot, and Captain Keppel of the Royal Navy received secret instructions to convoy Lieutenant-Colonel Worge with Forbes's regiment[302] and two companies of the Sixty-sixth to the West Coast.[303] Within three weeks the troops were embarked at Kinsale, and by the 28th of December Keppel's squadron was lying off Goree. On the following day the ships opened fire on the French batteries, and at nightfall the island surrendered, yielding up over three hundred prisoners and nearly an hundred guns. So with little trouble were gained the West African settlements of the French.

1759.
Jan. 13.
Jan. 15.

But even before Keppel had received his instructions six more battalions[304] were under orders for foreign service; and his squadron had hardly sailed before another fleet of transports was gathering at Portsmouth. Major-General Peregrine Hopson, who had been Governor at Nova Scotia in the difficult years that preceded the outbreak of war, was appointed to the chief command, and Colonel Barrington, a junior officer, was, despite the honourable protests of his brother, the Secretary-at-War, selected to be his second. The expedition was delayed beyond the date fixed for its departure by bad weather, but at length on the 12th of November the transports, escorted by eight ships of the line under Commodore Hughes, got under way and sailed with a fair wind to the west. On the 3rd of January 1759 they reached Barbados, the time-honoured base of all British operations in the West Indies, and there was Commodore Moore waiting with two more ships of the line to join them and to take command of the fleet. After ten days' stay they again sailed away north-westward before the trade-wind. Astern of them the mountains of St. Vincent hung distant like a faint blue cloud; ahead of them two tall peaks, shaped like gigantic sugar-loaves, rose higher and higher from the sea, and marked the southern end of St. Lucia. Then St. Lucia came abeam, a rugged mass of volcanic mountains shrouded heavily in tropical forest, and another island rose up broad and blue not many leagues ahead, an island which the men crowded forward to see, for they were told that it was Martinique. Still the fleet held on; St. Lucia was left astern and Martinique loomed up larger and bolder ahead; then an islet like a pyramid was passed on the starboard hand, the Diamond Rock, not yet His Majesty's Ship; a little farther and the fleet was under the lee of the island; yet a little farther and the land shrank back to eastward into a deep inlet ringed about by lofty volcanic hills, and a few useless cannon-shot from a rocky islet near the entrance proclaimed that the French were ready for them in the Bay of Fort Royal.[305]

| Jan. 16. |
| Jan. 17. |

The ships lay off the bay until the next day, while Hopson thought out his plan of operations. The town and fortress of Fort Royal lies well within the bay on the northern shore, so Negro Point, which marks the entrance to the harbour to the north, was the spot selected for the landing. The ships next morning stood in and silenced two small batteries mounted at the Point, and in the afternoon the troops landed unopposed in a small bay adjacent to it. A camping ground was chosen in the only open space that could be found, between two ravines, and there the army passed the night formed up in square, to be ready against any sudden attack. At dawn of the next morning shots were heard, and the outposts reported that the enemy was advancing and entrenching a house close to the British position. The grenadiers were sent forward to dislodge them, and a smart skirmish ended in the retreat of the French. Hopson would fain have pushed more of his men into action, but the jungle was so dense that they could find no enemy. "Never was such a country," wrote the General plaintively, "the Highlands of Scotland for woods, mountains, and continued ravines are nothing to it."[306] As it was plainly out of the question to attempt to drag the heavy artillery before Fort Royal over such a country, it was decided to re-embark the troops forthwith.

Nearly one hundred men had been killed and wounded in the morning's skirmish, but the embarkation was accomplished without further loss.

Jan. 18.

On the following day the fleet coasted the island northward and by evening lay off St. Pierre, the second town in Martinique, which stood nestling in a little plain at the head of a shallow bay. The men-of-war stood in on the next morning to observe the defences of the place, and the fire of the French batteries from the heights to right and left soon convinced the Commodore that the town could not be taken without such damage to his ships as would disable them for further service. It was therefore resolved that Martinique should for the present be left alone, and that the expedition should proceed to Guadeloupe, which was not only the richest of the French Islands but the principal nest of French privateers in the West Indies. So the fleet steered northward once more past Dominica, where the white flag of the Bourbons yet floated over the fort of Roseau; while a single ship was sent forward with the chief military engineer on board to reconnoitre the town of Basseterre, which lies on the western or leeward coast a few miles to north of the most southerly point of Guadeloupe.

Jan. 23.
Jan. 24.
Jan.

The engineer returned with no very encouraging report. The town though lying on an open roadstead was well fortified, and all the approaches to it along the coast were well protected, while the fort of Basseterre, situated on a lofty eminence at the southern end, was declared to be impregnable by the attack of ships alone. Moore, however, was resolute that the town could and should be taken, and at ten o'clock on the morning of the 23rd the ships of the line and bomb-ketches opened a heavy fire on the fort and batteries. In a few hours the town, crammed with the sugar and rum of the past harvest, was burning furiously, and by nightfall every battery was silenced and the town was a heap of blackened ruins. At dawn of the morrow the troops were landed, to find the elaborate lines of defence inland deserted and every gun spiked, while desultory shots from among the sugar-canes alone told of the presence of the enemy. The army encamped in Basseterre, but the firing from the cane-fields increased, and picquets and advanced posts were harassed to death by incessant alarms and petty attacks. Hopson sent a summons to the French Governor to surrender, but received only an answer of defiance. The Governor had in fact withdrawn his force some six miles from Basseterre to an impregnable position such as can be found only in a rugged, mountainous and untamed country. Each flank was covered by inaccessible hills clothed with impenetrable forest; in his front ran the river Galeon with high and precipitous banks, and beyond the river a gully so steep and sheer that the French themselves used ladders to cross it. The position was further strengthened by entrenchments and cannon. To attack it in front was impossible. The only practicable access was by a narrow road which led through dense forest upon one flank; and this was most carefully guarded. Here therefore the French commander lay, refusing to come to action but sending out small parties to worry the British outposts, in the hope that the climate would do the work of repelling his enemy for him.

Feb. 14.

Nor was he without good ground for such hope; for Hopson was in great doubt whether it would not be more expedient for him to re-embark. His own health was failing rapidly, and the men were beginning to fall down fast under the incessant work at the advanced posts and the fatigue of carrying provisions to them. From the day of landing it had been found necessary to push these advanced posts farther and farther inland and to make them stronger and stronger, until at last they embraced a circuit of fully three miles. By the end of January the men on the sick list numbered fifteen hundred, or fully a quarter of the force. Hopson sent six hundred invalids to Antigua in the hope of saving at least some of them, but therewith his efforts came to an end, nor could all the representations of Barrington stimulate him to further action. Yet new operations were by no means difficult either of conception or of execution. Guadeloupe is in reality not one island but two, being divided by a narrow strait known as the Salt River. It is very much of the shape of a butterfly with wings outspread, flying south; the western wing being known as Guadeloupe proper and the eastern as Grande Terre, while the Salt River runs in the place of the butterfly's body. Grande Terre, the most fertile part of the island, still lay open to attack, with an excellent harbour at Point à Pitre, of which the principal defence, Fort Louis, could be reached by the cannon of ships. Moore being fortunately independent of Hopson in respect of naval operations, sent ships round to Fort Louis, which speedily battered it into surrender, and installed therein a garrison of three hundred Highlanders and Marines. But even with this new base secured to him Hopson declined to move. He was indeed sick unto death, and on the 27th of February he died, leaving the command to devolve on Barrington.

March 6.
March 11.
March.

His death came none too soon, for the force was on the brink of destruction. The number of the dead cannot be ascertained, but over and above the six hundred invalids sent to Antigua there were more than sixteen hundred men on the sick list, and the remainder were succumbing so fast that sufficient men could hardly be found to do the daily duty. Barrington resolved to close this fatal period of inaction at once. The defences of the fort of Basseterre had already been repaired and rendered safe against attack, so the Sixty-third regiment was left to hold it while the remainder of the troops were embarked on board the transports. After five days of weary beating against the trade-wind a portion of the ships came to anchor before Fort Louis; but more than half of them had fallen to leeward. The next day was spent by Barrington in an open boat reconnoitring the coast, but on his return in the evening he was met by the bad news that a French squadron had been sighted to northward of Barbados and that Moore felt bound to fall back with his own squadron to Prince Rupert's Bay, Dominica, in order to cover Basseterre and the British Leeward Islands. Finally, as sickness had wrought little less havoc in the fleet than in the army, the Commodore begged for troops to make up the complement of his crews.

Few situations could have been more embarrassing than that in which Barrington now found himself. He loyally gave Moore three hundred soldiers for his ships, and watched the fleet on which his communications depended vanish from sight. Nearly if not quite half of his force had perished or was unfit for duty; while of the rest a part was isolated in Basseterre and fully one moiety was at sea, striving to beat into Point à Pitre. Fort Louis, the only strong position in which he could hope to wait in safety, was found to be untenable; and the French were already preparing to besiege it. Yet with a resolution which stamps him as no common man, he resolved despite all difficulties to begin offensive operations at once. He had at any rate transports though he had no men-of-war, and he resolved to use them; his plan being, if he failed to bring the enemy to action, to ravage the whole island and reduce it by starvation. The cultivated land in such a confusion of mountains could lie only in the valleys, and the settlements must needs lie at the mouths of those valleys where there was communication with other parts of the island by sea or by roads that followed the coast. The French had raised abundance of batteries and entrenchments to protect these settlements, but such multiplicity of defences necessarily implied dispersion of force. Barrington's troops, few though they might be, were at any rate to some extent concentrated; and it was in his power to embark men sufficient to overwhelm any one of these isolated settlements, and so to break up the defences in detail. The operations were not in fact difficult when once a man had thought out the method of conducting them, but it was precisely in this matter of thought that Hopson had failed.

| March 27. |
| March 29. |

A fortnight was occupied in strengthening the defences of Port Louis;

and on the 27th of March six hundred men were embarked under command of Colonel Crump and sent off to the south coast of Grande Terre, with orders to land between the towns of St. Anne and St. François, destroy both of them and ruin the batteries erected for their protection. Crump, an excellent officer, performed this duty punctually and with little loss; and on the 29th Barrington, guessing that the French would certainly have detached some of their troops from Gosier, a port a few miles to westward of St. Anne, sailed with three hundred men against it, and at dawn fell upon the enemy in their entrenchments. The troops, eager for work after long inaction, attacked with great spirit, drove the enemy out with little difficulty and slight loss, and then prepared to force their way back to Fort Louis by land. Barrington had ordered two separate sallies to be made by the garrison upon the lines erected by the French against the fort, but owing to some mistake one only was delivered. Nevertheless his own little detachment did the work unaided, captured a battery of twenty-four pounders which had been planted by the enemy to open on the fort on the next day, and returned to its quarters triumphant.

> **April 12.**
> **April 13.**

By this time the missing transports had succeeded in working into Point à Pitre; but to countervail this advantage there came news from Basseterre that the colonel in command, a valuable officer, had been killed, together with one or two of his men, by an accidental explosion, and that the French were constructing batteries to bombard the fort. Barrington appointed a new commander, with orders to sally forth and capture these batteries without more ado; and the task, since he had chosen the right men to execute it, was performed with little trouble or loss. Moreover, having now ruined the most important settlements in Grande Terre he resolved to apply the same principles of warfare to Guadeloupe. Accordingly on the 12th of April Brigadier Clavering, with thirteen hundred men and six guns, was sent off to a bay close to Arnouville,[307] where they landed unopposed, the enemy retiring to a strong position in rear of the river Licorne. This position was all-important to the French since it covered Mahault Bay, which was the port by which the Dutch supplied Guadeloupe with provisions from the island of St. Eustatia. It was so strong by nature that it needed little fortification by art; access to the river being barred by a mangrove swamp, across which there were but two narrow approaches, both of them protected by redoubts, palisaded entrenchments, and cannon. None the less Clavering determined to attack. Covered by a heavy fire of artillery the Fourth and Forty-second advanced against the French left, firing by platoons as coolly as if on parade, till the Highlanders drawing their claymores made a rush, and the Fourth dashing forward with the bayonet drove the French from the redoubt. Then pushing round to the rear of the entrenchments on the French right they forced the enemy to evacuate them also, and captured seventy prisoners. The French then retreated southward, setting fire to the cane-fields as they passed in order to check the British pursuit, and took post behind the river Lezarde, breaking down the bridge behind them. It was too late for Clavering to attack them on that day, for the only ford on the river was protected by a redoubt and four guns; but keeping up a fire of artillery all night in order to distract the enemy's attention, he passed a party in a canoe across the river below the position of the French, who no sooner saw their right flank turned than they retired with precipitation, abandoning all their guns. Following the coast southward to Petit Bourg, where they had prepared fortified lines and armed redoubts, the French again tried to make a stand; but Barrington had sent a bomb-vessel to await them off the coast, which opened fire with shell and drove them back once more, before they could withdraw their guns from the entrenchments.

| April 14. |
| April 18. |
| April 19. |
| May 1. |

Then and not till then did Clavering grant his men a halt after their hard work under the tropical sun; but on the 15th he was in motion again, and a detachment of a hundred men was sent to capture the next battery to southward at the town of Gouyave. The French, now thoroughly disheartened, waited only to fire one shot and then fled, leaving seven guns behind them, when the British having spiked the cannon retired to Petit Bourg. On the same day Colonel Crump was sent with seven hundred men to Mahault Bay, where he found the French defences abandoned. Having destroyed them, together with a vast quantity of stores, he marched to join Clavering at Petit Bourg and to help in the work of desolating the country round it. Heavy rain suspended operations during the two following days; but on the 18th the entire force, excepting a garrison of two hundred and fifty men which was left at Petit Bourg, renewed the advance southward upon St. Maries, where all the French troops in the island were assembled to oppose it. The French position was as usual strongly entrenched, but the paths that led to rear of it, being judged impassable, were left unguarded. A detachment was therefore sent to turn the entrenchments by these paths, and the artillery was hastened up to the front; but the guns had hardly opened fire when the French, perceiving the movement in their rear, deserted their fortifications and fled to another entrenched position on the heights beyond St. Maries. The British pursued; and, while the ground was clearing for the artillery to come into action, part of the infantry tried to force a way through the forest and precipices on the flank of the earthworks. The French, weary of finding position after position turned, left their fortified lines to meet this attack, whereupon Clavering instantly launched the remainder of his troops straight at the lines, and despite a heavy fire of artillery and musketry swept the enemy out of this last refuge. On the morrow the army entered the district of Capesterre, reputed the richest in the whole of the West Indies; and the inhabitants, dreading lest it should be overtaken by the fate of the rest, came and begged for terms. A capitulation was therefore granted on liberal conditions, and Guadeloupe, one of the wealthiest of the Antilles, with a harbour large enough to shelter the whole Navy of England from hurricanes, passed for the present to the Crown of Britain.

May 26.

The surrender came in the nick of time, for the ink of the signatures was hardly dry when news came of the arrival of General Beauharnais from Martinique with six hundred French regular troops and two thousand buccaneers. A day earlier this reinforcement would have saved Guadeloupe; but on hearing of the capitulation Beauharnais re-embarked his troops and sailed away. Nothing therefore remained for Barrington but to settle the administration, fortify the harbour, and leave a sufficient garrison to hold it. The island of Mariegalante, which had not been included in the capitulation, made some show of defiance but surrendered on the first display of force. Crump was installed as Governor; the Fourth, Sixty-third, and Sixty-fifth were left with him; the Thirty-eighth returned to its old quarters in the Leeward Islands, the Highlanders were shipped off to America, and in June Barrington, with the remnant of the Buffs, Sixty-first, and Sixty-fourth, returned to England.

So ended the campaign of Guadeloupe. The story is one which is little known, and the name of John Barrington is one of which few have heard; yet surely the achievements of himself and of his troops are such as should not be forgotten. Barrington took over from Hopson an army weakened by sickness, worn to death by defensive warfare of the most harassing kind, and disheartened by the consciousness that it was working to no purpose. He at once shifted his base for more active operations, only to find, to his great mortification, half of his force literally at sea, and the fleet taken from him for other duty. Yet he went to work at once; and knowing that he could not take the island by force reduced it to submission by cutting off and destroying its supplies. I have not hesitated to describe the petty engagements which followed, since there was not one which did not show forethought in the planning and skill in the execution. It is true that the French regular troops on the island were few, and that the enemy which deserted its entrenchments so readily was made up mainly of raw militia and armed civilians; but they never fought except in a strong position protected by artillery. It is true also that the actual work in the field was done by Crump and Clavering, two excellent officers, for Barrington was so much crippled by gout that he could hardly leave Fort Louis. Nevertheless the whole scheme of operations was Barrington's, and no man more cordially acknowledged the fact than Clavering himself. The number of the British killed and wounded in action is unfortunately not to be ascertained, but judging by the casualties of the officers, of whom eleven were killed and twenty-one wounded, it was not very great. But it is not lead and steel that are most fatal in a tropical expedition, and it is not in killed and wounded that its cost must be reckoned. The island had been conquered, but the climate had not; and the climate took its revenge. By the close of the seven months that remained of the year 1759 nearly eight hundred officers and men of the garrison had found their graves in Guadeloupe.

AUTHORITIES.—For the expeditions to Cancalle Bay and Cherbourg, see *Account by an officer of the late expedition*. Entick also gives details from the official documents. For the operations at Goree, see *State Papers* (Record Office), *C. O., Col. Corres.*, Sierra Leone, 2, 3. For Guadeloupe, see *State Papers, C. O.*, America and West Indies, 100, 101; W. O., *Orig. Corres.*, 26. Entick again gives a confused statement.

CHAPTER III

It was late in November before Parliament reassembled, and listened to a speech from the throne, jubilant over the captures of Louisburg, Fort Frontenac, and Senegal, but modestly deploring the inevitable expense of the war. The Commons, however, were practically unanimous in allowing a free hand to Pitt, though the minister himself was startled when he was brought face to face with the estimates. Those for the Army were introduced a week later, and showed but a slight increase in the British Establishment, the total number of men not exceeding eighty-five thousand. Yet the main operations of the coming year were to be conducted on a grander scale than before, while at the same time provision was needed to make good the enormous waste caused by tropical expeditions. Two new regiments only were formed before the actual opening of the operations of 1759, one of them, Colonel Eyre Coote's,[308] serving as a reminder that concurrently with all other enterprises there was progressing the struggle, which shall presently be narrated, for the mastery of the East Indies.

Pitt's principal effort, as in the previous year, was directed against Canada, and the operations prescribed were little less complicated than those of the last campaign. In the first place a direct attack was to be made upon Quebec, for which purpose Amherst was to make over ten battalions to General Wolfe. In the second, the attempt to penetrate into Canada by way of Ticonderoga and Crown Point was to be renewed. Amherst himself was to take this duty upon him, Abercromby having been rightly recalled; and it was hoped that he might join Wolfe in the capital of Canada or at least make a powerful diversion in his favour. At the same time Amherst was ordered to secure Oswego and Pittsburg, and empowered to undertake any further operations that he pleased, without prejudice to the main objects of the campaign. The General having already twenty-three battalions of the King's troops in America, it was reckoned that, with the regiments to be forwarded to him from the West Indies by Hopson, he would possess a sufficient force for the work. No fresh battalions therefore were sent to him from England.[309]

The selection of James Wolfe for the command of the expedition against

Quebec came as a surprise to many. He was now thirty-two years of age, and had held a commission ever since he was fourteen, attaining the rank of captain at seventeen and of major at twenty. He had served in Flanders and distinguished himself as brigade-major at Lauffeld, but it was as Lieutenant-Colonel in command of the Twentieth Foot that he had shown himself most competent. He was an admirable regimental officer, enthusiastic over his profession and well acquainted with its duties, a stern disciplinarian yet devoted to his men, and a refined and educated gentleman. In short he was a commanding officer who could be trusted to raise the tone of any corps.[310] He had attracted Pitt's notice by his constant though fruitless advocacy of action in the abortive descent on Rochefort in 1757, and had come prominently before the public eye by his behaviour at Louisburg. His relations with Amherst, however, appear not to have been very friendly, nor to have been improved by his return home from Cape Breton in 1758; indeed Wolfe was reprimanded as soon as he arrived in England for returning without the King's orders, under misconception of his letter of service.[311] It was possibly under the sting of this censure that he wrote to Pitt declaring his readiness to serve in America and "particularly in the river St. Lawrence"; but be that as it may he received the appointment. There is an anecdote that he filled the great minister with dismay by some extraordinary gasconnade at a dinner to which he had been invited shortly before his departure; but even if, in a moment of elation,[312] he may have given way to excited talk for a time, yet such outbursts were not usual with him, for he was the quietest and most modest of men. The real objection to his appointment was the state of his health. He had never been strong and was a martyr to rheumatism and stone, but he was as courageous against pain as against the bullets of the enemy; in fact, like King William the Third, he was never so happy as when under fire. For the rest nature had cursed him with a countenance of singular ugliness, his portraits showing a profile that runs in a ridiculous curve from the forehead to the tip of the nose, and recedes in as ridiculous a curve from the nose to the neck. A shock of red hair tied in a queue, and a tall, lank, ungainly figure added neither grace nor beauty to his appearance; but within that unhandsome frame lay a passionate attachment to the British soldier, and an indomitable spirit against difficulty and danger.

February.
May.

It was the middle of February when Wolfe sailed from England in H.M.S. *Neptune*, the flag-ship of a fleet of twenty-one sail under Admirals Saunders, Holmes, and Durell. The voyage was long and tedious, and when at last Louisburg was reached the harbour was found to be blocked with ice, so that the fleet was obliged to make for Halifax. From thence Durell was detached, too late as was presently proved, to the mouth of the St. Lawrence to intercept certain transports that were expected with supplies from France; Holmes was sent to convoy the troops that were to sail from New York; and in May the entire armament for the reduction of Quebec was assembled at Louisburg. Wolfe had been led to expect a force of twelve thousand men; but the regiments which should have been detached from Guadeloupe could not yet be spared, and those drawn from the garrisons of Nova Scotia had been reduced considerably beneath their proper strength by sickness during the winter. The quality of the troops, however, was excellent, and on this Wolfe counted to make good a serious numerical deficiency. The force was distributed into three brigades, under Brigadiers Monckton, Townsend, and Murray, all three of them men of youth, energy, and talent, well qualified to serve under such a commander as Wolfe.[313] The grenadiers of the army were, as had now become usual, massed together and organised in two divisions, those of the regiments in garrison at Louisburg being known as the Louisburg grenadiers.[314] Another separate corps was composed of the best marksmen in the several regiments, and was called the Light Infantry, while six companies of Provincial rangers furnished a proportion of irregular troops. The whole strength of the force was thus brought up to about eight thousand five hundred men. A fortnight sufficed for the final arrangements, for Amherst and his staff had spared no pains to provide all that was necessary; [315] and on the 6th of June the last division of transports, amid a roar of cheering from the men, sailed out of Louisburg for the St. Lawrence.

The French commanders meanwhile had been anxiously making their preparations for defence. There could be no doubt that the British would make at least a double attack upon Canada, from Lake Champlain on the south and Lake Ontario on the west, and every able-bodied man in the colony was called out to repel it. No sooner had the dispositions been settled than news came of the intended advance by the St. Lawrence, which threw the whole colony into consternation. Five regular battalions and the militia from every part of Canada were summoned, together with a thousand Indians, to Quebec; and after much debate Montcalm, who held the command of the troops under the Governor of the city, decided on his scheme of defence. Quebec with its fortifications stands on the north bank of the St. Lawrence, being situated on a rocky headland which marks the contraction of the river from a width of fifteen or twenty miles to a strait scarcely exceeding one. Immediately to northward of this ridge the river St. Charles flows down to the St. Lawrence; and seven miles to eastward of the St. Charles the shore is cut by the rocky gorge through which pours the cataract of the Montmorenci. It was between these two streams that Montcalm disposed his army, his right resting on the St. Charles, his left on the Montmorenci, with his headquarters on the little river of Beauport midway between the two, and his front to the St. Lawrence. All along the border of the great river were thrown up entrenchments, batteries, and redoubts. From Montmorenci to Beauport abrupt and rocky heights raised these defences too high above the water to be reached by the cannon of ships. From Beauport to the St. Charles stretched broad flats of mud, which were commanded by batteries both afloat and ashore, as well as by the guns of Quebec. On the walls of the city itself were mounted over one hundred cannon; a bridge of boats with a strong bridge-head on the eastern side preserved the communication between city and camp; and for the defence of the river itself there was a floating battery of twelve heavy guns besides several gun-boats and fire-ships. The vessels of the convoy that Durell had failed to intercept, together with the frigates that escorted them, were sent up the river beyond Quebec to be out of harm's way; and the sailors were taken to man the batteries ashore. Thus strongly entrenched with fourteen thousand men of one description and another, and firm in the belief that no foreign ship would dare to attempt the intricate navigation of the St. Lawrence, Montcalm waited for the British to come.

June.

It was not until the 21st of June that the first mast-heads of the fleet were seen. For days the British had been groping their way up the river, helped partly by a captured Canadian pilot, more often by their own skill and experience. "Damn me if there are not a thousand places in the Thames fifty times more hazardous than this," growled an old skipper on one of the transports, as he waived the pilot contemptuously aside. So the great fleet crept up the stream, ships of the line passing where the French had feared to take a coasting schooner, and at last on the 26th of June the whole was anchored safely off the southern shore of the Isle of Orleans, a few miles below Quebec. No single mishap had marred this masterly and superb feat of pilotage.

June 27.
June 28.
June 29.
July.

The troops landed without resistance next day on the Isle of Orleans, and on the same afternoon a sudden squall drove many of the ships ashore and destroyed several of the flat-boats prepared for the disembarkation. The storm raised high hopes of providential deliverance in the French, which, however, were speedily dashed, for the tempest subsided as suddenly as it had arisen. On the morrow therefore the Governor of Quebec resolved to launch his fire-ships down the river upon the fleet. The attempt was duly made, but the ships were ill-handled and the service ill-executed. The British sailors coolly rowed out, grappled the burning vessels and towed them ashore, while the troops, formed up in order of battle, gazed at the most imposing display of fireworks that they had ever seen. Meanwhile Wolfe reconnoitred the French lines and the city, but could see no possible opening for a successful attack. One thing alone seemed feasible, to occupy the heights of Point Lévis over against Quebec on the southern shore, and to fire across this, the narrowest part of the river, upon the city. Monckton's brigade accordingly entrenched itself on these heights, threw up batteries, and on the 12th of July opened a fire which wrought havoc among the buildings of Quebec. But however this cannonade might afflict the nerves of the inhabitants, it could contribute little, as Wolfe well knew, to advance the real work in hand.

Accordingly, while the batteries on Point Lévis were constructing, the English General resolved to see whether a vulnerable point could be found on Montcalm's left flank. On the 8th of July, leaving a detachment to hold the camp on the Isle of Orleans, he sent Townsend's and Murray's brigades across to the northern bank of the St. Lawrence, where they proceeded to entrench themselves on the eastern side of the Montmorenci. The movement was highly perilous, since it divided his force into three portions, no one of which could support the other; but the French kept themselves rigidly on the defensive, though the British lay but a gunshot from them across the rocky gorge of the Montmorenci and annoyed their camp not a little with their artillery. Still Wolfe could accomplish nothing decisive. The news that Amherst was advancing against Ticonderoga did indeed discourage the Canadians and increase desertion among them; but in all other respects the operations before Quebec had come to a deadlock.

| July 18. |
| July 28. |

Now, however, the fleet which had already vanquished the difficulties in the navigation of the St. Lawrence once more came forward to show the way. It was the opinion of the French that no vessel could pass the batteries of Quebec without destruction; but on the night of the 18th of July H.M.S. *Sutherland*, of fifty guns, with several smaller vessels, sailed safely up the river, covered by the fire of the guns on Point Lévis, destroyed some small craft which they found there and anchored above the town. This was the first menace of an attempt to take Quebec in reverse, and obliged Montcalm to detach six hundred men from the camp of Beauport to defend the few accessible points between the city and Cap Rouge, some eight miles above it. Wolfe took advantage of the movement also to send a detachment to ravage the country to westward of Quebec; but though he thus added a fourth to the three isolated divisions into which he had broken up his army, Montcalm still declined to move. A second attempt was indeed made to destroy the British vessels by fire-ships, which was frustrated like the first by the coolness and gallantry of the British sailors; but beyond this French aggression would not go. Montcalm was resolved to play the part of Fabius, and he seemed likely to play it with success.

The season was now wearing on, and Wolfe was not a whit nearer to his object than at his first disembarkation. Mortified by his ill-success he now resolved to attack Montcalm's camp in front. The hazard was desperate, for, after leaving troops to hold Point Lévis and the entrenchments on the Montmorenci, he could raise little more than five thousand men with which to attack a force of more than double his strength in a very formidable position. A mile to westward of the falls of the Montmorenci there is a strand about a furlong wide at high water and half a mile wide at low tide, between that river and the foot of the cliffs. The French had built redoubts on this strand above high-water mark, which were commanded, though Wolfe could not see it, by the fire of musketry from the entrenchments above. Wolfe's hope was that by the capture of one of these redoubts he might tempt the French down to regain it and so bring on a general action, or at least find an opportunity of reconnoitring the entrenched camp itself. Moreover, below the falls of the Montmorenci was a ford, by which some at least of his troops on that river could join in the attack, and so diminish in some degree the disparity of numbers. But Wolfe held the Canadian militia in such contempt that he was not afraid to pit against them, at whatever odds, the valour of his own disciplined soldiers.

| July 31. |

Accordingly on the morning of the 31st of July H.M.S. *Centurion* stood in close to the Montmorenci, dropped her anchor and opened fire on the redoubts. Two armed transports followed her and likewise opened fire on the nearest redoubt, stranding as the tide ebbed till at last they lay high and dry on the mud. Simultaneously the batteries on the other side of the Montmorenci opened a furious fire upon the flank of Montcalm's entrenchments, and at eleven o'clock a number of boats filled with troops rowed across from Point Lévis and hovered about the river opposite Beauport as if to attack at that point. Time, however, showed Montcalm where real danger was to be apprehended, and he concentrated the whole of his twelve thousand men between Beauport and the Montmorenci. At half-past five the British batteries afloat and ashore opened fire with redoubled fury, and the boats made a dash for the shore. Unfortunately some of them grounded on a ledge short of the flats, which caused some confusion and delay, but eventually all of them reached the strand and set the men ashore. Thirteen companies of grenadiers were the first to land, and after them two hundred men of the Sixtieth; while some distance behind them the Fifteenth and Fraser's Highlanders followed in

259

support. No sooner were they ashore than the grenadiers, the most trusted troops in the army, for some reason got out of hand. Despite the efforts of their officers they would not wait for the supports to form up, but made a rush in the greatest disorder and confusion for the redoubt and drove the French from it. Instantly a tremendous fire was poured upon them from the entrenchments above. The grenadiers recoiled for a moment; then recovering themselves they ran forward again and made a mad effort to struggle up the steep, slippery grass of the ascent, but only to roll down by scores, killed or wounded by the hail of musketry from the French lines. Where the affair would have ended it is hard to say, had not the clouds of a summer's storm, which had hung over the river all the afternoon, suddenly burst just at that moment in a deluge of rain. All ammunition on both sides was drenched, so that further firing became impossible, while the grassy slope became so treacherous that it was hopeless to attempt to climb it. Wolfe, seeing that everything was gone wrong, ordered a retreat; and the troops fell back and re-embarked, the grenadiers and Sixtieth having lost five hundred officers and men, or well-nigh half of their numbers, in killed, wounded, and missing.

| August 5. |

Wolfe was highly indignant over the misbehaviour of the grenadiers, and rebuked them sharply in general orders for their impetuous, irregular, and unsoldierlike proceedings. The French, on the other hand, were naturally much elated, and flattered themselves that the campaign was virtually at an end. Nor was Wolfe of a very different opinion. It is said, indeed, that he conceived the idea of leaving a part of his troops in a fortified position before Quebec, to be ready for a new attempt in the following spring. Meanwhile for the present he fell back on the tactics, which Barrington had so successfully employed at Guadeloupe, of laying waste all the settlements round about Quebec, with the object of provoking desertion among the militia and exhausting the colony generally. Montcalm, however, was not to be enticed from his lines; he had Indians with him sufficient to make hideous reprisals for Wolfe's desolation, and Canada was not to be won by the burning of villages. Wolfe, therefore, now shifted his operations to the point whither the enterprise of the fleet had led him, above and on the reverse side of Quebec. With every fair wind more and more ships had braved the fire of the batteries and passed through it in safety; and now a flotilla of flat-boats dared the same passage, while twelve hundred men under Brigadier Murray marched overland up the south bank of the St. Lawrence to do service in them. This movement compelled Montcalm to withdraw another fifteen hundred men from the camp at Beauport, to check any attempt at a landing above the city. The duty thus imposed upon this small body of French was most arduous, since it involved anxious watching of fifteen or twenty miles of the shore. So well was it performed, however, under the direction of Bougainville, an officer afterwards famous as the great navigator, that it was only after two repulses that Murray succeeded in burning a large magazine of French stores. The alarm caused by this stroke was so great that Montcalm hastened from Beauport to take command in person; but when he arrived the British had already retired, content with their success.

None the less the French from the highest to the lowest now grew seriously uneasy. Their army was on short rations. All its supplies were drawn from the districts of Three Rivers and Montreal; and, from want of transport overland, these were perforce sent down the river where the British ships lay ready to intercept them. Now was seen the error of sending the frigates up the river and allowing the British squadron to assemble by small detachments above Quebec; but it was too late to repair it. The British fleet had discovered the true method of reducing the city by severing its communications both above and below. The only hope for the French was that winter might drive the shipping from the St. Lawrence and put an end to the campaign, before Quebec should be starved out.

| June 15. |
| July. |
| July 24. |

Meanwhile Amherst's operations to south and west began likewise to tell upon the situation. Taking advantage of the latitude allowed to him by Pitt, he determined to add the reduction of Niagara to the enterprises prescribed to him. This duty he assigned to Brigadier Prideaux with five thousand men;[316] Brigadier Stanwix was entrusted with the relief of Pittsburg; and Amherst in person took charge of the grand advance by Lakes George and Champlain. The operations of Prideaux and Stanwix were to be conducted in combination; for it was intended that while Prideaux was engaged with Niagara, Stanwix should push a force northward against the French posts on Lake Erie, and thence on to Niagara itself, thus releasing Prideaux for an advance to the St. Lawrence. Prideaux was the first to take the field. His force having been assembled on the Mohawk at Senectady, he moved up the stream, left a strong garrison at Fort Stanwix to guard the Great Carrying-place, and moved forward by Lake Oneida and the river Onandaga to Oswego. There leaving nearly half of his force under Colonel Haldimand to secure his retreat, he embarked with the rest on the lake for Niagara. The fort stood in the angle formed by the river Niagara and Lake Ontario, and was garrisoned by some six hundred men. Prideaux at once laid siege in form, though the trenches were at first so unskilfully laid out by the engineers as to require almost total reconstruction. At last, however, the batteries opened fire. Prideaux was unluckily killed almost immediately by the premature explosion of a shell from one of his own guns, but Sir William Johnson, who had joined the force with a party of Indians, took command in his place and pushed the siege with great energy. The fort after two or three weeks of battering was in extremity; when a party of thirteen hundred French rangers and Indians, which had been summoned from the work of harassing the British on the Ohio to the relief of Niagara, appeared on the scene in the very nick of time. Johnson rose worthily to the occasion. Leaving a third of his force in the trenches and yet another third to guard his boats, he sallied forth with the remainder to meet the relieving force, and after a brisk engagement routed it completely. The survivors fled hurriedly back to Lake Erie, burned Venango and the posts on the lake and retired to Detroit. Niagara surrendered on the evening of the same day, and thus were accomplished at a stroke the most important objects to be gained by Stanwix and Prideaux. The whole region of the Upper Ohio was left in undisputed possession of the British, and the French posts of the West were hopelessly cut off from Canada. Now, therefore, the ground was open for an advance on Montreal by Lake Ontario; and Amherst lost no time in sending General Gage to take command of Prideaux's force, with orders to attack the French post of La Galette, at the head of the rapids of the St. Lawrence, and thence to push on as close as possible to Montreal. "Now is the time," wrote Amherst to him, "and we must make use of it."[317]

> July 21.
> July 26.
> August.

Amherst himself had assembled his army at the end of June at the usual rendezvous by the head of Lake George. His force consisted of about eleven thousand five hundred men, five thousand of them Provincials and the remainder British.[318] As was now the rule, he had massed the grenadiers of the army into one corps, and had formed also a body of Light Infantry which he had equipped appropriately for its work.[319] It was not, however, until the 21st of July that the troops were embarked, and that a flotilla little less imposing than Abercromby's set sail with a fair wind over Lake George. It was drawn up in four columns, the light troops and Provincials on either flank, the regular troops in the right centre and the artillery and baggage in the left centre. An advanced and a rear-guard in line covered the head and tail of the columns, and an armed sloop followed in rear of all. Before dark they had reached the Narrows, and at daybreak of the following morning the force disembarked and marched, meeting with little resistance, by the route of Abercromby's second advance to Ticonderoga. The entrenchments which had foiled the British in the previous year had been reconstructed but were found to be deserted; Bourlamaque, the French commander, having withdrawn his garrison, some thirty-five hundred men only, into the fort. Amherst brought up his artillery to lay siege in form, but on the night of the 26th a loud explosion announced that the French had abandoned Ticonderoga and blown up the works. It was, however, but one bastion that had been destroyed, so Amherst at once repaired the damage and made preparations for advance on Crown Point. On the 1st of August he learned that Bourlamaque had abandoned this fortress also, and fallen back to the strong position of Isle aux Noix at the northern outlet of Lake Champlain. Amherst was now brought to a standstill, for the French had four armed vessels on the lake, and it was necessary for him to build vessels likewise for the protection of the flotilla before he could advance farther. He at once set about this work, concurrently with the erection of a strong fort at Crown Point, but unfortunately he began too late. Amherst was above all a methodical man, whose principle was to make good each step gained before he attempted to move again. Possibly he had not anticipated so easy an advance to Crown Point, but, be that as it may, he had made no provision for advancing beyond it, and when at last, by the middle of September, his ships were ready, the season was too far advanced for further operations. He tried to stir up Gage to hasten to the attack on La Galette, but without success. In fact by the middle of August the campaign of the armies of the south and west was virtually closed.

| August. |

Nevertheless for the moment the news of Amherst's advance to Crown Point caused great alarm in Quebec, and Montcalm felt himself obliged to send Lévis, one of his best officers, to superintend the defence of Montreal. Gradually, however, as Amherst's inaction was prolonged, the garrison regained confidence; and meanwhile deep discouragement fell on the British. On the 20th of August Wolfe, who was much exhausted by hard work, anxiety, and mortification, fell seriously ill and was compelled to delegate the conduct of operations to a council of his brigadiers. Several plans were propounded to them, all of which they rejected in favour of an attempt to gain a footing on the ridge above the city, cut off Montcalm's supplies from Montreal, and compel him to fight or surrender. The course was that which had been marked out by the fleet from the moment that the ships had passed above Quebec. It was indeed both difficult and hazardous, but it was the only plan that promised any hope of success; and the success, if attained, would be final. Wolfe accepted it forthwith and without demur. The army had lost over eight hundred men killed and wounded since the beginning of operations, and had been weakened still more seriously by disease; but the General was driven to desperation by sickness and disappointment and was ready to undertake any enterprise that commended itself to his officers. On the last day of August he was sufficiently recovered to go abroad once more, and on the

2nd of September he wrote to Pitt the story of his failure up to that day and of his resolutions for the future, all in a strain of dejection that sank almost to despair.

| Sept. 3. |

On the following day the troops were skilfully withdrawn without loss from the camp on the Montmorenci. On the night of the 4th a flotilla of flat-boats passed successfully above the town with the baggage and stores, and on the 5th seven battalions marched westward overland from Point Lévis and embarked, together with Wolfe himself, on Admiral Holmes' ships. Montcalm thereupon reinforced Bougainville to a strength of three thousand men and charged him to watch the movements of the fleet with the utmost vigilance. Bougainville's headquarters were at Cap Rouge, with detached fortified posts at Sillery, six miles down the river, at Samos yet farther down, and at Anse du Foulon, now called Wolfe's Cove, a mile and a half above Quebec. It was by this last that Wolfe, searching the heights for mile after mile with his telescope, perceived a narrow path running up the face of the precipice. From the path he turned his glass to the post above it, and seeing but ten or twelve tents concluded that the guard was not numerous and might be overpowered. There then was a way found for the ascent of the cliffs from the river: the next problem was how to turn the discovery to good account.

On the morning of the 7th of September Holmes' squadron weighed anchor and sailed up to Cap Rouge. The French instantly turned out to man their entrenchments; and Wolfe, having kept them in suspense for a sufficient time, ordered the troops into the boats and directed them to row up and down as if in search of a landing-place. The succeeding days were employed in a series of similar feints, the ships drifting daily up to Cap Rouge with the flood tide and dropping down to Quebec with the ebb, till Bougainville, who followed every movement with increasing anxiety and bewilderment, fairly wore out his troops with incessant marching to and fro.

| Sept. 12. |

At last on the 12th of September Wolfe's opportunity presented itself. Two deserters came in from Bougainville's camp with intelligence that at next ebb-tide a convoy of provisions would pass down the river to Quebec. Wolfe sent orders to Colonel Burton, who was in command of the standing camps, that all the men which he could spare from them should march at nightfall along the southern bank of the river, and wait at a chosen place for embarkation. As night fell Admiral Saunders moved out of the basin of Orleans with the main fleet and ranged the ships along the length of the camp at Beauport. The boats were then lowered and manned by marines, sailors, and such few soldiers as had been left below Quebec, while the ships opened fire on the beach as if to clear it for a landing. Montcalm, completely deceived, massed the whole of his troops at Beauport, and kept them under arms to repel the threatened attack. Meanwhile Holmes' squadron, with boats moored alongside the transports, lay quietly anchored off Cap Rouge, nor showed sign of life until late dusk, when seventeen hundred men[320] took their places in the boats and drifted with the tide for some little distance up the stream. Bougainville marked the movement and made no doubt that attack was designed upon his headquarters. Night fell, dark and moonless, and all was quiet. Monsieur Vergor, who commanded the post at Anse du Foulon, gave leave to most of his guard of Canadians to go harvesting, and saw no reason why he should not himself go comfortably to bed. Bougainville remained on the alert, doubtless impatient for the tide to turn, which would carry the British away from his quarters and leave him in peace. He did not know that Wolfe was even then on board the flag-ship making his final arrangements for the morrow's battle, and that he had handed the portrait of his betrothed to Captain John Jervis[321] of H.M.S. *Porcupine*, to be returned to her in the event of his death.

| Sept. 13. |

At length at two o'clock in the morning the tide ebbed. Two lanterns rose flickering to the maintop shrouds of the *Sutherland*; Wolfe and his officers stepped into their boat, and with the whole flotilla astern of them dropped silently down the river. After a due interval the sloops and frigates followed, with the second division of troops on board;[322] and Bougainville with a sigh of relief resolved not to harass his men by a fruitless march after them. For full two hours the boats pursued their way, when the silence was broken by the challenge of a French sentry. "France," answered a Highland officer who had learned the French tongue on foreign service. "What regiment?" pursued the sentry. "The Queen's" (*de la Reine*) replied the officer, naming a corps that formed part of Bougainville's force. The sentry, knowing that a convoy of provisions was expected, allowed the boats to pass; for though Bougainville had, as a matter of fact, countermanded the convoy, the guards had not been apprised of the countermand. Off Samos another sentry, visible not a pistol-shot away from the boats, again challenged. "Provision-boats," answered the same officer, "don't make a noise or the English will hear." Once more the boats were suffered to pass. Presently they rounded the headland of Anse du Foulon, and there no sentry was to be seen. The leading boats were carried by the current somewhat below the intended landing-place, and the troops disembarked below the path, on a narrow strand at the foot of the heights. Then twenty-four men of the Light Infantry, who had volunteered for a certain unknown but dangerous service under Colonel Howe, slung their muskets about them, threw themselves upon the face of the cliff, and began to drag themselves through the two hundred feet of stunted bush that separated them from the enemy.

The dawn was just breaking as they reached the top, and through the dim light they could distinguish the group of tents that composed Vergor's encampment. Instantly they dashed at them; and the French, utterly surprised, at once took to their heels. Vergor, who was reputed a coward, stood firm and fired his pistols; and the report of three of the British muskets, together with the cheers of Howe's forlorn hope, gave Wolfe the signal for which he waited. He uttered the word to advance, and the rest of the troops swarmed up the cliff to their comrades as best they could. The zigzag path which had first attracted Wolfe's eye was found to be obstructed by trenches and abatis, but these obstacles were cleared away and the ascent made easier. Presently the report of cannon was heard from up the river: the batteries of Sillery and Samos were firing at the rearmost of the boats and at Holmes' squadron. Howe and his Light Infantry were detached to silence them, which they effectually did; and meanwhile the disembarkation proceeded rapidly. As fast as the boats were emptied they went back to fetch the second division from the ships and Burton's men from the opposite shore. Before the sun was well up the whole force of forty-five hundred men had accomplished the ascent, and was filing across the plain at the summit of the heights.

Wolfe went forward to reconnoitre. The ground on which he stood formed part of the high plateau which ends in the promontory of Quebec. About a mile to eastward of the landing-place was a tract of grass, known as the plains of Abraham, fairly level ground for the most part, though broken by patches of corn and clumps of bushes, and bounded on the south by the heights of the St. Lawrence and to north by those of the St. Charles. On these plains, where the plateau is less than a mile wide, Wolfe chose his position for the expected battle. His situation, despite the skilful execution of the movement which brought his army across Montcalm's line of communication, was no secure nor enviable one, for besides Montcalm's army and the garrison of Quebec in his front, he had also to reckon with Bougainville's detachment in his rear. His only chance of success was that the French should allow him to beat them in detail, that, in fact, they should bring out their main army and give him opportunity to crush it in front, before Bougainville should have time to operate effectively in his rear. But there was no reason why the French should do anything of the kind; and Wolfe's dispositions needed to be regulated accordingly. The extent of the ground was too great to permit order of battle in more than one line; and it was in one line that he prepared to meet the main force from the side of Quebec. The right wing rested on the brink of the heights above the St. Lawrence, and here was stationed a single platoon of the Twenty-eighth. Next it, in succession from right to left, stood the Thirty-fifth, three companies of the Louisburg grenadiers,[323] the remainder of the Twenty-eighth, the Forty-third, Forty-seventh, Fraser's Highlanders, and the Fifty-eighth. Straight through the centre of the position, midway between the Forty-seventh and Fraser's, ran the road from Sillery to Quebec, and here was posted a single light field-gun[324] which had been dragged up from Wolfe's Cove. On the extreme left, beyond the flank of the Fifty-eighth, ran the road from Sainte Foy to Quebec, with a few scattered houses on the south side and patches of bushes and coppice beyond it. The line, being three ranks deep, was not long enough to rest its left on this road, much less on the heights above the St. Charles, so the Fifteenth foot was thrown back *en potence* to prevent the turning of the left flank. The second battalion of the Sixtieth and the Forty-eighth Foot were stationed in rear, the one on the left and the other on the right, in eight subdivisions, with wide intervals. Two companies of the Fifty-eighth were left to guard the landing-place, the third battalion of the Sixtieth was detached to the right rear to preserve communication with it; and finally Howe's Light Infantry occupied a wood far in rear, evidently to hold Bougainville in check. Monckton commanded the right and Murray the left of the fighting line, while Townsend took charge of the scattered troops which did duty for a reserve. Wolfe in person remained with Monckton's brigade. [325] Probably he anticipated that Montcalm would attempt to turn his right and so cut off his retreat.

Meanwhile Montcalm had passed a troubled night. The false attack of the fleet on Beauport had kept him in continual anxiety; and he was still more disquieted at daybreak to hear the sound of the cannon of Samos and Sillery above the city. He sent an officer to the Governor's quarters in Quebec for information, but received no answer; so at six o'clock he rode up to look for himself, when on reaching the right of his camp he caught sight, over the St. Charles, of an ominous band of scarlet stretched across the heights two miles away. His countenance fell. "This is a serious business," he said, and he despatched an aide-de-camp at full gallop to bring up the troops from the right and centre of the camp of Beauport. The men, only lately relieved from the manning of the entrenchments, got under arms and streamed away in hot haste across the bridge of the St. Charles and through the narrow streets of the city—Indians, Canadians, and regulars all alike stirred by the sudden approach of danger. Further reconnaissance filled Montcalm with still greater dismay. It was not a mere detachment, but practically the entire British army that had found its way to the heights between him and Montreal. Meanwhile Vaudreuil, the Governor of Quebec, who was also Commander-in-Chief, was not to be found; and there was unity neither of direction nor of obedience. Montcalm applied to Ramesay, who commanded the garrison of Quebec, for twenty-five field-guns which were mounted in one of the batteries: Ramesay declared that he needed them for his own defence and would spare but three. Then there was anxious waiting for the troops from the left of Beauport's camp, which for some reason never came. All was confusion, perplexity, and distraction.

In such circumstances Montcalm appears to have succumbed to nervous strain and to have lost his wits. He held a hasty council of war with his principal officers and decided to fight at once. He was afraid, it seems, lest Wolfe should be reinforced or lest he might entrench himself. Yet there was no occasion for extreme haste. Another two hours would have sufficed, if not to bring up the missing troops from Beauport, at all events to procure more guns and to send a messenger by a safe route to concert measures with Bougainville; and the day was yet young. The supplies of the French were failing, it is true, but their army was not starving; and from whence was Wolfe himself, with Bougainville in his rear, to draw his supplies even supposing that he did entrench himself? The British had two days' provisions with them, but for all further supply they must depend on a single zigzag path wide enough for but one man abreast. Even supposing that Montcalm could not succeed in obtaining the thirty field-guns for which he asked, and which if obtained would almost inevitably have blasted the British army off the field, there was nothing to prevent him from manœuvring with a superior force to keep the British under arms until nightfall, while his Indians and irregulars, of whom he had abundance, harried the British right flank in front and rear under shelter of the scrub, and hindered the bringing up of further stores. What would have been the condition of Wolfe's army on the following morning after a second night under arms, and what opening might there not have been for successful attack? But it was not to be. Whether Montcalm was spurred on by the impatience of his own half-distracted force, or whether he simply gave way to nervous exhaustion, must remain uncertain. At any rate he resolved with the five thousand troops that were with him to accept battle at once.

By nine o'clock his line of battle was formed, some six hundred yards from the British position. On his right, resting on the road to Sainte Foy was a battalion of Canadian militia, and next to it in succession the regular regiments of Bèarn and La Sarre. Next to these, in column on either side of the road to Sillery, were the regiments of Guienne and Languedoc, and to their left regiment Roussillon and another battalion of militia. On the extreme right and left some two thousand Indians and Canadians swarmed forward in skirmishing order in advance of the line of battle. It was with the fire of these sharpshooters that the action began. There was good cover for them not only on the flanks but also among the scattered bushes in the front. Wolfe threw out skirmishers to meet them, and the fusillade became lively, especially on the British left, where Townsend's men began to fall fast. So severe became this pressure on the left that Townsend, alarmed for his flank, brought up the second battalion of the Sixtieth to the left of the Fifty-eighth, detailed part of them to drive the Canadians from the houses by the road and doubled the remainder back *en potence* in line with the Fifteenth; while at the same time the Light Infantry was called up in support of the Fifteenth to strengthen the flank still further. Thus before the action was well begun the rear-guard and half of the reserve was practically absorbed in the fighting line. On the British right, where the French sharpshooters could not get round the flank, their fire was by no means so deadly; but it does not appear that either of these attacks formed part of any settled plan of Montcalm, for by throwing the mass of his skirmishers against the British left he might have made them very formidable.

Meanwhile Montcalm's three field-guns had opened fire, and were answered by the single gun on the Sillery road with great effect. So the minutes dragged on, until at a little before ten the French line advanced with loud shouts to the true attack, the regulars in the centre moving steadily, a long streak of white edged on either hand with red and with blue, and the militia striving to move as steadily on the flanks. The English, who until now had been lying down, then sprang to their feet and stood steady with recovered arms. At a range of two hundred yards the French muskets opened fire but with little effect, while much confusion and delay was caused by the Canadian militia who, true to their instincts as skirmishers, threw themselves flat on the ground to reload. Wolfe was shot through the wrist, but he merely wrapped his handkerchief round the wound, and called to the men to be steady and reserve their fire. The French recovered their order somewhat and again came on, filling the air with their cries, while the British stood calm, silent and immovable, knowing their chief and trusting him.[326] Nearer and nearer drew the parti-coloured line, gayer and gayer as the blue and scarlet facings on the white coats came into view, brighter and brighter as the detail of metal buttons and accoutrements cleared themselves from the distance, till at length the time was come. Thirty-five yards only separated the opposing arrays, when the word rang out, the still red line sprang into life, the recovered muskets leaped forward into a long bristling bar, and with one deafening crash, the most perfect volley ever fired on battlefield burst forth as if from a single monstrous weapon, from end to end of the British line. A dense bank of smoke blotted the French from sight, and from behind it there rose a horrible din of clattering arms, and savage oaths and agonised cries. The sharp clink of ramrods broke in upon the sound as the British reloaded; and when the smoke rolled away, the gay line was seen to be shivered to fragments, while the bright coats strewed the ground like swathes of gaudy flowers. There was hardly a bullet of that volley that had not struck home.

Montcalm, himself unhurt and conspicuous on a black charger, galloped frantically up and down his shattered ranks in a vain effort to restore order. Wolfe gave the order to advance, and after one more volley the scarlet line strode forward with bayonet and claymore to complete the rout. There was nothing to stop the British, nothing even to gall them except the fire of a few sharpshooters hidden in the scrub. Wolfe himself led them at the head of the Twenty-eighth. A bullet struck him in the groin, but he paused not a moment and was still striding on, when another ball passed through his lungs. He staggered forward, still vainly striving to keep on his feet. "Support me, support me," he gasped to an officer who was close to him, "lest my gallant fellows should see me fall." Two or three men fell out and carried him to the rear, but his fall was noticed by few; and the victorious line pressed on. Some of the sharpshooters continued to fire from behind the shrubs and required to be driven out. Others taking cover nearer to the town opened a biting fire on the Highlanders who, charging as usual with the claymore only, suffered much loss in the attempt to force so wily an enemy from the bush. But other regiments came up and did the work for them with the musket, and thenceforward no further stand was made by the French, but Montcalm's whole force broke up and fled in wild confusion towards the town. He himself, borne away in the rush of the fugitives, was shot through the body, but being supported in the saddle rode in through the gates. "It is nothing, nothing," he called to the shrieking women who saw the red stains on his white uniform; "don't distress yourselves over me, good people." He was lifted from his horse and borne into a surgeon's house to die. The panic among the French increased. Their chief was dying, his second mortally wounded; and among the terrified mob that fled by the St. Charles there rose a cry to destroy the bridge of boats, lest the English should break into the camp of Beauport. This insane movement, which would have sacrificed the whole of the fugitives who had not yet crossed the river, was checked by one or two officers who still kept their wits about them; but none the less the French were not only beaten but demoralised, and the victory of the British was complete.

But the victors also had lost the services both of their General and his second. Monckton had been severely wounded by a musket-shot which for the present disabled him from duty, and Wolfe had been carried to the rear more dead than alive. He begged his bearers to set him down, and refused to see a surgeon. "There is no need," he said, "it is all over with me"; and he sank into unconsciousness. "How they run," cried out one of the attendants, as he watched the French flying before the red-coats. "Who run?" asked Wolfe, waking suddenly to life. "The enemy, Sir, they give way everywhere." "Go one of you to Colonel Burton," ordered the dying General with great earnestness, "and tell him to march Webb's regiment[327] down to Charles

River to cut off the retreat from the bridge." He ceased, and turned on his side. "Now, God be praised, I will die in peace," he murmured; and so died.

With his death and the disabling of Monckton the command devolved upon Townsend, who had no sooner assumed it than he found the rear of the army threatened by Bougainville. Turning upon this new enemy with two battalions and two field-guns he soon forced him to retire; and then, the pursuit being ended, he proceeded to entrench himself on the battlefield. The losses of the British were trifling compared with the magnitude of the success, amounting to no more than six hundred and thirty of all ranks killed and wounded.[328] The chief sufferers were the Highlanders, during their onslaught with the claymore, and the Fifteenth, Fifty-eighth and second battalion of the Sixtieth, who bore the brunt of the sharpshooting on the left flank. Before midnight the entrenchments had made good progress, and cannon had been brought up to defend them. A battery also had been mounted at the northern angle of the town, and the French hospital, full of sick and wounded men, had been taken. Nothing is said of the exhaustion of the troops, who had been on duty continuously for at least thirty hours.

Meanwhile utter confusion reigned in the French camp. Vaudreuil called a council of war, and there was tumultuous debate. A messenger was sent to the dying Montcalm for advice, and returned with the reply that there were three courses open, to retreat up the river, to fight again, or to surrender the colony. There was much to be said for fighting, for with Bougainville's force the French could still bring superior numbers into the field; still more to be said for the defence of Quebec; but the demoralisation was too deep to permit any bold action. At nine o'clock in the evening Vaudreuil gave the order to retreat, and, the word once uttered, the entire French force streamed away in disorderly and disgraceful flight to the post of Jacques Cartier, thirty miles up the St. Lawrence. The only instructions left with the garrison of Quebec were to surrender as soon as provisions should fail. Well was it for Montcalm, always a brave and faithful soldier, that his deliverance came to him before the dawn of another day.

Townsend for his part pushed his trenches forward against Quebec with the greatest energy. The French, despite their precipitate retreat, were still superior force in his rear; and though certainly demoralised might rally on joining the unbeaten troops of Lévis, and imbibe new courage under the leadership of that excellent officer. It was therefore imperative to press the garrison hard while still overpowered by the despairing sense of its isolation. On the 17th of September the British ships of war moved up against the Lower Town, and a scarlet column approached the walls from the meadows of the St. Charles. The French drums beat to arms, but the Canadian militia refused to turn out, and the white flag was hoisted. An officer was sent to Townsend's quarters to gain time, if possible, by prolonging negotiations. Townsend's answer was peremptory: unless the town were surrendered by eleven o'clock, he would take it by storm; and on this Ramesay signed the capitulation. It was none too soon. Before the messenger with the signed articles had reached Townsend, Canadian horsemen arrived with provisions and with a cheering message that help was at hand; and on the very next morning Lévis marched out from Jacques Cartier, only to learn that he was just too late.

On the afternoon of the 18th the British entered the city, and during the following weeks were employed in strengthening the defences and making provision against the winter; for it had been decided that the fortress must be held at all risks. Monckton was still too far disabled to assume command; Townsend, fresh from the House of Commons, had no mind for such dreary duty as winter-quarters; so Brigadier Murray was left as Governor with a garrison of seven thousand five hundred men, his battalions being strengthened by drafts from the Sixty-second and Sixty-ninth, which were serving on board the fleet. At the end of October Admiral Saunders fired his farewell salute and dropped down the river with his fleet, carrying with him the embalmed remains of Wolfe, to be laid by his father's body in the parish church of Greenwich.

So ended the first stage of the conquest of Canada, with better fortune than might have been expected; for there is no gainsaying the fact that the concert of operations intended by Pitt and designed by Amherst had broken down. It should seem indeed that the scheme was too complex, that too much was attempted with the resources at command, that the combination of the various enterprises was too intricate to admit of complete success in a wild and distant country, where the campaigning season was so strictly bounded by the climate. Amherst's operations depended greatly on the help given to him by the Provincials, and the colonial assemblies whatever their good-will were always dilatory, while sometimes, as in the case of Pennsylvania, they were intolerably recalcitrant. Again, though drafts had been sent to the General to make good the losses of the previous campaign,[329] these were not nearly sufficient to fill the gaps made by the slaughter of Ticonderoga and the bitter cold of a Canadian winter. Significantly enough, also, no care had been taken to provide the garrison of Louisburg, most arctic of quarters, even with coverlets, so that the casualties in the winter were far greater than they should have been.[330] Again, it had been ordained that Hopson should reinforce Amherst when his work at Martinique was done, but this arrangement also had broken down; and the least forethought as to the waste of a tropical campaign would have shown that it should not have been reckoned on. The result was that Amherst and Wolfe found themselves with insufficient troops, and that as a natural consequence the former was obliged to cut the margin of his several operations too fine. The death of Prideaux, an excellent officer, was a great misfortune, though Johnson finished his work at Niagara efficiently enough. Stanwix also, after overcoming vast difficulties of transport, succeeded in penetrating to Pittsburg; but here the operations of both columns came to an end. The Ohio happened to be so low that Stanwix could not send up a battalion, as he had been bidden, to reinforce Gage for his advance to La Galette; and Gage, who was not a very enterprising man, to Amherst's great disappointment thought himself not strong enough to move in consequence. On Amherst's own failure to reach Montreal comment has already been passed; but it should be remembered that the whole burden of the preparations for Wolfe's expedition was laid upon him, and that Wolfe gratefully acknowledged the thoroughness of the work. Still the fact remains that the diversions from south and west were an almost total failure, and that Wolfe was consequently obliged to perform his difficult task unaided.

Fortune was against the British in that the weather delayed the assembling of Wolfe's army at Louisburg; for those few lost weeks might easily have made the entire difference to the campaign. Wolfe, with an inadequate force, was driven to his wits' end to solve the problem assigned to him; and it is quite incontestable that the credit for the fall of Quebec belongs rather to the Navy than to the Army. The names of Saunders and of Holmes are little remembered; and the fame of James Cook the master, whose skill and diligence did much to reveal the unknown channel of the St. Lawrence, is swallowed up in that of Captain James Cook the navigator. Still the fact remains unaltered. It was the audacity of Holmes and his squadron in running the gauntlet of the batteries of Quebec which first threatened the supplies and communications of the city, and forced Montcalm to weaken his main army by detaching Bougainville. It was the terrible restless energy of the same squadron, ever moving up and down the river, which wore out the limbs of the French soldiers and the nerves of their officers; and to the Navy fully as much as to the Army is due the praise for the movement that finally set Wolfe and his battalions on the heights of Abraham. But in truth this last most delicate and critical operation was so admirably thought out and executed by the officers of both services that it must abide for ever a masterpiece in its kind. The British Navy and Army working, as at Quebec, in concord and harmony under loyal and able chiefs, are indeed not easily baffled.

It still remains for enquiry why Wolfe did not take earlier advantage of the opportunities opened to him by the fleet; and even after allowance has been made for his constant illness, the answer is not readily found. The measures which led to the decisive action were, as has been told, taken on the advice of his brigadiers, and, if Montcalm had not succumbed to positive infatuation, would very likely have brought Wolfe to a court-martial. But if instead of wasting the whole of August in futile efforts below Quebec, Wolfe had shifted his operations forthwith to the west of the city, it seems at least probable that he could have attained his object without hazarding that desperate cast on the plains of Abraham. It would presumably have been open to him to gain the heights as he gained them ultimately, to have overwhelmed Bougainville's posts piecemeal, as was done as far as Sillery by a small detachment on the morning of the battle, and to have entrenched himself in the most suitable of them. Then having cut the French communications by land and water, he could have forced Montcalm either to abandon Quebec or to fight on his own terms. But it is easy to be wise after the event; and a brilliant success, however fortunate, is rightly held to cover all errors. Moreover, the praise for the perfection of drill and discipline which won the victory with a single volley is all Wolfe's own. Still it seems to be a fair criticism that the General was slow to perceive the real weakness of Montcalm's position and the vital spot laid open to him by the fleet for a deadly thrust. The consequence was that the work was but half done and, as shall now be seen, only narrowly escaped undoing.

CHAPTER IV

The city of Quebec when the British entered into possession was little better than a shapeless mass of ruins, having been reduced to that state by the guns of the fleet. The population was thoroughly demoralised, and given over to theft and pillage; liquor was abundant and the British soldier was thirsty; in fact it needed all Murray's firmness to restore any kind of order.[331] In December severe weather began in earnest, and the effects of bad quarters, bad food, insufficient clothing and insufficient fuel speedily made themselves felt. The sentries were relieved every hour, yet it was impossible to keep them free of frost-bite. The Highlanders despite their natural hardihood suffered more than their comrades, the kilt being but a sorry protection against a Canadian winter; and they were only relieved by a supply of long woollen hose knitted for them, perhaps as much for decency's as for charity's sake, by the nuns of the city. Still the men remained cheerful, for they were kept constantly at work cutting fuel and dragging it in sledges to their quarters, an errand on which they set forth always with muskets as well as with axes, from fear of Indians and bushrangers. Nevertheless their sufferings were great. Fifty men were frost-bitten on a single day while employed on this duty; three days later sixty-five more were similarly afflicted, and before Christmas there were over a hundred and fifty cases.[332] This, however, would have been a small matter but for the more deadly scourge that was added to it. The garrison was victualled entirely with salt provisions; it was impossible to procure fresh meat for the men; and scurvy grew and increased until there was hardly a soldier in the ranks, even among those reckoned fit for duty, who was wholly free from the disease.

With such a plague in his midst Murray might well feel apprehensive for the safety of Quebec against the enemy without the walls, for ever since the British occupation of the city the French had made no secret of their intention to recapture it. Murray had established two fortified posts a few miles to westward of Quebec at Sainte Foy and Old Lorette; while the French had established themselves at St. Augustine, only two days' march from the gates, from which position it was soon necessary to expel them. Petty skirmishes such as this were frequent, but ended always with so easy advantage to the

British that the troops began to think themselves invincible. Repeated intelligence, however, still arrived of French designs against Quebec, vague enough at first, but, as the winter wore on, gradually assuming more definite form. Lévis, the ablest officer left to the French since the fall of Montcalm, was in fact straining every nerve to organise and equip a force of overwhelming strength for the purpose. He had full information of the state of Murray's army and knew that he had but to bide his time for scurvy to do the best part of his work for him. At the end of March he heard that half of the British were on the sick-list, and the report was not far from the truth. By the middle of April Murray had barely three thousand men fit for duty, while no fewer than seven hundred were lying in the snow-drifts, waiting till spring should unbind the frozen ground to give them a grave.

| April 21. |
| April 26. |
| April 27. |

On the 17th of April Murray, learning that the preparations of the French were complete, occupied the mouth of Cap Rouge River to prevent a landing at that point. Four days later Lévis set out with about seven thousand men, half of them regular troops, and a fleet of bateaux escorted by two frigates and by several smaller craft. The river was not yet free from ice, the weather was bad, and navigation was difficult; but on the 26th the army, reinforced by the garrisons of several outlying stations to nearly nine thousand men, landed at St. Augustine and marched upon the British advanced posts. The British at once fell back from Cap Rouge and Old Lorette upon Sainte Foy. Lévis followed after them all night, despite the difficulties of half-thawed ice and driving rain and tempest, and at daybreak arrived before Sainte Foy to find every house occupied by the British and their cannon playing on his columns as they emerged from the forest. Murray, warned by the information of a French gunner, who had been picked up half dead from the floating ice in the St. Lawrence, had marched out with half of the garrison to cover the retreat of his advanced parties. The position which he occupied was strong, and Lévis being ignorant of the weakness of his numbers would not venture to attack, but resolved to wait until nightfall and then move round the British left flank. Murray therefore was able to retire in safety to Quebec, while Lévis occupied Sainte Foy and pushed his light troops forward to Sillery.

| April 28. |

Murray's position now was none of the pleasantest. The fortifications of Quebec were in no condition to withstand an energetic cannonade, and the ground was still frozen so hard that it was impossible for him to throw up entrenchments, as he had long desired, outside the walls. The only alternative open to him was to sally out and fight Lévis, at odds of one against two, and beat him if he could. Murray was young, daring and fired by the example of Wolfe; his army was, as he said, in the habit of beating the enemy;[333] and he had a fine train of artillery. He therefore resolved to go out and fight. Accordingly at half-past six on the morning of the 28th he marched out of Quebec at the head of all the troops that he could muster, a bare three thousand men, with three howitzers and twenty field-pieces, and drew them up on the ground which Montcalm had occupied on the famous 13th of September. The force was formed in one line of two brigades, the right or Burton's brigade consisting, from right to left, of the Fifteenth, Fifty-eighth, second battalion of the Sixtieth, and Forty-eighth regiments; the left or Fraser's brigade of the Forty-third, Forty-seventh, Fraser's Highlanders, and the Twenty-eighth. The Thirty-fifth and third battalion of the Sixtieth were posted in reserve in rear of the centre, while the Light Infantry and the Provincial rangers stood wide on the right and left flanks. The field-guns were distributed in pairs to each battalion.

Moving forward to reconnoitre, Murray perceived that the French line was not yet formed. That Lévis had chosen his ground was clear, for he had occupied two block-houses built by the British above Anse du Foulon at the southern edge of the plateau, as well as a house and a fortified windmill at the northern brink, and had extended his vanguard along the ridge between these two points. But the main body was still debouching in columns from Sillery Wood, a mile or more in rear, and two brigades only were as yet deployed by the block-house to form the French right wing. Thinking the opportunity favourable, Murray ordered an immediate advance; and his whole line moved forward, the men dragging their guns with them in the intervals between battalions. The ground was for the most part still covered with snow, which in some places was piled up in drifts and everywhere soft and sodden with rain; and the tramp of three thousand men soon turned the soil into a sea of mud. Arrived at the ground where Wolfe's army had stood, the line halted, and the guns unlimbering opened so destructive a fire on the French columns that Lévis ordered the battalions of his left to fall back to the woods. The manœuvre was not executed without confusion, and Murray, elated by his apparent success, ordered the line to renew its advance, inclining to its right. This movement, however, brought Burton's brigade on to low ground, where the melting snow was knee-deep and the guns could not be worked with effect. The British Light Infantry attacked the windmill and houses on the French left with great spirit, carried them in spite of a desperate resistance, and pressed on in pursuit of the retreating French. But now the battalions of the French left, no longer checked by the fire of artillery, dashed out of the woods in skirmishing order and falling on the rash pursuers fairly overwhelmed them. Over two hundred of the Light Infantry were killed and wounded, and the few survivors hurrying back in confusion upon Burton's brigade prevented it from firing on the advancing enemy. The French seized the opportunity to reform their broken ranks and the combat was hotly maintained for more than an hour, until ammunition for the British artillery failed, the tumbrils being immovably fixed in the snow-drifts.

On Murray's left his hasty advance was little less disastrous. The block-houses were indeed carried and held for a time, but the French fell back into the woods only to advance again in overwhelming force when the fire of the British artillery failed, and to extend themselves along the British front and flank. The two battalions of the reserve were called up and the fight was maintained with indomitable stubbornness; but with both flanks turned the efforts of the British were hopeless, and Murray gave the word to fall back. The men, though but two in three of them remained unhurt, were furious at the order. "Damn it, what is falling back but retreating!" they said; but there was no help for it. So first the left brigade and then the right retired, cursing as they went. Some of the regiments tried to carry off their guns with them, but finding this impossible owing to deep snow and mud spiked and abandoned them. The French followed in pursuit, hoping to cut them off from the city; but Lévis perceiving the orderliness of the retreat judged it more prudent to recall his troops, and Murray brought back the remnant of his force in safety to Quebec.

So ended the action of Sainte Foy after two hours of stern and bloody work. The loss of the British amounted to a thousand killed and wounded or a full third of the entire force. The Fifteenth, Twenty-eighth, and Highlanders[334] were, after the Light Infantry, the greatest sufferers, but in the attenuated state of the battalions it is probable that in seven out of the ten there fell at least one man in three. The loss of the French was admitted to have exceeded eight hundred. Altogether it was an unfortunate affair, though it cannot be called discreditable to the troops. Murray was misled by overweening confidence in his men and miscalculation of the spirit of the French. His past experience doubtless partly excused the mistake; but even if he had failed to grasp that Lévis was a man who could restore confidence to demoralised troops, he might at least have guessed that he would bring up fresh regiments, who had not learned to fear the red-coats, to meet him. As things were, he sacrificed the advantages of his position and of his superiority in artillery and found himself shut up within the miserable fortifications of Quebec, with his force reduced to twenty-four hundred men, nominally fit for duty, but in reality, to use the expressive words of one of them, "half-starved scorbutic skeletons."

May 9.
May 16.

278

Murray, however, rose to the emergency with a spirit worthy of a British officer. The troops were at first inclined to break loose from discipline, but Murray hanged the chief offender, staved in all the rum-barrels of the sutlers and quickly restored order. Then every soul of the garrison fell to work to strengthen the defences. Officers yoked themselves to cannon and plied pickaxe and spade, and the men with such an example before them strained themselves to the utmost. In a short time one hundred and fifty guns were mounted and at work on the walls of Quebec, while the French, however they might toil at their trenches in the stubborn soil of the plateau, had hardly brought up a single cannon to answer them. None the less incessant labour and bad food were telling heavily on the enfeebled strength of the garrison, when on the 9th of May the *Lowestoft* frigate sailed up to Quebec with the news that a squadron was at the mouth of the river and would arrive within a few days. The tidings put new heart into the besieged, though had Lévis ventured on an assault they would have found it hard to repel him. On the 15th two more British men-of-war arrived at Quebec, and next morning two frigates sailed up above the city, attacked and destroyed Lévis' ships and with them the French supplies of food and ammunition. That same evening Lévis raised the siege and retreated with precipitation, leaving behind him forty guns, the whole of his material for the siege, and every man of his sick and wounded. Murray marched at dawn to fall upon his rear, but though he captured many stragglers failed to overtake the main body. Thus Quebec was saved; and the advent of spring, together with a supply of fresh provisions, soon turned Murray's sickly battalions into an army fit for service in the field.

During these miserable months of cold, privation, and disease Amherst had been maturing his plans for a decisive campaign. Pitt had enjoined the capture of Montreal upon him as the principal object, and had resolved to demolish the useless fortress of Louisburg, thereby releasing the garrison for active service.[335] The provincial assemblies were called upon once more to furnish large contingents of troops for a supreme effort, and the final blow was about to fall. Amherst's design was to invade Canada simultaneously from east, west, and south. Murray was to ascend the St. Lawrence from Quebec; Brigadier Haviland was to break in by Lake Champlain; and Amherst himself was to lead the main army down the St. Lawrence from Lake Ontario. Of the three lines of advance Amherst's was not only the longest but the most difficult and dangerous, owing to the rapids which obstruct the navigation of the St. Lawrence; but on the other hand the movement would cut off the retreat of the French army to westward and force it back upon Montreal, where Haviland and Murray would close in upon it and fairly throttle it. The plan was delicate in the extreme and called for the greatest nicety of calculation, for the three armies must start from three different points hundreds of miles apart without possibility of inter-communication, and yet arrive at their goal together, lest the French should concentrate and overwhelm Murray's or Haviland's corps in detail. The principal French posts for barring the lines of advance were Île aux Noix at the head of Lake Ontario, Sorel on the eastern side of Montreal, and La Galette at the head of the rapids of the St. Lawrence.

The year opened ill for Amherst. In March he was compelled to send thirteen hundred men[336] to the south to quell a rising of Cherokee Indians; and he had not long communicated his instructions to Murray when he received tidings of the defeat of Sainte Foy. He at once summoned two battalions from Louisburg to reinforce Murray, but it was not until late in June that he was relieved by news of the safety of Quebec. The provincial governments also were as usual a sore trial and the cause of much vexatious delay;[337] but Amherst was a man of tenacity and patience who never lost sight of his object nor relaxed his industry for a moment. At length, when midsummer was fully past, the net which he had woven began to close round the French.

| July. |
| August 4. |

Murray was the first to move. His garrison had rapidly recovered health and strength, and by July he was able to pick out twenty-two hundred men for the advance on Montreal, while still leaving seventeen hundred behind him for the garrison of Quebec. On the 14th of July his little column embarked in thirty-two vessels with a number of boats and bateaux, and on the following day set sail up the St. Lawrence, leaving Lord Rollo to follow with the Twenty-second and Fortieth Regiments, which had arrived from Louisburg. Murray advanced slowly, skirmishing with small parties of the enemy which hovered about the flotilla on the shore, and disarming the inhabitants as he passed. On the 4th of August he reached Three Rivers, where lay a detachment of the French army; but without delaying to attack it, he passed on to Sorel, where Bourlamaque and M. Dumas with some four thousand men were entrenched along both banks of the river. These officers had been instructed to follow up the flotilla as it moved, so British and French alike advanced towards Montreal, where Lévis lay with the main French army. Murray, meanwhile, by rigour towards the recalcitrant and lenity towards the submissive, persuaded half of Bourlamaque's militia to yield up its arms and take an oath of neutrality. By the 24th, being within nine leagues of Montreal, he sent out a party to seek news of Haviland, and then moving up to Île Sainte Thérése, just below Montreal, he encamped and awaited the coming of his colleagues.

Haviland, meanwhile, had embarked in the third week of August at Crown Point, with two battalions of regulars, and with Provincials and Indians sufficient to raise his force to thirty-four hundred men. Four days brought him to Bougainville's position at Île aux Noix, where he landed, erected batteries, and opened fire on the fort; while at the same time a party of rangers dragged three guns to the rear of the position and turned them upon Bougainville's sloops of war, which got under way in all haste and stranded in the next bend of the river. Thus Bougainville's communications with the next post, St. John's, down the river Richelieu, were severed, and, as Amherst had foreseen,[338] he was compelled to abandon the island. He joined M. Roquemaure at St. John's with infinite difficulty by a night march through the forest; and both officers falling back from St. John's and Chambly waited with Bourlamaque on the banks of the St. Lawrence, where their force melted away fast through desertion. Haviland opened communications with Murray, and both awaited the approach of Amherst.

The main army had assembled at Oswego during July, Amherst himself arriving on the 9th, but it was not until the first week of August that the last of the appointed regiments appeared at the rendezvous. The force consisted of eight weak battalions of British, numbering less than six thousand men, with four thousand five hundred Provincials and seven hundred Indians, or about eleven thousand in all. The flotilla for the transport of the army was made up of nearly eight hundred whale-boats and bateaux, and was escorted by gun-boats. On the 10th of August the entire force was embarked and by the 15th it had reached Oswegatchie or La Galette, on the site of the present Ogdensburg. Here a French brig of ten guns was attacked and captured by the gun-boats, and the flotilla pursued its way among the Thousand Islands. On an islet at the head of the rapids stood a French post named Fort Lévis, with a garrison of three hundred men, which Amherst forthwith invested, and after three days' cannonade reduced to surrender. Repair of the fort and of his boats detained him until the 30th, and on the 31st the expedition entered upon the most critical of its work, the descent of the rapids. On the 1st of September the flotilla was compelled to proceed in single file, but all went well until the 4th, when the most dangerous of the rapids was reached. On that day over sixty boats were wrecked or damaged and eighty-four men were drowned: but the passage was accomplished without molestation from the enemy, though large numbers of Canadians were on the watch on the banks. The next day was consumed in repairs, and on the 6th, the last rapid having been passed, the boats glided down to La Chine, nine miles from Montreal, on the left bank of the St. Lawrence. Here the army landed unopposed, marched straight upon Montreal and encamped beneath the walls on the eastern side: while Haviland on the 8th arrived on the southern shore against Amherst's camp. Amherst was a little late, having been delayed by the resistance of Fort Lévis. Had he been content to ignore it and simply to cut it off from Montreal, he, Murray and Haviland would have met, punctual to a day, on the 29th of August. As it was the junction was sufficiently complete, and the work of the campaign was practically done.

| Sept. 8. |

Bougainville, Bourlamaque, and Roquemaure had crossed over to Montreal with the few regular troops remaining with them, for the whole of their militia had melted away, and even the regulars had been greatly reduced by desertion. Thus the army assembled at Montreal, the sole force that remained for the defence of Canada, amounted to barely twenty-five hundred men, demoralised in order, in spirit, and in discipline. Around the city lay an hostile army of seventeen thousand men; the fortifications were contemptible except for defence against Indians, and Amherst's cannon were already moving up from La Chine. The French Governor called a council of war, which resolved that resistance was hopeless. Articles of capitulation were accordingly drawn up, and carried on the 7th by Bougainville to Amherst. The condition on which the French laid greatest stress was that they should march out with the honours of war; but this Amherst flatly refused. The troops, he said, must lay down their arms and serve no further during the present war: the French had played so inhuman a part in stirring up the Indians to treachery and barbarity of every kind, that he was determined to make an example of them. It is probable that the General referred only to the massacre of the wounded after the defeats at Fort William Henry, Ticonderoga, and the Monongahela; but the reckoning to be paid went back to earlier times. There were the wrongs, the encroachment and the double-dealing of a full century to be redressed; and the time for payment was come. In vain the French pleaded for easier terms: Amherst, a man not easily turned from his purpose, remained inflexible. Accordingly on the 8th of September, despite expostulation which rose almost to the point of mutiny on the part of Lévis, the capitulation was signed, and half a continent passed into the hands of Great Britain.

Meanwhile, as if to crown the whole work and to redeem all past failings and misfortunes, the expedition against the Cherokee Indians had been brilliantly successful. Trifling though the affair may seem in comparison with Amherst's momentous operations in the north, it marked the banishment of the panic fear of Indians which had followed on the defeat of Braddock. The command was entrusted to Colonel Montgomery, and the force committed to him was four hundred of the First Royals, seven hundred of his own Highlanders, and a strong body of Provincials. Starting from Charlestown, Carolina, Montgomery marched up one hundred and fifty miles to the township of Ninety-six, so called because it was supposed to be ninety-six miles from the township of Keowee, and pushed forward thence for four days through dense forest and mountainous country without finding any sign of Indians. Concluding therefore that the Cherokees were unaware of his advance, he left all tents and baggage behind and made a forced march to surprise the savages before they could escape. The main body of the Indians, however, retired before he could reach them; and he could accomplish no more than the destruction of crops and villages, after which he returned to a fort on the frontier, having traversed no less than sixty miles over a most difficult country without a halt. It was then resolved to begin the work anew and to make a fresh advance into the forest. On this occasion the Indians lay in wait for the British in a wooded valley and burst upon them suddenly, as they had upon Braddock, with hideous whooping and howling, and a scattered but deadly fire of rifles. The grenadiers and Light Infantry at once plunged into the forest to engage them, while the Highlanders hastened round their rear to cut off their retreat; and after a sharp action of an hour the Indians were put to flight with great slaughter. This engagement cost the British over eighty men killed and wounded, twice as many as Amherst had lost by lead and steel during the whole of his advance from Oswego to Montreal. But the mere comparison of casualties is of small moment. The really weighty matter is that British officers had learned to face the difficulties which had been fatal to Braddock, and to overcome them with a light heart.

It now remained for Amherst to enforce the capitulation on the French posts of the west. The occupation of Detroit, Miamis, and Michillimackinac was entrusted to Rogers, the partisan, with his rangers, who in the course of the winter hauled down the ensign of the Bourbons and hoisted the British flag in its place. There was still to be trouble with these remote stations, but it was not to come immediately, nor directly from the French. The rest of the General's work was principally administrative. Generous terms were granted to the inhabitants, and every precaution was taken to protect them against the Indian allies of the British. Amherst issued a general order appealing to his troops not to disgrace their victory by any unsoldierlike behaviour or appearance of inhumanity; and the army responded to the appeal with a heartiness which amazed the Canadians. A month after the capitulation the General could report that British soldiers and Canadian peasants were joining their provisions and messing together, and that when he had ordered soldiers to leave their scattered quarters so as to be closer to their companies, the people had begged that they might not be moved.[339] Such was not the fashion in which the French were wont to treat a captured territory.

Here then for the present we may take leave of Amherst. Pitt, as shall presently be seen, had further tasks for him, which were to be executed as usual quietly and thoroughly. The fame of the man is lost in that of Wolfe, and yet it was he, not Wolfe, that was the conqueror of Canada. The criticism usually passed upon him is that he was sure but slow, and to some extent it is justified by facts. Yet it should be remembered that, when he took over the command, affairs in North America were in extreme confusion and disorder, and that the work assigned to him was, on a far larger and more formidable scale, that which had fallen to Cumberland in 1745. Braddock had started everything in the wrong direction. Not only had he quarrelled with the Provincials and failed to instruct his troops aright, but he had deliberately forced them to follow wrong methods. Loudoun, again, had not improved relations with the provincial assemblies either by his correspondence with them or by his military operations. Finally Abercromby's imbecility at Ticonderoga had sacrificed hundreds of valuable lives, disgusted the colonists, and heightened the reputation gained by the French at the Monongahela. Then Amherst took the whole of the confused business in hand, and from that moment all went smoothly and well; so smoothly indeed that people quite forgot that it had ever gone otherwise. Yet his difficulties with the Provincials were not less than those of his predecessors nor less trying to his patience than to theirs; nay, even the good-will of the colonists was sometimes as embarrassing to him as their obstruction. It must not be forgotten, moreover, that the atmosphere of young communities, such as were then the North American colonies, is most noxious to discipline. Americans, as their latest military effort has proved, do not yet understand the meaning of the term; the colonists of Australia and New Zealand, which have no such religious traditions as America, have but the vaguest conception of its significance. Thus when Amherst returned from the conquest of Louisburg to Boston, not all his efforts could prevent the inhabitants of that godly city from filling his men with rum; and the same spirit of indiscipline doubtless haunted the army through all the long and dreary months of winter-quarters. There was, again, the additional complication that in the matter of forest-fighting the British had much to learn from the Provincials; and it fell to Amherst to teach his troops greater freedom and independence in action without simultaneous relaxation of discipline. He overcame all these obstacles, however, in his quiet, methodical way. Discipline never failed; for Amherst, though no martinet, could be inexorably severe. Special corps of light troops and of marksmen were organised, and the drill of the whole army was modified to suit new conditions. It was in fact Amherst who showed the way to the reform afterwards carried out by Sir John Moore at Shorncliffe, of reducing the depth of the ranks to two men only. Such a formation would have diminished Wolfe's difficulties and materially have strengthened his dispositions on the plains of Abraham: but apparently so important an innovation never occurred to him. Amherst never fought a great action, so his improvements were never put to the test; but this does not impair his credit as a soldier of forethought and originality.

But the most remarkable quality in Amherst was his talent for organisation. The difficulties of transport in the Canada of his day were appalling. "Canada," says the American historian Parkman, "was fortified with vast outworks of defence in the savage forests, marshes, and mountains that encompassed her, where the thoroughfares were streams choked with fallen trees and obstructed by cataracts. Never was the problem of moving troops encumbered by artillery and baggage a more difficult one. The question was less how to fight an enemy than how to get at him." It was just this problem which Amherst's industry and perseverance had power to solve. We read of his launching forth on to Lake George with a flotilla of eight hundred boats and an army of eleven thousand men, and all sounds simple and straightforward enough. Yet these boats, setting aside the original task of building and collecting them, had to make several journeys to carry the necessary stores and provisions from Albany to the head of the lake, while every one of them, together with its load, required to be hauled overland from three to six miles through forest and swamp from the carrying-place on the Mohawk to Wood Creek. The same provision against the same difficulties were necessary on a smaller scale for Prideaux's attack on Niagara, and, under conditions of special embarrassment, for Stanwix's advance to the Ohio; while over and above this, there was marine transport and all necessaries for the expedition to Quebec to be provided, so as to enable Wolfe to proceed on his mission fully equipped and without delay. Add to this burden of work endless correspondence with the various provinces, as well as constant friction, obstruction, and general dilatoriness, and it becomes apparent that for all his slowness Amherst accomplished no small feat when he achieved the conquest of Canada in two campaigns.

The whole problem was in truth one of organisation, and Amherst was the man to solve it, for he was a great military administrator. Cautious undoubtedly he was in the field, but it would be absurd to contend that a man who took ten thousand men down the rapids of the St. Lawrence, with the dry comment that the said rapids were "more frightful than dangerous,"[340] was wanting in enterprise or audacity. His career as a general in the field was short, and his crowning campaign, having achieved its end without a general action, has little fame. Such is the penalty of bloodless operations, though they be the masterpiece of a mighty genius. Austerlitz is a name familiar to thousands who know nothing of the capitulation of Ulm. So Amherst to the majority of Englishmen is but a name: as though it were a small thing for a colonel taken straight from the classic fields of Flanders to cross the Atlantic to a savage wilderness, assume command of disheartened troops and the direction of discordant colonists, and quietly and deliberately to organise victory. He was the greatest military administrator produced by England since the death of Marlborough, and remained the greatest until the rise of Wellington.

AUTHORITIES.—The history of the French in Canada and of the long struggle between them and the English for the mastery of the continent has been admirably written in a series of volumes by Francis Parkman. Following in his footsteps through the original papers in the Record Office (C.O., *America and West Indies*, vols. lxiii., lxv., lxxiv.-lxxvi., lxxxi.-xciv., xcix.; W. O. *Orig. Corres.*, vols. xiii.-xv.), through the *Bouquet and Haldimand Papers*, and through other English material, I have found little or nothing to glean, while the information which he has gathered from American sources is most valuable. The histories of Mante and Entick give a general account of the operations. Knox's *Journal* is one of the most valuable sources of information. Other authorities will be found given in detail by Parkman. Readers who are familiar with his works will have no difficulty in apprehending my obligations to him, which I wish to acknowledge to the full.

CHAPTER V

1755.

It is now time to return to the subject of India, which, as will be remembered, was dropped at the conclusion of the truce between France and England in January 1755. Two days after the signing of the articles, Governor Saunders left Madras for Europe, and was followed a month later by M. Godeheu. It is not likely that the departure of the two signatories of the treaty wrought any great influence on the subsequent proceedings of the East India Company; but certain it is that before the instrument was a month old the infraction of its provisions was already begun. It was in fact impossible to observe the truce. Its object seems to have been to terminate hostilities in the Carnatic alone; but it was not to be expected that, while Bussy was exerting his vast ability and energy at Aurungabad for the promotion of French interests, the British could sit with folded hands in submission to the article which bound French and English alike "not to interfere in any difference which might arise between the princes of the country." The British had their puppet as well as the French, and having used him for their own purposes could not suddenly desert him, the less so inasmuch as the Nabob Mohammed Ali had neither resources of his own nor the wits whereby to provide himself with them. When therefore Mohammed Ali begged for a British force to reduce Madura and Tinnevelly, which he conceived to be his tributaries, and to collect his tribute for him, the authorities at Madras assented without hesitation. It was, in fact, unusual, not to say impossible, for Indian tribute to be levied except by means of an armed force; and, since Mohammed Ali had no troops of his own, it might be maintained, at least with some show of reason, that the furnishing of a small army for so innocent a purpose was not an act of war.

February.

Accordingly at the beginning of February twenty-five hundred men, one-fifth of them Europeans, were placed under command of Colonel Heron, an officer lately arrived from England, who proceeded to perform the duty assigned to him. It is unnecessary to enter into details of his operations. Suffice it that he succeeded not only in occupying both Madura and Tinnevelly, but in demoralising his troops and insulting the religious prejudices of the people by scandalous pillage of a pagoda. Mohammed Ali made over the government of the subdued territory to his brother Maphuze

Khan, and in June Heron, having done his work, encamped before Trichinopoly. From thence he was summoned to Madras to be tried by court-martial for accepting bribes and for malversation of funds, and was dismissed from the Company's service.

The French lost no time in protesting against this expedition as a violation of the treaty, and with not the less vigour that they were extremely jealous of the reuniting of Madura and Tinnevelly, which had long been severed from the sway of Arcot, to the dominions of Mohammed Ali. The protest was of course answered by indignant disclaimer of any sinister purpose; and M. de Leyrit, the Governor of Pondicherry, thought it more profitable to waste no further words in argument, but simply to follow the British example. An opportunity for doing so soon presented itself. The chieftain of a tract of country known as Terriore, about thirty miles north of Trichinopoly, had for some time past evaded payment of his tributary dues to Mysore. Now the Mysoreans on retiring from Trichinopoly had appointed the French their agents to watch over their interests in the Carnatic; and M. de Leyrit accordingly sent fifteen hundred men under M. Maissin into Terriore to enforce discharge of the arrears of this revenue. Maissin having fulfilled his mission with ease and success led his army eastward to Palamcotah, on territory which the British claimed to be subject to Mohammed Ali. The authorities at Madras threatened to stop him by force if he did not desist; and, De Leyrit giving way, war was for the present averted. But since both sides had now infringed the treaty, it was plain that the renewal of hostilities could not long be deferred.

| 1756. |

The rest of the year passed away without serious trouble; but, however the suspension of arms might be observed in the south, there could be no safety for the Carnatic while Bussy remained at Aurungabad, virtually viceroy of the Deccan. He had been now installed therein since 1751, wielding his great powers with consummate tact and address in the face of intrigue, jealousy, and even conspiracy; nay, he had turned the most formidable of the combinations against him into a means of increasing his influence and of gaining nearly five hundred miles of the eastern coast, from the Chilka Lake southward, for the government of Pondicherry. It is true that this vast tract, which was known as the Northern Sirkars, had for the most part been restored to its native owners under the terms of the treaty, but it was still held by France pending the ratification of the articles, which was not expected to arrive until the middle of 1756; and it was always possible that so degrading a concession might be repudiated at Versailles. Moreover, whatever the fate of the negotiations, the cardinal fact remained that Bussy continued always at the court of the Viceroy of the Deccan, and that it was vital to the British that his power should be undermined—that, in fact, Salabad Jung should be persuaded or forced to dismiss him. The first idea at Madras was to send a force to the assistance of the Mahratta, Balajee Rao, who had frequently carried on hostilities against Salabad Jung; for which duty Clive, who had returned to India with the rank of Lieutenant-Colonel and Governor of Fort St. David, volunteered his services. Another officer, however, was preferred to him, who died before the work could be begun; and the authorities at Bombay, from which side the operations were to be conducted, allowed the project to drop. Native intrigue nevertheless wrought effectually for the British what they could not do for themselves; and in May the feeble Salabad Jung was prevailed upon to dismiss Bussy and the French troops from his service. But Bussy had still an army with him, and had shown himself not less formidable in the field than in the council-chamber; so his enemies, to decide the matter, applied to Madras for a body of troops to assist in the expulsion of the French. No invitation could have been more pleasing. A force of eighteen hundred men was at once ordered for the service, when in the middle of July came tidings from Bengal which demanded the presence of every British soldier that could be spared from the coast of Coromandel.

May.
May 9.
June.

The provinces of Bengal, Orissa, and Behar had since 1735 been governed by a prince known to the English as Allaverdy Khan, who, like all other viceroys of the Moguls, had become virtually independent. At his death the sovereignty descended, according to his own nomination, to his great nephew Surajah Dowlah, a youth who had early discovered propensities towards cruelty, intemperance, and debauchery such as are rare even in Oriental despots. Surajah Dowlah had always hated the English, and his hatred was not lessened after his succession by the fact that the most formidable of his competitors for the throne had received asylum and permission to deposit his treasures and his family at Madras. At the beginning of April the authorities at Calcutta received warning that the renewal of war with France was inevitable, and accordingly set about the repair of the fortifications of the settlement. Surajah Dowlah, not only irritated but alarmed lest such preparations should be levelled against himself, sent a message to the Governor requiring that the work should cease and that the newly-erected defences should be destroyed. The authorities answered by tendering explanations; but the angry Nabob heard them only to reject them, and ordered his army to march against the fort and factory of Cossimbazar. The place was in no condition to make any defence, and Surajah Dowlah having received its surrender pursued his march upon Calcutta. There the authorities, uninured to such trials as Madras, had weakly endeavoured to appease the wrath of the Nabob by desisting from further work on the fortifications: nor was it until too late that they discovered that their only safety lay in resistance. Letters were hurriedly despatched to Bombay and Madras for reinforcements, though with little hope that these would reach Calcutta in time. Appeals for aid were addressed also to the French at Chandernagore and to the Dutch at Chinsura, but were rejected by both parties, and by the French in particular with studied insolence. By the 16th of June the Nabob's army was before the city. Fort William, the principal defence, was abandoned as untenable, and the British resolved to confine their resistance to the streets. On the 18th the enemy attacked and were gallantly beaten back; but on the 19th they succeeded in carrying the principal batteries: and it was then determined, while there was yet time, to embark the women and children on the shipping in the Hooghly. The resolution was executed with a haste and disorder which soon turned to panic, and there was a general rush to escape. The Governor, who so far had shown firmness and courage, embarked with the rest, and the scanty remnant of Europeans left behind in Calcutta was compelled to capitulate. The tragedy that ensued is well known—how one hundred and forty-six Europeans were packed during the insufferable heat of a summer's night into a room not twenty feet square and with but two small windows; how the unhappy creatures strove for a time to fight with order and discipline against suffocation; how the effort proved, as it could not but prove, beyond their powers, and gave place to a succession of mad struggles for life, renewed and renewed again through hour after hour till at length they were closed by the slow mercy of death; and how when the corpses were cleared away from the door in the morning thirty-three ghastly figures staggered out from among them to tell to their countrymen the tale of the Black Hole of Calcutta.

July.

The Nabob then occupied himself with the plunder of the city and in writing inflated accounts of his conquest to Delhi; which done he left a garrison of three thousand men in Calcutta and departed with his army on the 2nd of July. On his way he extorted large contributions from Chandernagore and Chinsura as the price of their immunity, and so returned to his capital of Moorshedebad.

July 20.
August.
December.

It was not until the 15th of July that the news of the fall of Cossimbazar reached Madras. Two hundred and thirty Europeans under Major Kilpatrick were promptly shipped off to the Hooghly, and arrived at Fulta, five-and-twenty miles below Calcutta, on the 2nd of August. But there was long hesitation as to the expediency of sending further reinforcements to Bengal. News was daily expected of declaration of war with France, and it was held by many of the Council that it would be wiser policy to send aid to Salabad Jung and to complete the discomfiture of Bussy while there was yet time. Fortunately wider and less selfish views prevailed, and ultimately it was decided to send every ship and man that could be spared to the Hooghly. There was still longer debate over the selection of a commander, but the choice finally fell upon Clive, though he was subordinated to Admiral Watson, who commanded the British squadron then lying at Madras. The force entrusted to him consisted of nine hundred Europeans, two hundred and fifty of which were of the Thirty-ninth regiment, and fifteen hundred Sepoys. Thus at last on the 15th of October the transports sailed under convoy of Admiral Watson's four ships of the line, though, owing to divers misfortunes, it was Christmas before the bulk of the fleet arrived at Fulta. Even then two ships, the one containing two hundred European troops, the other the great part of the field-artillery, were still missing.

| Dec. 29. |

Even more discouraging was the condition of Kilpatrick's detachment which, being perforce encamped on unhealthy ground, had buried over one hundred men and could supply but thirty that were fit for duty. Still there was nothing to be gained by delay, so on the 27th of December the fleet sailed up the river and on the 29th anchored at Mayapore, two miles below the fort of Budge Budge. Here, contrary to Clive's opinion, Watson insisted that the troops should march against the fort overland. Five hundred Europeans and the whole of the Sepoys were accordingly disembarked, and after a most difficult march arrived at the place appointed for camp, a large hollow situated between two villages a mile and a half to north-east of Budge Budge. The men being greatly fatigued were permitted to leave their arms in the hollow and to lay themselves down wherever they thought best; and with inexcusable neglect not a sentry was posted. It so happened that Monichund, the officer left by Surajah Dowlah at Calcutta, had that very day reached Budge Budge with thirty-five hundred men, where on receiving intelligence of Clive's dispositions he laid his plans to attack him at nightfall. The British troops had not been long asleep when they were awaked by the fire of musketry and found the enemy upon them. Instantly they rushed to the hollow for their arms, the artillerymen deserting their guns and flying back with the infantry to take shelter. Clive, always cool and collected, called to his men to stand, knowing that the slightest retrograde movement would produce a panic, and detached two platoons from two different points to make a counter-attack. The British then recovered themselves, the artillerymen returned to their guns, and Clive was able to form his line in order for a general advance. Before the action could become general a round shot passing close to Monichund's turban caused that officer to give a hasty signal for retreat; and so Clive's army was saved, though, indeed, it was by no fault but his own that it had been endangered. H.M.S. *Kent* then sailed up and silenced the guns of Budge Budge; and on the following night a drunken sailor, who chanced to blunder into the fort, made the discovery that it had been abandoned by the enemy.

| Dec. 30. |
| 1757. |
| Jan. 12. |
| Feb. 2. |
| Feb. 3. |

On the 30th the fleet pursued its way up to Alighur, where Clive again landed with the army to march on Calcutta, while the ships engaged the enemy at Fort William. The Nabob's troops soon deserted both fort and town, and the fort was occupied, before Clive could reach it, by a detachment under Captain Eyre Coote of the Thirty-ninth Foot, who had sailed from England with two companies of his regiment in the previous November. It was then resolved to recapture Hooghly before the Nabob could advance from Moorshedabad; and accordingly three hundred and fifty of the Thirty-ninth with a due proportion of Sepoys were detached for the purpose, who took the town by storm with trifling loss and a week later returned to Calcutta. Meanwhile news arrived of the outbreak of war between France and England; and the Company fearing lest the French troops at Chandernagore, who numbered three hundred Europeans with a train of artillery, might join the Nabob, endeavoured to come to terms with him. The attempt was vain. Surajah Dowlah, irritated by the attack on Hooghly, collected an army of forty thousand men and moved steadily upon Calcutta. On the 2nd of February his advanced guard came into sight; whereupon Clive, who had taken up a position at the northern end of the town, marched out as if to attack. He decided, however, to wait for a more favourable moment; and on the following day the whole of the Nabob's army was encamped along the eastern side of the town, beside the entrenchment that bore the name of the Mahratta Ditch.

| Feb. 4. |

Even then, though the French had not joined Surajah Dowlah, Clive was loth to encounter his army without reinforcements, and made a last effort at negotiation; but, on the return of his commissioners without success, he decided to make an attempt upon the enemy's camp on the morrow. At midnight six hundred sailors were landed from the men-of-war, and with these, six hundred and fifty European infantry, a hundred gunners with six guns, and eight hundred Sepoys Clive started before dawn for the Nabob's encampment. His advance was made in a long column of three men abreast, with the artillery in rear; and day had just broken when he struck against the enemy's advanced posts and drove them back. With the coming of the light there came also a dense fog, through which the column continued to move forward, successfully repulsing an attack of the enemy's cavalry as it went, until a causeway was reached, running at right angles to the line of march, which led to the Nabob's quarters within the Mahratta Ditch. There the head of the column changed direction to the right, as it had been bidden, but in the perplexity caused by the fog found itself under the fire of the British field-guns in the rear, and broke up to seek shelter. This movement misled the rear of the column; and very soon the entire force was in hopeless confusion. The enemy opening fire with their cannon increased the disorder; and Clive had much ado to keep his men together. Finally when the fog lifted he found himself surrounded by the enemy's cavalry; and though he succeeded in driving them off he was obliged, owing to the fatigue of his troops, to abandon the attack and return to camp. His losses amounted to one hundred Europeans and fifty Sepoys killed and wounded, against which there seemed little gain to be set. The men indeed were not a little disheartened, and complained with some bitterness of the rashness of their leader.

| Feb. 9. |
| March. |
| June 4. |
| June 13. |

But if the British were discouraged, much more so was the Nabob. Blind and uncertain though the action had been, he had lost six hundred men and five hundred horses, while the idea of a British force calmly perambulating his camp was utterly distasteful and disquieting to him. Five days later he concluded a treaty whereby he agreed to restore all property taken at Calcutta and to revive all other privileges formerly granted to the British; an agreement which was expanded forty-eight hours afterwards into an offensive and defensive alliance. Clive then proposed to attack the French at Chandernagore, but this the Nabob positively forbade. In March, however, reinforcements of three companies of infantry and one of artillery arrived from Bombay, and Clive resolved to make the attack notwithstanding the Nabob's prohibition. On the 7th of March the army began its march up the river; the siege was opened a week later, and the fort, which held no very strong garrison, was soon forced to capitulate. This defiance of his wishes increased at once the Nabob's dread of the British and his anxiety to evade the obligations of the treaty. The miserable creature writhed under the masterful spirit of Clive. He made overtures to Bussy, to the Mahrattas, to any one whom he thought able to help him out of his difficulties: sometimes he threatened the English, sometimes he apologised to them; and Clive, thoroughly distrustful of this abject ally, determined to keep the whole of his army in Bengal to watch him and hold him to his obligations. Meanwhile aid suddenly reached the British from an unexpected source. The followers of the Nabob, alienated by his folly, his insults, and his caprice, began to fall away from him. Discontent ripened into disaffection, and disaffection into conspiracy. Overtures were presently made to the authorities at Calcutta to join in a plot for the overthrow of Surajah Dowlah and for the setting up of Meer Jaffier, hitherto his commander-in-chief but now foremost among the conspirators, in his place. Long negotiations followed, which have become famous for the blot which, rightly or wrongly, they have left upon the memory of Clive. Finally Meer Jaffier signed the treaty which bound the English to win for him the throne of Bengal, Orissa, and Behar, and engaged himself in return to make over to them all French factories within those provinces, as well as a slight accession of territory about Calcutta, and to give compensation for the damage inflicted by Surajah Dowlah. Meer Jaffier, however, had displayed considerable irresolution during the negotiations, and the secret of the conspiracy had already begun to leak out, so that it became necessary to clench the arrangement by immediate action. Accordingly on the 13th of June, Clive, who had been throughout the leading and deciding spirit, set his force in motion from Chandernagore upon Moorshedabad, and on the following day sent a letter to the Nabob which amounted virtually to a declaration of war.

Before the letter arrived Surajah Dowlah had awaked to his peril and sent emissaries to treat with Meer Jaffier; nay, throwing off all royal state he visited his former vassal in person to entreat humbly for reconciliation. Meer Jaffier yielded; the agreement between the two men was ratified by the usual oaths on the Koran; and Surajah Dowlah, returning a defiant answer to Clive, ordered the whole of his army to assemble some twelve miles due south of Moorshedabad at the village of Plassey.

| June. |

Meanwhile Clive continued his advance up the Hooghly, the Europeans travelling by water in boats, the Sepoys marching along the western bank. His force consisted in all of nine hundred Europeans, two hundred half-bred Portuguese and twenty-one hundred Sepoys, with ten guns. On the 16th he halted at Paltee, on the Cossimbazar river above its junction with the Jelingeer, and sent forward Major Eyre Coote to secure the fort of Cutwa, twelve miles farther up, which commanded the passage of the river. The governor of the fort was one of the conspirators against Surajah Dowlah, but he met Coote's overtures with defiance, and on the deployment of the British force for attack set fire to the defences and retired together with his garrison. Clive's force encamped in the plain of Cutwa that night; but the behaviour of the Governor was calculated to disquiet him, for Meer Jaffier's letters only reported vaguely that he himself, though reconciled to the Nabob, intended none the less to abide by the treaty with the British. Distrusting so ambiguous a declaration Clive decided not to cross the river into what was called the Island of Cossimbazar,[341] until his doubts should be resolved. On the 20th further letters arrived from Meer Jaffier tending somewhat to allay Clive's misgivings as to his good faith, but holding out little hope of assistance in the coming operations; while simultaneously there came a letter from one of Clive's agents which gave some reason for doubting Meer Jaffier's sincerity. Much perplexed Clive summoned a council of war, and put it to the twenty officers therein assembled whether it would be better to cross the river and attack the Nabob at all hazards, or to halt at Cutwa, where supplies were abundant, until the close of the rainy season, and meanwhile to invoke the assistance of the Mahrattas. He gave his own opinion first in favour of remaining at Cutwa, and was followed by thirteen of the officers, including so bold a soldier as Kilpatrick. Coote and six more, however, gave their votes for immediate action or return to Calcutta. Clive broke up the council, retired alone into an adjoining grove for an hour, and on his return issued orders to cross the river on the morrow.

| June 23. |

At sunrise of the 22nd the army began the passage of the river, and by four in the afternoon it stood on the eastern bank. Here another letter reached Clive from Meer Jaffier, giving information as to the intended movements of the Nabob. Clive's answer was that he should advance to Plassey at once, and on the following morning to Daoodpoor, six miles beyond it; and that if Meer Jaffier failed to meet him there, he would make peace with Surajah Dowlah. The troops accordingly proceeded on their way, Europeans by water, Sepoys by land; but owing to the slow progress of the boats against the stream, it was one o'clock in the morning before they had traversed the fifteen miles to the village of Plassey. Here they were surprised to learn from the continued din of drums and cymbals that the Nabob's army was close at hand; for they had expected to meet with it farther north. Solaced by this rude music the men lay down in a mango-grove to sleep; but the officers that slept were few, and Clive was not one of them.

The grove of Plassey extended north and south for a length of about half a mile, with a width of about three hundred yards. The trees were planted in regular rows, and the whole was surrounded by a slight bank and by a ditch beyond it, choked with weeds and brambles. The grove lay at an acute angle to the river, the northern corner being fifty yards and the southern two hundred yards from the bank. A little to the northward of it and on the edge of the river stood a hunting-house of the Nabob, surrounded by a garden and wall. A mile to northward of this house the river makes a huge bend to the south-west in the form of a horse-shoe, containing a peninsula of about a mile in diameter, which shrinks at its neck to a width of some five hundred yards from stream to stream. About three hundred yards to south of this peninsula an entrenchment had been thrown up, which ran for above a furlong straight inland and parallel to the grove, and then turned off at an obtuse angle to the north-eastward for about three miles. The whole of the Nabob's army was encamped within this entrenchment and the peninsula, and the angle itself was defended by a redoubt. Some three hundred yards to the east of the redoubt, but outside the entrenchment, stood a hillock covered with trees; half a mile to southward of this hillock lay a small tank, and yet a hundred yards farther south a second and much larger tank, both of them surrounded by a mound of earth.

At dawn the Nabob's forces began to stream by many outlets from the camp towards the grove, a mighty host of thirty-five thousand foot, eighteen thousand horse, and fifty pieces of artillery. The cannon were for the most part of large calibre and were carried, together with their crews and ammunition, on large stages, which were tugged by forty or fifty yoke of oxen in front and propelled by elephants from behind. Forty or fifty French adventurers under M. St. Frais, who had formerly been of the garrison of Chandernagore, took post with four light field-guns at the larger tank, which was nearest to the grove; while two heavy guns under a native officer were posted to St. Frais's right and between him and the river. In support of these advanced parties were five thousand horse and seven thousand foot under the Nabob's most faithful general, Meer Murdeen. The rest of the hostile army extended itself in a huge curve from the hillock before the entrenchments to within half a mile of the southern angle of the grove. Thus the British could not advance against the force in their front without exposing themselves to overwhelming attack on their right flank.

Clive watched these dispositions from the hunting-house, and was surprised at the numbers and confidence of the enemy. But knowing that his only chance was to assume a bold face, he drew his troops out of the grove and formed them in a single line, with their left resting on the hunting-house and their front towards the nearest tank. The European battalion occupied the centre of the line. It mustered on that day about seven hundred men, partly of the Company's troops, since numbered the Hundred and First to the Hundred and Third Regiments, and partly of the Thirty-ninth Foot, while one hundred half-bred Portuguese also were ranked within it. Three six-pounders were posted on each flank of this battalion, manned by fifty men of the Royal Artillery and as many seamen; and to right and left of these guns, twenty-one hundred Sepoys were drawn up in two equal divisions. The line extended for six hundred yards beyond the grove, but the enemy at this point was too remote to fall upon the British flank before dispositions could be made to meet them. Two more field-guns and two howitzers were posted two hundred yards in advance of the left division of Sepoys, under shelter of two brick-kilns. Therewith Clive's order of battle was complete; and the handful of three thousand men stood up to meet its fifty thousand enemies. Its strength lay in the group of white faces in the centre, and the strength of that group lay in the will of one man. It was the first time that British troops had faced such odds; but it was not to be the last.

At eight o'clock the action was opened by the firing of one of the French guns at the tank. The shot fell true, killing one man and wounding another of the British grenadier-company. Then the whole of the enemy's guns, from the tanks in front along the whole vast sweep of the curving line, opened a heavy and continuous fire. The British guns replied and with effect, but the loss of one of Clive's soldiers was ill compensated for by the fall of ten of the enemy; and after losing thirty men in the first half hour of the cannonade Clive ordered the whole of his force to fall back into the grove. So the little band of scarlet faced about, passed into the trees and vanished from sight; while wild yells of elation rose up from the enemies that ringed them about, and their whole line closing in nearer upon the grove renewed the cannonade with redoubled energy. The shot, however, did little damage, for the British had been ordered to lie down; and Clive's field-guns, firing through embrasures made in the bank, wrought greater destruction, at the closer range, than before. So the duel of artillery continued until eleven o'clock, when Clive called a council of officers, and decided that it would be best to maintain the position until nightfall, and at midnight to take the offensive and attack the enemy's camp.

Then by chance nature interposed, as at Crécy, to change the whole aspect of the fight. A heavy storm of rain swept over the plain, drenching both armies to the skin. The British had tarpaulins ready to cover their ammunition; but the enemy had taken no such precaution, and consequently most of their powder was damaged. Their fire began to slacken, while that of the British was as lively as ever. Nevertheless, believing that his adversary must be in the same predicament as himself, Meer Murdeen advanced from the tank towards the grove to drive the British from it. His troops were met by a deadly fire of grape, his cavalry was dispersed and he himself mortally wounded. The news of his fall shattered the shaken nerves of the unhappy Nabob, and in abject despair he sent for Meer Jaffier and besought earnestly for his help. He, the sovereign, flung his turban at the feet of his subject and cried, "Jaffier, that turban you must defend." And Jaffier, with the readiness of submissive gesture which graces Oriental duplicity, bowed his head and laid his hands upon his breast, swearing to render his utmost service. Then returning to his fellow-conspirators he forthwith despatched a letter to Clive, advising him to push forward at once, or at all events to attack the Nabob before next dawn. The messenger was afraid to deliver the letter while the fire continued; but Surajah Dowlah, as though aware that no faithful counsellor was left to him, turned to another of his leaders for help. This man, being also of the conspirators, advised him to order the army to fall back within the entrenchment and himself to retire to the capital, leaving the issue of the fight to his Generals. The wretched Nabob acted on this counsel, and mounting a camel set forth with an escort of two thousand horse for Moorshedabad. Thus it was that at about two o'clock the enemy's fire ceased, the teams were harnessed to the guns, and the whole host turning about flowed back slowly towards the entrenchments.

While all this was going forward, Clive, having resolved to make no offensive movement before night, had retired to the hunting-house to snatch a few minutes of sleep after the anxiety and fatigue of the previous day. He was roused by a message from Major Kilpatrick which brought him back speedily into the field. Despite the withdrawal of the Nabob's army St. Frais and his little party still held their position in the tank, and Kilpatrick, perceiving that the position was one from which the enemy's flank could be cannonaded during their retreat, sent word to Clive that he was about to attack it. Clive, waked abruptly from sleep, sharply reprimanded Kilpatrick for taking such a step without orders; but presently seeing that the Major was right, he took command of his two companies, and sending Kilpatrick to bring forward the rest of the army, himself led the advance against the tank.

St. Frais, aware that he could hold his ground no longer, thereupon limbered up, and retiring with perfect coolness to the redoubt at the angle of the entrenchment, made ready for action once more. Meanwhile, during the advance of the British, the southernmost division of the Nabob's army was observed to be holding aloof from the rest of the host and approaching nearer to the grove. These were the troops of Meer Jaffier, but their movement was misconstrued as a design upon the boats and baggage in the grove; and accordingly three platoons and a field-gun were detached to hold them in check. The division therefore retired slowly, but still remained significantly apart from the remainder of the host. But before this, the main body of the British had reached the tank, and planting their artillery on the mound opened fire on the enemy behind their entrenchments. Thereupon many of the Nabob's troops faced about again and moved out into the plain to meet them; the infantry opening a heavy fire, while the artillery likewise wheeled about to enter the fight anew. In effect it was at this moment that the true battle began, though the Nabob's force was by this time without leader or general. Clive perceived that his only chance was to press his attack home before the resistance to him could assume any organised form. He therefore pushed forward half of his infantry and artillery to the lesser tank, and the remainder to some rising ground a furlong to the left of it, at the same time detaching a hundred and fifty men to occupy a tank close to the entrenchments and to keep up a fire of musketry upon them. From these stations the firing was renewed at closer range than before and with admirable efficiency. The enemy suffered great loss, and the teams attached to their heavy artillery were so much cut up that the guns could not be brought into action. Nevertheless St. Frais's field-pieces at the redoubt were still well and regularly served; and the enemy, though lacking leadership, were able, under favour of the ground and of their immense superiority in numbers, to carry on the fight with some spirit in their own irregular fashion. The entrenchments themselves, the hillock to eastward of the redoubt, and every hollow or coign of vantage, were crammed with matchlockmen, while the cavalry hovered round, threatening continually to charge, though always kept at a distance by the British artillery. At length it dawned upon Clive that the isolated division of the Nabob's army by the grove must be that of Meer Jaffier, and that his flank and rear were safe. He resolved therefore to cut matters short. Two parties were detached to make simultaneous attack upon the redoubt on one side and the hillock on the other, while the main body moved up between them in support. The hillock was carried without the firing of a shot, and St. Frais, perceiving that he was now wholly unsupported, abandoned his guns and retired. At five o'clock the British were in possession of the Nabob's entrenchments and camp, and the battle of Plassey was won.

From a military standpoint the action has comparatively little interest, since the issue turned really on the good faith or, if the term be preferred, the ill-faith of the leading conspirators against Surajah Dowlah. The British could not advance until the enemy retired; it was a shower of rain that silenced the Nabob's artillery and began the discouragement which led to their retreat; and even then the British commander needed to be waked out of sleep to follow them. There were no such superb audacity of attack, no such bloody struggle, no such triumph of discipline over numbers, as were to be seen afterwards at Meeanee. The whole loss of the British amounted to but seven Europeans and sixteen Sepoys killed, thirteen Europeans and thirty-six Sepoys wounded. It was a small price to pay for dominion over the provinces of Bengal, Orissa, and Behar, for such and no less were the fruits of the victory. Yet it is not by the mere tale of the slaughtered and the maimed that such successes must be judged. The victory may have been easily won when the moment came for the actual clash of arms; but the main point is that the British were there to win it. The campaign of Plassey is less a study of military skill than of the iron will and unshaken nerve that could lead three thousand men against a host of unknown strength, and hold them undaunted, a single slender line, within a ring of fifty thousand enemies.

June 24.
1758.

The day's work did not end with the capture of the camp. Eyre Coote was sent forward with a detachment to keep the enemy moving, and the army encamped for the night at Daoodpoor. On the following day Meer Jaffier was saluted by Clive as Nabob of Bengal, Orissa, and Behar, after which he hastened with his troops to Moorshedabad, reaching the city on the same evening. Surajah Dowlah had fled before his arrival, but parties were sent out at once in search of him, and a few days later he was brought back and assassinated. On the 29th Clive likewise entered the city and formally installed Meer Jaffier on the throne. He then spent the succeeding months in dividing the spoils of the victory, of which the troops received no small share, and in securing that British interests should be paramount in the new possessions, or, to use plain language, that the Company should be the true sovereign and Meer Jaffier its puppet. On this part of his task I shall for the present dwell no further, except to mention that the agent selected by him to reside at the Court of Meer Jaffier was a young man of five-and-twenty, named Warren Hastings. The work was not fully accomplished for many months, nor was it until the following May that Clive was able to return to Calcutta, having left the greater number of his troops at Cossimbazar to keep watch over Moorshedabad. A month before his arrival events in Southern India had taken a ply which called for the appointment of the ablest possible man as ruler of Bengal; and in June Clive, at the request of the authorities at Calcutta, assumed the office of President. Before long his hand will again be seen busy in the direction of new conquests; but it is necessary first to trace the course of events in Southern India.

CHAPTER VI

It might have seemed that, with the recall of Dupleix and the dismissal of Bussy from the court of Salabad Jung, French ascendency in India was already shaken to its foundations. Such, however, was very far from the fact. On the news of Bussy's withdrawal the French governors both at Pondicherry and at Masulipatam had sent him reinforcements, which he contrived by rare skill and daring to join to his own troops, and to use so effectively that within three months of his dismissal he was re-established at Hyderabad with all his former titles, dignities, and honours. For the rest of the year he was fully occupied in the reassertion of his position at the Viceroy's court and of French influence in the Northern Sirkars, those provinces on the eastern seaboard which, as will be remembered, should by the treaty of 1755 have been restored to their native owners. The most dangerous enemy of the British, therefore, though not removed, was fully employed over his own affairs during the year 1756. No sooner was he free, however, than he was once again busy in mischief, reducing Vizagapatam and the British factories on the Godavery, until new intrigues at the Court of the Viceroy recalled him hurriedly to Hyderabad.

Still farther south, at Trichinopoly, matters remained for a time comparatively quiet. Major Caillaud, who commanded the garrison of the city, had received strict orders to abstain from all hostilities; while the French, though still in occupation of Seringham, had been so much weakened by the detachment of reinforcements for the help of Bussy, that until December 1756 they ceased to be formidable. In the following February, however, the dread of French intrigue at Madura and Tinnevelly had forced Caillaud to lead an expedition to both of these districts; and in April the necessity for collecting the revenues of the Nabob Mohammed Ali led the authorities at Madras to send a further expedition to Nellore on the river Pennar. This latter enterprise was unsuccessful, but has a distinct interest of its own for that it was entrusted to Lieutenant-Colonel Forde of the Thirty-ninth Foot, an officer who was soon to win for his name a place beside those of Clive and Lawrence. In this

his first command, however, he failed; and the French, though they had received orders to attempt nothing before the arrival of reinforcements, could not resist the temptation to take the field while the forces of Madras were divided between two points so remote as Tinnevelly and Nellore. M. d'Auteuil therefore seized the moment to collect four thousand men, one-fourth of them Europeans, together with a train of siege-artillery, and on the 14th of May appeared with this force before Trichinopoly. The position of the British garrison was never more critical during the whole course of the war than at this moment. The best of the troops were absent with Caillaud; and Captain Joseph Smith, who was left in command, had but seven hundred Sepoys and less than two hundred English with which to hold the fortifications and to guard five hundred French prisoners who were still within the walls. D'Auteuil, thinking to capture Trichinopoly at small cost, tried to scare Smith into surrender by bombardment and by incessant petty attacks, but Smith was not easily frightened and held his ground until the 25th. Then Caillaud appeared, having hastened back with all speed from Madura, and by extreme skill and perseverance passed his force by night unnoticed through the midst of the French camp into the city. D'Auteuil thereupon retired to Pondicherry, and Trichinopoly was once more in safety.

Sept.

Meanwhile the authorities at Madras had initiated a diversion in favour of Trichinopoly, to which the French answered by reprisals in kind; but the operations were of little interest or significance. In September a French squadron arrived which disembarked one thousand regular troops; but even after the arrival of this reinforcement the enemy's movements were of small importance. Indeed their inactivity at this period was no less surprising than welcome to the British, for the Presidency of Madras, in the face of their superior numbers, had been obliged to withdraw all its troops into garrison and to stand strictly on the defensive. The secret of the French forbearance was that the Governor of Pondicherry, having received positive orders from France to await the arrival of further succours, was fain to content himself with the reduction of a few of the outlying forts of the Carnatic. Thus the campaign of 1757 closed with the advantage to the French of the capture of Chittapett, a post thirty miles south of Arcot, and to the British of the acquisition of Madura.

1758.
April.

The year 1758 opened far more seriously for the British. At daybreak on the 28th of April a fleet of twelve sail was seen standing into the roadstead of Fort St. David and was presently recognised to be French. This was the long-expected armament on which the French had built all their hopes for the expulsion of the British from India, and it had consumed nearly twelve months in its passage. It had left Brest originally in March 1757 and had been driven back by foul weather. Then two line-of-battle ships had been taken from it for service in Canadian waters, and the squadron had waited till May for their place to be supplied by two French East Indiamen fitted out as ships of war. Then the Admiral, d'Aché, for all that a British fleet was hurrying after him, loitered on the voyage to Mauritius, and on leaving that island selected a course which kept him three months on his passage to Coromandel. At last, however, the squadron arrived in the roadstead of Fort St. David, having lost by that time between three and four hundred men through sickness. It carried on board Lally's regiment of infantry and fifty European artillerymen, together with Count Lally himself, who had been appointed to the supreme command of the French in India. Lally de Tollendal, or to give him his real name, O'Mullally of Tullindally (for he was of Irish extraction), was an officer who had been of the Irish brigade in the French service, and who enjoyed the credit of having suggested that movement of the artillery which had shattered the British column to defeat at Fontenoy. How far this training would avail him in India remained still to be seen.

| April 29. |

Lally's instructions from Versailles directed him first to besiege Fort St. David; and accordingly he himself sailed at once with three ships from that roadstead to Pondicherry to give the necessary orders, while the rest of the fleet worked down two miles to southward and dropped anchor off Cuddalore. But now the consequences of the long protraction of Admiral d'Aché's voyage began to reveal themselves. Commodore Stevens, who had left England with his squadron three months after him, had reached Madras five weeks before him, and joining with Admiral Pocock's squadron in the Hooghly had sailed with it on the 17th of April to intercept d'Aché. Pocock having missed the French squadron on his voyage south bore up to the northward, and on the morning of the 29th came in sight of it at its moorings before Cuddalore. D'Aché at once weighed anchor and stood out to sea; but owing to the heavy sailing of some of the English vessels it was not until the afternoon that Pocock could engage him, with seven ships against nine. The action that ensued though indecisive was decidedly to the disadvantage of the French. They lost six hundred men killed and wounded, while one of their ships of the line was so badly damaged that she was perforce run ashore and abandoned. The British ships lost little over a hundred men, though on the other hand their rigging was so much cut up that they were unable to pursue the enemy. Pocock therefore returned to Madras to refit, while the French fleet anchored some twenty miles north of Pondicherry in the roadstead of Alumparva.

April 30.
May 1.
May 6.

On the self-same day, under the energetic impulse of Lally, a thousand Europeans and as many French Sepoys under Count d'Estaing arrived before Fort St. David from Pondicherry and exchanged shots with the garrison. On the morrow M. de Soupire joined d'Estaing with additional troops and with siege-guns, and on the 1st of May appeared Lally himself, who immediately detached a force under d'Estaing against Cuddalore. The defences of this town were slight and the garrison consisted of five companies of Sepoys only, which were encumbered by the custody of fifty French prisoners. The fort accordingly capitulated on the 4th of May, on condition that the garrison should retire to Fort St. David with its arms, and that the French prisoners should be transported to neutral ground in the south until the fate of Fort St. David should be decided. Two days later d'Aché's squadron anchored again before Fort St. David and landed the troops from on board; and on the 15th the French began the erection of their first battery for the siege.

May 28.
June 2.

Lally had now the considerable force of twenty-five hundred Europeans and about the same number of Sepoys assembled before the town; but his difficulties none the less were very great. The authorities at Pondicherry were disloyal to him; the military chest was absolutely empty; and, long though his arrival had been expected, no preparation had been made for his transport and supplies. In his impatience for action, for he dreaded the return of Pocock from Madras, he had hurried the first detachment forward to Cuddalore without any transport or supplies whatever, with the result that the troops had been obliged to plunder the suburbs for food. Now, since no other means seemed open to him, he took the still more fatal step of impressing the natives for the work of carriage, without respect to custom, prejudice, or caste. For the moment, however, he was successful. The defences of Fort St. David were respectable, but the garrison was too weak in numbers to man them properly, and the quality of the troops was remarkably poor. The Sepoys numbered about sixteen hundred and the Europeans about six hundred; but of the latter less than half were effective, while two hundred and fifty out of the whole were sailors, recently landed from the frigates and most defective in discipline. Major Polier, who was in command, made the mistake of attempting to defend several outworks with an inadequate force, instead of destroying them and retiring into the main fortress. Lally was therefore able to drive the defenders from these outworks piecemeal; and his success sufficed to scare nearly the whole of the Sepoys into desertion. A ray of hope came for a moment to the garrison with the news that Pocock's squadron had arrived at

Pondicherry on its way from Madras, and that the French sailors had mutinied, refusing to put to sea until their wages were paid. But Lally, always energetic, contrived to find the necessary funds, and d'Aché set sail in time to prevent any communication between the fleet and Fort St. David. Finally the fort, though not yet breached, capitulated on the 2nd of June, and Lally's first great object was gained.

June 7.

The fall of Fort St. David gave great alarm at Madras, and with reason, for the defence had been discreditably feeble. Polier had formerly proved himself in repeated actions to be a gallant soldier; but making all allowance for the defects of his garrison, his conduct was not such as was to be expected from a countryman of Caillaud and a brother officer of Clive, Lawrence, and Kilpatrick. Moreover, Lally was not a man to be content with a single success. On the very day of the surrender he detached a force under d'Estaing against Devicotah, which was perforce abandoned by the British at his approach; and there was every reason to fear that his energy would now be bent towards the capture of Madras. The government therefore called in all its scattered garrisons in the Carnatic, maintaining only that of Trichinopoly, and concentrated them in Madras; thus adding two hundred and fifty Europeans and twenty-five hundred Sepoys to the strength of that city. On this same day Lally returned to Pondicherry with his army from Fort St. David and made triumphant entry. *Te Deum* was sung, and thanksgiving was followed by banquets and festivities—all at a time when the public treasury was empty.

June 18.

In fact, however Lally might long for it, there was no possibility for him yet to attack Madras. D'Aché, declaring that his duty summoned him to cruise off the coast of Ceylon, would not spare the fleet to aid in the enterprise against the seat of British power in the Carnatic, and actually sailed for the south on the 4th of June. For a march overland upon Madras Lally's army required equipment; and equipment meant money, which the authorities at Pondicherry averred that they could not supply. Acting therefore on the advice of a Jesuit priest, Lally resolved to march into Tanjore and to extort the cash which he needed from the Rajah. The civil authorities in alarm recalled d'Aché to protect Pondicherry, and on the day following his arrival Lally ordered out sixteen hundred European troops and a still larger number of Sepoys and started with them for the south.

June 25.

The march was one long succession of blunders and misfortunes. The harsh measures employed towards the natives on the advance to Fort St. David had alienated every man of them from taking service with the army; so the force started without transport. Gross excesses committed by the French troops in plundering the country drove the villagers to hide away all their cattle; hence neither transport nor supplies were to be obtained on the march. The soldiers were therefore of necessity turned loose to find provisions as best they might, and their discipline, already seriously impaired, went rapidly from bad to worse. When they entered Devicotah they had not tasted food for twelve hours; and finding that only rice in the husk awaited them there, they set fire to the huts within the fort and went near to kindling the magazines. It was not until they reached Carical, after traversing fully a hundred miles, that the troops at last received a real meal. Fresh follies marked the progress of the march. The town of Nagore was seized and its ransom farmed out to the captain of the French hussars, a corps which had only recently arrived in India and had distinguished itself above all others by violence and pillage. Ammunition again, for even this was not carried with the army, was extorted by force from the Dutch settlements of Negapatam and Tranquebar. Finally, two pagodas of peculiar sanctity were plundered, though to no advantage, and the Brahmins were blown from the muzzles of guns. Lally's difficulties were doubtless great, and his methods were those honoured and to be honoured by his countrymen in many a campaign past and future; but it is hard to understand how a man calling himself a soldier could deliberately have led from three to four thousand men for a distance of a hundred miles from his base without making the slightest provision for its subsistence, or the least effort to maintain its discipline.

| August. |
| Aug. 18. |

Lally's sins soon found him out. On his arrival at Carical seven thousand Tanjorines under the Rajah's general, Monacjee, advanced to Trivalore to oppose him; and this force was soon afterwards swelled not only by native allies but by five hundred British Sepoys and ten English gunners, who had been lent by Caillaud from Trichinopoly. Monacjee fell back before Lally step by step to the city of Tanjore, but his cavalry never ceased to harass the French foraging-parties, to drive off the cattle which they had collected, and to intercept supplies. Some days were spent in fruitless negotiation, and on the 2nd of August Lally's batteries opened fire on the city; whereupon Caillaud immediately sent to the Rajah a further reinforcement of five hundred of his best Sepoys. On the 8th disquieting intelligence reached Lally of the defeat of a French squadron by the British, and of a British occupation of Carical, the only port from which his army, already much distressed by want of stores and ammunition, could possibly be relieved. On the 10th, having with difficulty repelled a sortie of the garrison, he raised the siege and retreated towards Carical, leaving three heavy guns behind him. Instantly the

Tanjorines were after him, hovering about him on every side during his march, swooping down on stragglers and cutting off supplies. The sufferings of the French troops were frightful. It was only with the greatest difficulty that Lally brought them through to Carical, to find on his arrival that the British fleet was anchored at the mouth of the river.

| Aug. 28. |
| Sept. |

For on the 2nd of August Pocock had again engaged d'Aché, though with inferior numbers, and after an action of two hours had so battered the French squadron that it had crowded all sail to escape and taken refuge under the guns of Pondicherry. Moreover, d'Aché was so much disheartened that he not only refused to meet the British again, but announced his intention of returning to Mauritius. Lally had received intimation of this resolve during his retreat to Carical, and had despatched Count d'Estaing to d'Aché to protest against it. On arriving with his army at Pondicherry from Carical he repeated his remonstrances, but in vain. D'Aché had secured thirty thousand pounds by illegal capture of certain Dutch ships in Pondicherry roads, and this he was content to leave with his colleagues; but he was resolute as to his departure from the coast, and on the 2nd of September he sailed away.

| Oct. 4. |

Whatever Lally's indignation against d'Aché for this desertion, it must be confessed that his operations had been little more successful than the Admiral's. He had injured both the health and the discipline of his troops by the raid into Tanjore, and had failed to extract more than a trifling sum from the Rajah. The money taken by d'Aché, however, furnished him with sufficient funds to initiate preparations for a march on Madras; and since the British had seized the opportunity of his own absence to recapture some of the scattered forts in the Carnatic, he despatched three several expeditions to Trinomalee, Carangooly, and Trivatore to clear the way to Arcot, ordering them to concentrate about thirty-five miles south-east of Arcot, at Wandewash. The several columns having done their work, he joined the united force in person at Wandewash and marched with it on Arcot, which having no British garrison surrendered without resistance. There now remained but two posts in the occupation of the British between him and Madras, Conjeveram on the direct road from Arcot to Madras, and Chingleput on the river Paliar, neither of them strongly garrisoned and both therefore easy of capture. Failing, however, to appreciate the importance of these two forts, and finding that his stock of ready money was exhausted, Lally sent his troops into cantonments, and returned to Pondicherry to collect funds. Thereby he threw away his last chance of worsting the British in India.

The authorities at Madras accepted his successes in the Carnatic as the inevitable consequence of the fall of Fort St. David, and were therefore little dismayed. Nevertheless the situation had been apprehended to be serious; and early in August appeal had been made to Bengal for assistance. It was refused. Clive was not indifferent to the peril of the sister Presidency, but he had matured designs of his own for a diversion in favour of the Carnatic, which, as shall presently be seen, was brilliantly executed. Madras being thus thrown on her own resources, the authorities resolved at the end of August to recall Caillaud and all the European troops from Trichinopoly, and to leave Captain Joseph Smith in charge of that city with two thousand Sepoys only. After some inevitable delay Caillaud embarked at Negapatam, and on the 25th of September arrived safely with one hundred and eighty men at Madras. A few days before, a still more welcome reinforcement had been received in the shape of Colonel Draper's regiment,[342] eight hundred and fifty strong, with Draper himself, lately an officer of the First Guards, in command. Such an accession of strength made it possible to profit by Lally's omission to capture Chingleput. That post covered a district which, being rich in supplies, would spare Madras the exhaustion of the stock which had been laid up for the expected siege; and in view of its importance the troops at Conjeveram were withdrawn to it, and the garrison gradually strengthened to a force of one hundred Europeans and twelve hundred Sepoys. Further, it was determined to hire a contingent of Mahrattas and of Tanjorines so as to harass the enemy's convoys and lines of communication during the siege.

These preparations were well completed some time before Lally was ready to move. That General was indeed concentrating all the strength of France for his great effort against Madras, but in blind pursuance of this object he had removed the most dangerous enemy of the British from the post in which, of all others, he would have been most formidable. In plain words, he had recalled Bussy, with his army, from the court of Salabad Jung and from the administration of the Deccan. Further, he had ordered him to entrust the occupation of the Northern Sirkars to M. Conflans, an officer who was only just arrived from Europe, together with the smallest possible force that would enable him to maintain it. Bussy obeyed, but in perplexity and despair; for it was hard for him to abandon the work at which he had toiled for so long with unwearied zeal and unvarying success; and it was scarcely to be expected that he should feel cordially towards this new and impulsive commander who, whatever his merits, possessed not a quarter of his own ability. Lally on his side entertained decided antipathy towards Bussy. He looked upon the French authorities in India generally as a pack of rogues, wherein he was not far wrong, but in including Bussy with the common herd he was very far from right. He therefore treated Bussy's supplications to return to Hyderabad as designed merely for the thwarting of his own enterprise, and disregarded them accordingly. The junior officers of the army, with a sounder appreciation of Bussy's powers, generously petitioned that he might rank as their superior, to which request Lally, though with no very good grace, was forced to accede. Thus, for one preliminary disadvantage, there was little prospect of hearty accord and co-operation in the French camp. Then there was the deficiency of funds to be faced, which was only overcome by subscriptions from the private purses of Lally and other officers; though Bussy, the wealthiest of all, declined, if Lally is to be believed, to contribute a farthing. Finally, there were endless troubles over the matter of transport, for which Lally had no one but himself to thank; and, what with one embarrassment and another, it was the end of November before the French troops were fairly on the march for Madras.

| Dec. |
| Dec. 13. |

Lally's force comprised in all twenty-three hundred Europeans, both horse and foot, and five thousand Sepoys. The main body moved from Arcot along the direct road by Conjeveram, and a large detachment followed the bank of the Paliar upon Chingleput. Lally in person joined this latter column on the 4th of December, but having reconnoitred Chingleput decided to leave it in his rear, and to continue his march northward to Madras. The defending force collected by the British in that city amounted to seventeen hundred and fifty Europeans and twenty-two hundred Sepoys, the whole under command of Colonel Stringer Lawrence. The Colonel drew the greater part of these troops into the field to watch the French movements, failing back slowly before them as they advanced; and on the 13th Lally's entire force encamped in the plain, rather more than a mile to south-west of Fort St. George. Nearer approach to the fort was barred by two rivers, the more northerly of them, called the Triplicane, entering the sea about a thousand yards south of the glacis; the other, known as the North River, washing the actual foot of the glacis, but turning from thence abruptly southward to join the Triplicane and flow with it into the sea. Lally therefore passed round to the other side of Fort St. George, the British evacuating the outer posts before him as he advanced, and established himself in the Black Town on the north-western front of the fort, and thence along its northern side to the sea. With his right thus resting on the town and his left on the beach, he prepared to open the siege of Madras.

| Dec. 14. |

The Black Town was rich, and the French troops, with the indiscipline now become habitual to them, fell at once to indiscriminate plunder, with the result that in a short time a great many of them were reeling drunk. Colonel Draper thereupon proposed a sortie in force, and the suggestion was approved as tending to raise the spirit of the garrison. Accordingly, at eleven o'clock on the following morning, Draper with five hundred men and two guns marched out from the western ravelin of the fort, and holding his course westward for some distance turned north into the streets of the Black Town to attack the French right, while Major Brereton with another hundred men followed a route parallel to him, but nearer to the fort, in order to cover his retreat. By some mistake Draper's black drummers began to beat the Grenadiers' March directly they entered the town, and so gave the alarm. The French formed in a cross street to receive the attack, but in the confusion mistook the line of the British advance and awaited them at the head of the wrong street, too far to the westward. Draper therefore came up full on their left flank, poured in a volley, and bringing up his guns opened fire with grape. In a few minutes the whole of the French had taken refuge in the adjoining houses, and Draper, ordering his guns to cease fire, rushed forward to secure four cannon which the French had brought with them. The French officer in charge of them offered to surrender both himself and his guns, when Draper, looking behind him, found that he was followed by but four men, the rest having, like the enemy, fled for shelter to the houses. Had the British done their duty Draper's attack would probably have put an end to the siege then and there; but as things were, the French, hearing the guns cease, quickly rallied, and streaming out of the houses in superior numbers opened a destructive fire. Draper was obliged to abandon the guns and order a retreat, the French following after him in hot pursuit. His position was critical, for he could not retire by the route of his advance, but was obliged to take a road leading to the northern face of the fort. The way was blocked by a stagnant arm of the North River with but one bridge; and it lay within the power of Lally's regiment, on the left of the French position, to reach this bridge before him and so to cut off his retreat. Bussy, however, who was in command on the French left, either through jealousy, or possibly because his men were too much intoxicated to move, took no advantage of this opportunity. Brereton came up in time to cover Draper's retreat, and the British re-entered the fort in safety. They had lost over two hundred men in killed, wounded, and prisoners in this abortive attack; and though the French had suffered as great a loss, yet they were victorious whereas the British were demoralised. Had Lally's regiment done its duty Madras would probably have fallen in a few days. So ended an episode most thoroughly discreditable to both parties.

1759.
Jan.
Feb.

310

Lally now began the construction of batteries over against the north and north-western fronts of the fort, from the Black Town to the sea. Meanwhile Caillaud was despatched to Tanjore to obtain troops from the Rajah; and Captain Preston, who commanded the garrison at Chingleput, never ceased to harass the French by constant petty attacks and threatening of their communications. At length, on the 2nd of January, the French batteries opened fire, which they continued throughout the month, but with no very great effect. The indiscipline which Lally had permitted during his earlier operations told heavily upon the efficiency of the besieging force; and everything moved slowly and with friction. At length, on the 30th of January, a British ship arrived to hearten the garrison with ammunition and specie, both of which were sorely needed; and on the 7th of February Caillaud, after endless difficulties at Tanjore, joined Preston at Chingleput and increased his force by thirteen hundred Sepoys and two thousand Tanjorine horse. Though half of the Sepoys and the whole of the horse were worth little, yet this growth of numbers in his rear, and the knowledge that Pocock's squadron was on its way from Bombay to relieve Madras, forced Lally to take strong measures against Chingleput. Accordingly, on the 9th of February, he detached a force of nine hundred Europeans, twelve hundred Sepoys and five hundred native horse, with eight field-pieces, to attack Caillaud in earnest. The action was hot, and Caillaud only with the greatest difficulty succeeded in holding his own; but ultimately the French were repulsed, and Chingleput, that terrible thorn, remained still rankling in Lally's side. His position was now desperate. Supplies, money, ammunition, all were failing, and his troops, both native and European, were melting away by desertion. He had succeeded in battering a breach in the fort, but his officers were averse to attempt an assault. Finally, on the 16th the arrival of Pocock's squadron, at once relieving Madras and threatening Pondicherry, brought his darling project to an end. By the morning of the 17th he was in full march for Arcot, leaving fifty-two guns, all his stores and ammunition, and forty sick and wounded men behind him.

So ended the siege of Madras, the last offensive movement of the French in India. It had cost the garrison thirty-three officers, five hundred and eighty Europeans and three hundred Sepoys killed, wounded and prisoners, while over four hundred more of the Sepoys had deserted. Happily Pocock's squadron brought reinforcements which made good the loss of Europeans. The casualties in the French army remain unknown, but, whether they were considerable or not, the survivors were at any rate demoralised. Lally retired with bitter rage in his heart against the authorities at Pondicherry, to whose apathy and self-seeking he attributed his failure. Doubtless if they had seconded his efforts loyally and truly, his difficulties would have been infinitely less, and his chances of success proportionately greater. But even if the hasty and masterful temper which estranged them from him be excused, nothing can palliate his two cardinal errors as a soldier; first, the omission to secure Chingleput while yet the capture was easy, and secondly the neglect to enforce discipline among all ranks of his army. Violence without strength, energy without foresight, imperiousness without ascendency—such are not the qualities that go to make a great leader in the field.

1758.

And meanwhile the counterstroke prepared by Clive had fallen once and was about to fall again with redoubled force. Affairs in Bengal in the autumn of 1758 stood on no very sure footing. Meer Jaffier was not wholly resigned to his puppet-hood; but his nobles were disaffected, his treasury was empty, and he was threatened on his northern frontier by invasion from Oude; so he was obliged reluctantly to throw himself upon the protection of Clive. So unstable a condition of affairs presented no ideal moment for weakening the small force on which British influence in those provinces might depend; but Clive, perceiving that Bussy's withdrawal from Hyderabad gave him a chance to substitute British for French ascendency at the court of the Deccan, determined at all hazards to seize it. The ruler of one district of the Northern Sirkars, the Rajah Anunderaj, had already risen in revolt against the French, seized Vizagapatam, and appealed to Madras for assistance. An agent was sent to concert operations with him; and Clive, making up a force of five hundred European infantry and artillery, one hundred Lascars and two thousand Sepoys, together with six field-guns and as many battering pieces, shipped them off from Calcutta at the end of September. The command was entrusted to Lieutenant-Colonel Forde.

Dec.
Dec. 9.

The voyage was protracted by foul weather, and it was not until the 20th of October that the expedition reached Vizagapatam, from which it marched to join Anunderaj's troops at Cossimcotah. Here more delay was caused by the unwillingness of the Rajah to fulfil his engagement to pay the British troops; but at length on the 1st of December the force advanced and on the 3rd came in sight of the enemy, who were encamped forty miles north of Rajahmundry within sight of the fort of Peddapore and astride of the high road to the south. The French force, which was commanded by M. Conflans, consisted of five hundred Europeans, six thousand Sepoys and a quantity of native levies. Forde's army, on his side, had received the accession of five hundred worthless horse and a rabble of five thousand foot, chiefly armed with pikes and bows, which represented the contingent of Anunderaj. On the 6th Forde advanced along the high road to within four miles of Conflans, but each officer thought the other too strong to be attacked. Inaction continued until the 8th, when both commanders simultaneously framed independent designs for extricating themselves from the deadlock. Conflans's plan was to send six guns with a sufficient force to a height which commanded the British camp, and which Forde had omitted to occupy. Forde, for his part, had decided to make a detour of three miles to Condore, from which he could turn Conflans's position and regain the high road to Rajahmundry. At four o'clock on the morning of the 9th, accordingly, Forde marched away with his own troops only, while the Rajah's army, which though warned was unready to move, remained in the camp. Forde had not proceeded far before he heard the sound of Conflans's guns in his rear and received piteous messages from the Rajah for assistance. Turning back he met the Rajah's rabble in full flight and rallied them; after which the whole force pursued its march and at eight o'clock arrived at Condore.

Conflans, flattering himself that he had defeated Forde's entire army, followed him quickly, with the idea of preventing his return to his former camp; and in his haste to advance allowed his line to fall into disorder. His European battalion was in his centre, with thirteen field-pieces distributed on its flanks, while his right and left wings were composed each of three thousand Sepoys with some unwieldly native cannon. Forde formed his line in much the same order. In his centre he posted the British, now represented by the Hundred-and-First and Hundred-and-Second Foot, with six guns on their flanks, and his Sepoys, in two divisions each of nine hundred men, on either wing; and he bade the Rajah's troops keep out of the way in the rear. He then advanced under a heavy cannonade from the enemy for some distance before Condore, and halted with his centre in rear of a field of Indian corn, which entirely concealed the Europeans, but left the Sepoys uncovered on the plain on either hand. These Sepoys, being from Bengal, were dressed in scarlet instead of in the white clothing worn by their brethren in the hotter climate of the south. The French had never seen the scarlet except on the bodies of European troops, and Forde was fully aware of the fact; for he ordered the Sepoys to furl the old-fashioned Company flags, which they still carried, as also their regimental colours, that they might be the more easily mistaken for a regular battalion of British.

In the ardour of their advance the enemy's infantry out-marched their guns and moved forward without them. Their line, from its superiority in numbers, far outflanked the British on both wings; but as it drew nearer, the French battalion in the centre suddenly inclined to the right towards Forde's left wing of Sepoys. Conflans had swallowed the bait laid for him by Forde.

The French battalion evidently mistook the Sepoys for Europeans, for before engaging them it dressed its ranks, and then opened fire by platoons at a distance of two hundred yards. Long though this range was for the old musket, the Sepoys seeing Europeans in front and natives menacing their flank hardly stood to deliver a feeble volley, but immediately broke, despite all the efforts of Forde, and fled away pursued by the enemy's horse. Conflans at once detached several platoons of his Europeans to join in the pursuit; when to his dismay a second line of scarlet filed steadily up from behind the Indian corn to the ground whereon the Sepoys had stood, halted and fronted as coolly as if on parade, and then with equal coolness opened fire by volleys of divisions from the left.[343] The first volley brought down half of the French grenadiers, and by the time that the fifth and last division had pulled trigger the whole of Conflans's European battalion was broken up, and flying back in disorder to its guns, half a mile in rear.

Forde, unable to curb the eagerness of his men, allowed them to pursue in succession of divisions, the left leading; but every division marched too fast to preserve order excepting the fourth, which was kept well in hand by Captain Yorke as a rallying-point in case of mishap. But no mishap was to come. The French rallied behind their cannon, but had not time to fire more than a round or two when the British fell upon them, drove them from their batteries and captured every gun. The Sepoys and native levies of the French made little or no stand after the defeat of their Europeans, and the British Sepoys of the right, together with some rallied fugitives from the left, advanced to join their victorious comrades. No sooner were they come than Forde made fresh dispositions, and marched on without losing a moment to attack Conflans's camp. The remnants of the French battalion, which were posted in a hollow way before it, made some faint show of resistance; but seeing the British guns coming forward, turned to the right about and fled, with the British in hot pursuit. Many of the fugitives threw down their arms and surrendered; the rest, together with the remainder of the French army, ran away in hopeless confusion. Conflans, after sending off his military chest and four field-guns, jumped on a horse and galloped away, not stopping except to change horses till he reached Rajahmundry, forty miles distant. Of his Europeans seventy-six officers and men were killed, many wounded, and fifty-six taken. Thirty cannon, seven mortars, and the whole of his baggage and transport were captured. The British loss amounted to no more than forty Europeans and over two hundred Sepoys killed and wounded. Had the Rajah's cavalry been of the slightest value, the losses of the French would have been far greater; but Forde's promptness in following up his first success made his victory sufficiently complete. This brilliant little action marked the rise of yet another great leader among the British in India.

The British battalion being much fatigued was halted after the engagement in the French camp, but on the same evening Captain Knox with the right wing of Sepoys was sent forward to Rajahmundry. On the following day a further reinforcement of Sepoys joined him; and the French, still under the influence of panic, evacuated the fort. Knox at once entered it, and turning the guns on to the fugitives, though far out of range, set them running once more. Thus Rajahmundry, the gate and barrier of the district of Vizagapatam, passed into the hands of the British, with all its artillery, ammunition, and stores. Forde arrived there with the rest of the army on the 11th, eager to pursue his success by an advance on Masulipatam. This, the most important town and the centre of French influence in the province, was doubly important to the enemy as a base from which they might at any time recover their lost territory. Forde, however, was in want of money, for which he had relied on the promises of Anunderaj. The Rajah, as is the way of his kind, now refused either to supply funds or to set his rabble in motion to accompany him. At length after six weeks of negotiation this deplorable potentate was induced, partly by favourable terms of repayment, partly by a severe fright, to fulfil his undertaking; but fifty precious days had been lost, and the French had gained time to recover themselves.

On the 28th of January Forde resumed his march, and on the 6th of February occupied Ellore, forty-eight miles north of Masulipatam. Here again he was compelled to halt by the dilatoriness of the Rajah in sending forward supplies; but he was not on that account idle. Conflans, having got the better of his panic after Condore, had replaced garrisons in Narsipore and Concal, two outlying strongholds to the north of Masulipatam, and had organised an army of observation, consisting of two hundred and fifty Europeans and two thousand Sepoys, under M. du Rocher. The dispositions of this latter force were so faulty as to leave Narsipore in isolation, and Forde lost no time in sending Captain Knox with a detachment of Sepoys to capture it. The French commander of the post was no sooner warned of Knox's approach then he evacuated Narsipore and joined the army of du Rocher. Then came more delay; and it was the 1st of March before Forde was again able to move. Two days later Concal was taken, though most gallantly defended by a French sergeant; and on the 6th Forde came in sight of Masulipatam. Conflans occupied a strong position before the town, which he might have held with advantage; but his heart failed him, and he retired within the fortifications.

The defences of Masulipatam had been improved by the French since their entry into possession in 1751, and now formed an irregular parallelogram, open on the south side, where a broad estuary furnished sufficient natural protection, and closed on the three other sides by mud walls faced with brick and strengthened by eleven bastions: there was also a wet ditch and a narrow palisaded space between ditch and parapet, but no glacis. On the landward side the fort was surrounded everywhere by a heavy swamp, the road to the town being carried on a causeway to the main gate on the north-west front. This causeway was covered for a distance of a hundred and twenty yards from the wall by a parapet ending in a ravelin, which commanded the whole length of the road. The only sound ground within reach of the fort was to be found on some sandhills to east and west of it; of which those on the eastern side, being within eight hundred yards of the wall, were selected by Forde for his position. Regular approaches for a formal siege were out of the question for so small a force, so Forde was fain to begin the erection of batteries on the sandhills, to play on the works from thence as best they could. The whole of the eighteen ensuing days were devoted to the work of construction, the siege-guns being landed from ships which had followed the movements of the army along the coast. During this short period it seemed as though fate had laid itself out to raise every possible obstacle against Forde's success. No sooner had he invested Masulipatam than du Rocher's army of observation woke to sudden activity, and moved round upon Rajahmundry and the British communications with the north. The officer in charge of that fort, being unable to make any defence, was obliged to send away to safer custody a large sum in specie which had been received from Bengal; and thus Forde's supply of ready money was cut off. Du Rocher then advanced a little to the northward of Rajahmundry, vowing vengeance against Anunderaj's country, and so terrified the pusillanimous Rajah that he declined to employ either his money or his credit for the service of the British army. Forde was left absolutely penniless. He had already borrowed all the prize-money of his officers and even of his men, and knew not whither to turn for cash for the payment of his troops. The soldiers became apprehensive and discontented, and on the 19th the whole of the Europeans turned out with their arms in open mutiny, and threatened to march away. With great difficulty Forde persuaded them to return; and the men, once conciliated, went back to work with all their former ardour. But the batteries had not been completed two days when news arrived that the Viceroy, Salabad Jung, was arrived at the river Kistnah, not more than forty miles away, with an army of forty thousand men, to expel the intruders who had dared to invade the provinces under his suzerainty. Messengers arrived from him requiring Anunderaj to quit the British immediately and to repair to his standard; and the terrified Rajah actually started to return to his own country. He was only with difficulty recalled by Forde's representations that his one chance of retreat was to remain with the British. In the faint hope of gaining time Forde proposed to open negotiations with Salabad Jung, who to his great relief consented to receive his emissary and undertook for the present to advance no farther. Here, therefore, was a respite, though not such as could be counted on for long endurance.

Meanwhile, ever since the 25th of March, Forde's batteries had maintained a hot fire; and, though the damage done to the works by day had been regularly repaired by the besieged at night, three of the bastions had been sufficiently ruined to give foothold to a storming party. But now the weather changed, and on the 5th of April the southern monsoon broke with a flood of rain that soaked the morass around the fort to its deepest. On the morrow the storm ceased, but the day was ushered in by the gloomiest of tidings for Forde. Salabad Jung was advancing from the Kistnah, and du Rocher was on the point of junction with him. Finally, on the same evening, the artillery-officers reported that but two days ammunition was left for the batteries. Here, therefore, was the climax. Before Forde was a fortress with a garrison of greater strength than his own army; behind him was a force which outnumbered his own by more than ten to one; his communications were cut, and his ammunition and his funds were exhausted. It was open to him to embark and retire ignominiously by sea, or to stake all on a single desperate venture. He chose the bolder course and resolved to storm the fort.

During the progress of the siege it had been remarked that at the south-western corner of the fort, adjoining the sound, no ditch had been constructed; the ground without being a mere waste of mire, which might well be accounted a more difficult obstacle than any ditch. Natives, however, had more than once been seen traversing this quagmire; and Captains Yorke and Knox on making trial of it found it to be stiff and heavy indeed, but not more than knee-deep. This, therefore, was a point at which at least a false attack could be made, and Forde resolved to take advantage of it. Another point at which a feint might be directed was the ravelin outside the main gate. The true attack must of necessity be delivered against the front which had been damaged by the batteries; and the north-east bastion, known as the Chameleon, was the place selected. The necessary dispositions were quickly settled. The Rajah's troops were some of them to guard the camp, and the rest to make a demonstration against the ravelin. Captain Knox with seven hundred Sepoys was to conduct the feint attack upon the south-west angle, and the remainder of the troops were detailed for the true assault on the Chameleon bastion. The Europeans, who numbered but three hundred and forty-six, including the gunners, and thirty sailors borrowed from the ships, were told off into two divisions, the first under Captain Callendar, the second under Captain Yorke; while of the seven hundred remaining Sepoys part formed a third division under Captain Macleane, and the remainder a reserve under Forde himself. It was ordered that both the true and false attacks should begin simultaneously at midnight, when the tide would be at ebb and no more than three feet of water in the ditch; and the last stroke of the gongs within the fort was to be the signal for the storming parties to advance.

| April 7. |
| April 8. |

All through daylight of the 7th of April the British batteries maintained a fierce fire, playing impartially upon the three bastions of the eastern front. At length night came to silence the guns, and at ten o'clock the troops fell in for the assault. Knox having the longer distance to traverse was the first to move off, and his column presently disappeared into the darkness. The minutes flew by, and the time came for the advance of the European troops; but Captain Callendar, the leader of the first division, was not to be found. There was anxious enquiry and search, but the missing officer could not be discovered; and at length, after a precious half-hour had been lost, Captain Fischer took his place and the column marched off without him. The men were still struggling through the morass towards the Chameleon bastion when the sound of firing told them that Knox, punctual to a second, had opened his false attack. Quickening their speed as best they might, they plunged heavily on, knee-deep in mire over the swamp, waist-deep in mud and water through the ditch; when, just as Fischer's column reached the palisade, a sharp fire from the breach and from the bastions on either hand showed that they were discovered. All the more eagerly Fischer's men hewed and hacked at the palisade; while Yorke's division engaged the St. John's bastion to his left and Macleane the Small-gate bastion to his right. The men fell fast, but presently the palisades were cleared away, and the first division swarming up the breach swept the French out of the Chameleon bastion. Fischer halted for the arrival of Yorke with the second division, and then the two officers parted, Fischer to the right to clear the northern, and Yorke to the left to clear the eastern face of the fort.

Finding a field-gun with its ammunition in the Chameleon bastion, Yorke at once trained it along the rampart to southward, and was preparing to follow in the same direction himself, when he observed a party of French Sepoys advancing between the rampart and the buildings of the town to reinforce the Chameleon bastion. Instantly he ran down, and seizing the officer at their head bade them lay down their arms and surrender. Startled beyond all thought of resistance they obeyed, and were at once sent back to the captured bastion; while Yorke, taking the way by which they had advanced, pressed on against the St. John's bastion. The French guard, which had sought shelter within the angles from the raking fire of Yorke's field-gun, fired upon him and struck down not a few of his men, but surrendered immediately afterwards. They too were sent back to the Chameleon bastion, where the Sepoys took charge of them; and Yorke pursued his way to the next bastion to southward, named the Dutch bastion, where the same scene was repeated and a fresh consignment of prisoners was sent back to the custody of the Sepoys. The François bastion, the most southerly of all, alone remained untaken, and Yorke was eager to prosecute his success; but now the men hung back. The division had been not a little thinned by previous losses and by the detachment of guards for prisoners and for the captured bastions; and the handful of men that remained with the Captain began to wonder where such work was going to end. By threats and exhortations Yorke after a time induced them to follow him; but while passing an expense-magazine a little way beyond the Dutch bastion, one of the men caught sight of powder-barrels within it and cried out "A mine, a mine." Immediately every man rushed back in panic to the Chameleon bastion; and Yorke was left alone, with his black drummers by his side vainly beating the Grenadiers' March. Fortunately the guards in the captured bastions stood fast; and Yorke returning to the fugitives, who were on the point of leaving the fort, stopped the panic by threatening death to the first man who attempted to run. Rallying thirty-six men he went back to complete his work; but the delay had given the French in the François bastion time to train a gun upon the line of his advance. Waiting until his party was come within close range they fired, killed sixteen of them outright and wounded several more, including Yorke himself, who was brought to the ground with a ball in each thigh. The survivors picked him up and carried him off; but with his fall the attack in that quarter came, for the time, to an end.

Fischer meanwhile had been even more successful on the northern front. He cleared the two first bastions without difficulty, and on reaching the third, by the causeway, seized the gate and cut off the troops in the ravelin from the fort. Captain Callendar, the missing officer, suddenly appeared, no man knew from whence, in the middle of the affair, but was instantly shot dead; and Fischer was still pushing on, when he received orders from Forde to halt. Conflans throughout the attack had remained by the south front of the fort, quite at his wits' end, and adding to the general confusion by a succession of contradictory orders. Knox's attack distracted him on one side, the Rajah's troops made an unearthly din by the ravelin, and the true assault on the eastern front fairly broke his spirits down. At the very moment when Yorke's men were returning discomfited from the François bastion, he sent a messenger to Forde, offering to surrender on honourable terms. Forde was far too shrewd to betray his own weakness. He replied that he could hear of nothing but surrender at discretion; and Conflans, concluding his position to be hopeless, acceded. Five hundred Europeans and two thousand French Sepoys laid down their arms, and the British were masters of Masulipatam.

So ended this daring and marvellous adventure, with the loss to the British of but eighty-six Europeans and two hundred Sepoys killed and wounded. Salabad Jung was within fifteen miles, and du Rocher even nearer at the time of the assault; but the victory was sufficient to paralyse them also. The Viceroy quickly consented to open negotiations, and though he haggled, after the manner of his race, for a whole month, finally concluded a treaty whereby he granted to the British eighty miles of the coast, and engaged himself not only never to entertain French troops again, but even to compel such as remained to evacuate the Sirkars. Thus not only was the district secured, but French influence was displaced in favour of British at the court of Hyderabad. Such were the prizes gained by the will, resource, and resolution of one man, who had strength to rend the toils that fate had woven about him just when they seemed to have closed upon him for ever.

CHAPTER VII

Lally's failure before Madras could not fail to raise British reputation and to depress that of the French; and sundry petty chieftains who had long been wavering in the Carnatic, now threw in their lot definitely with the victors. Nevertheless the British success could be but negative unless the territory adjacent to Madras were at once recovered and protected; and to this task the authorities wisely addressed themselves without delay. The reinforcements which had already arrived, together with two companies lately returned from Bengal, left the British with a force of eleven hundred Europeans, fifteen hundred Sepoys, and three thousand native irregulars fit to take the field; but, owing to the difficulty of collecting transport and supplies, the troops were not in a position to advance until the 6th of March. Meanwhile Lally had moved his army eastward from Arcot to Conjeveram, whence he returned himself to Pondicherry, leaving M. de Soupire in command with orders not to risk a general action. On the British side also the command had changed hands owing to the failing health both of Draper and of Lawrence, and had passed to Major Brereton of Draper's regiment.

For fully three weeks the two hostile armies remained in sight of each other, de Soupire waiting to be attacked, and Brereton rightly declining to engage him except on the open plain. The capture of Conjeveram was important to the British, since the fort would cover such districts as they had already regained, and so liberate their army for service farther afield. At length Brereton determined to dislodge de Soupire, if possible, by threatening his communications south of the Paliar; so marching upon Wandewash, the most important French station between Madras and Pondicherry, he broke ground before it as if for a formal siege. De Soupire made no attempt to follow him, but finding himself pressed for money and supplies left a small garrison in Conjeveram and retired to Arcot, well content to be able to reach it without hazard of an action. Brereton thereupon made a forced march upon Conjeveram, and before de Soupire was aware that he had moved from Wandewash, had taken the fort, with little difficulty, by storm.

Lally, who at the news of the siege of Wandewash had advanced northward from Pondicherry, halted on hearing of the capture of Conjeveram, and finally took up a position seven miles to westward of the fortress. There Major Monson, who had taken the command from Brereton, thrice offered him battle; but Lally declined, and after a few weeks withdrew from the field, distributing his troops into cantonments at Arcot, Covrepauk, Carangooly, and Chittapett. In truth his army was rapidly going from bad to worse. A recent exchange of prisoners had restored to him five hundred French soldiers, who, having lived an idle and by no means uncomfortable life in custody of the British for five years, were very far from eager to resume hard work in the field. Their discontent soon extended itself to their comrades, and spread not the less rapidly since all alike were irregularly paid. Indeed, the garrisons both at Arcot and Covrepauk offered to betray these stations to the British for money, though, their hearts failing them at the last moment, they renounced their bargain. But events had begun to turn steadily against the French, while the British gathered strength on every side. At the end of June two hundred recruits arrived from England, and brought news that Colonel Eyre Coote was likewise on his way to Madras with his own battalion, one thousand strong, which had been lately raised in England. Brereton, who was once again in command, seized the opportunity afforded by his own strength and by French disaffection to make a dash upon Covrepauk, which surrendered almost without resistance. The flood-tide of British power was crawling slowly but surely to the south.

July.

Meanwhile disquieting symptoms had been observed in another quarter, from which British influence had for some years suffered little trouble. There was intelligence of a Dutch armament fitting out at Batavia for the Bay of Bengal, which, although nominally designed merely to reinforce the Dutch garrisons, could not, from the known jealousy of the Dutch over the British successes in Bengal, be credited with any very friendly intentions. Admiral Pocock, who was cruising off Pondicherry in daily expectation of a French squadron, had already picked up transports with five companies of Coote's regiment, and had received permission to keep these troops to man his ships pending the engagement, for which he waited, with Admiral d'Aché. A sight of the Dutch fleet at Negapatam, however, convinced him that the troops would be needed ashore; and he accordingly sent them to Madras, recommending that at least a part of them should be forwarded to Bengal. It will presently be seen that Pocock acted with admirable judgment and foresight.

| August. |
| Sept. 10. |

This complication added not a little to the anxiety of the British, though some relief was afforded by news of Lally's continued troubles with his troops. At the beginning of August his own regiment, which was in garrison at Chittapett, broke into open mutiny and marched out of the fort with the avowed intention of joining the British. Their officers followed them, and by promises to discharge the arrears of their pay, now several months overdue, succeeded in conciliating most of them; but sixty men persisted in their resolution and deliberately carried it out. The authorities at Madras seized the moment to order an advance on Wandewash; but before the troops could march there came fresh important intelligence. D'Aché had arrived off the coast and had for the third time been engaged by Pocock; and the action though severe had ended indecisively in the retirement of the French squadron to Pondicherry. It was therefore uncertain what reinforcements might have been landed for the defence of Wandewash; besides which, as a further ground for caution, there were uncomfortable signs of renewed French intrigue at Hyderabad. But Brereton, knowing that Eyre Coote must shortly arrive to take the command from him, was burning to advance; and the authorities had not the heart to bid him halt. Accordingly, after some delay owing to heavy rain, Brereton marched from Conjeveram, with fifteen hundred European and twenty-five hundred native infantry, besides cavalry and artillery, and, misled by false information as to the strength of the French garrison, attacked Wandewash with a thousand British only. Though successful at the outset he was eventually repulsed with a loss of two hundred men. The reverse was unfortunate at so critical a time, but luckily was insufficient to shake the confidence of the British troops in themselves.

In any case, moreover, Lally was in no position to take advantage of his success. D'Aché, though personally a brave man, was so much chagrined by his third failure that he sailed, in defiance of all protests, to Mauritius, leaving Pocock master of the sea. His desertion was a hard blow to Lally, for the indiscipline of his troops was ever increasing. In despair of help from other quarters he reverted to that from which he had at first so hastily withdrawn, the court of Hyderabad; though affairs there had altered greatly since the departure of Bussy. Salabad Jung had been won to the British cause by the storm of Masulipatam; his brother Nizam Ali had always been Bussy's worst enemy; but there was still a third brother, Basalut Jung, who hated his brethren and had shown a friendly disposition towards Pondicherry. Him Bussy now approached with the offer of the Nabobship of the Carnatic, if he would join the French with a body of native troops. The terms were agreed upon; Basalut Jung began to advance along the Pennar; and Bussy was on his way to him with five hundred Europeans, when he was recalled by the outbreak of a dangerous mutiny of the garrison which he had left behind him at Wandewash. Turning back, he succeeded by payment of six months' arrears in reducing the men to obedience; but the incident was fatal to his negotiations with Basalut Jung; and after a few days of fruitless haggling he returned to Arcot, with no accession to his force but a few irregular levies of horse and foot.

Nov. 24.
Nov. 29.
Dec. 12.

Foiled in this direction Lally in despair determined to make a diversion in the south, and sent a force of nine hundred Europeans and a thousand Sepoys under M. Crillon to alarm Trichinopoly, while he himself marched northward to join Bussy at Arcot. Crillon duly succeeded in capturing the island of Seringham, and left a battalion of French there to keep the city in awe; but Lally's rash division of his force between points so distant as Arcot and Trichinopoly gave the British an opportunity which they did not fail to grasp. Coote with the remainder of his regiment, in all six hundred men, had arrived at Madras, and though compelled to send two hundred men forthwith to Bengal, had been able to make good the deficiency with about the same number of exchanged prisoners who had arrived from Pondicherry. On the 21st of November Coote arrived at the British camp at Conjeveram, where he was joined two days later by the newly arrived troops. He had already made up his mind to attack Wandewash; but to conceal his intentions he despatched one detachment under Brereton to seize the fort of Trivatore on the road, sent another detachment with the heavy artillery to Chingleput, and himself marched upon Arcot. Brereton captured Trivatore without difficulty, and advancing forthwith upon Wandewash drove in the French outposts and began to construct batteries. Coote thereupon joined him instantly by forced marches; on the 29th his batteries opened, and on the same day Wandewash surrendered. Without delay Coote pushed on to Carangooly, five-and-thirty miles to eastward, and took that also after a few days of siege. Then calling in all detachments to him, he on the 12th of December reunited his entire force at Wandewash.

Dec. 19.

Now Lally perceived the evil consequences of his diversion in the south. The capture of Wandewash and of the other posts retrieved at once any reputation that the British might have lost by Crillon's success at Seringham, while the possession of these forts was a solid gain to his enemy. He therefore hastily recalled Crillon, bidding him leave three hundred men only in

Seringham and join him with the rest of his troops at Arcot. Meanwhile Bussy's irregular horse from that city spread desolation on the north of the Paliar to within twenty miles of Madras itself. The terror of these marauding bands drove all the natives from the open country to take refuge in the hills; and Coote, who had moved up to within a few miles of Arcot, as if to intercept Crillon on his march, was compelled by lack of supplies and inclement weather to cross the Paliar and distribute his troops into cantonments. So ended for the present the disjointed and indecisive operations in the Carnatic for the year 1759.

```
Oct.
Nov.
```

During these latter months any hope that Lally might have built on diversion of the British forces to Bengal by the menaces of the Dutch, had already been dashed to the ground. The Dutch armament, so much suspected of Pocock, had sailed to the mouth of the Hooghly in October; and Meer Jaffier, weary of his subjection and dependence, had gone to Calcutta to concert with them the overthrow of the British in Bengal. The Dutch force consisted of seven hundred Europeans and eight hundred trained Malays on board the fleet; while at Chinsura, their settlement on the Hooghly, there were one hundred and fifty Dutch soldiers, as well as native levies, which by Meer Jaffier's connivance and help were daily increasing in number. To meet this danger Clive could raise in and about Calcutta but three hundred and thirty men of the Hundred-and-First, and twelve hundred Sepoys; but he was a man accustomed to face heavy odds. Summoning to him every man that could be spared from outlying stations, he called out the militia for the defence of Calcutta, organised two tiny bodies of volunteers, both horse and foot, ordered the British ships to sail up the Hooghly, and strengthened the batteries that commanded the river. At the beginning of November Forde and Knox arrived fresh from the triumph of Masulipatam, in time to furnish Clive with two admirable commanders. To Knox was assigned the command of the batteries, and to Forde that of the troops in the field.

```
Nov. 24.
```

In the second week of November the Dutch addressed a long letter of remonstrance and complaint to Calcutta, and shortly afterwards followed it up by seizing some small British vessels and burning the British agent's house at Fulta; after which they weighed anchor and stood up the river. Clive thereupon ordered Forde to move forward by Serampore upon Chinsura. Forde started accordingly with one hundred of the Hundred-and-First, four hundred Sepoys and four guns, and on the 23rd encamped in the suburbs of Chandernagore, three miles distant from Chinsura. The Dutch on the same evening sent one hundred and twenty Europeans and three hundred Sepoys from Chinsura to take up a position in the ruins of Chandernagore and bar his further advance. These Forde attacked and utterly defeated on the following morning, capturing their guns and pursuing them to the walls of Chinsura. Thus one part of the Dutch force was disposed of, which, had it waited for the co-operation of the troops on the river might have placed Forde between two fires.

On the evening of the fight Knox joined the Colonel and raised his force to three hundred and twenty European infantry, fifty volunteer cavalry, eight hundred Sepoys, and one hundred native cavalry; with which Forde faced about to deal with the rest of the enemy. The Dutch squadron, for want of pilots, had moved but slowly up the river, but on the 21st it anchored just below the British batteries, and landed the troops on the western bank, with orders to march to Chinsura; which done, the ships dropped down the stream again to Melancholy Point. There on the following day Clive's armed East Indiamen under Captain Wilson attacked them, three ships against seven, and captured six of them on the spot, leaving only one to escape and to fall an easy prey to two British men-of-war that had arrived at the mouth of the river. This splendid little action cut off the Dutch troops from their base and ensured that any reverse must be fatal to them. Nor was that reverse long in coming. On the same evening Forde learned that the Dutch army would come up with him on the morrow, and wrote to Clive for instructions. Clive was playing whist when the letter reached him. He put down his cards, and without leaving the table wrote on the back of the letter, "Dear Forde, fight them immediately. I will send you the Order in Council to-morrow." Then taking up his hand again, he went on with the game.

| Nov. 25. |

Accordingly early in the morning of the 25th Forde took up a position midway between Chandernagore and Chinsura and astride of the road that connects them. His right rested on the village of Badara and his left on a mango-grove, both of which he occupied; while his front was covered by a broad, deep ravine behind which he posted his four guns. About ten o'clock the Dutch forces were seen approaching over the plain; and as soon as they were within range Forde's artillery opened fire. The Dutch advanced none the less with great firmness, until to their dismay they found themselves stopped by the ravine, of which they knew nothing. The leading files perforce halted abruptly, while the rear, not understanding the cause, pushed on and threw the whole body into confusion. Forde continued to ply them with artillery and musketry until they wavered, and then seized the moment to hurl his handful of European cavalry at them. This threw them into still greater disorder; and the native horse charging in their turn completed the rout. The entire force of the enemy, excepting sixty Dutchmen and two hundred and fifty Malays, was killed, wounded, or taken; and the Dutch settlements, humbled to the dust, sued not only for mercy but for protection. Clive used his opportunity so to shackle them that they could never again threaten British supremacy in Bengal; and the Dutch in Europe, being in alliance with England, disavowed the action of their fleet and paid compensation for the damage that it had done. Thus, far from diverting British troops from the principal conflict, the Dutch expedition served only to strengthen the foundations of British ascendency by the ruin of a still older rival than the French. In such fashion could Clive and Forde wrench profit out of adversity.

```
1760.
Jan. 8.
Jan. 13.
Jan. 15.
Jan. 21.
```

The death-blow to French rivalry also was now near at hand. On the 8th of January Crillon's force reached Arcot; and in the evening of the 11th, after three days of manœuvring, Lally divided his army into two columns, and leaving Bussy with one of them at Trivatore, made a forced march with the other upon Conjeveram. So effectively had his Mahratta cavalry screened his movements that Coote knew nothing of them, until he received a message from the officer commanding at Conjeveram itself. He at once made a forced march to save the fort, but on arriving found that Lally had been content with the plunder of the town and had marched to rejoin Bussy at Trivatore. Taking five hundred Europeans, a thousand Sepoys, and six hundred and fifty French and Mahratta horse, Lally left Trivatore on the 14th and marched on Wandewash, which had been his true object from the first. Coote received intelligence of his departure on the same evening, and on the following day marched also by the direct road to the same point. Lally meanwhile, anxious to recapture the post before Coote's arrival, had in the morning of the 15th attacked a small British detachment in the southern suburb and driven it with some difficulty into the fort; after which he began to erect batteries against the walls. On the 17th he learned from Bussy that Coote was advancing against him; by which time the British had actually arrived at Outramalore, about fifteen miles to north-east of Wandewash. Here Coote halted, being secure of his communications with Chingleput and Madras, and resolved not to risk an action until the French were ready to assault the fort. The French works meanwhile progressed but slowly; and it was not until the 20th that the batteries opened fire, Bussy's column having meanwhile joined Lally from Trivatore. On the next day Coote advanced to within seven miles of Wandewash, and on the 22nd, having directed that the rest of the army should immediately follow him, he went forward at sunrise with his cavalry to reconnoitre.

About seven o'clock Coote's advanced guard struck against an advanced party of Lally's native horse; and presently three thousand Mahratta cavalry came swarming over the plain in his front. Coote brought up a couple of guns masked behind his own cavalry, and wheeling his squadrons outwards, right and left, when within close range, opened a fire which sent the Mahrattas flying back with heavy loss. Then halting the main body of his army he went forward to examine the French camp. He found it marked out in two lines about two miles to the east of the fort and facing eastward, the left flank of each line being covered by a large tank. In advance of their left front were two smaller tanks, of which the foremost had been turned into an entrenchment and armed with cannon, so as to enfilade the whole front of the camp and command the plain beyond it. Leaving the advanced guard halted where it stood, he returned and brought up his main army, formed in two lines, in order of battle before the camp. Finding after a short halt that no notice was taken by Lally, he caused the whole force to file to its right across the French front towards the foot of a mountain, which stood about two miles to northward of the fort. As soon as the leading files had reached some stony ground, impassable by cavalry, close to the mountain's base, Coote again halted and fronted, at a distance of about a mile and a half from the enemy. Seeing that this movement also passed unnoticed, he ordered the army to file along the skirt of the mountain round the French left flank. By thus coasting the hill until he came opposite to the fort he would be able to form his line with his left resting on the mountain and his right covered by the fire of the fort, thus at once securing communications with the garrison and threatening the French flank and rear.

Before this masterly manœuvre could be fully completed, Lally came hurriedly out of his camp; and presently the whole of the French army was observed to be in motion. Coote thereupon desisted from his movement round their left flank, halted his filing columns, and fronting them to the left, formed his line of battle obliquely to the enemy. Lally was thus compelled to cancel his preconcerted dispositions, to change front from east to north-east, and, while still resting his left on the entrenched tank, to move forward his right in order to bring his line parallel to that of the British.[344] None the less this tank remained the pivot of his position. His army was formed in a single line in the following order. On the extreme right were three hundred European cavalry; next to them stood Regiment Lorraine, four hundred strong; next to Lorraine the European Regiment of India formed the centre; and to the left of the centre stood Regiment Lally with its left flank resting on the entrenched tank, the entrenchment itself being manned by marines, with four guns. Three guns were also posted between the tank and Lally's regiment, and as many more in the intervals between the different corps of the line, making sixteen guns in all. The smaller tank, which by the change of disposition was now in rear of the entrenched tank, was held by four hundred native infantry; while nine hundred Sepoys were ranged on a ridge before the camp. The total force drawn out for the action amounted to twenty-two hundred and fifty Europeans,[345] cavalry and infantry, and thirteen hundred Sepoys; some five hundred men more of both nationalities being left in the batteries before Wandewash. The Mahratta horse, having tasted the fire of the British artillery earlier in the day, had no relish for further share in the action.

Coote's army was drawn up in three lines. The first line was composed of four European battalions, with a battalion of nine hundred Sepoys on either flank. Of the Europeans, Draper's regiment held the right; the Hundred-and-Second, in two weak battalions, the centre; and Coote's the left. Three field-guns were posted in the intervals on each flank of Draper's and of Coote's, and two more with an escort of two companies of Sepoys were detached a little in advance of the left of the first line. The second line was made up of three hundred European grenadiers in the centre, with a fieldpiece and a body of two hundred Sepoys on each flank. The third line consisted entirely of cavalry, eighty Europeans forming the centre, with natives on either flank. The total force in the field was nineteen hundred and eighty Europeans, twenty-one hundred Sepoys, and twelve hundred and fifty native horse, with sixteen guns.

In this order the British advanced; but before they arrived within cannon-shot Lally caught up his squadron of European hussars, and making a wide sweep over the plain came down with it upon the cavalry in the British third line. Coote's native cavalry at once broke and fled away, and the left divisions of Sepoys, while changing front to meet the attack, showed signs of wavering; but the weak squadron of British horse stood firm, and the two detached guns of the left front under Captain Barker coming into action at short range in the nick of time, brought down ten or fifteen men and horses at their first fire. The French horse thereupon broke despite all Lally's efforts to stop them, and would not be rallied until they had galloped far to the rear. During this attack the British halted, while the French batteries fired wildly and unsteadily with grape, though their enemy was not yet within range of round shot. Coote coolly continued his advance until his guns could play effectively, and then opened a most destructive fire. Lally finding his men impatient under the punishment placed himself at their head, and gave the word to move forward. Coote thereupon halted the whole of his force excepting the Europeans of the first and second lines, and advanced to meet him with these alone. Like Forde at Condore he staked everything on the defeat of the French regular troops.

Coote, true to the English rule, intended to reserve his volley for close range; but some few Africans who were mingled in the ranks of the British opened fire without command, and this disorder was only with difficulty prevented from spreading to the whole line. Coote, galloping from right to left of the line, actually received two or three bullets through his clothes. Order being restored, he took up his station on the left by his own regiment; and at about one o'clock the fire of musketry became general. Coote's regiment had fired but two rounds, when Lally formed Regiment Lorraine on the French right into a column of twelve men abreast, and ordered it to charge with the bayonet. Anticipating Wellington's tactics of a later day Coote met column with line, reserved his fire until the French were within fifty yards, and then poured in a volley which tore the front and flanks of Lorraine to tatters. None the less the gallant Frenchmen, unchecked by their losses, pressed on the faster; and in another minute the two regiments had closed and were fighting furiously hand to hand. The column broke by sheer weight through the small fragment of line opposed to it; but the remainder of Coote's closed instantly upon its flanks; and after a short struggle Lorraine, already much shattered by the volley, broke up in confusion and ran back to the camp, with the British in hot pursuit, carrying dismay into the ranks of the Sepoys. Coote paused only to order his regiment to be reformed, and galloped away to see how things fared with Draper on the right.

As he passed, a flash and a dense cloud of smoke shot up from the entrenched tank, followed by a roar which rose loud above the din of battle. A lucky shot from the British guns had blown up a tumbril of French ammunition. The commander of the entrenchment was killed, eighty of his men were slain or disabled around him, and the rest of his force, abandoning the guns, fled in panic to the French right, followed by the Sepoys from the smaller tank in rear. Coote instantly ordered Draper's regiment to advance and occupy the entrenchment; but Bussy, who commanded on the French left, brought forward Lally's regiment to threaten their flank as they advanced, and forced them to fetch a compass and file away to their right. Bussy thus gained time to rally some of the fugitives and to re-occupy the tank with a couple of platoons; but Draper's men, with Major Brereton at their head, moved too fast to allow him to complete his dispositions, and coming down impetuously upon the north face of the tank swept the French headlong out of it. Brereton fell mortally wounded in the attack, but bade his men leave him and push on. The leading files hurried round to the southern face of the tank, opened fire on the gunners posted between Lally's regiment and the parapet, and drove them from their guns; while the rest hurriedly formed up on their left to resist any attempt upon the eastern face. Bussy did all that a gallant man could do, but the odds were too great for him; and he could hope for no help, since all the rest of the line was hotly engaged. He wheeled Lally's regiment round at right angles to the line to meet the fire on its flank, and detached a couple of platoons from his left against the western face of the tank; but his men shrank from the British fire and would not come to close quarters. Then two of Draper's guns came up, and opening on the right flank of Lally's regiment raked it through and through. As a last chance Bussy placed himself at the head of his wavering troops and led them straight at the southern face of the tank; but his horse was shot under him, and on looking round he saw but twenty men following him, the rest having no heart for the conflict. Two platoons of Draper's at once doubled round to cut them off, while Major Monson came up with part of the grenadiers of the second line to support Draper's attack. Bussy and his devoted little band were surrounded and made prisoners, and the whole of Lally's regiment was captured or dispersed.

The battalions of the centre on both sides had throughout kept up a continual fire at long range; but when the French Regiment of India perceived both its flanks to be uncovered, it faced about and retreated, hastily indeed but in good order. Lally had some time before attempted to bring forward the Sepoys from the ridge, but they had refused to move; and the Mahrattas took themselves off when they saw how the day was going. Nothing was left to Lally but his few squadrons of French horse, which came forward nobly to save his army. A few men of Regiment Lorraine, heartened by their appearance, harnessed the teams to three field-guns and joined with the cavalry in covering the retreat. The British squadron was too weak to attack, and Coote's native horse refused to face the French cavalry; so Lally was able to set fire to his camp, collect the men from his batteries, and to retire in better order than his officers had dared to hope.

None the less the victory was sufficiently complete. Two hundred of the Frenchmen lay dead on the field, as many more were wounded, and one hundred and sixty were taken, so that Lally's loss amounted to close on six hundred Europeans. Besides this, twenty-four guns were taken, together with all the tents, stores, and baggage that remained unburnt. Against this the British had lost but sixty-three killed and one hundred and twenty-four wounded, Draper's being the regiment that suffered most severely. The native troops had few casualties, for practically none but Europeans were engaged. The speedy defeat of the French was doubtless due to the explosion which gave away the key of their position; and there can be no question but that this fortunate accident immensely simplified Coote's task for him. On the other hand, it may be asked why, seeing that this tank was the key of the position, Lally should have garrisoned it with sailors and marines, the worst instead of the best of his troops. It is improbable that, even without this stroke of luck, the ultimate issue of the action could have been different, especially if Lally's own figures as to the strength of his own force be accepted as correct. It is plain that he felt no great confidence in his troops, and that his distrust was justified. His cavalry would not stand by him in his first attack on Coote's rear; his artillery was unsteady; he did not venture to attack the British infantry except with column against line; he seems to have advanced in the first instance chiefly because his men chafed under the fire of the British artillery; and his attack on Coote's left was not only a failure in itself but took all the heart out of his Sepoys. Coote, on the other hand, felt perfect reliance on his troops, and proved it by advancing finally with his infantry only, leaving his guns to follow as they could. Moreover, he had the choicest of his troops, the grenadiers, still in reserve at the close of the action; so that it would have been open to him, after the defeat of Lorraine, to have turned these or his own regiment upon the flank of the French battalions in the centre, and to have rolled up their line from right to left instead of from left to right. In fact, from the moment that he forced Lally to come out and fight, the superiority of his troops assured him of victory; and it is probable that Lally himself was painfully aware of the fact. The tragic fate of the French commander a few years later made him an object of compassion to foe and friend, but it is plain that the disaster of Wandewash was principally of his own making. Bussy had begged him to desist from the siege on Coote's approach, but he would not, and was therefore unable to oppose his full strength to his enemy. Finally, though he wished to decline any engagement except a direct attack on his camp, he was out-manœuvred and compelled to fight on his adversary's terms. In the face of such facts, whatever our sympathy with a gallant and unfortunate man, it is idle to ascribe his defeat to mere accident, although that defeat was a mortal blow to French domination in India.

| Jan. 29. |
| Feb. 9. |
| Feb. 29. |
| April 5. |

Lally on the next day fell back to Chittapett, and sending the Mahrattas and native troops to Arcot retired to Gingee to cover Pondicherry. Coote on learning of his withdrawal from Chittapett determined to attack that post, while yet he might, with his whole army; and after a few hours' cannonade compelled it to surrender. Then instead of following Lally up further, he bent himself, after the fashion of Amherst, to systematic reduction of all the minor posts held by the French. Arcot, the first object chosen, fell after a siege of a few days; Timery, a few miles to south-east of Arcot, fell at the same time; Trinomalee surrendered on the last day of February; Permacoil and Alumparva were taken after some resistance early in March. Coote, however, was wounded at Permacoil; and the capture of Carical, the one French station left on the coast, was entrusted to Major Monson, who speedily effected it with the help of Admiral Cornish's squadron, which had arrived on the coast six weeks before. The possession of Carical was of importance, since, being an outlet from the rich country of Tanjore, it could have kept Pondicherry supplied with provisions; while it was also a port wherein a French squadron could obtain not only victuals but also intelligence before proceeding to Pondicherry. Lally, amid all his preparations for defence, in his heart gave up the capital for lost after its fall.

| July 17. |
| August. |

On the 7th of April Coote re-assumed command, and drawing a chain of posts around Pondicherry from Alumparva to Chillumbrum, closed in slowly upon the doomed city. Lally had allowed him to capture far too many of his men piecemeal in different garrisons; but he now called in all French troops from Trichinopoly and other posts in the south, and entered into an agreement with Hyder Ali, then commander of the forces at Mysore, engaging to concede large tracts of territory in return for the services of eight thousand men. This accession of strength to the enemy hampered Coote not a little for the moment, the more so since a detachment which he sent to check the advance of the Mysoreans was totally defeated. But the relief to Lally was short-lived; for dearth of provisions and unwillingness to be attached to the losing side soon caused his new allies to withdraw. Even so, however, the British force was not strong enough to undertake a regular siege of Pondicherry, and Coote was obliged to content himself with a mere blockade.

| Sept. 2. |
| Sept. 4. |
| 1761. |
| April 5. |

At length reinforcements arrived for the Company's troops, together with half a regiment of Morris's Highlanders[346] under Major Hector Munro. Three men-of-war also came with the transports, raising the squadron before Pondicherry to seventeen sail. Lally, rightly guessing that more vigorous operations would follow on this increase of the British force, devised a plan of extreme skill and daring for the surprise of their camp; but fortune was as usual against him. His combinations miscarried; and his troops after showing conspicuous gallantry were repulsed. From that day the end drew rapidly near. Coote indeed forsook the siege for a time on finding that Colonel Monson had been promoted over his head, but was soon obliged to take command again on the disabling of Monson by a wound. It would be of no profit to linger over the dying agony of Pondicherry. Lally, despite shameful disloyalty and opposition from the civil authorities, resolved to fight on to the end, trusting that d'Aché might come with his squadron to his relief; and his regular troops worked for him with a fidelity and devotion worthy of the best traditions of France. Once there came a gleam of hope. On the last day of 1760 a sudden hurricane burst over the city and harbour which overwhelmed three of the British ships with all hands on board, drove three more of them ashore, and ruined all the works of the besiegers. But the surviving ships returned within a week to resume the blockade, and no d'Aché arrived to interrupt them. The British works were repaired and pushed forward; and on the 15th of January the garrison, being on the brink of starvation, surrendered. A few weeks sufficed to reduce the few isolated fortresses which were still held by French garrisons; and on the 5th of April the white flag of the Bourbons had ceased to fly in India.

So after fifteen years of strange vicissitude ended the long struggle of French and English for empire in the East. That the result was due as much to the shortcomings of the French Government as to the prowess of her adversary is unquestionable; for the corruption and mismanagement both at Versailles and at Pondicherry were sufficient to wreck any empire. Still the failure of the French was due to something more than mere maladministration. Though no people is so patriotic where the soil of their own country is at stake, Frenchmen once passed across the sea appear to be cursed with a fatal tendency to jealousy, distrust, and disunion. In Canada as in India the same forces were always at work to undermine French influence and neutralise French success. Individual Frenchmen are found wielding vast power and authority with consummate ability; yet such men are always alone; not one of them can command the loyal service of his countrymen. Even Dupleix, the Napoleon of India, was thwarted at every turn by his subordinates; for Bussy may be considered to have held practically an independent command. Again, setting aside individuals of brilliant talent, the general average of capacity was lower on the French side. It may have been that ability was by some strange coincidence absent; or that commanders had no power or were too jealous to select the ablest of their subordinates for important work; or indeed that capable subalterns found the acceptance of a great trust too thankless at the hands of such superiors. In any case the result remains the same. There are Dupleix, Bussy, and Paradis on one side, and on the other Clive, Saunders, Lawrence, Forde, Coote, Brereton, Caillaud, Kilpatrick, Knox,—captains, lieutenants and ensigns innumerable, all prepared to accept independent command and yet to work loyally for the common cause. Before long there will have to be told a story of administrative cupidity and corruption in Calcutta as shameful as ever disgraced Pondicherry; and yet always young officers come forward to undertake the most perilous work and to carry it to a successful end. Such a contrast points to a distinction between the two nations which is more deeply rooted than in mere accidents of administration. Partly no doubt the victory of the British was due to the traditions that kept archer and man-at-arms together at Crecy, and may be ascribed to peculiarities of social and political organisation. But beyond this there appears to be something in the national character which makes it difficult for a Frenchman, outside the borders of France, to assume high station without dangerous exaggeration of his self-esteem; while the Briton, for all his energetic and imperious nature, has the grim humour and the deep melancholy of his kind, ever whispering to him of the vanity of great place.

AUTHORITIES.—Orme's *Military Transactions* continues to be the chief authority though it unfortunately closes without giving account of Forde's action at Badara. The actions of Wandewash, Condore and Badara are described at length in Colonel Malleson's *Decisive Battles of India*, where the authorities are quoted. The French side of the story is presented by the same author in his *History of the French in India*, based chiefly on the memoirs of Lally and Bussy. Wilks's *History of Mysore*, the *Memoirs of Stringer Lawrence*, and the *Biographies of Clive* by Malleson and Malcolm are also of value.

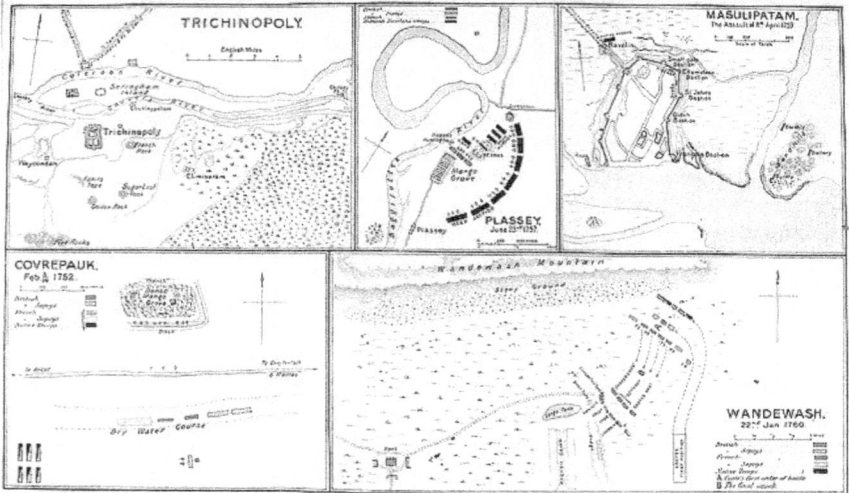

Walker & Boutall del.

To face Page 474.

TRICHINOPOLY.

COVREPAUK, Feb. $\frac{3}{14}$ 1752.

PLASSEY, June 23rd 1757.

MASULIPATAM, The Assault of 8th April 1759.

WANDEWASH, 22nd Jan. 1760.

CHAPTER VIII

For convenience of arrangement I have followed the conquests both of Canada and of India without interruption to their close. In the earlier stages of the war, when England had not yet succeeded in obtaining for herself the minister that she desired, it was possible and in the fitness of narrative to turn from enterprise to enterprise, fitfully undertaken, insufficiently provided for, and committed to the wrong hands for execution; since all were symptoms of one organic disorder. While the heart of England beat weak, palpitating and intermittent, it could not but fail to drive the blood to the extremities, and leave them cold and paralysed. But when, under the treatment of Pitt, the heart revives and throbs with strength and regularity, then we can watch member after member tingling with new life and waking to new power; and the action of each may be traced independently, for while their energy continues, it is certain that the heart must be vigorous and sound. Since, however, that work is now done, it behoves us to return, after long digression, to England and to Pitt, and to take up the study where it was laid down, in the spring of 1759.

| 1759. |

With the mighty enterprises, even now not yet wholly told, of that year in memory, it is remarkable to note that the estimates for 1759 showed little sign of what was to come. The British Establishment was set down at but eighty-five thousand men, or one thousand more than in the previous year; and the fact is the more extraordinary in that, ever since the previous winter, the French had been preparing for an invasion of Great Britain at three different points with sixty-three thousand men. Vast numbers of flat-bottomed boats had been collected at Dunkirk, Brest and Havre de Grace; and the menace was serious, for the regular troops left in England were but few, and the country was crowded with French prisoners. Pitt, while reposing his chief trust in the navy, was sufficiently disquieted in January to offer special terms to recruits who would enlist for short service within the kingdom only; and in May he called out the newly-embodied militia. Yet only two new regiments of regulars were raised during the first half of the year. The first of these, Eyre Coote's, has already been seen at Wandewash; the second demands lengthier notice since it signified a new departure. Mention has already been made of the addition of light troops to certain regiments of cavalry: it was now determined to form a complete regiment of Light Dragoons; which service

337

was entrusted to Colonel George Augustus Elliott,[347] an officer who was to become famous for his defence of Gibraltar, though not before his regiment had already won fame both for him and for itself. Its actions will come before us very soon, so for the present it will suffice to say that Elliott's Light Dragoons are still with us, retaining the original number of their precedence, as the Fifteenth Hussars.

Such additions were trifling enough if in view of no more than the danger of invasion, but, seeing that Pitt abated not one jot of his aggressive designs, they were of astonishing insignificance. With the nature and extent of those designs the reader has already been in great part acquainted; but it will be convenient to recall the military situation in all parts of the world in the spring of 1759. Goree had already surrendered and was occupied by a British garrison; Barrington was busy over the conquest of Guadaloupe; in America Amherst was organising his expedition against Ticonderoga and Crown Point, Forbes was struggling with the first difficulties of his advance to Fort Duquêsne, and Wolfe was on his way to Quebec; in India Lally had lately raised the siege of Madras and liberated the garrison for work in the field, Forde had lately fought Condore and was advancing on Masulipatam, and Clive was at Moorshedabad securing the fruits of his victory at Plassey. Lastly, ten thousand British troops were about to enter on their first campaign under Prince Ferdinand of Brunswick. Yet it never occurred to Pitt to recall one man of them, notwithstanding the peril of invasion. It may be asked why the ten thousand, being so near home, were not summoned from Germany, and of what possible service they could have been on the Continent. The answer, which has already been hinted at, will occur readily to those who have had the patience to follow me so far, who have seen Guadeloupe worried into submission by a handful of sickly troops, and watched Montreal and Pondicherry drop at last into British hands like fruit ripe for the plucking. Pitt spoke but half the truth when he spoke of conquering America in Germany; it was not only America, but the East and West Indies, in a word the British Empire. The war in Germany was in fact nothing more than a diversion on a grand scale, and it is as such that it must now be followed. The French likewise pursued their idea of a diversion when they threatened a descent upon the shores of Great Britain. It was a plan which they had employed with some success in the days of King William and of Queen Anne, but it had not saved them from Marlborough at Oudenarde, and it was not to deliver them from the busy designs of Pitt.

Before entering on the campaigns of Prince Ferdinand it is indispensable to attempt to grasp the general purport of the operations on either side. The French had invaded Germany primarily to take vengeance upon Prussia for King Frederick's scornful treatment of Madame de Pompadour. Frederick, being already occupied with the Saxons and Austrians to the south and with the Russians on his flank to the eastward, could hardly have escaped disaster with the French pressing on his other flank from the west. He had indeed, in 1758, with the swiftness that characterised his operations, made a dash upon the French and hurled them back at Rossbach, and within a month dealt the Austrians as severe a buffet at Leuthen with the same army. But to defeat two armies at two points over two hundred miles apart within a few weeks, was a strain that could not be repeated; and it was primarily to guard Frederick's right or western flank that Ferdinand's army was called into being. So far as Frederick was concerned it quite fulfilled its purpose; but in the eyes of England its mission was somewhat different. Under the Duke of Cumberland the force had been called an army of observation, to secure the frontiers of Hanover; and Cumberland, despite Frederick's warnings, had endeavoured to cover Hanover by holding the line of the Weser, with results that were seen at Hastenbeck. Under Ferdinand the army became an Allied Army for active operations in concert with King Frederick;[348] but none the less its chief function was to cover Hanover, Hesse-Cassel, and Brunswick. For the French army, being lax in discipline, behaved with shameful inhumanity towards the inhabitants of German territory during this war; and there was always apprehension lest the rulers of Hesse and Brunswick, from sheer compassion towards their suffering people, should withdraw from the Alliance.

Throughout the operations about to come under our notice the French acted with at least two armies, jointly superior to Ferdinand's in numbers, along two different lines. The northern army was known as the Army of the Rhine, its base being Wesel on the Lower Rhine, an outlying possession of King Frederick's, which had perforce been abandoned by him at the opening of the war, and which despite Ferdinand's efforts could never be recovered. This army was destined to advance into Westphalia, and thence, if possible, into Hanover; and a glance at the map will show that its simplest line of advance was by the river Lippe. The second or southern army of the French was known as the Army of the Main; having provided itself with a base on that river by the treacherous capture of Frankfort.[349] This was one of the many unscrupulous actions whereby the French made themselves loathed in Europe; for Frankfort being an Imperial Free Town was held always to be neutral. Still the thing was done; and thereby was secured to the Army of the Main, which had begun life as the Army of the Upper Rhine, not only an excellent base but a sure means of retreat. For the Allies, even if they defeated it, could not bar its way to the Rhine until Frankfort should be first besieged and captured, which could not but be a very arduous undertaking. The primary function of this second army was the invasion of Hesse.

Ferdinand's task, with an inferior force, was in its essence defensive. For him the supremely important thing was to retain possession of the line of the Weser, on which waterway he depended for his supplies alike from Germany and from England. Thus, roughly speaking, the field of operations lay between the Rhine on the one side and the Weser on the other, with the sea and the Main for northern and southern boundaries; and the normal front of the French would be to the east and of the Allies to the west. But it must be remembered that in addition to the army operating from Wesel against Ferdinand's front there was another operating from Frankfort upon his left or southern flank; while there was always the further danger that the Saxons might elude a Prussian corps of observation, which was posted to check them, on the south-east, and steal in upon Ferdinand's left rear. To defeat these combinations it was of vital importance to Ferdinand to hold in particular two fortresses—Münster in Westphalia, since the French, if they took it, could push on unhindered to the Weser and cut off his supplies; and Lippstadt on the Upper Lippe, which secured communications between Münster and Cassel, or in other words between Westphalia and Hesse, and contrariwise impeded the joint action of the two French armies. For the rest it will be useful to take note of three rivers which barred the advance of the French northward from Frankfort to Cassel and beyond: namely, counting from south to north, the Ohm, the Eder, and the Diemel. With the last in particular, as the final barrier between Hesse and Westphalia, we shall have much to do; so the reader would do well to grasp its position once for all, not neglecting its relation to the neighbouring waters of the Lippe and the Weser.

End of March.
April 13.

At the close of the campaign of 1758 Ferdinand's winter quarters extended from Coesfeld, a little to westward of Münster, through Münster, Lippstadt and Paderborn to the Diemel, his front facing thus somewhat to south of south-east. The French army of the Rhine under Marshal Contades was cantoned along that river from Wesel southward almost to Coblentz; while the army of the Main, under the Prince of Soubise, the defeated General of Rossbach, lay just to north of the river about Frankfort. Ferdinand's first trouble was with an advance of the Austrians upon his left flank by the river Werra. This he headed back by a rapid march to Fulda; and, being freed from this danger, he resolved to turn this enforced movement to southward to account by making a bold stroke upon Frankfort, so as, if possible, to paralyse the operations of the French on that side by snatching from them their base. Unfortunately for him, the incapable Soubise had been recalled to command the army for invasion of England, and Marshal Broglie, who had succeeded him, had entrenched himself in a strong position at Bergen, a little to the north of Frankfort. There on the 13th of April, just five days after the storm of

Masulipatam, Ferdinand boldly attacked him,[350] but was repulsed with a loss of over two thousand men, and compelled to fall back to Ziegenhain, on the road to Cassel. His audacious attempt to cripple one French army, before the campaign had even been opened, had failed.

```
May.
May 27.
May 29.
```

After this alarm the French employed themselves busily in entrenching themselves on the Main. Prince Henry of Prussia, by King Frederick's direction, marched northward to relieve Ferdinand from further trouble from the Austrians; and the enemy made little movement during the ensuing month. On the 25th of April Contades arrived at Düsseldorf from Paris with an approved plan of campaign in his pocket, and proceeded to distribute the army of the Rhine into four corps, two of them about Wesel, a third at Düsseldorf, and a fourth about Cologne. This grouping, as Contades intended, left Ferdinand in doubt whether his main design was aimed at Westphalia or Hesse. The corps which guarded Westphalia included the British contingent under Lord George Sackville, who had been appointed to the command on the death of the Duke of Marlborough in the previous year, and it lay a little to the west of Münster, under the orders of the Hanoverian General von Spörcke. That officer growing uneasy over Contades's movements, Ferdinand on the 16th of May marched from Ziegenhain, leaving sixteen thousand men under General von Imhoff to protect Hesse, and on the 24th, having effected his junction with Spörcke, cantoned his troops along the Lippe from Coesfeld to Hamm. Meanwhile Contades, detaching a corps of fifteen thousand men under Count d'Armentières to threaten Münster, marched southward from Düsseldorf upon Giessen, there to join Broglie and begin operations against Hesse. Ferdinand, in the faint hope of recalling him to the Rhine, despatched a corps under the Hereditary Prince of Brunswick, a most brilliant officer, to alarm the French garrisons at Düsseldorf and other points on the river; but Contades, adhering to his purpose, pushed forward an advanced corps under M. de Noailles from Giessen to Marburg, evidently intent on prosecuting his march to the north. Contades was in overwhelming force. Noailles's corps at Marburg numbered twenty thousand men, his own at Giessen close on sixty thousand, while Broglie's reserve-corps at Friedberg, a little to the south of Giessen, included close on twenty thousand more. He now sent Broglie forward by Fritzlar upon Cassel, while he himself continued his march due north through Waldeck upon Corbach. Imhoff, fearful of being cut off and unable to defend Cassel, fell back towards Lippstadt; and Broglie having left a force to occupy Cassel, turned westward to rejoin Contades. On the 14th of June the whole were again assembled together, Contades' corps lying a little to the south of Paderborn, and Broglie's at Stadtbergen.

| June 11. |
| June 18. |

These movements caused Ferdinand the deepest anxiety. On the 11th of June he concentrated and marched eastward to Büren, where he halted and picked up Imhoff's corps; but even so he was weaker than the enemy, for though he had recalled the Hereditary Prince from Düsseldorf, he had been obliged to leave nine thousand men under General Wangenheim at Dülmen, to watch d'Armentières's designs against Münster. But worse was to come; for on the 18th Broglie's corps, moving up to the right of Contades's, began to edge Ferdinand's left wing back to the westward. Ferdinand, accepting the inevitable, fell back on Lippstadt and crossed the Lippe to Rietberg. His embarrassment was now extreme. He could not divine whether the enemy designed to besiege Lippstadt or Münster or both, or whether they meant to force a battle upon him against greatly superior numbers. He was inclined to risk a battle, seeing that, for all that he could do to prevent it, both fortresses might be taken before his eyes; in which case he must needs cross to the east side of the Weser. So critical did he consider the position that he wrote to King George the Second for instructions, and begged that ships might be ready to transport the garrison in case it should be necessary to evacuate Emden. The King's answer showed the Guelphic loyalty and courage at its noblest. He said that since Ferdinand was inclined to hazard an action he also was ready to take the risk, but that he left his General an absolutely free hand, only assuring him that his confidence in him would be unabated, whatever the result; and, lest Ferdinand should be in any doubt, he caused a second letter to be written to him to the same effect, but in stronger terms even than the first.
[351]

| June 29. |
| July 3. |
| July 8. |
| July 10. |
| July 14. |

Meanwhile Contades marched up to Paderborn and halted for some days, keeping Ferdinand still in doubt as to his intentions. At last on the 29th he moved northward and pushed his light troops forward to Bielefeld, showing plainly that his true aim was the capture either of Hameln or of Minden on the Weser. Ferdinand therefore recalled Wangenheim's corps from Dülmen to the main army; whereupon, as he had expected, d'Armentières at once advanced to besiege Münster. On the same day Ferdinand himself moved northward and encamped parallel to Contades at Diessen, comforting himself with the reflection that though his enemies might be nearer to Minden than he, he at any rate was nearer to his food-supplies than they.[352] It was, however, extremely difficult for him to obtain intelligence of the French movements, since the two armies were separated by a broad chain of wooded hills; and he consequently hesitated for some days before he decided, on false information of a French advance, to move towards Osnabrück. His intention was to turn eastward from thence, and to take up a position which would render it perilous for the French to attempt the siege either of Hameln or Minden. He had made, however, but one march from Osnabrück when he received the news that Broglie had surprised Minden on the day before, and that the French had thus secured a bridge over the Weser and free access into Hanover. This was a most unpleasant surprise for Ferdinand. For a day he hesitated whether or not to return to Münster, and then decided to fall back to the Lower Weser, so as to save his magazine at Nienburg, and, since the French had set the example of lawlessness at Frankfort, to occupy the Imperial Free Town of Bremen. On the 14th of July accordingly his headquarters were fixed at Stolzenau, between Nienburg and Minden on the Weser, and a detachment was sent to Bremen.

July 17.

Meanwhile Contades proceeded to reap the fruit of his very successful movements. Part of his light troops seized upon Osnabrück, and the rest were sent to levy contributions in Hanover; M. de Chevreuse was detached with three thousand men to besiege Lippstadt; d'Armentières continued to besiege Münster; Broglie's corps crossed the Weser on the 14th to invest Hameln; and on the 16th Contades with the main army debouched into the basin of Minden, and pushed a part of his army as far to the northward as Petershagen. Ferdinand, though he could bring but forty-five thousand men into the field against sixty thousand, advanced southward next day to offer him battle; but Contades retired without awaiting his arrival and withdrew to an unassailable position immediately to south of Minden. If he could hold Ferdinand inactive while his several detachments did their work, it was of no profit to him to hazard a general action.

July.

So far Contades's operations had been masterly. He had taken Cassel, the capital of Hesse, and had invested both Lippstadt and Münster; he had further taken Minden and invested Hameln; and thus he bade fair to possess himself of the line of the Weser and to carry the war straight into Hanover. Ferdinand's position was most critical, and was not rendered more pleasant to him by a series of uncomplimentary messages from Frederick the Great. But Contades, from the moment that he declined battle, seems to have taken leave, possibly from excessive confidence, of all energy and ability. His position was, it is true, impregnable. His army lay immediately to the south of Minden, communicating by three bridges with Broglie's corps on the other side of the Weser. His right rested on the town and the river, his left on a mass of wooded hills—the end of the range that had separated his army from Ferdinand's— and the whole of his front was covered by a wide morass, through which ran a brook called the Bastau. But though unassailable from any point, the position had conspicuous defects. In the first place, it did not leave the army free to move in all directions; and in the second, it necessitated the detachment of troops to the south to maintain communication through Gohfeld and Hervorden with the French base at Cassel. It was for Ferdinand, by skilful use of these defects, to entice Contades from his pinfold to meet him in the open field.

| July 28. |
| July. |

Returning to camp at Petershagen after Contades's withdrawal to Minden, Ferdinand's first step was to push his picquets forward into a chain of villages that lay in his front: Todtenhausen on the bank of the Weser, Fredewald immediately to west of Todtenhausen, Stemmern and Holthausen somewhat in advance of Fredewald, and Nord Hemmern, Sud Hemmern, and Hille still farther to south and west. The occupation of Hille brought his advanced posts to the western edge of the morass that covered Contades's front, and to the head of the one causeway that led across it. On the 22nd Wangenheim's corps, about ten thousand strong, was pushed forward to Todtenhausen, where it remained conspicuous, in advance of the army. In the midst of these movements came the bad news of the fall of Münster, which enabled d'Armentières to march from thence to besiege Lippstadt, and Chevreuse to return with his detachment to Minden; but this misfortune only quickened Ferdinand to action. On the 27th the Hereditary Prince marched with six thousand men south-westward towards Lübbecke, and on the following day drove from it a body of French irregulars which was stationed there for the protection of Contades's left flank. Then turning eastward he pursued his march against the French communications. Simultaneously, on the 28th, General Dreve led the garrison of Bremen against Osnabrück, retook it, and hastened eastward to join the Hereditary Prince. The junction effected, the two pressed on towards Hervorden, and on the 31st established themselves astride of the road by which all Contades's supplies must be brought up from the south.

Here, therefore, was a menace in his rear to make the French General uneasy in his position behind the morass; and now Ferdinand added a temptation in his front to induce him the more readily to quit it. On the 29th the Prince, leaving Wangenheim's corps isolated about Todtenhausen, led the whole of the rest of the army a short march to the south-west, and encamped between Fredewald and Hille. Headquarters were at Hille, under guard of the Twelfth and Twentieth Regiments of the British Foot, for the red-coats held the place of honour on the right of the line; and picquets were pushed on to Sud Hemmern, Hartum, and Hahlen, villages on the eastern side of Hille, by the border of the morass. Finally, from two to three thousand men were ordered to Lübbecke to maintain communication with the Hereditary Prince. Such dispositions might well have appeared hazardous; but Ferdinand had thought them out in every detail. Wangenheim's corps, though isolated, was strongly entrenched, with several guns; while his position covered the only outlet by which the French could debouch from behind the marsh. Thereby two important objects were gained. First, the safe passage of convoys from the Lower Weser was assured; and secondly, it was made certain that, before Contades could deploy to attack Wangenheim in force, Ferdinand with the main army would have time either to fall upon his flank or simply to join his own left to Wangenheim's right. To ensure the swift execution of this latter critical movement, Ferdinand directed all Generals to acquaint themselves carefully with the ground, and in particular with the outlets that led from his position to the open plain before Minden.

Contades meanwhile reasoned, as Ferdinand had hoped and intended, in a very different fashion. The Allied army was, to his mind, dispersed in every direction. Ten thousand men were with the Hereditary Prince at Gohfeld; at least two thousand more at Lübbecke; Ferdinand himself, with the greater portion of the army, seemed so anxious to be within supporting distance of the Prince that he had left Wangenheim in the air; while even Wangenheim's corps was not united, but had detached a few battalions across the river to keep an eye on Broglie. Still the interruption of his own communications with Cassel was troublesome; and it would be well to put an end to that and to all other difficulties by a decisive blow and a brilliant victory. He therefore despatched the Duke of Brissac with eight thousand men to Gohfeld to hold the Hereditary Prince in check, threw eight bridges over the Bastau for the passage of his troops across it in as many columns, and ordered Broglie to be ready to cross the Weser with his corps to form a ninth column upon his right. The total force which he could bring into the plain of Minden was fifty-one thousand men with one hundred and sixty-two guns. Against it, if all went well, Ferdinand could oppose forty-one thousand men and one hundred and seventy guns.

| Aug. 1. |

A fresh gale was blowing from the south-west which drowned the stroke of the clocks of Minden, as midnight closed the last day of July and ushered in the first of August. Already the French camp was all alert in the darkness, and the columns were moving off, not without confusion, to the bridges of the

345

Bastau. An hour later two white-coated deserters were brought in by a picquet to the Prince of Anhalt, General Officer of the day in the Allied army, with the important intelligence that the whole French army was in motion. Ferdinand had seen signs of some stir on the previous evening, and had directed that, on the observance of the slightest movement at the advanced posts, information should be brought to him at once. Yet two o'clock came, and three o'clock, before a belated messenger arrived at headquarters from Anhalt with the news. Instantly Ferdinand called the whole of his troops to arms, and ordered them to march to their appointed positions. His orders had already been issued, and were clear and precise enough. The advance was to be in eight columns, and the formation for battle, as usual, with infantry in the centre and cavalry on each flank. The first or right-hand column consisted of twenty-four squadrons of cavalry under Lord George Sackville, fifteen of them being British squadrons of the Blues, First and Third Dragoon Guards, Scots Greys, and Tenth Dragoons. The second was made up entirely of German artillery; and the third under Major-General von Spörcke comprised the Twelfth, Twentieth, Twenty-third, Twenty-fifth, Thirty-seventh, and Fifty-first regiments of the British Line. Seven out of the eight columns were formed and marched off with great promptitude; but in Sackville's column all was confusion and delay. Some of the regiments were ready and others were not; and Sackville himself was not to be found. It was no good beginning for the British cavalry.

Having given the alarm Ferdinand hastened, with a single staff-officer accompanying him, to see for himself how matters stood. It is not difficult to conceive of his anxiety. Owing to the unpardonable neglect of Anhalt the French had gained two hours upon him; and now, when the army had been at last set in motion, the cavalry of his right wing was not moving with the rest. There was therefore every likelihood that the village of Hahlen, on which he had intended to rest his right flank, might be occupied by the French before Sackville could be there to prevent them. Instantly galloping away to Hartum he ordered the picquets stationed therein to move at once to Hahlen, and then hurried back with all speed to the latter village, only to learn the bad news that it was already in possession of the French. Meanwhile not a word had come from Wangenheim, who, for aught he knew, might be in serious difficulties. Despatching his solitary aide-de-camp to Todtenhausen to ascertain how matters were going on the left, he galloped on alone with his groom into the plain of Minden. The wind was blowing so furiously that not a sound even of cannon could be heard in the direction of the Weser; but before long he caught sight of the French advancing on Kuttenhausen, and of a dense cloud of smoke rising before Todtenhausen. Evidently Wangenheim was hotly engaged. But meanwhile from windward there came the roar of a furious cannonade about Hille, where the causeway issued from the western end of the morass. This could only be a diversion, for Ferdinand had already sealed up the outlet of the causeway with five hundred men and two guns; but to make assurance still surer he now ordered two more guns and the detachment from Lübbecke to Hille, and sent information to the Hereditary Prince of what was passing. Then, galloping for a moment to the left, Ferdinand satisfied himself that his columns were advancing, and turned back in the teeth of the wind to Hahlen. There once again the stupidity of the Prince of Anhalt had set matters wrong. He had duly brought up the picquets from Hartum before Hahlen, as directed, but had halted instead of clearing the French out of the village, and had thereby delayed the deployment of the whole of Spörcke's column. He was bidden to take the village at once, which he did without difficulty; but having done so this hopeless officer proceeded to instal himself and his picquets as if to stay there for ever.[353]

After the occupation of Hahlen, however, matters on the right began to adjust themselves. Ferdinand ordered Captain Foy's battery to the front of the village to cover the formation of the troops, and was soon satisfied by the admirable working of these British guns that all was safe in that quarter. Meanwhile his aide-de-camp returned from Todtenhausen with intelligence that Wangenheim was holding his own, though the enemy had gained ground on his right, where his flank was uncovered. Probably few commanders have passed through two worse hours than did Ferdinand at the opening of the battle of Minden.

Fortunately for him the French had not executed their own manœuvres without confusion and delay. It was one defect of Contades's position that he could not debouch from behind the morass by daylight, since he would have brought Ferdinand down instantly upon his flank; and the indiscipline of the French army among both officers and men was not calculated to favour orderly movement in the dark. Broglie, a capable officer, had crossed the river, taken up his appointed position on the right, and made his dispositions to fall upon Wangenheim, punctually and in good order; but he dared not attack until the rest of the army was formed, so contented himself with a simple duel of artillery. The rest of the columns shuffled here and there in helplessness and confusion; and it was not until Broglie had waited for two full hours that most of them were at last deployed in some kind of order. The French line-of-battle was convex in form, following, as it were, the contour of the walls of Minden, with the right resting on the Weser and the left on the morass. Broglie's corps on the right was drawn up in two lines, the first of infantry, the second of cavalry, with two powerful batteries in advance. On his left stood half of the infantry of Contades's army in two lines, with thirty-four guns before them. Next to these, in the centre, were fifty-five squadrons of cavalry in two lines, with a third line of eighteen more in reserve; and next to this mass of horse stood the left wing, composed of the rest of the infantry in two lines, with thirty guns. Thus to all intent the French line-of-battle consisted of a centre of cavalry with wings of infantry; but the left wing of infantry was late in arriving at its position, and its tardiness was not without effect on the issue of the action.

Observing the excellent practice of Foy's battery before Hahlen, Ferdinand had already sent Macbean's British battery to join it and ordered Hase's Hanoverian brigade of heavy guns to the same position. Then seeing Spörcke's column of British infantry in the act of deployment, he sent orders that its advance, when the time should come, should be made with drums beating. The order was either misdelivered or misunderstood, for to his surprise the leading British brigade shook itself up and began to advance forthwith. A flight of aides-de-camp galloped off to stop them; and the line of scarlet halted behind a belt of fir-wood to await the formation of the rest of the army. In the first line of Spörcke's division stood, counting from right to left, the Twelfth, Thirty-seventh, and Twenty-third, under Brigadier Waldegrave; and in the second, which extended beyond the first on each flank, the Twentieth, Fifty-first, and Twenty-fifth, under Brigadier Kingsley, Hardenberg's Hanoverian battalion, and two battalions of Hanoverian guards. There then they stood for a few minutes, while the second line, which was only partially deployed, hastened to complete the evolution; when suddenly to the general amazement the drums again began to roll, and the first line stepped off once more, advancing rapidly but in perfect order, straight upon the French horse. The second line, though its formation was still incomplete, stepped off likewise in rear of its comrades, deploying as it moved, and therefore of necessity dropping somewhat in rear. And so the nine battalions, with the leading brigade far in advance, swung proudly forward into a cross-fire of more than sixty cannon, alone and unsupported from the rest of the line.

No aide-de-camp, gallop though he might, could stop them now; and their majestic bearing showed that they would not easily be stopped by an enemy. The British, being on the right, were the more exposed to destruction, for the French batteries on their left were too remote to maintain a really deadly fire; but what signified a cross-fire and three lines of horse to regiments that had fought at Dettingen and Fontenoy? For nearly two hundred yards of the advance the French guns tore great gaps in their ranks; but they passed through the tempest of shot unbroken and untamed, and pressed on with the same majestic steadiness against the huge motionless bank of the French horse. Then at last the wall of men and horses started into life, and eleven squadrons coming forward from the rest bore straight down upon them. The scarlet battalions stood firm until the enemy were within ten yards of them; then pouring in one volley which strewed the ground with men and horses, they hurled the squadrons back in confused fragments upon their comrades, and continued their advance. Ferdinand, perceiving the disorder of the French, sent an aide-de-camp at full speed to Lord George Sackville to bring up the British cavalry and complete the rout. Sackville disputed the meaning of the order for a time, and then advancing his squadrons for a short distance, as if to obey it, brought them once more to a halt. A second messenger came up in hot haste to ask why the cavalry of the right did not come on, but Sackville remained stationary, and the opportunity was lost.

Then shamed and indignant at their defeat the French horse rallied. Four brigades of infantry and thirty-two guns came forward from the French left to enfilade the audacious British foot; and Ferdinand, since Sackville would not move, advanced Phillips's brigade of heavy guns in order to parry, if possible, this flanking attack. Then the second line of the French horse came thundering down, eager to retrieve their defeat, upon the nine isolated battalions. For a moment the lines of scarlet seemed to waver under this triple attack; but recovering themselves they closed up their ranks and met the charging squadrons with a storm of musketry which blasted them off the field. Then turning with equal fierceness upon the French infantry they beat them also back with terrible loss. Again an aide-de-camp flew from Ferdinand's side to Sackville, adjuring him to bring up the British squadrons only, if no more, to make good the success; but it was not jealousy of the foreign squadrons under his command that kept Sackville back. The messenger delivered his order; but not a squadron moved. Meanwhile Ferdinand had hurried forward fresh battalions on his right to save the British from annihilation; and now the third line of French horse, the Gendarmerie and the Carbineers, essayed a third attack upon the nine dauntless battalions and actually broke through the first line; but was shattered to pieces by the second and sent the way of its fellows. A fourth messenger was sent to Sackville, but with no result. Ferdinand's impatience waxed hot. "When is that cavalry coming?" he kept exclaiming. "Has no one seen that cavalry of the right wing?" But no cavalry came. "Good God! is there no means of getting that cavalry to advance," he ejaculated in desperation, and sent a fifth messenger to bring up Lord Granby with the squadrons of Sackville's second line only. Granby was about to execute the order, when Sackville rode up and forbade him; and then, as if still in doubt as to these repeated orders, Sackville trotted up to Ferdinand and asked what they might mean. "My Lord," Ferdinand is said to have answered, calmly, but with such contempt as may be imagined, "the opportunity is now passed."

Nevertheless the astonishing attack of the British infantry had virtually gained the day. Ferdinand's line had gained time to form and to join with Wangenheim's; and the guns of the Allies coming up gradually in increasing force silenced the inferior artillery of the French. Ferdinand's left wing then took the offensive, and the German cavalry by a brilliant charge dispersed the whole of the infantry opposed to them. Between nine and ten o'clock the struggle was practically over. The French were completely beaten, and retreating rapidly under the guns of Minden to their pinfold behind the marsh. Had Sackville's cavalry come forward when it was bidden, it might have cut the flying French squadrons to pieces, barred the retreat of most if not all of the French left wing, and turned the victory into one of the greatest of all time. As things happened, it fell to Foy and Macbean of the British Artillery to gather the laurels of the pursuit. Hard though they had worked all day, these officers limbered up their guns and moved with astonishing rapidity along the border of the marsh, halting from time to time to pound the retreating masses of the enemy; till at last they unlimbered for good opposite the bridges of the Bastau and punished the fugitives so heavily that they would not be rallied until they had fled far beyond their camp.

Meanwhile the Hereditary Prince had engaged the Duke of Brissac at Gohfeld and defeated him, so that the French communications with Hervorden and Paderborn were hopelessly severed. The news of this misfortune seems to have smitten Contades almost with panic. Had he chosen to fall back by the line of his advance he could hardly have been stopped by the inferior force of the Hereditary Prince, and he would have found supplies and a good position at Hervorden. But his defeat had crushed all spirit out of him. Abandoning his communications with Paderborn he crossed the Weser in the night, broke down the bridge of Minden, burned his bridges of boats, and retired through a difficult and distressing country to Cassel, with an army not only beaten but demoralised.

MINDEN,

Aug. 1st 1759.

The Action at the moment of the attack of the British Infantry.

British
Allies
French

0   100   200   400 Yards.

Walker & Boutall del.

To face page 494.

MINDEN. Aug. 1st 1759.
The Action at the moment of the attack of the British Infantry.

So ended the battle of Minden, a day at once of pride and disgrace to the British. The losses of the Allies amounted to twenty-six hundred killed and wounded, of which the share of the British amounted to close on fourteen hundred men.[354] Of the six devoted regiments who went into action four thousand four hundred and thirty-four strong, seventy-eight officers and twelve hundred and fifty-two men, or about thirty per cent, were killed or wounded; while the Hanoverian battalions with them, being on the left or sheltered flank, lost but twelve per cent. The heaviest sufferers were the Twelfth, which lost three hundred and two, and the Twentieth, which lost three hundred and twenty-two of all ranks; these regiments holding the place of honour on the right of the first and second lines. The casualties of the French were acknowledged in the official lists to amount to seven thousand, though the letters of Broglie and Contades state the numbers at from ten to eleven thousand; and the defeated army lost in addition the greater part of its baggage, seventeen standards and colours, and forty-three guns. From a military standpoint the most remarkable feature in the action was the skill with which Ferdinand contrived to entice his adversary into the field, reflecting perhaps even more credit on his judgment of men than on his knowledge of his profession. Once drawn from behind the morass into the plain, Contades made singularly feeble and meaningless dispositions: and the formation of his line with cavalry in the centre and infantry on the flanks was, in the circumstances, simply grotesque. He seems indeed to have had no very clear idea as to what he really meant to do. If he had designed to overwhelm Wangenheim's isolated corps—and no doubt he had some vague notion of the kind—the obvious course was to launch Broglie straight at him independently, and himself to protect Broglie's flank with the main army. What he actually did was to turn Broglie's corps into the right wing of an united army, and so practically to fetter it for all decisive action. On the other hand, all preconcerted arrangements on both sides were upset by the extraordinary attack of the British infantry, a feat of gallantry and endurance that stands, so far as I know, absolutely without a parallel. "I never thought," said Contades bitterly, "to see a single line of infantry break through three lines of cavalry ranked in order of battle, and tumble them to ruin." "Never," grimly wrote Westphalen, the chief of Ferdinand's staff, "were so many boots and saddles seen on a battlefield as opposite to the English and the Hanoverian Guards." Next to this attack the feature that seems to have attracted most attention among both contemporary and modern critics, was the remarkable efficiency of the British artillery. The handling of the artillery generally at Minden, which was entrusted to the Count of Lippe-Bückeburg, was very greatly admired: but Westphalen, who passed lightly over the deeds of the infantry, went out of his way to write that, though every battery had done well, the English batteries had done wonders. And indeed some British guns which were attached to Wangenheim's corps on the left earned not less praise than those of Foy and Macbean on the right. The palm of the cavalry fell to the Germans, and in particular to a few squadrons of Prussian dragoons lent by Frederick the Great, which earned it brilliantly. It would have fallen to the British but for Sackville.

The part played by this deplorable man did not end with the battle. Ferdinand in general orders made scathing allusion to his conduct without mentioning his name; and Sackville was presently superseded and sent home.

There he was tried by court-martial and pronounced unfit to serve the King in any military capacity whatever—a hard sentence but probably no more than just. Sackville was admitted to be an extremely able man; and as he had passed through Fontenoy and been wounded in that action, it is not easy to call him a coward. But the courage of some men is not the same on every day; and the evidence produced at the court-martial shows, I think, too plainly that on the day of Minden Sackville's courage failed him.[355] The King published the sentence of his dismissal from the Army in a special order, with very severe but not undeserved comment; and Lord George Sackville henceforth disappears from British battlefields. But we shall meet with him again as a Minister of War, and the meeting will not be a pleasant one.

| Aug. 2. |
| Aug. 5. |
| Aug. 18. |
| Aug. 24. |
| Aug. 25. |
| Sept. 19. |

On the day following the battle the Hereditary Prince crossed the Weser in pursuit of the French, and overtaking their rear-guard at Einbeck captured many prisoners and much spoil, but failed to arrest the retreat of the main body. Contades, therefore, succeeded in bringing his troops back to Cassel, half starved, worn out by hard marching, and utterly demoralised by indiscipline and pillage. D'Armentières, on hearing of his chief's defeat, raised the siege of Lippstadt and marched eastward to meet him. Ferdinand meanwhile, having received the surrender of Minden, advanced by Bielefeld and Paderborn south-eastward upon Corbach, so as to turn Contades's left flank. On the 18th Contades, seeing his communications endangered, evacuated Cassel and retired by forced marches to Marburg, where he took up a strong position. Cassel capitulated to the Allies on the following day; and Ferdinand, while still pursuing his march southward, detached seven thousand men to recapture Münster. Marshal d'Estrées then arrived to supersede Contades; but little came of this change of command. Renewed menace from the westward upon the French communications forced him to withdraw from the line of the Ohm and Lahn, and to fall back to Giessen. Ferdinand at once laid siege to Marburg, which fell within a week, and finally on the 19th of September he encamped at Kroffdorf, a little to north-west of Giessen, over against the French camp.

Meanwhile the siege of Münster had gone ill for the Allies, and had been turned into a blockade. Ferdinand, after sending additional troops thither, found himself too weak to attempt further operations until the fall of the town; and during this interval Broglie, who had been appointed to the supreme command, had received a reinforcement of ten thousand Würtembergers. Thus strengthened he tried incessantly with a detached corps of twenty thousand men to interrupt Ferdinand's communications with Cassel, but in vain; and finally the Hereditary Prince attacked this corps at Fulda, defeated it signally, and then turning upon Broglie's right flank forced him to retire to Friedberg. Ferdinand then blockaded Giessen; but at this point further operations were stayed. Ever since his disastrous defeat by the Russians at Kunersdorf in August, Frederick the Great had pressed Ferdinand for reinforcements; and the detachment of twelve thousand troops to the King not only rendered the Prince powerless for further aggression, but obliged him also to raise the blockade of Giessen. In January 1760 both armies retired into winter-quarters. The French occupied much the same ground as at the beginning of the campaign; and the Allies likewise were distributed into two divisions, the army of Westphalia extending from Münster through Paderborn to the Weser, the army of Hesse from Marburg eastward to the Werra. Thus ended the campaign of 1759, leaving both parties in occupation of the same territory as at its beginning; but it had branded the French with the discredit of a great defeat, and had heightened in the Allies their contempt for their enemy and their confidence in their chief.

CHAPTER IX

1759.

Never in the whole course of her history had come to England such a year of triumph as 1759. Opening with the capture of Goree in January, its later months had brought one unbroken tale of success, of Madras saved and Masulipatam taken in India, of Quebec captured in Canada, of Minden won in Germany, of one French fleet worsted by Boscawen off the Portuguese coast, of another defeated by Hawke in the romantic action of Quiberon Bay. Such was the story with which King George the Second met his Parliament for the last time in his life; and Pitt did not fail to turn it to good account. A monument was voted to Wolfe in Westminster Abbey; thanks were given to Hawke, Saunders and Holmes of the Navy, and to Monckton, Murray and Townsend of the Army; and the military estimates were passed with little difficulty. It was ordered that Ferdinand's army should be augmented from Great Britain, Brunswick, and Hesse alike. The full number of national troops voted for the British Establishment exceeded one hundred thousand men; the embodied militia augmented this total by twenty thousand, and the German troops in the pay of England by fifty-five thousand more; while another twelve thousand men at home and abroad, which were borne on the Irish Establishment, raised it to close on one hundred and ninety thousand men. Before the campaign of 1760 was opened, the infantry of the British Line had increased to ninety-six regiments; England contributing one new corps, Wales one, Scotland five, and Ireland four, all of which were disbanded at the close of the war.[356] To these there were added later in the year six new regiments of Light Dragoons. The first was formed in August under Colonel John Burgoyne, which took rank as the Sixteenth Dragoons, and is now known to us as the Sixteenth Lancers; the second, created in October by Lord Aberdour, soon perished and left no mark behind it; and the third was raised under rather remarkable conditions by Colonel John Hale in November. Colonel Hale, originally of the Blues and later of the Forty-third Foot, was the officer who brought back the despatches reporting the victory of Quebec. Finding on his arrival in England in October that there was still some alarm of a French invasion, he volunteered to form a regiment of the footmen and chairmen of London and to lead them against the best household troops of France; an offer which so delighted Pitt that he reported it to the House of Commons. Finally, he engaged himself to raise a strong regiment of light dragoons without levy-money for men or horses, promising that any men or horses objected to on review by the inspecting officer should be replaced without expense to the country, and that the whole corps should be completed within two months. The offer was accepted, and the regiment was raised at the sole expense of the officers within the space, as it is said, of seventeen days. The number was not inappropriate; for though first known, during the few years while Aberdour's lasted, as the Eighteenth, this regiment, still conspicuous by the white facings and the badge of skull and crossbones which Hale selected for it, remains with us as the Seventeenth Lancers. The three remaining corps, which raised the number of regiments of dragoons to twenty-one, were too short-lived to merit more than mere mention.[357]

1760.
Feb.

The menace of French invasion was rather ludicrously realised in February by a descent of the French privateer, Thurot, with five ships upon Carrickfergus. Landing about a thousand troops, he received the surrender of the town after a skirmish with the garrison, plundered it, contrary to the terms of the capitulation, and re-embarked. His squadron, however, was almost immediately caught by three British men-of-war, when after a short action Thurot was killed and every one of his ships captured. This tragic termination to Thurot's escapade relieved the general tension, and restored the country's confidence.

So foolish a raid was not likely to produce any change in Pitt's preparations for the reinforcement of Ferdinand, who needed to be specially strengthened after the disasters that had befallen King Frederick at Kunersdorf and at Maxen. In January it was decided to send three more regiments of British cavalry to Germany; and a few weeks later the number was increased to five. In May a further reinforcement of six battalions and two regiments of Highlanders was promised, and in June two additional regiments of cavalry; making up a total of close on ten thousand men.[358] The troops were shipped to the Weser instead of, as heretofore, to Emden, and seem to have been despatched with commendable promptitude; for the six regiments of foot, though only warned for service on the 1st of May, were actually reviewed by Ferdinand in his camp at Fritzlar on the 17th of June, and were declared by him to be in a most satisfactory condition.[359]

May.
June 20.
June 22.
June 24.
July.

The campaign of 1759 having been prolonged so far into the winter,

Ferdinand gave his army rest until late in May. At length on the 20th he called the infantry of the army of Hesse from its cantonments, and posted the main body under his own command at Fritzlar, with one corps advanced to Hersfeld on the Fulda to protect his left, and a second under General Imhoff at Kirchhain, on the Ohm. It was his intention that, in case of the enemy's advance, Imhoff should call in the detachment from Hersfeld to Homberg, a little to the south of Kirchhain on a bend of the Ohm, where there was a position, before long to be better known to us, in which he could bar the way to a far superior force. Simultaneously the army of Westphalia moved to its line of the previous year, from Coesfeld eastward to Hamm. In these positions the Allies remained for nearly a month before the French made the least sign of movement; when at last the army of the Lower Rhine under the Count of St. Germain assembled at Düsseldorf, and crossing the Rhine advanced to Dortmund. From this centre it was open to St. Germain to advance either northward against Münster or eastward against Lippstadt; but it was tolerably evident that his real design was to join the army of the Main, and to operate against the right flank of the Allied army of Hesse. At about the same time Broglie concentrated the army of the Main a little to the east of Giessen, and began his advance northward. The Hereditary Prince at once fell back from Hersfeld with his detachment towards the Ohm, while Ferdinand moved southward as far as Ziegenhain to join Imhoff, with every intention of making Broglie fight him before he advanced another mile. To his infinite disgust, however, he learned that Imhoff had abandoned the position entrusted to him, and had ordered the whole of the advanced corps back to Kirchhain. Thus the most effective barrier in Hesse was opened to the French; Ferdinand perforce halted; and Broglie pushed on without delay to Homberg, whence turning eastward he encamped in the face of Ferdinand's army at Neustadt. In this situation both armies remained for a whole fortnight inactive, though not two hours' march apart, neither daring to attack the other, and each waiting for the other to make the next movement.

| July 8. |
| July 10. |

Broglie brought the deadlock to an end. Sending orders to St. Germain to march from Dortmund on the 4th of July, and to meet him at Corbach, he marched on the night of the 7th north-westward upon Frankenberg. Ferdinand on learning of his movements next day marched also northward with all speed, pushing forward a strong advanced corps under the Hereditary Prince by way of Sachsenhausen upon Corbach, to bar the outlet of the defile through which Broglie's army must pass into the plain, and so to hinder his junction with St. Germain. The French, however, had gained too long a start. St. Germain, though he distressed his troops terribly by the speed of his march, succeeded in passing through the defile from the north; and Broglie, hastening up from the south, found his troops forming in order of battle just as the Hereditary Prince debouched into the plain from Sachsenhausen. As not more than ten thousand of the French were yet deployed, the Prince attacked; but was soon driven back by superior numbers as the rest of the French came up, and finally retired with the loss of five hundred men and fifteen guns, seven of which last were British. It fell to the British infantry with the Prince, the Fifth, Twenty-fourth, Fiftieth, and Fifty-first regiments, to cover the retreat; but so hard were they pressed that the Prince only extricated them by putting himself at the head of two squadrons of the First and Third Dragoon Guards, and leading them to a desperate charge. Fortunately the squadrons responded superbly,[360] and so the rear-guard was saved; but the Prince had received an unpleasant reverse, and the French had secured their first object with signal success.

July 12.

The Allied army of Westphalia, under General von Spörcke, arrived on the scene in obedience to orders two days after the action, and was posted at Volksmarsen on the Diemel to protect Ferdinand's right; and then once more the two hosts remained motionless and face to face, the French at Corbach, the Allies at Sachsenhausen. Ferdinand's total force was sixty-six thousand men only, while that of the French numbered one hundred and thirty thousand;[361] yet such was the difference in the quality of the two armies that Broglie dared not act except with extreme caution. His principal object was to envelope Ferdinand's right and cut him off from Westphalia at the line of the Diemel; and Ferdinand accordingly resolved to distract Broglie's attention to the opposite flank.

July 15.
July 16.

Having intelligence that a party of the enemy under General Glaubitz, consisting of six battalions, a regiment of Hussars, and a number of light troops, was on its way to Ziegenhain from Marburg, evidently with the object of disturbing his communications, Ferdinand, on the night of the 14th, detached the Hereditary Prince to take command of six battalions which were lying at Fritzlar, and to attack it. Accordingly on the following morning the Prince marched rapidly southward, being joined on the way by a regiment of German hussars, and by the Fifteenth Light Dragoons, which had just arrived from England. On reaching the vicinity of Ziegenhain, he found that Glaubitz was encamped farther to the west, near the village of Emsdorff. His troops being exhausted by a long march, the Prince halted for the night at Treysa, and continuing his advance early on the morrow, picked up two more bodies of irregulars, horse and foot, which were on their way to him, and pushed on with his mounted troops only, to reconnoitre the enemy's position. He found the French posted at the mouth of a gorge in the mountains, fronting to north-east, astride of the two roads that lead from Kirchhain to Fritzlar and to Ziegenhain. Their right lay in rear of the village of Erxdorff, and their left in front of the village of Emsdorff, resting on a forest some three miles long. The Prince and General Lückner, who was with him, entered the forest, but found neither picquets nor sentries; they pushed forward through the corn-fields to within half a mile of the camp, but saw neither vedettes, nor patrols, nor so much as a main-guard; nay, Erxdorff itself, though within less than a mile of the camp, was not occupied. They stole back well content with what they had seen.

Waiting till eleven o'clock for his infantry to join him, the Prince posted one battalion, Lückner's regiment of hussars and the Fifteenth Light Dragoons, in a hollow a mile before Erxdorff; then taking the five remaining battalions, together with the irregular troops and four guns, he fetched a compass through the forest and came in full upon the enemy's left flank. The French were completely surprised. Two battalions had barely time to form towards the forest before the Prince's infantry came upon them, poured in a volley which laid three hundred men low, and drove back the rest upon Glaubitz's remaining infantry, which was falling in hurriedly in rear of the camp. Simultaneously Lückner, at the sound of the firing, came galloping up on the French right with his cavalry; whereupon the entire French force abandoned its camp and retired through the woods in their rear towards Langenstein. Here they rallied; but Lückner's single battalion hurried on beyond them to bar their way over the Ohm to westward, while the Fifteenth, pressing on along their flank, stationed itself across the road to Amöneberg, and charging full upon them headed them back from that side. With some difficulty the French repelled the attack, and turning about to south-eastward made for a wood not far away, hoping to pass through it and so to escape to the south. But on arriving at the southern edge of the wood they found every outlet blocked by the Prince's mounted irregulars. Perforce they turned back through the wood again and emerged on to the open ground on its western side, trusting that some marshy ground, which lay in the way of the Prince's cavalry, would secure them from further pursuit. But they had not marched over the plain for more than a mile before the hussars and light dragoons were upon them again, and the Fifteenth for the second time crashed single-handed into the midst of them, cutting them down by scores and capturing one battalion complete. With great difficulty the remnant of the French beat back their pursuers and continued the retreat: half of them had been killed or captured, or had dropped down unable to march farther, but the rest struggled gallantly on. Reaching an open wood they again halted and formed for action. The Prince, still close at their heels with his cavalry, thereupon surrounded them and summoned them to surrender; and the French commander, despairing of further resistance in the exhausted state of his troops, was obliged to yield.

So ended the action which is still commemorated on the appointments of the Fifteenth Hussars by the name of Emsdorff. The French camp had been surprised at noon; and the last fragment of their force capitulated at six o'clock in the evening, having striven manfully but in vain to shake off the implacable enemy that had hunted them for nearly twenty miles. The loss of the French in killed and wounded is unknown, though it must have been considerable, but the prisoners taken numbered twenty-six hundred, while nine colours and five guns were also captured. The total loss of the Prince's troops did not exceed one hundred and eighty-six men and one hundred and eighty-one horses, of which one hundred and twenty-five men and one hundred and sixty-eight horses belonged to the Fifteenth. It was the Fifteenth, in fact, that did all the fighting. The other regiments engaged did not lose twenty men apiece. The infantry could not keep pace with the pursuit after they reached Langenstein, and the two other corps of cavalry, though they did excellent work in heading back the enemy, never came to close quarters. Lückner's hussars did not lose a man nor a horse, and of the mounted irregulars but twenty-three men and horses were killed or wounded. It was the Fifteenth alone, a young regiment that had never been under fire, which thrice charged five times its numbers of French infantry and rode through them; and the success of the action was ascribed to them and to them only. Their gallantry indeed was the amazement of the whole army.[362] The tradition of charging home, as shall be seen in due time both in Flanders and in Spain, remained with the regiment, and doubtless remains with it to this day.

| July 23. |
| July 25-27. |
| July 29. |
| July 30. |

This brilliant exploit was some compensation to the Allies for past mishaps; but a week later Broglie sought to turn the scale by more serious operations. On the 23rd he divided his army into three corps, of which he sent one round Ferdinand's left flank under Prince Xavier of Saxony to threaten Cassel, and a second to force back Spörcke on his right from Volksmarsen, while the main body under his own command advanced to Sachsenhausen. Perforce Ferdinand retreated north-westward to Kalle, his rear-guard being incessantly and severely engaged throughout the movement; whereupon Broglie, seeing the way to be clear, detached a corps under the Chevalier de

Muy, who had recently arrived to relieve the Count of St. Germain, across the Diemel to Warburg, in order to cut off the Allies from Westphalia. The Marshal himself meanwhile moved up parallel to Ferdinand on the eastern side towards Kalle, and Prince Xavier pressed still closer upon Cassel. It being evident to Ferdinand that either Cassel or Westphalia must be abandoned, he detached a force under General Kielmansegge to strengthen the garrison of Cassel and resolved to attack de Muy. Accordingly, on the afternoon of the 29th Spörcke's corps crossed the Diemel to Liebenau, followed on the same evening by that of the Hereditary Prince; and on the 30th their combined force, not exceeding in all fourteen thousand men, encamped between Liebenau and Corbeke with its left on the Diemel, facing west. At dawn of the same morning Broglie's army debouched from several quarters simultaneously against the Allied camp at Kalle, but drew off after some hours of cannonade; and Ferdinand, satisfied through other signs that this demonstration was intended only to cover the movement of the French towards Cassel, resolved to pass the Diemel without delay and to deliver his stroke against de Muy.

Spörcke and the Hereditary Prince had meanwhile reconnoitred de Muy's position and had recommended that their own corps should turn its left flank, while Ferdinand with the main army advanced against its front. De Muy, with about twenty thousand men, occupied a high ridge across a bend of the Diemel, facing north-east, with his right resting on Warburg and his left near the village of Ochsendorf. To his left rear rose a circular hill crowned by a tower, and on his left front lay a village named Poppenheim. It was arranged that the corps of Spörcke and the Hereditary Prince should advance westward in two columns from Corbeke and form up in three lines between the tower and Poppenheim, so as to fall on de Muy's left flank and rear, while Ferdinand crossing the Diemel at Liebenau should attack his centre and right. As the camp between Liebenau and Corbeke lay about ten miles from de Muy's, and as Ferdinand's camp lay some fifteen miles to the south of the Diemel from Liebenau, the operation called for extreme nicety in the execution.

| July 31. |

At nine o'clock on the evening of the 30th Ferdinand's army marched from Kalle, and at six o'clock on the following morning the heads of his columns passed the Diemel and debouched on the heights of Corbeke. They arrived, however, at later than the appointed hour. The passage of the Diemel had caused much delay; and not all the haste of officers nor the eagerness of men could bring the army forward the quicker. At seven o'clock Spörcke and the Hereditary Prince, after much anxious waiting, decided to march from Corbeke before more time should be lost. The northern column, which included the right wing of all three arms, moved by Gross Eider and Ochsendorf upon the tower; the southern, composed of the left wing, by Klein Eider and Poppenheim. Both columns were led by British troops—the northern by the Royal Dragoons, whose place was on the extreme right of the first line, while the British grenadiers, massed in two battalions under Colonels Maxwell and Daulhatt,[363] marched at the head of the infantry. The southern was headed by the Seventh Dragoons, with Keith's and Campbell's Highlanders[364] following them to cover the grenadiers in second line.

At half-past one the Hereditary Prince, having posted his artillery on the outskirts of Ochsendorf and Poppenheim, opened fire as the signal for attack; and at the same time the British grenadiers began to file through Ochsendorf. Certain French battalions, which de Muy had thrown back *en potence* to protect his left flank, thereupon retired without firing, until it was perceived that the Allies were making for the steep hill in rear of the French position. Then one battalion of Regiment Bourbonnois deliberately faced about and marched off to occupy the hill. To permit such a thing would have been to derange the whole of the plans of the Allies, so it was necessary to prevent it at any cost. Colonel Beckwith with ten grenadiers ran forward, keeping out of sight of the French, to reach the hill before them; the Prince himself with thirty more hurried after him; and with this handful of men, all panting and breathless, they crowned the crest of the height. Bourbonnois arriving on the scene a little later found itself greeted by a sharp fire, and, being unable to see the numbers opposed to it, halted for ten minutes to allow its second battalion to come up. The delay gave time for Daulhatt's entire battalion of grenadiers to join Beckwith's little party; and then the two battalions of Bourbonnois attacked in earnest, and the combat between French and British, at odds of two against one, became most fierce and stubborn. The disparity of numbers however, was too great; and Daulhatt's men after a gallant struggle were beginning to give way, when Maxwell's battalion came up in the nick of time to support them. This reinforcement redressed the balance of the fight; Daulhatt's men speedily rallied, and the contest for the hill was renewed. The French, however, prepared to send fresh battalions in support of Bourbonnois, and the situation of the British became critical; for a battery of artillery, which was on its way to the hill to support them, got into difficulties in a defile near Ochsendorf and blocked the advance of the rest of the northern column. Fortunately it was extricated, though none too soon, and being brought up to the hill was speedily in action; while the head of the southern column likewise coming up took the French reinforcements in flank and drove them back in disorder. The Royals and Seventh Dragoons were then let loose upon the broken French battalions, completing their discomfiture and taking many prisoners.

So far the turning movement had succeeded; but its success was not yet assured, for only a portion of the southern column was yet formed for action, and the troops on the field were becoming exhausted. De Muy might yet have hoped to turn the scale in his left, when his attention was suddenly called to the advance of troops upon his front. After desperate but fruitless efforts it had been found that the infantry of Ferdinand's army could not hope to arrive in time to take part in the action. The British battalions, urged by General Waldegrave, struggled manfully to get forward, but the day was hot, and the ground was difficult and in many places marshy: the men would not fall out, but they dropped down insensible from fatigue in spite of themselves. Ferdinand therefore ordered Lord Granby, who had succeeded to Sackville, to advance with the twenty-two squadrons of British cavalry and the British artillery alone. Away therefore they started at the trot, the guns accompanying them at a speed which amazed all beholders.[365] Two hours of trotting brought them at last within sight of the enemy; and Granby at once turned them upon the cavalry of de Muy's right wing. The pace was checked for a brief moment as the squadrons formed in two lines for the attack. In the first line from right to left were the First, Third, and Second Dragoon Guards, in one brigade, the Blues, Seventh, and Sixth Dragoon Guards in another; in the second line were the Greys, Tenth, Sixth, and Eleventh Dragoons. Then the advance was resumed, Granby riding at the head of the Blues, his own regiment, and well in front of all. His hat flew from his head, revealing a bald head which shone conspicuous in the sun, as the trot grew into gallop and the lines came thundering on. The French squadrons wavered for a moment, and then, with the exception of three only, turned and fled without awaiting the shock. The scarlet ranks promptly wheeled round upon the flank and rear of the French infantry; whereupon the three French squadrons that had stood firm plunged gallantly down on the flank of the King's Dragoon Guards, and overthrew them. But the Blues quickly came up to liberate their comrades; and the devoted little band of Frenchmen was cut to pieces. The French infantry, finding itself now attacked on both flanks, broke and fled; and the whole of de Muy's men, horse and foot, rushed down to the Diemel, and, without even looking for the bridges, threw down their arms and splashed frantically through the fords. A party of French irregulars in Warburg tried likewise to escape, but was caught by the cavalry and well-nigh annihilated. Finally, the British batteries came down to the river at a gallop, unlimbered on the bank, and played on the fugitives so destructively as wholly to prevent them from reforming. Granby presently crossed the river in pursuit with ten squadrons; and the fragments of de Muy's corps retired in disorder to Volksmarsen. Thus brilliantly ended the action of Warburg.

The loss of the French was set down at from six to eight thousand men, killed, wounded, and taken, while twelve guns remained as trophies in the hands of the victors. The Allies lost just over twelve hundred men, of whom no less than two hundred and forty belonged to Maxwell's grenadiers; Daulhatt's battalion also suffering very severely. The losses of the cavalry were trifling. Altogether the action was a brilliant little affair, well designed and, despite the tardiness of Ferdinand's arrival, well executed. For the British it redeemed the character of the cavalry which had been so shamefully sacrificed by Sackville at Minden; since it was evidently the recollection of that disgrace which spurred Granby on to so rapid an advance and so headlong an attack. For Ferdinand the victory effectually opened the way into Westphalia.

| Aug. 10. |

Meanwhile it had been found impossible to defend Cassel against Broglie's overwhelming numbers; and the town was accordingly abandoned. It was no fault of Ferdinand's that Hesse was thus laid at the mercy of the French; indeed, with an army weaker in numbers by one-half than his enemy's, he had done well to save Westphalia. He now took up a position along the Diemel from Trendelburg to Stadtbergen, so as to seal up every passage over the river, while Broglie posted his main army over against him on the opposite bank. The Marshal's superiority in numbers, however, enabled him, while holding the Allies in check with the bulk of his army, to detach independent corps for minor operations, though he took even such enterprises in hand with redoubled caution after the lessons of Emsdorff and Warburg. His first essay was the reduction of Ziegenhain, which surrendered after a siege of ten days; and concurrently he moved a corps under Prince Xavier eastward against Münden, which occupied Göttingen and pushed detachments forward as far north as Nordheim and Einbeck. This latter movement carried the war unpleasantly far into Hanoverian territory; but Ferdinand none the less remained immovable on the Diemel. Broglie thereupon broke up his camp on that river and shifted his position eastward to Immenhausen, to support the operations of Prince Xavier. This placed Ferdinand in an awkward dilemma. He had sent a few troops to Beverungen on the Weser to check Xavier's advanced parties; but this detachment, though it had done its work well, was not strong enough to make head against an invasion in real force. Moreover Einbeck was disagreeably near to the border of his brother's dominions of Brunswick, which he would fain have saved from invasion if he could. Yet he could not move to the east bank of the Weser without uncovering Lippstadt, the one fortress which enabled him to prevent the perfect concert of the French armies of the Rhine and Main. In fact the situation was one of extreme trial and embarrassment.

| Sept. |

Ferdinand, whose light troops and irregulars were never idle while they could make mischief, first tried the effect of a raid with a flying column upon Broglie's communications with Frankfort; but this enterprise, though it alarmed the French and somewhat threw back their preparations, only partially achieved its object. On the other hand, it was always open to Ferdinand to stay where he was till want of forage should compel Broglie to retire; but this, though an infallible method, was slow, and would mean that the country would be converted into a desert, through which it would be impossible to follow the French during their retreat. He therefore resolved to make a diversion by carrying the war suddenly to the Rhine. Broglie, in his anxiety to invade Hanover and Brunswick, had denuded Wesel of the greater part of its garrison. If Ferdinand could snatch Wesel, the base of the Army of the Rhine, from him, the diversion would be a telling stroke indeed.[366]

| Sept. 23. |
| Oct. 1-2. |
| October. |

All through the first days of September Ferdinand's preparations for this undertaking went steadily and silently forward; and on the 22nd a powerful train of siege-artillery, under the Count of Lippe-Bückeburg, marched away for Wesel, followed three days later by the Hereditary Prince with about ten thousand Hanoverians and Hessians. The Count was to conduct the siege and the Prince to cover it. Broglie, on learning of their departure, at once detached a strong corps under the Marquis of Castries to follow them; to which Ferdinand retorted by sending to the Prince one Hanoverian and ten British battalions, together with a Hessian regiment and three British regiments of cavalry.[367] Meanwhile the Prince's advanced parties had crossed the Rhine below Wesel on the 29th of September, and had surprised two or three small garrisons. The commandant of Wesel thereupon broke down the bridge which connected it with the western bank of the Rhine; and none too soon, for on the 30th the Prince came up and invested the fortress. The siege, however, progressed but slowly owing to rain and stormy weather; and meanwhile Castries was advancing by forced marches, despite the dreadful state of the roads, along a route full fifty miles south of the Prince's, to the Rhine. On the 12th of October he crossed the river at Cologne and pushed on without delay to Rheinberg, where he was joined by reinforcements from Brabant. Considering the unspeakable difficulties of foul weather and almost impassable roads, this march of Castries stands out as a very fine feat of resolution and endurance.

The advance of French troops from the side of Brabant was a complication which neither Ferdinand nor the Hereditary Prince had foreseen. In fact it almost deprived the advance to Wesel of the character of a diversion.

365

Castries had in Rheinberg thirty battalions and thirty-eight squadrons besides irregular troops, and was expecting further reinforcements; whereas the Prince, weakened by the absence of men in the trenches before Wesel, could muster but twenty-one battalions and twenty-two squadrons to meet him. It was open to the Prince either to fight against superior numbers or to retreat; and he elected to fight. Castries had taken up a position behind the Eugenian Canal, facing north-west, with his right resting on Rheinberg, and with the abbey of Kloster Kampen, on the northern side of the canal, before his left front. Immediately before his left, but on his own side of the canal, stood the village of Kampenbröck, consisting of several scattered houses with gardens, ditches, and hedges. In front and to the left, or western, side of Kampenbröck was a morass covered by a straggling wood of sparse and stunted trees, through which were cut paths to a bridge that connected the village with the abbey on the other side of the canal. Across this bridge lay the Prince's only way to penetrate into the French camp; and Castries had been careful to guard the passage by posting no less than two thousand irregular troops in and about the abbey. The only possible chance for the Prince lay in an attack by surprise.

Waiting until the 15th to collect his troops, the Prince marched from before Wesel in dead silence at one hour before midnight. The force was disposed in five divisions. The Fifteenth Light Dragoons, Royal and Inniskilling Dragoons, and Prussian hussars formed the advanced guard; then came the support, of two battalions of Highlanders and as many of British grenadiers; then the main body of the Twentieth and Twenty-fifth British Foot, with eight Hanoverian battalions, all under command of General Waldegrave; then the reserve, of the Eleventh, Twenty-third, Thirty-third and Fifty-first British Foot, with three German battalions, under General Howard; then a rear-guard of the Tenth British Dragoons and ten German squadrons.

Oct. 16.

At three o'clock on the morning of the 16th the advanced parties of the Allies come upon the outposts of the French irregulars, a mile and a half beyond Kloster Kampen. Despite the strict orders of the Prince one or two shots were fired, but fortunately without alarming the enemy; and the Allies pursued their march unmolested to the bridge, thus cutting off the irregulars in the abbey from the French main body. These isolated troops were then attacked and utterly dispersed; and while the musketry was still crackling loud round the abbey's walls the Prince stealing silently on with the British grenadiers penetrated into the wood and into the village of Kampenbröck, so quietly and yet so swiftly that he was in possession before the enemy were aware of his presence. The French in camp had, however, been alarmed by the firing, and some of the principal officers had turned the men out and gone forward to the wood to reconnoitre. One of these, the Chevalier d'Assas, on his way to visit the picquets of his regiment, suddenly found himself among the British grenadiers, but distinguishing no one but the Prince in the darkness advanced towards him with the words, "Sir, you are my prisoner." "On the contrary," answered the Prince, "you are mine, for these are my grenadiers"; and as he spoke the men closed round d'Assas with bayonets fixed. "Auvergne, Auvergne, the enemy is on us,"[368] shouted d'Assas to his regiment without a moment's hesitation at the top of his voice; and before the words were out of his mouth a dozen bayonets pierced through his body and laid him dead on the ground. None the less the devotion of the gallant man sufficed to save the French army. Regiment Auvergne came down at once to d'Assas' call; Castries hastily brought down two more battalions to support it; and three more battalions arrived directly after to protect their flank. The supports of the Allies came up in their turn; and the fight swayed furiously backward and forward until daylight, when the French brought up additional battalions from their right. The reserves of the Allies were promptly and frequently summoned, but through some mistake were not to be found. Still the little force of British and Hanoverians fought desperately on, until the Prince himself fell wounded from his horse; and then, their ammunition being exhausted, they yielded to superior numbers in front and flank and suddenly gave way. The French broke their ranks with loud cries of exultation for the pursuit, when the Fifteenth Light Dragoons swooped down upon them, charging home as their custom is, broke up two battalions completely, and drove the rest flying back in confusion upon their comrades. The French cavalry now came forward in overwhelming numbers and handled the British squadrons very roughly; but the charge of the Fifteenth had given the infantry time to rally, and to make their retreat in good order. The reserve appeared at Kloster Kampen in time to cover the retiring troops, and by noon the fight of Kloster Kampen was over.

The loss of the Allies amounted to nearly twelve hundred killed and wounded and sixteen hundred prisoners, in addition to which one gun and one British colour were captured. That of the French was as heavy and heavier, amounting to twenty-seven hundred killed and wounded and three hundred prisoners. The struggle was unusually stubborn and murderous, and the fire of the British was so rapid and deadly that three French brigades were almost wiped out of existence.[369] Yet it is said that after this action the Hereditary Prince would never take British troops under his command again.[370] He admitted that General Waldegrave did wonders in the combat,[371] but he complained of the behaviour of his troops, though Waldegrave bore witness that not a man retired until his ammunition was exhausted. It may have been that the Prince was irritated by the failure of the reserve to arrive when it was wanted; but no blame is imputed to any one for this mischance, which appears to have been due simply to bad luck. Mauvillon, who is always very frank in his criticism of the British, says flatly that he does not believe in their misconduct on this occasion; and as the only extant list of casualties, though very far from complete, shows that they lost five hundred killed and wounded, it should seem that the Prince's strictures were ill deserved. It was hard, too, that he should have forgotten all that they had done for him at Emsdorff and at Warburg, to say nothing of the fact that the heroic charge of the Fifteenth probably saved his force from total destruction at Kloster Kampen itself. Whether he himself should have hazarded such an action against odds of two to one, with the French bringing up reinforcements from the west, is another question; for it was not as though the fall of Wesel were likely to ensue speedily even if Castries were beaten, while the diversion had proved to be no diversion whatever. On the other hand, the destruction of his corps, or of the best part of it, would have been a severe blow to Ferdinand. Nevertheless the stake, if he should win it, was worth winning; though if he could have foreseen what was immediately before him he would probably have hesitated to play so desperate a game.

October.

After the action he retreated northward to Büderich, to find that the bridge which he had thrown over the Rhine had been swept away by floods, and that he could go no farther. His situation was now desperate, for not only was his retreat cut off, but his ammunition was exhausted. Still, wounded though he was, he faced his difficulties with his usual energy, entrenched himself among his waggons, reconstructed his bridge, and on the 18th crossed the river unmolested, picking up the troops from before Wesel on the eastern bank. Castries followed him as he retreated eastward, thereby forcing him to remain in Westphalia for the protection of Lippstadt and Münster, though the Prince none the less made shift to detach a portion of his force to the assistance of Ferdinand.

| Aug. 15 and |
| Nov. 3. |

For to Ferdinand also the failure before Wesel was a serious matter. Any further stroke upon the French was impossible; and the utmost for which he could hope was to drive them out of Hesse and to hold Westphalia safe. He made an effort to expel the French from Göttingen, but without success; and at last, driven to desperation by three months of continuous rain, he cantoned a force in winter-quarters before the town and closed the campaign, leaving the French in possession of Hesse, of the Principality of Göttingen, and of the defiles of Münden, which gave them free ingress into Hanover and Brunswick. His own headquarters were fixed at Warburg; those of the French at Cassel. Despite all his efforts, superior numbers had told heavily against him; and though he had fired a *feu de joie* for the capture of Montreal, he probably found less consolation in this than in the victories of his master Frederick at Leignitz and Torgau, and in the expulsion of his enemies' forces from Saxony.

CHAPTER X

1760.

Meanwhile on the 20th of November Parliament had met to hear his first speech from a new king. For on the 25th of October, just before the coming of the news of Kloster Kampen, King George the Second had died suddenly, having lived to see the glories of Queen Anne's reign brought back by Pitt, and the fame of Blenheim and Oudenarde revived not only by Minden and Warburg but by Wandewash and Quebec. George the Third struck a new and strange note in his speech from the throne. "Born and educated in England," he said—and the words were of his own insertion—"I glory in the name of Briton"; and the phrase fell pleasantly on ears that did not love the sound of Hanover; though what this sudden outburst of insular patriotism on the King's part might portend to his German allies was not yet revealed. The estimates for the Army were passed with little difficulty, though the Establishment showed a considerable increase. The new regiments that appeared on the list, indeed, were few, for a system had been initiated of raising an indefinite number of independent companies; but these were gradually combined into regiments, and before the campaign opened there was already a corps numbered the hundredth of the Line.[372] The total number of men voted on the British Establishment was one hundred and four thousand; besides which the embodied militia was increased from eighteen to twenty-seven thousand, making, together with the troops on the Irish Establishment, over one hundred and forty thousand men raised in the British possessions alone. Adding the mercenary forces of Hanover, Hesse, and Brunswick, the number of soldiers in British pay fell little short of two hundred thousand.

1761.

Yet for the present no considerable reinforcement was despatched to Ferdinand. A battalion from each regiment of Guards had indeed been sent to him late in the past campaign, together with the usual drafts to fill up vacancies. But Pitt had another enterprise in hand as a diversion in Ferdinand's favour. A scheme of the kind had indeed been on the point of execution in the autumn of 1760; and eight thousand men had actually been embarked for a secret expedition under General Kingsley, but had been returned to the shore on receipt of the news of Kloster Kampen.[373] In January, however, the same regiments were again warned for service under

Major-General Hodgson,[374] and on the 29th of March they sailed from Spithead under convoy of ten ships of the line, besides smaller vessels, under Admiral Keppel, for their unknown destination.[375]

April.
April 22.

On the 7th of April the fleet anchored off the island of Belleisle on the French coast, and on the following day sailed round it looking for an undefended point. Finally Port La Maria on the south-eastern side was selected; the troops were shifted into flat-bottomed boats, and an attempt was made to storm some French entrenchments which covered the landing-place. But the ground was so steep that only sixty men of the Thirty-seventh succeeded in making their way to the top of the heights above the sea, and these after a gallant attempt to hold their ground were overpowered by superior numbers. The attempt was therefore abandoned, and the troops were re-embarked, having lost about five hundred men, killed, wounded, and taken. The island was in fact so strong by nature, and so skilfully fortified by art, that Keppel despaired of a successful descent.[376] The commanders, however, decided that, if feint attacks were made on La Maria and Sauzon some footing might be obtained by ascending the rocks between them, which being judged inaccessible had been left undefended. The attempt was accordingly made on the 22nd and was brilliantly successful. The grenadier-company of the Nineteenth contrived to scramble up the rocks and to hold its own on the summit until reinforced, when the men charged with the bayonet, drove back the enemy and captured three guns. The French then retired into the fortress of Palais and proceeded to strengthen the defences; while Hodgson, to his infinite mortification, was obliged to lie idle for a fortnight, being unable to land his heavy artillery owing to continual gales. At length on the 2nd of May ground was broken, and on the 13th the entrenchments were carried by storm. The French thereupon retired into the citadel, which after a most gallant defence was compelled on the 7th of June to surrender. The losses of the British throughout the whole of the operations were about seven hundred killed and wounded. Thus Belleisle was secured as a place of refreshment for the fleet while engaged in the weary work of blockading the French coast.

Feb.

Any hopes that might have been built on the value of this expedition as a help to Ferdinand were very speedily dissipated. Ferdinand himself had sought, while it was yet mid-winter, to make good the losses of the past campaign by a bold stroke for the recapture of Hesse. Moving out of his winter-quarters on the 11th of February he distributed his army into three columns. The left or eastern column, under Spörcke, was designed to march to the Werra and Unstrut, and to join with a detachment of Prussians in an attack upon the Saxons in that quarter; the main or central army, under Ferdinand himself, was to march to the Eder; and the right or westward column, which was composed of the troops cantoned in Westphalia under the Hereditary Prince, was to advance on Fritzlar, while a separate corps was detached to attempt the capture of Marburg.

March 20.
March 21.
March.

Spörcke for his part did his work well and gained a brilliant little victory at Langensalza; but the rest of the scheme went to wreck. Broglie on learning of Ferdinand's movements left a garrison in Cassel and retreated first to Hersfeld, behind the Eder, and finally to the Main. But meanwhile the Hereditary Prince had been delayed for two invaluable days by unexpected resistance at Fritzlar; and Ferdinand, though he had driven the enemy for the moment from Hesse, had left Cassel, Ziegenhain, and Marburg, invested indeed but untaken, behind him. He dared not linger to master these places one after another, for the whole country was laid waste, and the strain of hauling all supplies from the Weser was intolerable. The road from Beverungen to the central column of the army was paved with dead horses, the corpses tracing the whole line of the advance. He was therefore obliged to hasten on to a district where supplies were still obtainable, trusting that good fortune would throw the strong places into his hands before it was too late. But it was not to be. Broglie quickly concentrated his troops on the Main, summoned twelve thousand men from the Lower Rhine and advanced northward to Giessen; whereupon Ferdinand, who had penetrated as far south as the Ohm, was compelled to fall back to the Eder. On the following day the Hereditary Prince was attacked by superior numbers at Grünberg and compelled to retreat with loss of two thousand prisoners; and this misfortune neutralised all the advantages so far gained by the enterprise. Ferdinand, therefore, raised the siege of Cassel and fell back with all speed by forced marches; for Broglie had now eighty thousand troops against his own twenty thousand. Arrived at his old position to north of the Diemel he dispersed his troops once more into winter-quarters. His stroke had failed; and the operations are interesting chiefly as exemplifying the futility, in those days of slow communication, of an advance into an enemy's country, unless at least one fortress were first captured as a place of arms. It is easier to understand the reason for the laborious sieges of Marlborough and Wellington when it is observed that Ferdinand, though he drove the French before him from end to end of Hesse in a few weeks, was obliged to abandon the whole of it and to retreat because he had left Cassel uncaptured in his rear.

The Allies had suffered so terribly from hardship and exposure during this winter's expedition that it was two months before they were again fit to take the field;[377] and the French, partly from the same cause, partly owing to the magnitude of their preparations, needed little less time than they. The Court of Versailles had, in fact, resolved to make a gigantic effort and to close the war forthwith by employment of an overwhelming force. The army of the Rhine was raised to one hundred thousand men, under the Prince of Soubise, and that of the Main to sixty thousand men under Broglie. Soubise was to advance from the Rhine against Ferdinand early in May; thus forcing the Prince either to abandon Westphalia, together with Münster and Lippstadt, in order to gain time for recuperation of his army, or to march with his troops, still weakened and exhausted by the winter's campaign, to fight him. His task in fact was simply to keep Ferdinand's army in motion until Broglie's troops were refreshed, and ready to advance either into Hanover or to Hameln on the Weser. When Broglie thus occupied the attention of Ferdinand, Soubise would find himself with a free hand in a free field. The weak point of the plan was that the two French armies were to act independently, and that the stronger of them was entrusted to Soubise, an incompetent commander but a favourite with Madame de Pompadour. But in any case the outlook for Ferdinand was formidable, since at the very most he could muster but ninety-three thousand men against one hundred and sixty thousand of the French.

April.
May 14.

Soubise duly arrived at Frankfort on the 13th of April and summoned Broglie to discuss matters with him. Then, instead of taking the field early in May, he remained motionless behind the Rhine on various pretexts until the beginning of June. Further, he determined, contrary to the advice given to him at Versailles, to pursue operations to the south of the Lippe, and between that river and the Ruhr, in order to effect a junction with Broglie. The motives that may have dictated this resolution are unknown; but it was conjectured that he shrank from engaging so formidable an adversary as Ferdinand without a colleague to share the risk and responsibility. Meanwhile Ferdinand, selecting the least exhausted of his troops, sent a corps under the Hereditary Prince to Nottuln, a little to the west of Münster, to watch Soubise, and by great exertions contrived within ten weeks to render both his army and his transport fit to take the field. Soubise's army was known to be encumbered by a vast train of baggage; one troop of Horse Guards, for instance, with a strength of one hundred and forty men, travelling with no fewer than twelve hundred horses attached to it. So all the forage about Münster was destroyed, the inhabitants and their herds being provided for by the King's commissaries, and every step was taken to embarrass the French in their advance to the east.

June.
July 1-2.
July 3.
July 4.
July 6.

At length on the 13th of June Soubise crossed the Rhine at Wesel, and arrived ten days later at Unna, a few miles to eastward of Dortmund, where he entrenched himself, with his front to the east. Ferdinand thereupon concentrated his army on the 19th at Paderborn, leaving twenty thousand men under Spörcke on the Diemel to watch Broglie, and a smaller corps of observation before Göttingen. On the 20th he marched westward, and on the 28th encamped over against Soubise, where he was joined by the corps of the Hereditary Prince. Finding that the French position was too formidable to be attacked, he determined on a bold stroke, made a forced march of thirty hours round Soubise's left flank by Camen, and appeared suddenly at Dortmund full in his rear and across his line of communication. The movement left Soubise free to unite with Broglie; but this was rather an advantage than otherwise to Ferdinand, since the two commanders being on bad terms might neutralise each other, whereas each of them independently was at the head of a stronger army than Ferdinand's. On the 4th of July Ferdinand advanced against the rear of Soubise's camp; whereupon the French General at once moved on, always with the Allies close at his heels, to Soest, where Broglie came to concert with him the junction of the two armies.

July 10.
July.

Broglie himself had on the 29th of June advanced to the Diemel and obliged Spörcke to abandon Warburg and to retreat, not without loss of part of his artillery. He had then turned westward upon Paderborn, which he had occupied, and thence to Soest, where his army joined that of Soubise on the 10th of July. The joint strength of the two armies at Soest, after deducting the detachments made from both of them, was just about one hundred thousand men. Ferdinand's force, after the arrival of Spörcke, who had made his way to him from the Diemel with all haste, amounted to no more than sixty thousand men. Even with such odds against him, however, Ferdinand stood firm, refusing to cross to the north bank of the Lippe and abandon Lippstadt, as the French commanders had hoped. He was determined that they should fight him for Lippstadt; and they, knowing their adversary, were not too eager to hazard the venture.

After sundry small changes and shiftings of position between the 7th and 11th of July Ferdinand made the following dispositions. General von Spörcke with about eight thousand men was left on the north bank of the Lippe at Hersfeld, to watch Prince Xavier of Saxony, who lay with a corps in the

374

vicinity of Paderborn. The main army was encamped on the south bank of the Lippe, with its left resting on the river; from whence the left wing extended to the village of Kirchdünckern on the Ase, a brook impassable except by bridges. Vellinghausen, Ferdinand's headquarters, lay midway between the Ase and the Lippe at the foot of a declivity called the Dünckerberg. From the Lippe to Vellinghausen the ground was occupied by Wutgenau's corps, of seven battalions and five squadrons, all of them German troops. From Vellinghausen to Kirchdünckern the heights were held by Granby's corps, consisting of two battalions of British grenadiers, the Fifth, Twelfth, Twenty-fourth and Thirty-seventh Foot under Brigadier Sandford, Keith's and Campbell's Highlanders, six foreign battalions, the Greys, Seventh and Eleventh Dragoons in one brigade under General Harvey, and eight foreign squadrons, together with a regiment of Hanoverian artillery. From the Ase the position was prolonged to the right along a similar line of heights by the villages of Sud Dünckern and Wambeln to the rear of Werle at Budberg, the whole of the front being covered by a marshy brook called the Salzbach. From the Ase to Wambeln the ground was occupied by Anhalt's corps of ten German battalions and the First, Sixth, and Tenth British Dragoons; to the right of Anhalt stood Conway's corps, of three battalions of British Guards with their grenadiers massed into a fourth battalion, Townsend's brigade of the Eighth, Twentieth, Twenty-fifth, and Fiftieth Foot, and the First, Third, and Seventh Dragoon Guards; to the right of Conway stood Howard's corps, consisting of Cavendish's brigade of the Eleventh, Twenty-fifth, Twenty-third, and Fifty-first Foot, two German battalions, the British light batteries and two brigades of Hessian artillery; and finally the extreme right from Wambeln to Hilbeck was held by the Hereditary Prince's corps of twenty-five battalions and twenty-four squadrons of Germans. The Salzbach was an obstacle well-nigh insuperable, the only passage by which the French could cross it being by the village of Scheidingen, opposite to Conway's corps, where an old redoubt, dating from the days of Turenne, still remained to bar the way. The weak point of the position was its right flank which, though more or less protected by marshy ground, lay practically in the air, and could have been turned with little difficulty.

| July 15. |

The plan of the French commanders, though it took no advantage of this defect, was not ill conceived. Broglie was to attack the corps of Wutgenau and Granby, but particularly that of Granby between the Lippe and the Ase, with his whole force; while Soubise kept the rest of the Allies distracted by an attack on Scheidingen, at the same time sending a cloud of light troops round the right flank of the Allies to Hamm, five miles in their rear, so as to create confusion and embarrass their retreat. The attack was fixed for the 13th but was deferred for two days; and it was not until the evening of the 15th that Ferdinand was apprised of the advance of the French in force against his left. For some reason Wutgenau's corps had been encamped a thousand yards in rear of its position in the line of battle; and although it had received orders at noon, in consequence of suspicious movements by the French, to strike tents and march forward, yet this order had been cancelled. Thus Broglie's attack came upon it as a complete surprise. Granby's corps had only just time to seize its arms and turn out, leaving the tents standing; the Highlanders indeed hardly emerging from their tents before the French guns opened fire on them. Yet there was no confusion, and Granby's dispositions were so good that he was able to hold his own till Wutgenau's troops came up. The two corps then made a fine defence until darkness put an end to the combat; but none the less the French had succeeded in taking Nordel, a village on Granby's right front, and had made good their footing in Vellinghausen.

Meanwhile Soubise had not yet moved forward against Scheidingen. The time fixed by the Marshals for their decisive attack has been, in fact, the early hours of the 16th, so that Broglie's advance had been premature. He excused himself by saying that he had intended only to drive in the outposts of the Allies, but that he had been encouraged by his unexpected success to bring forward more troops to hold the ground that he had gained, and that he had accordingly appealed to Soubise to hasten his movements likewise. Had Broglie really pushed his attack home he would probably have succeeded, for the Allies were too weak to stop him and were, moreover, short of ammunition. But the Marshal was too timid a man to take responsibility on his own shoulders; so instead of making a bold attempt to carry the Dünckerberg, which if successful must have forced Ferdinand to retreat, he stopped short at Vellinghausen, leaving the Allies in their position unmoved.

| July 16. |

The night passed uneasily in the Allied camp. Between the Lippe and the Ase skirmishing never ceased. The road to Hamm was full of waggons going and returning with loads of ammunition; Anhalt's corps, together with all the British of Howard's corps, was streaming across the Ase to reinforce Granby; and Conway's and the Hereditary Prince's were extending themselves leftward to cover the ground thus left vacant. For Ferdinand knew Broglie to be his most dangerous antagonist, and was determined to stop him at all costs by fresh troops. Broglie, on his side, was equally busy replacing the battalions that had already been engaged; and the dawn was no sooner come than his columns deployed and attacked in earnest. The ground was so much broken up by hedges and ditches that in many places the troops engaged, though no more than one hundred and fifty yards apart, were unable to see each other, and fired furiously, not without destructive effect, at every puff of smoke that betrayed an enemy's presence. From four until eight o'clock this fusillade continued, neither side gaining or losing an inch of ground, until at last it slackened from the sheer exhaustion of the men, after more than twelve hours of intermittent action.

Meanwhile Broglie looked anxiously for Soubise's demonstration against the Allied centre and right, but he looked in vain. Soubise, though he did indeed bring forward troops against Scheidingen, made but a faint attack, often renewed with unchangeable feebleness and as often repulsed. Then after half an hour's respite, the fire opened again on the Allied left. Spörcke had detached six battalions to Wutgenau from Hersfeld; and the arrival of fresh troops infused new life into the engagement. Broglie too showed symptoms of reviving energy, for two French batteries were observed in motion towards a height opposite the Dünckerberg, from which they might have made havoc of Granby's corps. Ferdinand ordered that the height should be carried at all costs; and Maxwell's grenadiers, Keith's and Campbell's Highlanders and four foreign battalions advanced forthwith to storm it. The French were so much exhausted that they appear hardly to have awaited the attack. They broke and fled precipitately, abandoning their dead, their wounded, and several guns. Maxwell's grenadiers alone made four battalions prisoners; and Broglie, disheartened by his failure and by the apathy of Soubise, gave the word to retreat. The ground was too much broken for the action of cavalry; so he was able to draw off his troops with little loss indeed, but not without shame and disgrace.

| July. |

Thus ended the battle of Vellinghausen, one of the feeblest ever fought by the French army. The losses were not great on either side for the numbers engaged. Those of the French were reckoned at from five to six thousand men, besides eight colours and nineteen guns; those of the Allies did not reach the figure of sixteen hundred men, of whom over nine-tenths belonged to the corps to the north of the Ase. The brunt of the fighting fell of course on Granby's troops; but the casualties of the British with him little exceeded four hundred men, while those of the British in other parts of the field did not amount to fifty. The victory was in fact trifling except for its moral effects; but these were sufficient. The French were humbled at the failure of a hundred thousand men against fifty thousand; and Broglie and Soubise, who had left the camp with embraces, returned to it sworn enemies, each bitterly reproaching the other for the loss of the battle. Lastly, Broglie, who possessed some military talent and had hitherto been anxious to bring his enemy to action, came to the conclusion that a general engagement with Ferdinand was a thing henceforth not to be courted but to be shunned.

| July 27. |
| August. |
| Aug. 16. |
| Aug. 22. |
| Aug. 28. |

The remainder of the campaign is reckoned to be the finest example of Ferdinand's skill as a general; but it is impossible in this place to sketch it in more than the faintest outline. After the action, Soubise made up Broglie's army to forty thousand men, and therewith the two commanders separated; Broglie marching on Paderborn for operations against Hanover and Hesse, while Soubise made for Wesel to threaten Westphalia. The Hereditary Prince was detached to follow Soubise and to harass his rear-guard, while Ferdinand marched some thirty miles eastward to Büren, to be ready to move into Hesse and threaten Broglie's communications with Frankfort. At the same time Granby's corps was sent forward to Stadtberg, to drive back a French corps under Stainville, which covered Hesse at the line of the Diemel. At Büren Ferdinand remained, with his eye always on Lippstadt, until the 10th of August; when, Stainville having been forced back to Cassel and Soubise to the Rhine, both at a safe distance from the precious fortress on the Lippe, he marched away to keep watch over Broglie's army. That officer had used his time to advance to Höxter, aiming at the capture of Hameln and the mastery of the line of the Weser, and had detached a corps under Prince Xavier of Saxony into the Principality of Göttingen. Ferdinand by swift marches brought his army to northward of Broglie's at Reilenkirchen, thus heading him back from Hameln; while a separate corps, which he had sent across the Weser, attacked the French detachments about Göttingen. The Hereditary Prince, finding nothing to fear from Soubise, also returned from the Rhine to threaten Broglie from the south. The Marshal thereupon crossed the Weser; and Ferdinand, for all his unwillingness to move to the east bank of the river, perforce followed him; carefully avoiding an engagement, however, lest Soubise should seize the opportunity to march on Lippstadt. Soubise, finding himself unwatched, moved eastward again towards Hanover; whereupon the Hereditary Prince flew back to look after him, and Ferdinand retiring with the rest of the army to the Diemel, advanced against Broglie's communications with Marburg and Frankfort. This movement brought Broglie back hurriedly to Cassel; whereupon Ferdinand retired quietly to Geismar on the Diemel, having accomplished his object of occupying Broglie's attention for weeks and of rendering his movements absolutely purposeless, without the risk of an action.

| Sept. 20. |

It was a whole fortnight before Broglie ventured to return to the east side of the Weser, having meanwhile reinforced Stainville's army for the protection of Hesse, and furnished him with most careful instructions for his guidance. No sooner was the Marshal's back turned, than Ferdinand made a sudden dash upon Stainville just to south of the Diemel, and though he failed to inflict any great damage on him, forced him to retire to Cassel and brought Broglie back in all haste from Hanover. Meanwhile the lethargic Soubise had made a diversion towards the sea, had actually taken Emden, and was threatening Bremen. The Hereditary Prince was as usual despatched to hunt him back to the Rhine; and Ferdinand's communications with Holland were restored.

October 10.

There still remained some weeks, however, before the campaign could be closed; and Broglie, despite all Ferdinand's activity, was strong enough to detach a corps under Prince Xavier into Brunswick, which captured Wolfenbüttel and bade fair to capture Brunswick itself. The loss of these two fortresses would have been serious, since the French could have turned them into bases of operations for the next campaign, when Ferdinand would have found it impossible to attend both to Brunswick and to Lippstadt. He therefore hastened northward at once from the Diemel to save his brother's capital; whereupon Prince Xavier, though Ferdinand had travelled no further than Hameln on his way, at once withdrew from before Brunswick and evacuated Wolfenbüttel. Much relieved at the news of this deliverance, Ferdinand halted at Hameln until November, when Soubise went into winter-quarters. He then made a final effort to drive Broglie from the eastern bank of the Weser, but succeeded only in thrusting him back for a short distance from his northernmost post at Einbeck. Broglie then went into winter-quarters along the Leine from Göttingen to Nordheim, and the Allies followed his example; their chain of posts running from Münster along the line of the Lippe and Diemel, and eastward through the Sollinger Forest to Ferdinand's headquarters at Hildesheim.

So ended this most arduous campaign, in which, though overmatched by two to one, Ferdinand had won a victory on the battlefield and lost little or no territory. The exertion demanded from his troops by incessant and severe marches told heavily upon their efficiency, and the more so since many of the men had been already much weakened by the winter's campaign in Hesse. The waste of the army was in fact appalling, amounting to no fewer than five-and-twenty thousand out of ninety-five thousand men. Of these some few had been killed in action, considerably more had deserted, still more had been invalided, and fully one-half had died of hardship and disease. It was only at such a price that Ferdinand could make one army do the work of two; and the task would have been beyond even his ability had not one of the commanders matched against him been utterly incompetent, and the other hampered by constant interference from Versailles. The extreme laxity of discipline among the French also helped him not a little, and served to heighten the moral superiority of his own troops. But, making all such allowance in his favour, the campaign remains memorable in the annals of war for the consummate skill with which Ferdinand kept two armies, jointly of double his strength, continually in motion for six months, without permitting them to reap the slightest advantage from their operations.

CHAPTER XI

Before the campaign closed in Germany, the great Minister who had revealed to England for the first time the plenitude of her strength in arms, and had turned that strength to such mighty enterprises, was fallen from power. The accession of the new King had brought with it a steady increase in the ascendency of John, Earl of Bute, long a trusted member of his household and now his chief adviser and friend. Blameless in private life and by no means lacking in culture or accomplishments, Bute was both in council and debate a man of distressing mediocrity. Possessing neither sense of the ridiculous nor knowledge of his own limitations, and exalted by mere accident to a position of great influence, he interpreted the caprice of fortune as the reward of merit and aimed at once at the highest office. He was, in fact, one of the many men who, finding it no great exertion to climb up the winding stairs of a cathedral tower, press on, ducking, stooping, and crawling to the top, to find when they reach it that they dare not look down. Being weak as well as ambitious he was compelled to fall back on intrigue in default of ability to help him upward, and having succeeded in displacing Lord Holderness as Secretary of State in March 1761, he turned next to the ousting of Pitt himself. The opportunity soon came. The French Court, weary of the war, approached Pitt with proposals for peace. Resolved, as he said, that no Peace of Utrecht should again sully the annals of England, Pitt not only made large demands for the benefit of Britain, but insisted that even a separate peace between Britain and France should not deter King George from giving aid to the King of Prussia. Curiously enough the negotiation was broken off owing precisely to one of the most disgraceful concessions made at the Peace of Utrecht. The Bourbon King of Spain, Charles the Third, who had succeeded to the throne in 1759, cultivated the friendship of the Bourbon King of France; and the result was a secret treaty of alliance between them, which presently became famous as the Family Compact. Pitt no sooner obtained an inkling of this agreement than he put an end to negotiations with France, and advocated immediate declaration of war against Spain. As shall presently be seen, he made his preparations, which were effective enough; but above all he desired to strike at Spain while she was still unready for war. The Cabinet, however, was alarmed at so bold a measure, being too blind to see that in such a case aggression is the truest precaution. Many of the ministry had only with difficulty been persuaded to second Pitt in the lofty language which he had held towards France; and Bute, who abhorred all interference with affairs on the Continent, was a leader among the dissentients. Lord Temple alone stood by his great chief, so Pitt, unable to prevail, resigned, and his solitary supporter with him. All power passed into the hands of Bute; and within three months Spain, having gained the time that she needed for her military preparations, assumed so offensive a tone that Bute, as Pitt had predicted, was to his huge vexation obliged to declare war against her himself. Such is the fashion in which politicians make difficulties for generals.

```
1761.
June.
```

Fortunately the designs of Pitt for the new year against both France and Spain were fully matured, and the means of executing them were ready to hand. In June 1761 two new regiments[378] had been either raised or formed out of existing independent companies, and thirteen more had been added in August and October,[379] thus bringing the number of regiments of the Line up to one hundred and fifteen. The total number of men voted by Parliament for 1762 was little short of one hundred and fifty thousand men, making with the German mercenaries a total of two hundred and fifteen thousand men in British pay. There were thus men in abundance for any enterprise; and the sphere of operations had been marked out by Pitt. The conquest of Canada having been completed by the end of 1760, there was no object in leaving a large number of troops unemployed in America; and as early as in January 1761 Pitt had written to Amherst that some of them would be required in the autumn for the conquest of Dominica, St. Lucia, and Martinique. Amherst was therefore instructed to send two thousand men forthwith to Guadeloupe; to concert with the Governor the means of taking the two first of the islands mentioned; and to despatch six thousand more men rather later in the year for the capture of Martinique.[380] Accordingly in the first days of June 1761 transports from America began to drop singly into Guadeloupe, the fleet having been dispersed by a storm. By the 3rd of June four ships had arrived, together with Lord Rollo, who had been appointed by Amherst to take the command; and on the following day the whole of these, together with one ship more from Guadeloupe itself, made sail under escort of Sir J. Douglas's squadron to beat back against the trade-wind to Dominica.[381] By noon of the 6th they had arrived before Roseau, where the inhabitants were summoned to surrender. The French replied by manning their batteries and other defences, which included four separate lines of entrenchments, ranged one above another. Rollo landed his men and entered the town; when reflecting that the enemy might be reinforced in the night he resolved, though it was already late, to storm the entrenchments forthwith. He attacked accordingly, and drove out the French in confusion with trifling loss to himself. The French commander and his second being both taken prisoners, no further resistance was made; and on the following day Dominica swore allegiance to King George.

Therewith the operations in the West Indies for the time ceased, though the preparations continued always; but, notwithstanding all possible secrecy, the French in Martinique got wind of the intended attack on that island, and took measures for their defence. Their force was not wholly contemptible in so mountainous a country, for it included twelve hundred regular troops, seven thousand local militia, and four thousand hired privateersmen.[382] The neighbouring English islands did what they could to help the mother country. Antigua sent negroes and part of her old garrison, the Thirty-eighth Foot, which had never left her since Queen Anne's day; and Barbados raised five hundred negroes and as many white men, which were the more acceptable since that island was, as usual, the rendezvous for the expedition.[383] The first troops to arrive in Carlisle Bay were a detachment from Belleisle,[384] where, as well as in America, regiments had been lying idle; and on Christmas Eve appeared the main army from America under command of General Monckton. This was made up of eleven different regiments,[385] besides a few companies of American rangers. In all, the force entrusted to Monckton must have amounted to fully eight thousand men.

| 1762. |
| January. |
| Jan. 24. |

On the 5th of January the transports weighed anchor and sailed away to leeward, under escort of Admiral Rodney's fleet, past the Pitons of St. Lucia, past the port of Castries and the bay which Rodney was twenty years later to make famous, and on the 7th anchored in St. Ann's Bay, just round the southern extremity of Martinique, on the western side. Two brigades were then landed in the Anse d'Arlet, a bay farther up the western coast, from which they marched to the south of the bay that forms the harbour of Fort Royal, but, finding the road impracticable for transport of cannon, were re-embarked. On the 16th the entire army was landed without loss of a man at Case Navire, a little to the north of Negro Point. This Point forms the northern headland of the harbour, and had at its foot a road leading due east over the mountains to the capital town of Fort Royal,[386] some three miles away. The way was blocked by deep gullies and ravines; while the French had erected redoubts at every point of vantage, as well as batteries on a hill beyond, named Morne Tortenson. Monckton was thus compelled to erect batteries to silence the French guns before he could advance farther. By the 24th this work was complete, and at daybreak a general attack was made under the fire of the batteries upon the French defences on Morne Tortenson, a party being at the same time detached to turn the enemy's right flank. The turning movement was completely successful; and the redoubts by the sea, on the enemy's left, having been carried, the troops stormed post after post, until at nine o'clock they were in possession not only of the detached redoubts but of the entire position of Morne Tortenson, with its guns and entrenchments. The French retired in great confusion, some to Fort Royal and some to Morne Grenier, a still higher hill to the north of Morne Tortenson. Simultaneously two brigades under Brigadiers Haviland and Walsh attacked other French posts to the north of Morne Tortenson and, after great difficulty owing to the steepness of the ground, succeeded in driving them also back to Morne Grenier. The losses of the British in this action amounted to thirty-three officers and three hundred and fifty men killed and wounded.

Jan. 25.

On the following day Monckton, being now within range, began to throw up batteries against the citadel of Fort Royal, but finding himself much annoyed by the French batteries on Morne Grenier to his left, decided that these must first be silenced. Fortunately the enemy saved him from further trouble by taking the offensive. On the afternoon of the 27th they suddenly debouched in three columns from Morne Grenier upon Haviland's brigade and the Light Infantry of the army, on Monckton's left, and with unexpected temerity ventured to attack. Unhappily for them, one column exposed its flank to the Highlanders and was almost instantly routed. The two remaining columns thereupon gave way, and the whole fled back to Morne Grenier with the British in eager chase. Such was the impetuosity of the pursuers that they plunged down into the intervening ravine after the French, and swarming up Morne Grenier "by every path, road, and passage where men could run, walk, or creep,"[387] hunted the fugitives headlong before them. Night came on, but the British officers would not stop until they had cleared every Frenchman off the hill and captured all the works and cannon. Monckton at once sent off more troops to support the pursuers, and by one o'clock in the morning of the 28th Morne Grenier was securely occupied, at a cost of little more than one hundred British killed and wounded. The batteries on Morne Tortenson were then completed, new batteries were constructed within four hundred yards of the citadel, and on the 3rd of February Fort Royal surrendered. Nine days more sufficed to reduce the rest of the Island, and by the 12th of February Monckton's work was done.[388]

| Feb. 26- |
| March 3. |
| June. |

He at once shipped off detachments to St. Lucia, Grenada, and St. Vincent, which islands fell without resistance, and had made his arrangements for the capture of Tobago also, when he received orders requiring the presence of his troops elsewhere. War had been declared against Spain; Lord Albemarle had been appointed to command an expedition against Havanna; and Amherst had been directed not only to embark four thousand men from America to join him, but to collect eight thousand more for an attack on Louisiana.[389] The stroke meditated by Pitt three months before was now about to fall. In February 1762 Albemarle's troops embarked; and on the 5th of March he sailed with four regiments only,[390] under convoy of Admiral Sir George Pocock, to pick up the remainder of his forces in the West Indies. On the 20th of April he arrived at Barbados, and on the 25th at Fort Royal, Martinique, where he took over from Monckton what he termed "the remains of a very fine army," much reduced by sickness, which brought his force to a strength of twelve thousand men of all ranks.[391] Thence continuing his voyage he came on the 6th of June into sight of Havanna. Twelve sail of the line were detached to the mouth of the harbour to block in the Spanish fleet, and on the following day the troops were landed safely a little to the northward of the city. On the 8th the army advanced westward, brushing away a force of militia that stood in its path, and on the same day arrived before the principal defences of Havanna.

July.

The entrance to the harbour of Havanna lies through a channel about two hundred yards wide, which was defended by two forts at its mouth, Fort Moro on the northern shore, and Fort Puntal opposite to it, the town also being situated on the southern shore. On the north side the ground rises rather abruptly from the harbour into a ridge known as the Cavannos, at the end of which stands Fort Moro, abutting on the open sea. A detached redoubt on these heights was carried without difficulty on the 11th of June, and, Fort Moro being found after reconnaissance to be surrounded with impenetrable brushwood, the construction of a battery was begun under cover of the trees. The work progressed slowly, for the soil was thin, while the Spanish ships in the harbour caused the besiegers no slight annoyance; so on the 13th a part of the British force was landed at Chorera, on the other side of the harbour. It was not until July that the British batteries could open a really effective fire, but by the 15th, with the help of the fleet, the enemy's guns were for the time silenced; and since trenches were impossible in ground so rocky, approaches to Fort Moro were made of gabions and cotton-bales. Still the work made little progress, for the climate had begun to tell on the troops, and little more than half of the men were fit for duty. Meanwhile the garrison of Fort Moro continued to defend itself with the greatest obstinacy, due in part to its confidence in the strength of the fort. The ditch at the point of attack was seventy feet deep from the edge of the counterscarp, except in one place, where a narrow ridge of rock made it possible to reach the wall of the fort without scaling-ladders. The only way to surmount such an obstacle was to sink a shaft and blow the counterscarp into the ditch, but powder was already running short; and Albemarle grew extremely anxious over the issue of his operations.

July 30.

At length on the 27th Colonel Burton arrived from America with three thousand men of the Forty-sixth, Fifty-eighth, Gorham's rangers and Provincial troops, having lost five hundred men captured by the French on the voyage. Three days later the mine under the counterscarp was sprung with success, and Fort Moro was carried by storm with trifling loss, the Spaniards offering but little resistance. New batteries were then pushed forward along the shore at the foot of the Cavannos in order to play on the town. On the 10th of August these opened fire and on the same evening silenced Fort Puntal. The Spaniards then proposed a capitulation; and Albemarle, in consideration of their defence, granted them the honours of war, being in truth devoutly thankful to obtain possession of Havanna on any terms. His army was melting away rapidly from disease; there was indeed one brigade of four battalions which could not muster twenty men fit for duty. Albemarle hastened to ship it back to America; but Amherst could spare no more troops to replace these, having already reduced his garrison to a strength of less than four thousand men.[392] Albemarle hoped that rest and better quarters might restore the health of the army after the work of the siege was done; but on the contrary sickness increased. The losses actually caused by the enemy's fire during the siege were rather less than a thousand men killed and wounded, yet by the 18th of October the British had buried over five thousand men dead from sickness alone.[393] Nor did the transfer of the troops from Cuba to America serve to abate the plague among them; for the hapless brigade first shipped off by Albemarle lost three hundred and sixty men within a month after its return. Yet at any rate Cuba was taken, and Cuba in those days was reckoned a prize little less rich than India.

June 27.
Sept. 18.

The virtual destruction of the army before Havanna put all ideas of an attack on Louisiana out of the question; and the French seized the opportunity offered by the removal of so many troops from Canada to send a small squadron and fifteen hundred troops against Newfoundland. The British garrison being only one hundred strong could offer no resistance, and the island was accordingly surrendered. Amherst, however, sent his brother with a sufficient force to recover it; and the French after a short defence capitulated as prisoners of war. As Amherst's losses did not exceed fifty men, and the captured French garrison numbered six hundred, the enemy gained little by this brief occupation of Newfoundland.

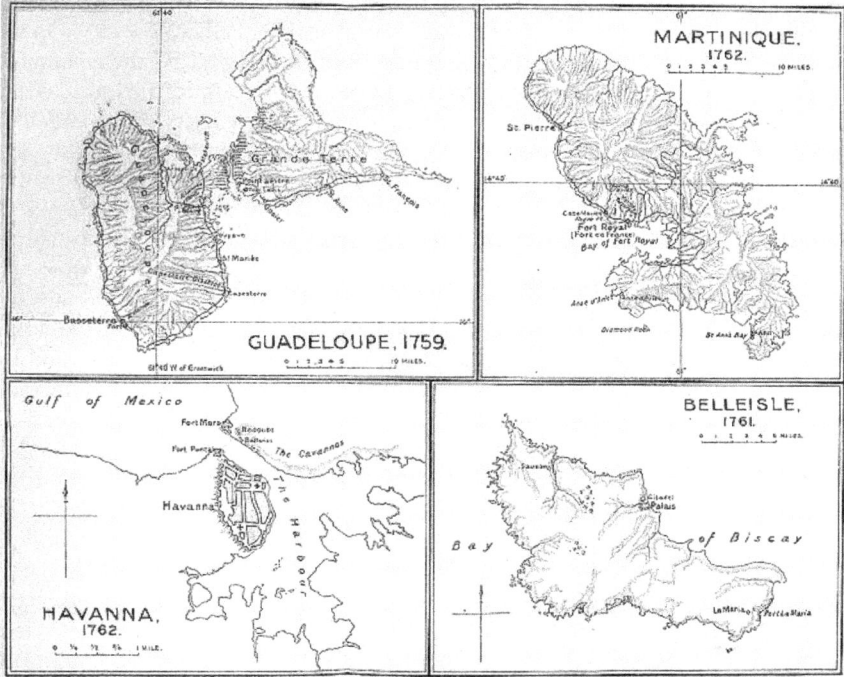

Walker & Boutall del.

To face page 544.

GUADELOUPE, 1759.
HAVANNA, 1762.

MARTINIQUE, 1762.
BELLEISLE, 1761.

| Aug. 1. |
| Sept. 24. |
| Sept. 25. |
| Oct. 4. |
| Oct. 5. |

But in India also there were troops lying idle since the fall of Pondicherry, which could be employed against Spain. In June Admiral Cornish received secret orders for an expedition, which he communicated to the authorities at Calcutta; and on the 1st of August the fleet sailed away to eastward with a force of one thousand Europeans, half of them of Draper's regiment, and two thousand Sepoys, under General Draper. On the 24th of September, after much delay owing to stormy weather and the extremely defective condition of Cornish's ships, the expedition entered the bay of Manila and anchored off Fort Cavita. Draper decided not to waste time in reducing the fort, so landed his troops unopposed on the following day through a heavy surf, about a mile and a half from the walls of the city. On the 26th he seized a detached fort which had been abandoned by the Spaniards within two hundred yards of the glacis, and began to construct a battery, while the ships sailed up to draw the fire of the town upon themselves. On the 30th a storeship arrived with entrenching tools, but was driven ashore on the very same evening by a gale, and there lay hard and fast. By singular good fortune, however, she had taken the ground at a point where she served exactly to screen the rear of Draper's camp from the Spanish cannon, while her stores were landed with greater speed and safety than would have been possible had she remained afloat; for the gale continued for several days and forbade the passage of boats through the surf. Four days later the battery and the ships opened a furious fire, which in four hours silenced the enemy's guns, and by the next day had made a practicable breach. That night the Spaniards made a sally upon the British position with a thousand Indians, who, despite their ferocity and daring, were driven back with heavy loss; and at dawn of the 6th Draper's regiment and a party of sailors attacked the breach and carried the fortifications with little difficulty. Thereupon Manila, with the island of Luzon and its dependencies, surrendered to the British, paying four million dollars for ransom of the town and of the property contained therein. Thus fell Manila within ten days of the arrival of the British; but the siege though short was attended by much difficulty and hardship. Regular approaches were impracticable owing to the incessant rain; while the surf made the landing of troops and stores a matter of extreme labour and peril. Had not the defences of the town been for the most part feeble and the spirit of the garrison feebler still, the capture of the Philippines would have been no such simple matter. The story of Manila is, however, interesting as a comment on Wentworth's proceedings at Carthagena, justifying to the full Vernon's predilection for a direct assault at the earliest possible moment in all operations against the Spaniard.

| Aug. 26. |

Yet another expedition brought the British face to face with their new enemy on more familiar ground than Luzon. The Spaniards, on the pretext of Portuguese friendship with England, in April invaded Portugal, overran the country as far as the Douro from the north, and threw another force against Almeida from the east. The injured kingdom appealed to England for help;

and in May orders were sent to Belleisle for the despatch of four regiments of infantry,[394] together with the detachment of the Sixteenth Light Dragoons, to Portugal. Two more regiments were added from Ireland,[395] bringing the total up to about seven thousand men; and simultaneously a number of British officers were sent to take up commands in the Portuguese army. Unfortunately there was some trouble over the selection of a commander; and though the two regiments from Ireland were actually in the Tagus by the first week in May, it was not until June that the rest of the troops arrived, with the Count of Lippe-Bückeburg, the famous artillerist, as Commander-in-Chief of the Allied forces, and Lord Loudoun in command of the British. The operations that followed were so trifling and of so short duration that they are unworthy of detailed mention. The Spaniards captured Almeida early in August; and Bückeburg was obliged to stand on the defensive and cover Lisbon at the line of the Tagus. Two brilliant little affairs, however, served to lift an officer, who so far was little known, into a prominence which was one day to be disastrous to himself and to England. This was Brigadier-General John Burgoyne, Colonel of the Sixteenth Light Dragoons, who with four hundred troopers of his regiment surprised the town of Valencia de Alcantara after a forced march of forty-five miles, annihilated a regiment of Spanish infantry and captured several prisoners. Not content with this, he a month later surprised the camp of another party of Spaniards at Villa Velha, on the south bank of the Tagus, dispersed it with considerable loss and captured six guns, at a cost of but one man killed and ten wounded. Such affairs, which in Ferdinand's army were so common as seldom to be noticed, made Burgoyne and the Sixteenth[396] the heroes of this short campaign; but though the regiment has lived the rest of its life according to this beginning, Burgoyne's career will end for us twenty years hence at Saratoga.

From these scattered enterprises against Spain I return to Ferdinand's last campaign against the old enemy in Germany. We left the contending parties in their winter-quarters, the French army of the Rhine cantoned along the river from Cleve to Cologne; the army of the Main extending from Altenkirchen, a little to north of Treves, north-eastward to Cassel and from Cassel south-eastward to Langensalza; and the Allies, facing almost due south, stretched from Münster to Halberstadt. The whole situation was, however, changed in various respects. The French had resolved to throw their principal strength into the army of the Main, which was accordingly raised to eighty thousand men under the command of Soubise and Marshal d'Estrées; Broglie having been recalled to France. The army of the Rhine was reduced proportionately to thirty thousand men under the Prince of Condé. The total numbers of the French, though less than in previous years, still remained far superior to Ferdinand's; but, on the other hand, owing to the change of ministry in

England and the reopening of negotiations by Bute, the Court of Versailles was content to hold the ground already gained without attempt at further conquest. Soubise and d'Estrées were therefore instructed to cling fast to Cassel and Göttingen, to spare the district between the Rhine and the Lahn with a view to winter-quarters, and to destroy the forage between the Eder and the Diemel so as to prevent Ferdinand from manœuvring on their flanks and rear.

Ferdinand on his side, though still outmatched by the armies opposed to him, was relatively stronger in numbers than in any previous year, having a nominal total of ninety-five thousand men ready for the field. Winter-quarters were little disturbed during the early months of 1762, the country having been so much devastated that neither side could move, from lack of forage, until the green corn was already grown high. Towards the end of May both armies began to concentrate; and Ferdinand, though much delayed by the negligence of the British Ministry in recruiting the British regiments to their right strength, determined to be first in the field.

| June 18. |
| June 22. |

Having detached a strong corps under the Hereditary Prince to watch the movements of Condé, he concentrated at Brakel, a little to the east of Paderborn, and advanced to the Diemel, where he posted the main army about Corbeke, with Granby's corps to westward of it at Warburg. Hearing at the same time that the French had left a corps under Prince Xavier on the east of the Weser to invade Hanover, he detached General Lückner with a small force across the river to keep an eye on him, sending also parties to seize the Castle of Zappaburg, some few miles to south-east, to secure communications with Lückner, and to occupy the passes leading from the south of the Diemel into Hesse. Meanwhile, on the 22nd of June, Soubise and d'Estrées moved northward from Cassel with the main body of the army as far as Gröbenstein, fixed their headquarters at Wilhelmsthal and halted. The design of this movement is unintelligible unless, as is conjectured by one writer,[397] they wished simply to amuse themselves at the castle of Wilhelmsthal; but in any case they neglected all necessary precautions. Their right flank rested on the large forest known as the Reinhardswald, and might have been rendered absolutely secure by the occupation of the Zappaburg, which commanded every road through that forest; yet they had suffered this important post to fall into Ferdinand's hands. Again, the occupation of the passes to the south of the Diemel would have secured their front; but here also they had allowed the Allies to be before them. None the less there they remained, careless of all consequences, at Wilhelmsthal; while to tempt an active enemy still farther, they stationed a corps under M. de Castries before their right front at

Carlsdorff, in absolute isolation from their main body. Ferdinand saw his opportunity, and though he could bring but fifty thousand men against their seventy thousand, resolved to strike at once.

June 23.

On the 23rd he recalled Lückner from across the Weser to Gottesbühren, a little to the north of the Zappaburg; and on hearing of his safe arrival at eight o'clock of the same evening, ordered the whole army to be under arms at midnight. For Lückner's corps was but one of the toils which he was preparing to draw around the unsuspecting French; and the places for the rest had already been chosen. Spörcke, with twelve battalions of Hanoverians and several squadrons, was to advance from the left of the main body, turn a little to the eastward upon Humme after crossing the Diemel, and, marching from thence southward, was to fall upon the right flank and rear of Castries' corps at Hombrechsen. Lückner, with six battalions and seven squadrons, was to march south-west from Gottesbühren through the Zappaburg to Udenhausen, and form up to the left of Spörcke on Castries' right rear. Colonel Riedesel was to push forward from the Zappaburg with a body of irregulars to Hohenkirch, on the south and left of Lückner. Meanwhile Ferdinand was to advance with the main body in five columns between Liebenau and Sielen, upon the front of the French principal army, while Granby should move south upon Zierenberg and fall upon its left flank. Supposing that every corps fulfilled its duty exactly in respect of time and place, there was good hope that the entire force of the French might be destroyed.

June 24.

Riedesel and Lückner were punctually in their appointed places at seven o'clock on the morning of the 24th. Spörcke's two columns, on emerging from the Reinhardswald at five o'clock, found only two vedettes before them on the heights of Hombrechsen, and ascended those heights unopposed. Then, however, not seeing Castries' corps, which, as it chanced, was hidden from them by a wood, they turned to their left instead of to their right, and advanced unconsciously towards the front of the French main army. The startled vedettes galloped back to give the alarm; and Castries hurriedly calling his men to arms prepared to retreat. Pushing forward his cavalry right and left to screen his movements from Spörcke and from Riedesel, Castries quickly set his infantry in order for march; and having contrived to hold Spörcke at bay for an hour, began his retreat upon Wilhelmsthal and Cassel. Lückner came up as he had been bidden at Udenhausen, but meeting part of Spörcke's corps on its march in the wrong direction was fired upon by it; and in the confusion Castries was able to make his escape. Riedesel being weak in numbers could not stop him, though he fell furiously with his hussars upon the rear-guard and cut one regiment of French infantry to pieces; but except for this loss Castries retired with little damage. Thus, as so often happens, failed the most important detail of Ferdinand's elaborate combinations.

Meanwhile the French main army, startled out of its sleep by the sound of the guns about Hombrechsen, was in absolute confusion. Fortunately for the Marshals, the unlucky mistake as to Lückner's corps which had saved Castries, saved them also, since it checked Spörcke's advance against their right. Breaking up their camp with amazing rapidity, they formed upon the heights and hastened their baggage away towards Cassel. Lückner, awake to the miscarriage of the turning movement on the French right, now begged Kielmansegge, who commanded the left column of Spörcke's corps, to hasten with him to Hohenkirchen, from whence a cross way to westward would enable them to bar every road between Wilhelmsthal and Cassel. But Kielmansegge persisted in attacking the right flank of the French main body, despite the fact that it was covered by a brook running through a swampy valley; and before he could effect his passage over this obstacle, the opportunity for cutting off the French retreat was lost.

Meanwhile the troops under Ferdinand in the centre advanced against the French front, though very slowly. Spörcke's right column formed up on their left, but being out of its right place hampered the advance of the rest and caused lamentable delay. The French main army, having cleared its baggage out of the way, was falling back in several columns towards Wilhelmsthal, when the appearance of Granby on their left showed them the full extent of their peril. The flower of the French infantry was then collected under M. de Stainville and thrown out on the left to cover the retreat of the main body at any cost; and now the action began in earnest. Taking up a strong position in a wood Stainville prepared to do his utmost. Granby's infantry consisted of three battalions of British Guards, the British grenadiers in three battalions, and the Fifth and Eighth Foot,—some of the finest troops in the British Army —but the fight was long and stubborn. Stainville appears at first to have taken the offensive and to have fallen upon the head of Granby's columns before the whole of his troops had come up, but to have been gradually forced back as more and more of the British battalions advanced into action. French and English came to close quarters, guns were taken and retaken, and for a time two British cannon remained in the hands of the French. Granby, however, seems to have got the upper hand at last, to have surrounded the wood on two sides and to have made his dispositions for surrounding it on all sides, when Ferdinand's troops at last came up on Stainville's rear and put an end to the conflict. The gallant Frenchman's corps was nearly annihilated; fifteen hundred men were killed and wounded, nearly three thousand surrendered to the Fifth Foot alone,[398] and two battalions only made good their escape. The

Allied army advanced a little to the south of Wilhelmsthal; and so the action came to an end.

The losses of the Allies were small, reaching but seven hundred men killed and wounded, of which four hundred and fifty belonged to Granby's corps. The result of the action was in fact a great disappointment, due partly to the mistakes of Spörcke and Kielmansegge, partly to the extreme slowness of Ferdinand's advance in the centre. The main body of the Allies indeed seems to have taken five hours to move from Gröbenstein to Wilhelmsthal, a distance of little more than four miles; and the fact would appear to indicate considerable clumsiness on the part of some officer or officers in the handling of their men. Still the fact remained that forty thousand men had attacked seventy thousand and driven them back in confusion; and the French were not a little shamefaced and discouraged over their defeat.

| July 1. |
| July 24. |
| Aug. 30. |

On the night of the action Soubise and d'Estrées fell back across the Fulda and took up a position between Cassel and Lutternberg. Ferdinand therefore ordered Granby's corps to a position near Cassel and sent forward a detachment to clear the enemy from the north bank of the Eder; whereupon the French evacuated Fritzlar and retiring across the Fulda took post upon its eastern bank. Both armies remained in this position until the 1st of July, Ferdinand trying always to force the French back, but obliged to act with caution, since Prince Xavier's Saxons had joined the French at Lutternberg and might at any time give trouble on the eastern side of the Weser. Finally on the 24th he boldly attacked the French right at Lutternberg and completely defeated it.[399] The French thereupon fell back to Melsungen on the Fulda, while Ferdinand took up a position opposite to them on the western bank of the river and threatened their communications with Frankfort. The Marshals then summoned Condé from the Rhine, but Ferdinand continued to press their communications so hard that at length they evacuated Göttingen and retreated by Hersfeld and Fulda to Vilbel, a little to the north of Frankfort; Ferdinand marching parallel with them on their western flank to the Nidda, in the hope, which was disappointed, of preventing their junction with Condé. So far he had done well, for he had for the present driven the French armies from Hesse.

| Sept. 7. |
| Sept. 15. |

Meanwhile Condé, obedient to orders, had marched towards Frankfort, joining Soubise a little to the south of Friedberg on the 30th of August. The Hereditary Prince, who had followed him closely all the way from the Rhine, attacked him on the same day, apparently in ignorance of the presence of Soubise's army, and was repulsed with considerable loss. For the next few days the two armies remained inactive, Ferdinand between the Nidder and Nidda with his headquarters at Staden, facing south-west, and the French opposite to him between Friedburg and Butzbach. Such a position, while forces were so unequal, could not continue long; and on the 7th of September the French moved northward by Giessen towards the Eder. Ferdinand, divining that their design was to cut him off from Cassel, which it was his own intention to besiege, at once hurried northward to stop them. It was a race between the two armies. The French travelled due north by Giessen and Marburg, crossing the Lahn above the latter town. Ferdinand made for Homberg on the north bank of the Ohm, and turning north-westward from thence marched on by Kirchhain and Wetter, where he overtook the French advanced guard. On the following day he offered battle; but Soubise declined, and, turning to the right about, repassed the Lahn and encamped along the line of the Ohm, with his left at Marburg and his right over against Homberg. Ferdinand thereupon took post in full sight of the enemy on the opposite bank of the river, with his left at Homberg and his right extended beyond Kirchhain. This was the position from which he had intended Imhoff to cover Hesse in 1760; and he had no intention now of allowing the French to break through it to Cassel, for he had made up his mind to recover Cassel for himself.

The valley of the Ohm south-eastward from Kirchhain is about eleven hundred yards broad, rising gradually on the east bank of the river to a height called the Galgenberg, and on the western bank to a steep basaltic hill known as the Amöneberg. The Ohm itself between these hills is from twenty to thirty feet wide and from five to seven feet deep, flowing between steep banks. Just to the south of the Amöneberg was a stone bridge by which stood a water-mill, consisting of a massive court with a group of houses. The steep sides of the Amöneberg frown close to it on the northern hand; but to westward the ground rises in a gentle slope, through which a hollow road, covered by an old redoubt, ran down to the mill. The town and castle of the Amöneberg itself was surrounded with a wall and towers strong enough, on the south and south-western sides, to defy all but heavy artillery. The bridge with the mill and the castle beyond it were for some reason neglected by the Allies. There had been some attempt to secure the bridge itself, and a redoubt had been begun on Ferdinand's side of the river for its defence; but the breastwork was not above three feet high and as many feet thick, so that it could be commanded by an enemy's fire, and the more easily since the western or French bank of the river was the higher. The court of the mill was occupied by but thirteen men; the old redoubt appears not to have been occupied at all; and the garrison of the castle of Amöneberg consisted of a single battalion of irregulars only. Yet the Amöneberg was an advanced post over against the enemy's left wing and on the enemy's side of the river; and the possession of the bridge was of vital importance to the Allies, not only to ensure communication with that advanced post, but to bar the advance of the French across the Ohm and to secure to Ferdinand the means of taking the offensive. The carelessness which allowed these points to remain so slenderly guarded is therefore almost inexplicable.

| Sept. 21. |

The French were not slow to take advantage of the opening thus afforded to them. On the night of the 20th they invested the castle of the Amöneberg so closely that not a man of the garrison could pass through their lines, and, driving the thirteen men from the mill, occupied the court as well as the old redoubt with light troops. This done they waited till morning, and at six o'clock, under cover of a dense mist, opened a heavy fire on the bridge and on the unfinished redoubt beyond it. The men in that redoubt, two hundred Hanoverians, resisted stoutly, in order to gain time for their supports to come up and for their artillery on the Galgenberg to answer the French batteries. The corps in occupation of the ground immediately before the Brückemühle (for so the mill was named) was Zastrow's of seven battalions, seven squadrons and six guns; while Wangenheim's corps of about the same strength lay on his left, and Granby's[400] on the heights of Kirchhain to his right. Ferdinand on hearing the sound of the firing hastened to the scene of action and found the redoubt still safe, the two hundred Hanoverians having held it stubbornly for two hours until relieved by Zastrow. But meanwhile the French brought forward more guns behind the veil of the mist; and presently thirty pieces of cannon were playing furiously upon the redoubt, while the infantry under cover of the fire renewed their attack on the bridge. Zastrow continued to feed the redoubt with fresh troops, and so held his ground; but the full significance of the attack was not realised until at ten o'clock the mist rolled away, when it was seen by the French dispositions that the enemy was bent upon carrying the bridge at any cost. Then at last Ferdinand ordered up Granby's corps from Kirchhain to Zastrow's assistance.

| Sept. 22. |

Meanwhile the fight waxed hotter. The superiority of the French in artillery made itself felt; nine out of twelve of Zastrow's guns were dismounted by noon, and the rest were silent for want of ammunition. At length at four o'clock the British Guards and the Highlanders arrived; and twelve German field-pieces attached to Granby's corps came also into action.

The French likewise brought up reinforcements and the combat became livelier than ever. So far the reliefs for the garrison in the redoubt had marched down in regular order, but the fire of the French artillery was now so terrible that the men were ordered to creep down singly and dispersed, as best they could. British Guards replaced Hanoverians, and Hessians replaced British Guards; regiment after regiment taking its turn to send men to certain destruction. So the fight wore on till the dusk lowered down and the flashes of the guns turned from yellow to orange and from orange to red. The Hessians piled up the corpses of the dead into a rampart and fired on, for the redoubt though untenable must be held at any cost. At seven o'clock the French by a desperate effort carried the passage of the bridge and fought their way close up to the redoubt, but they were met by the same dogged resistance and repulsed; and at eight o'clock, after fourteen hours of severe fighting, they abandoned the attack. Zastrow's and Granby's corps bivouacked about the bridge, and Ferdinand took up his quarters in the mill; but on the next day, none the less, the French after several unsuccessful assaults forced the garrison of Amöneberg to an honourable capitulation.

The loss of the Allies in this action was about seven hundred and fifty killed and wounded, more than a third of whom were British; the Scots Guards suffering more heavily than any corps of the troops engaged. The loss of the French rose to twelve hundred men, and the failure of their attack decided the fate of Hesse. Ferdinand, who on his advance southward had left behind a force to blockade Cassel, was able within three weeks to spare troops enough for a regular siege. On the 16th of October the trenches were opened, and on the 1st of November the town surrendered. A few days later came the news that preliminaries of a treaty had been signed. For despite all the successes of the year nothing could deter Bute from his resolution to make peace; and, indeed, knowledge of this fact had latterly made English commanders negligent and British troops backward in the field.[401] So with the fall of Cassel the war came to an end.

The terms, including as they did the cession by the French of India, except Pondicherry and Chandernagore, of French America, Canada, Tobago, Dominica and St. Vincent, might not seem unfavourable to England. But it was reasonably thought at the time that Goree and Martinique should have been added, though Bute was in such haste to bring the war to an end that it was only as an afterthought that he exacted the cession of Florida by Spain in exchange for Havanna. But the true blot on the treaty was the desertion of Frederick the Great and the conclusion of a separate peace, an exhibition of selfishness and folly which recalled the Peace of Utrecht. Nevertheless Frederick was able to insist on the conditions from which he had from the first resolved not to recede, namely the retention of all that he had taken from Austria in Silesia. In February 1763 the peace was finally concluded, and Frederick entered Berlin with Ferdinand of Brunswick, who had through five campaigns guarded his right flank, appropriately seated at his right side.

The story of the war in Germany should not be closed without some few words as to Ferdinand, who, little though we know of him, was the greatest commander that led British troops to victory in Europe between Marlborough and Wellington. It was no small feat to have fought through five campaigns successfully, always with one army against two, and with at most four men against five. It is true that the conception of his most skilful movements may often be traced to Westphalen, the chief of his staff; but it is not every commander who knows when to take advice and how to act on it, or is so sure of the confidence of his troops that he can trust them always to make the best of it. Moreover, he was confronted, though in a smaller degree, with many of the difficulties that afflicted Marlborough. His army was not an army of Allies, though generally so styled, but a mercenary army of German troops in the pay of England. So far he had the advantage of the great Duke; but his force was compounded of several different elements, British, Hanoverians, Hessians, Brunswickers and Bückeburgers, who were divided by not a little jealousy as to their respective precedence, privileges, and superiority. Of all of these the British gave him the most trouble. Their insular contempt for all foreigners was heightened by the knowledge that their comrades were mercenaries paid by their own nation; and they claimed the best quarters, the post of danger and the post of honour on all occasions. In one respect perhaps they did show superiority to the rest of the army, namely when actually on the field of battle; for beyond all doubt theirs is the chief credit for the success at Minden, at Warburg, at Emsdorff, at Wilhelmsthal, and in a lesser degree at Vellinghausen. In every action indeed they did well, and at Minden and Emsdorff they accomplished what probably no other troops in the army would have attempted. But there were scores of minor actions fought during these campaigns by German troops only, which could be matched against any other of their achievements; and there were grave defects which marred not a little the general efficiency of the British. In the first place there was a large number of British officers of all ranks from the general to the ensign who, though brave enough, knew nothing of their duty. In the second, as Turenne had noticed a century earlier in Flanders, they were extremely negligent in the matter of outposts, patrols, and guards, owing partly to inexperience, partly to their more luxurious life at home, and partly to the contempt of danger and the spirit of gambling which is so strong in the race. Frequently Ferdinand, though quite alive to the valour of British troops in action, dared not trust them as advanced parties; whereupon the red-coats themselves, quite confident of their own sufficiency, grumbled because the foremost place was not given to them. Such jealousies as these gave endless trouble; and the disposition of the various corps, particularly of Granby's division of the Guards and Blues, required careful study as a matter not of military exigency but of policy and tact, lest the various nationalities in the army should fall at variance and take to fighting among themselves. Lastly, the British soldiers, taken as a whole, were men of inferior character to the Germans and of less experience in war; and by loose behaviour in quarters and on the march they set a bad example, which came ill from the men that looked down on all the rest of the army.

Such were the troubles which hampered Ferdinand and his staff at every turn; yet under his guidance the machine worked always with the least possible friction and the greatest development of power. He was in fact not only a great soldier but a great governor and leader of men. He combined patience, tact, and self-control with a genial and hearty courtesy, he had the faculty of selecting good men for his instruments, and above all he worked without fear or favour in noble singleness of purpose for the common cause.

Of his merits as a General his campaigns speak sufficiently; and it is only necessary to add that their history was thought worthy of official study and compilation fifty years ago by the Prussian General Staff. British troops may feel proud to have so served under so able a soldier and so great and gallant a man in the campaigns which they fought in Germany for the conquest of their own empire.

AUTHORITIES.—For the expedition to Belleisle there is little beyond the official papers in the Record Office, *W.O., Orig. Corres.*, vol. xxi., and the accounts to be found in such histories as Entick's. The like is true of the operations in Portugal, except that few original papers are to be found in the Record Office. As to Martinique there is again little besides the Official Papers, C. O., *America and West Indies*, vol. cii., with the letter in the Bouquet Papers already quoted. For Havanna there is a printed account of the siege, and the original papers in *C. O., America and West Indies, Havanna*. For Manila, see *Admiral's despatches, East Indies*, and the account in Entick. The *Annual Register* is also a source of information in default of better in all the above expeditions.

For Ferdinand's campaigns, the most readable account is that of Mauvillon, being written in German of rare clearness and simplicity. There are also the histories of Tempelhof and Archenholtz, *La Vie Militaire de Ferdinand*, *Mémoires de Bourcet*, and Westphalen's *Feldzüge Herzogs Ferdinand*, in which last is printed every document that came to Ferdinand's headquarters, besides a great many more, with quotations from all other writers on the subject—an exhaustive work of six huge volumes, without an index. Ferdinand's original letters, with some from Granby and other officers, will be found in the Record Office, *F. O. Mil. Auxiliary Expeditions*, vols. xxviii.-xxxi., xxxiii., xxxiv., xxxvii.-xliv., xlix., l. The letters in the Belvoir Papers, *Hist. Manuscript Commission*, are disappointing.

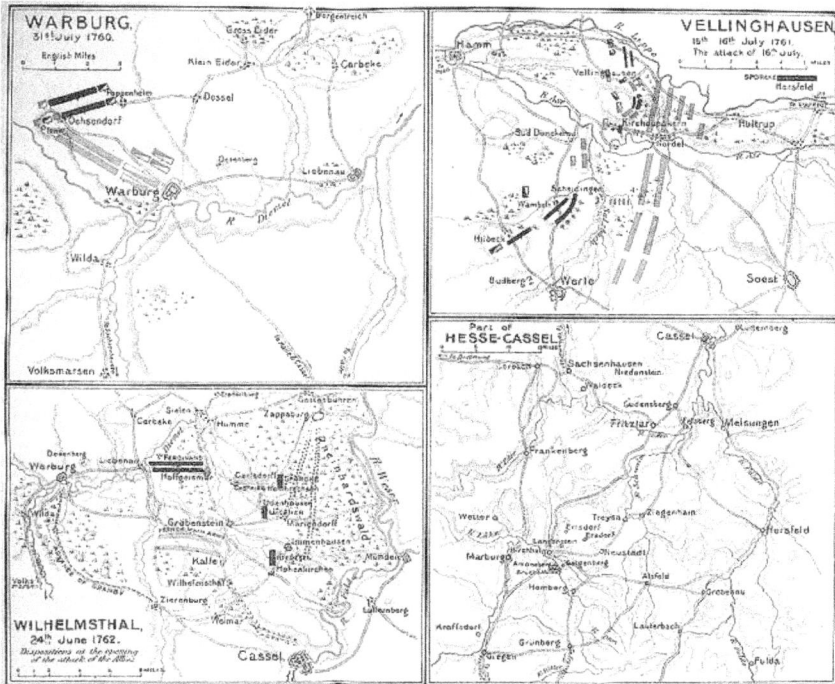

Walker & Boutall, del.

To face page 560.

WARBURG, 31st July 1760.
WILHELMSTHAL, 24th June 1762.
Dispositions at the opening
of the attack of the Allies.

VELLINGHAUSEN,
15th 16th July 1761.
The attack of 16th July.
Part of HESSE-CASSEL

400

CHAPTER XII

I have followed with little interruption the long tale of hostilities which opened with the declaration of war with Spain and closed with the Peace of Fontainebleau; for despite the brief truce made by the Peace of Aix-la-Chapelle, the armies of England and France were eternally in collision either in the far east or the far west, so that to all intent the struggle resolved itself into one long war. Little though she knew it, England, when she entered wantonly and with a light heart upon the attack on the Spanish Main, had really set herself to wrestle with the French for the empire of the world. For nearly seventeen years she waited for the man who would carry her victorious through the contest; and at last he appeared. The instant change which came over the spirit of the nation when he assumed command has already been shown in the narrative of the operations. It remains only to study more closely the conduct of the war in the departments at home, and to trace the progress, not only in the organisation and training of the various branches of the Army, but also in the general administration.

The war with Spain opened, as will be remembered, while the nation had not yet ceased to rail at the iniquity of a standing Army, when the ascendency of the civilian element at the War Office was overpowering, and when the attitude of the ordinary citizen towards the soldier was unfriendly even to aggression. These evils, as may be guessed, did not pass away at once, even though the obnoxious red-coats were embarked or embarking for foreign service. In 1741 there was a general refusal of innkeepers to supply soldiers with food and forage, owing to the dearth caused by a winter of extraordinary severity. Such refusal was not unreasonable; and it was proposed to meet the difficulty by a new clause in the Mutiny Act. It will hardly be believed that one member of the House of Commons made this suggestion a pretext for urging that the Mutiny Act should be dispensed with altogether, his argument being that if the system of billets should break down it would be necessary to build barracks, which would result in the subjection of the country to military government.[402] Two years later again[403] advantage was taken of an address to the King respecting his hired Hessian troops, to insert words, designed evidently for purposes of insult only, referring to, the burthensome and useless army at home. Nor did such amenities end even after the warning of 1745, for the Peace of Aix-la-Chapelle, which left the air still electric with

401

war, was no sooner signed than the old foolish arguments against a standing Army reappeared in the House of Lords, propped by such stable epigrams as "To a free state an army is like drams to a constitution." Yet the full measure of the intoxicant which was distilled for the ruin of the nation was a niggardly draught of nineteen thousand men. These childish outbursts continued until 1754, when they ceased, at any rate until the close of the war, having served their mischievous purpose in keeping alive old animosities which common patriotism and common sense would have buried without ceremony. The ill-will of publicans and of municipalities continued likewise unabated for a few years,[404] but rapidly dwindled away before more generous feelings; and unreasonable complaints from this quarter almost disappear from the correspondence of the War Office after Dettingen.

The War Office itself was slower to mend its ways. The Secretary-at-War was quite equal to such petty jobbery as procuring the promotion of sergeants and corporals; but for all other purposes the Office showed itself at first to be utterly and hopelessly inefficient. Glimpses of maladministration have already been seen in the account of the expedition to Carthagena; but the blindness and ignorance of the officials became still more patent when Lord Stair's force was despatched to the Netherlands. The Office had not been at the pains to keep even its records in order. Not a soul seems to have known what were the rules as to allowances for forage, baggage, and the like, for troops embarking on active service; and the officials were obliged to apply to old officers who had served with Marlborough to gather precedents on such purely departmental matters as these.[405] From such beginnings it is not difficult to judge of that which must have come after.

The Office of Ordnance also was at the outset as badly disorganised as the War Office. Its shortcomings have already been shown in the matter of the train sent out to Carthagena; but even a year after the departure of Cathcart it seems to have made no improvement. Transports destined for the West Indies in 1741 were obliged to put in at Cork because the water shipped at Spithead was undrinkable, and the provisions supplied for the men unfit to eat.[406] Stair, again, was despatched to the Netherlands without artillery or engineers, a deficiency which brought his force into immense contempt with the French; and when he asked for siege-guns he found that all England could afford him was but twenty twenty-four pounders.[407] Small arms again were so scarce that, when the king rearmed the infantry, it was necessary to purchase ten thousand muskets and bayonets abroad.[408] In Scotland again the inquiries of Hawley and Handasyde revealed not less flagrant neglect.[409] But this was by no means all. The general condition of the national defences both at home and abroad was most alarming; and the result was that at the opening of 1743 there was a regular panic among all the seaports, great and small, on the coast of England. Frantic applications poured into the Office of Ordnance for guns, carriages, and ammunition. It seems to have been the custom for the minor ports to erect batteries at their own expense, and to apply to the Government for their armament; so that the blame for these shortcomings must rest in part upon local authorities. But there is no such excuse for carelessness in respect of regular strongholds, such as Pendennis Castle, where forty-six guns were found to be in charge of a master-gunner ninety years of age, aided by a single assistant. It was not until 1756, when ministers should have been looking after Minorca, that the Government suddenly took the alarm and threw up lines of defence at Chatham, Portsea, and Plymouth Dock.[410]

Colonial stations, for which the British Government was responsible, were in little better order. Newfoundland was in a deplorable condition,[411] and Gibraltar even worse; nor could all the representations of officers procure attention for them. As late as in May 1757, even after the actual fall of Minorca, Governor Lord Tyrawley wrote furiously of the state of affairs at the Rock. There had been total stagnation for many years; letters had not been answered; requests often repeated had remained unheeded. The guns mounted on the fortress were too short, the spare carriages were too few, the palisades better fitted for hen-coops than for fortifications; in fact the defences were reduced to dangerous weakness by years of systematic neglect.[412] At St. Kitts, again, the Thirty-eighth Foot, which for years had formed the standing garrison, was in a miserable condition; not forty per cent of the men were fit for service; their clothing was in rags; they had neither hats nor shoes nor cartridge-boxes nor swords.[413] Nor were the self-governing colonies more careful than the mother country. Wealthy West Indian Islands, notwithstanding the incessant warnings of their governors, found themselves at the outbreak of the war in dangerous want of arms and ammunition; and there was a rush of all the colonies both in the West Indies and in America for guns and stores, which ought to have been ready in their own magazines.[414] British carelessness, aggravated by the evil example of factious politicians in the mother country, and by the spectacle of such a creature as Newcastle in high place, had well-nigh stripped the empire of its defences.

As to the Army itself, enough has been said in the account of the operations to show how unstable, despite the abundance of individual heroism, were the foundations upon which it rested. The interference of civilian administrators and of irresponsible politicians with military discipline had wrought mischief untold. Officers could not be brought to do duty with their regiments. Stair found the difficulty insuperable; so also did Hawley; so even did Cumberland in Scotland; while in the garrison of Minorca the evil transcended all bounds. Thus both the *personnel* and *matériel* of the Army were nearly ruined, the former by persistent jobbery and meddling on the part of civil officials, the latter by the equally persistent carping of factious critics in the House of Commons, which forbade the presentation of estimates for necessary works. The military system was in fact a chaos; and it was only by the strenuous efforts of two men, who strangely enough abominated each other, that this chaos was reduced to order.

The first of these two was Cumberland. Though in many respects a martinet of a narrow type, and no great commander in the field, Cumberland was an able man, a strong man, and an administrator. He it was who first took the Army seriously in hand and set himself to reduce it to discipline. He began during his first campaign by teaching the officers that they must obey. Hitherto it seems that they had taken the field as if they were going to a picnic, after the fashion of the French, travelling comfortably if not luxuriously, and neglecting all duties except that of displaying gallantry in action. Cumberland quickly put a stop to this. The number of wheeled carriages, even for general officers, was strictly limited, and two only, one for the colonel and one for the sutler, were allowed in each regiment; while in order to reduce baggage still further, it was ordered that no officer under the rank of brigadier-general should appear either in camp or in quarters, on or off duty, except in his regimental coat, old or new.[415] Such orders may appear ludicrous at the present day, but they point to a tightening of the reins of discipline that was very sorely needed. Cumberland, too, was impatient of useless officers. He disliked the system of purchase[416] and chafed at the retention of old colonels, some so unfit for duty as to be confined in a mad-house, whose permanent presence on the active list prevented the advancement of deserving officers.[417] His own selections were not always fortunate, as witness Hawley and Braddock, but he was fully alive to the merit of such men as Ligonier, Wolfe, and Conway, to whom, though not of his school, he gladly gave promotion.

But it is after the close of the first war, when the Duke had returned to be Commander-in-Chief in time of peace, that his work is seen to greatest advantage. The whole tone of the War Office is changed. The Secretary-at-War almost reverts to his old position of clerk to the Commander-in-Chief. Military authority is predominant in military matters, and "Secretary-at-War's leave of absence" becomes a thing of the past. The functionary, who not many years before was ready to perpetrate a job for any officer with vote or interest, suddenly develops virtuous scruples and objects to the once familiar phrase, as he never grants leave without the King's signature.[418] But it is less by isolated examples, such as this, than by a general alteration in the methods of transacting business, that the Duke's hand may be traced. There is no longer the indiscriminate correspondence with every rank of officer; but due regard is paid to the rights of superior officers as channels of communication and discipline, and to the authority of the Commander-in-Chief as the supreme motive power. In fact, a work of great and beneficial reform is seen to accomplish itself imperceptibly through the will and influence of a single strong man; and Cumberland's services herein have never received the recognition that they deserve. The Duke, indeed, with all his foibles and prejudices was no ordinary man; and it is no surprise to one who has followed his administrative work to find that Horace Walpole ranked him with his father, Sir Robert Walpole, with Granville, Mansfield, and Pitt as one of the five great men that he had known. It is no disparagement of other members of the Royal Family to say that he was the ablest man which it has produced during the two centuries of its reign in England.

The other man who raised the tone of the Army beyond estimation was of course Pitt. His share in the work, however, was very different in its nature from Cumberland's; though, without the preliminary reforms of Cumberland, his influence could hardly have been so successful as it was. Pitt's instincts respecting military administration, as distinct from the statesman's choice of a theatre of war, were thoroughly sound. He was for allowing officers to do their work, and for backing them loyally as they did it. Thus when in 1750 George Townsend, afterwards Wolfe's brigadier, proposed a clause in the Mutiny Bill to prevent non-commissioned officers or privates from being punished except by sentence of court-martial, Pitt crushed him with words which deserve to be remembered. "We," he said, "have no business with the conduct of the Army, nor with their complaints one against another. If we give ear to any such complaint we shall either destroy all discipline, or the House will be despised of officers and detested of soldiers." Cumberland himself would have asked for no severer criticism than this; and yet Pitt, though perhaps unconsciously, was probably more obnoxious in his military even than in his political views to Cumberland. The Duke, as has been repeatedly illustrated, was a soldier of the rigidest German type. "He was as angry," to use Walpole's happy phrase, "at an officer's infringing the minutest precept of the military rubric as at his deserting his post, and was as intent on establishing the form of spatterdashes and cockades as on taking a town or securing an advantageous situation." In other words, he lacked that sense of proportion in matters of discipline which distinguishes the disciplinarian from the martinet. Now, despite the influence of Cumberland, there was growing up in the Army a school of officers quite as strict as he was in needful matters of discipline, but less rigid, less narrow, and more humane—officers who looked upon their men not as marionettes to be dressed and undressed, used up and thrown away, but as human flesh and blood, with good feelings that could be played on, good understandings that could be instructed, self-respect that needed only to be cultivated, and high instincts that waited only to be evoked. Such an officer, as his regimental orders can prove, was Wolfe, who contrived to turn even the work of road-making in Scotland to excellent disciplinary account; and indeed I am disposed to think that this same road-making, first begun under the direction of the mild and gentle Wade, had much to do with the foundation of the new school. The officers were brought very much more into contact with their men off parade, being obliged to supervise them while at work and to enjoin on them conciliatory bearing and behaviour towards the inhabitants; and the men, on their side, were happy and well-conducted, for they were kept constantly employed and received a welcome addition to their pay. It must be remembered that the gulf fixed between officer and man at that time was much wider than at present. Nowadays it is nothing for the subalterns of the smartest regiment of cavalry to pull off their coats and work with their men at the unshipping of horses from a transport; then it was almost painful to men to see their officers lay their hand to any but officer's work. A sergeant of Murray's garrison at Quebec describes the labours of his officers when hauling up the guns almost with tears. Such things were not seemly for gentlemen to do. But beyond all doubt the new school introduced a healthier feeling between officers and men, having the courage to utter its sentiments in print. "Never beat your men," says an officer's manual of the year 1760; "it is unmanly. I have too often seen a brave, honest old soldier banged and battered at the caprice of an arrogant officer." And then follows a protest against picketting, tying neck and heels, the wooden horse and other punishments of torture, which were never inflicted by court-martial, but by the authority of officers only.[419] Such teaching was not in accordance with the system of Cumberland as expounded by himself or by his favourites Braddock and Hawley.

Yet it was to officers of this new school that Pitt, when he could have his way, preferred to entrust his work, partly perhaps on account of their youth and vigour, but more probably owing to their freedom from the fetters of pipeclay. Amherst, though he maintained an excellent tone among his troops, was hardly a perfect representative of the school, but Howe and Wolfe were pre-eminently of it, as were likewise such of Wolfe's pupils as Monckton and Murray. India seems spontaneously to have produced men who commanded in virtue of personal ascendency, though the only training of Lawrence, Forde, and Coote had been that of regimental officers. Still these men, though appointed by sheer force of circumstances and by no nomination of Pitt's, served to confirm the correctness of his judgment.

By giving scope to this new stamp of officer Pitt rendered the Army signal service, apart from the spirit which he infused into it, as into every body of Englishmen, of energy and adventure. He was too good a master for men to be willing to return to him, unless they had fulfilled their mission or exhausted every effort to fulfil it. It is possible even that the raids on the French coast, which are a blot on his fame as a minister of war, might have been more successful (though they could never have been profitable) could he have appointed commanders of his own choice. But in truth the work of Pitt as a designer of campaigns and operations of war was by no means flawless. He had skill in thinking out how a body of men could be passed rapidly on from enterprise to enterprise, as from Guadeloupe to Canada, from Canada back to Martinique, from Martinique to Havanna, and from Havanna, as he hoped, to Louisiana. But he never made sufficient allowance for the waste of men in the process, nor, apparently, for the loss of life entailed by maintaining large garrisons in tropical territory. In some respects, too, the military administration was little better in his day than in Newcastle's. Notwithstanding the warning given by the terrible losses of the troops during the occupation of Louisburg, no proper care was taken to provide them with special clothing in subsequent winters in Canada; while the arrangements for the hospitals in Germany were so deficient that few of the invalids of the campaign of 1760 ever rejoined their regiments.[420] Hodgson, again, before starting for Belleisle, complained bitterly of his want of officers and of the inadequacy of the preparations made by the Office of Ordnance. These abuses were, it is true, due to the shortcomings of departments only, and therefore must not be charged against a minister who bore the burden, not only of the direction of the war, but of foreign affairs also on his shoulders; but it is, I think, a reproach to Pitt's military administration that he did not appreciate the importance of husbanding the lives of his troops. The British soldier, to put the matter in its least sentimental and most brutally practical light, has always been a most expensive article; no prodigality can be more ruinous than the careless squandering of his life, no economy so false as the grudging of his comfort. But this failing in Pitt, serious though it be, is far outweighed by the profound policy which converted the militia into an efficient force for defence against invasion, thus liberating the regular army for purposes of conquest; and by the military insight which kept King Frederick subsidised, and Prince Ferdinand's army afoot as auxiliary to Frederick, thus turning the whole war in Europe into a diversion in England's favour. Nor was this policy wholly selfish, for loudly though the Prussians still complain of the withdrawal of Pitt's subsidies by Bute, Pitt remained in office long enough to tide Frederick over the deadliest of his peril, and so to establish the corner-stone of the present German Empire. Yet even these achievements pale before the mighty genius and the lofty enthusiasm which called the English-speaking people to arms on both sides the Atlantic to wrest from France the possession of the world. The minister of war is swallowed up in the statesman of the Empire.

The next subject of inquiry is the manner of raising that Army, large beyond precedent in English history, which was accumulated by the end of the war. It will be remembered that the regiments of cavalry rose to thirty-two, and that in the infantry of the Line the numbered regiments were one hundred and twenty-four, besides two corps of Highlanders (which for some reason were known by titles of a different kind) and the brigade of Guards, making altogether a total little short of one hundred and fifty battalions. To provide recruits for such a force on the ordinary terms was impossible; and the struggle with France had hardly begun before recourse was made to the system of short service. In the session of 1743-44 was passed the first of a series of Recruiting Acts on the model of those which had been passed under Queen Anne. The bounty offered to volunteers was four pounds, while parish-officers were empowered to impress unemployed men, for each of which they received a reward of one pound and the parish of three pounds. The standard for recruits was fixed at five feet five inches; and it was enacted that every volunteer or enlisted man should be entitled to his discharge at the end of three years. In the following session the Act was somewhat altered. The bounty to volunteers was abolished; the gift to the parish was reduced to two pounds; the standard was lowered by one inch, and the term of service was extended to five years. But as yet of course the real drain on the supply of Englishmen was not begun.

After the treaty of Aix-la-Chapelle an effort was made in the House of Commons to establish the principle of short service in time of peace. In February 1750 Mr. Thomas Pitt, a kinsman of the Great Commoner, brought forward a bill to enact that soldiers should henceforward be enlisted for ten years, and that the price of discharge should be fixed at three pounds. The scheme was opposed on the ground that men would always claim discharge after receiving their new clothing, and so defraud the colonel; that the country would be filled with idle vagabonds; and that the Pretender's adherents would take advantage of the measure to obtain military training, which would later be turned against England herself. One speaker, who supported the bill, thought ten years too long a term; and Colonel Henry Conway, an officer of much promise, while approving the principle contended that the bill as it stood would be useless, since no man would enlist for service in Ireland or the Colonies without a bounty, nor accept smaller bounty than the cost of his discharge. More than one member who took part in the debate deplored the system of enlisting men for life, which by depriving them of hope made them idle and disorderly; but all agreed that the limitation of the term of service must inevitably lead to increased expense, since it would entail the need of a larger number of recruits. The expense of recruiting fell at that time of course on the officers, pay being allowed for a few fictitious men on the muster-rolls, and the proceeds turned into a recruiting fund. While this practice lasted, it was futile to speak of enlisting more recruits, for the officers simply could not afford it. It was useless to urge, as Conway and Oglethorpe did, that the expense of recruiting at ordinary times should be borne not by the regiment but by the public; for this would have meant an augmentation in the military estimates which was not to be thought of for a moment. So after a useful debate the bill was defeated by one hundred and fifty-four to ninety-two.[421]

On the renewal of the war a Recruiting Act identical with that of 1744-45 was passed; but in the following year (1756-57) a bounty of three pounds was again offered to volunteers, who were also allowed to take service for three years only. With this latter Act the measures sanctioned by Parliament came to an end, and though this particular enactment was passed, as usual, for one year only, I conceive that it must have been renewed annually to the close of the war.[422] There were of course the usual abuses in the enforcement of these Acts, abuses which rose to a grave height towards the end of the war. The country was so much exhausted in 1762 that the standard was reduced to five feet two inches,[423] by which time men made a regular living by hanging about the recruiting officers, ready to accompany them before a justice and to swear that some hapless creature had taken the King's bounty.[424] Practically there was impressment for the army as for the navy; and indeed as early as in 1744 the newspapers speak openly of a general press made in Southwark for the Army and marines, with the satisfactory result of a haul of two hundred men.[425] Nor was impressment without its usual romantic consequences. On one of the ships of Admiral Boscawen's squadron in 1748 was a marine named James Gray, who was duly landed with the rest for the siege of Pondicherry. In the course of the siege Gray had the misfortune to be wounded, apparently by splinters, receiving six wounds in one leg, five in the other and a bullet in the groin. This last hurt the injured marine did not submit to the doctors, contriving to extract the bullet without assistance, and so to make a good recovery. In due time Gray returned to England; and then there came a petition to the Duke of Cumberland setting forth that James Gray was in a reality a woman named Hannah Snell. Her sweetheart had been impressed, so she had enlisted and followed him to India, braving all the misery of the voyage and the hardships of the siege to be with him; but all had been to no purpose, for the sweetheart had died, leaving her alone, maimed, friendless and penniless. It is satisfactory to learn that Cumberland at once obtained for her a pension of thirty pounds a year from the King's own bounty.[426]

It should be remembered, meanwhile, that since the Highlands had been thrown open, the old recruiting grounds had been considerably enlarged, and that the prospect of bearing arms had attracted great numbers of Highlanders to the ranks. Exclusive of the Forty-second there were at least a dozen Highland battalions on the list in 1762. Irish Catholics again were admitted to the Army, at any rate in America, and distinguished themselves particularly in the Twenty-eighth Regiment at Quebec, where Wolfe himself charged at their head.[427] But to what other shifts the Government may have resorted I have unfortunately been unable to discover. It is more than probable that several corps were formed under peculiar conditions of service. At least one whole regiment of Highlanders, the Duke of Sutherland's, was raised explicitly for three years only or till the close of the war;[428] and the same principle was doubtless extended to other cases. Private enterprise also came to the help of the country. Very early in the war a society was formed in London to promote the enlistment of marines; and after Minden the Common Council of London opened subscriptions to encourage recruiting, and promised to admit men so enlisted to trade within the city forthwith, if discharged with a good character on the close of the war.[429] Then again there were regiments like Hale's and Granby's Light Dragoons which were raised by patriotic officers without cost to the country; and it is probable that these were not solitary examples. Similar advantages of economy seem to have dictated the creation in 1760 and the following years of innumerable independent companies, which after a few months of isolated existence were sorted together into regiments. The history of this system is exceedingly obscure, but it appears to have amounted practically to the offer of a commission to every man who could or would raise a hundred recruits. It was adopted amid considerable difference of opinion, and was not a success, the men so enlisted being generally unfit to carry a musket.[430] Speaking broadly, it may be asserted that during this war the ranks were filled by compulsion far more than by attraction, and by compulsion so ruthless that recruits would resort to self-mutilation to escape service.

An interesting experiment in the inner organisation of the recruiting service was instituted by advice of Lord Stair, namely the formation of two extra companies of infantry and one extra troop of cavalry for all regiments on active service. The object was to maintain a depot at home to refill all vacancies in the ranks abroad, and so to obviate the necessity of sending back recruiting officers from abroad to England. The plan did not at first commend itself to the King, and Stair was obliged to urge it repeatedly before he could obtain for it a trial; but the suggestion seems to have been approved by Cumberland, and to have been put into practice for a time, though the additional companies were presently amalgamated into distinct regiments.[431] Therewith the whole system of the feeding of regiments abroad fell back on the old plan of drafting; and during the Seven Years' War regiments at home, particularly the dragoons,[432] were raised to a considerable strength to serve simply as recruiting depots for regiments abroad. From a regimental standpoint the story of the war is one of drafting, drafting, drafting, with of course all the vices that had been condemned by Marlborough attendant on the practice. The garrisons of captured places suffered terribly from this evil, particularly in the West Indies, where service was still abominated by the men. There was no such reluctance to go to the East Indies, where there was some prospect of spoil; and men and officers gladly took advantage of the opportunity afforded to them not only to go to India, but to stay there in the Company's service after their regiments had been recalled.[433] But the West Indies were held in horror and loathing. It became more and more the practice to pardon deserters and bad characters on their accepting service in that unpopular quarter, though even so there were men who preferred to take a thousand lashes.[434] As the operations in the West Indies grew wider of extent, resort was made as usual to drafting; whereupon the colonels, to whom it fell to supply the drafts, of course seized the opportunity to rid themselves of their worst men, heedless of the unhappy corps to which they consigned them.[435] The government of a captured island in the Antilles on such terms was no very enviable post.

But the British Isles were by no means the only recruiting ground of the Army during this long struggle. Braddock as early as in 1755 was ordered to fill up his regiments with recruits from America; and the system, as has already been seen, was carried farther and farther as the war progressed. There were at first considerable difficulties, which the British Government attempted to meet by proclaiming that two hundred acres of land should be granted free of rent for ten years to all recruits, after the close of the war.[436] It should seem, however, that this temptation was of small effect, for the Americans enjoyed all the British prejudice against a red-coat, and at first drew little distinction between a soldier and a negro. The Sixtieth in particular found great obstruction to recruiting in Pennsylvania; the lawyers, justices, and people at large being violently opposed to enlistment[437] even for short terms of three or four years. Violent controversies raged over the recruiting of indented servants, the "white servants" or white slaves to which I have already referred; their owners pleading not without reason that, having paid for the passage of these men, they were entitled to consider them as their own property, or, to use their own phrase, as "bought servants." This difficulty was settled by providing for compensation to the owners for loss of such men; but even so the most serious obstacles remained unremoved. In New Jersey, for instance, the justices would persuade recruits not to be attested, or would grant warrants against them for fictitious debts and throw them into gaol until the regiment that sought them had marched away. Finally in 1760 Amherst wrote that, though his battalions were seven thousand men below the proper strength, he could obtain no recruits owing to the vast bounty offered by the provincial authorities to their own troops. These facts should not be forgotten in view of the far greater contest between mother country and colonies which lies close ahead of us. The colonists boasted constantly, and not without just cause, of the sacrifices which they had made throughout the war; but they overlooked the incessant difficulties which they threw in the way of the King's commanders.[438]

Intimately connected with the subject of recruiting is the general condition of the private soldier. There was little or no alteration in his pay or allowances during the period under review; and such changes as there were tended if anything rather to his disadvantage. It appears that the War Office had not yet learned that the rigid rules applicable to service at home were impossible of enforcement abroad, and either through blindness or ignorance insisted that all additional burdens, imposed by differences of climate and remoteness from civilisation, must be borne by the soldier. The mutiny roused at Louisburg by excessive stoppages from the pay of the men has already been related; but so dangerous a warning even as this produced no result, for the grievance remained unredressed and led to a second mutiny of the troops in Canada in 1763.[439] The meanness of the Government in respect of such matters was indescribable. It would not even supply extra blankets for the garrison of Quebec, but decided that the price must be deducted from each soldier's pay, and this although recruits were already hardly obtainable for garrisons abroad.[440] Not an official, notwithstanding the repeated representations of military officers, seems to have been capable of devising a new system to cover new conditions. The old formulæ were stretched and stretched again till they became a mere confusion of rents and patches, barely sufficient to cover the nakedness of maladministration.

It is true that the Government was not wholly to blame; it was rather that spirit of carping and meddlesome criticism in the Commons which in these days has led to what is called legislation by reference, with the result that few Acts of Parliament are intelligible without a complete body of the Statutes of the past century to elucidate them. In mortal dread of distasteful discussion of the military estimates, the civil authorities clothed every possible grant of money in the garment of pay for so many men, and made it over to regimental officers to do their best or worst with it. Hence arose a chaos of strange terms which are the bewilderment and despair of every student. The mysteries of the "recruiting-fund" have already been laid bare, and the veil which shrouds the "widow's man" has likewise been lifted; but the list is unfortunately far longer than this. As though widow's men were not sufficient, there were also "contingent men," fictitious men kept on the rolls of every company that their pay might discharge the contingent expenses of the captain.[441] Then there was an item known as "grass-money," an allowance of similar nature, but of so complicated a description that it can be shown only in tabulated form.[442] There were also curious devices whereby the foot-soldier likewise was provided with certain necessary portions of his equipment. Then there was yet another source of regimental income called the stock-purse, which applied originally to dragoons only, and was made up partly from the recruiting fund, partly from the vacant pay of men when the troop was below its established strength, and partly from the value of cast horses. The fund so collected was placed in the hands of the agent, to defray contingent expenses and current cost of recruiting. As all horses were cast at the age of fourteen, and as four horses, at a price not exceeding twenty guineas apiece, were replaced every year irrespective of those lost by death or accident, it may be imagined that a stroke of bad luck might reduce a troop to ruin. All this, however, was part of the system which made the Army pay for itself, and was therefore preserved in defiance of the trouble and confusion to which it inevitably led. It may now be understood why officers who loved their regiments frequently bequeathed large sums of money to the regimental funds, to enable their successors to secure good recruits and to uphold the fair name of the corps.

Thus it is sufficiently evident that the Army, notwithstanding the wild ravings in Parliament, did far more for itself than the country did for it; though there are signs that as an institution it was gradually finding acceptance with the nation. In 1740 the nickname of "lobster" for a soldier, which thirty or forty years ago was common enough, first made its appearance, curiously enough with the Christian name of Thomas prefixed to it.[443] Then in the same year Parliament called for and printed a return of the officers of the Army, which was continued yearly and ripened into the annual Army List.[444] Another change also helped to give regiments a surer identity in the popular mind, namely the substitution of a number for the colonel's name for the distinction of corps from corps. This reform crept in during July 1753;[445] but it was many years before the colonel's name was altogether discarded, while the numbers did not find a place on the buttons until 1767. Then, to pass to minuter matters, sufficient deference was paid to the popular love of military music to relieve the colonels in part of the burden of hiring bandsmen, who, in some regiments at any rate, were after 1749 enlisted as soldiers and placed under military discipline.[446] In the cavalry, where the trumpeters supplied six or eight men more or less skilled in the playing of a wind-instrument, the issue of horns and bassoons to these sufficed more cheaply to form a band of music;[447] but the main burden of supporting a band has always lain, as it still lies, upon the officers. Private enterprise, which thus forced military musicians upon the country, strove also to impose another modern fashion, but without success. After his march to Fort Duquêsne General Forbes caused a medal to be struck, of extremely florid design, and authorised such of his officers as might desire it to wear the same in gold suspended from their necks by a blue ribbon.[448] The hint, however, was not taken at home,—possibly the fame of it never reached official ears,— and though a medal might have increased the flow of recruits and reconciled men to service beyond sea, not one was issued. Ferdinand of Brunswick received the Garter, and Amherst the red ribbon of the Bath, but nothing was done to commemorate for lesser men the share that they had taken in the conquest of an empire.

I turn now to consideration of the military progress in the three combatant branches of the Army. In the Cavalry an early change, which has been perpetuated by certain regimental titles to the present day, was the conversion of the three senior regiments of Horse into Dragoons, with the names which they still retain of the First, Second, and Third Dragoon Guards. This was done in December 1746 and was apparently part of a general scheme of economy; for at precisely the same time the Third and Fourth troops of the Life Guards were disbanded, and two troops only reserved, together with two troops of Horse Grenadier Guards.[449] But there seems also to have been somewhat of a craze for dragoons at the moment,[450] first because their pay was small, and secondly, because Frederick the Great, in imitation of the Austrians, had made greater mobility the rule for all cavalry. In truth the old distinctions between Horse and Dragoons were disappearing fast and becoming very much a question of names. The French indeed still made it a rule not to place dragoons in the line of battle; but the horse in their army was distinguished by being heavily clad in defensive armour. Ligonier, who loved the cavalry above all arms, boldly advised the disregard of all fanciful differences, and the issue of defensive armour to the British dragoons; but his recommendation remained unnoticed for twelve years, when, in a true spirit of pedantry, cuirasses and iron skull-caps were given in 1758 to the Blues and in 1760 to the Third and Fourth Horse, or to give them their present names, the Sixth and Seventh Dragoon Guards.[451] Another defect noted by Ligonier in the organisation of the cavalry was the extreme weakness of the British squadrons as compared with the French; for remedy of which he purposed to raise the strength of troops of horse to fifty and of dragoons to seventy-five troopers. Such a reform would have been valuable as a return to Cromwell's system of making the units strong enough to provide full employment for the officers; but the authorities settled the question in a far more simple fashion by ordaining that three troops, instead of two as heretofore, should be the strength of a squadron on service.[452] The country has waited long for Ligonier's suggestion to be adopted, and it is only within very recent years, if now, that it has at last grasped the soundness of the principle.

More important as a step forward was the institution of Light Dragoons, begun, as has been told, by the establishment first of light troops and later of complete light regiments. The example in this case came from a corps formed during the Scottish rebellion of 1745, the Duke of Kingston's Light Dragoons, which did so good service that, though disbanded after Culloden, it was at once reformed as the Duke of Cumberland's own. As such it distinguished itself greatly at Lauffeld, and Cumberland pleaded hard that it might be spared after the Peace of Aix-la-Chapelle; but with the usual blindness it was disbanded, and thus a regiment of quite unusual value and promise was sacrificed.[453] Happily the Fifteenth Light Dragoons made a most brilliant beginning for the new branch of the cavalry, and assured its success. The light dragoons were distinguished by wearing a helmet of lacquered copper or leather, and were armed with carbine, bayonet, pistol, and sword, carrying also entrenching tools in their holsters. Their horses are described as of the nag or hunter kind, standing from fourteen hands three inches to fifteen hands one inch; and their saddlery was lighter than that of the ordinary dragoon. Being intended for employment as irregular troops they were known from the first in England as hussars;[454] but though they received special training in horsemanship and in firing, even at a gallop, from the saddle, they had little or no instruction in the duties of reconnaissance, which were the peculiar function of the hussar. Nothing could be more characteristic of the difference between the true and the false light cavalry than the behaviour of the Fifteenth at Emsdorff, who charged through and through the French infantry without hesitation, while the Prussian hussars, never coming to close quarters, lost not a man nor a horse. Fortunately it was not the true hussar that was most sorely needed on that day.

For the rest, before the opening of the war the old system of manœuvre by turning every horse in his own ground had given place to that by wheeling of small divisions, although the ranks were still formed three deep. It does not appear that the drill introduced by Frederick the Great for field-movements was adopted either in whole or in part, though possibly it may have been practised by individual colonels. Shock-action our cavalry did not need to learn from Frederick, having learned it already of Marlborough; but our squadrons seem as usual to have been prone to their besetting sin of unwillingness to rally after a successful charge. It was this wild galloping forward that wrecked Ligonier's heroic regiments at Lauffeld. On the other hand, Granby's squadrons, for all their leader's impetuosity, seem to have been well in hand at Warburg, and to have done their work with spirit and yet subject to control. But a trot of two hours before coming into action had probably rubbed the keen edge off both horses and men.

Passing next to the Artillery we approach the most remarkable development observable during this period in the whole Army. Notwithstanding the early disgraces at Carthagena and the shortcomings of the Office of Ordnance, the gunners after 1741 are found to raise the reputation of their corps steadily in all parts of the world. Their place as yet was still on the left of the line, yielding precedence to the whole of the rest of the Army, but they were entitling themselves to a higher station. This sudden change is doubtless in great measure attributable to the foundation of the Academy at Woolwich, with an allowance at first of two hundred pounds, which after a few months was increased to a thousand pounds, a year.[455] In 1744 the forty gentlemen cadets were formed into a single company, and their pay was raised from one shilling to sixteenpence a day; their number also was increased to forty-eight, and from thenceforth the cadet-company stood as the senior company of the corps.[456] The growth of the Royal Regiment in numbers in itself is remarkable. In 1741 it possessed but three marching companies, but from that year onwards it was constantly increased by one, two, or four companies, until in 1757 it consisted of twenty-four companies in two battalions and in 1761 of thirty-one companies in three battalions, or close on thirty-two hundred of all ranks. Finally, in 1760, a warrant was issued for the formation of a distinct regiment of Royal Irish Artillery.

At first the gunners are seen at work principally with the battalion guns, light three-pounders or six-pounders, which though attached to the infantry were served by artillerymen;[457] but they are always distinguished, whether at Fontenoy or before Trichinopoly, by the rapidity and accuracy of their fire. In Germany, however, we find the guns before Minden scientifically concentrated and handled in large masses by the skill of the Count of Lippe-Bückeburg; and there the British batteries win the admiration of the most critical artillerists in Europe, and their officers the special praise of Ferdinand of Brunswick himself. The influence of the Academy had told early; but it is a still more significant fact that British Artillery officers, not obtaining their commissions by purchase, did not rise to command without knowledge of their work. The variety of guns issued for the field was very great, and though three-pounders seem to have given place in the Seven Years' War to light six-pounders as the lightest ordnance employed,[458] yet there were also heavy six-pounders, light and heavy twelve-pounders, howitzers and twenty-four pounders. It was probably the light six-pounders that amazed the whole army at Warburg by advancing at the gallop, a feat which was the more remarkable since drivers and horses were still hired, and not part and parcel of the corps as at present.[459] Finally, Mauvillon bears witness that the British guns were kept far the cleanest and in the most perfect order of any in the whole Allied army.

Of the Engineers it is impossible to speak as favourably; indeed it is almost an extreme assumption to assert their existence except in name. A school of engineering was founded in 1741; and the small establishment of engineers as fixed in 1717 having been largely increased in 1756 was finally reorganised with a strength of sixty-one officers in 1759.[460] There seem to have been no men, except a strong company of miners, which, however, was borne on the strength of the Royal Artillery.[461] The results of the school were singularly small compared with those of the Academy at Woolwich. Wentworth possessed one efficient engineer at Carthagena, but Stair had not even one in the Low Countries, and was obliged to engage Dutch and Austrian officers;[462] while the engineers employed with Boscawen at Pondicherry, Abercromby at Ticonderoga, and Hodgson at Belleisle were all alike inefficient. The fact is less remarkable when it is remembered that the sea obviates the necessity for the fortification of inland towns in England. In truth the French engineers, in respect both of the skill of the officers and the organisation of the men, seem to have stood far above the rest of Europe,[463] while the British probably stood lowest of all.

Lastly we come to the Infantry. Attention has already been called to the reforms initiated by Howe, Washington, Forbes, Bouquet, and Amherst, which, though still too much advanced to receive welcome at home, were to be realised by Sir John Moore forty years later. The great characteristic of the British infantry throughout the war is the excellence of their fire-discipline and the deadly accuracy of their fire. It is curious, therefore, to read in the most popular military handbook of the time[464] that it was precisely in the matter of fire-discipline that the British were reckoned defective, so defective that they were accounted inferior to the Dutch and were obliged to comfort themselves with the reflection that the Dutch were naturally more phlegmatic of temperament. The author is careful to point out that Dutch superiority lay in discipline only, so it is reasonable to infer that the British improved rapidly in this respect during the war. And such indeed is the conclusion to be drawn from the study of the various actions. At Dettingen the fire though deadly was unsteady; at Fontenoy it was nearly perfect; at Minden, where the British stood motionless until the French cavalry was within ten paces, it was quite admirable; at Quebec it was simply superlative. It is commonly supposed that this improvement was due to the adoption of Prussian methods, but I can find no ground for the assumption. The Prussian manual and firing exercise did indeed find its way to the First Guards in 1756;[465] and there still exists record of a petition from some aged pensioners against the cruelty of an ensign who drilled them every day through the winter in the Prussian exercise, though they had hardly clothes to cover their nakedness;[466] but this has no bearing on the action of Fontenoy in 1745. The truth is that in the matter of attack the British had nothing to learn from the Prussians, either in the cavalry or the infantry. Marlborough had taught them the superiority of shock-action and platoon-fire long before Frederick the Great was born; and all that the Prussian school had to teach, apart from this and from the discipline which went to its perfect execution, was the precision of march learned from pendulum and pace-stick, and certain undeniable improvements in the manœuvre of a regiment or battalion. It has been suggested, indeed,[467] that a Prussian column at Fontenoy might have manœuvred its way to victory by sheer perfection of drill and discipline; but this begs the question whether they would have preserved their order as admirably as the British during the advance. Certainly it is hardly conceivable that even Prussian regiments could have behaved more perfectly under very heavy fire and in the presence of an overwhelming force of cavalry than the six British battalions at Minden.

But the most important changes in the infantry were akin to those in the cavalry. The first was the practice of massing the grenadiers of the army into battalions, which though forbidden by the King as an Austrian innovation when first proposed by Stair,[468] was ultimately adopted both in America and in Germany. The next was the introduction of light troops for the work of skirmishing and for such rapid movements and special duties as were committed in the cavalry to hussars. In the British Army the first representatives of this class of infantry were the Highlanders, who for this reason were armed with short muskets or carbines and were drawn up outside the line in the formal order of battle. Stair[469] had begged for Highlanders in their native dress as early as in 1742, and to his influence probably was due their presence at Fontenoy. During the Seven Years' War, as has been seen, they were employed in every quarter of the globe and did excellent service. Amherst, however, and Wolfe after him, were not content with Highlanders only, but formed those bodies of marksmen, often armed with rifles, which prepared the way for the Light Companies and the complete corps of Light Infantry and Riflemen that were to follow at a later day. Indeed, there was actually a regiment (which during its short life took precedence as ninetieth of the Line) that was called Morgan's Light Infantry. This was probably an imitation from some continental model; but the British had found a far better model for their own purposes in America.

In truth, though there were lessons which the British might learn with profit from foreign nations, both as to what they should imitate and what they should avoid, the best of their instruction was that which they gained from their own hard experience in lands remote from Europe. The influence of

King Frederick the Great was perverted in great measure for ill to the Army. The King and Cumberland had both of them a passion for minute details of dress, facings, lace, buttons, cockades, and the like, and were dear lovers of the tight clothing and inelasticity of movement which characterised the Prussian school. There can be no doubt, on the other hand, that strict insistence on cleanliness and smartness is indispensable, and that correctness and uniformity of dress are valuable aids to discipline and to *esprit de corps*. Such little distinctions as that the coats of Horse should be lapelled to the skirt and of Dragoons to the waist, while those of Light Dragoons should be without lapels of any kind, are harmless in themselves, and give men a pride and an interest in their branch of the service; but the powdering of hair, the docking of the old-fashioned serviceable coats, and the straitening of every article of raiment were no gain to efficiency, no improvement to health, and in the eyes of Englishmen, at first, no embellishment as to appearance.[470] Had the King turned his thoughts to diminishing the weight on a soldier's back, [471] or devising suitable equipment for tropical climates, he might have saved lives untold; but many years were still to elapse before such simple matters as these were to receive due notice. The beautiful accuracy of drill enjoined by Frederick was turned to good account by the British on many fields in Europe and in India; but his excellent discipline on active service both on and off duty was by no means so faithfully copied, as Ferdinand of Brunswick found out to his cost.[472] Yet at any rate the British had an example of the worst that they must eschew in the armies of the French. Therein "there was no discipline, no subordination, no order on the march, in the camp or even in the battlefield. The very subalterns had their mistresses with them, and officers often left their men to accompany them on the march in their carriages. Everything that could contribute to the luxury of the officers was found in the French camp.... At one time there were twelve thousand waggons accompanying Soubise's army which belonged to sutlers and shopkeepers, though the army was not fifty thousand strong.... Balls were given in camp and officers often left their posts to dance a minuet. They laughed at the orders of their leaders and only obeyed when it suited them."[473] From such folly and disgrace as this Cumberland's attachment to the stricter models of Germany delivered the Army; but its best lessons came not from Germany but from America, not from Frederick the Great but from Howe, Washington, Wolfe, Bouquet, and Amherst.

Lightning Source UK Ltd.
Milton Keynes UK
UKHW010641120922
408721UK00002B/402

9 783752 353396